SING TO
SILENT STONES

VIOLET'S WAR

David Snell

Hornet Books

Sing to Silent Stones:
Violet's War

This edition first published 2016 by
Hornet Books
Text © David Snell
This work © Hornet Books Ltd
Paperback ISBN 978 0 9934 3534 8

Editor: David Roberts
Proof-reader: Matthew White

Printed in the UK by CPI

www.hornetbooks.com

Sing to Silent Stones was previously
published in one volume in 2011

For Frank Balfour, who perished in the Great War. For his son Frank, my father-in-law, who fought behind the lines in the Second World War, and for his mother, Violet, who I came to think of as my own granny. For my brave and beautiful mother, Pat, who ferried bombers in the war and trained bomb aimers. Most of all for my dear father, Eric, who served three tours in Bomber Command, and was in the skies over wartime Berlin at just nineteen years of age.

For the men and women of the French Resistance who perished in a senseless massacre in the Forest of Orleans, days before the end of hostilities. For the men, women, boys and girls who fought in all those wars. They were not, in the main, soldiers. They were people from all walks of life, all religions and all races who did their duty and got caught up in events of their time, beyond their control.

The title for 'Sing to Silent Stones' comes from the lines of silent gravestones in northern France, with the larks singing down at them from the sky.

David Snell
byoh@yahoo.co.uk

Special thanks to:-
Linda Snell, Naomi Snell, Cynthia Scott, Pauline Holsgrove, Mark Neeter, Jacqui Freeman, Gisela Hunting, Naomi Handford-Jones, Moira Houghton, Birgit Muller and Michel et Annie Fouilleul for all their help and encouragement. Very special thanks to Joan McConnell-Wood for her enthusiastic support and for her insights into just what life was like in the period.

Prologue: January 1919

The whoop of delight from the small boy hurtling down the hill on his sledge cracked through the still of the snowbound landscape, to be returned in an echo that buried itself in its plush whiteness. Behind him, framed against the clear sky and set solidly into the hill, stood his farmhouse home, its stone walls defying the elements, its mullioned windows set deep within their reveals. Even the roof was stone slated, and in places their very weight had depressed between the thick hewn rafters, creating undulations into which the mosses and lichens, now hidden by the snow, gathered and flourished. In front, beyond the driveway, there was a wide pond fed by a stream coming from further up the hill around to the back of the house. Come spring the rising trout that congregated there would break the limpid blackness of its peat waters but now, in the stillness of winter, the snow lay on its surface ice, creating a flat table of white. From its outfall a shimmering cloak of ice draped the huge rocks, reflecting the colours of the small boy as he flashed past.

The boy neared the last large boulder that stood proud from the ground, covered now in its mantle of snow. A lonely sentinel of pre-history upon which he would often clamber and play and which, in many games, featured as the last stand of some great warrior of his imagination. He was not the first and he would not be the last to grace this timeless landscape and this small boy was as much a part of the scenery as the rocks and the house.

As he neared the river, the ground became rougher and the sledge began to bottom, jarring him and throwing the sledge off line until, as he came up to the old willows at its edge, it veered sharply and dumped him giggling and happy at the foot of one of the gnarled old trees. At rising four years old he was a strong and healthy boy with a wide grin and an open look that endeared him to most. The hair beneath his cap was medium brown and wayward but now, even in the cold of this day, the sweat of his joyous exertions held it firm to his forehead. He lifted his cap and pushed it back with his mittened hand. Like most small boys of the day, even in the worst of weather he was wearing grey shorts with grey socks that should have reached his red and chapped knees but which in his case were almost always down around his ankles or the top of his sturdy lace-up boots. The top half of his torso was better prepared for the weather with a dark blue buttoned-up jacket and matching cap over his grey pullover. Around his neck he wore the bright red scarf knitted and given to him by his aunt for Christmas.

He sat up and brushed himself down before the snow could melt into his clothing. Dusting the snow from one of the gnarls in the tree butt he sat up on it, looking back up the tracks in the snow curving past his last violent swerve to run straight and parallel up the hill to where a second figure now departed. The boy stood as the sledge got nearer and called encouragement to his playmate, waving his arms in the air. "Come on George!" George raised one arm in greeting and swerved off line. The right side runner struck a large stone and the sledge slewed around, dumping its rider to roll on down the hill, gathering snow as he went. The sledge, upside down but relieved of its burden, overtook the rolling figure and slithered silently down the hill.

"Are you alright?" shouted the first boy as he trudged through the snow towards the now prone figure.

George rolled over on to his back and lay there laughing for a few moments before the cold and damp made him sit up and start to brush the snow from his clothing. He was about seven years old, and unlike the first boy he wore long trousers tucked into his socks, affording him better respite from the cold. "Course I'm alright Frank. That was great wasn't it?"

Frank retrieved the sledge and dragged it over to George, who was by now standing and beating the remaining snow from himself. "Shall we do it again George?"

"Cor, let's get me breath back first." He took the guide rope from Frank and dragged his sledge over to the trees and sat down on the gnarl. Frank stood in front of him expectantly.

A call rang down the hill, breaking into the younger boy's excited thoughts and he turned back to look up to the house. It was a woman's voice but not his mother's. Kate. It was Auntie Katie's and she was calling his name from in front of the house, looking down the hill to see where he was. "It's my mum and she's calling for you," said George. "Doesn't look as if I've got to go."

Frank waved and shouted back up at her. She saw him and shouted again, motioning for him to come up to the house. "Aah, I wanted another go."

"You'd best go. I'll wait here for a bit and then I'll come on up."

Frank shrugged his shoulders and started up the hill, dragging the sledge behind him, trying to keep its runners in the same tracks as before, imagining as he did all sorts of ills that would befall him if it strayed. He rounded the curve of the hill, in front of the house, lost in his game.

Then play deserted him as he noticed for the first time a strange black motor car in the driveway. Its driver leant against the front wing smoking a cigarette, looking down the hill at him as he approached.

"Hello," said Frank, smiling up at the man and past him at the motor car. "Cor can I have a look inside please sir?" He made as if to mount the running board.

"Hold up boy," the man said. "Don't you go putting all that wet and dirt on there. I've only just brushed it off. Besides which you're wanted in the house and if I was you I'd get in there sharpish."

Frank pulled back and with a wry grin trudged off around the back of the house towards the storm porch door. He pushed it open, dropped on to the cill and began to unlace his boots and take them off. Picking them up, he put them in line with the others, stood up, hung his hat and coat on the row of hooks and entered the kitchen with his damp socks hanging off his feet and flapping as he walked. Sleepy socks his mother called them.

It was a large kitchen, which in truth served as the principle living room for the house and the main point of congregation for the family. To the right of the door that he had entered there was a large cooking range, upon which a kettle always simmered. The floor was flagged in polished stone, producing an uneven surface which meant that generations before the dressers and cabinets which lined the other walls had been propped up by wedges to level them. In the centre of the room, similarly propped, stood a huge wooden table at which his Auntie Kate sat, her back to him. She turned as he entered. "Ah there you are Frank."

Her face was red and puffy and he wondered if she had been crying. "Come here," she whispered, opening her arms and beckoning him towards her as she stood up.

He ran to her and she put her hands on his shoulders and looked down into his face. He saw then that he was right. She had been crying. She was doing her best not to do so now but the tears were starting again, even as she pushed his tousled hair back off his forehead and cupped his chin in her hand.

"Frank," she said. "Frank you've got to be a very brave boy now." She sat again and held the boy in front, looking into his face.

"Mummy..."

She checked and looked away and then back into his face. "Florrie is in the parlour and you must go in there and be a very brave boy. And remember how much we all love you."

"Of course I know you love me," said Frank. "Why have you been crying Auntie Kate?"

She didn't answer but instead busied herself with tidying him up as best as she could, tucking his loose shirt tails back into his grey shorts and telling him to pull his socks up. She crossed to the sink, wrung out a cloth, and cupping his face again wiped it clean. She searched around for a brush but couldn't see one so pushed her open fingers through his hair to make some order of it, then held him away and looked down at him. "You'll have to do," she said as she took hold of his hand and led him gently through the door and across the large stone-flagged hall to the parlour. Here she stopped, and after glancing down at him once more, knocked quietly.

He wondered at her knocking. Why hadn't they just gone in?

"Come in," said his mother's voice. Kate pushed open the door to reveal Frank's mother on the couch. He ran to her and sat down beside her, pushing up to her and looking into her face. Her cheeks were all puffy and red and he realised that she too had been crying. Her eyes filled even as she looked down at him trying to smile. His father, standing behind the couch, put his hands down on each of their shoulders. Kate moved around to stand with him. Frank looked up and noticed, for the first time, that the chair nearest the fire was occupied by a strange lady.

She was a handsome woman, not that that meant much to a small boy. Of medium height, she was dressed in a long dark skirt and a white blouse, over which she still wore a dark matching cape. Her legs were crossed elegantly in front of her as she leaned slightly forward in the chair. Her hair, the same colour as his own, was crimped and waved in perfect place, unlike his mother's which normally flew free. What fascinated him the most, however, was that over her dark cape she wore a fox stole with its head fastened to its rear, its tail hanging loose. Fierce teeth were visible in its open mouth and its little dark glass eyes twinkled brightly in the fire's light, brought to life by the movement of the woman's body and the flickering flames.

Her grey eyes stared steadily at him and he squirmed in their gaze, aware that she was gathering every detail about him. He began to appreciate the atmosphere in the room, to wonder at what was happening and why this stranger was here.

"Frank?" said the stranger in an enquiring tone, looking up at the man behind the couch. His father nodded back at her. Frank started at her voice. It made his name sound the same as when the Vicar said it, clipped and not stretched out by the familiar Devon vowels.

"Frank," his father interjected quickly. "Your mother... that is Florrie," he corrected with a glance at the stranger. "Florrie has summat to say to you and you must listen well and be a strong and a brave boy, like I knows you can be."

Frank stared up, trying to understand precisely what his father was talking about. He turned back to his mother, looking into her eyes, waiting for the news which he was to be so brave about and which with all the tension, was beginning to send a chill of fear through him.

She smiled down at him through her tears, gathered him closer and stroked his hair back from his forehead. "Frank," she said, looking deep into his enquiring eyes. "Frank you're a big boy now and you know that we've loved you and we always will." She stopped and turned towards the woman in the chair, who nodded back to her and motioned for her to carry on. "Frank. There's something we have to tell you. Something I should have... something I meant to tell you... and it concerns this lady here." She hesitated, darting a look to each of the other adults in the room. Each one returned her glance with a mixture of pity and anticipation.

She gathered herself together and continued. "She's your mother, Frank. Your real mother, and she's come here today to meet you again and..." She faltered once more, looking beseechingly at the woman and then back up to her husband before continuing. "A... a long time ago you was born to this lady, who couldn't keep you and so you was brought here to us and we agreed to raise you as our own... until... until the time came when she could..."

She choked into her tears and her husband, his voice shaking and rough, took over and continued, "...until she could take you back wiv her to live, Frank. And that's why she's cum here now. It's time for you to go and live wiv her."

Frank stared up at him, unable to understand what they were

all really saying. He didn't want to understand. Why should he? It couldn't be true. Mum had always been Mum... and Dad... and Kate and Lizzie and George and... and... and they all... they were his family. Not this strange woman with her fancy clothes and funny accent. They were his family. There had to be a mistake. There just had to be. It would all be all right in a minute. They'd all laugh at the joke they had played on him and everything would be all right. His look bounced from one face to another and back again. He waited for the smiles to break out on their faces, but they didn't come. They just carried on looking down at him with pity and with tears welling in their eyes, or, in the case of his mother, coursing freely down her flushed cheeks.

The woman stood. She walked to the front of the fire, coughed and turned back to Frank. "Frank, your mother..." She paused, raising her finger to her lips as if to stem the words, before continuing. "Your foster parents are telling you the truth. You are my son."

"I'm not!" he cried. "I'm not am I Mum? You're my Mum and Dad aren't you, and she can't make me... I don't want to go with her. Tell her Dad! Tell her to go away!"

"I'll not go away Frank," said the woman, raising her voice slightly to be heard above his pleas. "I've always loved you but... but I couldn't have you until now when..." Her voice tailed off in the face of the enmity flaring from the little boy's face. She turned from it, looking at each of the adults in turn, desperate pleading in her eyes, tears springing unwelcome. They numbly returned her look, waiting for her to continue. The room fell silent, the only sound seeming to be the crackle and fizzle of the logs on the fire and the barely perceptible ticking of the large clock on the mantle. The woman turned to the fire, weeping quietly into her handkerchief.

"It's true," said a voice, breaking the tension. A startled Frank switched from observing the woman to stare at Florrie, who continued: "Oh Frank. Frank, I've always meant to tell you but there just never was a right time. I tried at Christmas when I knew Miss

Violet was coming soon... I tried but I could never find the words. You've always been such a happy lad and every time I went to... but Frank it's true. She's always loved you Frank... I know that... I've always known that. We've all loved you and we always will... we always will..." She drew herself up, seeming to gain strength from some inner source. "But we promised and she has the right Frank. She has the right to... to take you back to her own and we can't... no we mustn't stop her... even though it's near breaking my heart."

He recognised that strength in her. He had seen it before and sheltered within it. Why then, he wondered, wouldn't she use that strength to let him stay? Why wouldn't she tell this woman that he was her son and that he could stay? His mind raced, the thoughts and fears tumbling about within it beginning to displace all reason. Panic welled up in his chest like a hot lump and his eyes began to bulge and stare. She held him now at arm's length and looked down at him, with the love in her turning more and more into determination to carry through what she perceived to be her duty.

"Frank," she said in a soft and gentle voice that still left no doubt that it was to be obeyed. "You have to be strong and you have to do this for me... and for your... for Joe. We love you but she is... she is your mother and you have to understand and you have to obey her... and me in what we want you to do now. I know it's a shock to you and I'm so..." she swallowed hard. "I'm so sorry that I've let this happen. After all this time I'd put the truth out of my mind but it's the truth... the truth nonetheless... and there's nought that'll gainsay it."

"But Mum," he pleaded, reaching out for her. She avoided his grasp.

"No. That's an end Frank," she said firmly. "You have to listen and you mustn't make this harder for me and for all of us than it needs to be."

The boy seemed to crumple up now and he fell against her sobbing. How could his whole world have turned so bad in just a few minutes? What was happening? Why couldn't he just go outside and play in the snow again as if this... this horrible lady had never come? Thoughts tumbled about in his head, obliterating their own rationale, reducing him to shuddering blind panic.

Florrie laid him back into the sofa and stood up to face the woman. "He's a good boy Miss Violet. He'll be all right, but please can you leave him 'till morning whilst we pack his things and see to his bits and pieces... say our goodbyes like. Please let him rest 'till morning and then I promise you he'll come with you... I promise."

Violet stepped forward, took her hand and clasped it in both of hers. "Of course he can my dear," she said softly. "I've waited years for this moment and I can wait one more night. I'm staying at the Green Dragon for tonight and I'll come back in the morning." She cocked her head slightly to one side and bit her bottom lip as if thinking, shaking her head almost imperceptibly. "I know how hard this is for you all and I can see that everybody, perhaps including me, needs to calm down and take stock." She smiled a strained smile, looking around at each of the faces for some support. "And in the morning... well in the morning... well you know." She let go of Florrie's hand and looked away from her at Frank, who had turned his face to look up at them.

"I mean you no harm Frank," she said softly. "I'm sure that things will look better in the morning. I'll see you then and we'll talk in the taxi on the way to the station. You'd like to ride in the taxi and go on a train, wouldn't you Frank?"

"I want to stay here," retorted Frank, burying his face in the sofa.

"Now then Frank," said his father. "There's no call for rudeness. You apologise to the lady."

"I won't, I won't!" shouted Frank, raising himself to crouch on all fours, clearly desperate that all around him seemed to be deserting him. "You can't make me. You can't!" He flung himself back, face down on the sofa, sobbing bitterly.

A look of pain and anger flicked across Joe's face but it was quickly replaced by kindly concern. He leant over the back of the sofa gently, shaking the little boy's shoulder, and said quietly, "I may not be your

real father my boy, but I've been a father to you and this ain't no way
to behave... I knows you don't mean it."

"Perhaps I could have a few moments with Frank, please, before
I go," said Violet suddenly, with as much cheer as she could muster.
"Just a little while. I won't stay much longer... I know..."

Florrie dragged her eyes away from the sight of the small boy
weeping on the couch. She put her hand on Violet's shoulder
reassuringly. "Yes certainly," she said, then turned to her husband
and to Kate, who had stood there all this time stricken dumb with
grief. "Come on my loves. We'll go into the kitchen and leave them
to talk... and mind Frank, we're only in the other room. You stay
here and talk to the lady... talk to your mother. We'll be across in the
kitchen."

She waited while her husband and Kate joined her before the
three of them went from the room, closing the door softly.

The boy sat up on the couch and stared at the closed door. Then,
as if feeling exposed, he moved across to the arm end, where Florrie
had been seated, and looked up at the cause of all his misery who
stood in front of him, wringing her hands. She turned away to look
into the fire, coughed discreetly and then sat back on the edge of the
chair looking intently at him. She didn't speak. She just seemed to
study his face. To look deep into it as if seeking something that he felt
was not entirely to do with him.

"You look like him," she said softly. "The same eyes. The same
direct look. Even the same anger. You certainly are Frank's son."

"I am Frank. That's my name... Frank."

She smiled now. A wry smile which served to break the tension for
them both but which he still didn't understand. "I meant Frank your
father. Your daddy's name was Frank and I named you after him."

"My daddy's in the kitchen," said the boy. "His name's Joe."

"Joe is not your father, Frank. That's what we've been trying to tell
you. Oh yes, he's been a father to you but he's not your real father.
That was Frank... Frank Balfour."

"Well why's he not here then," said Frank in triumph. "You're fibbin' aren't you?"

She looked straight at him now. "Your father was a fine man and you would have loved him... as I did. But he went to war many years ago... before you were born, and he died there and I was alone and... well... I couldn't keep you then."

The boy looked up, interested now in spite of himself. "Was he a hero? Did he get any medals?"

She laughed softly now. "No he didn't get any medals. Leastwise not that I know of," said Violet, amused at the boy's ability to rise above his miserable condition and let fly his obvious and vivid imagination. "But he was a hero. They all were heroes in that war."

"I'd have got tons and tons of medals," said the boy, fantasising.

"I'm sure you would have," said Violet, but the irony in her voice went over the boy's head. "So Frank," she continued in a lighter tone. "Tell me about you. What do you get up to? What games do you play and what will you be."

Being invited into his favourite world of fantasy and imagination was unwittingly the best tack she could possibly have taken. For a moment, Frank was able to forget the cause and object of his misery and indulge himself. "I'm going to be in the army and... I'm going to be a General and tell all of the other soldiers what to do... and I'm going to kill loads and loads of Germans."

She laughed lightly. "Wait Frank. The war's over now you know. You don't have to kill anyone anymore."

For a second he looked almost crestfallen, but then the visionary light lit in his eyes again. "Then I'll go to another country and fight them and be ever so brave... the bravest in the world." He stopped and considered his future glory, revelling in his increasing importance.

"I will take you to other countries Frank."

The boy suddenly realised the trap he was walking into and sought to recover the situation.

"There's no need 'cause I'm alright here and... anyway I've

got to go to school soon." A light turned on in his mind as he realised he had stumbled on the real reason he couldn't go with this stranger. "I can't go with you because I've got to go to school soon and my mummy says that school is very important." He drew himself up and sat erect and important on the sofa, staring triumphantly up at the woman.

"I know it's important and I'm pleased that you feel it so, but Frank, there are many schools and do you imagine that the one in your village is the only one you can go to?"

He slumped a little, disappointed that he still hadn't won, but not yet prepared to admit defeat. "There's no need to move me 'cause I'll be alright here. I will and... and you can visit me here 'stead of me goin' wiv you."

"Maybe Frank," she said. "But would you achieve all you could? I doubt it." She stopped, realising that to continue on this theme would be to denigrate the family in the other room and she had no wish to do that and no wish to give the boy issues on which to defend the status quo. "Oh Frank, there's so much out there for you to see and so much which I can show you. I know you fear me... hate me a little now perhaps, but I promise you Frank I only wish the best for you and I know that Florrie and Joe feel the same. Much as it hurts, they know it's right for you to come with me." She was warming to her theme now and she continued. "You can always come back to see them. There's no need for you to lose touch. That wouldn't be fair after all these years... you would see them all again."

"I don't want to go," said Frank, and Violet's heart sank at the loss of momentum. "I want to stay with Mum and Dad and Lizzie."

"Of course you'll miss them Frank," said Violet, pretending not to notice his statement. "But you would always be there in their thoughts and you can write to them of your adventures. There's a great big world out there and you have to get ready to meet it sometime. First we have to go to London and then we will be going to France. You'd like that, wouldn't you?" She glanced up at the clock above the fire. "Look, I've got to get to the Green Dragon and I think your mum... Florrie will want to be with you and... I really must leave now... I'll be back in the morning at about 10 o'clock to pick you up."

"I don't want to go," Frank repeated, clasping his hands together between his knees.

She stared at him for a moment, seeking to explore the mind of this little boy. "But you are going, aren't you Frank? You are coming with me and I think you know it, don't you?" Her heart rose with triumph as his eyes betrayed his inner thirst for adventure. He folded his arms and looked away from her to stare down into the fire, sniffing slightly from his crying but crying no longer.

She stood, straightening her dress and turning to the oval mirror to the right of the fireplace to adjust her hair before replacing her hat. She pursed her lips and examined her make-up for any smudges caused by the emotions of the past few hours, then turned and smiled down at the small boy. He sat still, staring into the fire, lost in his tumbling thoughts trapped between adventure and the comfort of his familiar surroundings, his mind jumping from scene to scene conjured up in his imagination.

"Frank," she said quietly. And then again to break into his thoughts. "Frank. Could you please tell them that I'm ready to leave now."

He looked up at her and then rose from the sofa and went quietly across to the door. He opened it and then turned back to look at her.

"It's true Frank," she said softly. "It's all true and I'm proud of you. Oh so proud of you and, I hope... I know we'll learn to love each other Frank. I know it."

He nodded almost imperceptibly and looked back at this woman who had only just come into his life, and yet even after these few minutes seemed strangely familiar. It was almost as if he had always known her. Always known that mouth with its perfect, even teeth. Those grey eyes at once so direct and yet so caring. Had he but looked into the mirror he would have seen much of it reflected on his own face.

"What is your name?" he asked.

"Violet. Violet Matthews." She waited for the follow-up question but it never came and he turned and left the room, pulling the door shut behind him.

Left alone, Violet looked around at the homely room and began to notice the furniture and pictures for the first time. The door from the hall came into the room to the left of the large stone fireplace, with its rough hewn mantle, above which the clock ticked. To the right of the fire was the chair upon which she had sat, and into the reveal there was a display cabinet topped by the oval mirror she had just used. She peered in at the books. Shakespeare. Haggard. Verne. All were there, but in such neat order that she doubted that they had ever been opened, let alone read. On most of the other shelves there were colourful ornaments of no value other than to the memory of their purchase. In front of the fire was the large sofa upon which Florrie and Frank had sat, their impressions remaining in the plumpness of the cushions. On the wall beyond that there was another dresser, and above that were framed pictures of what she imagined were Joe's parents looking down into the warm and cosy room. She avoided their stern if long dead remonstration and looked out through the window and down the hill to where she had first glimpsed the boy as he answered the summons to the house, not knowing or guessing then what was to befall. All was white and still. She noticed the taxi and realised that the driver would be pretty chilly after all the time she had been. I must apologise to him as soon as I get out there, she thought, and I'll have to give him something extra for his trouble.

The door opened and Florrie came into the room. Violet looked at her. A homely woman in her flowered dress and white apron, her face kindly, if a little ruddy, with blue eyes that would normally twinkle with the joy and certainty of life but which now were set deep from the puffy aftermath of crying. She pushed the damp curls of blonde hair from her brow and struggled to form the semblance of a smile in defiance of her obvious distress. A strong woman who

Violet knew would always inspire the loyalty and love she had seen demonstrated today.

Violet stood before her. "He's a fine boy," she said quietly. "A fine boy and you've certainly put your mark on him. I know he'll always respect and love you and you must know that... that I will make sure that he always remembers and thinks of you."

"I meant to tell him so often," said Florrie, wringing her hands. "I meant to tell him but I just didn't... even when I got your letter and I knew the time was coming I couldn't ever seem to bring myself to tell him. And then, what with Christmas an' all... now look what I've done... look at the misery that today has brought us all."

"There now," said Violet. "There was never a reason to tell him before, and though today must have been a shock to him the news he had to hear would always have had the same result. He's a strong boy and he won't dwell too long on his sadness. It's you I feel for Florrie, you and Joe." She shook her head. "Funny isn't it? After all these years and this time it's me who needs to comfort you."

Florrie straightened and looked Violet straight in the eye. "Me and Joe will be fine," she said. "We've known... we've always known... ever since you first came here that this day would come... and now it's here." Violet glimpsed once more the strength in the woman as Florrie continued. "We have Lizzie now. We never thought we would have a child of our own... and we have our family... it'll be hard but we've got to pull together, and if Frank ever needs us we'll be here for him... for you too if needs be." She put her hand out to Violet and Violet didn't hesitate. She reached out and drew Florrie to her and they stayed like that for some moments in a silent and comforting embrace.

At length, Florrie stood away and Violet straightened herself. They smiled at each other. Not the happy smiles of people sharing a joke but the wan smiles of two people sharing adversity. "I must be off," said Violet. "I'll be back at around 10 o'clock tomorrow morning. Will that be... will that be all right?"

"We'll be ready," said Florrie. She turned, opened the door and ushered Violet through into the hall. "Frank... Joe!" she called through to the kitchen. They came out into the hall, followed by Kate carrying Lizzie in her arms. George hung back looking at them all. "Miss Matthews is going now."

Joe moved forward to offer his hand to the departing guest and pushed Frank in front of him. "Say goodbye to the lady now, Frank."

Frank offered his hand and Violet smiled down at him. "See you in the morning Frank. See you in the morning."

A cloud passed over Frank's face and he withdrew his hand. Florrie nudged him and he looked up to her quickly, then back at Violet. He offered his hand again silently. Violet took it and held it for a moment, then she smiled at the rest of the grouping and turned out of the front door, held open now by Joe, to step down into the snow-covered driveway. The driver, seeing her coming, made his way around the motor car to open the rear door for her as she settled herself in the seat, apologising for leaving him so long. He muttered his understanding, shut the door and walked back around to the front of the vehicle. He picked up the crank handle and carefully inserted it, swinging it once. The engine sprang into life and the driver stood up, a contented and proud smile on his face, to stow it. He nodded to the assembled onlookers at the front door and got into the driver's seat. Joe lifted his arm, beckoning, and ran out and around to him, crunching in the snow as he went. "There's no need to turn around," he said. "If'n you go all around the back of the house you'll come out there." He pointed behind the car to the left of the house and stood back as it started off, before crossing behind it to re-join his family.

The car disappeared behind the house and then came back on the other side and slowly went down the driveway. Violet turned in her seat to look through the rear window at the small group huddling on the doorstep.

She turned from the window to think back over all that had led up to this moment.

September 1913

Violet lifted her skirts and tripped lightly up the five steps to the black-panelled door of her father's office. '*Walter Matthews & Son Property Sales & Management*' was etched grandly on the brass nameplate to the left of the door, but you had to look quite carefully to make all of it out as years of cleaning had gradually blurred the lettering. Her father, Ernest, was the '*& Son*' bit of the firm. Some years before, his own father had died quite suddenly and now, in his mid-forties, the responsibility and seriousness of his standing in life was weighing heavily on him. A physically empty marriage due to his wife, Elsie's, constant infirmities had removed much of the humour from his world with the result that, with little or no other emotional or intellectual outlets, he devoted almost his entire waking life to his work... with one exception. His only child, Violet.

Violet was the light that shone through the murk of his existence, the beacon of real life and the promise of life to come. He had been indifferent to children, and indeed he had taken very little notice at all of his daughter as a baby. Oh yes, he had shown the requisite interest when she was presented to him on weekends or before her bed time, but that was about all.

Then one summer's Sunday afternoon, when she was about eighteen months old, he was sitting in the garden reading the newspaper. It was a dreamy hot day and his attention had been distracted by this little girl, his little girl, dressed in a blue and white dress with matching bonnet, wandering alone through the garden with a flower in her hand. He'd watched fascinated as she tottered through the miniature box maze just below the terrace, singing tunelessly and unselfconsciously to herself, seemingly unaware of his presence. Suddenly she'd noticed him, proffering him her flower and calling out, "Daddee!" Ernest had put down his paper, uncrossed his legs and leant forward to study this little vision as she grinned and raised her arms above her head, very nearly overbalancing. He made to rise but sat back down again as she giggled and recovered herself, calling out to him once more.

He was smitten. It was as if a bolt of lightning had hit him. He loved this little creature from that moment forth with a passion that no other emotion in his life would ever really supplant. Oh, he wasn't blind to her faults... far from it, he saw them perhaps more clearly than others. God knows he had many of the same faults himself, but the intensity of their love for each other transcended stricture. At home he showed his love for her in a demonstrative way, which was out of character with his normal public persona, and, when she was young, he would often be seen carrying her in his arms or bouncing her on his knee, laughing happily.

In public, however, he was strictly conventional and she recognised at a very early age the segmentation that he applied to his life. For him, his public profile and the way he was judged by his peers were all important and she learnt from his example; something that was to stand her in good stead in later life.

As the little girl grew up into a young woman and as his wife's indisposition progressed, Violet took over more and more of the duties that would normally be hers. With this responsibility came the bonus of a far greater freedom of association than other young ladies of her age. However, her father felt that by and large his faith in her was rewarded, and anyway, and in truth, with the help of Alice their maid, she did manage to run their home with an efficiency that allowed him his own escape from domestic involvement.

Violet opened the heavy door and stepped into the front office.

Her father's secretary, Miss Crabb, looked up briefly from the lines of accounts that she was tallying. "Morning Miss Violet."

"Good morning," Violet replied. "How are you this morning?"

"Fine thank you," said Miss Crabb, bending once more into her work as Violet swept past and on towards the stairs leading up to her father's office.

"Is he available?" she called back.

"Yes Miss Violet," Miss Crabb answered, her back to the figure disappearing up the stairs. "But don't be too long, he's got an appointment with Alderman Peters in fifteen minutes."

Violet was halfway up the stairs before she noticed the desk at the rear of the front office, partially hidden by the staircase, and the young man sitting, looking with undisguised interest at her.

Early twenties, laughing green eyes, with dark blonde hair only barely tamed by the dressing that sought to confine it to its centre parting. He was probably about six feet tall, she guessed... taller than most men... a big man at any rate, with a smile that sat naturally on his face, the laughter lines bearing testimony to its frequency. His large hands, seeming more suited to manual labour, held a fragile pen over the inventories he had been filling in before her entrance had distracted him.

For his part, the object of her interest returned her study, observing the young woman on the stairs above him. Her face betrayed the plumpness of youth with a hint of greater beauty to come in later life, but the openness of her expression and her flawless skin made up for any imperfections. Striking wide set grey eyes... brown hair pinned up leaving her neck bare... in the conventional sense, he thought, she certainly was not beautiful but she was, nevertheless, damned attractive.

"Hello," he said, the timbre of his voice confirming all of her impressions.

"Hello," she replied. "I haven't seen you here before, have I?"

"That is Mr Balfour, Miss Violet," Miss Crabb said, without turning round. "He's recently come to work for your father... and this, Mr Balfour, is Miss Violet Matthews."

Her words seemed to break the spell that had brought Violet's progress up the stairs to a halt as they stared at each other, his direct look bringing a flush to her face. "Pleased to meet you Mr Balfour," she said. "I hope you enjoy working here."

"Oh I'm sure I will do Miss Matthews. I'm sure I will." She smiled down at him and then, humming quietly to herself, continued up to the top landing and knocked at her father's door.

"Come," came the reply, muffled by the door. She opened it and went in, shutting it behind her.

"Hallo daddy dearest," she trilled as she entered, before her face took on a look of mock disgust. "Oh no, you've been smoking those awful things again, haven't you?" She waved her arms in a theatrical attempt to clear the fug whilst crossing to the window and sliding the sash up and open.

The wind rushed into the room, scattering the papers on her father's desk and forcing him to throw himself across it to prevent them all going. "For God's sake, Violet, look what you're doing girl. Shut that damned window!" he shouted.

"Oh I'm so sorry daddy," she cried as she pulled down the sash. "I wasn't thinking. I was only trying to clear the air... anyway it's your fault for smoking those horrible things."

"It's my office and I'll smoke what I damned well wish if you don't mind miss. That's the trouble with you Violet. You never do think things through, do you?" He busied himself with trying to make some order of the chaos, but then caught sight of her standing by the window, a miserable expression of regret on her face. He knew she was sorry. He could sense her disappointment that what had been planned was not going right for her and, as usual, he softened. "Oh well, never mind this time. I know you meant well."

"I didn't mean to upset you," wailed Violet, crossing the office to help him retrieve the papers, pushing the piles into some semblance of order.

"No not that... you don't know which ones go where," Ernest cried out in exasperation. "Leave them to me. I'll do it in a minute. Now what did you want dear?"

"I came to tell you that mother's feeling better and that she'll be up for tea this evening and if you can make it home it would be so lovely and it would cheer her up immensely. Oh you can come, can't you daddy?"

Ernest could think of nothing more depressing than to spend a mealtime with his wife complaining and feeling unwell again at the slightest excuse, but he knew too how much Violet tried to keep up the semblance of a normal family home... to herself as well as to others. He smiled up at her. "Yes of course my dear. I should be home by 6 o'clock."

"But that's too late, daddy," she pleaded. "Couldn't you make it home by 5 o'clock this evening. Just this once. Please. For me and for mother."

He sighed and looked seriously at his daughter. "I have business to conduct with Alderman Peters this afternoon. He is due in a few minutes and it will probably take until at least 5 o'clock, if not beyond. All I can promise is that I will try to get home as soon as my business is concluded."

This last was delivered in a voice that brooked no argument. She recognised that her intrusion into the work segment of his life was over and that any further discussion would threaten to pass the limit of his tolerance.

She sighed and smiled back at him. "Well I'm sure you'll do your very best daddy and we'll see you at the house later." She bent down to his now re-seated figure, kissing him lightly on the cheek. "I must dash," she said, making for the door, but on reaching it she turned. "I've just met your new young man Mr Balfour. He seems awfully nice. You didn't tell me about him."

"I didn't need to young woman!" her father retorted. "Don't you go disturbing my staff... especially junior staff such as he."

She accepted his admonishment with a mock curtsy and left the room.

......

Frank Balfour came out of the West End offices, where he had been delivering some documents. He glanced up at the October sky, then stood on tiptoe to peer back inside and look at the clock on the wall. Quarter past four. By the time he got back, Miss Crabb would have left work and he wouldn't be able to get access as Mr Matthews was also out that afternoon. 'Ah well,' he thought. 'I might just as well stay up West and look about a bit before going back to my lodgings.' He stood in contemplation for a while before making the decision to walk up St. James Street, along Jermyn Street and then up to Piccadilly to see what was going on.

In Jermyn Street, he paused outside a shop selling gentlemen's shirts and idly looked in. He needed a new shirt but he certainly couldn't afford one from here. He turned to walk on but a shop assistant, standing just inside the doorway, had seen his interest and pulled open the door as Frank passed to enquire whether he could be of service.

"I don't think so thank you," said an abashed Frank. "I'm afraid that your prices will be too high for the pocket of a humble clerk."

"Well that's where you are absolutely wrong sir," said the assistant smiling. "Our shirts are indeed of the finest quality but we have a selection at very reasonable prices for gentlemen such as yourself. Come on in and have a look."

Twenty minutes later, Frank continued his walk down Jermyn Street, only now he had two new shirts and four new collars neatly wrapped in brown paper and tied up with string under his arm. He stopped outside a pie shop as its warm aromas came out to him and, after a moment's hesitation, went in and bought a meat pie, which he took out to eat on his way.

It started to rain and he searched for shelter. Across the street was a shop with a deep display foyer. He pulled up his jacket and ran across and in, pretending to admire the produce whilst he ate his pie. When he had finished, he took out a handkerchief and wiped his mouth. He folded it neatly before putting it carefully away in his coat pocket, and then looked around wondering what to do with the waste paper. The shop assistant, within whose foyer he was standing, had obviously drawn the conclusion that at the finish of the pie there would be rubbish to dispose of and he now made his presence perfectly apparent. Frank would not have dropped it anyway, but still felt quite guilty under his gaze. He looked out to see if the rain had stopped. It had, and a backward glance into the shop confirmed that it was time to leave. He waved cheerily as he did so, walking off in the direction of Regent Street, which he crossed before continuing on to the Haymarket. Here he stopped to consider his next move and then, on seeing that there was a cart just down the road collecting rubbish, he turned down towards Trafalgar Square.

He reached the cart and threw in the paper and was just about to turn back towards Piccadilly when he heard the noise of shouting and singing coming from the direction of the square and decided to investigate. As he neared the square, he realised that what he could hear was the sound of a demonstration of some sort. On even closer approach, he recognised that they were suffragettes standing in a tight group of about twenty, holding their placards and singing bravely, their backs to the National Gallery. Cat-calling men surrounded them, and in the square and beyond them a line of policemen, with truncheons drawn, were silently awaiting instructions. Suddenly a whistle blew and the policemen rushed at the women and started to manhandle them. The singing stopped, to be replaced with shouts and screams as the women were thrown to the ground and then dragged off to the waiting vans. Those still free began to scatter and run, only to be cornered by the men standing around and bounced back into the arms of the policemen.

A small group of women broke free from their tormentors and ran towards Whitcombe Street, where Frank was now standing against a small alcove in the wall, and as they got closer he recognised Violet amongst them. Her face was flushed and fearful and her cape, torn at the clasp, flapped uselessly off one shoulder. Her blouse was ripped at the arm, with a nasty scratch bleeding into the torn material. As the leading women passed him, Frank stood smartly back and then, just as quickly, stepped forward again to grab Violet, whirling her around and into the alcove, trapping her arms in his embrace even as a posse of policemen started up the street towards them. "Quiet," he hissed. "It's me, Frank Balfour... Frank Balfour from your father's office." She stared at him, her anger turning to recognition and then back to anger as she squirmed in his arms. "Miss Violet," he commanded. "Be still. Pretend we are together. Quick now, they're coming." Hurriedly he straightened her cape over her shoulders, pushed her hair back roughly into place and turned her around. "Deep breath now Miss Violet," he ordered. "Take my arm. We are out walking together. We are not part of the demonstration."

She turned to object but he paid no attention and instead patted her hand as he turned to face the oncoming policemen, adopting an open and enquiring gaze as they came up to them. Violet tried desperately to contain herself and still her heaving bosom. "Evening Officer," Frank called to one, who slowed down and looked enquiringly at them. "They went that way." He pointed up the street.

Another stopped, his hands on his hips, his body bent slightly forward as he fought, red faced, for breath. He raised his head and looked at the couple, his eyes narrowing in suspicion. "Come on Tim they're getting away!" one of his colleagues shouted from further up the road. He turned away from Violet, shaking his head. Frank tightened his grip on her arm and pulled her closer. The policeman took his hands off his hips and straightened, willing himself to run once more. "Coming," he shouted, and with one last look he turned and ran after his mates.

Frank waited until he was out of hearing and then breathed an audible sigh of relief. "Phew, I thought he was going to rumble us. Are you alright Miss Violet?"

Her anger now resurfaced and turned on the nearest recipient, who happened to be the man who had so recently and roughly saved her. "Of course I'm alright," she said imperiously, brushing her skirts down furiously. "Why shouldn't I be? You had no business detaining me like that. Kindly let me go."

Frank studied the angry young woman in front of him, his amusement rapidly failing in the face of this betrayal. "Certainly Miss Violet," he said icily. "If that will be all miss, I'll be getting along... and you can go and join your friends in the lock-up."

The angry face turned up to his, wavered and then crumpled. Her eyes filled and her bottom lip quivered. "Oh Mr Balfour, I'm so sorry. I was so angry and now I'm being beastly to you when... when you're only trying to help." Her voice broke in a rising tide of tears.

"Hush now." He dug into his coat pocket and took out his handkerchief to wipe her face, tenderly dabbing the tears from her cheeks. She took the handkerchief from him and blew her nose on it, then folded it and handed it back. He took it, looking down at the damp material as if wondering quite what to do with the now soiled object, a slight smile playing on his lips. She gazed at him for a moment and then, realising what she had done, started to laugh.

"Well Miss Violet," he said cheerfully. "We'd better be getting you home now, hadn't we? I think perhaps that you've done enough demonstrating and fighting for today."

The anger flared anew in Violet and she shouted at him. "That's what you'd like, is it? For all of us little women to just give up the fight and buckle to!"

"Hold up, Miss Violet. Hold up," he protested, his hands held aloft in surrender. "All I meant was that you've done your bit for today. There'll be another day, I've no doubt... no doubt at all."

The fury died once more in her and she apologised again. "Oh I'm so sorry, Mr Balfour. I'm being ungrateful and ungracious. It's just that... it's just that our struggle is such a hard one and we really can't give up now."

"That's quite all right, Miss Violet," he soothed, smiling in amusement at this mercurial young woman standing in front of him, tired, beaten, yet still inwardly bristling with indignation. He took her elbow to go and then realised that, in all the commotion, he had dropped his package. It languished in a filthy puddle, the paper undone and bearing the footprint of the policeman. A collar waved forlornly from the wreckage. "Oh dear, there go my new shirts," he moaned quietly. He bent down to retrieve the dripping parcel, but as he picked it up the paper parted and the shirts tumbled back into the mire.

Violet looked down at his new shirts lying in the dirty water. "Oh Mr Balfour, I'm so, so sorry. Your new shirts ruined... all ruined. Oh I must repay you... I'll get you some new ones or... or I'll have these washed." She bent down and picked up the dripping garments and stood holding them up to him.

As he stood there looking at her, her hair falling out, the cape once more slipping off her shoulder and her outstretched arms holding the filthy shirts, he started to laugh. At first it was a chuckle, but then it grew and at the end he was laughing wholeheartedly and pointing speechlessly at her.

For a moment she just watched him, but then she too started to giggle and then laugh outright. Soon the two of them were standing there roaring with laughter and holding their sides, their mirth only increasing when she once more dropped the shirts.

After a while, the laughter died down and he bent down, still chuckling, and gathered the soiled shirts into a bundle. "We'd better be getting along Miss Violet," he said as he stood up. "Your father will be worried for you and I've got to get back." She nodded silently, still trying to stifle a giggle as he led her down the street towards the square and searched for a suitable bus to take them north and home by means of various changes.

It was late when the final motor-bus crossed the Great North Road into Ballards Lane. Frank looked down at Violet's sleeping head resting on his shoulder and gently shook her. "Miss Violet. Miss Violet. We're nearly here. Nearly home. Wake up now."

She looked up bleary-eyed and blinking, seeming to forget where she was. Then she smiled, sat up straight in her seat, pushed her hair back into position and tried to adjust her cape. "I want to thank you for all of your kindness, Mr Balfour. Thank you for seeing me home safely." She looked down at his lap where the ruined shirts lay. "And I'm so sorry about your shirts. I will make recompense, I promise."

Frank cleared his throat. "Err, Miss Violet, I take it that Mr Matthews is not to know of your little outing."

"I think that would be best, don't you?" she said, returning his look as they alighted from the bus.

They walked in silence down Etchingham Park Road to her front gate. For a moment, the two of them stood looking around themselves, not sure of what to say or do next, but then he put out his hand for hers and shook it politely. "Good night Miss Violet. In you go now, and mind you pay some attention to that scratch on your arm."

She shook his hand. His grip was firm yet tender, and the pressure it exerted was comforting. "Good night Mr Balfour." She turned and walked through the gates, up the path and round towards the rear of the house. At the corner, she turned and looked back at him standing there, half hidden in the shade of the tree by the front gate. She walked quickly back to him. "Here," she whispered, "give me those shirts and I'll see what can be done for them." He handed her the package without a word and she ran back up the path. She waved. He waved back and then she turned and ran out of sight.

....

Late on Sunday afternoon the following week, Frank sat in a tearoom, hunched over his newspaper, reading intently as he stirred his tea. The spoon chinked against the cup edge as he digested the news. An old gentleman at the adjoining table coughed and looked meaningfully at him. He stopped stirring, put down the spoon and raised the cup to his lips, still staring into his newspaper. 'Loyalists resentful of Home Rule proposals', he read, shaking his head. It'll come to violence he supposed... would that there were another way... but...

He turned the page and read of the Kaiser and his military build-up. The seeds of war were being sewn, but none yet read the full runes. He folded the paper and put it down with a sigh. Enough of depressing news he decided, as he addressed himself to the teacake on his plate. He picked it up and took a bite, feeling the smooth warmth of the melted butter as it escaped from the corners of his mouth.

"Hello," said a woman's voice. "Mr Balfour."

He looked up in surprise and stood quickly, knocking the table and spilling his tea into the saucer. "Hallo Miss Violet," he spluttered, desperately reaching for the napkin and swallowing hard to clear his mouth. The teacake caught in his throat and refused to budge downwards, adding to his discomfort. "I'm sorry Miss Violet," he said, recovering his composure. "You startled me." He gestured to the spare seat at his table. "Do sit down. Tea?"

"Yes please," she said, "and there really is no need to be sorry Mr Balfour, it is I who have disturbed you in the middle of your tea."

He moved around the table, pulled back the chair for her to sit, settled her in it and then went back to his seat, motioning to the waitress.

"Another pot of tea please... for the lady," he called to the approaching girl as he sat himself down again. She nodded in reply and went back to prepare it. "Well what brings you in here, Miss Violet?"

"You do," she replied, giggling as she handed over the neatly wrapped parcel she was carrying and which he had failed to notice in the excitement of her arrival.

"Ah, the shirts I presume?"

"You presume correctly sir, as promised. As good as new, I'll warrant... well almost. Actually I couldn't quite get the mark of that policeman's big boot off the back of one of them, so don't take you coat off when you wear it."

"He's probably convinced to this day that we were up to no good at all. Still, we fooled him, didn't we?"

"We certainly did. Or rather you did Mr Balfour. You were so calm and assured and I was so ungrateful and horrid."

"You could never be horrid for me Miss Violet," he said, more tenderly than prudently, "...and please Miss Violet when we are alone... please call me Frank."

"Frank," she repeated. "Frank. Such a nice, strong name." She knew of course that his name was Frank, but now she savoured it like new and wonderful knowledge. "And you may call me Violet," she said brightly. "And we shall be such friends, shan't we Frank?"

"We will indeed," he said, "but between ourselves only I fear, for I doubt your father would approve."

"You leave my father to me," she said laughingly. "But in the meantime our friendship will be our secret." They both laughed and turned their attention to the tea that was by now arriving.

They chatted on for some time, breaking into laughter at frequent intervals, oblivious of the disapproving glares of the occupant of the adjoining table, until at length Frank made to stand, saying, "It's getting late... Violet." He spoke her name without the title for the first time and it felt strange... as if he had mistaken his station in life.

She felt his unease and moved to counter it by standing too and saying brightly, "Heavens yes, Frank, I was so engrossed that I forgot the time. You must forgive me."

"There you go again, Violet," he said, more confident now in the use of the name, "apologising again and all for nought. I've enjoyed our talk and I'd be honoured if you'd allow me to walk you home again." He crossed to the rear of the shop to pay for the teas and then re-joined Violet at the door and held it open for her as she passed through, bobbing under his outstretched arm with a mocking "Thank you kind sir."

Out in the street, the early November sky was dark and foreboding and a chill wind blew up her shawl and pinned her skirts against her legs. Around their feet the dry leaves of autumn swirled and rustled in mad circles before joining their compatriots in ever-increasing drifts. She shivered and he pulled her shawl down and back around her shoulders, feeling as he did the smooth outline of her upper arms. He proffered his arm to her and she took it as they bent into the wind to make their way back down the street towards Etchingham Park Road and her home.

Turning the corner, they came out of the wind and relaxed a bit, slowing their walk as if eager to extend their time together. "Where do you live Frank," she asked.

"Oh I have a room in a large house in Long Lane," he replied. "It's not much but I'm afraid it's all I can afford at the moment."

"Oh your family house isn't near here then?"

"No," he answered. "There's no family house as such. I was brought up by my aunt in Kent after the death of my parents."

"Oh I'm so sorry. I didn't mean to pry."

He laughed lightly, turning to face her. "What did I say? You're always saying sorry when there's really no need. My parents died when I was very young and I can hardly remember them really. My aunt raised me and my grandmother left me enough money to study and give me a grounding in life... which I'm now using to advantage in your father's offices." She nodded sagely, recognising for the first time that he did indeed have the trace of a country accent. "I'll not amount to much but my folks always dreamt of me being important... being in an office instead of working on the farms like all of my cousins."

"You must miss them," she said quietly. "You must feel terribly alone here without them all."

"Not really," he said. "Least not lately." He looked straight at her in the deepening gloom and in spite of herself, she felt her cheeks flush.

She railed against this betrayal of her inner feelings, hoping against hope that it did not show, yet still conscious of the thrill that ran through her. "But you must miss the countryside at least," she said in a voice that she prayed did not hint at the emotion within her.

"I miss it all right," he said. "Not so much now, but more in the spring and summer. The country can be a cold and uncomfortable place in the winter you know."

"I expect it depends on who you're with," she said, blushing again at her boldness, glad now that the gathering dark could not betray her.

They had reached the gates of her house and she turned to him. "Thank you so much for a lovely evening, Frank." She held out her hand for him to shake. "And thank you for the tea. We must do it again some time."

"I'd like that Violet," he said. "I'd like that very much."

"Well good night Frank." She walked up the path towards the door. He called softly after her. "Thank you for the shirts."

"Don't mention it," she whispered back, and then she was gone.

Unseen by either of them, the curtains in the front room twitched as the hand holding them aside in the dark was removed.

Frank stood for a moment in contemplation of the empty path, then shrugged his shoulders, hunched back into the cold and retreated back up the road.

Violet came into the hall, singing gaily as she took off her shawl, and looked at herself in the large mirror. Picking up the silver hair brush, which was always left on the dresser, she brushed her hair back into shape, placing the pins in her mouth as she released them. She started as a figure came from the darkened front room but then relaxed again. "Oh it's you daddy," she said through a mouthful of pins. "What are you doing in the front room all in the dark?"

"What am I doing, miss? What am I doing? It is more a case of what are you doing. Out at all times with men. Who was he, may I ask?"

"I am not out at all times with men," she said, feeling a hot surge of temper rising within. "A gentleman saw me safe home to the gate in the dark and that's all there is to it father." She always called him father when she was angry. He knew it and it only served to inflame his anger.

"Let's have less of that, miss," he said sternly. "A father has a right to know what his daughter is getting up to and with whom."

"Well this daughter is not getting up to anything wrong, sir," she said, raising her voice.

"Who's that out there?" came the voice of her mother from the drawing room.

It broke the tension and she turned from her father. "Only me mother," she called lightly. She glanced at her father and crossed to the door. "And daddy," she said as she entered. "How are you this evening?" Her father followed her to the door, muttered something inaudible and left.

Violet glanced back at the closing door and then turned back to her mother, sitting by the fire, a rug around her legs and another around her shoulders. "I thought for a moment the two of you were arguing."

"No mother," Violet lied. "Daddy was only asking where I'd been and I was telling him."

"Have you been anywhere nice dear?"

"Only to the tea rooms at the top mother dearest."

"What and back alone in the dark?" exclaimed her mother.

"No," Violet laughed. "A kind gentleman acquaintance walked me home."

"Oh good," said her mother relieved. "You can't be too careful you know. There are so many ruffians around."

"Don't worry mother. I know how to take care of myself. I'm a big girl now. Now, how are you more to the point? Have you had your tea? Is there anything I can get you or has Alice been looking in after you? Violet had always been adept at changing the subject with her mother, especially if it was back to her favourite subject... herself and her ailments.

"Alice brought me some tea a little while ago now, but I'd really like to go to my room if you'd help me please my dear. I've got such a headache and this chill is going right through me." She passed her hand over her forehead, sighed deeply and looked up expectantly at her daughter.

"Certainly mummy dearest. Let's get you upstairs." She helped her mother to her feet, folded the two rugs and tucked them under her arm, picked up the book she had been reading and guided her towards the door.

Elsie stopped halfway and turned back to her seat. "My glasses. I've left my glasses on the table beside my chair."

"I'll fetch them. Stand there a moment." Violet retrieved the glasses and led her mother through the door and across the hall to the foot of the stairs.

The kitchen door opened and Alice came out. "Ah there you are Ma'am," she said, wiping her hands on her pinafore. "I've lit a nice fire in your room and put a warmer in your bed. I'll bring you up some supper shortly."

"Thank you Alice," Elsie said weakly. "Thank you so much. Violet will help me to my room, won't you my dear?"

"Of course mother... that's where we're going. Now up the steps. One at a time now."

Ernest emerged from the front room, where he had been reading, and watched the two of them slowly mounting the stairs. "Goodnight Elsie," he called as he retreated back into his room.

"Good night Ernest, my dear," his wife called back without realising that her words no longer found a recipient.

In the bedroom, Violet sat her mother down on the armchair by the fire and placed one rug over her legs and another over her thin shoulders. "Is there anything more that you need mother dearest," she said soothingly. "I'll get Alice to bring you some warm water to wash with shortly and she can help you into bed."

"Thank you darling," her mother said weakly. She closed her eyes and turned her face to the warmth of the fire as Violet drew the curtains and stole from the room.

Downstairs, she knocked softly on the front room door and entered. Her father was sitting in his chair reading some papers he had brought from the office. He looked up as she entered and then back down at his papers. "Oh it's you, is it?"

She crossed the room and knelt down in front of him. "Sorry I shouted."

He pulled a wry face. "Sorry I shouted," he repeated. She smiled secretly to herself and rested her head into his lap. He put his hand on her hair and toyed with it. She closed her eyes.

....

Frank opened the door of the office and walked down the steps. 1 o'clock. He had half an hour for lunch. Better make the most of it. He hurried along the street towards the tea rooms. 'Lord I'm famished,' he thought. 'I should have had breakfast this morning instead of lying there in bed until it was too late. Serves me right.'

"Hello Frank."

He stopped. Violet stood in front of him, smiling up at him. "Hello Miss... Violet. How lovely to see you again so soon."

"Oh I'm just up here doing a bit of shopping for the kitchen. I saw you coming down the road and... well, what are you doing now?"

"It's my lunch break. I've got half an hour and then I must be back or face the high jump. I... err... I was just going in here. Umm... would you like to join me for a cup of tea?"

"I'd love to." She swung her basket on to the other arm and taking his, the two of them marched up to the shop door, and in.

They sat at the same table they had occupied the night before and he ordered tea for them both and a pasty for himself. "You're sure you don't want anything to eat?"

"No thanks, Frank. Alice will be making something for me and...

well I only came out for a little while." She shuffled with the basket
on her lap and he noticed that there was little or nothing in it. She
looked up at him. "Err Frank...". She put the basket down on the
floor beside her. "Frank, I was wondering... that is unless you've got
something else on. I was wondering if you would like to come to a
recital at the hall on Friday. It's for a good cause... the British Red
Cross Society and well..."

"I'd be delighted."

"You would?" She grinned broadly. "Oh that's marvellous. Oh I am
so pleased."

"What time is it?"

"I think it's about quarter past one. Why? Do you have to get back
now. I thought you had half an hour."

"No Violet," he said laughing. "I meant what time is the recital?"

She clapped her hands to her face in mock embarrassment, looking
over them at him. "Oh I'm sorry, I thought you meant... 7 o'clock."

"Shall I pick you up at your home?"

The smile left her face as the innocence of their association was
compromised and replaced by the recognition of the difficulties that
lay ahead. "No I... I think it would be better if I met you either here
or at the hall."

He looked across at her intently and went as if to speak. Then
thinking the better of it, shrugged his shoulders and addressed the
pasty, which had just arrived.

She leant forward, her expression concerned. "Look Frank, it's not
that... it's not that... well the truth is daddy..."

Frank swallowed his mouthful and wiped his lips with his napkin.
"I understand Miss Violet. Honestly I do."

"No you don't!" She was angry now at the tension that had arisen
between them, reinforced by his use of her title. She looked around
at the other occupants, some of whom had noticed her raised voice,
then turned back to him, bending forward and speaking softly. "My
father would be wary of me seeing any man, whoever it was. I... I'm

still his little girl. It would not be good for you right now if... well now do you understand?"

He put down his pasty, wiped his hands on the napkin and reached across to her hand lying on the table. "I'm sorry. I thought... well I thought..."

"Then you thought wrong, Frank."

"I thought wrong," he said in feigned humility. "Beggin' yer pardon miss." He tugged his forelock and they both laughed and chatted on for some time. After a while he stopped, looked up at the clock and gasped. "Oh my God, look at the time. I must be getting back."

She followed his look and got to her feet. "You go. I'll pay for this." He started to protest but she cut him short. "Go! You'll be late. Go."

He made for the door. "Friday, six-thirty, here?" she called.

"Six-thirty here? Right, see you then." And he was gone.

Over the following weeks, Frank began to get quite accustomed to apparently bumping into Violet by sheer chance on his lunch outings, but then they admitted that chance had nothing to do with it and it became a regular habit. Violet began to take her lunch with him at the tea rooms, explaining to Alice that as she was up in the town anyway she might just as well take her midday meal there.

On those occasions when Frank had to make trips to the City or the West End, and had sufficient notice, they would arrange to meet and she would accompany him. Sometimes that meant staying out until late in the evenings, although she always made sure, after that first night at the tea rooms, that he stopped just short of her house in order to avoid being seen.

Nevertheless, it did not go beyond the notice of her family, and Alice, that her routines had changed, and on more than one occasion she was challenged. To Alice she simply smiled and winked and that was the end of the matter, but she had to tell her father a white lie... well it wasn't so much of a lie, she reasoned. She told him that she was involved in the Red Cross, which was indeed true as she had indeed become a member of that organisation as well as the St.

John's Brigade, both of which were organised from the local church hall.

What she didn't say was that Frank, too, had enrolled at her instigation and that the two of them attended the meetings together. Twice a week Violet would be hugely amused by the attention he received from the young ladies, who made up the majority of the membership. In the bandaging and splinting demonstrations he got fairly used to spending most of the evening lying prone on the floor, being attended to by a bevy of excited females, and on those occasions when he could be persuaded to wear his reservists uniform to add some authenticity to the proceedings, the hall would resound to joyous laughter.

As the year drew towards its close, they began to be recognised as a couple, and in the small society which revolved around the hall, they began to be invited to functions as such. Most times an invitation would be made and graciously accepted in person, but occasionally they were delivered to the house, addressed to the two of them, making it necessary for Violet to make doubly certain that she was always around to intercept the post.

It wasn't that they wanted to deceive her family, it was just that they both felt that at this stage, to advertise their friendship wouldn't be helpful. They were helped, of course, by the fact that Ernest and Elsie had almost totally withdrawn from Finchley society. "How is your dear mother?" Violet would be asked. "Is she any better?"

"No better, I'm afraid," Violet would reply, "but you know..."

"And your father?"

Violet would smile knowingly and grimace. "Work," she would say, shaking her head.

"Ah yes, work," the enquirer would agree, and the ritual encounter would be over unless followed up by, "Still, nice of you to have the company of dear Mr Balfour", to which statement Frank would smile obligingly before the two of them quickly made their excuses, stifling their obvious amusement.

"It's obvious they'd all love to tell your father about us, if only they could," Frank once remarked.

"But how can they," Violet replied laughing. "Daddy's always working and mother... well she hasn't been out in years."

"That doesn't mean that one of them might not come into the office... and then what?"

Violet laughed and grabbed his arm. "We're friends... we have the same interests. We meet in the company of others... what harm are we doing?"

"None at all," he replied. "None at all."

"Well then, let's not worry about it then," she said lightly. Frank pursed his lips and nodded and the moment passed.

....

In the raw December air, Frank and Violet stood together, hand in hand, watching and listening to the band playing Christmas carols. They struck up 'Hark the Herald' and Frank joined in, singing lustily in a rich tenor voice. Violet watched him as he sang. A fine man, she thought... kind and gentle yet strong and dependable. She always felt safe with him.

It would be difficult, if not impossible, for her father to accept any man who might want to take away his daughter, let alone an employee of his with no particular background and very little to offer. They were both good men, her father and this man who stood beside her singing joyfully. Still she had learnt from her father how to partition her life and that was certainly serving her in good stead now. Oh yes, Frank was from another class and some of the things he did rankled with her. At times his accent seemed broader and she watched for the reaction of others... but they never seemed to notice. If they were eating out, his table manners and the gusto with which he ate his food sometimes brought a grimace of distaste from her and she balked at the thought of her father's reaction, were he to see it. Frank, on catching her glance, would shrug his shoulders and smile apologetically, a strange lop-sided smile halfway between 'sorry' and 'what the hell'.

She squeezed his hand gently and he responded as he sang. 'What is it that I do so like in this man,' she pondered. He is from a totally different background... and so what? He's a good man. Oh how I wish we could bring things out into the open. After Christmas. Yes, after Christmas I'll broach the subject with both Frank and my father.

Frank was going away to the country to be with his relatives, and her parents were having it at home with Ernest's sister and her husband. "I do hope that you have a nice time in the country for Christmas, Frank," she said as the hymn finished. "I shall miss our little outings."

"Just the outings?" said Frank pretending offence. "Not me I suppose?"

"Silly... of course I'll miss you Frank. That's what I meant and you well know it." She dug him playfully in the ribs. "And I've got a present for you. Do you want to open it now here with me or would you rather open it when you're away?"

"Here with you. And you can open yours... which I just happen to have here in my pocket." He reached into his coat and took out a small packet that he handed to her.

She took it smiling delightedly and led him across to a bench where she sat, motioning him to sit beside her. "And here, Frank Balfour, is my Christmas present to you." She handed him a small, round leather box that he took and looked down at, wondering. "Go on open it," she said excitedly.

"No. You first."

"Oh all right. I tell you what, we'll both open them together." She carefully began opening the small parcel as he watched. He waited until she had nearly got it open and then began to prise the lid open, looking all the while at what she was doing. "Oh Frank, they're lovely," she said. "You shouldn't have. They must have cost far too much!"

She held out three dainty handkerchiefs with a monogrammed 'V' in the corner and looked up at him.

He smiled and then gasped as he flipped open the box to reveal a set of collar studs and cuff links with the letter 'F' engraved upon them. "My God Violet, they're gold aren't they?"

"Yes... and before you say a word Frank, you deserve them and I can afford them. I have my allowance you know and I can't think of a nicer person on which to spend for this Christmas. Besides, I bet these handkerchiefs cost a pretty penny... I shall treasure them all my life."

"And I these," said Frank. He bent across and kissed her on the lips, then pulled back quickly, looking around guiltily to see if they had been seen. Nobody seemed to have taken any notice. "I'm sorry Violet," he said ashamed. "I shouldn't have done that. Please forgive my impertinence."

Violet smiled warmly back at him. "Nonsense Frank Balfour, you should have done that some time ago. Here..." She leant forward and kissed him back. At first he just sat stock still, but then his arm went around her and they kissed passionately, oblivious to all around them. Eventually they parted, staring at each other in wonder. Over her shoulder he noticed a small boy staring at them intently and she followed his gaze. The boy stuck out his tongue and ran off, leaving Frank and Violet collapsed into each other's arms, laughing happily.

....

Christmas passed slowly for Violet, even as she dutifully went through all the motions of entertaining and being with her family. On the Monday, her father was glad when he was able to re-open the office, and Violet knew that Frank would, therefore, be back at work. Nevertheless, much as she longed to see him, she was kept busy entertaining her uncle and aunt until they finally left on the Wednesday. No sooner had their cab disappeared round the corner than she announced to Alice and her mother that she was off to see daddy in the office. She practically ran down the road to Ballards Lane and up the steps to the office, barely pausing to compose herself before entering. She took a deep breath and pushed open the door, looking straightaway at Frank's desk whilst cheerily saying, "Good afternoon Miss Crabb. I do hope you had a nice Christmas."

Frank looked up at the sound of her voice, unable to conceal his look of delight, thankfully seen only by Violet, as Miss Crabb had her back to him. "Very nice thank you Miss Violet," replied Miss Crabb, "...and you?"

"Yes thank you... busy but enjoyable." She passed by Miss Crabb who, having finished this ritual banter, put her head back into her books and presumed that she would go on up to her father. Instead, Violet stopped at Frank's desk and addressed him. "Good afternoon Mr Balfour. I do hope that you too had a good Christmas."

"Very nice thank you Miss Violet," he said, smiling at her as they conducted a conversation which had little or nothing to do with the actual words spoken. "Mind, I did miss some dear friends."

"Oh how sad," she said, trying to sound concerned. "From the tea rooms I've no doubt. Still you'll be able to make their re-acquaintance this evening, I feel sure."

"No doubt at all Miss Violet. No doubt at all."

She grinned secretly at him, and with a final "Oh I'm so pleased" breezed up the steps to her father's office, knocked and entered.

....

In the weeks and months that followed, they continued to meet secretly at the tea rooms or the park. The slight unease that he had felt with her at the onset of their friendship had long since disappeared, and as they spent more time together he began to learn from her and adopt her more gentle mannerisms. Their friendship grew ever more important for them both and she pressed him for his consent to approach her father, seeking his blessing for their meetings. Frank was at first reluctant. Not because of any denial of the strength of his, as yet undeclared, feelings for her but more for fear of a reaction that would of course jeopardise his job and curtail their outings. By the middle of March, however, the evenings were getting lighter and it became increasingly difficult for him to be able to walk her home unseen. He agreed that they should broach the subject with her father and she made up her mind to talk to him on a Sunday afternoon, after which Frank was to turn up at the house and speak to Ernest before taking her out.

The Sunday came and Violet, as usual on the family's return from church, helped Alice in the kitchen with the lunch, which passed off normally, although Violet's mother was taken ill halfway through the meal and had to retire to her room. Ernest, although not a man for family occasions, was nevertheless a stickler for a traditional Sunday lunch, which for him meant roast beef with all the trimmings, and he showed some exasperation as it was interrupted by his wife's departure.

Violet waited until everything had settled down and she was alone with her father before speaking. "Daddy," she began. "I have been seeing someone and I... that is he and I would like your approval to continue to see each other." She stopped and looked down the table to where her father sat toying with his meal.

He put the forkful of food into his mouth and chewed silently, looking all the while down at his plate as if contemplating the next morsel. The silence in the room became noticeable, but Violet waited while he finished chewing and swallowed. He put down his knife and fork to the side of his plate and picked up his glass of red wine to take a sip, before gently putting it back down. "And who may I ask is this man?"

"It is Frank Balfour daddy... your clerk."

"My clerk! My clerk!" His explosion of contemptuous anger, coupled with a desire not to sound too loud, caused his voice to take on a hissing tone. "You've been seeing one of my employees?"

"Not just one of your employees daddy," she said in admonishment, her voice rising to his obvious annoyance. "Frank happens to be an employee of yours... yes, but he's more than just that."

"He's a man with no background, no real prospects and no real means of keeping the likes of you miss," said Ernest with barely concealed disdain.

"He's a good man daddy. I have become very fond of him and I would only ask that you respect my opinion of him."

"And do you respect my opinion miss? Do you accept my opinion that this affair should go no further. Why... why... for God's sake can't you see girl that he's not of our class, nor ever shall be?"

She quailed at the ferocity of his attack, but it was not for nothing that they were father and daughter and the temper within her drove her back on to the attack. "I have told you of my friendship for a decent man who has done much to elevate himself from humble beginnings father. I hope and pray that you can accept that friendship."

"And how far would this affair between you get if I was to terminate his employment? You seem to forget miss that I not only provide his living but that I also provide yours." He warmed to his subject now. "I have a right to demand that this relationship cease forthwith."

"You could indeed do that father," she said coldly, and he instantly recognised the use of the formality. "You could indeed do that, but you would lose the love of a daughter. Are you prepared to risk that?"

"Are you prepared to throw away all that you have... all I've given you for this... this man who can hardly keep himself, let alone you?"

"It is not I who will make that choice father, but you. I have merely asked to be able to associate with a good man... a friend. There is nothing more to it at present. It is you who is being unreasonable."

Ernest's mind churned. The time he had perhaps unknowingly dreaded for years had come. Was he prepared to risk the love of his only daughter... one had to uphold standards. Ah yes but... principles were one thing. He hesitated before committing himself to the next step, thinking quickly whilst eating another mouthful of what now seemed a tasteless meal. How old was she now? Nineteen or thereabouts... a woman now. He thought about his life and how empty it would be without her, about the house and the running of it as Violet waited for his answer, hardly daring to breathe. He cleared his throat. "What are his intentions towards you exactly?"

"We have not made any plans yet daddy." Ernest registered the renewed use of the familiar 'daddy' as she continued. "We simply enjoy each other's company at the present and that is as far as it goes. Whether it will develop further has to be seen."

The chink of light was there! He had time to discourage this unfortunate association and perhaps... perhaps in due time it would cease of its own accord. God knows she must eventually see through the fellow. He cleared his throat again. "I do not." He paused then continued. "No, I cannot agree that this affair is correct and I will not alter my position on that. I will allow this man to call for you, but as your friend and without any granting of approval."

"Oh thank you daddy," she gushed. "That's all we ask. Oh I know that you'll grow to like him, I just know it."

He held his hand up to silence her. "I have said to you that I do not approve and that is my position. I will make that clear to this young man when I see him. Is that understood?" She nodded silently and he continued. "In the matter of his employment, I will wish to keep your relationship with this man separate from that fact, otherwise I shall be forced to consider his position. Do I make myself clear?"

It was far from what she had hoped for, but a long way removed from that which she had feared. She decided that this was enough for today and that it was best that matters rested there, so she said quietly. "I understand daddy dearest. I understand. Frank is coming here to pick me up this afternoon at about 3 o'clock. Would you wish to speak with him then or would you rather wait until another day?"

"I will speak to Mr Balfour in my own time if you please," he said, and then, as if wishing to dismiss the subject, "Is Alice ready to bring in the dessert or is she still with your mother?

"I'll see to that," Violet said. "I expect that she's busy with mother." She wiped her mouth on her napkin, folded it neatly and picked up her plate with her father's and left the room.

Ernest, left alone in the room, sat and stared out into the garden. He had suspected that there was someone. He had even seen the figure of a man when she had returned one night as he watched from the darkened front room. What he had not imagined was that this someone would be an employee of his and he considered the implications. Would this man now expect preferential treatment at the office? Would he take advantage of the situation in an endeavour to improve his status within the company? He damned well would not, he thought. The man was a good worker, but he was only a clerk and he possessed no qualifications whatsoever for advancement beyond that state... not within his company at least. He would see to it that this affair withered on the vine. In the meantime, there was little point risking the loss of his daughter's affections for something which might not in any event progress.

Violet came back into the dining room and the meal continued more or less normally to its conclusion, in almost complete silence.

As she left the dining room, Violet resolved that she should head off Frank at the front door when he called that afternoon and busied herself with getting ready to leave as soon as he arrived. She watched for him coming down the road and when she saw him, quickly put on her hat and coat and met him at the front door before he could even ring the bell. "Hallo Frank," she said cheerfully as she pulled the door shut after her, took his arm and turned him around to guide him back down the path to the gate and out into the road.

"Do I get the feeling you're trying to get me away from here," said Frank, half amused and half annoyed.

"You do sir," said Violet, continuing to propel him away from the house. "I've spoken to daddy and I honestly think it would be best to leave it at that for now."

"You mean he didn't take too kindly to the idea of us being friends?"

"Oh I think if he thought it was just a friendship he wouldn't mind really," she said. "But I think he is looking ahead."

"And are we... looking ahead I mean?" asked Frank playfully.

"Why Frank Balfour, I don't know what you mean," Violet replied coquettishly, and they both laughed as they continued up the street.

....

Ernest entered his office the next day in his usual manner with a perfunctory "Good morning" to Miss Crabb as he strode to the stairs and up to his office. However, just before entering, he called down to Frank and asked him to come up to his office immediately, before pulling the door shut with a bang.

Frank looked up and across to return Miss Crabb's quizzical stare with his own questioning glance. He put down his pen, stood, adjusted his jacket and walked upstairs. At the top he knocked, waited for the command to enter and went in.

Ernest was sitting at his desk, but with the chair turned around looking out of the window, his back to Frank. He said nothing, and after what seemed like an age of silence Frank was forced to say, "You asked to see me sir."

The seated figure remained still, seemingly preoccupied with something outside and well beyond Frank's vision. Then he said curtly. "Yes. I do wish to see you young man." He swung round and fixed Frank with a glare. Frank stood, not knowing whether to move forwards towards the desk or back to the door as he waited for the next words from his employer. "I understand you've been seeing my daughter?"

"We've become friends, yes sir," said Frank, becoming bolder now that the original intimidatory tactic was over.

"I am very fond of Violet."

"You sir, will refer to my daughter in the confines of this office as Miss Violet. Is that understood?"

"Perfectly sir," said Frank, with a heavy emphasis on the salutation.

"I do not approve of this liaison Mr Balfour. I do not approve at all and I have made my position clear to my daughter." He leant forward over his desk and fixed Frank with a cold stare. "Do I make myself clear sir?"

"Do I take it sir that you are forbidding Miss Violet to see me?" Frank asked.

Ernest remained quiet for a moment. Then his posture visibly slackened and he shook his head slowly. "You know, full well, sir, that I am not prepared to risk the loss of my daughter's affections. That does not mean however that I am prepared to condone your association with her and it does not mean that I will not take all necessary steps to make sure that she sees the error of her ways." He stood behind his desk and leant forward, balancing on his knuckles. "Good God man, do you not see that this affair is as misguided as it is mismatched?"

"I fear sir that you have misjudged me and my intentions towards Miss Violet, for whom I hold a great affection."

"Oh you hold a great affection for her, do you?" said Ernest, his voice full of heavy sarcasm as he sat back down. "And does this affection extend to being able to support my daughter in the manner and status of her accustom."

"I regret sir that I am not a man of many means, but I do hope for advancement..."

He was interrupted by a triumphant explosion from Ernest. "Ah!... and there's the nub of it sir!... your hope of advancement. Is that the reasoning behind this attachment to my daughter? Is it, eh? Tell me that."

"Sir," said Frank, "if you feel that to be the truth then I will offer you my resignation right here and now."

This last seemed to deflate Ernest and he sat back into his chair. "What exactly is your relationship, may I ask, with my daughter?"

"We are friends who enjoy many things together sir," said Frank candidly. "We have not taken matters any further than the pursuance of that friendship... but I must warn you that I hope to one day earn the love of your daughter."

"It would be more to the point if you earned enough to support my daughter if that were the case, but we both know the likelihood of that, don't we?"

Frank pulled himself upright and stared defiantly at the older man. "I think we both understand each other's position fully sir. Do I take it that you will require my resignation?"

"You take nothing of the sort," snorted Ernest. "I have acquainted you with my feelings and for now we will leave it at that. I require that you continue to perform your duties and I require also that your relationship with my daughter... for the short time that it persists, does not affect your work or judgement within this office. Do I make myself clear?"

"Perfectly sir. Will that be all sir?"

"That will be all," said Ernest, picking up the sheaf of papers on his desk and turning away from the younger man. For a moment, Frank considered the dismissive gesture, then he shook his head and walked to the door and out.

Outside he stood for a moment to catch his breath before descending the stairs to his desk, studiously ignoring Miss Crabb's enquiring gaze.

....

"What happened?" said Violet, taking his arm as he joined her on the corner at lunchtime.

"I'll tell you in a minute," said Frank, looking back over his shoulder at the office door, half expecting, half dreading its opening. He took

her arm and propelled her, protesting, along the street in his hurry
to get away.

It was a warm day and she'd packed a few goodies in a small
basket so that they could lunch in the park. The birds were singing
in the trees as the weak sunshine brightened up the spring air, and
as they neared the park other couples converged with them on the
gates, fanning out then along the various paths, looking for a suitable
bench or pitch on which to picnic. They slowed down as they reached
the anonymity of the open spaces and Violet was able to catch her
breath sufficiently to ask him once again what had occurred with
her father.

"Well, I've still got a job for the time being but he's not best pleased."

"Oh dear, I'm so sorry Frank. I'd hoped he would have calmed
down a bit since our chat but it would appear not."

"Never mind, the point is that we've told him of our friendship and
we don't have to skulk about any more. The rest is up to him."

"We don't skulk about you fool," she said digging him playfully in
the ribs. "Come on, let's go over there by the trees and put the rug on
the ground." They walked up the slope to the group of silver birch
trees. "Oh I do hope it's not too damp. What do you think?" she said,
afraid that perhaps her plans would not work out.

"I think that it's all right. It's a bit damp but I don't think it'll
come through as long as you don't mind having to dry out the rug
afterwards." He put down the basket and took the rug from her,
spreading it out on the ground. They both sat down and turned to
the business of eating, looking across, as they did, to observe other
couples similarly engaged.

"It's fun to watch other people, isn't it?"

"Yes. I wonder if they have the same problems as us."

"The truth is," she said, rolling across to him and looking up into
his serious face, "that all of them will have problems of one sort or
another... that's life."

"I suppose so." He shrugged his shoulders in that engaging habit she had by now got used to. "Anyway, it's not us who's got the problem, is it?"

"No it isn't, unless it is to decide who's having that last cake. Now that is a problem. An insoluble one if ever I came across one."

"No it's not," she giggled, reaching across and snatching it up. She broke it in half, handing one half to him with a grin, and the two of them sat there happily munching and chatting until it was time to clear up and get him back to the office. She walked him back, her arm in his, the basket now empty apart from the rug. As they neared the steps to the offices, the door at the top opened and Ernest came out. Frank stiffened visibly and stopped in his tracks. Violet held fast to his arm as Ernest came down the steps, his face expressionless.

"Hallo daddy. Are you going home now? If you are I'll walk with you."

"You'll be late Mr Balfour," he said without displaying any recognition of their togetherness.

"Yes sir. Sorry sir." Frank disengaged her arm from his. "Thank you for a lovely lunch time," he said graciously. He turned, briefly nodded to his employer and then ran up the steps and in.

As the door closed, Violet planted herself in front of her father, the basket held two-handed in front of her. "Daddy that was not called for." Ernest snorted and marched off down the street towards home. For the second time that day, Violet found herself trailing in the wake of one man in her life wishing to distance himself from the other.

April 1914

"You will come, won't you? Say you will. Oh please say you will."

"But Violet," he protested. "I'd be out of place at a suffragette march. All those women and me... in the middle of them all. I'd feel a fool. Couldn't I just wait around for you to finish and walk you home afterwards?"

"Why Frank Balfour. You old coward. You told me you believe in our cause, so why can't you give us your physical as well as your moral support?"

"It's just that... oh well, all right then I'll do it... but I shall feel uncomfortable. I'm not the demonstrating sort you know."

"We don't go there to feel comfortable Frank. We go there to advance our cause."

"Well at the first sign of any trouble, we're leaving. Is that clear?"

"Perfectly, and thank you Frank. It means so much to me that you will share my beliefs and stand with us." She stood on tiptoe and kissed him on his lips, then she stood away. "Well, if we're going we'd better get going. Come on, you'll enjoy yourself I promise, and we'll be back for tea and then tonight's recital in the church hall."

A bus arrived and they both got on and took seats close to the front, behind an elderly couple who sat stiffly in their seats staring straight ahead without talking. Violet giggled at Frank and he shot her a look as if to quiet her. The conductor approached. "Two tickets to Enfield please," said Frank to his enquiring look.

They settled down to the journey, chatting happily about the evening ahead. "Mrs Stuart has asked me if I will help with the teas this evening and I've said yes," said Violet. "You won't mind if I leave you a bit before the interval in order to help, will you?"

"Not a bit, as long as I don't get stuck with that Miss Jones again. I can't stand her simpering silly conversation."

"I'll ask her to give me a hand and that will solve that. Ah, here we are, and there are our friends all ready for the march."

She motioned to a group of about ten women standing on the corner and made as if to rise from her seat. The old couple in front of them saw from the banners being held the purpose of the event and tutted to each other, turning round and staring at them both as they rose.

"If you ask me sir, a man should have better things to do than to associate with such silly ideas," said the man.

"I didn't ask you sir," said Frank, "..and I had no intention of doing so."

The older man snorted in anger and his wife clutched his arm in horror. "How dare you speak to my husband like that," she cried shrilly.

"He was the one who started the conversation, madam," said Frank. "I have the right to voice my opinion. Good day to you. Come Violet, let us join our friends." He stood in the aisle and held out his hand to Violet to assist her. She took his arm and left her seat, feeling as proud of her man as any woman could.

On alighting from the bus, they walked across to the little group where Violet introduced Frank to her friends. "Right then," said their leader. "Let's get going. We are to march down the street to the market square and then line up and declare our position. There is no intention to confront the authorities in any particular fashion on this day, but if we are faced with any hostility I suggest that we disperse as quickly as possible. Our aim today is to bring our message to our sisters and to make people think."

They formed up in a group four abreast and the women started to sing and hoisted their banners aloft. Passers-by stopped and stared at them as they marched off down the road, but there was little or none of the animosity that Frank had witnessed at the Trafalgar Square demonstration. Instead, there was some amusement and, in some cases bemusement, that something such as this was in their town rather than far off in the city. Frank relaxed and began to enjoy the walk with Violet on his arm, joining in with the singing, even if at times he had to mouth the words he was unsure of.

The march passed off peacefully and they approached the square, with its little open market house, in good spirits and formed a group at the base. Two policemen stood about twenty yards away in front of the church and observed them, obviously waiting for instructions, and various passers-by stopped to look inquisitively at their small gathering. Suddenly Frank noticed Violet's father amongst the onlookers, and as he recognised them, he came across to them.

"Is this the sort of thing you persuade my daughter into Balfour?"

Violet stepped forward quickly before Frank could answer. "Daddy," she cried happily. "Have you come to join us too?"

"Certainly not Violet," he retorted. "Whatever are you thinking of, associating with this rabble?"

"Now then Mr Matthews, there's no cause to insult these good people," said Frank at last, stung into a defence.

"No cause eh. No cause. You bring my daughter out to illegal gatherings and you say there's no cause. Why..."

"Frank hasn't brought me out to anything father," shouted Violet above their voices. "I have persuaded him to accompany me. This is my belief and he lends me support in it."

"What on earth is a man doing consorting with suffragettes? It beggars belief. It really does!"

Frank ignored the insult and instead stared over Ernest's shoulder at the policemen, who had now been joined by several others. He tugged at Violet's arm. "Violet," he said urgently. "It looks as if there might be trouble and... well you did promise that at the first sign..."

Violet turned and looked at the policemen and then called across to their leader. "Hazel! They seem to be working up to something. What shall we do?"

Hazel looked in the direction of the opposition and then hastily called everybody together. "It looks as if we're in for some trouble ladies... and gentlemen," she added, nodding at Frank and Ernest.

"Not me, I'm no part of your silliness!" Ernest exploded. He hurried across and away from them, calling over his shoulder for Violet to follow him, and when she didn't, stood impotently at the other side of the square looking red faced and angry.

Hazel watched his departure with some amusement, as did they all, and Violet felt a twinge of sympathy for her father being the butt of such amusement. "I suggest that when they ask us to disperse we do so. I feel that we have made our point today and that confrontation would be counter-productive. Are we agreed?"

"Agreed" came the chorus of response, except for one old lady dressed in black with a high lace collar and a wide-brimmed hat.

"Why should we give way to them? I say that we should stay," she called out shrilly.

"Not today Doris. Please let us leave it at this today and not cause any animosity. Please... for today?"

"Oh all right then, but mark my words, it doesn't always do to appease."

"I know dear, but the idea was that for today we would bring our message to the townspeople and I feel that we have achieved that."

"I must ask you people to disperse immediately," said a gruff voice and they all turned their attention from Doris to the policeman who had crossed the road to address them.

"We are just going," said Hazel. "Ready ladies? Thank you for your support all of you... and Violet's young man of course. If only there were more like him. Eh girls?" Violet positively brimmed with pride.

....

Spring gave way to summer and the talk in all the cafes and amongst people with an interest in politics revolved around the two prominent issues: Ulster and the looming threat of war in Europe. In late June, the heir to the Austro-Hungarian throne was assassinated in Sarajevo and the talk began to turn to the inevitability rather than the probability of war. Time and time again Frank tried to talk to Violet about the seriousness of the situation, knowing that if war was declared he would certainly be called up and that, as a reservist, he might well be required even earlier. Violet seemed not to want to understand the implications and refused to contemplate the suspension of their relationship for what to her seemed relatively unimportant events in far off lands.

They had never actually discussed the depth of their feelings for each other, but Frank realised that he was rapidly falling in love with this intriguing young woman. What had started out as innocent friendship was becoming ever more important to them both. As it did, the content of her father's lecture to him back in March began to weigh heavily upon him and he began to recognise the truth in what the older man had said. How indeed could he ever hope to provide for her in his current circumstances?

Violet, of course, now knew full well that she loved Frank, despite the relative shortness of their acquaintance. She waited for him to declare his feelings for her, and in the meantime was happy to see him whenever she could and to share his life with him as far as was possible given the continued coolness of her father towards their association.

As the evenings grew longer, they took to walking in the park and he would tell her of his life back in Kent. She listened as he described how he had won a scholarship to Kent College. How his family had scrimped and saved to enable him to take it up, and the deep feelings of isolation that he'd experienced as the poor farm boy thrown in amongst his hostile betters. He told her of joining the school's Officer Training Corps and repeated to her that, as a reservist, he would probably be amongst the first to be called up when the war was entered. She listened but she didn't really hear, refusing to contemplate the full import of his words. For her life revolved around Finchley and the world was a place that could never touch her.

With the news from Europe getting grimmer, Frank resolved one last time to try and make her understand. He suggested a picnic at Muswell Hill, where they could spend the day looking out over London and he could try to explain all of his feelings to her and sow the seeds for the break he knew must come. Violet jumped at the opportunity and entered into the spirit of the occasion by baking a whole stack of different cakes and packing the wicker hamper with all sorts of goodies.

Came the day and he arrived at the house to pick her up, with her all ready and waiting for him in the hallway with everything packed. "By God Violet, we'll need a pack horse to carry it all."

"Nonsense," she replied laughing. "You carry the hamper and I'll manage this bag with the rugs in. We'll get along fine."

"You're sure you can manage that?" he said concerned.

"Of course I can silly. See it's not that heavy." She handed him the bag and he hefted it in his strong arms. It was indeed not as heavy as it looked and he handed it back to her with a smile as they set off on their outing.

Later that afternoon, lying on the rug after their picnic, he turned to her and said, "Violet, I have to talk to you seriously."

"Of course you do Frank, dear. Of course you do," she laughed. "Don't you always talk to me seriously?"

"I mean seriously about us." She stopped laughing and paid attention to him, expecting him to declare his feelings for her at last.

Frank looked into the distance and continued. "I have become very fond of you Violet and I enjoy our meetings and outings... but I have to tell you that I am not a man of means and I have very little to offer a young lady such as yourself."

"Fi! Frank Balfour. Do you think I'm just after you for your money?" she said, digging him in the ribs and failing to see that what he was saying would lead up to exactly the opposite of her hopes. "I don't want to talk about money. It's vulgar and it's such a lovely day. Let's talk about something nice."

He perceived that this tack wasn't working so he tried another. "I believe that war is imminent, you know, and I feel that I must enlist. I shall be away for some time."

"Nonsense Frank Balfour. If anybody has the stupidity to declare war on England they had better watch out. And if you go, we'll win all the sooner and you'll be back before you know it and I shall be waving the flag for my hero."

"Violet, I'm trying to be serious," he said exasperated.

"No you're not Frank... you're trying to upset me and spoil my day and it's not fair. Now come on, I'll race you down the hill and back up again." She stood up, took hold of his arm, hauled him to his feet, picked up her skirts showing her pretty legs and started to run down the grass. He watched her go. The moment had been missed and would not come again that day. He shrugged his shoulders and ran after her, catching her up and then overtaking. At the bottom of the slope he waited for her to arrive and just as she did, he started back up to their rug, leaving her trailing behind.

He reached the starting point and flopped down on the rug waiting for her return. Eventually she came panting up the hill, complaining bitterly at his beating her. She dropped on to the rug beside him where they both lay, red faced and blowing from their exertions, laughing happily between gasps for breath.

'Ah well I tried,' he thought, 'but for now there's nothing for it but to make the best of today and to try another time.'

The following Tuesday evening, Frank arrived at the house to collect Violet in order to attend brigade classes and, to his dismay, she was not yet ready. Alice, who had opened the door to him, asked him to wait in the hallway and he stood uncomfortably, hoping against hope that he would be spared the embarrassment of having to come face to face with his employer, who he knew full well was in the adjoining drawing room. But his hopes were dashed as the door opened and Ernest emerged. "A word with you please, Mr Balfour," he announced, before turning and walking back into the room, obviously not thinking for one moment that his command would not be obeyed. He stood by the open door as Frank passed him and motioned him to one of the leather chairs in the bay. Ernest shut the door firmly, crossed the room and sat down in the other chair. He was silent for a moment but then he said. "What do you make of this business in the news Balfour?"

It wasn't the question or the topic of conversation that Frank had been expecting and he had to think fast in order to give an answer. He coughed politely and leant back in the chair. "Well sir," he began. "I take it that you are referring to the Sarajevo affair and what has followed?"

"Quite so. Bad business eh? It's certainly going to make a mess of all of our lives."

"It does rather depend on the reaction of the Austrians sir. But I do fear that it means war."

Ernest leant forward and across to Frank. "And what is your position in that eventuality."

"My position is quite straightforward sir," Frank replied without hesitation. "I am a reservist and shall enlist. I have endeavoured to warn Violet... that is Miss Violet... of this but I fear..."

The older man cut him short. "I believe Balfour that you owe it to my daughter to desist in this affair before any further harm is done. You have little or nothing to offer her in the way of property and prospects and now you are effectively planning to leave." He waved his arm in the air as if to brush away any misconception. "I don't mean that I disagree with your principles. Far from it. I have to say that I admire them... but..." He left the question open.

Frank cleared his throat. "I have indeed been considering my position since our last talk sir and I have to say that I recognise the merit in your argument."

Ernest didn't respond. He was the fisherman. The bait was being taken. The strike was imminent. He looked across at this troubled young man. A half decent fellow, he thought. The moment passed.

Half decent or not, the truth was that he had probably come as far as he was going to in life and if all he could ever offer his daughter was life in rooms with a herd of dirty brats around her skirts and the bailiffs around the corner, that was simply not good enough... no sir, not for his Violet.

Frank sat there mulling it over in his mind. The turmoil showed on his face and his brow furrowed. "I have attempted to discuss the situation with Violet sir," he said. "She is not always that easy to get through to. When she doesn't want to hear something, she doesn't hear it."

"Now there's the truth," said Ernest, raising his eyes to the heavens. "But as a man it's your responsibility."

Frank stood up, pulled his jacket down and turned to Ernest. "I thank you for your time sir. I will think on our conversation and act upon it as I see fit."

He turned towards the door. Ernest stood and crossed the room ahead of him to open the door. He held out his hand to Frank and shook his, saying, "Good luck Balfour. I know that you'll do the correct thing and I wish you well."

"Thank you sir," said Frank and he turned into the hall just as Violet came down the stairs.

"Sorry to keep you Frank," she called, and then, seeing her father and Frank shaking hands, a broad smile broke out on her face. "Oh I'm so pleased to see the two of you are getting along together. Come Frank we'll be late." She took his arm and led him to the front door and out. "Bye daddy," she shouted to the closing door. "See you later."

......

My dearest Violet,

I am writing this letter in haste as I am leaving for the station on my way to enlist.

For some time I have been trying to tell you that, fond of you as I am, I cannot hope to offer you anything more than my friendship. I do not feel that it would be fair to take any further advantage of you and I feel that it is best that I leave now.

It is almost certain that war will now be declared and I have told you of where I feel my duty lies. Please find it in your heart to forgive me for my cowardice in not telling you this face to face.

I have discussed the situation with your father and he agrees that this course of action is the best one for us both. I shall always treasure our friendship and I wish you all the luck and the love in the world.

Regards

Frank"

Violet sat quite still in the chair in the front room and read the letter again and again through the tears welling in her eyes. "Oh Frank. Oh Frank you fool," she said aloud. "You fool."

The tears flowed freely down her cheeks and she reached into her pocket and took out a handkerchief. She wiped her eyes and then, seeing the monogrammed 'V' on it, burst out crying once more. At length she stopped and pulled herself together, looked out into the late July morning and read the letter yet again.

After a time she stood up and folded the letter neatly. She put it into her skirt pocket, left the room and hurried upstairs. Fifteen minutes later she came back down the stairs dressed to go out, carrying a large overnight bag in one hand and a sealed envelope in the other. She tucked the envelope into the corner of the mirror, where she was certain it would be seen, and left the house.

......

"All change. All change!" the Station Master called as he walked importantly down the platform in his smart uniform. "All change!" He reached the carriage in which Violet sat, looking anxiously out of the open window. "Tenterden miss. This train stops here."

"Oh dear," said Violet, gathering up her bags and alighting on to the platform. "When's the next one to Rolvenden?"

"Not another one now miss," said the man with that relish reserved for the giving of bad news to hapless members of the public by officialdom. "You'd be quicker off walking if it's the station you want. The station's nowhere near Rolvenden itself you know. Where are you making for?"

"Pudding Cake Lane."

"Oh well, that's only about half a mile up the hill from Rolvenden Station. Nowhere near the village itself."

"So when's the next train to Rolvenden Station?"

"Not 'till tomorrow morning miss. Like I say, you'll be better walking."

Violet picked up her bags and started to walk off the platform. "Tickets please," shouted the man stopping her in her tracks. She put down the bag and fished in her pocket for the ticket. He punched it slowly and deliberately and handed it ceremoniously back to her. She looked at it and then back at him. "Used tickets in the bin there please miss," he said, motioning towards the platform gate.

"Which way do I go?"

"Straight up Station Road... here... to the High Street and turn right. Go along the High Street to the end of town and down the hill. Keep going straight. Don't take the Cranbrook Road. Cross the railway line at the bottom of the hill and then go up the hill to near enough its brow and you'll see it on your left."

"Thank you," said Violet, picking up her bag again and starting up the hill.

"Who are you looking for up there," the Station Master called out.

"Mrs Long," she called back, stopping.

"Mrs Long. Mrs Long," he mused as she shuffled, impatient to be off.

"Jesse Long," she said helpfully. "Mrs Jesse Long." She put down the heavy bag.

The penny seemed to drop. "Ah you mean Jesse Long," he said.

"Precisely," said Violet, relieved that this particular conversation seemed to be nearing a climax.

"Funny you should ask about her. Her nephew Frank came through yesterday. He wasn't very talkative though."

"Thank you so much," said Violet. She picked up her bag and trudged up the hill, past the church to the High Street. On her left was the Vine public house and she could see through the windows that it was fairly full, with young men drinking and singing. Outside, union flags were flying and she guessed that the situation in Europe had deteriorated even further. She knew of the Austrian ultimatum to Serbia and a woman on the train had told her of the Kaisers' reported anger at London's attempts at mediation. It was July 31st. Half the world held its breath whilst the other half celebrated. "Oh God I hope I'm in time," Violet muttered out loud as she hurried on down the High Street, past all the little shops set back and down from the road behind wide pavements and grassy verges planted grandly with plane trees, as if in pretension of a London street. No, not like a London street she thought, for here they had air to breathe and space to grow in.

Reaching the end of the town by the Rye Road she noticed another public house full of young men making merry. She shook her head in despair. What on earth are they doing? What is at about men that makes them revel in the thought of war. She knew for certain that Frank, for all his damned enthusiasm about enlisting, would not be revelling. He for one would take the step he was taking with a cool head, not inflamed and bolstered by alcohol.

It was a warm evening and she stopped to rest for a moment, putting her bag on the ground beside her. A cart drawn by a small coloured horse came down the High Street towards her, driven by an old man wearing a battered felt hat and smoking a long straight pipe, which he held between his teeth in such a manner as to give his face an upward twist. He drew to a halt beside her and touched the brim of his hat. "Need a lift miss?" he said. "Where're you goin' to now?"

"Pudding Cake Lane," she replied. "Are you going near there?"

"No miss, I'm going as far as the station if that'll help any."

"I would be most grateful," said Violet, picking up her bag and slinging it into the back of the cart. "Where shall I go?"

"Sit on the tail if'n I were you... and hold tight."

Violet clambered up on to the tail of the cart with as much dignity as she could maintain and, at a cluck from the driver to the horse, it moved off slowly down the hill. Violet swung her legs loosely over the tail of the cart and watched the scenery passing by. She noticed the strange-shaped buildings that she would later learn were oast houses. Round brick buildings with tall conical roofs, finishing in a hood of white-painted wood with a vane on the very top. They were set in groups of two to four close by the farmhouses, which slept there in the sun of that summer's evening. As the cart passed each one, dogs tumbled out of their yards to bark, running alongside until they deemed it to be out of their territory. They neared the bottom of the hill and the railway crossing, where the old man turned the horse into the yard by the station and stopped. "Far as I go miss," he said as he climbed out of the cart and came round to the back. She handed him her bag and he put it on the ground and held out his hand to help her off.

She took his hand and jumped down. "Thank you kind sir. Thank you very much."

"You're welcome miss," he said, and then walked off into the station yard without a backward glance. Violet looked around and up at the hill she was about to climb, took a deep breath, picked up her bag and set off.

Just after the level crossing the road crossed a small stream and she leant on the wall and looked down into the slowly moving waters. She was not used to clear water and was amazed at the fact that she could see fish swimming in the current. All she had known before was the canal with its opaque brown reflecting the sky, giving no hint of what lay below. In the fields on either side of the road sheep grazed, their well-grown lambs gambolling around them. Further up along the stream where the valley sheltered them, the fields changed and she could make out the verdant darkness of the hop gardens. The air smelt clean but heavy with the scents of a late summer's evening. It had been a long day and she realised that she was getting tired and not a little hungry.

She turned to tackle the hill, determined now to make it to the top and the junction of the lane before stopping again. Impatient as she was to reach her destination, she began to think of what she had done and what was ahead of her. Would her father come after her? No, he probably wouldn't know where to go unless he too thought of enquiring at Frank's old rooms, as she had. No he wouldn't... would he? He might. Well, let him then. He had caused this situation to a large extent. Frank was a good man and daddy had given him no encouragement or help. He had done all in his power to frustrate their relationship and now... well he could stew in his own juice for a while.

But what about Frank, she thought. What would his reaction be? She passed a little cottage on the left with hanging baskets spilling cascades of colour down its neatly whitewashed walls. Would he be pleased to see her? Was she making a mistake about her belief in his real feelings towards her? He had never declared his love. What if she were wrong and he didn't care for her? God, that would be embarrassing. She paused briefly and stood there holding her bag and thinking. No! She'd come this far and she would go on, she thought, starting once more up the hill. He owed her a full explanation and she wasn't going to be fobbed off with a short, curt letter from somebody who she had cared for and who she believed cared for her. He would have to tell her face to face... like a man... if he really didn't want to see her again.

She reached the corner of the lane and put the bag down for a breather. Lilac Cottage was the name of the house she was searching for. Lilac Cottage, Pudding Cake Lane. What a wonderful and emotive address. She could hardly wait to see if the reality fulfilled the dream.

She walked on down the lane, pleased now to be walking on the flat rather than uphill. The lane had hedges on either side and she couldn't really see what lay beyond. A yellowhammer sat on the top of a wild rose singing his song of "Little bit of bread and no cheese" and a yaffle laughed in the distance... sounds she heard but would only identify much later when they became familiar.

A row of small cottages came into view on the left. White painted to the lower floors with clay tile hanging to the upper floors and tiled roofs. The first one had no name that she could see and the middle one was called Rose Cottage so she presumed that the last one was the one she sought. Violet put her bag down to gather herself together, wiping her brow with one of the handkerchiefs he had given her and adjusting her dress, which had gone awry. Then she took a deep breath, opened the little gate, walked down the pathway to the front door and knocked.

A large woman in her mid forties answered the door. She was dressed in a long skirt with a cream-coloured blouse blooming out over her ample bosom and buttoned up to the lace collar at her neck. Her greying hair was piled up on top of her head in a bun, but what immediately struck Violet were her eyes. They were the same colour as Frank's and bore the same laughter lines around them. Violet knew that she was at the right house.

"Yes love," said the woman in a deep and resonant voice, which again reminded Violet of Frank when he was singing. "Can I help you?"

"I'm Violet. Is... is Frank here please?"

The woman smiled a knowing smile that spoke of warmth and welcome. Violet knew that here, on this doorstep, whatever happened, she had found a friend. "I'm Jesse. Frank's auntie," she said, stating for Violet what was now quite obvious. "He's in the back garden under the apple tree having a drink and I fancy he'll be pleased to see you my dear."

"Oh thank God," said Violet. "Thank God I'm in time." Her eyes... damn them, she thought, welled with tears. Jesse opened her arms and Violet stepped into the warmest embrace she could have ever imagined... a feminine embrace such as she had only dreamt of through the long years of her mother's infirmity.

After a while, Jesse released her and stood her back. She reached into her skirt pocket for a clean handkerchief and wiped Violet's eyes, for all the world as a mother would a child's, pressing her hair into place, stroking her cheek and saying quietly, "Come this way my love and I'll show you where he's at." She led Violet through the little house and out to the back door. "Down the path under the tree. I'll leave you two for a bit. I was just going to make a pot of tea... now I'll set an extra cup. Don't worry now my love," she whispered. "He'll be pleased to see you. There's no doubt of that."

Violet reluctantly let go of the hand that had brought her, in the space of a few minutes, more female support than she had ever had in life, and walked down the path. Frank was sitting with his back towards her, looking out down the hill across towards Tenterden. "Frank," she whispered. "Frank."

He turned in his chair and looked at her, his mouth open with wonder. Then he seemed to recover himself, standing so quickly that he knocked the chair over. "Violet!" he almost shouted. "My God Violet it's you. It can't be... it is. Oh Violet I'm so sorry, so very sorry. Oh God, I'm so pleased to see you."

He opened his arms. She ran into them and this time the embrace she received was the one she had come for. This embrace spelt love. The love between man and woman. She turned her face up to his and he kissed her and she kissed him back, moaning softly. "Frank... oh Frank."

"Here we are. A cup of tea. I expect you're in need of this my dear... Oh I'm sorry, I seem to be interrupting something," Jesse chuckled knowingly as she swerved past the entwined couple and put the tray on the table. "Come on now Frank, let the lady have a sit down and something to drink."

Frank released Violet but she kept hold of his hand. With his other he stooped and righted the fallen chair, setting it beside another. The two of them sat down together, still holding hands, and Violet turned to Jesse. "Thank you Mrs Long. Thank you very much."

"Mrs Long she says," laughed Jesse. "Come on love, there's no need to stand on ceremony here. My name is Jesse to you."

"Well thank you Jesse. Thank you very much for making me feel so welcome."

"Of course you're welcome my love... his lordship was so miserable just now.. I've never seen anyone so welcome. I'll leave you two to talk now and I'll do supper." She turned back to the kitchen door, singing happily to herself.

Frank turned to Violet. "I... Violet I... oh you shouldn't have come. It... I'll be off soon. It would have been..."

"Shut up Frank Balfour," she said. "If you think I've come here to be sent away again you're wrong. If you think I care one jot about your so-called prospects you're wrong." She reached across to him and stroked the back of his neck. "I care about you Frank Balfour and I think you care about me."

"Of course I care about you Violet. I love you!"

He had said it! She heard it. He had said it! "I love you too Frank," Violet whispered.

She loves me too, he thought... I must have said it then. I've said it! I've told her. He looked across at her shyly and she smiled back at him. A happy open smile of contentment. A dark cloud of doubt impinged upon his thoughts and he blurted out. "But Violet I've signed on for foreign service and I'm on standby awaiting my call-up."

"Then what we'll do Frank Balfour is enjoy the next few days and, when, and if you have to go, I'll go home to sort things out with my father... and when my hero comes home I'll be waiting for him."

"Violet," he persisted. "You're under age. You're not yet twenty-one and if your father continues to disapprove he can force you to stop seeing me."

"Then he'll force me to stop loving him. I'll not lose you Frank Balfour, I simply won't. Now there's enough."

"Yes miss... certainly miss," he said, touching his forelock, and they both dissolved into laughter. In the kitchen, Jesse heard them and smiled to herself. Maybe, she thought. Maybe. But there was a lot more to divide them than there was to bind them. Still, if it sent her Frank off to this blessed war in a better frame of mind, then all to the good.

......

"Pinch, punch, first of the month and no return." Violet ran off down the hill with Frank in hot pursuit, but he caught her just as she reached the stile by the stream and threw one leg over. She giggled as he pulled her back and held her tight while he got his breath. Then he kissed her. She turned fully and stepped down from the stile, still locked in his embrace, her lips still fastened on his. A hot sensation crept through her body and into her loins and she pushed herself against him, feeling his response. He broke off the kiss and held her close with his head over her shoulder, his lips close to her ear. "Violet, oh Violet," he moaned. "We mustn't. We mustn't." He tried to prise himself from her grip but she held him tight.

"Frank," she whispered, passion overtaking reason. "Frank, I love you." She pushed herself into him and he kissed her again, feeling the surge within him and the aching hardness at his crotch. He picked her up and stepped up on to the first rung of the stile, swung one leg over and then the other one, dismounting on the other side with her still held in his arms. Across the open corner of the field, he carried her before laying her on the bank of the river, under the alder trees sighing and rustling in the summer's breeze. Gently at first, but then with increasing urgency, he covered her body with his own.

The clothing between them could not hide his arousal and almost instinctively she pushed herself up into him, wanting to be part of, to be one with this man. Frank pushed himself up on his wrists and looked down at her. She smiled back at him. "Is this what you want?" he asked gently.

She made no reply as such, except to reach down and undo the buttons of her blouse, revealing and releasing her firm breasts, the pink nipples standing erect. He looked into her eyes and then back down at her breasts. Arching down, he took one of the buds in his lips and teased it with his tongue. She reached down her sides, and taking her skirts in her hands pulled them up. He shifted his weight then reached down, pulled her drawers aside and released his belt. His member burst free and she glanced down at it quickly before he lowered himself again and hid it from view.

Gently at first, he pushed at her opening and she responded by pushing up against him. Then he thrust deep within her, pausing only at her gasped intake of breath. "Have I hurt you," he asked gently of her closed eyes.

"No Frank. You could never hurt me," she breathed as she pulled him down and kissed his face. Slowly at first, he began to move within her, then faster. She pushed up against him and then to his surprise began to make rhythmical whimpering noises, transferring her grip to his buttocks in an effort to pull him within her. At length her cries became almost continuous and he released within her in a gasp of pure joy, which she responded to with a yell as she too climaxed.

He collapsed back down on to her, panting from the exertion, only to feel her begin to move her loins once more. He felt the hardness coming back and soon he too was moving against her, and as he came again he cried out and then rolled off her, as the touch of her became too much to bear.

For a while they lay side by side breathing hard. Her hand stole across the gap between them, took his and held it. After a while she raised herself into a sitting position, pulled her skirts down over her knees and looked down at him lying there beside her. His trousers were halfway down his thighs and she looked with wonder at his glistening penis lying flaccid over his thigh, small now and shrinking further. The enormity of what they had done, what she had instigated, struck her. She had not planned this. Instinct had dictated her actions but her mind had controlled them. 'The animal in me took control,' she reasoned, as a feeling of revulsion... no, no, how could she feel that. She corrected herself... shame... what would he think of her... how could she? She hugged her knees and buried her head in her skirts, unwilling to risk looking into his eyes. Her mind raced as she tried to blot out... to extinguish that which had happened. 'It wasn't my fault,' she told herself. It was... it was my fault. I'm no better than a beast in the field.

Now and in later months, she asked and would ask herself so many times what had led to this. Was it the element of the unspoken fear that he was going to war and might not return? Was it her own baseness? The real answer would never come, except that it was her love for this man at that moment... that she had given in to her desire to be one with him.

She raised her head and looked up, hoping against hope that the turmoil of thought tumbling around in her brain did not show on her flushed face, unaware of the fact that once more she was staring at his parts. He pulled at his trousers. "Have you no shame woman?" he said in mock disapproval.

His voice brought her back to the dawning reality and she covered up her confusion by reaching her hand across to him. He squirmed out of her grasp, misinterpreting her move. "Nay I can't take any more," he said.

"I was a virgin," she whispered.

"I never doubted it my darling," he said softly.

She hugged her knees again as the silent tears began to flow from her eyes, cascading down her cheeks to drop on to her skirt. Why, she reasoned. Why? Instinct? "What must you think of me?" she sobbed, burying her face once more. "I'm a shameless hussy."

Frank raised himself up and rolled over to her, despite the fact that his actions served to move his trousers even further down his legs. "No! No, I won't hear you say that Violet!" he cried, appalled at the enormity of what they had done... the consequences of which seemed now to crash in upon them both, reducing their thoughts to a scrambling panic. "Oh I'm sorry Violet. It's all my fault. I should have stopped."

He threw his arm around her and dragged her down to cradle her body in his embrace and she pulled herself into a tight foetal position, rocking slightly as she buried her head in his chest. For some long while they lay thus, neither of them speaking, each of them taking comfort from the other's closeness. The panic in her subsided in his embrace, to be replaced by a feeling of warmth that seemed to steal through her body. She snuggled closer, relaxing her tight grip on her knees to lie with him full length, her head resting on his breast as his arms enfolded her. 'This is my man,' she thought clearly. 'This is the man I want... the man who will be taken from me soon but who I will wait for. We are one now.' For a moment, the shame crept back and she felt her face redden. No! No. What was done could not now be undone. 'He loves me. I love him.' Guiltily, she tried to recall their love-making, to remember the delicious sensations that had coursed through her.

"I'm so sorry Violet," he murmured. "So sorry... If I could..."

"Hush now Frank," she whispered. "We did wrong but... it was the most wonderful thing that has happened in my life and I shall always remember it and I shall always love you."

"But Violet, I..."

She reached across to put her finger to his lip. "Shhh." She opened her eyes and looked down at their two bodies, noticing his naked whiteness. She giggled and he raised his head to look questioningly at her. "Your... your bottom..." She laughed openly now and he turned from her face to follow her pointing finger, gasping in embarrassment as he realised his exposure. He grabbed his trousers and pulled, lifting himself off the ground on his elbows as he struggled with them.

Violet sat away from him watching, torn between embarrassment and mirth... between sneaking another look at him and a wish not to compound what they had done by her continued forwardness. Control seemed to flood back into her being. What was done was done... best now to forget... no, she could never forget it... to put it aside and get on with things. He stood and she reached up her hand to him as he finished buckling his belt. "Come on Frank, help me up. We'd better get going before we're discovered." He reached down and hauled her to her feet, pulling her close to him as she buttoned her blouse.

For a moment the two of them stood inches apart, looking with faint embarrassment into each other's eyes, but then Violet smiled a shy smile and stood on tiptoe to kiss his lips. His brow furrowed but he returned her kiss, wondering at her forgiveness for what he saw as his inexcusable actions.

She bent to undo the laces and slip her boots off. "Turn away for a moment whilst I... well turn away," she indicated, twiddling her finger in a circle. Frank turned and stared out across the field as she lifted her skirts up to her waist and waded into the water, holding them up with one hand as she splashed herself.

She was so calm. He was amazed at how calm she was. After what they'd just done most women would, he imagined, be mortified beyond reason... would hate him for the shame he had brought upon them. She had been ashamed, he knew that full well, but now... now there seemed little to be ashamed of. It was past and he would always... 'God I love this woman,' he thought.

"All right," she called, and he turned and held out his hand to her as she came from the water, guiding her across to a knoll where she sat brushing off her feet before putting her boots back on. I can't go back to the cottage just yet, she thought as she tied the laces. She looked up at him, still standing awkwardly, shyly glancing at her as she finished dressing. "What shall we do now," she said. "It does seem to me that it will be difficult to top what has gone already, but we must do something."

He swallowed hard trying to recover his thoughts and then coughed, deliberately concentrating on making his voice sound as normal as possible. "Why don't we go into town. I could show it to you and we could find out the latest news."

There was no need to go back up the hill to the cottage. If they were going into town they could walk along the banks of the stream, through the hop gardens and on through the fields to the railway crossing. In any event, neither of them could have faced Jesse right then and both needed time to recover their thoughts.

As they went, he pointed out landmarks to her and named the various flowers on the banks. Mallow flowers. Pink striated trumpets amidst their spatulated green leaves. Vivid yellow Kingcups standing proudly at the water's edge like giant versions of the buttercups she was used to. All was wonder to her, all was beauty, and it seemed as if the world was a new place which she was here to discover.

The shame she had briefly felt was now gone. Never had she felt so alive, so whole. What was supposed to have been lost was a great find. Her virtue was gone, but feelings and senses had been discovered and heightened that would forever be with her.

"What will you say to your father when you see him?" Frank asked.

"I shall tell him that I came to visit you here, to say goodbye properly, and that as far as I am concerned, goodbye is for now only."

"Do you think he would give his consent for us to marry?" he whispered in a worried tone.

"Why Frank Balfour, you haven't asked me yet!" she said, skipping away from him.

"I'm asking Violet. Would you marry me if you could?"

"Why yes kind sir!" She ran back to him and kissed him full on the lips. She broke away and looked at him seriously. "Like a shot."

"We'd need your father's consent as you're under age. What if he won't give it?"

"Then we'll have to wait. Anyway, I'm twenty in November and you'll be away for some months and..." Her voice tailed off as the imminence of their parting suddenly dawned on her. "Oh Frank, do you really have to go?"

He took her hand. "Violet, I have to go. I told you I would go if there was war. I'm a reservist. Oh I know I've speeded things up a bit by signing now, but I'll be back I promise."

"I've given myself to you Frank Balfour," she said firmly. "Freely and with love and I..." She turned away for an instant and then turned to look him full in the face. "I regret nothing."

Frank stared back at her, wonder written all over his face. "I don't deserve..."

"Nonsense, Frank Balfour," she admonished. "I'll not hear of you talking like that. You are the only man I want," she laughed mischievously. "Anyway, no other man would want me now."

"Any man would want you Violet," he said firmly. "You're..." He stopped, putting his hands to his head and she turned to him.

"What's the matter Frank?"

"Violet, what if... what if you have a baby? God I never thought of it."

"You can't have a baby from the first time."

"Do you think that's true?"

"It must be. I heard Alice say it to a friend of hers. Anyway, you'll be back, and if I am..." She quelled the rising tide of panic that seemed to well up within, turning from him to hide her fears. "I'm not and I won't be... you'll see. Now come on Frank and show me your town."

They crossed the railway and walked up the hill to the town, barely talking as they went, each one lost in their own thoughts, content for now to simply be hand in hand. "I walked as far as here and then

I got a ride in the back of a cart down to the station," she told him as they reached the Rye Road. "Let's walk on the other side of the road by those pretty cottages. Oh what lovely gardens. Look at those paths with the flowers either side. It's so beautiful. How could you bear to leave it?"

"I found a flower more beautiful in Finchley and its name was Violet."

She turned to him, wonder in her face. "Oh Frank, you are so... oh I'm so lucky to have found you. And to think we nearly lost each other. I'll never quite forgive daddy you know."

"How so?"

"Well he could have helped. He could have given you a better job if he was so worried about your ability to keep me... well couldn't he?"

"Your father did what he thought was best. Sometimes people do things and they... they just don't get it right. You can't hate him Violet. He's your father and he loves you."

"I don't hate him," she said, looking down at the ground as she walked beside him. "I'm just... I'm just very angry with him for... well for driving you away."

"He didn't drive me away. I went because I knew he was right and that I do indeed have very little to offer you."

"Are we having our first row?" she said, stopping in front of him and looking up into his face.

He smiled down at her. This young woman that he loved... that he had just made love to. "Nay we're not love. I'm just talking."

"Well talk sense then, Frank Balfour. You have everything to offer me that I want, and if necessary we'll live here in the country and you'll work and I'll work and we'll make it together, just you wait and see."

She meant what she said.

Now more than ever she felt absolutely certain of herself. This was her life and she would live it and all around her would come to understand... after all, she reasoned, if daddy hadn't been so unkind to poor Frank then she wouldn't have had to run away and all this wouldn't have happened.

They neared the White Lion opposite Station Road. The pavement was wide here and the lunchtime drinkers spilled out on to it, the talk all of war on every lip. Frank and Violet listened and learnt that the Kaiser had that day declared war on Russia. The wheel had turned another ratchet, and with mounting horror they observed the crude bravado of the young men. "Why do you men so revel in war," she whispered fearfully in his ear.

"Some do," said Frank. "Some don't think about it. Some... perhaps me as well, see it as a way of giving some meaning to their lives. Without you it would have filled a vacuum... given my life some sort of purpose. Now with you, I dread it."

He shivered and turned away and the two of them walked on down the High Street in silence. Opposite the town hall they stopped. The union flag flew proudly from it and a throng of local dignitaries were gathered on its first floor balcony. "I would always have to have gone you know Violet. If not at first, then some day." He turned to her and held her, looking down into her upturned face. "I will be back... I promise."

"And I'll be here for you Frank, I promise, or at my parent's house waiting for you if Jesse sends me word. Come let's go back. Jesse will wonder where we've got to and what we've got up to."

"I hope she don't find out."

"Why Frank Balfour! Anyway, it's I hope she *doesn't* find out."

"Sorry miss."

......

August 2nd dawned bright and the occupants of Lilac Cottage were up and about fairly early. For Jesse, Sunday meant church and her church was in Rolvenden village, some one- and-a-half miles away, so she was usually picked up by a friend, Brian Gooch, who drove her there in a small buggy drawn by a dark bay pony. This large and homely woman had never had children of her own and would have spent her life alone, following the death of her husband from polio, were it not for the tragic death of both her sister and brother-in-law that had left her with Frank. Many a person faced with that much sorrow would have folded in on themselves and become bitter at life, but for Jesse that was not possible and she had sought to provide Frank with a stable and loving home background, supported by her unswerving belief in God.

She had been helped in the earlier years by Frank's grandmother, who had arranged for her life tenancy of the cottage and provided the money for his further education when he had achieved the scholarship to Kent College. That he was to go outside the community for his education and outside his class had caused many a tongue to wag, and the predictions of his downfall had been rife. The fact that he had now been visited by a posh-looking lady from London, reported at length to all by the station master, was causing considerable further interest which, for some, threatened to supplant even the talk of war.

Brian stopped the buggy outside the church gate and waited whilst Frank assisted the two ladies down and proudly escorted them in, one on each arm, acknowledging the looks and greetings of the various locals. The service was reflective, the sermon dwelling on the coming war with a call to uplift the spirits and frequent reference to duty and honour. Both Violet and Jesse were glad when it was all over. For them both, their visit to the church had been an attempt to rationalise their ambivalent feelings, and for it to merely act as a reminder of all that they had wished to forget for a while proved a disappointment. Nevertheless, they thanked the vicar as they left the church and got back into the buggy for the journey home.

They travelled in silence as far as the end of the village street by The Bull, where the road turned right and went on down the hill towards Tenterden and home. But as the buggy picked up speed,

Violet roused herself. "Come on you lot," she said. "Let's not dwell on it. It's a lovely day. It's a Sunday. My first in the country here with you. Let's be happy and forget for a while."

"Good idea," said Jesse, reaching across to squeeze Violet's hand. She started to sing a country tune that Violet didn't know but soon picked up. Then Frank joined in with Brian and the little buggy went down the hill with all four occupants singing away. In the gardens of the little cottages the tenants looked up and smiled and waved as they passed.

The Sunday meal was well on the way in the oven when they got back and Violet could smell the roasting lamb with the added oily aroma of fresh rosemary. "Mint sauce," said Jesse. "Do you know how to make it my dear?"

"Mint I suppose," said Violet. "I don't really know. But I'd love to make it. May I?"

"You gather some mint. Frank will show you where. Then wash it and chop it finely and mix it with a little vinegar from that jar over there and add sugar from that jar there on the table."

"How much sugar?"

"Oh well, you just add it to taste. You'll know when it's enough. Now you do that and I'll wash the spinach."

Frank handed a trug to Violet and the two of them went out into the garden to where the mint was. He stood back and watched her as she knelt down to pick. She looked back up at him and smiled. "I've never been quite so happy in all my life Frank."

Sunday drifted on, and after lunch they all sat out in the garden and Jesse fell asleep in her chair, snoring loudly. Frank looked affectionately at this contented woman and then across at Violet, who was herself nodding off. He felt complete, although not at ease with a nagging feeling of dread that he seemed unable to dispel.

Monday morning came and Violet awoke in Frank's bed and sat up to look out through the small dormer window framed with yellow climbing roses. Out across the valley she could see right up the hill to the church in Tenterden, and to the left she could just make out the tip of the spire of the next church of St. Michael's. Frank had given up his bed for her and had slept downstairs since her arrival, but she had a sneaking wish that he had remained with her. She blushed at the thought and felt again the delicious memory of their love-making.

There was a knock at the front door and she wondered who was there that early on a Bank Holiday. She slipped out of bed, dropped her nightshift to the floor and went over to the wash stand. She washed herself and combed her hair, leaving it loose and down before slipping her dress over her head. Then she descended the stairs into the living room area, pushing open the small door and holding on to it from the last step. Frank stood in the centre of the room with a piece of paper in his hand. Jesse stood next to him holding on to his arm, staring at it.

"What is it? said Violet. "What's happened?"

Jesse walked over to the armchair and sat down. Frank turned to Violet. He held out the paper to her. "It's come Violet," he said in a voice breaking with emotion. "I'm to go today. I have to be in Chatham by 6 o'clock this evening to report to my regiment."

Violet stood there and looked at him. It can't be, she thought. Not now when we are so happy. She looked away from him at Jesse sitting there in the chair, staring bleakly at the floor, and a chill ran right through her. No, this was it. This was the moment that she had hoped would never happen. She stepped into the room and crossed to Frank to hold him tight, her mind racing. Today. He was going today.

She held back the tears. She had to be brave. She swallowed hard and then, taking his hand, led him across to Jesse. She picked up Jesse's hand and the three of them stayed silent for a while, hand in hand within their own thoughts. After a while, Violet broke the silence. "Frank, you're going away... we may not see you for a little while but we have you now... until... we all have each other. Let's make it a good day and look forward to when we will be together again... please."

Frank raised his gaze from its blank contemplation of the floor and looked into the earnest face of the girl he loved. He saw the steel within her, the resolve she had, and he responded with a broad grin. "She's right Jesse. Let's not be sad. Let's have a good day and look forward to Christmas when I'll be back for sure and we can all be together again."

The day went by quite quickly, however much they wished to stretch it into eternity. After lunch, Frank changed into his uniform and then suggested that Violet and he should go for a walk before he had to go to the station, where special trains were apparently running.

The two of them walked down the lane to its end and on to the footpath leading to Rolvenden Layne. Through fields they wandered in silence, neither wishing to break the illusion of normality by speaking and perhaps giving away their true fears. Eventually she had to speak. "Frank, I will always love you and I will be here for your return."

He stopped and sat down on the grass, pulling her down beside him, where they sat looking out into the field. "There is something I want to say Violet," he said in a serious tone. "I'm going to war and I intend to come back but..."

"Of course you'll come back."

"I will come back... but if I don't..."

"I won't hear of it. I won't Frank. Now there's an end."

"Violet, you must listen to me this time... I shall say this just once and then it's done." He lifted his finger to her lips to silence any further interruption. "If I don't come back, remember I love you, but don't waste your life on my memory. Promise me that."

"But Frank," she protested.

"Promise me," he commanded.

"I promise," she said. "But it's a waste of a promise 'cause you are coming back Frank Balfour... you are. Anyway, there isn't a war yet and there might not be."

"There will be," he said ruefully. "There will be." He turned to her and kissed her and they lay back in the early afternoon sun just holding each other. "I'll write to you whenever I can," he said. He sat up. "Where will I write? Will I write to your home or... what should we do?"

"Write to Jesse and she can send them to me or I'll visit her."

When they got back to the cottage, Jesse was in the lounge with Frank's kit bag, and as they walked up the front path she opened the door. "I've asked Brian to be here at 3 o'clock to give us all a lift into town and see you off at the station," she said. "That gives us a few minutes to check you've got everything."

"I don't really think I need that much Jesse," he said. "I don't expect I'll be able to take many personal things with me."

"Is there room for me in there?" Violet joked and they all laughed... the strained laughs of people desperately trying to keep up their spirits.

Brian pulled up outside and called in to them. Frank led the two women out of the cottage and up into the buggy before climbing in himself. "This is very good of you," he said, putting his arm around Brian's shoulder.

"It's all right," Brian replied. "It's the least I can do, and if you don't get the job done quickly I expect I'll 'ave to be following you shortly."

"Let's hope you don't have to," said Frank, and the two women, listening from the back, thought 'Amen to that.'

At the station the train was already in, its engine puffing quietly away, its carriages waiting, their doors open to the platform, along which stood huddled groups, each surrounding a uniformed man. Brian silently helped the two women off and guided them through to the platform gate. He turned to Frank and held out his hand. "Good luck Frank," he said quietly, covering Frank's hand with his other hand in a double grip. "Keep safe."

Frank nodded his thanks, unwilling to speak for fear of betraying his emotions. He turned and walked across to where Violet and Jesse stood alone on the platform. Violet had been staring at the train, almost hating it for being there. She turned to Frank, a huge lump in her throat, as he reached out for and held her hand.

"Well Frank... you take care now my boy," whispered Jesse. "Come back safe to me... to us both." She cuddled into Frank as Violet stared at them, her vision now clouded by oncoming tears, a yawning pit seeming to open up within her very being. Jesse stepped back and put her hand on Violet's shoulder. "Say your goodbyes my loves," she whispered, her voice croaking with grief. She turned away and walked to the back of the platform, leaving them alone.

Frank took Violet in his arms, looking down into her upturned face. Nothing was said but volumes were spoken as all about them seemed to recede and their world shrank to their own entwinement.

"All aboard. All aboard. This train for Maidstone!" shouted the station master, blowing his whistle.

The spell was broken. Frank stood back from Violet and picked up his kit bag as Jesse hurried over to him and swept him into her arms again, whispering "Take care my lovely boy. Take care." She released him, took his hand and Violet's and put them together.

Violet's eyes widened in terror and Frank stared at her, torn between one last embrace and the move he knew he now must make. "I'd better get in," he said, his voice sounding strange even to himself, but not, he hoped, to Violet. He swung his kit bag through the open door, got in, shut it and slid the window down. He reached out both hands to Violet and they stood there dreading the movement of the train. The whistle blew once more and the train puffed a cloud of steam and smoke and started. Violet moved along the platform sideways with it, but as it gathered speed had to release one of his hands. Still she held the other until, at last, he let go and she stopped, looking down the platform at his receding face. The tears coursed down her face, and as the train rounded the bend and went out of sight she turned sobbing into the waiting arms of Jesse, who held her, letting her cry.

Along the platform similar scenes were being enacted and, as the train finally disappeared, small silent groups turned and made their way to the gate. Eventually Jesse guided the still sobbing Violet back to the buggy where Brian, his face sombre, helped them up and in. He mounted, clucked to the pony and they drove back to the cottage in silence.

Frank hung out of the window for as long as he could, looking after the diminishing figure of Violet standing there on the platform, waving her arms in the air. When he could no longer see her and the smoke from the engine finally obscured his view as it turned the corner he stood back, slid up the window and sat down. In other windows, men were doing likewise, manfully and deliberately setting the sadness of their partings behind them and replacing it with the anticipation of what was to come.

A figure stirred at the opposite corner of the compartment. "Frank?" Frank peered across and was delighted to see Keith, a friend from Tenterden and their early days at school together. Keith smiled as Frank recognised him. "Hallo Frank. I thought it was you."

Frank moved across to sit beside him. "Keith," he said, noticing for the first time that his friend was also in uniform.

Keith smiled wanly at him. "So you've answered the King's call, have you?"

"I have," said Frank. "Although I'm having my doubts now. Has anything more happened? Do you know why we're being called up when there's no war yet?"

"The Kaiser's apparently declared war on France and our lot have warned him to leave Belgium alone and mobilised the Navy. As far as I know there's no general mobilisation, but reserves are being called up... the likes of you and me."

"I expect they'll all back down and we can go home," said Frank, more in hope than expectation.

"No, they've started fighting in Russia already," said Keith sadly. "I expect we'll declare war in the next few days... then there'll be a rush to join up and that's why they want us there first."

"Mayhap you're right," mused Frank. Where are you bound for now?"

"Chatham. You?"

"Same."

For a while they travelled in silence, each deep within his own thoughts, yet grateful for the company of the other. At each station, more and more soldiers joined the train, filling the carriage with their chatter and, as home receded, Frank and Keith felt themselves drawn into the general excitement.

By the time they reached Maidstone, where they had to change for Chatham, they too were excitedly exchanging information and stories with their fellow travellers.

They dismounted the train as soldiers; caught up and eager for what lay ahead.

......

Violet couldn't sleep at all that night. She lay awake in Frank's bed wondering where he was, how he was faring and thinking about what she must do. She decided that she really should go home and face her father. Besides, she was worried about her mother. Would daddy have told her of her elopement, or would she not realise that she had gone?

In the morning she got up, washed and dressed and went downstairs for breakfast. Jesse was already there in the kitchen, cooking some bacon in the large black pan. "Would you like a fresh egg with this my love?" she said. "Did you sleep well?"

"Not really," said Violet, "and yes please, I'd love an egg." She sat down at the table. Jesse broke an egg into the deep fat. It bubbled and crisped at the edges and she spooned it on to the plate, placed the bacon beside it and handed it to Violet. "Thank you," said Violet as she started to eat. "Jesse," she said between mouthfuls. "I think that I should be going home now that Frank's gone. My parents will be worried and I have things to sort out."

"I thought as much my dear. That's why I've done you a good breakfast to keep you going 'till you get home."

Violet smiled. She might have known. "I will keep in touch you know Jesse, and Frank has said that he will write to me through you. Would you mind sending his letters on to me?"

"Not at all my love, and whenever you need me I'll be here. I do hope your father will let you visit properly next time and you don't have to come away from them like you did. They must've worried you know."

"I know, and that's why I must go to them today. But it is so hard to leave here." Jesse placed her hand on her shoulder and squeezed it reassuringly as Violet cocked her head over to acknowledge the touch.

After she had finished eating, Violet went back up to finish packing and then she was ready to leave. Jesse was all sorrow at her going now and upset that there was no transport available for her as Brian had gone to Hastings. But Violet told her that she was happy to walk, and after much hugging and kissing she set off down the lane towards Rolvenden Station. The walk downhill didn't take that long, but by the time she got there she was quite tired. She bought her ticket and stood alone on the platform thinking of her loss and trying to come to terms with the nagging sensation of having left something behind. Her thoughts were broken by the arrival of the train. She waited for it to come to rest before picking up her bag and taking a seat by the window so that she could look out over the fields that she and Frank had walked. As the train crossed the road and rounded the bend, she craned her neck to look as far up the valley as she could, guiltily imagining and searching for the spot where they had made love. The tears sprang to her eyes once more as she remembered those blissful few days and she dabbed them with her handkerchief.

The train drew into Tenterden and she sat there looking out blankly. The station master was standing on the platform talking to a gentleman who seemed familiar, and as the man turned his face towards her she recognised her father. Winding down the window she shouted out to him, and on seeing her he abruptly ceased his conversation and ran down the platform to her. "Violet, what on earth are you doing?" he yelled through the window at her. "Where are you going?"

"I'm going home daddy," she replied "Are you coming?"

"Not before I've had a few words with that man Balfour first, if you don't mind miss," he virtually bellowed.

"You'll have to wait daddy. He's gone to the army."

"Has he now? Well at least he's done that thing right, the bounder. You do know, I suppose, that unless the Germans respond to our government's ultimatum by midnight tonight, we're at war?"

She gasped and the tears flooded once more into her eyes. "Oh daddy. Oh daddy." Ernest rolled his eyes skywards and then opened the carriage door and got in beside her. The whistle blew and the train departed.

......

"Who's that?" came a whisper in the night.

"It's me. Frank."

"What the hell are you doing out there?"

"I'm having a pee if you don't mind," said Frank.

"Well don't get it shot off will you," said a voice from deep within the tent.

"All right, all right," said Frank. "Settle down now lads, the fun's over. Get some bloody sleep while you can... you may meet the Boche in the morning." He scrambled back through the tent flap and settled down on his bedroll.

"Right ho, Corporal. Nighty nighty then."

"Go to sleep Tim, you silly bastard," said Frank, laughing to himself as he settled himself down and pulled the bedroll over. He lay there awake in the dark. He was still unused to sleeping in such close proximity to other men. The constant sounds they made, farting, snoring, coughing and sometimes talking in their sleep. He thought of Violet. Had she gone home and what would the reaction of her parents have been when she got home? He wondered if she'd got his letter, hastily scribbled and sent as they departed for the continent. No, she couldn't have done yet as he'd sent it to Jesse, who would have to send it on. Since then he hadn't had time, and in any case he doubted that at the moment he would be allowed to send anything uncensored. And besides, what he wanted to say he wouldn't want read by others.

The march north from Boulogne had been an incredible experience. At times it had seemed like a country ramble for the boys club, as apart from the inconvenience of their arms and equipment, anything less like war would be difficult to imagine. Peasants working in the fields had watched them, waving as if they were a passing carnival. In the villages, as they passed through, they had been greeted warmly and plied with food and wine, which only served to heighten the almost holiday-like atmosphere of the occasion. Some of the younger soldiers had even kept a tally of the number of times they had been kissed by pretty girls on the trip, and the earlier parts of the evenings had been given over to a loud and cheerful comparison of scores. Frank smiled to himself in the dark at the memory. He turned over and pulled the thin roll up to his neck. Gradually the sounds of his compatriots became rhythmical and he dropped off into a fitful sleep.

Bugles and a call to arms woke him roughly just after first light and he and the other men tumbled out of the tent. They rushed around getting dressed and picking up all of their arms and ammunition as a Sergeant came running down towards them, gesticulating wildly. "Get your men ready Corporal. They're coming. Get to the end of town." He ran on past them, shouting and rousing other men stumbling from their tents.

"Who's coming?" Frank called after him.

"Boche!" the man screamed back at him.

A thrill of fear ran through Frank and he turned to his men. "Come on!" he shouted. "Look sharp there, I think we're under attack."

"What about the tent?" called Tim from within, as he tried desperately to stuff his belongings into his kit bag.

"Leave it! Grab your weapons and come on," Frank yelled, aware now of the distant crump of exploding ordinance.

In the next tent, Keith, his friend, also a Corporal, was getting his men together. "We'll come with you Frank," he called.

"Best hurry then, we're off," Frank shouted in reply. He turned back to his men. "Come on! Leave that! Grab your weapons and follow me!"

Keith's lot joined them, shouting "We're here, let's go!", and they all ran out of the copse in which they had been camped, down towards the end of the small town. Ahead as they ran, the sounds of gunfire grew louder, and as they rounded a corner they came across a Sergeant and three other men crouching behind a small wall, firing out into the distance. Frank ducked back and down, motioning those following to keep out of sight. Keith joined him and they peered out at the surrounding countryside, trying to locate the enemy positions from the incoming fire.

Across the street, Frank could see that there was a higher wall at the back of the garden of a small house. He pointed it out to Keith. "I reckon that's our best position. We can cover the whole street from there and it's elevated enough for us not to be fired down upon. We'll cover you and your chaps while you get over, and once you're there you can cover us as we come across."

"Righto," said Keith. He called to his men to follow him and they ran, swerving from side to side across to the wall whilst Frank and his chaps poured covering fire in the direction of the open countryside.

Puffs of dirt rising in spurts from the road indicated that the running men were being fired at, but they all got across.

Frank looked at each of his men in turn. "Right mates, we've got to get over there now and the enemy's aware of our position so look lively now... run fast and zig zag. All right?"

"All right Corp," said Tim. The others nodded and made ready.

"On my shout go," said Frank. "Go!", and they ran like hell across the open space with the bullets whining past them, kicking up sections of the road. The wall that had seemed to be just across the street now seemed miles away, but eventually they made it and Frank rolled the last bit, his helmet banging on the stones as he spun round to scramble behind it and look back to check that they'd all made it. A pit opened up in his stomach as he saw that one young lad, Paul he thought it was, hadn't. He lay there lifeless, for all the world as if he had decided to lie down in the road with his rifle still held in his outstretched hand. That is, until one noticed the trickle of blood from his head and the helmet that had been cast aside by the force of the bullet that had taken his life.

"Shall we get him Corp?" said Tim. "We can't just leave him there, can we?"

"No point," said Frank quietly. "He's gone. There's no point in risking our necks for him now." Bullets pinged off the wall and he rolled across to peer through a chink to see what was happening. In the far distance he could see figures running and men and horses moving artillery into position. The lines of men seemed to thicken and take on some order and Frank realised that they were massing for an attack on the town itself. A large puff and then a plume of smoke in the distance was followed by the shriek of the shells as they passed over their heads and crashed into the buildings behind them, showering Frank and his men with stones and rubble.

"Jesus Christ," said Keith, "we can't match that can we?"

"Not with rifles we can't," said Frank, shaking his head. "Where are our big guns?"

"At the other end of town of course," said Tim, "protecting the big wigs no doubt."

"Well sod this," said Frank. "We can't stay here, can we? Where's that bloody Sergeant. "Sarge!" he shouted. "Are you over there?"

"Here," shouted the Sergeant. "What do you want?"

"What do we do Sarge... we can't stay here, can we?"

"Hold there whilst I get orders," he shouted back. They watched as he crawled along behind the low wall back towards the corner of the street. Another round of shells slammed into the house behind him. For an instant the building seemed to flex itself, almost as if stretching after a long sleep, but then it simply burst open and the walls fell outwards, burying him completely. All they could see was the broken side of the house lying over where he had been and the cloud of dust rising into the August sky. Yet another round hit the position the Sergeant had just left and scattered the men still there like rag dolls. Two lay still and broken but one still lived. He lay in the open road near Paul's body, crying pitifully, his arms waving vainly in the air.

"What the hell do we do now Corporal?" shouted Tim.

"I don't know," said Frank. "What do you reckon Keith?"

"I reckon, my old mate, that this is not a healthy place to be and that we're next in the firing line if we don't move."

Frank nodded in agreement. "Right lads, fall back to those buildings beyond there and keep that bloody wall between you and those guns for Christ's sake or you're done... I'll stay 'till you're there. When you're safe, shout and I'll come."

Keith put his hand on Frank's shoulder. "I'll stay with you. Go on men, get back there and keep low."

The others ran, doubled up, back to the houses and in through an open door. Frank watched them go and then looked across to the middle of the road to where the wounded man lay crying. "We can't leave that poor bastard there can we Keith?"

"Oh shit," said Keith, pushing back his helmet and wiping his brow. "I had a horrible feeling you'd turn out to be a hero. Don't you know that's dangerous?"

Frank laughed. "You cover me and I'll get him over here", and then without waiting for an answer he darted out across the road to where the young man lay, skittling down to lie beside him. The boy turned his head as he arrived and his face, contorted with pain, relaxed a little as he recognised help. He reached out to Frank and grabbed his arm. "Can you move at all?" Frank shouted above the increasing din of battle.

"No," came the croaking reply. "Nothing seems to work down there."

"Right, give me your hands," Frank yelled. "For God's sake don't let go or I'll have to leave you here."

He tried shuffling backwards on his belly whilst holding on to the boy but could make no headway. "Come on," Keith called.

"Oh sod it!" Frank cursed, and then with a quick glance in the direction of the enemy he stood quickly, grabbing the boy around the armpits to reverse, doubled up, back across the road. The boy screamed all the way and Frank noticed with horror that his legs seemed to simply follow as if attached only by the trousers, leaving a trail of blood on the grey of the tarmac road. Hands clutched at his waist as Keith took hold of him and pulled them both behind the wall.

For a moment, Frank lay back to catch his breath but then he sat up. "Right Keith, let's get the hell out of here." He turned to the young man. "All right mate, let's get..." He stopped and looked into the lifeless face, its lips drawn now into a permanent grimace, the eyes staring out into space, dulling and unseeing. "Oh bugger," he whispered. "You poor little bugger."

Keith put his hand on Frank's arm. "Time to go Frank. Let's get the hell out of here." He called back to the houses. "Are you lot still there?"

"Yes," came the reply. "What're you waiting for?"

"We're coming. Cover us. Come on Frank, time to go old son." Keith tugged at Frank's arm.

He was still staring down into the face of the young dead boy, but at the touch he roused himself, closed the boy's eyelids and turned to Keith. "This is not going to be as simple as we thought, is it?"

Keith shook his head sorrowfully. "Come on Frank, let's go."

Frank nodded and knelt into a starting position. "Coming in!" he shouted, and the two of them dashed, doubled up back to the houses, diving through the open door to land in a heap just beyond their crouching friends.

"What now Corp?" asked a soldier.

Frank looked at Keith. "What do you reckon?"

Keith grimaced. "I reckon this whole area's going to be reduced to rubble any minute."

"So do I. I reckon we should drop back to that row of houses through there and then move back further in the town." Keith nodded. "Right," said Frank. "Pick up your gear and let's get the hell out of here!" Without further ado, they all picked up and ran across the street to the next row of houses, barely stopping as Keith kicked in the front door for them to run on through, just as the houses on the other side exploded in a pile of dust and rubble. "Keep on going!" Frank screamed as they all ran down the garden and across its rear wall to the next row. Frank, this time, kicked in the door and they bundled into the kitchen of the little house to find an old woman and a young boy crouched under the table, looking up at them in horror. "Oh bloody hell," Frank swore. "I didn't know there'd be civilians here. What do we do Keith, leave them or take them?"

"I don't know for Christ's sake," Keith roared. He turned to the couple. "You come with us?" He gestured at them, pointing first at himself, then at them and the door. The old woman shook her head and motioned for them to go, waving her hand as if urgently dismissing them. "She wants to stay I think Frank," he said. "Let's go."

Frank hesitated but then he shrugged his shoulders. "Let's go!" he
repeated. He held the front door and waved the men through. For a
moment he stood there gazing down at the couple, but then he rushed
out to follow his men and on down towards their headquarters at the
other end of town, thankful for every building that they could put
between them and the enemy.

If they were expecting order and assistance at the Town Hall,
which had been commandeered as headquarters, they were to be
sorely disappointed, for as they approached they could see that to
all intents and purposes the building was deserted. One lone vehicle
filled to capacity with files and paperwork stood outside, its engine
running, its driver impatient to be off. A staff Sergeant ran from the
building as they arrived, making for the open door of the small lorry.
Frank held his arm and he turned, clearly annoyed at this detention.
"What are we to do Sergeant?"

"Get the hell out of this town," said his captive, pulling himself
loose. "We're leaving... they've taken Mons and we're to head south
and regroup." He shook himself free from Frank's grasp and ran
across to the vehicle and jumped in, pulling the door shut as it jerked
forward and away before Frank or his band could do anything to
stop it.

"Damn and blast!" yelled Keith. "The bloody swine's just left us to
rot."

"Regroup," said Tim. "Doesn't he mean retreat."

"No mate. Retreat means you're beaten and running and the
Generals have to admit to failure. Regroup means a tactical
repositioning and they come out with their arses intact."

"Sounds the bloody same to me" was the almost universal chorus.

Frank stood looking after the departing vehicle. "What do you
think, Frank?" Keith asked quietly.

Frank turned and then stirred into action. "Right. We're going to
get out of this mess chaps, and like the man said, we'd better go
south. Search around and see if you can find us some food first... and

fill every billy you've got with good water. I reckon we'll need that. Meet back here in five minutes."

It was a sorry scene that they joined later. The road at the southern end of the small town was by then clogged with men and machinery, all desperate to get clear of the advancing enemy. Frightened men who for the first time had seen other men die and had faced death themselves. Lost in a foreign land and to all intents and purposes left to their own devices. The proud British Expeditionary Force, which was supposed to be home victorious before Christmas, was in tatters and in full retreat.

Throughout that long and wearisome march, Frank and Keith managed to keep their little group together. They marched along with men from their own regiment, with Frenchmen and men from the remnants of the Belgian army. Lines of tired men carrying their arms and equipment. Marching on either side of the road to allow the horse-drawn wagons and the occasional motor vehicle to pass through the middle. Three whole armies in retreat, with the German army snapping at their heels. Across the Sambre and on to the Somme, where at this, the last natural barrier before Paris, they turned and dug in.

......

My darling Violet,

Once again I seem to be writing to you in haste, but please forgive me as I have to post this letter now as we are off soon.

I have thought of you every day since I left. How did your father accept you on your return? I presume that you did go home. Oh my love I miss you, and the worst of it all is that I cannot hear from you and only have to imagine what is happening with you.

I live for the time when we are home again and I can be with you. When I close my eyes at night I remember our times together and in particular the time we spent in Kent. I do not think that I have ever felt such a thrill in my life as when, sitting in Jesse's garden, I turned and there you were. I am sending this to Jesse with a short note so that she can send it on to you. My darling I wish that I could bring it to you myself.

Our commanding officer thinks that the war will all be over by Christmas. I do hope so because if we can arrange it I would love you to have Christmas with Jesse and me at Lilac Cottage.

I have to go now my darling. I will write again as soon as I am able. Take care of yourself. All my love forever.

Frank

It was dated 12th August, but Violet was reading the letter at the end of the month nearly a full week after Frank had begun the march south following the fall of Mons. News was beginning to trickle through that all was not well with the British Expeditionary Force and the papers were full of exhortations for young men to join up.

Violet sighed and then read the letter again, sitting there in the same chair in which she had read his previous letter. The only difference was that this time she could not pack her things to seek him out because she simply didn't know where he was. The worst aspect of war, she thought, was that the separations were so complete. In normal circumstances, if you were apart from someone you loved you would at least know where they were or have some clear idea of their situation. Whereas now... well, he didn't really know where she was and she had no idea at all about where he was save a shrewd idea that he was on the continent and involved in the fighting. For the first time, it hit her that he was actually in danger and she felt her hands go clammy at the thought.

She sat quite still and mentally pulled herself together. This wouldn't do. She had to remain calm and she had to keep up her spirits... for his sake as well as for her own. She looked again at the letter and smiled. He didn't write a very good letter, did he? It was funny, when he was with her in Kent he had been able to express himself quite clearly, yet put a pen and paper in front of him and it came out all stilted and formal. Still, the message was there clear enough... he loved her and one day they would be back together. She put aside the letter and looked at the accompanying one from Jesse.

My dear Violet,

I enclose the letter for you that Frank has sent to me. In his letter to me he says that he is off soon but he does not say where. If he says more in your letter I expect you will let me know, but Brian says that they have to be careful as there are spies everywhere. Who would have thought it in England?

Brian tells me that your father met you at the station in Tenterden. That nosy old station master told him when he was down there the other day. I do hope he was not that angry with you, but in another way I was glad that you had a companion for your journey. Speaking of which, I heard that Frank was not alone on his train as a friend from his school, Keith, was with him. It makes me pleased to know that he has a friend from home.

The garden is looking lovely this August but the cottage seems empty without you two, even though you were only here a short while. I pray for the day, quite soon I hope, when we are together again.

Well that is all for now my love. Take care and write to me as soon as you can.

Love Jesse

Violet smiled secretly to herself. Hearing from Jesse brought it all back. Those days in the country. Days of learning. Days of love. She thought of their love-making and the memory made her tummy roll over. She rubbed it thoughtfully. She had been feeling   of late. Probably a bug she had picked up, she thought, or the fact that deep within her there was an emptiness and an unspoken fear.

"Violet. Violet," came a call to break into her thoughts. It came from the sitting room. Her mother.

"Coming mother." She folded the letters into her pocket and

hurried through. "I looked in just a while ago and you were asleep."

"Have you been away again Violet?" her mother asked.

"No mother. I've been back for some time now. I was only away for a little while."

"Oh good. Only your father seemed so agitated while you were away. Did you go anywhere nice?"

"Only to the country mother... to see some dear friends."

"That's nice dear. That's nice." She nodded her head and dozed off again. Violet rearranged her mother's shawl and stole from the room. In the hall, a sudden feeling of nausea came over her. She stopped and leant against the wall, waiting for it to pass before gathering herself together to go upstairs to write to Jesse.

Through the open door of the kitchen Alice had seen her, and as Violet went up the stairs she turned back down to her cooking shaking her head.

October 1914

"Ready lads?" Frank whispered.

"Ready as we can be Frank," said Keith. "But if it's all the same to you would you mind if I stayed here and tidied the place up for your return?"

"Fix bayonets" came the order down the line and the metallic clunk of the rings going home ran down the line and on into the distance.

Frank smiled at his friend. They had stayed together now ever since their meeting on the train, and even though Frank had been made Sergeant their friendship had grown. Adversity and danger forged links between them that bordered on love. Each held within his pocket the names and addresses of the loved ones of the other. Neither had considered what would happen if they both bought it.

Frank talked of Violet all the time to Keith, who by now felt as if he knew her almost as well as if he'd actually met her. For his part, Keith had become enamoured of a girl they had both gone to school with called Rosie and who he had ended up working in the hop gardens with. A big blonde girl with a ready smile and a ready kiss. On nights when Frank lay trying to picture Violet, shyly thinking of their illicit passion, Keith would be chuckling to himself and remembering rolls in the grass with Rosie... frantic couplings with little if any preamble, accompanied by giggling and laughter. Keith had no doubt that when he got back he would eventually marry Rosie, but he had no illusions either that she would remain faithful to him. When opportunity came, Rosie would laugh and roll in the grass with whoever was available. For Keith, her very amorality was her appeal, and if he had the chance to tumble a French girl, or any other for that matter whilst he was away... well he wouldn't think twice.

In stark contrast, the thought of anyone else but Violet left Frank cold. He had made a pact with her and he would keep that pact whatever. He had received one letter from Violet, sent on by Jesse, so he knew now that she was back at her home. He knew also that relations with her father were strained, but in a funny sort of way was glad that she was there with her family in the support and environment she was used to... especially whilst he was helpless to assist.

They had dug in after the flight from Mons and a sort of stalemate had evolved around the Somme north of Paris, where the system of trenches and dugouts had become home for them. Day after day and night after night were spent in an endless repetition of checking weapons and ammunition, keeping a watch out for any enemy movement and generally trying to keep as healthy as possible in the atrocious conditions. When the sun shone, the vapours given off by the rubbish and effluent of so many men threatened to overpower them, and when it rained their environment turned into a quagmire of filthy stinking mud that clogged up everything. Footwear became heavy. Puttees shrank in the wet, cutting off the blood supply to feet already damaged with trench foot, and movement around the dugout became unbearable. Water leaked into everything and gathered in disgusting pools, attracting midges and flies, which in the warmth of the autumn flew around biting any and all exposed areas of skin, driving up tempers.

In places where the trenches were only a short distance from the enemy they had to face the constant danger of snipers, and the only way to alleviate this was to dig deeper unless they wanted to go everywhere doubled up. The deeper they dug the more they collected water and the more the cycle of problems expanded.

Now on this chill morning they were all lined up with orders to advance on a given signal, in an attempt to break this stalemate and push the Germans back.

It was quieter now. An unearthly silence after the bombardments of the night when shells had shrieked and wailed like demons across the night sky. Upon everybody lay the fear of what the push could bring, tempered with the earnest desire to do something... anything to alter their current conditions. "A change is as good as rest," Tim had pronounced.

Frank looked down the line of men he had grown to know so well. Keith first. How he wished now that they had kept more in touch when they were home in England. In the years leading up to the war they had barely spoken a word other than general greetings, yet here... here he could not imagine life without this man. He resolved that when they got home he would never let time lie between them for too long. Tim. The irrepressible Tim. What could one say? Always cheerful, always with a quip on his lips, the one who had kept their spirits up and their sense of humour alive. He looked on down the line. John, Andy... the other John, David... the line went on, out of sight beyond the curve of the trench. All of them had become so much a part of him that the thought of their loss was as strange to him as would be the cutting off of a limb.

They waited there in the growing light of the autumn morning. Silent now. Their very silence probably warning the Germans of their coming. A whistle blew in the distance, followed almost immediately by one a little closer, and so on down the line until the one held by their own Captain also blew and they launched themselves up the ladders and over the top. Almost immediately they were met with rifle fire. Tim reached the top of the trench ladder and then just slid back lifeless, a puzzled look on his face and a purple-red hole in his forehead. Frank saw him go back but kept on running. Keith's broad back was in front of him, and to his left he could see David pushing forward, a grim look on his face. A machine gun stuttered in front of them and Keith and Frank hurled themselves to the ground, scrabbling for any cover that the undulations and ridges of previous shellfire had made. David seemed to watch them, wondering. Then he too fell to the ground between them, but sideways, his legs buckling and flying from under him, his rifle falling from his grasp as he raised his hands in the air in a sort of mock token of surrender.

A gurgling red froth came from his mouth. He jerked spasmodically round in a half circle and then stopped, his neck arched back, his eyes wide and staring, before his head fell forwards, burying his face in the mud.

Frank and Keith watched this macabre dance in silent terror before a shout from the Captain, kneeling on the ground just ahead of them, brought them back. He was waving them forward. Frank raised himself out of the mud and gathered his strength and thoughts for the next move. He reached over David's body to touch Keith. "All right Keith?" he yelled.

"All right? What the hell do you mean all right? This is bloody murder and that bastard wants us to go on!" he shouted back over the deafening roar of battle.

"We don't have a bloody choice, do we mate?"

Keith looked at him and smiled wanly. "All right let's do it." He turned and waved at the men behind them. "Come on lads!" he cried. They scrabbled to their feet and, yelling wildly, rushed forward towards the guns. Smoke was everywhere and the sound of guns firing and men screaming in anger and pain filled their senses. Like ravening beasts they descended upon a group of frightened forward German gunners, scattering and shooting them down as they ran. As they passed they stabbed down with their bayonets, and in a continuation of the movement withdrew and ran on in their killing rage. Coils of barbed wire curled over and caught them but they rushed on, tearing their uniforms, ripping great gashes in their legs as they dragged errant sections with them. Beyond the wire the Captain lay face down in the mud, his pistol still clasped in his outstretched hand, seeming to point the way like some ludicrous signpost.

Keith disappeared over a ridge and Frank veered to the right and found himself alone for a moment in the mist and smoke. He heard gunfire ahead and ran towards it, shouting for his friends. He topped the ridge of a shell crater and stopped, exposed on its rim. A chattering burst of machine gun fire seemed to break into his very consciousness and he felt punching sensations in his legs and side. Still he stood there, rifle in hand, firing blindly forward to where he perceived the gunfire to be coming from. He tried to hold his rifle straight. He tried to stand up straight, cursing himself at his inability to do so. He sought to fire forwards, but for some stupid reason he could only point his rifle at the ground, and then he realised with surprise that he was bent over it with the barrel in the mud and his waist resting over the butt. 'What the hell are you doing,' he thought. Stand up straight for Christ's sake. He jerked himself into what he believed to be an upright position, dropping the gun in the process, and was surprised to find that, far from being upright, he had only contrived to lie face up and head down into the shell hole.

A sudden griping spasm of pain ripped through his stomach and he clutched himself. It felt wet. He raised his hands so that he could see them and saw dark blood on them... and shit. It looked like shit. 'How the hell did shit get on my stomach,' he thought, and then all reason fled from him as he doubled up with another searing spasm of pain that felt as if a red-hot poker had been thrust deep into his very being. He heard a strange sound. A high piercing sound that wavered up and down and he listened to that sound for some time before realising that he was making it. 'Oh Jesus Christ,' he thought from beyond the pain. 'I'm dying... no I can't... I won't.' His mind raced. He jerked his body again in a vain effort to stand but his legs were both shattered at the knees and he only succeeded in slipping further into the hole, ending up in a heap at the bottom, up against something soft. It moved slightly and let out a low moaning sound. For a moment Frank lay there, his eyes shut firmly against the pain, but then he opened them to look sideways and up, to see that he was lying against a young German soldier who sat clutching a gaping, bloody wound in his side. He made no move against him and the two lay there beside each other.

A coldness was creeping through Frank's lower body now, moving up his torso in a welcome extinguishing of his pain. He lay there looking up into the brightening morning sky with a strange peace coming over him.

The young German boy coughed horribly and blood appeared at the corners of his mouth. He looked down at Frank, and in a voice barely audible whispered, "Ich habe große angst."

Frank reached up and took his enemy's hand. The boy's breathing became shallower and he lapsed into unconsciousness. Frank followed him.

"Frank. Frank," Violet called softly. He awoke and looked at her.

"Violet you've come."

"Of course I've come, silly. Here, rest your head." He moved slightly to rest his head on her lap. She put her hand on his head and stroked his hair. "Rest now my love."

Keith found Frank later that morning on his way back. He nearly passed straight by, but something about the two bodies caught his eye. The body of the German boy was sitting there, his head lolling into his chest, with Frank's head resting on his lap. The boy held fast to one of Frank's hands and his other hand rested on Frank's head, the fingers frozen in the act of stroking his hair.

......

Ernest sat in the dining room, the newspaper propped up in front on the cruet set whilst he cracked open his egg. He peeled off the top and scooped out the white left in it, whilst still staring at the paper. He read that Paris had been saved and that British and French troops had occupied Ypres. 'Our boys are doing well,' he thought. The image of Frank Balfour's face crossed his mind. 'Damned swine,' he thought, 'taking my daughter from me.' Violet and he had co-existed in the house since her return, but she seemed odd and at times distant from him. He longed for her to sit beside him again and for their hands to entwine in that quiet comfort that he remembered.

The journey back in the train had been a frosty one, with her all upset at the fact that her blessed Frank had gone off and that war had been declared. He, on the other hand, had been seething at the interruption in his programme and not a little disappointed that he had been unable to give the bounder a piece of his mind. Damn it all, he'd enticed his daughter to disobey and desert him!

Once home, she had resumed the position of the dutiful daughter and fulfilled the role around the household that she had occupied before her departure. No complaints there. The business of her elopement was not raised again, and both of them seemed at pains not to mention it further. She had, though, not seemed very well in herself and he wondered if she was sickening for something. Probably pining for that bloody man Balfour, he thought.

The letterbox clacked and he made a mental note that the postman had been.

In the hall, Violet saw the letters come through the box and stooped to pick them up, sorting through them and removing one addressed to her before putting the others on the dresser by the mirror for her father to pick up on his way out to work. She looked down at the envelope in her hand. It was from an army source. She could see that from the envelope, but the writing on the front wasn't Frank's.

She climbed the stairs, opening the envelope as she went, and stopped at the half landing as she freed the letter and opened it to read.

Ernest was just wiping his face with his napkin and preparing to leave for work when he heard the long drawn out scream from the hallway and the sound of someone falling. He stood up quickly, knocking his chair backwards and catching the tablecloth as he rushed from the room, oblivious to the damage. Out in the hall, Violet was lying on her back at the foot of the stairs with her legs still pointing up them, her skirts all awry and her face the colour of ash. She seemed to have fainted but he could see no other damage as he rushed to her side and cradled her head, calling her name.

Alice came running out of the kitchen and stopped, clutching her hands to her mouth in horror. "Get me a doctor!" shouted Ernest. "Quick, hurry now."

She needed no further urging and ran out of the house and down the road towards Doctor Crowe's house, leaving the front door wide open. Ernest sat on the floor with Violet's head in his lap, looking out of the door agitatedly awaiting the doctor while stroking his daughter's face. It seemed ages to him, but it wasn't that long before Alice came running back through the door, calling back to the doctor running up the garden path with his coat open and his bag in his hand.

"Quick Crowe," Ernest shouted as he came through the door. "She's fallen down the stairs. Help her please."

"All right," said Crowe, putting down his bag and kneeling by the girl. "Let me look at her." He felt down her limbs, looking for broken bones as Ernest stood up and aside, looking down at her and wringing his hands.

"Is she all right?"

"She's had a nasty fall... but I don't think anything's broken," mused the doctor. "We'd better get her upstairs to her bed and I'll have a proper look at her. Here, give me a hand will you Matthews, and you too Alice. Let's get her upstairs."

The three of them picked up her lifeless form and carried it upstairs as gently as they could to lay her on her bed. Crowe knelt down beside it and started to examine her properly and then, aware of the other two still standing in the room, he turned to them. "Would you mind old chap... giving me a moment? I won't be long I promise."

"Of course, of course. So sorry. Come Alice, we'll leave the doctor to his business." He ushered her from the room. "I'll be just outside." Crowe nodded and turned back to his patient.

Ernest closed the door. He glanced at Alice standing there, pale-faced and shaking. "You go downstairs and make some tea for us all please Alice," he said quietly. She nodded and ran down the stairs.

For a moment he watched her go, then he turned and looked out of the landing window at the garden beyond. He sighed and turned back in, glancing at the bedroom door and then along the corridor to his wife's room. Had she heard? No, she couldn't have. He put his hands behind his back and paced up and down, his head low as he stared at the carpet.

Alice appeared at the foot of the stairs with a tray in her hands. "Where do you want this sir?" she called up.

"Put it in the front room please Alice."

What seemed an eternity later, the bedroom door opened and the doctor came out. "Is she all right," said Ernest clutching his arm.

"Nothing serious... look old chap, is there somewhere we could have a word?"

"Certainly. Oh what a relief... you're sure she's all right?"

"Quite sure, but I need to have a word with you."

"Eh... yes down here. Come into the front room. I've had some tea put in there. I expect you'll need some. So good of you to come." Ernest was aware that he was gabbling on, but his nervousness and relief needed some expression and he constantly repeated his thanks as he showed the doctor down the stairs and into the front room. He shut the door behind him as they entered. "Please take a seat doctor." Crowe remained standing, looking out through the front window, his back to Ernest. "Are you sure everything's all right doctor?" Ernest said tentatively, aware now of the doctor's own unease.

Crowe turned, a grave look on his face. "Sit down old chap," he said, motioning Ernest into one of his own chairs. Ernest meekly followed his command and sat looking up at the man expectantly. "Your daughter... Violet is fine. No damage at all from the fall."

"Oh thank God," said Ernest, making as if to rise but sinking back as the doctor held his hand out motioning him to stay seated.

"Your daughter is pregnant, Matthews."

"What!" Ernest exploded.

"Pregnant, I'm afraid... about three months I'd say. Oh it's all right, the baby's not harmed, but the mother will need to rest for a few days to get over the shock."

Ernest sat there poleaxed. Pregnant? Violet pregnant? How? When? He stared into space, his mind racing around thinking of the implications. Thinking of the damned culprit! Well he would be made to pay for forcing his unwelcome attentions to his daughter, he thought. He'd not be allowed to leave his daughter with his child and escape his responsibilities. The doctor coughed and held out a letter to him.

"I think you'd better read this."

Ernest took the letter, blankly staring at the man. Then he unfolded it and read.

Dear Miss Matthews,

I am very sorry to have to tell you that Frank was killed yesterday fighting bravely in battle. I found his body.

He was my friend and I shall miss him more than I can say. He told me of you and his love for you and we had promised each other that if either of us was killed we would tell our loved ones.

I cannot tell you how sad I am at his loss and I know that this letter will cause you much pain. I am sorry. One day I hope that we can meet and I can tell you of him and his last moments.

Yours

in sympathy

Keith Pitts (Cpl)

Ernest put down the letter. The doctor looked down at the beaten man. "I think I'd better be going now," he said, concern in his voice. "I think we'll keep this between us and say nothing to anyone for now, eh? Except of course Violet. You need to talk to her and I will need to see her again tomorrow."

Ernest said nothing. He just nodded in agreement, showed the doctor to the door, and when he left shut it quietly and went back alone into the front room.

Ernest stepped into the bedroom and stood just inside the door, looking over at Violet. His face was grave. A small muscle twitched in his temple and he put his hand up to feel it. 'I must remain calm,' he thought. 'This business has to be sorted out and sorted out properly.'

He watched his daughter lying there looking over at him, her face expressionless. She had been thus for nearly two days now. Crowe said that there was nothing wrong with her physically, but that the shock that had rendered her senseless at the time of the accident would take some time to wear off. Some time. How much time? Damn it, the girl was pregnant. Pregnant. Pregnant. He repeated the word like a chant in his mind. His Violet was with child and unwed and now... now with Balfour dead in France, would not be. Oh he hadn't wanted Balfour before, but by Christ he could do with the bugger now.

He looked down at her. There she was. The same daughter he had loved. In the same body yet... now she was occupied by... had been violated by... He shuddered. It was no longer his child's body but the body possessed by another man and now host to that man's child. Where was she? He swallowed hard and tried not to allow the feeling of revulsion that swept over him. 'My little girl. My little girl. She's here. She's here. Oh God!'

What would the neighbours think? Crowe wouldn't say a word, he knew that, but soon it would become apparent. Alice. Did she know? Did she guess? Oh God, what the hell would all his business associates say? Serves him right for giving the girl her head, they'd say. Bad lot the Matthews'. He couldn't stand that. As soon as she was well enough he would have to make arrangements, and this time she would obey him. She did not have her majority yet, and by God he would not have the reputation he and his father had built up in this town destroyed.

He moved closer and studied her ashen face. Void now of emotion, her unseeing eyes staring into the distance. "How are you feeling?" he whispered, moving closer and sitting on the bed beside her. She nodded but made no sound. Well at least she understood him. He stroked her forehead. "I'll leave you alone. We'll talk later. Oh, your mother's been asking after you. I've told her you had a fall and must be left quiet."

He bent down to kiss her cheek, stood, looked briefly around the room and then left, closing the door quietly behind him. He had things to arrange.

Leaving the house later that morning he turned right, not left as he usually would to go to the office, and instead walked down to Doctor Crowe's house. He knocked at the door with the small brass nameplate beside it. 'Not as bright as ours at the office,' he thought, but clearer. He could hear the approaching footsteps and the door opened to reveal the doctor standing there in just his shirt. "Ah Matthews. Come on in man, it's chilly out there. Come on in. We'll talk in my study."

He led the way through. A small room with just a desk and two leather-bound chairs, but with the walls covered on every surface with shelves laden with books. A small fire was burning in the arched iron grate, set into its surround of ochre tiles, and above the mantle was the only decoration in the room, a Highland scene.

"Sit you down," said Crowe. "Sit you down." Ernest took a chair and the doctor closed the door and sat in the other one, leaning forward slightly to talk to his friend. "I've been making some enquiries about the situation and I may have come up with a solution if it's acceptable to you."

"I'm grateful for all your trouble Crowe. Damned grateful."

"Well, I've the name of a lady who will take your daughter in until the birth of the child. And, I think, I can then suggest a placement of the infant, which will remove the problem and allow your family... that is you and your daughter, to get on with your lives. I take it that the three of us are the only ones who know."

"As far as I can tell. Mind, I've not spoken to Violet about it as such. Do you think she realises the full import of her situation?"

"I've told her but I have to admit she made little response and I cannot be sure she fully understood. Perhaps that's for the best at the moment. After all, you don't know what she'd do or say... for that matter, who to."

"God forbid. I cannot let this out. My business relies on my reputation. This would kill it off."

"Well it's important that we act quickly then and, if I may say so, with the girl in shock, if we act quickly she may be more amenable."

"Quite so," said Ernest.

"Well I can arrange for you to meet this... eh, shall we say... chaperone, this afternoon. It's a Miss Court, she's the sister of one of my nurses. Quite discreet I can assure you. She lives in a cottage in the country near Gloucester, but she's visiting her up here at the moment. Due to go back next week so that should be splendid."

"I can't thank you enough Crowe," said Ernest, reaching forward for the man's hand. "You've been so understanding."

"Well we professionals must stick together now, mustn't we? After all you... eh... well you handled that other business for me a few years back and... well you know old man."

Ernest smiled for the first time. "Quite so. Quite forgotten about that, don't you know." He coughed and stood up. "When should I come to meet this lady?"

"Oh not here," said Crowe. "I've arranged for you to meet her at the hospital... more private if you see what I mean. If you don't take to the lady that will be as far as it goes."

"Oh I'll take to the lady I'm sure. She sounds a Godsend. Err... you were saying about... well about afterwards?"

"Yes. Well there are... shall we say... channels for this sort of thing. You're not alone in this predicament and there are... well networks which place children suitably."

"How do you mean suitably?"

"I mean that there are families which will take the child and look after it properly."

"I have no real interest in the child. No bastard child of Balfour's is of interest to me."

"It is your grandchild old man. Surely you are interested in its welfare?"

"Not really. I confess that at the present time I have no interest other than in concealing this situation and resolving it."

Crowe nodded his understanding. "These families will take on the infant and foster it for a monthly payment... rising as the child grows up, of course."

"Of course."

"The child remains in your legal custody and can be reclaimed at any time."

"I cannot say that prospect delights me, I'm sure," said Ernest, standing. "I will come to the hospital at what time?"

"About half past three. Ask for me and I'll introduce you." Crowe opened the door and stood back to allow Ernest to leave the room, following him to the front door. "I'll see you later," he said as he shut the door.

Ernest made his way back down the street, past his house and on to the office. Might as well get some work done today, he thought. This affair is taking enough time as it is. He passed a news stand. "Income Tax Doubled". Oh good, he thought. Business is down and they double the taxes. He admonished himself almost immediately. No, he mustn't think like that. Young men were giving their lives for this war. Young men like... like Balfour. He banished the vision from his mind. Don't lose the anger, he thought. Don't weaken.

......

"I've come to see Doctor Crowe."

"Doctor Crowe. Doctor Crowe," the porter mused. "Ah yes, Doctor Crowe. He'll be at the end of that corridor there. The last door on the left."

Ernest thanked him and strode purposefully down the corridor. He knocked at the door. "Come in," said Crowe's voice. He opened the door and went in.

Crowe was sitting behind his desk and, in front of it, on one of the two uncomfortable-looking chairs usually reserved for patients was a middle-aged woman. She remained seated with her hands clasped demurely in her lap, seemingly oblivious to the intrusion. Crowe stood and came around the desk to shake Ernest's hand. "Come in and meet Miss Court."

Ernest moved in front of the woman and held his hand out, but let it fall again as she kept hers firmly in her lap. Crowe put his hand on his shoulder, guided him to the other chair and then went back around to his own and sat down. He leaned forward on the desk. "Well now. This... this... err... Miss Court, is Mr Matthews. The gentleman I was telling you about."

Ernest studied the woman. She was skinny and drawn. A spinster if ever he had seen one. Fiftyish and already dried up like an old apple well past its storage. Her hair, grey and fine, was dragged back from her thin face and held tightly within the confines of her hat. Her nose was aquiline and there was a discernible dewdrop at the end, which she dabbed with her handkerchief whilst she kept her thin lips pursed in an expression of distaste.

But it was her eyes which caught his attention. They looked for all the world like the little false eyes of a stuffed ferret he had seen in a shop window. Dark and fierce and set deep into her sallow, wrinkled face. God, he thought. Poor Violet.

Poor Violet be damned! She'd brought this upon herself. She'd sowed the seeds all right. Now she had to reap the harvest. A small smile played on his lips at the non-intentional aptness of the metaphor. Miss Court saw the smile, and taking it for a greeting on his part forced her face into what she imagined was a smile. It only served to enhance her ugliness and show her little sharp teeth, reinforcing his impression of the ferret.

"I presume Doctor Crowe has informed you of my... my daughter's... situation?" said Ernest.

"He has," said Miss Court in a thin, reedy voice which again did nothing to dispel his impressions.

"Miss Court," Crowe interjected, "is prepared to accommodate your daughter at her home until the birth of the child and then to escort her to a farm in Devon, where the child is to be kept. We have discussed a level of remuneration for this and I have set it out here on this paper."

He passed a sheet of paper with figures tabled on it to Ernest, who picked it up and scanned the contents. He nodded his agreement to Crowe, who continued. "As for the upkeep of the child when it's fostered, I have agreed the figures set out on this paper." He handed over another sheet to Ernest, who again read it, nodded his agreement and passed both sheets back to him.

"When will you wish my daughter to accompany you?" said Ernest to the woman.

"I leave for home at the end of next week," said Miss Court. "That is Friday the 17th of November. I shall take the girl with me if that is your wish."

"It is," Ernest replied without hesitation. "I need to talk to her, but she will be ready to travel then... will she doctor?"

"Physically yes, but her mental state is, as you know, one of anguish."

Ernest turned back to the woman. "I do not wish my daughter to suffer unduly, but at the same time I do not wish this arrangement to go wrong and for the... for the situation to become public knowledge."

"I understand," said Miss Court. "You may rely on my discretion and you may rely on me to fulfil your wishes. Might I ask that payment is made monthly to this account." She handed Ernest a note. He glanced at it briefly, folded it quietly and put it in his top pocket.

"I think that concludes our business for the present," he said briskly, relieved that it was in fact nearly over. "Where would you suggest we meet on Friday?"

"Bring her to Paddington station for the 2.10 train to Gloucester. I will meet you in the waiting room at say a quarter to two... and bring her ticket."

......

Ernest knocked quietly at Violet's door.

"Come in," she called. He entered. "Oh it's you daddy."

She was sitting in a chair by the window, looking out into the evening sky, a blanket around her shoulders. She looked pale and drawn, and for the first time ever she resembled her mother. God that that man had brought his daughter to this, Ernest thought.

"How are you feeling?"

"Black and blue all over... as if I'd been hit by a train. And... and empty... lost and very alone."

"How can you be alone when you have your family?"

She turned, showing her tear-stained face pale in the fading light. "I loved him daddy. I truly loved him... even though you hated him. I loved him... I..."

"I know my dear but... well he has obviously taken advantage of you, hasn't he?"

"Taken advantage? What do you mean, taken advantage?"

"I mean... well I mean your... your condition."

She looked up at him quizzically. "My condition? You... you mean all these bruises?"

He looked down at her horrified, the realisation coming to him that she had no idea what he was talking about. A pounding began in his temple as he knelt down in front of her, taking her hand in his. "Violet, you are pregnant."

She snatched her hand from his, looking up at him as if he were mad. She shook her head. "Pregnant. No I can't be. Pregnant. How?"

"I would have thought you should ask yourself that question my dear. But you are definitely with child."

"Pregnant." She repeated the loathsome word.

He persisted. "Yes Violet, pregnant. You are going to have a baby and presumably Frank Balfour is to blame."

"Father, Frank is dead. Don't you understand, he's dead... killed in the war."

"I know dear. I know. But before that... it must be him... he... he must have forced himself upon you... and... now... now he's gone and..."

The full truth struck her at last and she flushed scarlet and turned her face away from him. Shame and... What was it? Disgust? No it couldn't be. The memory of her passion rushed back to her and she felt the colour drain just as fast from her face and an empty well opening in her stomach. Tears sprang into her eyes. Feelings welled within her in conflicting circles of triumph and despair. "Oh Frank!" she wailed loudly. Ernest patted her arm and motioned for her to be quiet but she ignored him. "Frank. Oh Frank!" She bent her head and sobbed, muttering his name all the while.

"Violet," Ernest said, shaking her arm gently. "Violet we have to talk about this. We have to decide what to do." She looked up at him, wondering, as he continued. "We have to decide what to do about the baby. You're not married and with... with Balfour de... with him gone we're going to have to do something. We've both got our reputations to think of. You're only nineteen..."

"I'm nearly twenty."

"What's the difference Violet? You have no means of support other than me... and with an illegitimate baby no prospects whatsoever..."

She started to cry again, the full horror... the full shame of her situation showing on her face. She turned her head away from him, unable to look him in the eye. "Oh daddy, what shall I do? What shall I become?"

"You shall become my daughter again. That's what you shall become. I've spoken to people and I've arranged for you to stay with a lady in Gloucestershire until the birth... and for a family to foster the child when it's born."

She turned back to him, her face flushed. "You've arranged all that without consulting me?"

He saw the danger of her annoyance spoiling all his plans. He reached out to her with both hands and cupped her face, holding it and staring straight into her eyes. "Now listen Violet. You've not been well. You had a terrible fall. I had to do something... I had to."

"But why? Why can't... why can't I... could I not...?"

"No Violet, you could not. You know that you could not." He thought quickly. "Frank would not want you to be shamed, would he?" He waited as his words hit home and she crumpled in his hands, nodding her head in mute agreement. He reached up and stroked her hair. "There now my love, it's for the best. It's for the best."

"Are you angry with me daddy? Do you hate me?"

"No darling. I could never hate you. I'm upset and hurt, but that's to be expected. After all... no it doesn't matter now. All that does matter is that we do the right thing from now on and keep our own council, even to your mother. Is that understood? Nobody must know of this other than the two of us... and Doctor Crowe."

"Does he know?"

"Of course he does Violet. How else would I know? He told me... he told you actually but you don't seem to have understood."

"He would have married me you know. He did... we did love each other."

Ernest hid his grimace of distaste by pulling her down to him and holding her. No point in pushing the issue now, he thought. But damn the man. Damn the man to hell!

......

The week had flown by for Ernest and now here he was at Paddington with Violet. The explanations and inventions he had had to make in the last few days had left him quite exhausted. First there was Elsie. "Why was Violet going away again?" she had wanted to know. "If she wasn't well after her accident, surely she would recover better at home," she had pleaded.

"No," he had insisted. "The doctor felt that she needed to rest in the country air and he had arranged it for her."

"But surely the air was good enough here in Finchley, where she was at home with her family," Elsie had persisted. In the end, and thank God this time, her own infirmities had once more overwhelmed her and she had taken to her bed and ceased her questioning.

And Alice? He wasn't sure about Alice. She hadn't said anything, but the looks she gave made him feel that she knew or suspected more than she let on.

Violet was the strangest one in all of this. She had simply gone into a shell following their talk and seemed to act as if she were in some sort of a dream. He had half expected her to change her mind and threaten to defy him. He had a speech all ready in his mind whereby he would lay the law down, threaten her support and warn her of her lack of a majority. But it hadn't been needed at all. She had merely listened to what he had said when he had confirmed the arrangements and meekly packed her suitcases ready for this day.

And here they were at the station. Half past one. They were early. Time to get her luggage properly marked up and put on the train by the porter before meeting Miss Court in the waiting room. He wondered at Violet's reaction to Miss Court. She would instinctively dislike her of course... it was difficult not to. But would she say or do anything? If her behaviour over the past week was anything to go by, the answer was no. She now seemed drained of all emotional reaction or feeling. Could she have really been in love with that bounder Balfour, he thought, or was Crowe wrong and the fall had affected her? Either way it was not the Violet he knew and loved who was accompanying him on this sad occasion. Would that the girl who returned next year was the daughter he knew.

They walked into the waiting room and Ernest looked around for Miss Court. Violet stood there beside him, holding on to his arm, showing no interest at all in the surroundings or any anticipation of their meeting. Miss Court sat primly on a bench at the far end and Ernest guided Violet over to her. "Good afternoon Miss Court. May I introduce my daughter Violet."

The spinster looked at this fallen young woman in front of her. The barren and withered observing the flowering and fruiting. "Pleased I'm sure," she said with no pleasure at all in her voice. Violet merely nodded at her and then turned her face to her father's. He thought he saw a flicker of emotion, a plea... but then her face resumed its set and vacant expression. The moment was gone.

"Well, best be getting to the train then," said Miss Court. "Might as well make sure of a good seat. Where's your luggage?"

"Oh her trunks are on the train. This is all she has to carry," Ernest answered on Violet's behalf. He held up Violet's travelling bag to the woman. She wrinkled her nose, wiped the dewdrop off, picked up her own bag and made for the exit.

"Here let me..." Ernest's voice tailed off at her disdainful look. They followed her on to the platform and found two opposite seats near the centre of the train. Miss Court settled herself in the forward-facing one and Violet went to the other. She checked as Ernest tugged her arm. "Goodbye my love," he said bending to kiss her on the cheek. She accepted his kiss and then took her seat. Miss Court wrinkled her nose in obvious distaste.

Ernest stood on the platform until the train had gone. Violet had stared hard at him as it left, and for two pins he would have plucked her from the train there and then. But the moment passed. Thank God, he thought.

He watched and waited until the train was completely out of sight. He had never felt so empty in his life. A gaping hole had opened up in his heart at the strange sense of his betrayal of the one thing in life he loved. He turned back and resolved to work late that night and every night. He would fill the emptiness with the one thing he knew... work.

......

Spring in the forest was a wonderful sight and Violet, heavy as she now was, would walk deep within it for much of the day when the weather was fine. Even if it threatened to rain, she would often still go to get out of the house she had occupied with Miss Court, her jailer, since before Christmas.

Christmas! Now there was a joke. Nothing at all changed for Christmas in Miss Court's house, save that they had attended church on Christmas Eve. Other than that, the day had been just like always, with the house cold and silent except for the ticking of the clock in the hall, signalling the passing of time and the endless uselessness of Miss Court's existence.

Ernest and her mother had sent Christmas greetings with a small parcel containing a locket with a likeness of them both. Miss Court had wrinkled her nose and expressed her contempt for the giving and receiving of presents. Violet had guessed as much, so did not disappoint her by even attempting to get her one. She was sure she wasn't the first young lady to take refuge in this interesting condition and she certainly wouldn't be the last. Quite frankly, she didn't care and simply waited her time out and served her sentence.

Happily, their paths very rarely crossed, and when they did Miss Court made it abundantly clear that she disapproved of her. She had once made a reference to Violet about 'You sort of girls' and Violet picked her up on it, asking what precisely she meant by it. She frostily advised her that she was performing a service for her, but that that did not extend to offering any approval for promiscuous or licentious behaviour. Violet realised that to argue with the dried up old hag was pointless and dropped the matter.

She tried to think of the baby growing within her. Frank's baby. She tried to love it, but knowing what was planned for it tried also to put that love to the back of her mind. She had no means of supporting herself, let alone a baby, and she recognised that events were out of her control. At times, she allowed her mind to form half-baked schemes to take the child and run off with it when the time came. But she knew that, attractive as it seemed, the practicalities left a lot to be desired and very soon reality came crashing back in on her thoughts. Time and time again she analysed her feelings. Shame? Perhaps. It was, after all, not the sort of behaviour expected of a young lady of her class. But she couldn't really feel shame as such. She felt wronged in some way... oh not by Frank, but it seemed to her that fate had tricked her into this position and taken away all of her dreams. Propriety was no stranger to her, and she knew that to parade her condition would not be right. Society had its rules and she could flout them to an extent, but not that much.

The local doctor was attending her. Mrs Matthews, as she was known. He came regularly to the house to examine her, as did the local midwife, Mrs Buffin, a relative of Miss Court's. Violet guessed that she probably knew the truth of her marital status, but she never mentioned it in the course of her visits. Somebody less alike to her relative could not be imagined. She was a huge jolly woman with a red face and a ready laugh who had brought so many souls into the world that she had lost count. Although she was married, she had never had one of her own, maintaining that she had children all over the place by different fathers, an innuendo that never failed to wrinkle Miss Court's nose; which in turn, never failed to delight Mrs Buffin.

It was calculated that Violet was due to give birth in late April, but the knowledgeable Mrs Buffin reckoned that she wouldn't go full term. She could see the sadness and the loss in the face of the young woman and the frailty it brought about. She was quite right, of course, and it was only the 15th day of the month when Violet woke up early one morning to realise that her waters had broken. She rose from her bed and called out to Miss Court, who immediately ordered her back to her room, told her to lie down and be quiet, and sent her pale-faced and timid maid down the road to fetch Mrs Buffin.

By the time Mrs Buffin got there, Violet was well into labour and was by then quite frightened at being alone. The midwife chided Miss Court for her lack of care and sent her off to arrange for hot water. Then she came back to Violet and sat first on the bed beside her to calm her down. "There now my love," she said, stroking Violet's brow. "No need to worry... Buffin's here. You're doing fine. Now let's have a little look and a feel of you."

Her matter-of-fact cheerfulness eased Violet's nerves, and by the time the doctor got there everything was prepared and Violet was having regular contractions, with Mrs Buffin sitting beside her holding her hand as she kept up a steady flow of encouragement and advice.

The next few hours for Violet were a whirl of pain and effort, where time stood still and all the world for her seemed concentrated on her labours. At the final push, which released the baby from her, she called out Frank's name and the doctor, thinking that she had named him thus, presented him to her, still bloody but wrapped in a shawl, as her baby Frank.

She lay there on the bed with the little thing beside her, touching him, examining him. Oblivious now to the ministrations of the doctor and midwife still busy with her, she looked at him and tears rolled silently down her face. Frank. Her little Frank. Hers and Frank's baby... and she was soon to be parted from him. He was perfect, she thought. "Oh Frank," she called out loud. "Oh Frank."

"There now my love," soothed Mrs Buffin. "He's fine. No need to worry so. Little baby Frank is a fine young boy." She picked him up and showed him again, naked this time, to Violet as she lay there. He was indeed a fine young boy, she thought.

Mrs Buffin turned away with the child. "No! No! Not yet! Please not yet! Violet screamed and reached out to him.

"Hush love. I'm just going to clean him up a little and dress him. I'll bring him back in a minute." Violet relaxed a little but refused to take her eyes off the child. Miss Court came into the room, wrinkling up her nose as usual, this time at the odours of the birth and the baby. Violet visibly stiffened on the bed, gave a strangled cry and reached out for the baby as Mrs Buffin ushered the old woman out again. "You don't like her very much do you?"

"She wants to take my baby away."

"Her? What would she want with a baby?"

"You know don't you?" said Violet quietly.

"I know that you have a beautiful baby boy."

"His father was Frank. Frank is dead. He died in the war. They want me to give him away."

Mrs Buffin looked across at the doctor packing away his things in his case on the other side of the bedroom. He didn't appear to have heard what Violet had said, but she put her fingers to her lips and motioned for her to be quiet. The doctor finished packing his bag and turned to her. "Well I'll be off now, Mrs Buffin. Thank you for your help as usual. Eh... goodbye Mrs Matthews. Mrs Buffin will look after things here now, but I'll be on call if you need me." He doffed his hat, put it on and left the room.

Mrs Buffin watched him go then turned to Violet. "Now then my love, no need to tell the whole world of your problems, is there?"

"I'm to give him away. I can't keep him they say."

"I know my love," said Mrs Buffin. "I'm so sorry my dear, but perhaps it's for the best. After all, how would you manage with a baby if your people won't support you?"

"I could try. I could get a job."

"As what my love? What can you do where you could keep a baby?"

Violet thought for a while. "I can't do anything, can I? Even if I could, how could I work and keep a child?"

"Now listen my love. How old are you?"

"Twenty. Why?"

"Let the child go to where it's arranged. Make it clear in your own mind that you will reclaim him one day and then make your life until you can."

"Would that be possible?"

"Of course it will... and there's another thing to consider."

"What is that?" said Violet, thinking that there was something wrong.

Mrs Buffin saw her reaction. "No love. Nothing wrong. What I was going to say is that with this war on and your young man having already given his life for it... well... you're a young and healthy girl and there's plenty you can do to make... I was going to say amends, but that ain't right. What I mean to say is that there's plenty you can do to help those young boys over there."

"How so?"

"Well there's war work. They're asking for women to come forward to do the men's jobs while they're away and they need nurses desperately for one. You could do that, and after the war you could come back... you'd be over twenty-one, the baby would be safe and you'd have... well sort of avenged his father's death." She sat on the edge of the bed looking down at the young girl. She noticed her look of interest and stood up. "You think on it. I'll just gee up the old crow out there." She smiled and winked at her, then stood and left the room, closing the door firmly behind her.

Outside on the landing, Miss Court stood impatiently waiting. "What on earth did you do that for? Throwing me out of a room in my own house?"

"You nearly bloody blew it my dear, that's what. I needed to have a word with her, otherwise she would have upset everything."

"What do I care of that? The baby's born now. I've done my bit."

"Your bit was to keep her until the baby was born and then take it to its foster home."

"Well what of it," said Miss Court crossly.

"Do you think her father went to all this trouble... and paid all that money to get her out of the way, only for her to turn up six months later with a bastard?" Miss Court stood with her tight mouth closed. "No. She came here to keep her accident hushed up, and if she goes back with a child it's all for nought. What on earth do you think her father would say?"

"He could say what he likes. I've done my bit."

"And how many more young ladies would you have to visit... eh... tell me that?"

Miss Court wiped her nose and sniffed. "Well what do we do to stop her?"

"I've had a chat with her. I've told her that she can get the child back when she's ready and of age."

"And did she accept that?"

"I think so, but I'll keep on with the suggestion as long as you don't upset things. This one's a bit different to the last one you know. I reckon that she and her young man were serious."

"I don't really care. When we've got our money in full she can do what she likes. To me they're all shameless whores and serves them right."

"To you and to me they're a source of income we sorely need." Mrs Buffin turned on her heel and left the old woman to go back into Violet's room.

Early the next morning, after a fitful night during which she had for the first time fed the baby at her breast, assisted by the ever cheerful Mrs Buffin, Violet awoke. She looked out of the window at the forest rising up the hill on the other side of the valley and recalled the months when she had watched its changing face. Dark and forbidding in the winter's gloom, she had felt imprisoned by its marching hordes of trees and the constant driving rain of those first months. Then, as if by magic, she had awoken one morning to a fairytale land of glistening whiteness. The trees, decorated and transformed with a pristine gift from the skies, no longer seemed to threaten and she had wandered amongst them filled with delight, laughing as they shook themselves free in flurries of white dust. Now in spring the larches were already showing their tiny bright green paint brushes of growth and the monotonous *chink chink* of the male great tit proclaiming his territory heralded new life and new hope. But to who? Beyond the forest the world still tore itself apart and men still spilled their lives in useless combat... and here... here she had brought life into the world, which she was soon to put aside. She smiled a tired smile and turned away from the window to the cradle on the other side of the room. He was quiet. She got up and crossed the room and looked in at the sleeping baby.

All that Mrs Buffin had said to her repeated and rolled around in her mind. It needn't be forever... there was work to do... she did have important things to sort out before... 'To think that I once thought of killing myself,' she thought. 'That would have killed this little mite. Oh thank God I didn't. Frank would never have forgiven me for killing his baby. Giving him away was bad enough, but it wasn't going to be forever. I promise you Frank. And you Frank.'

......

The taxi made its way up the long driveway, with Violet sitting in the back seat holding young Frank in her arms. On the seat beside her, Miss Court sat looking straight ahead, taking no notice of the surroundings whatsoever.

Violet, on the other hand, was taking a particular interest as she gazed out at the countryside. Her heart was in her mouth at the thought of parting from her baby and a rising tide of dread threatened to swamp her, but she had thought things through and knew that after all, this was the best option. Deep down this was what she wanted too. She knew that in her heart, even though she chastised herself for thinking thus.

The wheels of the taxi scrunched on the gravel driveway as it rounded the corner of the drive and pulled up in front of the large stone farmhouse. To the right of the driveway was a large pond, its waters reflecting the blue sky and clouds above.

The taxi stopped and Violet turned to Miss Court. "Miss Court, I appreciate that your duty was to accompany me here and presumably make sure that my father's wishes were accomplished, but we are here and I have decided to go through with this. I would prefer therefore that you remained in the car whilst I talk to Mr and Mrs Pope."

"Well I never..." Miss Court exploded, before any further comment was stifled by a withering look of disdain from Violet.

"Thank you Miss Court. I knew you'd understand," said Violet with scarcely concealed triumph.

The door of the large farmhouse was open now and a man and woman in their mid twenties stood on the step, smiling broadly. Violet had never met these people before but felt on first sight that she would like them and that if anyone was to look after her baby Frank these should be the ones. She got out of the taxi carrying the baby and the driver came around to assist her. "Not the suitcases," said Violet. "I'm going on to the station afterwards... just that bag." She pointed and he picked it up with a slightly puzzled look on his face and handed it to the man, who had come forward.

The woman now stepped down from the door and came forward to Violet, who found herself in an open embrace, baby and all. "Welcome my loves. I'm Florrie and this is my husband Joe. And who's this little fellow then? She bent down and tickled the baby under his chin, smiling and making little clucking noises.

"This is Frank," Violet replied, trying to appear calm and in control. "Shall we go inside and talk?"

"Yes of course. Oh I'm sorry, I'm that excited. Silly me. Come on in now all of you."

She rushed ahead and up the steps to the front door, turning and beckoning Violet to follow. "In here my loves, here in the parlour.

There's a nice warm fire for you." She positively bubbled with scarcely suppressed joy. "Take the bag up to the baby's room," she called to Joe.

"Righto," said Joe, coming through the door. "Eh, what about the lady in the taxi?"

"She'll stay in the taxi," Violet called from the open door of the parlour. Florrie looked at Joe and the understanding between two close people told them that this was none of their business. Joe shut the front door.

Out in the taxi, Miss Court, who had imagined that the invitation she had clearly heard would upset Violet's plans for her, seethed helplessly.

Florrie watched Joe for a moment as he mounted the stairs, then she turned and went into the parlour. Violet was standing by the fire, holding the baby and looking earnestly down into his sleeping face. She looked up as she came into the room and Florrie saw that there were tears in her eyes, which dripped down on to the baby's face, causing him to flinch slightly but not to awaken. "Now then love," said Florrie, crossing the room to her. "Don't upset yourself."

"I'm sorry," said Violet, trying to wipe the tears from her eyes with one hand whilst still cradling the baby. "I was going to be so strong, but now it's come to it I don't know that I'm able..."

"Why should you my love? Nobody has to be strong all the time. Here, sit down here with Florrie and let's talk about this."

She sat on the couch and motioned to Violet to join her. Florrie moved closer and put one arm around her shoulder, reaching across with her other hand to gently stroke the sleeping baby's face.

"I love this little thing, even though he's only been with me a few short weeks," sobbed Violet. "But now... now I have to give him up and I don't know how..." She wept freely now, and Florrie held her close. "Frank's his name," Violet managed through the tears. "It was his father's name. He... he was killed... in the war. He would... we were to be married but..."

"Oh you poor love," said Florrie, holding her even tighter and looking down at the baby. "The poor little mite."

Violet pulled herself together and sat more upright. Florrie shifted a little, but left her hand resting on her shoulder. A good woman, thought Violet. A kind woman who would look after her Frank until... until she could take him back. Did she want him back? 'I must do,' she reasoned. 'Of course I do but not now... not now.' She needed to... to try and make sense of all of this and poor Frank's death. Oh God, make it not too long. Please God, make things right. Why does it have to hurt so much? Why should doing the right thing... the thing all about her felt was right, hurt so much?

"Do you have any other children Florrie?" she asked.

"No love. Not yet leastways. We keep on trying but... maybe someday God willing. In the meantime, there's a home for this little fellow for as long as you want."

"Thank you. I plan to make my life... I have to do some things first... I can't... you understand don't you... I... I..." She turned her face away from Florrie's, unable to look her straight in the eye. "I will have him back you know. I will..."

"I know my love. I know. We'll love him 'till you're ready. He'll be here."

"I have to see my father first and then... well I haven't made my mind up completely but... oh I mustn't bother you with all my silly problems."

"Course you can my love. Course you can."

"I know but I'm not going to. I have... I have a train to catch but..."

"Oh... oh we thought you might like to stay for a while... sort of... well... you know love."

Violet stood and Florrie followed her up. "Thank you for your kindness Florrie, but the taxi is waiting outside with that awful woman in it and I must make my way soon or I shall lose my resolve. Where do you want me to put him?"

"Would you like to see the room Joe's prepared for him? He's so proud of it and I'd like you to think of him, when you're gone, in his own little room."

"Oh yes please." She followed Florrie out of the room and up the wide staircase to the first floor and into a little room at the front of the house, next to what was obviously Joe and Florrie's bedroom. The room was decorated beautifully in a pale blue and Joe, or someone quite talented, had painted a little frieze of childish pictures at the dado. In the corner was a wooden cot with its crisp white and clean bedding turned down, all ready to receive its new occupant. Violet smiled her appreciation and unwrapped the shawl from the baby. Florrie took it and folded it as she lowered him into the cot and tucked him in.

The horror of the situation, so out of place in the warmth and beauty of this lovely household, threatened to engulf Violet. She blinked and swallowed hard. "His things are in the bag..." Her voice sounded stretched and strange and she paused, her eyes darting around, seeking to focus on something, to latch on to some reality. "He's feeding from the bottle. He shouldn't need feeding again for another hour." She turned to Florrie, concern in her face. "You do know how to use one, do you?"

"Yes dear of course," said Florrie, clutching her arm and squeezing it affectionately "...and the doctor will be calling around this afternoon to check on everything. I warned him of your coming."

"Oh I'm sorry, I didn't mean to question you. I'm sure you know as well as I do what to do but... well you know, I'm sure."

"I've nephews and nieces all over and I'm a farmer's wife you know. There's not much we don't know about how to bring up small creatures. Even ones as precious as this little mite."

Violet smiled through her tears, wishing with all her heart that she could stay longer, not just to be with her baby but to bask in the warmth and comfort of this happy house and this lovely woman. She steeled herself, wiping her eyes with the backs of her hands. She had made the decision and she had to carry it through. Outside through the window, she could see the taxi waiting patiently on the drive with its far from patient occupant. She bent down and kissed the still sleeping infant, her mind begging him to wake and reach up for her, forbidding her to go. The child slept on and Florrie reached forward and took her hand to guide her from the room, leaving the door ajar. "I will write as often as I can," said Violet, "...and... forgive me, can you write? I'm sorry to ask but... oh you must think me so rude."

"I can a little but not well. Enough to let you know how he is."

"Oh please do. Please let me know... let me know... oh..." Her resolve broke and she dissolved into tears, throwing herself on to Florrie and sobbing on to her shoulder. Florrie held her, patting her back as she would a small child. "I'm sorry," Violet sobbed. "I didn't mean to be so strong."

"Hush now my love. There's nothing at all to be sorry for. He'll be all right and so will you be. You mark Florrie's words."

"Thank you." Violet half turned away, mopping her eyes with her handkerchief with the monogrammed 'V', which thankfully Florrie did not comment on. "Thank you so much for everything."

"Thank you too my dear. You were the one bearing the gift." She smiled up at the younger woman and Violet knew for the second time in her life just exactly what she'd missed in female companionship. Again they embraced, as Violet willed herself to take the next step, forcing the courage back into herself as Florrie held her. She straightened, releasing herself from the embrace and clutching Florrie's hands in hers. "Is there anywhere I can clean up and put my face straight? I don't want that old... Miss Court to see me like this."

Florrie winked at Violet. "Course there is my darling. In here... in here." She led the way into her bedroom and indicated the stool by the wide dressing table. Violet sat and looked into the mirror.

"Oh God, what a mess!" She reached into her bag and took out her make-up and lipstick to repair the damage. Florrie took up a brush and stood behind her, brushing her hair. Violet allowed her eyes to close briefly, but then applied herself to her task. Miss Court was not going to get the satisfaction of seeing her tears. Not if she could help it. Eventually, the peace of the moment was over and she stood and faced Florrie, composed now and ready to depart. She smiled and they hugged each other again briefly, for all the world as if they were old friends rather than two people who had only just met.

By the time Florrie and Joe showed a smiling Violet out of the door to the taxi nobody, least of all Miss Court, would have guessed at the emotion that had gone before. Violet kissed Florrie warmly on the cheek and shook Joe's hand. Then she marched resolutely to the taxi and got in. "Bye-bye," she called, waving as the taxi started off. "The station please driver. I'm so sorry to have kept you."

"That's all right miss," the driver called back to her as he observed her in the mirror and wondered at the full story behind all he had seen.

Violet made no acknowledgement of Miss Court, who sat there a trifle disappointed at the younger woman's composure. The taxi sped down the driveway with Violet looking out of the rear window, still waving.

On the doorstep, Joe hugged his wife joyfully before they both went back inside and crept upstairs to look in wonder at their new charge.

At the station, Violet arranged for her bags to be taken to the London express whilst Miss Court stood by the taxi expectantly. "Goodbye," said Violet curtly as the porter wheeled her luggage away. She turned on her heel, leaving the old woman to find her own way to the Gloucester train and home.

Violet sat alone in her compartment for most of the journey. She felt so different. Something was missing... as if she had forgotten something. Yet in the midst of all this she felt a strange relief.

The guilt was hidden. The shame was gone. She was a normal young lady again. Could anyone tell from looking at her what had befallen her? It was difficult to imagine that everyone could not but see her story in her face. She chided herself for her feelings of relief. What would Frank have thought of her giving up her... giving up their baby? She turned her face to the window, seeing her reflection dimly in the smoke-stained glass. The face that looked back at her looked to her the same as it had always. Frank would have approved, she reasoned. He would not have wanted me to be reviled. He would want the best for his son, and in the circumstances she had given him the best.

Florrie would love him as her own, she knew, and she could always reclaim him in the future.

She looked up again at her reflection. No real intention there, she realised shamefully, despite her protestations. The feeling of relief was too real to dismiss. One guilt was replaced by another, and the two of them left a wound which would take years to heal.

......

Ernest stood on the concourse under the clock, looking down the platform at the passengers alighting and hurrying through the steam towards the gate. He searched amongst them for Violet. What would she be like? Surely she would look the same. Oh please God she would be the same girl she was before this terrible event.

He had of course been informed of the birth of his grandson by Miss Court and had to admit to mixed feelings on hearing of it. His first thoughts were fear at what Violet had gone through. Was she all right, and how had she stood up to the birth so far from home and apart from all those she knew and loved? The poor child must have felt so alone.

And then there was the child itself. A boy... and healthy by all accounts. His grandson. He wondered at it. A bastard, yes, but his line nevertheless. What would he be like, this offshoot of his... still no need to think about it. It was a bastard and that was that. He had done his best for it, and from all the reports and accounts Crowe had given him the Popes would prove excellent carers. That was as much as could be expected... surely?

There had been letters for Violet whilst she was away. One was undoubtedly from Balfour. He could tell by the handwriting. The other was from Kent, and he presumed from the woman who had connived at their association and all it had led to. He had put the letters away. The affair had been ended and he saw no reason to open old wounds. Violet was coming home alone and unburdened and he must see to it that she put this whole unfortunate business behind her and got on with her life.

He dreaded a scene with her in public. How had she taken the loss of the child? Would she be distraught or would she be calm and reasonable? He searched once more along the platform. No sight of her yet. He noticed the number of young men in uniform who had alighted from the train and were obviously on their way to join up or perhaps to re-join their regiments. The war was now pervading all aspects of life in the country, not least by the reduction in the number of young men available for quite ordinary jobs. In many cases, these were being taken over by women and it was becoming quite usual to see females delivering goods or doing quite heavy manual tasks one would have thought quite beyond them. Why, he'd even heard of women working in factories and in munitions production.

In his own office, he had been totally unable to find a suitable man to take Balfour's place and had had to employ a woman to undertake his work. So far he had to admit that she had performed her duties quite admirably, and there didn't seem to be any friction with old Miss Crabb. He flinched inwardly at the way he'd had to lie to her about Violet's absence. Oh he had poured forth his oft repeated words about her having had an accident and having gone to the country to recover, but she knew him too well. She had stood there while he said the words and just turned away with an "If you say so sir." It'd made him feel about one inch tall, but knew that he had to leave it at that or face further inquisition.

He saw Violet coming down the platform at last and waved to her. She didn't acknowledge his wave but turned instead to the porter wheeling her luggage and indicated his whereabouts. Ernest felt deflated already. In his heart he had known that she might be cool to him, but he had hoped otherwise. It was perfectly obvious as she walked up to him and greeted him formally that they were both going to have to work quite hard to heal the wound they shared. "Hello father," she said, confirming his worst fears by the use of the formal address.

"Hallo darling," he replied, trying to act normally as he bent to kiss her cheek. She proffered it to him but made no reciprocal move. "Good journey?"

"Tiring," was her only comment. "Where do you want the man to take my luggage?"

"Oh I've got a motor car over there." He pointed to the loading area beyond all the platforms and the porter, an elderly man who looked well past this sort of thing, made his way over, followed by the two of them walking side by side but not arm in arm.

"Which one sir?" said the porter as he reached the kerb.

"That one over there," Ernest indicated to a new-looking motor car, handsomely black as most were, but with its top down, revealing the spacious interior and leather-bound seating.

"A new motor car father," enquired Violet quietly, surprising him with her interest. "I thought you said that business would suffer because of the war."

He looked a little sheepish. "It did, but I've been devoting a lot of energies to it recently and the war does of course have its good sides for business."

"How so?"

He was so pleased that a conversation seemed to be flowing normally that he lost his caution. She was talking to him. "Well the war means that there's property to dispose of. Property to buy. There's a lot of business to do out there."

Violet stopped short of the motor car and watched the porter open the luggage rack and start to put the cases in. Ernest stopped with her, pleased and happy at this turn of events. He looked at her and was frozen by her look of contempt. "Do you mean to tell me that you can ostentatiously profit from the misery and death of fine young men without any qualm or conscience?"

He stiffened at her admonishment and looked guiltily about to see if anyone had heard her strictures. The only one who could have was the porter, but he showed no sign of it and continued to heave the trunks laboriously on to the rack.

"I think father that at least you should help him," said Violet. "He is an old man doing this job no doubt because there are none younger to perform it."

Ernest accepted her command and moved forward to help the man, who turned to him as he reached for the straps. "Thank you sir. Very kind sir."

The two of them heaved the luggage on and strapped it. Ernest reached into his pocket and handed the chap a sixpence. The old man took it and muttered his thanks, looking up at Violet. Ernest looked at Violet, and in the face of her look of disapproval reached back into his pocket. He took his hand out. There was a half crown in it. He looked at it possessively for a moment before glancing back at Violet and handing it over. "Thank you sir," said the old man, doffing his hat and wiping his brow. He smiled to reveal broken and stained teeth. "Thank you miss," he said with the accent on the 'you', before shuffling off with his trolley.

"Really Violet, do you have to embarrass me so in public," Ernest hissed in anger.

"I fear that you have embarrassed yourself father," she replied, getting into the rear of the motor car. "There is a war on and we must all pull together you know."

He snapped then. "Pull together! Does that mean the last months of me paying for your indiscretions? The continuing payment for the upkeep of..." He stopped himself, fighting to control his anger. "Violet why are we arguing? We haven't seen each other for months and here we are fighting with each other. Do we have to?"

"If you are going to throw things in my face every time we speak or disagree then yes, life is going to be difficult between us. Frank gave his life for this war and you just display your profit from it." Ernest made as if to respond but she carried on. "Well those fine women you entrusted me to made damned sure your requirements were carried out, I can assure you, but they also sowed seeds in my mind which I am going to fulfil, and you daddy dearest are going to help me."

"If by that Violet you mean I am to go back on all I have arranged... and which I may say you agreed to, then you have another think coming. I will not go back on my decision," he said, desperately trying to recover control of the situation. "I cannot condone the child and neither will I have him in my house. It is fostered out suitably and that, as far as I am concerned, is the end of the matter."

"Of course it is father. I have no means or intention of going back on it."

He was almost glad of the use of the word 'father' now. 'Daddy dearest' had sounded so mocking. "You don't have to... but you will one day. Make amends they said. Put something back they said. Young men like yours fighting and dying they said. Plenty to do. Help needed. Well I thought about it and I realised that there has to be some purpose in all of this."

"I am afraid I cannot see your point," said Ernest, moving forward to start the engine.

Violet shouted above the noise as it started. "The point is I am resolved to do what I can to help the men suffering in this war, and you daddy are going to help me do that."

"What do you expect me to do?" Ernest said as he got into the driving seat, slipping the vehicle into gear and moving off.

"I expect you to support me in my intention to volunteer for war work and hopefully nursing. I expect you to help me train as a nurse and support me in that work."

"Well if that's all," he said, quite relieved at the turn of events, his temper cooling. "I don't think we've much to argue about apart from the fact that I will not countenance having your illegitimate child under my roof."

"That's as maybe father, but neither of us can deny his existence forever, I fear."

The rest of the journey home was made in silence, and it was not until they turned into Etchingham Park Road that he said to her, "Your mother is excited at your return and recovery. Please do nothing to disappoint her. She and all others, including Alice, believe that you went to the country to recover from your fall and I suggest, miss, that you do nothing to gainsay that."

"Of course father. We'll keep up our little pretence. Just like all of the other families whose daughters have to go to the country for a while. Who do we think we're fooling?"

"I don't care about others. I am stating what we will continue to abide by. Do I make myself clear?"

"Perfectly daddy dearest."

"And stop calling me daddy dearest!"

They pulled up to the house and drove in on the new driveway he had had constructed since his purchase of the motor car, and which had necessitated the removal of the lovely tree at the gate. Alice came out and went straight around to Violet's side, enquiring about her and chattering excitedly as she followed her in, carrying her bag. One look at her convinced Violet that Alice knew the real reason for her absence, but unless invited to comment never would. "Your mother's in here," she said preceding Violet into the lounge, where a fire was lit despite the warm spring air. "Here she is Mrs Matthews. Miss Violet is home safe and well. I'll leave the two of you alone and fetch some tea."

Violet crossed the room to her mother's chair and knelt down in front of it. Her mother looked at her smiling. She reached out and cupped her chin in her thin hand. "Are you better now my love?" she asked with tears in her eyes. "You were so ill when you left that I could not talk to you."

"I'm fine mother. Fully recovered," Violet assured her. "But how are you?"

"The same my dear. The same as I was, the same as I'll be."

"Nonsense mother, you'll be better soon. What have you been doing lately?"

"Nothing really my dear. Nothing... when do I ever do anything except sit here and wait? I read the newspapers now and then but it is so depressing, isn't it? Have you heard of this new atrocity by the Germans? Poisonous gas. How cowardly. And now I see that there is another big battle taking place at... where was it now... Geeps or some such name."

"Ypres mother. Ypres in Belgium. You're very well informed."

"That's it. Funny name, isn't it? Do you remember that young man who worked for your father? Yes the one who used to call here for you sometimes. He went to the war, didn't he? We haven't heard from him, I do hope he's all right."

A chasm seemed to open up beneath Violet and a pain struck deep into her heart. She dropped her head for a moment so that her mother didn't see. Regaining her composure, she looked up at her, hoping that the tears she felt in her eyes were not showing. "He died in the war mother," she said quietly.

"Oh I'm so sorry. Your father didn't mention it. Oh what a pity, he seemed such a nice young man."

"He was mother. He was."

Alice entered with a tray. "Here's the tea. Three cups, as I thought maybe Mr Matthews would be joining you." She put it down on the small table just in front of Mrs Matthews. "I'll leave you alone. I expect you've plenty to talk about."

"Thank you Alice," they both said in unison, and Violet stood and went over to attend to the pouring just as her father entered the room.

"Oh there you are dearest," said his wife. "Isn't it lovely to have Violet back and looking so well after her terrible illness?"

"Yes, isn't it?" he said, looking across at Violet. She glanced up at him from her attention to the tea. He could detect no particular message in her look so he took a seat and awaited the cup of tea, which was duly passed to him.

"Violet's just told me that that nice young man who used to work for you was killed in the war," said Elsie.

Ernest stiffened and shot an alarmed look across at Violet who, seeing that he thought she had betrayed their secret quickly, said, "Mother has been reading the newspapers about the war and she asked me about Mr Balfour. You remember don't you daddy, he went to war right at the beginning and he was killed fighting for his country. Surely you remember him?"

Ernest saw the lie of the land here and knew that although she had not divulged anything she was going to push home this particular barb for all it was worth. "Like so many men have," he intoned. "Like so many have." And he stared into his cup as he stirred.

Violet sat down with her cup in the chair opposite her mother. "That's why I might have to go away again mother," she said with a concerned look.

"Oh surely not dear. You've only just got home."

Ernest made as if to speak but was cut short by Violet's look as she continued. "This war is no longer just a war for men to fight mother... we women have to fight too, in our own way."

"Don't be silly dear," said Elsie, smiling indulgently. "Women can't fight in wars."

"No we can't, and I don't mean fight in that sense. What I mean is... and daddy has agreed to support me in this... what I mean is that we have to do our bit to help in whatever way we can."

"Well I'm not well enough dear, I'm sure you know that."

"Oh I don't mean you mother," said Violet, slightly exasperated at her mother's insistence at bringing everything back down to her own infirmity. "What I mean is that I... with daddy's help, am going to find a way of training to be a nurse so that I can help those poor young men..." She looked down at the newspaper. "...those poor young men like the ones you have been telling me about.

"Oh would you? Oh how splendid," said Elsie. "Oh Ernest, I expect you've put her up to this and I'm proud of you both."

Violet flashed a look of triumph at Ernest, and he had the good grace to acknowledge it with a slight smile.

......

Violet trudged along the street in the pale warmth of the early morning sun. A very different Violet to the wayward girl that had caught the train to Kent what now seemed an eternity ago. Gone were the lace-collared dresses and smart boots and instead her dress was one of utility, with a long dark skirt and a plain blouse. On her head, in lieu of the pretty hats she had worn before, was a cap into which she had tucked her hair, and in her heavy bag were dark overalls into which she would shortly slip.

As she neared the factory gates, the crowd of similarly dressed young and middle-aged women grew greater and groupings of friends formed as they marched. Cheery "Good mornings" gave way to laughter and the general hubbub that carried them all in a stream through the gates.

"Morning my lady," called an older woman smiling a great smile that only served to show that she had no teeth. "And how's my lady this fine morning?"

"Very well Queenie, thank you," Violet responded with a smile. "Nice to see that the weather is kind, so you'll not catch your death dressed like that."

The older woman looked down at her vast bosom, barely concealed by the low cut bodice, and laughed out loud. "Them's me warmers and they've warmed a few I can tell yer."

Violet laughed gaily as she was swept on through the gates and in. Once through, the crush lessened and she peeled off to the changing rooms to put on her overalls and pin back some errant hair that had escaped in the melee.

The whistle blew and she hurried to her station. The next twelve hours, give or take a few short breaks, would be taken up with picking up the bars of heavy metal that lay in a constantly replenished pile beside her and placing them on the drill table. She then had to pull down hard on the machine to drill holes in the punched positions before lugging the bar off and on to another pile that others cleared away as fast as she could make it. When she'd first started, the strain of bending down to pick up the heavy metal had been an enormous shock, but now, some months later, she was developing the muscles and techniques necessary for this kind of work, and although tired and exhausted when she went home each night she didn't feel half as bad.

She still had to put up with the taunts of the other women about her class, but in the main they were good-humoured and she was learning to give as good as she got. The earthy language and attitude of her fellow workers had been a bit strange to her at first, but of late she had found herself, much against her better nature she reasoned, joining in their banter. Nor was she always completely alone in class terms. There were one or two other young ladies of her type who had heeded the calls in the newspapers to help with the war effort. But the very fact that in the main these others had either proved incapable of doing the job or had given it up in despair after a very short while gained Violet respect and a grudging admiration.

She tried not to think about Frank or the baby too much and she certainly didn't make the mistake of mentioning either of them to anyone else. As a result, her workmates all assumed her virginity and made constant and crude references to it, along with advice on how to rectify the situation. She accepted the fact that her starting work at the factory in the first place, just after her return from Gloucester, had rescued her from a period of extreme depression. Truth to tell as well, she welcomed the way she was able to use her tiredness as a shield against her inner feelings, subsuming her whole life into the daily timetable of work and exhausted sleep.

She and her father had never spoken of the child since her return. She, because to do so would be too painful, and he, because he instinctively realised that she would not want it raised as a constant barrier between them. He understood only too well that her very involvement in her work was an attempt to hide away her true feelings. 'God knows,' he thought, 'I use the self same tactic and it works... after a fashion.'

But would she have behaved thus if she'd never met that bloody man? Would she be doing this to herself, pushing her young body and mind to the limits of endurance if she were not trying to bury the guilt? She would have done something... that was how she was, but to dedicate herself so totally to the concept of a war she had never envisaged, never totally understood? No, she would not have gone this far. Damn the man to hell. Damn him!

......

Doctor Crowe opened his door to reveal Violet standing there, looking fit and well but very serious. "Good morning Doctor Crowe," she said. "May I please have a word with you? I'm sorry to bother you on a Sunday."

He froze. God this was an awkward situation. Damn Matthews for letting his daughter loose on him. "If it's about..." No it couldn't be, he thought... surely not.

"It's not. May we please talk?"

"Certainly. Err yes, please come in. I... I don't have to be at the hospital until later. We'll talk in my study. Through here."

He showed her into the room in which he and Ernest had spoken previously. "Take a seat please, Miss Matthews."

She sat and looked around the room. She had no doubt that this is where her fate had been discussed, but that wasn't why she was here now.

"I'll come straight to the point Doctor Crowe. Since my return from the country..." She looked up at him deliberately and was pleased to see that his face showed signs of agitation. "Since my return from the country I have been working at the munitions factory down the road, but I really wish to get into nursing and I would welcome your advice and help."

He looked at this determined young woman. "Eh, have you any training in this field?"

"Not formally of course, but I am a member of both the Red Cross and the St. John's Brigade. We were... I was, even before the war. Lately I have been assisting with bandage classes at the factory and I have passed the first aid and proficiency tests."

"Good, but I should warn you that the job of a nurse is an arduous and difficult one... are you sure?"

"Doctor Crowe, I am aware of the difficult nature of the work and I am aware also that you think of me as an ineffectual young lady with no particular aptitude, but I am sincere and I'm asking you for your help. Will you give it?"

"But my dear Miss Matthews, you have no real experience of these matters."

"Sir, the men who are fighting and dying in their thousands in France and Belgium have for the most part no experience, yet they still carry out their duties. For my part I know that I can be of help."

He observed this young lady before him. How old was she? Twenty... something like that. The mother of a bastard child. A girl of certain strength of character he had no doubt, in spite of that. He thought for a bit and she waited for him to deliberate. "What does your father think?"

"My father supports me in this quest. I will be his contribution to the war effort."

He sat there quietly looking at her. A good-looking girl he thought. No wonder that blighter took a shine to her. She stared straight at him and he squirmed in his seat, uncomfortable in her gaze. Christ! Did she know about the other business her father had dealt with for him? Surely not. Still, he couldn't take the risk of offending Matthews, could he? He coughed. "Eh hem... there are the Voluntary Aid Detachments who are administered jointly by the Red Cross and St. John's. If you come to the hospital this afternoon at 4 o'clock precisely I will introduce you to the matron and she will advise you what to do."

"I thank you for your time Doctor Crowe," said Violet, standing. "Thank you very much. At four then." She turned to leave the room and he hurried past her to attend to the door.

......

"This is the young lady I was telling you about matron," said Crowe. Violet studied the woman by his side. A large woman, her appearance made even more formidable by the uniform she wore of a dark navy blue dress overlaid by a starched white apron, with a cap whose sheer sides further increased the aura of power. Her face was round and her cheeks betrayed a slightly unhealthy flush. All in all she could have looked frightening to a young girl, until one saw her eyes and the kindness within them. Undoubtedly a spinster, but not the dried up and withered sort that Miss Court had been; rather the type that had dedicated her life to a particular cause and found total satisfaction within that... and by her looks the odd glass of something strong.

"Miss...?"

"Matron. You will always refer to me as matron."

"Matron. Pleased to meet you matron. I do hope that Doctor Crowe has told you something about my wishes."

"If you mean, has he told me of what you want to do, then he has. We need all the help we can get here at the moment. We are a cottage hospital dealing mainly with cases who have been repatriated for convalescence and many of our trained nurses have had to go to other hospitals. I have some Special Service forms here for you to fill out. Registration takes six weeks on average... start tomorrow."

Violet was taken aback by the speed and apparent success of her mission. "I'm afraid that tomorrow will not be possible. I am working at the munitions factory and I have to give notice of my intentions."

The matron looked at the young woman in front of her, this time with a greater respect. "You're working in a factory. What in the offices?"

Violet showed her hands to the matron, now callused and ingrained with the nails all broken. She smiled. "No matron, I've been working on the machine floor, but I've been taking classes and have a proficiency in first aid and bandaging."

She studied the young lady before her. No ordinary being here, she thought. "Well miss, you'll have to do something about those hands before you start. Be here on Monday week ready for work."

"Monday week it is then. Thank you very much matron. Thank you very much."

"Don't thank me young lady, leastwise not yet. Wait until you see how difficult this work is before you thank me, although from the look of those hands I hazard you're no stranger to hard work. Monday week then?"

"Thank you. At what time?"

"5 o'clock."

"Thank you matron, I shall see you then." Violet turned to Doctor Crowe, thanked him and left the room.

Matron turned to the doctor, who had stood aside all this time amused at the interplay between these two women. She caught his look. "Not your usual brand of girl, doctor," she said knowingly.

"Usual brand... oh no. Oh no, you've got the wrong idea

there matron... she's not... well she's the daughter of a business acquaintance of mine who I am indebted to..." He stopped talking, knowing that with this particular female there was no point in continuing.

She smiled again broadly and left the room, giving him a knowing wink as she did. There was a story here. Not what she had originally supposed but a story nevertheless.

......

Five o'clock the following Monday week found Violet standing outside the matron's office, eager and ready for work. It was Monday the 14th of September and the news was all abroad regarding the fall of the city of Lille. Even at that early hour of the morning she had seen knots of people talking animatedly about it, huddled in groups with serious faces.

She knocked on matron's door and entered on her command. "Good morning matron."

Matron looked down at her watch and looked up approvingly. "Well, I see that you can be on time. Let's hope that's a good omen."

"I asked if I could help matron, and if that means being on time, I shall be."

"Good," said matron, rising to her feet and walking around the desk to meet her. "Come with me, we'll fix you up with something to wear first of all. Then I'll introduce you to the ward sister and she'll get you started." She marched off down the corridor at high speed, followed by Violet, and turned into a large store room, on the shelves of which dresses and parts of uniforms were stacked. For a second she studied Violet's figure, before diving into one of the piles to come up with a light grey dress, which she held up against Violet briefly before handing it to her and turning away for another foray. A triumphant snort and she turned back to Violet and thrust an apron and hat at her as she strode out of the room. "Sister will show you where to change. These will do for now. You can buy the proper things at Hobsons," she called as she marched down the corridor with Violet trying to keep up whilst clutching her bundle of clothing. They turned into a ward and matron marched straight into the sister's office. "Morning sister," she said to the nurse behind the desk, struggling to rise to her feet without knocking everything on it over. "This is..." She whirled round. "...who are you again?"

"Violet Matthews, matron."

"Yes, Violet Matthews. She's come to help out. She's applied to enrol as a VAD but you'll have plenty for her to do, doubtless, in the meantime?"

The door slammed shut on the departing back of the matron and the sister looked at Violet and smiled. "She's alright really. Just a bit overpowering at times. Well now, I see she's measured you up. We'd better get you dressed and ready for work." She showed Violet into a small room with a large white sink at one end, under the high window. "If you change in here I'll introduce you to Nurse Calcutt and you can learn the ropes with her for today. How much have you done before?"

"Oh not much I'm afraid, just the normal first aid test, but I'm willing to do all I can."

"Well what you can do is generally look after the welfare of the patients and change bedpans... that sort of thing. We won't expect you to do that much cleaning as there are cleaning staff, but there will be times I'm afraid when you'll just have to pitch in."

"That sounds perfect," said Violet as she reached down and started to take her dress off. The sister nodded approvingly and left her to her privacy. A short while later, Violet reappeared in the corridor and she led her into the ward, through large double doors which opened on to another world.

The ward was a long one, lined on either side by beds, each about three feet from their neighbour with a chair of dubious-looking comfort set in the gap. Some of the men were sitting on these, whilst others lay on their beds. "Are these all men who have been wounded in the war?" Violet whispered.

"Yes. This ward is mainly for those who have suffered wounding to limbs. There are other wards that you will be required to go on where they have received more serious injuries, but I think it's better that you start here." She caught sight of a nurse and hurried over to her. "Here's a volunteer come to help us out nurse. This is Miss..." She turned to Violet. "Do you know, I didn't pick up your name in all of matron's rush."

"Violet Matthews, sister."

"Miss Matthews." The sister turned to the nurse. "She's applied to become a VAD but is willing to help in the meantime. Show her the ropes today, if you could please dear." She patted Violet's shoulder and walked off down the ward, stopping to talk to one or two of the men as she did.

Violet looked at the nurse and smiled. "What would you like me to do?"

"Well you can take over from me here with this chap, Private Smith. He needs his bottom rubbed with spirits to prevent him getting sore, don't you my love?" She turned and smiled at the young man lying sallow-faced in the bed. "Nice new young lady to rub you better. Who's a lucky boy?"

Violet forced a smile and took over from her. She hadn't had any experience of rubbing men's buttocks before, but now wasn't the time to be squeamish. "Hallo Private Smith," she said as lightly as she could. "Roll over a bit and let's see what we can do." The man rolled to the right in the bed and lifted the bedclothes sufficiently for her to see his bottom with the tell-tale yellow-edged black marks of bedsores. Violet rubbed the spirits in soothingly for a while and the young man, flinching at first from the coldness, gradually relaxed as she continued. She finished that cheek, and before moving on to the other one said, "What about your heels, are they a bit sore?" She flipped the bedclothes further over and stopped short in horror at her mistake. The man had no legs below the knee, and only the stumps with their barely healed wounds and cross hatch of stitching showed. "Oh I'm so terribly sorry," she said. "You must think me dreadful... but I didn't know."

He chuckled. "Never mind Miss. You weren't to know, were you? Anywise, my heels will never be sore again, will they?"

Violet sighed and shook her head, relieved that he had taken her slip so well. "I suppose not, but let's have a look at that other cheek." When she had finished with him, she asked if there was anything he wanted and he asked for a bottle. "What do you mean bottle?" she said, thinking he meant drink.

"I need a pee miss."

The penny dropped. "Oh... I'll just fetch you one." She hurried over to the nurse. "Where do I get bottles from please, nurse?"

"In the store room, beside the toilets at the end there. Is that for Smith?"

"Yes."

"Well when he's done, mark it with one of the tags you'll find in there and leave it on the shelf above the sink. We have to check his urine for blood."

The rest of that first day was a whirlwind of bottles, bedpans and rubbing for Violet, and when it came to five o'clock in the evening and the sister came to her and told her that that was enough for one day, she was quite exhausted. "Where do you stay," asked the sister.

"I live at home with my parents in Finchley."

"Oh that's nice. Do you have a young man?"

"He... he died... in the war."

The sister put her arm around her shoulder. "Mine too," she said quietly.

So began what was for Violet the most fulfilling time she had spent since Frank's death. Being a voluntary worker, she wasn't expected to keep the regular hours of the normal nurses, but she agreed that she would work in the hospital six days a week, although that didn't necessarily mean that the day off that she got was a Sunday. In any event, when she did get Sunday off the day seemed shallow in comparison with the Sundays she remembered so fondly. Her mother now took most of her meals in her room, and her father always retired to his study for the afternoon, leaving her at a loose end, remembering the outings she and Frank had so enjoyed.

She volunteered for weekend work and gradually became more and more accepted and relied upon at the hospital. She loved it when one of the men called out "nurse" to her, even if it wasn't strictly true. It gave her a feeling of belonging and helped to fill the huge void that she would otherwise have felt. In the early days of the war, the regular nurses had resented the barely trained VADs and objected to their being referred to as 'nurse'. But at the small hospital which Violet was at, and elsewhere as the war progressed and swamped the whole medical establishment, rivalries fell away as it literally became all hands to the pump.

She began to get to know some of the men in her charge, their histories and their sufferings.

She never talked to them directly of Frank, but they more or less guessed at some loss on her part. As well as Smith, who had lost both legs below the knee and suffered internal wounds when a mine tore open a hole in the trench wall, there were three others who became favourites of hers.

Pike was a tall, handsome man with dark straight hair and thick black bushy eyebrows. He had dark twinkling eyes and, on the surface, he never seemed to let his terrible wounds bother him, even though the bullet that had ripped through him had removed much of his genital area. He had a tube that drained his urine into a bottle, which was normally kept in a small wire holder at the side of the bed. But he had started to walk around the ward and could often be seen chatting to one of his fellows with his bottle in his hand. The trouble was that every now and then he would stop for a chat, put his bottle down and then get up, forgetting about it. A great crash of breaking glass would be accompanied by his cry of dismay and Violet would run down the ward. "Oh not again, Ian."

"I'm sorry nurse," he would wail. "I've done it again."

"Never mind. We'll get you another one. Don't stand in it!" she'd invariably have to shout, as he always did and his mates would chuckle to themselves at his misfortune, forgetting for a moment their own troubles.

The tasks Violet was generally assigned to were those that dealt in the main with the welfare of the men, such as fetching and carrying the bottles and bedpans and the distribution of teas in the daytime and hot milk at night. Quite often Pike would help her on her rounds, holding his bottle in one hand as he balanced the cup of tea in the other.

In the bed next to Smith was Corporal Salmon, who had lost one leg and taken a bullet in his shoulder as he was being carried on the stretcher to the field hospital. He always exuded an air of ease, but from the workings in his face one could tell that inside he worried. All of the men worried about their futures. Would they indeed have one? At the moment they were heroes, but they all knew well enough that in time they would become burdens on society and their families, just like those from previous wars.

Opposite Salmon was the real joker in the group, Thomas. A huge man whose weight would have been repulsive were it not for the constant stream of jokes and self-deprecating innuendos which reduced all about him to helpless laughter. He had suffered chest wounds from a shell burst over his trench and had contracted a lung infection which had left him permanently breathless. This made walking difficult and consequently his weight had ballooned, until even the slightest effort left him red-faced and helpless.

Within a few short weeks, Violet found it hard to envisage a different life from the one she was leading. It provided such a focus for her that she began to forget that she was not really there in an official capacity, and it was with some worry therefore that she received a summons from matron one day to see her in her office at nine o'clock the following morning.

Violet knocked at the door and waited for the call to enter. What on earth could she want? God forbid that she wanted to dispense with her services. Please God no. The papers were full of stories of wounded men being shipped back from France. That meant that the small cottage hospitals had an important part to play in relieving the main hospitals of those men who were at the end of their treatment, prior to discharge or return to their units. 'Surely what I do,' she thought, 'is an important part of all that.'

"Come in."

She entered and matron indicated the chair in front of her desk. "Good morning Miss Matthews. Sit down please."

Violet sat. "You wanted to see me matron?"

"Yes, I've received notification of your acceptance as a VAD and I wanted to tell you that I am very pleased with what you've been doing here and to say that you are welcome to a position here."

"Oh thank God. I thought for one moment that you'd called me in to say that you didn't want me anymore."

"Why would I say that?"

"Well... I ... well I just... oh never mind. I'm so pleased you still want me," said Violet, clutching her chest and visibly trying to calm herself down.

Matron smiled. "I've had a report from sister, Miss Matthews. We need trained and experienced medical staff. But as well as that we also need staff such as yourself who can provide comfort for these poor boys. That is where you have excelled."

"I love them all," said Violet contemplatively. "Sometimes I think that's wrong of me but..."

"...But they replace one you would have loved."

Violet looked up across the desk at the older woman. A figure of authority, yet a woman still and now with a look of deep concern on her face. "You know?"

"I don't know any details my dear, but I do know suffering. I've seen enough in my years to know when someone is trying to submerge that suffering in their work."

"I do try not to show it."

"I know, and that is why we're so pleased with you because you have helped many of these men with the degree of your understanding. Now, to more important things. How is your training progressing, because for all we've been talking of it is important that you progress your medical skills."

"Well, I've been attending classes and am now quite proficient in many aspects of our work."

"Good. We are, as you know, a small hospital and we receive the patients after they have progressed through all of the other hospitals, both here and abroad. We are constantly receiving requests for trained nurses and experienced VADs from the bigger hospitals. They probably won't want to take you until you've had at least six months here with us in an official capacity, so we're not talking about immediately but..."

"But I'm happy here."

"There is a war on and we all have to be ready to serve where we are needed. Have you not thought of this before?"

"Well no I haven't... but I suppose I should. What must I do?"

"Nothing much really. I really just wanted to touch on the subject with you now that you are here in an official capacity. I expect you'll need your parents' consent. Would that be forthcoming?"

Violet leant back in her chair. "I don't think I'd have any trouble there. My father's supported my work here and it would seem on reflection to be a natural progression... I don't know I'll have to ask."

"Well then, let's just leave it there for the moment, shall we?"

"Yes thank you." Violet stood, still thinking. "Thank you matron, you've been most kind." She left the room, her mind in a turmoil.

......

"I'll not hear of it, do you hear!" shouted Ernest.

"Not hear of what dear?" said Elsie, coming into the lounge, supported by Alice. "For all your shouting the whole road has heard of it, whatever it is."

"Violet..." he indicated to Violet, sitting on the chair over by the fire, which was lit to take the chill off the September air. "Violet now tells me that there is a possibility that she will be asked to go away to another hospital, God knows where in the country!"

"I have asked your permission father to go and serve in the capacity which you have encouraged and supported," said Violet, standing and moving across the room to assist Alice with the seating of her mother in the other chair by the fire. "What is wrong with that?"

Elsie, seated now and with her customary rugs around her, looked up from her chair at Ernest standing there red-faced and angry. "What is wrong with it Ernest dear?" she enquired sweetly.

"What is wrong? A young woman away from her home. What is wrong, you ask!"

"I will be in a nurse's hostel wherever and whenever I go," said a clearly exasperated Violet.

"My dear, I cannot see what is wrong with that," said Elsie. "So many other young ladies are having to do the same. I was only reading the other day of..."

Ernest's explosive gasp of annoyance cut short her story and Violet took up the argument once more. "If I go... and it is a big 'if' at the moment. If I go, it will be in a proper VAD detachment assigned to a particular hospital."

"Her mother looked across at her daughter. "What about me and the house dear?" she enquired, realising suddenly that her main support was about to be taken away again.

Ernest raised his finger triumphantly and went to speak.

"I'll look after things here," said Alice, who had stayed in the room unnoticed by them all. "I'll be here whilst Miss Matthews is away."

Ernest lowered his hand, glowering across at her. "Well I see there's a conspiracy of women in this house... just as there seems to be everywhere. I give up. Do as you wish, only don't bring shame on us."

"The only shame on us would be if the whole family did nothing," said Violet as Ernest left the room, leaving the three women looking at each other in united victory.

It was probably the first time Violet had ever seen her mother stand up to Ernest, and for that brief moment she glimpsed the woman she must once have been.

......

The routine of the hospital and her home life moved into a pattern with Violet until she could hardly remember or imagine life without that structure. Men came and went, some back to their units, some to other convalescent homes, the lucky ones back to their families if they could cope with them.

In late November on a chilly morning, Violet walked as usual into the ward, her home from home and the repository of her affections now.

"Morning boys," she called as she walked into the ward. "How are we all this morning?"

"Morning nurse," said Smith. "Much better for seeing your face. Did you have a nice Sunday with your family?"

"Very nice thank you," said Violet, fussing with his bedclothes and tidying up the small table beside it with his few bits and pieces on it. "Where's Mr Pike? I need his help with the teas."

"He had to see the doctor earlier this morning nurse, and he's been gone to the toilet some time now."

"Oh well, if he's not out in a bit I'll check on him," she said, and she moved across to Thomas. "And how's the big man this morning?"

"Getting bigger nurse. For seeing you, if you know what I mean."

"Why Mr Thomas, shame on you. Me a respectable young lady and you a gentleman."

"I'm no gentleman. I can be gentle though, if that's what you want."

She laughed with him and at him. "What I want is for you to shift over so I can tidy up these bedclothes."

"Spoil sport," he said smiling. Then his face became serious. "Here nurse, I'm a bit worried about Pike. I think the doctor gave him some bad news this morning. Leastwise he came out looking very glum and he's been in the toilet a long time."

"I'll go and see what's keeping him." Violet walked off in the direction of the toilets, stopping to talk to some other men on the way and exchanging banter with them. She entered the toilets, calling out as she did. "Ian," she called, "...are you in there? Your mates have all been..." She stopped dead in her tracks, her hands held tight against her mouth to stifle any sound she might make. Pike was hanging from the window sash, with the cord from his dressing gown around his neck. His feet pointed balletically down to the floor and the tube ran from underneath his pyjamas down to the bottle, placed this time neatly on the floor beside the chair, which he had kicked over in order to hang himself.

Her eyes were drawn to his face. The eyes were closed as if in peace, but his mouth hung open and his tongue, swollen from his strangulation, protruded obscenely. "Oh you poor boy," she moaned, and she moved forward and cradled his hanging body, trying to lift it and relieve the strain on the noose. She couldn't move it, feeling in any case that her efforts were useless. She cupped her face in her hands and backed away to the wall and sobbed. For a while she stayed like that, but then she pushed herself away from the wall, wiped her eyes with the back of her hand and went to the door. As she got there, she bumped into a walking wounded soldier coming in. "Please could you get the sister," she said, trying desperately to maintain her composure. "There's been an accident."

For a moment he looked as if he was going to disobey her, standing on tiptoe as he tried to look beyond her into the toilets. She stood her ground, blocking his view, and he gave up, shrugging his shoulders as he turned and went down the ward to the sister's office. Violet remained on guard until the sister came hurrying up the ward. "What's the matter?" she called ahead as she approached. "Carter tells me there's been some sort of an accident. Is it Pike? Has he dropped his damned bottle again?" She stopped, seeing for the first time the tears rolling down Violet's face. "Oh my dear, what is it? What's happened?"

Violet slumped against the wall, motioning soundlessly behind, and the sister brushed past her and stopped dead at the sight of Pike's body. She gasped and then turned back to Violet and put her arms around her. "Oh my dear... oh that poor man... and you had to find him of all people. Oh I'm so sorry for you both." She guided Violet out of the doorway and closed it firmly behind her. "Stay here just a minute longer," she said, "and stop anybody else going in. I'll fetch help. Are you all right for a little while longer?"

"Yes," said Violet faintly, "only please get his poor body down from there."

"I will love. Hold on there." She hurried away down the ward and came back a few minutes later with Dr Crowe and another nurse wheeling a trolley.

Crowe acknowledged Violet with a nod and went in, followed by the sister. "Could you please come in nurses," he called. "We'll have to cut him down I'm afraid, so if the three of you can lift his body, I'll cut the cord and then we'll lay him on the trolley."

Violet and the other nurses supported the body whilst Crowe stood on the chair and cut the slackened cord. Gently they laid him on the trolley and Crowe got down to examine him. For a moment there was an expectant silence as he bent over the body, but then he straightened and pronounced, "Dead as a doornail I'm afraid. Poor chap. I had to give him the news this morning that his remaining private parts would have to come off. Obviously it disturbed his mind, poor chap... nice bloke by all accounts. He motioned to the sheet under the trolley. "Cover him up with that, and then one of you get him down to the mortuary."

"I'll do it," said Violet.

"I'll come with you," said the sister, throwing the sheet over him as Violet picked up his bottle, still attached to him, and laid it beside him under the covers. They pushed the trolley through the door and out into the ward, where a small crowd of wondering men had gathered. "Back to your beds," shouted the sister, clapping her hands together. "Come along now, there's good chaps." They backed away, muttering as Violet pushed the trolley down the ward with the sister guiding it.

As they drew level with Thomas, Violet tried not to look at him, but as fate has these things, the bottle slipped from under the sheet and crashed to the floor, spilling Pike's urine for the last time. Violet stopped pushing and looked across at Thomas. Huge tears were rolling down the big man's face, and his body shook with his sobs. Violet's tears now fell freely, and the sister hastily picked up the larger shards of the bottle, virtually throwing them on to the trolley which she now commandeered, pushing it with one hand whilst encircling Violet with the other to steer them through to the doors. "Nurse," she called back to the other girl as the doors swung shut. "Please clear the floor up as soon as possible. I'll go with Nurse Matthews."

......

"Is that you Violet?" Ernest called as he heard the door close. There was no reply, so he got up from his chair and went out into the hall. "Oh it's you. Are you all right? Only Crowe called in to tell us that you'd had a bad experience at the hospital."

"A young man... one of my patients committed suicide and I... I found him... I found him hanging... hanging there." She broke off, unable to continue, and slumped against the wall, mentally and physically exhausted. He reached out for her but she straightened up and ran upstairs to her room, leaving him staring up the empty stairs, a lump in his throat and tears in his eyes. Not for the young man. Not even for Violet, but for himself and the loss he felt. His daughter would once have thrown herself into his arms and found comfort there, and he would have gained comfort from her wants. But now... now she ran away and bore her grief alone and left him to do the same. Far from time healing, it seemed as if the secret they shared was driving a wedge between them.

He turned back into the lounge and walked across to Elsie. She looked up at him. "Is everything all right Ernest dear?"

"Yes Elsie. Violet's had a difficult day at the hospital but everything's all right now. She's taking a rest upstairs."

......

The next day at the hospital, the sister looked up and through her open office door as Violet arrived. "I didn't expect you in this morning, Nurse Matthews."

"Why not sister? It's my day on duty is it not?"

"Yes but... I thought my dear... that yesterday..."

"Yesterday, a young man died here. Many young men die here, and we have to look after and care for the living."

The sister looked into the resolute face of this young lady. She could see that the night had not been easy for her, that the speech she had just delivered had been rehearsed. The marks of grief still showed on her face and around her eyes, but there was a deeper grief, one which she sensed had little or nothing to do with the previous day's events but had been triggered by them. "Yes... well nurse you know where I am if you need me."

"Thank you sister," said Violet, who removed her coat.

"Oh you've got your new uniform. That's nice. Very smart. Your young men will be impressed. Hurry along now and cheer them up. God knows they need it."

Violet was indeed wearing her new VAD uniform, its smart but simple long-sleeved dress all but obliterated by the white apron, which stretched right around her slim body, complimenting the starched white cuffs and headgear. If she hadn't been feeling so awful about the events of the day before she would have marched proudly into the ward and done a twirl for them all but, as it was, she just walked in through the double doors trying not to dwell on her last passage through them and her sad mission.

"Good morning boys," she announced as brightly as she could, "and who's for a cup of tea?" She paused, inwardly cursing her stupidity. Her helper was usually Pike, as one of the few amongst them capable of walking. Now what would she do, and would her very remark bring their grief flooding back? These men, who had seen worse horrors than could be imagined on this earth and who had in all probability inflicted similar upon others, were amongst themselves a tight little unit of loyalty and friendship. The loss of one of their number and the manner of Pike's death was grievous to them.

"Would you like a hand nurse?"

She turned to see a new face. Well half a face really, for the rest of it and a goodly proportion of his head was swathed in bandages. A blue twinkling eye shone out of a probably handsome face and locks of blonde hair curled out from underneath the bandage. "Rogers nurse. Sapper Rogers." He held out his left hand to shake hers. From the awkward way he held her hand it was obvious that he had been right-handed and that the bandaged stump of his other arm was the one he would have used.

"Well thank you very much," said Violet. "Let's get that kettle on or these poor boys will die of thirst." She breathed a sigh of thanksgiving and led the young man out to the small side room and slipped the already full kettle on to the hot plate. "You watch this and let me know when it boils. I'll tidy up a few beds in the meantime."

She walked back into the ward and straight over to Thomas. "Good morning my love," she said, looking directly at him, determined to act naturally and not to let things get too sad.

"Good morning my lovely lady," he said. Then he leaned over in the bed and motioned her closer. "We're all right nurse. Don't worry about us. We've all been worried about you."

She stood bent down, listening to him but looking at the floor. Then she looked up straight into his eyes, willing the tears deep within hers to remain hidden. She leant forward and brushed a kiss on the big man's cheek. "Does that mean we're engaged," he quipped. "... now I've lost my virtue to you?"

"Why Mr Thomas, you do mock a lady," she replied, laughing as she pulled and tugged the bedclothes into what semblance of good hospital order she could, given their restraint and burden.

"Name the day my darling. Name the day." The spell of gloom was broken and she began to understand more the spirit and courage of these men and how they beat adversity and horror with their humour.

The days and weeks of 1915 ran on towards their end and Violet got more and more into the rhythm of her life at the hospital. The wounded kept on coming. Men broken in body and now, more and more as the horror continued, broken in mind. On duty at night she often had to rush down the ward to a patient reliving his experiences in his nightmares, and sometimes all she could do was to hold the young man in his bed to prevent him injuring himself further.

Thomas received notice that he was to be moved to a hospital in Sussex where they could address his breathing difficulties, and Smith was formally invalided out of the army with arrangements made for him to go back to his family. Their departure was a wrench for Violet, but she soon realised that the supply of patients was inexhaustible, and as she became more confident in the work, she was able to spread her affections and ministrations, learning not to concentrate her efforts with just a few souls. In turn, when there was a tragedy, as indeed there often was, she was able to bear it more easily. She never became, nor did any of them, completely inured to the pain and the suffering, but without some rationalisation of their feelings they would all have gone mad.

There was another row with her father as Christmas approached, and she informed him that she would be on duty for the majority of the holiday period. She hadn't had to volunteer, but had done so in recognition of the fact that many of the other nurses had families they wanted to be with. Unfortunately he took it as a personal affront, feeling that as she had been absent for the previous Christmas, she owed them her presence.

She realised now that they were partners in the crime of covering up baby Frank's existence and that the secret was creating a division between them which was growing, despite the fact that neither of them wished it to.

She had reached her majority in November, and if she had wished for things to be different she could have made them so. After all, if the secret was out then what would be the point of the continuation of the arrangements? But she didn't. She left things as they were, and the very fact that she did weighed heavily upon her until events pushed the problem once more into the background.

"Nurse!" called the sister as Violet walked past her door on Christmas Eve. "We've received an urgent request for nurses, from the hospitals on the coast, and I wondered if we could put your name forward?"

"Why... yes. Yes of course. Where would I go?"

"Probably Southampton. It looks as if they are expecting ships from Gallipoli and we have orders to clear the beds for an intake from them so they can handle things."

"Yes... well yes... yes of course. When would I go?"

"By the end of the month, I'm afraid. Is that alright?"

"Yes. Yes... I'm sorry, it's just a bit of a shock... I had been expecting...

I mean I've got used to being here but... yes that's fine. There are some things I have to clear up before I go and it isn't going to be easy."

......

Ernest sat in his chair, looking up at the determined face of his daughter standing in front of him. "I am decided on this father," she said.

"I know you are. I have said that I will not stand in your way, so what's the problem?"

"The problem is father, that I am likely to be away for some time."

"Well what of it? What's different? We see so little of you these days. What are you saying?"

"I can't go and leave things as they are between us."

"I don't understand what you mean."

She knelt down in front of him, taking his hands in hers and looking up into his face. "Don't you daddy?"

He looked into her earnest face staring straight into his. His daughter. 'My love,' he thought. 'My love.' He looked deeper into her suffering and seemed to find it there for the first time. The pain and the guilt that could not be assuaged, even by the absence of... especially with the absence of its cause. The child was hidden... the shame was gone, but the pain was with them both. "I love you Violet," he said, and he drew her up so that her arms rested on his lap.

"I love you too daddy, and I'm sorry. I'm so sorry."

"There's no need. It can't have been your fault. I'm sorry I doubted you."

"It was my fault daddy."

He stiffened but remained where he was, trapped by her kneeling form. "What do you mean... it can't have been... No, I won't hear of it. If he'd been a gentleman rather than..."

"But that's the problem daddy. You have to hear of it or we'll go on tearing each other apart. I loved him and... and I made him... it was my fault, my instigation. I have to face it, and if you're to forgive me you have to know."

"The bounder forces himself on you and you say it was your fault. Don't be ridiculous." He tore himself loose from her grasp and crossed to the window. She swivelled on her knees and then rose and sat in the chair he had vacated, staring at his back against the light of the window.

"Frank was an honourable man, but he was a man nevertheless. A simple man facing his departure for war. He took my love... I offered myself to him. The fault and the shame is mine, not his." There was a long silence, broken only by her realisation that he was crying. She rose and crossed to him, holding him from behind, feeling the sobs racking his body. He squirmed in her grip, but unwilling to face her relaxed finally and stood head down, weeping whilst she held him, her cheek pressed against his jacket. "I'm so sorry daddy. I never meant to hurt you. It was just that... there was such an impending sense of loss that... I always wonder if Frank guessed that he would never return."

He spoke now. His head down and his heart broken. "How could you do this to us. How could you betray me like this?"

"I cannot alter what has gone daddy. I can only seek to make amends, as I have been trying to do. Amends to Frank and now to you."

"What amends can you make to me for the ruination of all my hopes for you."

"None. None that you can know, except that I love you daddy and I need your love and support."

"I've supported you in what you've done since... since you came back. I've even agreed to your going away... but I'll..." He realised that he had turned to her and was standing there before her, his naked grief on his tear-stained face. He tried to turn away again, but she hugged him close and buried her face in his chest, crying openly now herself. "Oh I've missed you so much," he said as he stroked her hair. "My little girl."

"What are we going to do daddy?"

He pulled himself up, wiping his eyes briskly with the back of his hand. "We are going to make the very most of your time before you go away, and when you get back and this war's over we are going to decide what is the best for all of us."

"All of us?"

"All of us."

"Oh daddy, I'm sorry for everything."

"I know my darling but... but let's not go all over it again. Let's leave it 'till you get back."

"I love you daddy."

"I love you too, Violet. I always have and I always will."

February 1916

Steam hissed from each segment of the train, swirling into the cold night air as the lights of the station picked out the hurrying people in shades of grey and dirty yellow. Violet scurried along the platform, her bag in her hand, her cape drawn tightly round to keep out the damp chill. She passed through the gate and into a noisy throng of soldiers. Fresh-faced and bright in their smartly pressed uniforms, wide-eyed with keen anticipation for the adventure ahead, they called to each other like schoolboys on a seaside outing. Playfully they parted for her, bowing down and swearing their adoration as she swerved amongst them, smiling her thanks. She reached the other side of the crowd and turned to watch for a moment as they were marshalled into a semblance of order, ready to be marched off to the docks and the ships that would take them to their fate.

To the left of the entrance, away from the noise of the men on their way to war, a line of ambulances was drawn up, and from them wounded were being taken to the trains which would take them to hospitals throughout the land. Probably even to Finchley, thought Violet, wishing now that she too could be back there in familiar surroundings. Home seemed so very far away in this chill.

She crossed to one of the ambulances. "Hallo, I'm trying to get to The General. Are you going near there?"

"Yes nurse I am. Do you want a lift?"

"Oh yes please," said Violet, relieved that she had stumbled upon such luck. "Where would you like me to sit?"

"Up front with me, I should miss. You'll get all dirty in the back. My last clients seem to have made rather a mess, poor buggers... beggin' yer pardon miss."

"It's all right." She climbed into the front seat and sat there huddled into herself, trying to keep out the cold whilst she waited for his return.

She started as the door opened and the young driver leapt into his seat, the thick pebble glasses betraying the reason for him not being amongst those now leaving for the front. "You new here miss, or are you returning from leave?"

"I'm new here. Oh, not new to nursing but new down here. I've never been to Southampton before."

"Well you'll not get a chance to see much of it tonight. I'm afraid there's another push coming, mark my words. We've been told to clear the beds and that's a sure sign, believe me. If the Boche had nurses for spies they'd know everything we was planning before it 'appened just by looking at what went on in the 'ospitals."

"I expect so," said Violet, crouching down in an attempt to keep warm.

They arrived at the hospital and the driver pulled up in front. "Here's where I leave you my love. I've got to pick up some more customers and get them to that train before it goes. Good luck."

Violet dismounted and thanked him before hurrying up the steps and in. She pushed open the heavy doors, to be confronted by a hive of activity, not to say mayhem. Orderlies and nurses pushed beds and equipment around to the accompaniment of shouts and commands that rang down the long corridors. Across at a side door, more beds were being delivered and yet more orderlies were busily assembling them, whilst other nurses rushed past with great armfuls of bedding.

"What's going on?" Violet asked a nurse hurrying red-faced past her.

"They're coming," she said without stopping, and Violet, unwilling to lose this contact, hurried along beside her.

"Who's coming?"

"The ships have docked. They're coming. Get rid of your bag and help."

Violet watched the receding figure. She looked helplessly up and down the corridor, striving to find someone to direct her, but everybody seemed too busy to bother. She entered one of the wards leading off the corridor and went to the ward sister's office. It was empty so she took off her cape, folded it neatly and put it on top of her bag in the corner. Then she turned and walked through the double doors.

The ward was devoid of patients, but more and more beds were being wheeled in and placed barely two feet apart down both sides, with a double row down the middle. As they were positioned, nurses and VADs plonked the mattresses on them and proceeded to make them up. Violet took one look at the scene and then joined in, moving to the opposite side of a bed being made alone by a young blonde-haired nurse. "Here, let me join you," she said. The other nurse, too busy to reply, merely nodded and smiled and the two of them went through the mechanics of making the bed, and having done that moved on down the line to the next and then the next.

At length, all the beds that the ward could accommodate were made up and they all looked around exhausted. "Hallo, my name's Violet," said Violet, smiling at her new companion.

The other girl wiped her brow with the back of her hand. "Doris. Pleased to meet you."

"I've just arrived. What's going on exactly?"

"The ships are coming in. The ambulances will be bringing them in any moment. We got orders to clear the wards for the intake." She looked around. "Well I guess we're as ready as we can be. All we need now is the bodies."

A sister walked by inspecting their work, tweaking bed covers into the correct configuration, her face sour and humourless.

"Excuse me sister," said Violet. "I've just arrived. Do you know where I should report?"

The sister stopped in her progress and looked her up and down. "What are you?"

"VAD from Finchley sister. I've just arrived."

"More amateurs," said the sister disdainfully.

Violet felt a hotness in her chest and struggled to remain calm.

"Amateur or not sister," she said with an icy accentuation of the word 'sister'. "I am here at the request of the hospital to assist. May I please know where I should report."

The sister, taken aback by the lack of timidity in the reply, was for a moment at a loss for words. She opened her mouth as if to speak and then shut it again. She seemed to think, and her thoughts were obviously about how to make this young upstart suffer.

"Go with this nurse to the receiving rooms and then come and see me later when the intake is over." She turned on her heel and marched off.

Violet turned to Doris. "Whoops. Have I done the wrong thing?"

"You certainly have my love. You certainly have. She doesn't like VADs and you've certainly ruffled her feathers."

"Why doesn't she like VADs? We're only trying to help."

"Don't know I'm sure, but she won't even allow you to be referred to as 'nurse' in her hearing. You'll find she calls you miss."

Violet laughed. "She can call me Buckingham Palace for all I care, as long as she lets me get on with what I came for."

"I like you," said Doris. "But you're trouble. Now let's get down to the casualty."

She led the way down to the receiving room, pushing open the doors, even as they heard the sound of the ambulances arriving outside. A sister saw them and motioned them across to a line of narrow tables on the left-hand side of the room, beside each of which stood a pair of nurses wearing heavy rubberised aprons. "Hurry up nurses!" the sister called. "Get your aprons on and take that table." Violet looked around and spotted a row of hooks on the wall with two aprons left. She nodded mutely to the sister and crossed to them, handing one to Doris and donning the other herself before turning to see what was going on as she picked up one of the pairs of scissors laid on the table.

The outside doors opened and an icy blast of air rushed in, bringing with it the first of the orderlies burdened with a stretcher, which they placed on a table, beside which stood a doctor and the sister. Violet craned forward to see as the doctor bent over the wounded man, briefly assessing his injuries before ordering him to be carried across to the nurses, even as the doors opened yet again and another stretcher was brought in. She watched spellbound as the line of narrow tables was gradually occupied, and her heart leapt into her mouth at the realisation that the next one to be brought across would be hers.

Horrified, she stared at the man on the next table as the nurses proceeded to strip off the bandaging from the various wounds, much of which was obviously field dressing which had been on since the evacuation.

As the first patient was placed on her table, Violet could not help but look into the young boy's face as he stared up at her beseeching, knowing that the pain he was going through was as nothing to that which he was about to endure. She tore her eyes away from his desperate gaze and addressed the task in hand. The remains of his filthy uniform jacket were all that covered his upper torso. His trousers had long before been cut away and both legs were roughly splinted and bandaged up to his middle thighs, leaving his middle torso and private parts exposed when the thin blanket was removed. This was no time for embarrassment and Violet bent to the task of easing off the dressings, cutting carefully to remove the soiled packing as gently as she could.

"Not like that!" came a cry from the sister. "God we'll be here all night if we pretty about like that."

She brushed Violet aside, took hold of the dressing and pulled quickly. The boy gasped and fainted and the sister held aloft the bloodied and filthy mess before hurling it across the room to the open bin. "There are three-hundred more like this waiting for attention and we'll never get them in if you don't get on with it. Now clean him up and make him ready."

She stormed back across to the reception table, leaving Violet standing there feeling quite faint, staring down at the exposed wounds on the young soldier's legs.

A hand touched her shoulder. "Are you all right love?" She looked up and across into the concerned face of Doris. "Are you all right love, only we've got to get on with this."

She nodded her head, unable to speak. Her mind racing, she looked down again at the boy on her table. I can't she thought... No. No, I've got to. She pulled herself together. No, she was not going to give in. That would not be fair to this boy or any of the others. Frank... She hadn't thought of him for a while. Why not? Had he been like this? Was his suffering as bad... worse?

The wound, now open on the thigh, seemed to pulsate with a life of its own as the bubbles of gas-filled membrane vibrated with the workings of the boy's body and the movement of air all around him. Visible amongst the ravages of the gas gangrene were its obvious causes, strips of clothing, mud and even stones that had been trapped within dressings hastily applied in the evacuation. The smell of the putrefying flesh hit her, a smell she would remember for the rest of her life. She bent to her task, swabbing out the worst of the dirt and removing the remaining dressing. Doris nodded to an orderly and the still unconscious boy was taken off to the next section and another patient was placed on her table.

What she had experienced in the hospital in Finchley could in no way have ever prepared her for what she now saw constantly repeated in front of her. When the patients had been presented in Finchley, even those with appalling wounds had already received weeks or months of care and treatment in other hospitals. Here, she was looking at the immediate aftermath of battle, even though these poor souls had lain for days in the foetid holds of the overcrowded hospital ships.

The nurses on those ships had time only to attend to the haemorrhaging and immediate danger casualties, and most of the wounded remained more or less untreated between battlefield and

Blighty. Personal hygiene had been impossible on the battlefield, and the stench of sweat and body wastes mingled with all of the other odours was almost tactile. The next few hours were a nightmare. As one poor boy was taken off her table, another replaced him in an endless succession of misery. Bandaging came off easily in some cases, and in other cases with great difficulty. In the worst cases it often proved beneficial, as the very hardness of the tissue meant that a degree of healing had taken place. In one case of a heavily bandaged foot, the dressings came off so easily that before she was through to the flesh, Violet had a premonition of the horror to come. As the last of the binding came away, the mass of raw flesh, barely recognisable now as the foot of a human being, could be seen to be moving and Violet had to repress her involuntary gasp with the back of her hand as the first of the freed maggots fell from the wound on to the table. Guiltily she acknowledged the man's stare, smiling weakly at him before brushing out as many of the filthy creatures as she could and passing him on.

As the dressings were removed and the extent and nature of each man's injuries became apparent, the doctors and sisters on duty nodded them through to either a room on the right, where they were cleaned still further and redressed, or to the doors on the left, where they were lined up to wait for the operation that in most cases meant the amputation of destroyed and gangrenous limbs. Those who had internal wounds were rushed past the limb casualties straight into the theatre, where a line of operating tables could be seen. There they would gratefully receive the anaesthetic, gasping as the mask was placed over their mouths. Breathing deeply as the ether was dripped on to the gauze, slipping into a blessed unconsciousness that in too many cases was only the prelude to oblivion.

If the dressing's removal meant the onset of a haemorrhage, the cry of "Bleeding!" went up and other nurses would rush to assist with the pressure points to stem the flow. The patient would then be rushed through to the theatre for immediate suture, after which he would be returned for the remaining soiled dressings to be removed.

What astounded Violet in the midst of this carnage for the first time was the quietness of the wounded themselves. Most of the shouts and cries came from the nurses, doctors and orderlies issuing orders or calling for assistance. With the injuries they had, and given the suffering they were going through, in most cases without any pain relief at all, the soldiers stoically bore their pain. Occasionally there would be a cry as a dressing was finally whipped off, or a groan as they were turned over, but for the most part they maintained a dignified if shocked silence. Morphine injections were given to the ones suffering from the hopeless and unbearable pain of internal wounds, but for the most part aspirin was the only other relief available until or unless they required major surgery and an anaesthetic was employed.

After what seemed ages, the flow of bodies stopped and Violet and Doris were able to look at each other. Their hair hung lank and sweaty from beneath their head-dresses. Blood from their hands, as they had wiped their brows, smeared down their temples and gore soiled their cuffs and covered the aprons. Doris pulled the apron over her head and stood there in front of Violet. "Welcome to our little home. I do hope you'll be happy here."

Violet laughed as best she could through the exhaustion and horror of the past hours. She dropped into a mock curtsy. "I'm sure I will be. Thank you so much for my welcome."

Although their end of the line was now quiet and no more casualties were being brought, through the doors they could hear work continuing in the theatre. Violet nodded in that direction. "Do we have to go in there now?"

"No love, that's for qualified staff and doctors, besides which we're too dirty now. We're best getting a cup of tea and then going back up to the ward to bed the poor buggers down when they've finished with them."

"Right nurses, now get cleaned up and get something to drink," called the sister to the exhausted women standing around in little groups. "Get back to your wards then as quickly as you can and help out with bedding them all down."

Doris tugged at Violet's arm. She led the way out through the double doors on the right, and for the first time Violet could see what became of the patients who had been sent through these, rather than across to them and the other nurses. Here in this cold and draughty corridor the 'dead on arrival' patients were laid, awaiting transportation to the mortuary. Violet tried not to look at the faces of the poor wretches lying there in the cold, but her eyes seemed drawn to them. Some lay there peacefully, for all the world as if in sleep, but others had died with the grimace of agony frozen on their faces, lips curled back in a final silent scream. She shuddered and clutched her stomach. Doris put her arm around her shoulder. "Come on love, there's little we can do for these poor boys. Let's get a cup of tea."

They made their way with all of the other exhausted nurses to the staff rest area, and after a quick wash and tidy up as best they could, grabbed a cup of tea. Sitting there, cupping the warm brew in their hands, it would have been all too easy to fall asleep, but one by one they stood, stretched and began to make their way back to the wards.

"I don't even know where I'm supposed to go now," said Violet, "but my bag is in that awful sister's office and I'll have to come back with you to get it and then... well I suppose I'll have to find matron."

"Sister said to report to her when we'd finished," said Doris. "Come on, let's get down there and you can pick up your bag and tell sister you've to see matron. I do hope you get on my ward."

"Even if it means working with your sister?"

"Well you can't have everything, can you?"

As they got to the ward, the first of the patients were being wheeled and carried in from the dressing rooms and the theatre. The sister, standing in the open doorway to the ward, ushered Doris through and on to her duties.

Violet gestured into the office. "May I retrieve my luggage please sister, and then I'll report to matron if you could tell me where to find her."

"Matron is busy now miss. I suggest you replace those filthy cuffs and help out here, after which the nurses can show you to your quarters." She turned on her heel and marched off into the ward.

Violet shrugged her shoulders and went into the office to retrieve her bag and slip on some new cuffs. For the next two hours, she worked on the ward until, at last, Doris beckoned to her that their shift was over and led her to their quarters, a dormitory on the top floor, laid out much as the wards below. Doris, speechless with tiredness, simply pointed to a vacant bed before passing on to her own. Some nurses proceeded to undress and comb their hair, but most simply threw themselves on their beds and went straight off to sleep fully clothed.

The following morning after a hurried breakfast, Violet duly reported to the matron's office and was assigned to the ward she had worked on the night before. Any joy at the thought that she would be working with her new-found friend Doris was, however, short-lived as, on her arrival on the main ward, she was met by the sister and escorted instead to a side ward.

The double doors were blacked out and the whole area was darkened. Curtains were drawn at every window and heavy screening divided each bed from its neighbour. Violet's eyes took some time to adjust to the gloom and she peered through it at the beds as the sister explained to her that she was to attend to these men and to commence with bottles and bedpans. In the darkness she could make out two other nurses going quietly from bed to bed.

"What is this?" she whispered to the sister.

The older woman looked at her hard-faced and then turned and indicated the beds and their occupants. Her voice softened and Violet detected a note of sympathy as she said softly, "These are the unglamorous victims of this war."

"Unglamorous? What do you mean?"

"Facial and head injuries. The ones who cannot be seen."

Violet walked slowly across to the nearest bed. A man lay there in the dark. He was fully clothed, reclining there on the bed in the darkness, his uniform neatly pressed and complete except, of course, for his footwear. In the silence she could hear his breath rasping and bubbling, and as she moved further forward he dabbed the corner of his mouth area with a wad of absorbent dressing. The left side of his face was destroyed, a mass of twisted, barely healed flesh. The eye on that side had gone, as had the whole of the nose and his left lower jaw. The bubbling came from the slackly open hole that was the remains of his mouth and the two longitudinal creases that had been his nasal passages.

His remaining eye fixed on Violet's face. It stared up at her. Looking down at him, her mouth hanging open in sheer horror at the gargoyle before her, her thoughts tumbled about. God the poor man. How disgusting. She shot a glance back at the sister standing there, watching for her reaction. She had done this to her on purpose, hadn't she? 'She thought I would be unable to face them.' Anger. She felt anger at this woman. She had used this wretched man to get at her for her impudence last night. She looked straight into her eyes and the sister was surprised to see her unwavering look and the determined set of her jaw.

"Thank you sister." She turned back to the man on the bed and smiled broadly. "Now then, have you been up to the toilets already, or is there anything I can get you?"

The eye stared back up at her and the face twisted slightly as the broken muscles, which would have created a smile, twitched. The eye blinked quickly. The signal was received and understood. Sister turned and left the room.

As Violet continued on the ward through that day and the following days, she came across hopeless misery and terrible destruction of human life. The sister had been right. Here there certainly was no glamour in war, if there ever really had been in the first place. But it was worse than that. These men were injured and their injuries were no more or less honourably gained than any of the others, yet their very existence was almost denied. Throughout the land, war heroes displaying terrible injuries and loss of limbs were feted and applauded. A grateful populace showered money and presents upon them, and young girls were happy and proud to be seen in their company. Not so the facially disfigured. They were shunned and disregarded, shunted off into darkened side wards, hidden from public view. Even years after the war, the sight of one of these men would reduce a room to guilty silence and people would show offence at their very presence.

Violet was struck by the way they seemed to co-operate in some sort of supposed guilt at the nature of their injuries, and at night on those first days of her assignment she lay awake thinking of the gloomy ward and its quiet occupants. That they were quiet was understandable because many of them could not speak in any event, but why the darkness? Was it to hide them from themselves? There were no mirrors in the ward, and the drawn curtains prevented use of the windows as such. Was it to prevent them seeing the other occupants? She tried whilst on duty to act as normally as possible, but if she ever raised her voice to a normal speaking tone, the other nurses would stop what they were doing and look meaningfully at her, forcing her to moderate her voice to the more customary whisper.

Feeding the men with badly damaged mouth parts was the most difficult part of her job. In some cases they had to be fed by a tube directly into the gullet. In others it was a long, drawn out and messy affair accompanied by spluttering and gurgles as the poor men fought to breathe whilst swallowing as best they could. Violet patiently wiped their ruined faces and waited until they nodded their assent to the next attempt. She held their hands as they cried there in the dark. Cries which had no sound. Ravaged eyes that could shed no tears.

Often the only way she could tell that a man was crying was the spluttering from his breathing tubes and the shuddering of his body. If she saw this, she would stop whatever she was doing and rush across to be beside him and hold his hand, but many times in the darkness of the ward they lay there alone and unnoticed in their misery.

Unfortunately, that misery was often as the direct result of the visits of their relatives, wives or girlfriends. No matter how much preparation was made before they were finally ushered in, the almost inevitable result would be that they would break down in front of the poor man. In some cases they just stood there in shocked silence, but the majority had to be escorted from the room in a state of near collapse; that is, unless they had already fled.

When Violet escorted such cases from the darkened ward, they would turn to her for help as if it were they who were injured, but it was always the poor man that had been left behind in the dark that she felt for. Lying there wondering exactly what he looked like, or coming to terms with the realisation that he was marooned in a life he could never share.

Returning from assisting one such weeping female relative from the room about a month after she had started, Violet happened upon the sister. "Everything all right Miss Matthews?" she enquired.

"It will be sister. But I'm afraid that poor boy in there is pretty upset and I'd better get back to him."

"Miss Matthews," said the sister, calling her back. "Miss... Nurse Matthews I..." She seemed unable to continue. But she had said enough.

"Thank you sister," said Violet quietly as she turned away and made her way back into the ward.

May 1916-March 1917

In the first six months of 1916, the British sectors were relatively quiet as the Germans concentrated their efforts against the French at Verdun. Nevertheless, within that period huge numbers of British and Empire men were killed or wounded as part of the normal attrition of trench warfare.

For the hospitals, that meant a steady flow of casualties passing through the various stages of the medical chain, and at the Southampton hospitals the throughput of injured continued unabated. Unlike the small cottage hospital in Finchley, the men passed through this large hospital quite quickly, being transferred to other specialist hospitals or convalescent establishments as soon as they were capable of being moved. Fraternisation between the nurses and soldiers was strictly discouraged but, in any event, as most of the patients did not stay long, Violet was never able to form the friendships with individual patients that she had done in Finchley.

It was in the middle of June that the orders came through to clear the beds once more. As the ambulance driver had remarked, a watch on the hospitals would give away a great deal and so it proved, with the start of the British offensive on the Somme in the first week of July.

In the weeks before, when the hospital had been cleared as far as was possible, a calm descended on the wards, which in some ways reminded Violet of her days at Finchley, but they all knew that it was the calm before the storm. On the continent, all had been made ready for the offensive. Advance dressing stations were sandbagged off near the front and elaborate plans were laid for the injured to be passed from them to casualty clearing stations, thence by ambulance and hospital train to the base hospitals and the hospital ships bound for England. The trouble was that the casualty rate was fifty times greater than had been anticipated and the whole system was swamped in the first twenty-four hours, with no let-up in the days and weeks which followed.

The news flooding back to the hospitals on the coast filled them all with dread as to what they were about to receive, and when the first ships came in they were crowded with casualties to such a degree that the evacuation of Gallipoli, all those months before, paled into insignificance.

Violet found herself working once more in the receiving rooms, and when things got busier and busier, eventually ended up within the operating theatre itself.

Night after night and day after day the men would be wheeled through and into the theatre, where they would be quickly anaesthetised, sometimes by qualified staff but often, when the rush was on, by others who were simply judged to be competent. No consultation took place. The limbs were removed in quick succession and the bodies passed on for dressing as soon as the stitches were in. Even then it was not always the end of the story, for when the dreaded gangrene set in, the patient would often have to go back for more radical surgery.

On the ward, Violet and the other VADs were now accepted as being proficient enough to remove and replace dressings, as well as irrigate gangrenous wounds with Eusol. Day after day, Violet would approach the patients for their four-hourly treatment and see the look of dread on their faces. They knew what was coming. They knew only too well the pain the treatment involved and they knew too that, even if the killer could be prevented from entering their main bloodstream, the affected limbs would probably still be rendered useless by its ravages.

Once again life fell into a routine for Violet, and before she knew it another year was drawing to a close. A harsher than average winter had drawn the Somme offensive of 1916 to a stalemate, and the surgical cases began to be overtaken by the medical ones, with problems such as acute trench foot and frostbite being seen more and more.

Violet asked if she could go home for Christmas and was granted a full week's leave. She wrote to her parents that she would be coming, and her father replied saying how delighted they all were and how they were looking forward to it. She also wrote to Florrie, telling her what she was doing and asking for news of baby Frank, and the reply came around the middle of December. She picked the letter up as she was going off duty and happily that night she found herself more or less alone in the dormitory and was able to read it quietly to herself.

Dear Miss Matthews,

We got your letter the other week. It is very interesting to hear all that you are doing. You are very brave to be doing the good work you and all the other nurses are doing for our brave soldiers.

Little Frank is very well and brings us much joy. He is a lovely little boy. He is walking now and we are careful to watch him. At the moment he has a bit of a rash and a runny nose, but the doctor says that is normal and he is a fine healthy boy.

We have some wonderful news. I am going to have a baby in May of next year. Joe and me are very pleased. We have been trying for such a long time. The doctor says that it often happens that when two people care for a baby they fall for one of their own so we think that baby Frank has done the trick for us.

All our love and best wishes.

Kind regards

Florrie and Joe

Violet read the letter over and over. She sat on her bed holding it to her breast, dreaming of her lost child. She did not cry, but she sat there alone feeling very wretched. When oh when would the guilt end? All those who cared about her seemed to have forgiven her, but she was a very long way from forgiving herself.

She could rationalise the act of love that had led to the baby. This war and what she had witnessed bore testament to the brief moments that had to be treasured. What she could not however come to terms with was her own rejection of the child, for that is what, after all, it had been. She had not been prepared to face the ignominy of openly bearing and caring for the child and to stand up to her father and society. If she had done so, then maybe by now she would have gained acceptance. But instead, Frank's child, born of love and out of wedlock, had been pushed aside for her own vanity. 'I will make amends Frank,' she promised as she stared down at Florrie's letter... 'but give me time.'

Christmas at home was a joyous one, even if it was all too brief. Her mother seemed unusually well and officiated at each and every meal. She spent time in the kitchen with Alice and even accompanied Violet and Ernest to church on Christmas Day, walking proudly into the church with one on each arm, acknowledging the waves and smiles of greeting with broad smiles of her own.

Ernest was not a little gratified by this turn of events. His wife on his arm in public gave him a feeling of wholeness, which he had not felt for years, and the pride he had in Violet's uniform and calling only added to his joy.

The day after Boxing Day, on the Wednesday, Elsie, tired with all the exertions but happier and fitter than she had felt for ages, was finally persuaded to take an afternoon nap, leaving Violet and Ernest alone by the fire.

"How has it been my love?"

"Oh it's all right daddy. It's just that my life now seems so full of horror and pain."

"Oh my darling, I thought you and I had sorted things out."

She looked at him quizzically for a moment. "Oh no! Not me... I'm not talking of my life as such. I'm talking of what I've seen... the things I see every day." She stopped and looked down into the flames, her brow furrowed, her hand clenched in a ball and held against her mouth. She looked up at him. "I cannot tell you daddy what I've seen and it never seems to stop. Oh when will this war end?"

He leant forward in his chair and touched her knee. "Are you sure you want to carry on with this Violet?"

"What?"

"Are you sure you want to go on doing this?"

"Oh yes daddy. I'm sorry. It's just that... it's just that sometimes it really affects me. Take no notice, I'll be all right and... yes I will see this through to the end." She paused and deliberately sought to change the subject. "Frank's fine. I had a letter from Florrie... but there's no point in changing things until the war's at an end."

He squeezed her knee and sat back in his chair. "Well don't forget. If you feel you've had enough... nobody will blame you and you can come home with honour."

"Thank you daddy, and thank you for making this such a nice Christmas."

"Don't thank me. Thank your mother. She's the one who's done it all... well with Alice's help I grant you... but she deserves much of the credit."

The two of them went quiet and dozed in the chairs until late in the afternoon, when the door opened and Elsie and Alice brought in tea.

......

One night in late March, as the two of them sat on their beds, Doris announced to a very tired Violet that she was going to apply for service abroad.

Astonished, Violet looked up at her friend. "Are you really?"

"Yes, they need help over there because they can't get them all back here, you see... and the girls who were there are starting to come back now after their tours. Here, why don't you come Violet?" She sat up, her knees drawn up under her, looking expectantly at her.

"No I couldn't, you have to be over twenty-three, don't you? I'm not that 'till November."

"Me neither love, but they don't ask that much if you get my meaning. Oh come on, why don't you? The forms are in the sister's office."

"I'll think about it," said Violet. She dropped back on her bed, stared at the ceiling for a moment and then turned over and fell into an exhausted sleep.

The next morning as she passed by the sister's office, Doris ushered her in. "Where's sister?" asked Violet.

"She's not here. But these are." She held up the Foreign Service forms. "Come on, let's fill them in now and send them off."

"Oh all right," said Violet, more to shut her up than anything, and the two of them leant on the desk and carefully filled them out. When they'd finished, Doris put them in her skirt pocket to deliver later and Violet forgot all about them until a few weeks later, when she was informed that a selection committee would be sitting and that she was to attend.

"I can't do it Doris. Honestly I can't. If they ask me my age I'll blush and give the whole thing away. Anyway, surely they'll require my parents' consent?"

"Don't be silly love, course they won't. All they're interested in is what experience you've got and whether you'll be any good."

......

Ernest stood once more on the concourse at Waterloo, looking down a platform for Violet. How superbly different this was to that other time at Paddington. Then he had been dreading what was to happen, but now he was filled with excitement. She was coming home again on leave and he hadn't felt as happy in... well it seemed like years. She wouldn't be here for long, she had said, but by God he was going to make the very best of the whole time.

He looked around at the other people waiting for the train to arrive. A mixed crowd. Those waiting like him to greet someone, looking happy and expectant, their eyes alight, the smiles playing freely on their faces. Those waiting to see someone off trying to be cheerful, looking around with darting, haunted looks, the smiles immobile, frozen. Couples standing entwined and silent, hidden within the folds of the greatcoats that sought to protect and preserve them from the world that was about to part them.

The great engine approached the buffers, clouds of steam issuing forth, brakes squealing. Those waiting to greet arrivals surged forward, closer to the barrier expectantly, Ernest amongst them, leaving the departees isolated and exposed in their misery. He scanned the platform eagerly looking out for his Violet. She saw him first and waved. He waved back furiously, disavowing his normal reticence at any public display of emotion. He could hardly contain himself from rushing through the barrier, and as she passed through enveloped her in his arms and held her, rocking from side to side.

After a while, he put his hands on her shoulders and held her away, looking into her face. "How are you darling?"

"I'm fine daddy. Fine." She bent down to pick up her bag, which had been dropped in the greeting, but he stooped forward to take it and they bumped heads. They both recoiled, laughing and rubbing their foreheads. Eventually he retrieved the bag and she turned towards where the car would be parked. He took her shoulder and turned her back to the station entrance. "No car daddy?"

"No darling. Oh, I've still got it but there's no fuel for it nowadays and... well it's not done to... well you know... I'll get rid of it soon."

She squeezed his arm and held tight, walking in step with him happily. How different was the journey back home to that other time before last? Then much of it had been conducted in a stony silence, but now they chatted and laughed all the way. When the final bus dropped them off in Ballards Lane and they turned into Etchingham Park Road, they slowed their pace for Violet to savour the sights, smells and sounds of the familiar street. She noticed that many of the wrought iron railings and fences had gone, to be replaced with rough wooden fencing or young hedging plants, and remarked upon it.

"All gone. Yes even ours. Gone to make weapons I'm afraid. You'll not find much of anything metal around that's not been taken now."

She sighed. "Our men and boys. Even our fence. What more do we all have to give?"

He looked at her. Her face, no longer the face of a young and privileged girl, showed the lines of her experiences. The eyes still retained their sparkle and spirit, but they were set now in the hollows of sleepless nights and exhausted days. Here was the face of a young woman who had known life and seen things that perhaps he could only imagine at. The hand holding his was rough and bore the results of the sepsis that had crossed to her through tiny cuts and abrasions. In later years her fingers, like those of many of the other nurses, would be stiff and unwilling, a lasting legacy of their dedication. Ah well, he thought. Enough of that now. She was home, and for the days that she was here the war was a long way away.

They entered the house and Violet was amazed to see her mother standing there in the hall. For a moment they just stood looking at each other, but then Elsie crossed to her daughter. "Hallo my darling." She took her hand, and with the other traced the lines on Violet's face. The feel of the thin hand on her face, the strength in the grip of the other, were all new to Violet and she glanced questioningly across her mother's shoulder at her father standing there, beaming proudly at them both.

"Where's Alice?"

"She's not home yet dear. She gets home about 7 o'clock and she'll be delighted to see you no doubt."

"She's home at 7 o'clock? What do you mean?"

Her father stepped forward to speak, but Elsie held up her hand to stop him. "Alice works at the hospital... you know the one you worked at before you went away."

"Alice works... but why... how? Who looks after you?"

"Your father and I manage well enough together and... I've been feeling so much better recently and... well there's a war on you know and we all..."

"...We all have to do our bit," her father interrupted. "Now go with your mother and sit in the drawing room and I'll put the kettle on and bring you a cup of tea."

An almost spellbound Violet allowed herself to be led into the drawing room and sat down by her mother. My God, she thought. What a change. What a reversal of roles. Why, she had changed even from the woman who had been so difficult to recognise at Christmas. Her mother caught her look.

"I know. It's all strange to you. The truth is... the truth is that I just had to make the effort and... well... having made the effort I've felt better for it, even if I do get a little tired at times."

"But mother, how do you manage without Alice?"

"Oh I always have something ready for her when she gets in, poor thing. She works so hard you know. Well you would know wouldn't you, you did it."

"You mean you cook for Alice?"

"Yes dear. Of course I do. You can't expect her to work all day in the hospital and then to come home and cook for all of us, can you?"

"No indeed. Indeed you can't mother." Violet looked into the earnest face of her mother. Heavens what a change. She was not quite sure how to handle this situation... her mother being a capable being. She had not been thus for... for... well since she could remember. She smiled at her and her mother smiled back, seemingly oblivious to the full impact her new-found health was having.

The door opened and Ernest came in with a tray of tea and put it down on the coffee table. Violet moved to pour, but sat back again as her mother proceeded to attend to things. She glanced across at her father and he smiled and winked at her.

"A scone darling?" said her mother, interrupting their silent conversation. "Alice showed us how to make them and I think we're getting to be quite proficient, aren't we Ernest?"

"Yes indeed dearest," replied Ernest, and he beamed with pride at the wondering and silently shaken Violet.

"Now Violet, tell us what you've been doing and what's happening. How long are you staying and where are you off to next?"

"I'm here for one week mother and then I'm off to France."

There was a silence in the room. Violet held her breath, dreading a scene which would lead to questions about where and how and why. What if they knew about the age rule? Would they stand in her way? Her father coughed and broke the silence. "I'm... we're both so proud of you Violet and... well I think I speak for us both when I say that we will of course support you."

Violet looked from one to the other. Her father looked serious and his face betrayed the many emotions going on in his head. Her mother smiled openly across at her and nodded. Thank God, she thought, torn between happiness and total disbelief at the ease with which her mission had been accomplished. She had imagined all sorts of scenes, tantrums and pleadings against her going, but here they were wishing her bon voyage. Her mother rose from the chair, and it was all Violet could do to stop herself getting up to assist her. "If you'll excuse me darlings, I have to get supper started. You two stay in here and chat. Your father can tell me all about it later on, but I have to get things done before Alice comes home." She left the room and Ernest slipped into the chair she had vacated, opposite Violet.

She looked across at him, the questions all on her face, even if she could not bring herself to articulate them.

"I know," he said. "It's wonderful, isn't it?"

"When did it start?"

"Well you noticed the difference at Christmas, I'm sure... and just after you went back... well, she got up in the morning and announced that she'd read in the papers that people were being urged to give up their servants in order that they could assist in the war effort, and that she'd decided that that was what Alice should do."

"And what did Alice think of this?"

Ernest smiled. "Well, she was a bit taken aback at first because she really didn't have anywhere else to go. After all, this was her home. She was quite upset at your mother apparently planning to throw her out."

Violet laughed. "I expect she was. Poor Alice."

"Yes, but then your mother astounded us all by saying that she had spoken to Dr Crowe and that if Alice was willing she could start at the hospital the following week and continue to live here."

"And what did Alice think of all of this being arranged without her knowledge?"

"She was pleased. She had apparently been troubled, herself, about her lack of any contribution. The whole thing worked out quite nicely, don't you know."

"Well I don't know, actually daddy. It's all very strange and different to me."

"Well don't complain please."

"Oh no... no far from it, I think it's all wonderful and I'm so happy that you seem happier than I've ever seen you. How's work?"

"Fine. Fine. We've not lost any houses to the Zeppelins yet. Rents are sometimes a bit slow coming in with all the men being away. Business, of course, isn't very good but... well you just have to make the best, don't you?"

"Oh daddy, I'm so proud of you. I really am."

He shrugged his shoulders. "I don't see why. I've done nothing... not like you."

She smiled at him and they sat for a while without talking, allowing the peace of the moment to settle upon them. Eventually he broke the silence. "Have you heard again from Devon?"

She looked up at him. "No, not since the last time. I need to tell Florrie where I'm going, but I'm not sure where to tell her to write."

"Do you want me to find out if everything's all right?"

"Would you daddy? Tell her I've gone to France and I'll write from there."

"I'll do that." He looked across at her, her face troubled now. He wished he hadn't said anything, but he had and that was that. Better that than to leave it to fester, as it had before.

"Does mother know anything?"

"No she doesn't, and I feel that it's better that way at the moment. If she knew she would want to do something about it and really, although she copes awfully well here, she couldn't cope with a young child. When you're back or settled we'll tell her together."

She smiled and reached across to take his hand. He squeezed hers comfortingly and they sat there silent again, each within their own thoughts. How old would Frank be now, she thought. Coming up to two years old. He would be starting to talk soon. Was he all right? Of course he was. So much of him to miss. But miss it she must. Her father had obviously made up his mind to do something about things when she was back. Dear daddy, how he had changed. How they all had changed.

He sat across from her. A brave girl, he thought. A brave woman. The anger at her betrayal had long since disappeared and been replaced, if not with a complete understanding, by acceptance of what was. Should he give her the letters now? He looked across at her sitting there in front of him, her eyes closed as she dozed quietly. No. She was happy now. Why upset her just as she was leaving? There would be another time. He stole from the room, leaving her to sleep, and took her bag up to her bedroom.

"Supper's ready."

Violet stirred, stretched and woke up. "Oh I've been asleep. You shouldn't have let me."

"Nonsense," said Ernest. "You needed the sleep. Don't bother about changing, just rinse your hands and come straight in." He left the room and Violet went quickly up to her bedroom to wash her hands and comb her hair.

She entered the dining room. Her father was sitting at his place. He rose and indicated her to one of the three other set places, sitting as she sat. "Your mother's just bringing it in. She won't be long. She's so proud to be cooking for you."

"I know," said Violet. "I'm finding it all a bit strange I can tell you." She indicated the fourth setting. "Who's that for? Are we expecting company?"

He laughed. "No, not tonight. That's Alice's place. She'll be down in a minute. She's just getting changed out of her uniform."

Violet smiled happily and picked up her napkin. My, how things had changed, she thought. What a pity Frank hadn't lived to see it. But changed it was. And for the better.

May 1917

The truck rattled and bounced along the pot-holed road, with Violet clinging to an upright stanchion, despite the flapping canvas making the back of her hand red raw. Her bottom bumped up and down on the hard bench seat until it became almost too unbearable and she tried to raise herself off it, until the strain on her knees forced her to sit again. She had never been quite so uncomfortable in her life. Her kit bag, along with everybody else's, slithered and bounced about in the well of the vehicle but she, like them, had long since given up all hope of controlling it.

At every upright another nurse clung on with squeals and shouts as the vehicle lurched its way forward. Violet called across to Doris. "What a good idea of yours this was."

"Wonderful, isn't it? Remind me to shut up next time." They both laughed. A staccato of intermittent sounds, given the shaking they were receiving, and then screams as the vehicle hit a larger than average bump, literally flinging them into the air.

Eventually they determined that they were slowing down and gave a collective sigh of relief as the lorry came to a halt. The rear tarpaulin was undone and whisked sideways. The tailgate was let down by the driver and an old ammunition box placed to form a step.

"Good afternoon ladies," came the cheery voice of a young orderly, standing there looking up at them with a clipboard in his hand. "Welcome to Camiers Hotel."

He held out his free hand to each of them in turn as they dismounted, then he leapt nimbly up and started to hand down the kit bags, calling out the name on each as he did so. At length they were all standing in a bruised gaggle as the lorry rattled off.

'Camiers Base Hospital' announced the notice and directions board. Not a bit like they had imagined. A huge sprawl of marquees and tents laid out in neat lines almost as far as the eye could see, huddling into the windswept coastal plain of northern France.

"Bloody 'ell," said one of the other nurses. "I never knew we was goin' campin'."

Violet looked at Doris and put her hand on her shoulder. "A really good idea." Doris, lost for words, could only smile wanly.

An orderly marched across to them. "Right ladies, let me show you to your quarters," he called out as he approached, "and then you're to report to matron for her welcoming address and allocation to your wards. Follow me."

He strode in through the camp gates, turning right at the orderly tent and along the line of duckboards, past the tented wards laid out in lines to their left. The new arrivals followed as best they could, trying not to slip on the damp boarding as they clutched their unwieldy bags.

"What's all this nettin' I keep trippin' on?" asked the girl Rosie. The one who had spoken when they first arrived.

"Stops the boards shinin' at night."

"What's wrong wiv that?"

"Boche planes. They can pick 'em out in the moonlight."

"What! They surely don't bomb the hospital?" said Violet amazed. "Can't they see the red crosses?"

"Oh they sees them all right, but they don't care."

A shiver of fear went through them all and, for the first time, some of them realised that they might actually be in danger here, and not a few of them began to question their commitment. Their morale was further dampened when they crossed out of the main encampment to a field in which there were rows and rows of dirty white bell tents, some small and some larger.

"The small ones is for the sisters, the larger ones is for you ladies. Six to a tent now. Be back up at the orderly room for matron in half an hour."

"Where do we pee then?" said Rosie. "In an 'ole?"

He laughed lightly. "No course not. There's the nurses ablutions over there in that 'ut. All spick an' span. An' over there beyond that is the kitchens and your mess 'ut." He pointed and they all looked with dismay, thinking of long treks in the night across muddy fields, should they be caught short.

Violet pulled open the flap of a tent which was obviously unoccupied and stepped in. She could stand fully upright in the tent, which was a relief. Around the central pole six palliasses were arranged on the groundsheet, like so many hands on a clock. On each was a small pile of rough linen sheets and some thin army blankets. No other furniture was available except for a couple of dangerous-looking folding chairs stacked up against the tent pole. The canvas flapped lazily in the afternoon breeze.

Violet stood, trying to take it all in. Doris followed her in and stood with her, her hand on her shoulder, their kit bags on the floor beside them like lumpy dogs on leashes. They said nothing.

Rosie followed them in. "Bloody 'ell, it gets worse an' worse." She ducked her head out of the entrance flap and called to the departing orderly. "'ere you can't be serious. We'll freeze in 'ere in the winter."

He laughed and called back. "Na yer won't. It'll be long before then. It snowed at Easter." He waved and walked on.

Violet looked at the other girls who were now filing into the tent. She tugged at Doris, indicating two palliasses to the left of the tent, a bit away from the entrance but not too far so as to make it difficult to get in and out. "Let's take these two here." She knelt down, rolled over on to the bed and lay looking up at the tent roof. She jumped her hips up into the air and down again. Little or no resistance came from the filling of straw and sawdust. No comfort for her aching and bruised bottom would be found here.

The girl Rosie sauntered over to the bed on the other side of Violet and plonked her kit bag down beside it. "I do hope your ladyship don't mind slummin' it wiv me."

"Not at all," said Violet. "Make yourself at home."

"Make myself at 'ome, she says. Make myself at 'ome. Oh thank you so much your ladyship."

The other girls laughed nervously. Violet felt a flush of temper. Rosie continued. "On a tour of inspection are we?"

Violet sat up. "I'm here to work the same as you."

"Pah! What would your sort know about work? Bet you've never done any real work in yer life."

"Don't be silly Rosie," piped up the mousy girl who had taken the bed next to her. "She must have worked in an 'ospital to even be 'ere."

"Southampton, Finchley, and before that on the factory floor," said Violet. "Does that satisfy you?"

Rosie looked across at her, her face flushed and angry, spoiling for a fight. Then quite suddenly her demeanour visibly relaxed. She smiled and waved both of her hands in the air, shaking her head. "Sorry love, I was just feelin' ratty. I 'ad no call pickin' on you."

"Apology accepted. We're all tired and fed up."

"Sorry love."

"Don't mention it. Here, we'd better get going or we'll all be late on parade."

The address by matron was a litany of rules and regulations, mainly about the behaviour that would be expected of them and the fact that socialising with officers and men was discouraged, especially in uniform. The fact that they were also not allowed out of uniform in nearly all circumstances narrowed down the exceptions to the meaningless. If they did meet any officers or men by accident rather than design, the rule was that there had to be at least two and two and the strict curfew must be observed. "Remember you are in a foreign land in the middle of a war zone and any infringement of the rules will mean your immediate dispatch back to England."

"Cor there's 'ope for us yet," whispered Rosie, and Violet had to stifle a giggle.

Life for all of them in the Base Hospital, when they had settled in, revolved around a similar routine to that which Violet had become accustomed to in Southampton, with, of course, the main difference being the conditions in which they had to live and work. The wards were laid out in familiar pattern with beds down each side, but there the similarity ended. The flooring was of duckboards laid close together with ground sheeting below and above which, over time, became rucked up, making progress difficult and the movement of patients and beds well-nigh impossible. The sick and injured men lay in their beds, huddling against the draughts, beset by the constant flapping of the tent walls and the spluttering lanterns. At night, the lights made strange patterns and shapes on the tent, giving the impression of a medieval vision of hell. Only here the creatures moving about amongst the stricken were angels rather than tormenting demons.

The first flush of casualties from the Easter offensive had run through the system, and what was left on Violet's particular ward were the cases that were either on their way to recovery or far too ill to move. Those who were recovering sat around bored and disconsolate, awaiting their sending off to the convalescent hospitals and eventual return to the line. They had not been lucky enough to receive a wound sufficient for repatriation. Most knew that they would be back in the ward again if they were lucky and dead if they weren't.

Every week the doctors would make a ward round, accompanied by a sister, to mark up those who were to be sent home and those who had to stay. All of the nurses, and Violet was no exception, hated that day and the way the men would lie there hoping for a 'Blighty', looking up at their judges with beseeching eyes. If they got a ticket home, then the joy the recipient felt was as palpable as was the despair of those that didn't get one. In most cases the bad news was received in silence and the soldier kept his own council, but occasionally there were those who simply couldn't hide their disappointment. "I've had enough nurse," they would confide with tears in their eyes. "I've had enough."

This was not a war fought by a professional army. This was a war fought in the main by farmers, millers, shop boys and gentlemen. Ordinary men from all walks of civilian life who had answered the call of duty and found themselves in uniform.

Strange also was the existence of the nurses, camped there in the mud of France. When it rained, as it often did that summer, everything got damp, however much they tried. The very air seemed filled with the humid mud, to the point where they seemed to be almost breathing it in. Boots and hems were constantly covered in its gritty wetness, and even when cleaned their aprons and dresses retained the tell-tale staining.

When the sun shone it wasn't much better. Then the tent seemed to act as a draw for the damp ground beneath the groundsheet and the humidity levels left the walls running with moisture. Clothing and personal effects left in the kit bags would become musty, so they rigged up a system of lines which left dresses performing a ghostly dance in the hot dark air above where they lay. Boots, shoes and any other leather items seemed to act as a magnet for moulds and mildew. At night, if the noise of the rain on the roof didn't keep them from their much-needed sleep, then the proximity of six sweating bodies tossing and turning in their discomfort served them equally badly.

The summer also brought with it plagues of mosquitoes and biting insects, which found their way through every crevice and opening in the tents. Just as sleep would finally beckon Violet, she would hear the high whining hum of some ghastly creature coming to feast and would have to lie there swotting blindly in the dark, hoping against hope to catch the damned thing. But all too often the morning would show up the scene of its meal in long lines of angry red blotches.

The conditions under which they lived were brought into stark relief by the arrival of the Americans. Violet and the others watched with undisguised jealousy as their smart new huts were erected, complete with stoves and fitted out with proper beds and bedding. As if that weren't enough, the level of freedom the new arrivals enjoyed left them feeling very much the poor relations in all respects. Nothing illustrated this quite as well as the times when there was a concert at the machine gun school and they had to march there two by two in full uniform, like school girls out to church, whilst the American nurses drifted over there in the company of uniformed men, free to associate as they pleased. That they looked down on the British was never in dispute, but this public demonstration of their differences brought with it the seeds of much resentment.

July 1917

The rain beat down on the tent roof in a pallid imitation of the distant gunfire coming from the Machine Gun School. Pools of water seeped in under the eaves of the tent and Violet moved across and pushed the stones, kept there for the purpose, further under in an effort to persuade it to change direction. She sat on her bed and undid her boots, grimacing at the mud, which coated them and the first inches of her heavy skirt. Thank God for the new huts which were at last being erected in the next field. They had the Americans to thank for that. Well, that and public opinion at home fuelled by *The Times* newspaper's disgust at the contrast in their conditions.

She reached into her kit bag and took out the carefully tied bundle of letters that she kept there on the top. She put them on the bed beside her, spreading them out a little so as to let the moisture within them dissipate. Preserving paper was so difficult, and these treasures meant so much to her. Alone in the tent, she savoured the solitude. It was the one thing it was so difficult to get in the camp. Everywhere there were people, and moments of silent contemplation were almost impossible to come by. She sighed and took out the latest letter from her father.

He told her news of home and the 'home front'. Business continued to be difficult, but her father did not seem overly concerned and seemed to enjoy his new role as benefactor to the families incapable of paying their full rents. She savoured the thought of his change, but hoped that he would not take it so far as to bring ruin upon himself. He gave much emphasis to his employment of women in the office, and she smiled to herself at the memory of his outrage at the suffragettes demonstration. Dear daddy... Frank would like you now... no he always did. It was daddy who had... oh what was the point now.

She looked down at the bundle of letters beside her on the bed and ran her fingers lightly, lovingly over them. They brought her comfort but also revived those feelings of guilt that normally had so little time to surface. He would be two... no two years and four months old now. What was he like, this child of hers and Frank's? Would she ever be forgiven by him? Would she ever really forgive herself? He would be walking now, his little arms stretched out before him, his legs held apart to balance. His face, no doubt wreathed in smiles. The image blurred and tears, those damned tears, welled in her eyes. She lay back and closed her eyes.

"Readin' our love letters are we?" said a voice, breaking into her reverie.

She looked up at the voice. It was Rosie, the girl she'd had the spat with on their arrival.

They hadn't crossed swords since that day, and in point of fact a sort of grudging friendship had arisen. A good job too, because in the close proximity and privations of their existence, if there had been any enmity, life for all the occupants of the tent would have been well-nigh impossible. If any small argument did flare up, then those who were not involved would instinctively dampen it down. In any event, as far as Rosie was concerned, she had been in the wrong that day and Violet had more than proved herself in the intervening period.

"Not really, it's from my father."

"Oh no boyfriend then?"

"I did have but..." She looked down on the bed beside her and fingered the letters, free from their binding, lying scattered across the bed. Rosie followed her attention. On top was the fateful letter from Keith Pitts that she kept with the others, even though she could never bear to read it again.

"Why that's... What's..." Rosie bent down and swept up the letter before an astonished Violet could stop her. She held it aloft, pointing at the signature. "This is from my Keith. What are you doin' wiv a letter from my boyfriend?"

The colour drained from Violet's face. She felt naked, exposed as if in a strange dream.

"Your... Corporal Pitts is... is your..."

"Boyfriend. Yes he's my fella, and I want to know why he's writin' to you."

Violet struggled to retain her composure, her mind racing. How amazing. How cruel that life should play such a trick on her. Here, far from home in a foreign land, a girl she would normally have had nothing to do with, nothing in common... she slept in the bed next to her... a link with Frank she could never have imagined.

"Read the letter please Rosie."

"What?"

"I said read the letter please Rosie."

"Why?"

"Because when you have, you'll understand."

Rosie sat down on her bed, the letter in her hand. She looked carefully at it as if it was going to bite her, then back up at Violet, who nodded to her to continue.

"I don't read so fast." She sat there slowly reading the letter, mouthing the words as she read them. She stared into space, her eyes troubled... wondering... the letter in her lap. She looked across at Violet, the truth dawning on her. "Frank. Frank Balfour... he's talking about... It's you, isn't it? You're that lady... the one Frank fell for when he was up London."

"Yes Rosie. I'm the... Frank and I were... we loved each other but..."

Rosie continued to stare, seemingly unable to comprehend the full import of this amazing coincidence. Violet reached across to her. "Did you know my Frank?"

The blonde girl turned to her, seeing, as if for the first time, the stricken grief-filled face turned to her, begging information. "Of course I knew him love," she said gently as she moved across and sat beside Violet on her bed. "Know him? I went to school wiv him, worked in the fields wiv him. Played wiv him... and Keith. We were always together... up town, in the woods... at Jesse's house."

"You know Jesse?"

"Of course I do. Like I'm telling you, since we was kids. 'ere, I've even got a letter from Jesse. Yeah it's in my bag." She turned to face Violet. "Yeah, she said he was killed and how she'd written to you and how you never replied."

She wrote to me? I didn't get... I was ill after and I... I was ill."

She turned away from Rosie. Father! He must have hidden or destroyed the letter. Either that or it had never got there. No, it must have done. She would write to him immediately demanding that he send it on. If he had... oh what was the point. They'd made their peace now. Why bring it all up again? She'd simply tell him that she knew of the letter's existence and ask him to send it on. She wouldn't comment, she'd leave it unsaid. A hand touched her on the shoulder and she remembered Rosie.

"I'm sorry about your Frank. He was a lovely bloke, even if we didn't see much of 'im after he went off to that posh school. Keith still writes about 'im and how they was such mates an' all before... before he was killed."

"Is Keith all right?"

"Yes he's fine. Well he lost 'is arm. Well 'alf of it really, but he's fine. He's back 'ome in Kent safe and sound. Funny really, there's 'im safe at 'ome and there's me out 'ere in a bleedin' war. Sometimes I think it's the wrong way round, do you know what I mean?" She turned her excited face to Violet's and noticed that she was crying quietly to herself. "Ah come on love. Don't cry... 'ere, let Rosie give you a cuddle."

Once again Violet found comfort in the arms of another woman and again it was one she hardly knew. Doris, returning to her bed, stopped at the sight of the two of them sitting there intertwined, with Violet crying freely. "Bad news?"

"No, it's just that we've just found out that her boyfriend is one of my best mates."

"So what?" whispered Doris.

"So he died. Killed in the war."

"What just now?"

"No ages ago but... well it still 'urts... poor love."

Doris sat down on the palliasse and the three of them stayed there quietly for some time.

......

Violet was not confined in her duties to the ward she had started on and would often be allocated to one or other of the officer's wards. In addition, nurses were at times called upon to work in the Casualty Clearing Stations closer to the front. It was here, in the late summer of 1917, that she first met Armand, although at the time he was just one more patient to be attended to in the misery of the charnel house that the field hospital could become.

He was brought to the hospital near to death. A shell had exploded in the air above his trench and the shrapnel from it had scythed through a whole line of his men, sheltering with him, waiting to resist the advance they knew would follow the bombardment. All he remembered was a blinding flash, a terrible roaring sound in his head and then silence.

He regained consciousness on a stretcher outside the field hospital. His first impression was the feel of the rain beating down on his face and a strange inability to move. He wanted to sit up, but nothing in the event seemed to co-ordinate properly. The only limbs he could move were his arms, and they felt so heavy that they merely flopped down by his side and slipped off the stretcher. He could see the sky above him through the rain, feel the mud between his fingers, but all other sensation, all other feeling was lost to him.

He lay there, he knew not for how long, just staring up at the sky. For some reason, which escaped him, he felt at peace. He was aware of movement around him and the fact that he was not alone in his plight. There were other stretchers on the ground beside him, and from the sounds he could now interpret others beyond them.

A hand touched his face and smoothed the hair away from his forehead. It cupped his chin, and another wiped away the grime before moistening his lips with a clean cloth. A face swam into view. The face of a young woman with a starched white headdress barely concealing her thick brown hair. The face was upside down for him, but he could see her smile and the wide set eyes. "Comment tu t'appelle?"

"Je m'appelle Violet," she said, and then reaching the limit of her new-found French, she lapsed back into English. "Be still now and we'll look after you."

She stroked his brow again. The features and the name locked into his memory as he drifted back into unconsciousness. He seized upon them as a dream, which he held fast to whenever his brain came back into its higher states. A lighthouse on the voyage back to life.

In the operating tent, a huge shard of shrapnel was removed from his back, where it had destroyed his right kidney, causing the paralysis and merciful loss of feeling. The debris taken into the wound was pulled clear, and when the smaller splinters of jagged metal had been attended to, as far as was possible, he was bound up for transport to the Base Hospital.

Back at the main hospital they were alerted to the arrival of the ambulances by the sound of their horns as they trundled down the road almost nose to tail. Nurses looked out and then ran to their posts as the first casualties were brought in and allocated to the wards. Armand was installed in the officer's ward, and later that evening after returning in one of the ambulances, Violet, with Doris, set to, cleaning him up and changing him into the cream-coloured hospital gown which all bed-ridden patients were required to wear.

They were by now used to the filthy state of new inmates and the effects of the conditions endured in the trenches. Nothing, however, could ever completely inure one to the shock of seeing and smelling the result of weeks of sanitary deprivation and it took a strong stomach to attend to some of the poor wretches. It was also extremely hard work, especially as it was often necessary to be very careful about handling or moving the patient. Armand remained unconscious for the whole of this lengthy procedure, which was perhaps a good thing.

Violet stood for a while, looking down at the man in the bed. How tall was he? She guessed about 5'9", maybe a little bit more. He had dark thick hair with thick black eyebrows and a thick, surprisingly well cared for moustache. With his eyes closed in sleep, the most striking feature of his face was his nose. Large and important. A nose made for the enjoyment and savouring of wine, she thought. Good job he was a Frenchman. She sighed. Poor wretch. With the injuries he had, he'd probably never survive anyway. A pity. He looked such a nice man.

She left to get on with her duties and tidy up before a well-earned and much-needed rest.

A couple of days later, around lunchtime, a doctor came on to the ward and asked for a word with the sister. Violet was making beds at the end of the ward nearest to the sister's office, or rather the curtained-off area which sufficed as such. She didn't take much notice of their conversation and busied herself with her tasks, gathering up the pile of soiled linen into her arms and preparing to take it around the back to be collected for the laundry. As she got to just by the curtains, they swung open and sister came through them, nearly bumping into her. "Ah Nurse Matthews, have you nearly finished what you're doing?"

"Why yes sister. I've just finished these and I was going to start on bottles."

"The doctor here has got something to do over by the camp and he needs your help. Can you go with him for this afternoon?"

"Why... yes... yes of course. What is it about?"

"He'll tell you on the way. Run along now and get your coat and take a bag of bandages of various sizes with you. Meet him..." She turned to the doctor. "Where shall she meet you?"

He thought briefly and then suggested outside the orderly room. Violet nodded and went off in search of the bandages, wondering as she did what it was all about.

About half an hour later she was seated beside the doctor as he drove off, her bag clutched on her lap and his between her feet. "Where are we going doctor?"

"We are going to the main camp just behind the lines. There is a prisoner there who has..." He paused for a moment. "...who has hurt himself and we have to treat him."

"What do you mean, a German?"

"No, actually he's an Englishman."

"Well why on earth couldn't they bring him to the hospital?" she exclaimed, exasperated.

"Because he's under sentence of death."

A knot appeared in Violet's throat, together with a cold feeling in the pit of her stomach. She turned around towards him, a look of entire disbelief on her face. "Sentence of death? When?"

"Tomorrow I believe."

"And we're driving all the way over there instead of helping people live at the hospital?"

He stared straight ahead at the bumpy road, his face set in an angry frown. He said nothing for some minutes. Then he suddenly banged both his fists down on the wheel and shouted. "Stupid bloody war! Stupid bloody Generals! Stupid bloody orders!" He flashed a glance at her, then looked back at the road, unable to meet her amazed and incredulous look. He wrestled to keep control of the vehicle as it lurched from pothole to pothole, bouncing them both up and down on the hard seats. "I'm sorry but... well let's get this over with and get back as soon as possible, eh?"

There was little or nothing that Violet could say. Her mind raced with emotion and the anticipation of the scene to come. She dreaded arrival, yet was fascinated and appalled at the prospect. The doctor remained tight-lipped and said nothing further for the whole journey.

As they got nearer to the front, their progress was slowed still further by the traffic on the road.

Moving away from the front on one side of the road were lines of battle-weary men, their heads bowed, uniforms and equipment covered in mud, weapons held down. On the other side, moving the other way, were lines upon lines of marching men, their uniforms still showing rank and insignia, their rifles sloped proudly over their shoulders. The doctor wove the vehicle between the two lines, hooting his horn to clear the road.

They pulled into the camp, the sound of battle now very close and the reality of the war at its fighting point coming home to them. Mud everywhere was the dominant theme. It permeated everything they looked at. The tents were mud-coloured and mud-spattered. All of the vehicles and the piles of ammunition were covered in a brown film of mud. The men they could see were similarly coated, walking wide-legged and laboriously through it or struggling to remain on the slippery duckboards, huddled into their capes against the rain.

They came to a halt in front of the guard tent and the doctor motioned Violet to stay put whilst he made enquiries as to where to go. Violet's heart thumped wildly with fear at the coming ordeal. She stared through the windscreen at the dismal sight before her; a dun-coloured world of misery and hopelessness where not even a blade of grass dared show its head. Shattered trees stood testament to the passage of war, unable now to give shelter or shade.

Her morbid thoughts were interrupted by the doctor's return. He slipped the vehicle into gear, drove past the guardhouse and around to the right of it before pulling up in front of the cow shed that had been converted to the gaol. A small brick and stone building, windowless except for the barred section of the wooden door with a nearly flat roof of clay pantiles, from which the water now ran copiously, dropping into the rivulet it had created over time and then wandering out to add to the sea of mud.

They sat in silence in the truck for some time before the doctor said, "Well, I suppose we'd better get in there then." Violet nodded and pushed open her door. Duckboards had been laid through the mud leading up to the gaol and the doctor had endeavoured, as far as was possible, to park so that Violet could step straight on to them. She pulled her cape up and over her head as they saw the guard beckon them into the gaol. She put her foot out and then gasped with horror at the sight of a large round post standing in the open, away to her left. The doctor heard her exclamation, and seeing the object of her dismay dragged her back into the vehicle, leaning across her to pull the door shut again. The two of them sat there breathing heavily, Violet struck dumb with the sheer ghastliness of the situation, the doctor angry and upset at this betrayal of his calling. "God this is hideous," he hissed between clenched teeth. He looked across at Violet. "I'm so sorry. Are you all right?"

"Yes... yes I'm fine... I'm... I'll be all right... it's just..." She stopped and just raised her hands in a gesture of helplessness.

"I know. Let's get this over with. And both of us, let's try and be strong... for the sake of the poor blighter in there, if for no other reason. Eh?" She nodded her silent agreement. "Good girl," he said. "Let's go then."

She opened the cab door again, willing herself not to look in the direction of the stake. Gingerly she stepped down on to the planks, and clutching her cape with one hand and holding her bag with the other, she ran through the rain to the door. The doctor followed from the other side, tiptoeing through the mud, trying to keep as clean as possible. He made the plank and arrived at the door just behind her, where they both hesitated before making the final dive through the curtain of water and entering the gloomy interior. The door slammed shut as soon as they were in. Violet swung her wet cape off and it was taken by the guard.

For a moment they stood, adjusting to the light. The floor was bare earth. By the door there were two chairs and a small table, obviously for the use of the guards. In the centre there was a simple iron bed, such as would be found in the hospital, and on it underneath a thin blanket lay a man. As their eyes accustomed to the gloom, they could discern the still, drawn features, the skin like thin, stretched chamois leather over the jutting bones of his cheeks and brow. His eyes, dead, expressionless, such as one would see on a fishmonger's slab, stared straight up at the ceiling. For all the world he looked as if he were dead already, and were it not for the slight movement of his breathing, detectable under the blanket, they would have taken him as such. "What exactly is the problem?" the doctor whispered to the guard.

"The problem is he won't eat anyfink sir," said the guard in a normal speaking voice. "We've tried to force him but he just frows... begging yer pardon miss... he vomits it all up again."

"Is he drinking?"

"No sir, same game. We can't keep nuffing down 'im."

"What's his story?"

"Desertion in the face of the enemy sir! Just put darn 'is rifle and walked away. Never said nuffink since and 'asn't eaten nuffink for weeks now... nor drunk."

The doctor looked at Violet. A small muscle in the corner of his mouth twitched. He rolled his eyes skywards in a gesture of despair and turned back to the guard. "What are we expected to do for this man?"

"I don't know, I'm sure sir. We was just told you was comin'."

"Let's have a look at him then. Is he all right... he won't..."

"Oh no sir. He ain't got the energy. Not now anyways."

The doctor moved across to the bed, taking one of the chairs with him and sitting. He pulled the blankets down to the man's middle chest, took out the stethoscope from his bag and listened. There was no reaction, even when the unheated instrument touched the bare chest, with every rib visible through his strangely coloured, almost transparent skin.

"Here, help me roll him over please nurse," he said. Violet put down her bag and went over and helped to roll him over on his side. She stood there supporting him whilst the doctor listened. "All right, let him back down."

Violet gently eased him on to his back and then walked around to the other side of the bed.

"I s'pose they fought you could give 'im somefing to buck him up a bit like," said the guard as he sat himself down in the remaining chair by the door. "Waste of time though ain't it really?"

"I'll be the judge of that," said the doctor angrily.

"Quite sir! Quite. Didn't mean to... Yes sir!"

The doctor turned back round to Violet. He smiled slightly and jerked his head, indicating her to come closer, lowering his voice as she bent down to pick up his words. "This man is close to death."

She stared at him and then looked down at the man's face, the eyes still transfixed on the ceiling. A small tear started at the corner of his eye and then the other one. They ran down his cheeks silently, underneath his jaw line and on down his neck, where they disappeared into the mattress. The vacant expression didn't change one jot. Neither did the eyes blink at all, and in a moment the tears stopped, for all the world as if there were no more liquid left to sustain them.

"I think I'll give the fellow something to buck him up," said the doctor in a normal speaking voice. Violet started at its unexpected loudness. He reached down to his bag, picked it up and put it on his lap, hidden from the view of the guard behind him, who was, in any case, idly making patterns in the dirt of the floor with his rifle butt. He took out a small brown-ribbed bottle and filled a syringe from it. Violet looked hard across at him. He returned her stare directly and she nodded her understanding and silent assent.

"This will make you feel a lot better old chap." He lifted the man's shirt sleeve and quickly and efficiently gave him the injection.

The man half turned his head to look at him for the first time. He nodded imperceptibly and swallowed. The doctor put the syringe back into the bag and took out a clear bottle in an almost simultaneous movement. He dropped a little of the liquid into the man's mouth and then reached into his pocket, taking out a handkerchief, into which he poured half the contents. Putting it back into his pocket, he turned to the guard and held out the nearly empty bottle for him to see. "An elixir to pick him up... ease his throat and make it easier for him to swallow," he announced. "I'll leave it here for you in case he needs some more. Apart from that there's very little I can do."

He stood and packed his bag on the chair. Straightening up, he looked across at Violet's colourless face. "Ready nurse?" She forced herself to look away from the bed and up at the doctor. "Ready nurse?" he repeated. "There's little else we can do for this chap. We'd best be on our way."

"Yes. Yes of course. Sorry doctor, I'm coming." She reached down and touched the still face of the man on the bed. "Goodbye." There was no response and none was expected. The door opened and she looked up at the sound.

An officer stood in the doorway, his features and rank indistinguishable to them in the dark of the room looking out into the light. "Sorry, I wasn't here before doctor. I've only just been told of your arrival." He moved forward and shook the outstretched hand of the doctor. "Glad you could come. Bit worried about this chap here."

"Yes well, there's little I can do, but I've given him a little pick-me-up and I'm leaving this bottle for the guard. He may well sleep now for a while, but hopefully when he wakes up he'll feel better."

"Not for long though eh!" said the officer in a conspiratorial manner.

The doctor opened his mouth to speak. Violet, fearful of his reaction, coughed loudly, moving across to his side. She tugged at his arm. "We must get back to the hospital doctor." He looked at her, his face betraying the struggling emotions within, his eyes wide. For an eternity she wondered at his next move, but then he nodded to her in agreement and turned back to the officer. "Quite. Yes, there's nothing I can do here. I must get back to where we are needed. If you'll excuse me." He crossed to the guard standing to attention at the door and pressed the bottle into his hand. "Whenever he requires it. You understand?"

"Yes sir. Certainly sir."

"Well we must be off. Ready nurse?"

"Yes doctor." She moved to the door and the guard put down the bottle and held her cape out for her.

The officer strolled across the room to look idly down at the man lying on the bed as the doctor and Violet prepared to leave. "Damn me if the blighter don't look dead to me," he remarked.

Violet was halfway out of the door, preparing to dive through the water falling from the roof. She turned back to the doctor, her expression frightened and pleading. His face was an inscrutable mask apart from his eyes, which commanded her silence. He turned back to the bed. Violet stood just inside the doorway, watching the scene being played out in the gloom. The doctor knelt down and felt the man's pulse. He leaned over and put his ear to his chest and then stood with a loud sigh. "Poor bastard's heart has just given out, I'm afraid. He was near death when we got here and perhaps the stimulant was the last straw." He turned back to the man and closed his still staring eyes. "Sorry. I'll sign the report and send it on to you."

"Damn," said the officer.

"Quite," said the doctor. "Now I must be off." He joined Violet and the two of them ducked through and out of the door and ran along the duckboards to their vehicle.

For a while they sat there silently staring out through the windscreen at the still open door of the gaol. After what seemed an age, Violet broke the silence, still staring straight ahead. "Did you kill him?" she said quietly.

He didn't respond at first. Then just as quietly, "No. This war killed him."

There was another long silence. "I ask again. Did you kill him?"

"I... I gave him enough to... my intention was to alleviate his suffering rather than kill him but... but I didn't deliberately kill the poor blighter... he was to all intents and purposes dead already."

"I understand."

"You do?"

"Yes."

The journey back passed in complete silence. When they got back to the hospital, he pulled up outside and stopped. "Thank you for that nurse. I'm sorry you had to witness... there was no necessity for you to have come after all. Me neither for that matter. I'm afraid I was just told that the man had harmed himself and I didn't quite know what to expect."

She reached across and shook his hand. "Goodbye doctor."

"Goodbye nurse."

October 1917

"Why do you cry?"

Violet straightened up from tucking in the bedclothes, startled at the sound of the voice. "Oh you're awake. I'll fetch the doctors. They'll want to see you."

"Why do you cry. Is it for me? Do I die?"

"No! No it's...it's not you, it's me. I..."

"You have lost someone you love?"

"No... well yes, but not recently... it's just... no not now, lie still while I fetch the doctors to see you."

"So they can tell me all of the bad news?"

"So they can tell you what's wrong with you."

"Can't you tell me... Vi-o-let?"

His use of her name startled her and the way he pronounced it, splitting it up into its parts made it sound exotic. "You know my name?"

"Mais oui. You told me your name."

"When did I do that? You've been unconscious. You must have been awake before and heard someone talking to me... one of these chaps." She indicated the three other occupants of the curtained-off section of the ward.

He smiled and reached out his hand to her. She took it and held it, looking down at him. His face was unshaven, the prominent moustache sprouting from beneath his large nose, merging into the unwanted beard. His eyes were dark. So dark that unless one looked closely it was difficult to distinguish the pupils. Set deep in the dark hollows of his illness they still twinkled merrily. "Do you not remember telling me your name when I was lying outside in the rain?"

She looked again at him. "Why no... yes. You remembered from there. Surely not?"

"Surely yes. Your face... it looks more pretty this way up, I think."

She laughed. "I think monsieur that we are going to have to watch out for you. I will fetch the doctor now. You lie here quietly now whilst I'm gone."

"Am I able to move then?"

She paused and turned to him, the sadness on her face, embarrassed at his perception. "No... you cannot move yet... I'll fetch the doctor." He nodded. He understood. The news when it came would not be good."

He lay there thinking. How much time had he lost? How long had he been here, lying in this bed? A week? More? Strange to think that in a few short minutes he should be so lucid. He was aware that time had passed. He was aware too that he must have been on that ward for some days, even though looking around there was nothing that he had seen before. His eyes lighted on the chair beside the bed. His jacket, hung across the back, had been cleaned. No trousers, even though his worn boots were visible on the floor underneath. No trousers?

A doctor came down the ward, followed by Violet. "Ah monsieur. Comment allez vous?"

"Tres bien merci." He realised that the doctor had by now reached the limit of his knowledge of French. "I speak English if you would prefer?"

"Oh good." The doctor moved around to his side and picked up his wrist, checking the pulse, more for something to do than a genuine enquiry. Still looking down at his watch he continued. "I'm afraid old man that you've had a bit of a bad do."

"Pardon? A bit of a bad do? Qu'est que c'est. What is a bad do?"

"Sorry old man. What I mean to say is that you've had a nasty injury. You've been very ill you know and you're still not out of the woods." He finished with the pulse. Patently uncomfortable with his task and, in an effort to avoid having to look Armand straight in the eye, he pulled the bedclothes down a little and proceeded to listen to his chest. Armand observed the dressings around his middle to lower back for the first time.

"Out of the woods?"

"Sorry again old man. I mean that it will be some time before you are well again."

"Tell me please doctor. Have I lost my leg? I cannot move it."

"Your leg? Oh no, your legs are fine.. it's just..."

"Then where are my trousers?"

"Your trousers? Oh I see, you think that...yes, I suppose you would." He put down his stethoscope and at last addressed him directly. "You have sustained an injury to your back which has, I'm afraid, wrecked one of your kidneys. The right one actually. The other one's fine and you should be able to function quite well on that but you have been... indeed you still are fairly poorly."

"Fairly poorly?"

"Sorry. Doing it again old man, I mean you are not very well."

"I am paralysed?"

"No, not at all. Look, what's happened is that when the shrapnel went into your body it took with it parts of your clothing, mud and all manner of things and... well it's the infection caused by all that dirt that's the problem now."

"The soil of France will not kill me."

"Well the problem is old man that it might. It just might."

Armand looked up at him. "What is to be done?" He closed his eyes for a moment as an unexpected wave of pain and nausea washed over him. Violet moved forward and picked up his hand to feel his pulse. He interpreted this as simply a kind gesture and willed himself back into full control. "What shall we do?"

"Well, the nurses here will be changing your dressing at four-hourly intervals and keeping it irrigated to try to stop the spread of any infection. There's a drainage tube coming from your back to a bottle down here, and for the moment, apart from giving you painkillers when the pain is at its worst, it's really up to you."

"Up to me?"

"Well yes, really. It's your body that has got to fight off the infection with our help."

"And my legs and... the other... things. They are all right?"

"Absolutely fine old man." The doctor glanced across at Violet, embarrassed by this oblique reference in front of her, and then back at Armand. "No problems there at all old man," he whispered conspiratorially. "All your bodily functions are fine. Look, I'm sorry old man, I can't stay. I'll come back another time and talk to you, but for now you seem to be making a remarkable recovery. What you need to do is rest here under the care of the nurses whilst we decide what to do with you."

He replaced the bedclothes and patted Armand paternally on the shoulder. "Look after him nurse," he said cheerily.

"Yes sir, of course sir," said Violet, crossing from the foot of the bed to stand beside it.

The doctor turned just as he got to the door and came back. "Ah, there's a couple of other things I think I should mention old man. You took in quite a bit of shrapnel. We've... well we got most of it out but there are some bits which are a bit tricky."

"A bit tricky? I'm sorry, what is a bit tricky? Ca va dire quoi?"

"Difficult. Difficile. They're a bit far in and it would have been dangerous to remove them. Safer to leave them, don't you know."

"Oui. J'ais comprend."

"Good. We'll see you later old man." He left the room and Violet stood there silently beside the bed. Armand stared at the door then up at Violet. "Je suis fatigue... I am tired now."

"Of course you are. You sleep now. I'll sit here with you for a little while until you're asleep."

"My name is Armand."

"I know."

He closed his eyes and seemed to drift off to sleep. She sat there on the chair beside him, resting her arm on the bed. He could feel the weight of it against his body through the bedclothes. "How long have I been here?"

"A week."

"Thanks God for that. He kept calling me 'old man'. I thought maybe I had been here for some years." He chuckled to himself, his eyes still closed, and she giggled with him. There was silence for a while, and she thought he had dropped off to sleep. She rested her head down on to the bed and closed her own eyes with accumulated tiredness. He felt the new weight and warmth against him.

"Why were you crying?"

"Eh! What? Oh..." She raised her head off the bed. "Nothing. Nothing and everything. The war I suppose. Now go back to sleep."

"Oui mademoiselle." He closed his eyes and she sat there looking at him. Suddenly he spoke again without opening his eyes. "What is bodily functions?"

"Bodily functions means going to the toilet. Having control over those parts of... well you know."

"Ah bien."

She waited now until his even breathing indicated that he really was asleep and then stole from his side and went across to the bed opposite. He too was asleep, poor boy. She returned to the main ward, glancing back at the figure on the bed as she left. 'I like you Armand,' she thought. 'I hope you live.'

Whether he did or not hung in the balance for the remains of that summer. The sepsis that was always dreaded in wounds such as he had took hold with a vengeance. The lucidity that he had displayed when he first regained consciousness evaporated, and as the fever progressed he lapsed into nightmares and wild ramblings in his native French; way beyond her limited comprehension.

As the summer offensive continued into that wet autumn, with each side trying to gain the maximum advantage before the onset of winter, the hospital became extremely busy with horrendous casualties. The staff worked to the limit of their endurance, both physically and mentally, and it was with some relief that in the middle of all of this the new huts were made ready and at last they could sleep, whenever they had time, in more civilised conditions.

Through all of this Armand clung to life, drifting in and out of consciousness, at times hardly aware of where or who he was. The infection spread into his waterworks and the already alarming red of his urine gave way to an opaque greenish-yellow. For a time he hovered on the edge of life and Violet had more or less resigned herself to the fact that he would die. It was with some relief, therefore, that she noticed the first changes in his urine and a gradual return to clarity. Slowly the fever subsided and the angry swellings died down on most of his injuries, apart from those that still contained hidden metal. These never truly healed, and for the rest of his life a new abscess would sometimes erupt and weep for a while before slowly closing again.

With his gradual return to health his spirits returned, and it seemed that it was to Violet that he directed much of his attention and humour. Discouraged as it was, there was little that could be done to prevent friendships forming between the nurses and the long-stay patients, and although any overt favouritism was obviously not a good idea, and Violet did her best to hide any suggestion of it, their ease in each other's company began to be noticed. The relationship blossomed and grew into a friendship that gave her an entirely different perspective on her work, lightening its load and bringing with it a gaiety that she had neither felt nor shown for a long time.

"Are we going dancing tonight mademoiselle?"

"No, I don't think so kind sir. Nice of you to ask though. Now let's get on with this, can we?" Violet pulled down the bedclothes and folded them across the end of the bed and Armand, taking hold of the bed head, pulled himself into a sitting position and sat there expectantly.

"My, you two are cards," laughed Doris. "You're always larking about with each other."

"Larking? Larking? What is larking?"

"She means we're always laughing and playing the fool," said Violet.

"She thinks I am a fool. Pah, the woman is mad, no?"

"Quite mad," said Doris, "and I'll get madder still if you don't get that pyjama jacket off and use this water before it's cold."

"You are both so cruel to a poor hero of France."

"Poor hero... dirty one more like, if you don't get cleaned up."

"How can I wash in the presence of two beautiful maidens?"

"It never stopped you before. Anyway, there's nothing we haven't seen before, is there Violet?"

"Have you no shame?" mocked Armand.

"None at all," said Violet, opening his jacket and splashing the water on to his chest. She picked up the flannel and worked the soap into it. "Here Armand dear. You do it."

"Armand dear is it now?" said Doris. "Well ooh la la what do we 'ave 'ere." She grinned at them both and twirled around into a mock curtsey.

"Oh shut up Doris," said Violet laughing. "Come on now, we'd better get on." She turned back to Armand. "Now you get washed up and we'll be back in a few minutes to make your bed before the doctor comes to see you."

The two of them moved on, giggling. Armand watched them go. He sighed, looked heavenwards and then began the task of cleaning himself as far as he could without disturbing the heavy bandages that still swathed his lower torso.

Presently, the two girls returned. Doris took away the water whilst Violet busied herself with making his bed around him. "Got to look smart for the doctor."

"Why all the fuss today?"

"Because they're going to take off your bandages and have a look at how you're doing. Who knows, you may be able to go home soon."

"Home? You mean to another hospital, do you not?"

"I don't know. We'll have to wait and see what the doctor says first."

Armand looked pensive and turned away from Violet in order that she didn't guess at the trouble in his face. It did no good. It was late November now, and although they had only known each other for a few months, in that time she had come to understand him. That strange telepathy that can exist between two people existed between them. They spoke together in a mixture of her uneasy French and his fluent but non-colloquial English, but still there was rarely any misunderstanding.

"I would miss you."

"I would miss you too, but your family will be pleased to see you."

"I have no family. Well I have my sister who lives in the next village, but my parents are dead since six years now."

"Oh I'm sorry. What do you do? I mean what were you before the war?"

"I was... I still am a farmer. I grow asparagus."

"Asparagus, how interesting. We had asparagus once at home. I remember it was delicious but I had never thought of it being grown on farms. I thought it was something that some people grew in their gardens for a treat."

"In England maybe, but in France no. Here we are serious about our asparagus and all our food... and our love." He looked at her intently and she blushed.

"Armand, you are a wicked man."

"I am a useless invalid."

"You are not an invalid. You have not walked yet, but that is the next step. Now don't be silly. And get ready for the doctor."

......

Violet sat on the bridge, looking down into the waters below. She picked up the letter and began to read it.

My dear Violet,

I am glad to hear that you are well and that you have made some friends over there. Your mother and I think of you all the time and we are so proud of what you have been doing. Your mother has not been very well of late, but any visitor who happens by is regaled with her boasts about you.

Life has changed greatly here at home as the effects of this war come to everyone, including me. You will hardly recognise some things when you get home. Violet there is so much I want to say to you. I miss you terribly but I realise that my little girl is now a woman and you have your own life to lead. Christmas was a little sad without you though. Let us all hope that the New Year will bring peace at last.

I cannot say how sorry I am about the enclosed letters. Please find it in your heart to forgive me. I withheld them during your absence, I admit, but I would have given them to you before now. I thought of doing so when you were last home, but in the end decided not to, preferring not to risk upsetting you just before your departure. Forgive me my love. I have never opened them of course and I do hope that their contents will not overly upset you. It must have been a terrible shock to discover your mutual acquaintance, but in the end I hope it brings you comfort. I only really regret the separation we have had due to this war and take comfort in our reconciliation.

Take care my dearest Violet and write to me soon. All my love.

Daddy.

P.S. Write a little note to your mother next time. She would be so pleased.

England seemed so far away now. Her life had changed so much. Life itself had changed so much. Oh not in the superficial way her father had referred to. No, far more fundamentally. Before, when she was a child, her world had revolved around her home and her family and the certainties they provided. Then had come Frank. With him all horizons had been opened to her and her life had changed so dramatically as a result of... as a result of the baby. But in spite of that huge upheaval, the total difference in perspective that all that had caused, those changes had been additions to her life as it was. Now, what this war had done was to completely change the direction of all of her thoughts. It was as if... as if she had gone through the first part of her life from one starting point and then reached a point where instead of branching off in a new direction it was almost... it was almost as if she'd gone back to the very beginning and started again.

The past was still there. Oh yes, it always would be, and the responsibilities from that past remained and would need to be faced. But they were not now to be faced by the same girl who had inherited or created them. No certainty existed now in life. Nearly all of the participants in this war had come to realise that the values they had held previously were gone. The war itself, rather than any particular cause, had become the feature of their lives, and questions of morality, of right and wrong, fell away in its all-consuming progress. She had witnessed men dead and dying. Bodies torn apart. Minds destroyed within those broken bodies. How many of these men who went home would ever really be the same again? Even those who had remained untouched by injury went home taking with them the memories of those lost comrades and the fears they had shared. How many of her fellow nurses, like her, would return to lives of spinsterhood with all these fine men gone?

An eddy formed in the cold waters and traced its pattern downstream. She watched it. Frank had taught her in that short time... oh so long ago now, to appreciate the beauty of nature, and whenever she saw such a sight she thought of him. 'He will always be with me,' she thought. But why, oh why, was it harder and harder to picture his face?

Why was it fading from her memory? The more she tried to conjure his likeness in her mind the more it became confused with the faces of all the men she had seen and known in this war. Frank's face would be there in her thoughts for a moment, and then it would change and become Armand's or Pike's or the man in the condemned cell, or any combination of them all.

She sighed and took out the two letters that her father had enclosed. She looked at them both. Unopened, they lay there in her lap, waiting to reveal the words of a long dead lover and a near forgotten friend. She opened the one from Jesse first.

My dear Violet,

I know that by now you will have received the terrible news of Frank's death. I am finding it very difficult to come to terms with his loss and I know that you will be equally distraught. I wish that I could be with you so that we could share our grief.

Friends and neighbours have all called round to give their condolences and many of them who met you last August have asked to be remembered to you.

Words cannot express my sorrow. He was not my son yet he was as much a son to me as any woman could have. My life has lost much of its meaning, but what I have to say to you my dearest Violet is that your life must go on as Frank would have wished. Never forget my Frank, but do not waste the rest of your life on his memory. He would have wanted you to find another, and I guess that he may have told you so himself.

If you ever think of me and my little cottage then write to me or come and visit me. You are forever welcome.

All love,

Jesse

Through the tears that fell freely from her eyes, the signature of love swam before her. She lifted the paper to her nose and smelt the faint scent of Jesse; the comfort she had known so long ago in that first embrace on her doorstep. 'If I have wronged anyone in my life, I have wronged you,' Jesse, she thought. 'Whatever has transpired, you deserved more than this. That I should cut you out of my life is bad enough, but that I should leave you ignorant of Frank's child is despicable. Oh yes, I could say that I didn't get your letter, that I have been away. All valid excuses, but not enough. Not enough. How can I ever undo that wrong,' she thought.

She looked down at the other letter. A letter from a man who was dead. A letter written by a living man. He lived within this letter. He would say things in this letter which, though delayed beyond his death, came from his living being. She took a deep breath and opened it.

My darling Violet,

I am writing this letter to you as we prepare to advance tomorrow. Keith, my friend, is also writing to his sweetheart and we will be able to send the letters before we set off. The guns have been blazing over our heads all day now in preparation for our advance, and it may be difficult to write to you for a little while.

We have all been mightily fed up with our billets here and will be glad for a change of scenery and the end of this war. Many of our friends have been wounded, but Keith and I seem to have lucky charms. I do hope that when we get back we can all be together and that you can meet him. We were friends when I was a boy and it has been wonderful to make his acquaintance again, even if the surroundings are not very nice.

How are you? I miss you so much and I think often about our times together. We have known each other for such a short time and yet I feel as if you have always been a part of my life. Life is such a funny thing. If I hadn't come to Finchley to work for your father we would never have met. Now I cannot think of life without you.

But my darling Violet, I have to repeat what I told you in the field on the day I left. If I do not make it home from here, make your life with another. Make it for me.

I wish now that I had never got involved in this war. What is it for? It is not for me, or you? That is for certain. Sometimes I feel such a fool for letting myself be drawn into it.

I'm not a coward, but all of this seems so pointless now I have seen war at first hand.

Enough of this. I love you Violet and I long for the day when we are together again. I will write again as soon as I am able.

All my love forever,

Frank.

PS. Don't forget to write to Jesse. She's my only family apart from what you will be one day.

Once more the tears fell freely from her eyes, dropping on to the papers she held in her hand. This time the tears were not for her and her shame, but for Frank. His letter had hinted at his fear that his life could be ended, but was all about its continuation. How cruel that all of his dreams and hopes should come to an end in this terrible war. His death was no more terrible nor any less pointless than all of the other deaths she had witnessed, but now, having been in the forefront of the war, the true reality of it was known to her. No glorious battlefield valour could disguise the disgusting filth of young men pouring their life's blood into the mud.

In those final moments did he realise that he was dying? Was he afraid? Had he thought of her?

She looked back towards the hospital sprawled out in the fields behind her, put the letters in her skirt pocket and made her way back to the wards, where huts were now replacing the worn-out marquees. She paused before entering and adjusted herself, wiping her eyes with the back of her hand, hoping against hope that they did not betray her tears. She walked down the ward, quiet now in the late afternoon, towards Armand's bed. It was empty and she quickened her pace, wondering what could have befallen him, passing a figure in a wheelchair.

"Violet."

"Armand?"

"I am out of bed, as you will see."

"Oh Armand I didn't realise. I'm sorry."

"Sorry? For what? I am in this wheelchair from your efforts. You have made me well again."

"Don't be silly," she said, crossing to kneel in front of him, smiling up at him. "You did it yourself."

"I did it with your help my dear Violet. You and some other good friends... but you first of all." He reached forward to cup her face in his hand. "You have been crying."

"No. No I haven't. What makes you say that?"

"The tear stains on your face. This gives me a clue." He bent forward and brushed a kiss on her forehead. "Ma pauvre cherie."

"I had some letters."

"From your family? Do you have bad news?"

"They were sent by my father but they weren't from him." She squatted on the floor in front of him, her face pointing out to the window. "They were letters from... a man I loved and from his... well aunt, but she was more like his mother."

Armand was silent for a while as he rested his hand on her shoulder and studied her face in profile. When he spoke it was softly. "You loved this man. Do you not still love him?"

"He is dead. Killed in the early part of the war."

"And you have received the letter today?"

"My father... my father kept the letter from me."

"He kept the letter from you? But why?"

She didn't reply at first. Tears sprang into her eyes and she let them roll down her cheeks. She made as if to rise, but he leant forward and pressed her back down. "Tell me Violet. Let me help."

Her face dropped. "You will hate me."

"I could never hate you."

Who had said that to her before? Frank? Had Frank said that or her father? Which one was it, or was it both? She turned and faced him now, looking directly into his concerned eyes as she pushed aside the tears with her fingers.

"There was a baby... I had a baby by Frank and we were never married..." Her voice grew stronger now. She had crossed the bridge and the rest was easier. She could tell him all of it now. He would despise her anyway. There was nothing left to lose.

"He never knew. He never knew of his son and I gave the baby away... and denied him. There!" She rose now, unimpeded by him. "You know it all." She turned to face him, her head held high and defiant. "Now you can see what kind of woman I really am."

He looked at her long and hard as she stood there breathing heavily. She had rarely looked more beautiful to him as she did then, standing there proud within her perceived humiliation. "I know what kind of woman you are," he whispered softly.

She tossed her head. "Yes, the kind of woman who goes with a man outside marriage. The kind of woman who denies her own child. The kind of..."

"...the kind of woman who devotes her life to the care of others and me. A beautiful, gentle and brave woman."

She stared down at him. "You should hate me."

"I could never hate you. I could only love you as you must learn to love yourself."

"But..."

"...but nothing. You loved a man, a good man I think, and the war ruined all for you, as it has ruined all for many others."

She relaxed now and squatted once more in front of him, her back leaning against his legs and his hands resting on her shoulders, heedless of what would befall her if she was so discovered. She felt she wanted to talk of Frank for almost the first time since his death and found herself telling Armand all about their friendship and how it had turned to love. She told him of her father's disapproval and her flight to Frank in the dying days of peace. He sat there listening quietly. Occasionally he would gently squeeze her shoulder as if to reassure her, but he made no comment as she recounted her story until she got to the part about receiving the letter from Keith telling her of his death. "So you had the letter to tell you he was dead before you knew about the baby?"

"Yes. I read the letter and fainted... I fell down the stairs and they called the doctor. It was him who told my father that I was... that I was going to have a baby."

"You didn't know?"

"No. I had no idea."

"But if you and Frank were lovers..."

She turned up to him. "Oh no. We were not... we didn't..." She swallowed hard and drew herself up a little. "We made love just one time, the day before he went to war. It... it was bad of me... of us but... I tried to be ashamed all this time. I am ashamed but I cannot be sorry... do you understand?"

"I understand completely. Do you not imagine that all over the world in those days lovers and friends were telling each other goodbye? All of those poor people thinking that maybe they would never see each other again."

"I didn't want to believe that he wouldn't come back."

"And did you not think that perhaps what you did was for you a way to keep him, a way to make sure he stayed with you always?"

She looked at him now with wonder in her eyes. "I thought I was a bad woman. I thought I must be punished."

"Punished? Pah, for what? For being a lover. Ma cherie Violet, the whole world would have to be punished."

"I gave away the child. That is my real guilt. My father didn't like Frank because he was not a... because he was not rich or of our class." She faced him. "He was not an officer. He was a soldier, a sergeant."

"It does not matter. He was a man," Armand objected.

"But that's it, don't you see? When he died it began to matter. I felt that I had betrayed so much. My parents, myself... even Frank. I was the instigator... I chased him. I made him love me. I even... I even made him make love to me. It was all my fault."

"So you punished yourself?"

"Of course I punished myself, I was angry with him. I punished the child by banishing him from my life but still I loved him... I loved them both. I still do."

"Then you must make it right."

"How? How do I make amends... make it right?"

"You must take back the child of Frank and give him your love."

She sighed. "My father and I had a very strained relationship for some time, but before I came to France we... well we became friends again and agreed that when this war was over, we would change things."

"He has realised that you... especially you... cannot bury forever what has happened and that when you are strong you must face the truth."

Violet studied this man. That he had become her friend there was no doubt, but there was much more to him than she had realised. "You are very wise Armand."

"I am a simple paysan... a farmer."

"If you are simple then I am German."

"Your English is very good mein fraulein." They both laughed and then sat quietly, each in their own thoughts, content in each other's company.

December 1917

Christmas came around yet again with the war still raging... that same war that was supposed to be all over by the first Christmas. By now the thought was wearing a bit thin, but despite all that, a hope still persisted that this might be the last one of the war. Nobody could quite put their finger on it, but there was a feeling in the air that something was afoot. A feeling that despite the knowledge that the spring would bring fresh offensives on both sides, the steam was going out of the thing and an end had to come soon.

The Red Cross was receiving thousands of parcels and presents for the boys and great boxes of goodies, including not a little booze, were piled up ready for distribution. An air of expectancy and fun pertained, and the nurses reacted to it by decorating the wards wherever possible with paper chains and brightly coloured flags. Patients who were well enough joined in the festivities and made sure that their less well colleagues did not feel left out. The sight of a man lying back in his bed swathed in bandages, his face the colour of uncooked pastry or worse, yet with his bed decorated with brightly coloured branches of holly and ivy intertwined with tinsel, became quite a common one.

The only problem being that after Christmas when it all came down again, the contrast with the stark, cold and primitive conditions was enormous.

A concert was arranged for Christmas Eve, and all who could go began to get quite excited at the prospect.

Armand was by now able to get about in his wheelchair, and as he had been able to dispense with the tubes draining him it had been arranged that he would be able to go. That is, so long as he was attended the whole time by a nurse who could watch out for him getting too tired and return him to the ward if necessary. Of course Violet had immediately volunteered for the assignment, and the two of them made plans for the outing as if it were a private function to which the two of them alone were going.

Armand made sure that come the night he was all spruced up as far as was possible and that he had on his cleaned uniform jacket over his pyjamas. His hair was neatly cut and parted and his moustache trimmed to absolute perfection. He regarded himself in the mirror and then put it down and sighed. He half smiled to himself and let out a secret little chuckle. He was like a boy going out on his first date with a girl. He wondered at this delicious feeling of anticipation and excitement that he felt. Violet. Violet. What a lovely name for a lovely escort. He leant back trying to analyse his feelings for her. He hardly knew her. 'Nonsense. I know practically all there is to know about her. More, much more than anybody else in the hospital.' A wonderful girl... no a wonderful woman. Not French, but what did that matter? With all that had befallen him, nationalities no longer mattered.

Dare he hope that this young woman he had met by chance thought of him in the same vein? He was one of thousands of patients surrounded by these beautiful young nurses from all over Europe and America. All of the men must entertain the fantasy that they would persuade one of these angels to fall in love with them, but how real was that possibility?

She seemed to be content, even happy in his company, and it certainly did seem to him that she spent far more time with him than was strictly necessary. That this was the case had not gone unnoticed by his fellow inmates, who often referred to her arrival with comments such as, "Here comes Armand's private nurse."

He wanted to pursue the point with her but there was never the right opportunity, and besides, they were never really alone. Their conversations had usually to be conducted quietly so as not to be overheard by the occupants of the adjoining beds, and any touch that they made was, of necessity, furtive and hurried. The only exception had been the time when she had come back into the ward crying after receiving the letters from her dead lover, and he savoured the memory of that afternoon and the intimacies they had shared.

The evening of the concert came, and with it the ward was filled with orderlies, nurses and walking well patients ready to assist in the carrying or wheeling of those able to go. Those who were not either lay there quietly or waved as cheerily as they could to their departing friends, and all who did go made damned certain that they left the others with as much good cheer as they could.

An orderly came up to Armand and assisted him off the bed and into the wheelchair, tucking a rug around his legs. "Right ho matey, let's go," he said cheerfully as he prepared to wheel him out.

Armand held up his hand. "I wait for someone who is taking me."

The orderly shrugged his shoulders. "Never mind mate, I'll see to this fellow over here. Anyone special is it?"

"I think so."

He saw Violet approaching and smiled his greeting. The orderly noticed and nudged Armand. "I think so too matey," he said, laughing as he went across to the other patient. "I think so too."

"Good evening Armand," said Violet as she reached him. She bent down and brushed his cheek with a kiss.

"In my country we kiss four times, two on each cheek, when we meet."

"In my country we kiss once on the cheek and on the lips for... well for special friends or... lovers."

"Am I not special?" He looked up at her, his face a picture of innocent hurt.

She looked around quickly to see that nobody was watching and then bent down and briefly kissed his lips. "You are special," she said lightly as she moved around to the rear of the chair so that he would not see her blush. He smiled to himself and relaxed back into the chair as she wheeled it out into the chill night air.

"I wish we could be arm in arm instead of you being behind me like this," he said, turning back to look at her. She laughed and reached forward to touch the side of his neck. He reached up and held her hand briefly before she took it back to control the chair.

The concert passed off wonderfully, with jokes and singing turns raising the roof as they all joined in. Men who had lost so much threw themselves wholeheartedly into the business of enjoying themselves, forgetting for an evening the travails that lay ahead. Violet couldn't help thinking that for all the noise, the Germans themselves would be able to join in, and indeed throughout the hospital area even those confined to their beds were able to participate to some extent.

Armand and Violet left at the end, joined on the walkways by a large band of merrymakers still singing the songs they had just seen performed. They proceeded quietly amidst the throng, making their way back to their wards, but as they got to the main driveway and prepared to cross to his ward, he reached back and took hold of her hand on the bars. "I do not want to go back in at this time. Do you know somewhere quiet?"

She nodded silently and then steered the chair towards the main gate, out on to the lane and off to the right to the bridge, upon which she had sat and read the letters. Behind them they could still hear the sound of singing and laughter. She stopped by the bridge parapet and parked his wheelchair up against it. "Are you cold?"

"A little," he replied, "but not too bad."

"We won't stay long... otherwise you'll be ill again."

"Just a little time. It is good to be alone for a some time."

She laughed lightly. "I know what you mean. Always people and movement. That's why I come out here sometimes." She looked back at the hospital. "All those people... far from home... all of us."

He reached up and took her hand. "Thank you for taking me tonight."

"Thank you for accompanying me sir. She bent forward and kissed him softly on the lips, her hands resting on his shoulders.

"I wish I could stand."

"You probably can with my help."

"Help me then."

She transferred her grip to beneath his armpits, conscious now of her closeness to him. "When I say go, push up with your legs. Right... go." He pushed down with his legs. Muscles weakened by months of lack of use, nerve endings disconnected by the wound above his pelvic bones, shook as he tried to force himself upwards. She bent back slightly as she pulled upwards and he ended up on his feet, leaning heavily upon her, clasped in her embrace.

He placed his arms around her waist and the two of them stood there holding each other closely, breathing heavily in the cold air. "Happy Christmas Violet," he said softly.

"Happy Christmas Armand." She kissed him then and he responded. Not a passionate kiss. A tender kiss of yearning and comfort. His legs started to shake with their unaccustomed burden and she lowered him gently back into his chair.

He laughed grimly. "Your kiss makes me weak in the legs."

She laughed with him and turned the wheelchair back towards the ward. "Best get you back before you come to some real harm."

"Not with you my Violet."

February/March 1918

As he was by now well on the mend, Armand was moved to another ward, and although that meant that Violet was no longer strictly responsible for his nursing, she nevertheless spent much of her free time with him. In consequence, he was ribbed quite frequently about his private nurse. However, she made certain that their friendship did not interfere with her duties and, although a passing reference was made by the sister, nobody really took offence.

To the sister, Violet remarked that she was friends with Armand and that he had helped her greatly with overcoming a personal problem. Luckily she accepted that, but warned of antagonising other officers who could be jealous of Armand seemingly receiving attention they would cherish. Violet overcame that by becoming popular with many of the patients on her visits to the ward. She also took Doris and/or Rosie with her at times, and the little band of cheerful visitors became greatly appreciated and much looked forward to.

A terrible time on the front with the use of mustard gas meant that the hospital again became quite crowded, this time with men who had lost their sight or were horribly scarred and blistered by this evil. The disorientation of the sufferers and the damage caused to their lungs made pitiful wretches of all of them and Violet, despite what she had experienced, was physically and mentally exhausted at the end of each shift. At times she would have just liked to go straight to bed and sleep, but she felt the need to be with somebody she could talk to and she invariably found herself with Armand. The secrets they now shared of her life served to further bind them together, and she drew increasing comfort from his company.

It was therefore quite a shock when one afternoon she went to visit him as usual. "I have been told I am being transferred to a convalescent hospital," he said as she approached.

She stood in front of his bed, hand to her mouth, shock registering on her face. He had been in the hospital a long time; far longer than usual, due in no small part to an administrative mix-up between the French and British authorities. She had known in her heart that this moment must come, but she had always managed to put it to the back of her mind. "Oh Armand I... I shall miss you. I have come to..."

"I shall miss you too my Violet."

"When will you be going?"

"I do not know exactly. Very soon I think. They have to make the arrangements."

Her mind raced. Other patients had gone from her. Some had gone back home, some to other hospitals and some back into the war. Why was she so upset? Surely he was just another patient amongst the thousands that she had seen pass through? She was tired of this war, with its churning up of relationships. All that was constant in her life had been upset and replaced by this throughput of acquaintances. Smith, Pike, Thomas... Frank himself if it came to that... and now Armand. Why did it all have to be like this? Why couldn't she be allowed to keep something... someone from the wreckage surrounding her? She looked at him sitting there on the bed. Another friend about to pass out of her life forever. She burst into tears and ran from the ward, out and along to her hut, where she threw herself on her bed, face down, sobbing her heart out. She had had enough. Hadn't she been punished enough? What more did she have to suffer?

Rosie found her when she came off duty about half an hour later. She heard the crying as she entered the hut and thought at first that an animal had been hurt and trapped in the room. "What the 'ell's the matter luv? 'ave you 'urt yerself?" She sat down on the bed, leaning over Violet and holding her heaving shoulders.

"He's going," sobbed Violet, her head buried in her pillow, muffling the sound.

"Who's goin' luv?"

"Armand." She turned over, her tear-stained face looking up now at Rosie. "Armand's going to a convalescent hospital and I... he's my friend and I shall never see him again."

"Nonsense luv. If'n you wanner see 'im again an' he wants to see you then you'll see each uver. Now listen to Rosie, dry yer eyes, tidy yerself up an' go an' see 'im... I expect he's just as unhappy as you. All right?" She stroked Violet's face with the back of her hand, smoothing away the tears. "Fer a big girl you don't 'alf cry a lot."

Violet smiled up at her, opened her arms and Rosie sank down into them. They lay there cuddling for some time before Rosie got up. "Go on now. Go an' see 'im."

Violet walked back to Armand's ward, busier now that the evening changeover had occurred and teas were being brought round. She nodded at the nurse working on the ward, who looked over at her and then indicated Armand. "He wants to see you."

"I know. I won't be long." She walked up to Armand's bed. He was back in it now, lying there looking the other way so that he didn't see her approach. "Hallo Armand."

He turned over and smiled at her, holding his hand out from underneath the bedclothes. She looked over her shoulder at the nurses at the other end of the ward. They weren't looking their way. She moved closer to the bed, taking hold of his hand and standing close to hide their familiarity. "I'm sorry. I didn't mean to make a scene. It's just... it's just that I will miss you so."

"I am not leaving the world my Violet... not yet at least."

"I know but... well the war seems to take everything away from me."

"The war has brought us together. No?"

"I suppose it has but now... well now it's going to... oh I don't know. I don't know anything anymore. I'm so tired."

"Listen to me. Everybody knows the spring comes, and I have been here much longer than would be normal. They have to clear the hospital of people like me. You will become very busy again soon."

"I've had enough Armand."

"We have all had enough my love, but I think the end is nearly here, and when it is I would like to... how do you say... court you... that is if you'd let me."

She laughed now and was aware that she had done so out loud. She turned around and looked at the nurse, who smiled back at her and waved. "And what pray sir have you been doing for months now to me and all of the other girls?"

"What other girls? For me there has only been one girl and it is you... bien ecoute. Listen I will be taken tomorrow..."

"Tomorrow!" She gasped and held her hand to her mouth.

"Shh." He put his finger to his lips. "I am going to Le Chateau de Fontere. It is about forty kilometres from here. You can write to me there and you can even come and see me on your days off. No?"

"I will."

"Bien c'est ca, and I will be walking and standing properly when you come."

"What time do you go?"

"I have been told to be ready for 11 o'clock."

"I will be here."

......

In the weeks following Armand's departure, Violet felt completely lost and alone. The hospital received orders to clear the beds and they were all kept busy getting patients who could be moved up and away. Leave was cancelled so there was no chance of visiting Armand, and they had to make do with letters. A strange expectancy hung over everything as the winter broke and spring approached.

In March, the news came that the Russians had signed their own armistice with the Germans and it seemed only a matter of time before the full might of the German army would be focused on the western front. The question only remained as to where the blow would fall, and generals and administrators alike spent long hours deliberating over countless maps.

The planning for the coming battles included arrangements for field hospitals closer to the front, and then casualty clearing stations set up even closer to the lines, staffed with doctors and nurses with experience. Violet was allocated to a casualty clearing station about ten miles behind the lines, and in early March she once more found herself under canvas, only this time it was in a smaller tent which she shared with another nurse that she hadn't met before, called Marjorie.

The station basically consisted of two large marquees with huge red crosses painted on the roofs, around which clustered the smaller staff tents. The marquees were set out so as to directly adjoin each other at the ends, and the plan was that the wounded would be brought in at one end, where nurses and orderlies would remove their field dressings and clean them up sufficiently for them to pass through the screening curtains to the theatre section. Here, emergency operations and amputations would be carried out and they would be stabilised before being carried on stretchers through to the second marquee to await transportation by a fleet of ambulance vans standing ready to carry them back to either the field hospitals or directly to the hospital trains waiting to transport them on to the base hospitals.

All was made ready, but even in what was euphemistically known as a quiet spell the general level of warfare meant that the station was blooded soon after its incorporation. Evenings and night times were the busiest, for when darkness fell the medics could risk going out into no man's land to fetch the wounded, who had often lain there all day. Not long after dark therefore, the nurses would hear the approach of the ambulances and rush to their stations.

The system they had all set up seemed to work quite smoothly and they waited for the coming battle, confident that they would be able to handle things.

Their only worry was that in the event of an advance by the allies they would find themselves too far in the rear.

On the 21st of March, the German offensive began with a huge and sustained bombardment of high explosive and gas shells. At the station they could see the night sky lit up with flashes, and it was only a very short time before the first casualties were rushed in. That night, Violet had been allocated to the second marquee and was responsible for looking after the wounded as they came through, until they could be loaded into the ambulances by the teams of orderlies. As the stretchers were brought through, they were laid out in long lines, side by side, with just enough room for Violet and the other nurses to get between each one. There in the dark, lit only by the swinging lamps suspended from a rope slung from the two main spars and the flashes from the night sky beyond, Violet moved from patient to patient ministering to them and making sure that their dressings were secure. She carried with her a pan of water and a tin cup, from which she let each conscious man drink a little. They clamoured for more to slake their raging thirsts, but she had to limit their intake as she was never completely sure of the nature of the injuries and whether to give into their demands would prove harmful.

The ambulance drivers came up to the collection point at the end of the marquee and the orderlies picked up the wounded marked out for them and loaded them as gently as they could. As the men were carried out, Violet or another of the nurses would normally try to accompany the worst of the wounded in order to make sure that no fresh bleeding occurred.

"It seems as if the guns are getting louder," remarked Violet to one of the drivers.

"They're not getting louder nurse, they're getting nearer."

A thrill of fear ran through Violet. "What do you mean getting nearer?"

"I mean nurse, that the Boche have broken through our lines."

"Will they get here?"

"I don't know, but if they do I'd scarper quick if I was you and get on one of the ambulances. A Boche with his blood up would do 'orrible things to a young lady like yourself, beggin' your pardon."

Violet said nothing but cast an apprehensive eye towards the north and the sound of battle. The ambulance drove off, fully laden, and she wished that she too was leaving this place, which now felt insecure. She thought for a moment and then, before going back into the marquee, dived off into the blackness in the direction of her tent. She entered the tent and scooped up the small bag she had brought with her containing her precious things she could not - would not - lose, such as the small bundle of letters.

She had been gone from the main tent no more than a couple of minutes, but already she felt guilty at her absence. Hastily, she laced up the flap and ran back, stumbling over guy ropes which either lurked in the darkness or flashed bright in the flares and flashes of battle. As she neared the main tents, she became aware of a terrific howling noise. The very air seemed to thicken and vibrate. She threw herself flat on the ground, clutching her bag to her breast as a massive explosion reduced the first marquee to a crater and a straddling shell cut the remaining one in half, leaving just one tent pole supporting the remains of the canvas as it draped the edge of the steaming hole. Her ears seemed to reflect the sound around the inside of her head, bouncing it through her brain and reducing her to the level of a frightened animal scrabbling in the dirt, trying to bury herself from the horror as she lay panting in terror. Desperately she tried to gather her disorientated thoughts as she dared to raise her head to look across at the devastation laid out before her.

Her ears still screamed their protest at the noise and pressure, but through it she could just make out the shouts and screams of dying and wounded men and the calls of the few left to help. Panic was beginning to grip her as she stood up, clutching the bag to her breast with both hands. She wanted to run, but where to? An ambulance pulled up in a squeal of brakes to where the pick-up point had been and the driver got out. "Bloody 'ell," he shouted to nobody in particular. "Bloody 'ell." He looked up as Violet stumbled towards him. "'ere you alright nurse?"

She couldn't speak. Her eyes wide and bulging with terror, she ran now to where he stood and clutched his arm. In front of them lay the mangled remains of the wounded who had been lying there waiting for evacuation, and just beyond them, a little way from the edge of the crater, others lay on the ground stunned. Over where the first tent had been there was nothing except a huge hole, its edge decorated with the gruesome fruit of its destruction. Something white flapped on the edge of the crater and she gagged as she realised it was a nurse's apron.

"I should have been there," she whispered.

"I shouldn't if I was you miss, otherwise you'd be dead. Talkin' of which, this 'aint a healthy place to be. I'm off."

"Off? What about these poor people?"

He hesitated, looking back at her and then across at the men, then he shrugged his shoulders and muttered resignedly, "Bloody heroes everywhere." He gestured at the men on the floor. "I can take those six there if they're still alive and you, but you'd better get a move on. I reckon the Boche 'aint far away."

Violet ran towards the waiting ambulance and threw her bag in. She breathed deeply, drawing herself up to her full height and preparing herself... willing herself to remain in control. She ran over to the few bodies that seemed to be still intact and joined the driver. The first one they got to looked all right. He reached up as they got to him and tried to raise himself off the stretcher. "Hush, lie still," said Violet, pushing him gently back down. "Let's get you out of here." Summoning up all her reserves, she lifted her end of the heavy stretcher and the two of them struggled across to the ambulance and slid him in before returning to look for more. All in all they found only three more who were still alive, and by the time they got the last one into the ambulance Violet was very nearly exhausted.

The sound of rifle and machine gun fire seemed very close now and the driver could hear the shouts of the soldiers. Violet, a worrying trickle of blood visible in each ear, could by now hear very little. "I think we'd better be off my love," the driver shouted, gesticulating towards the van to make her understand. He ran around to his door but Violet got in the back with the wounded and did her best to comfort them and hold them still as the van bounced across the ground and on to the road leading roughly south to safety. As they reached it they were forced to stop by the sheer volume of men and machinery trying to come up the other way, rushing into battle in an attempt to hold the line. A detachment of splendidly mounted French cavalry galloped up the road towards them, splitting in two to pass them, their lances held erect and proud as they rode to battle. A body of tall men in mustard-coloured uniforms appeared in the headlights of the ambulance, crossing the road in front of them, their black faces briefly turning to them. White eyes and teeth glowed in the headlights... sharp steel glinted cruelly... and then they were gone, melting into the night off to their right.

The driver waited until they were clear, wondering which way to go. The road he had intended to take seemed to be where most of the sound of battle was coming from. Earlier in the day, however, he'd noticed a crossroads at the top of the rise straight ahead, and he figured that if they turned left there they might be able to get away from it all and then turn back a few miles on. He drove forwards searching for the junction, and when he found it, after a moment's hesitation, took it and was pleased when the road seemed to veer to the right, bringing them, by his calculations, on to a southerly heading.

For a while all seemed to be quiet and they felt that perhaps they had escaped the fighting. Until, quite suddenly, they turned a corner and practically ran into a whole column of marching American infantrymen, who, faced with the sudden appearance of the ambulance, dived for the ditches on either side and took up firing positions. One even popped off a shot in their general direction before the driver yelled out of the window, "British ambulance! British ambulance!"

"Hold yer fire men," came a shout in the dark, and a Sergeant rose from the ditch and sauntered over to them, followed by his inquisitive men. "Hi there fella. What the Sam hell are you doin' out here?"

"Lost Sarge. I've got wounded in the back and a shook-up nurse from the clearing station what got blown up. We need to get to the railhead or the base hospital and... well I reckon we're lost."

"You sure as hell are fella, and them Germans are hard on your heels. The road ahead is out and they've broken through our flank so you won't get around that way. If'n I was you I'd head on down here and take a left at the next junction and keep going down there just as far as you've got juice for."

"Thanks mate," said the driver, slipping the van into gear and starting to move forward.

"Keep the lights off 'till you git to the crossroads and turn the corner or you could attract fire!"

"Right o mate and ta," the driver called from the window as he drove off into the night, slowly now hanging his head out, watching for the road edge on one side. In the dark they went past the side turning and he had to reverse back. They turned left and, when he thought that they'd gone far enough, he thankfully put the lights back on. "Cor thank the Lord for that. I thought me eyes was goin' to pop out," he called back to Violet, who by now couldn't really hear his voice over the sound of the engine.

Could we stop just a moment and let me have a look at the chap over on the other side," she called.

He pulled over to the side of the road, got out and walked around the back to lower the tailgate. Violet jumped out and then climbed straight back in on the other side, making her way forward on hands and knees to the head of the wounded man. She felt for a pulse in his neck, but in the starlight she could see his eyes staring blindly into space and realised that the poor soul had died.

"I'm afraid he's gone," she whispered.

"Well we can't do anythin' for 'im 'ere. 'spect we'll have to just leave 'im be 'till we gets where we're goin'."

Violet crawled backwards out of the van and dropped on to the ground, and for a moment the two of them stood there looking towards the north and the sound and lights of fighting. "We'd best be off luv," said the driver, and then realising that she hadn't heard him repeated himself louder, adding, "Yer ears is bleedin' a bit miss. Probably the pressure of the blast."

He pointed to her ear and she put a hand up to it. It felt wet and she held her hand in front of her face to examine it as best she could in the darkness, rolling the stickiness in her finger tips. "I'm bleeding from my ears."

"That's what I was sayin' luv," he shouted. "Let's go... an' it might be best if you rode up front and helped me keep a look out." He pointed to the front seat, to his eyes and the road. She nodded her understanding and got into the passenger seat, sitting sideways in order to be able to keep an eye open for the men in the back.

All that night they drove onwards through the French countryside, and at last, as dawn approached, they entered a village. It seemed to be inhabited, although there was very little sign of life at that time of the morning. The driver pulled up in front of the fountain and the two of them got out and went around to the back of the van and dropped the tailgate.

Over by the fountain someone had left a tin cup, and she filled this and brought it round to the injured, climbing in beside them and holding their heads up to allow them to drink. "Thank you nurse," whispered the first one, unaware that by now Violet could no longer hear him. She saw his lips move and guessed at what he'd said.

"There we are. Soon have you in a proper hospital."

A door opened a crack in one of the small houses and an old woman peeped out, holding the door. Two small children clutched her skirts, peering fearfully across at the ambulance.

"Hey!" called the driver, scrambling to his feet and making his way across to them as the old woman brushed the children back and slammed the door shut. He stopped and turned around to Violet, watching from the back of the van. "They're frightened of us. See if you can speak to them luv."

Violet eased herself from the van and went across to the door. She knocked and waited. There was no response, so she knocked again and this time called out. "Hallo. We're English. English!"

Reassured, more by the female voice than by what she had said, the door opened a crack and the old woman peered out. Violet stood there, aware that she was being examined closely and aware too that she must have looked a terrible sight. Her hair had started to escape from the confines of her headgear and hung in loose tendrils. Streaks of dried blood ran down her cheeks from her ears and her uniform and apron were smeared with mud and the blood of the injured men in her care. "Mon dieu," muttered the woman, crossing herself.

"Hospital?" cried Violet. She stopped to think. "Ou est the hospital?" She pointed to the smeared Red Cross on her chest.

"La-bas. Tout droit. Cinq kilometres," the woman shouted, pointing to the road running off to the left of the square and holding up five fingers. She slammed the door shut and Violet turned and walked back to the ambulance.

"She says that it's down that road about five kilometres. What's that? About three miles?"

"'bout that. Let's go then. I could do with some breakfast!" the driver shouted to make himself heard.

"I don't think it can be our hospital. I don't recognise any of the scenery around here."

"Who cares so long as it's safe an' they serve a good breakfast." He put the tailgate back up, got back behind the wheel and waited while

Violet came round and climbed in beside him. Crashing the gears a little, he reversed away from the fountain and then moved off in the direction indicated by Violet.

Sure enough, after a few miles they could see a large chateau in front of them rising majestically above the surrounding trees, and joy of joys, the Red Cross flag flew from one of its turrets. "Well thank God for that," Violet whispered to herself. She leaned into the back. "Nearly there lads. Warm beds and breakfast for you." A chorus of approval came back at her, the sound jumbled up and indistinct but recognisable nevertheless.

The van turned in through the gates and Violet and the driver craned their necks to observe the huge chateau unfolding in front of them, its towering grey stone walls and blue-black roof planes mirrored in the limpid stillness of its surrounding moat. Small windows punctuated its fastness and brightly coloured curtains gently waved in the early morning breeze. They pulled up beneath a huge oak tree, beside two large camions that were parked there, the red crosses clearly visible on their sides. Nurses milled around the vehicles helping men in. Others walked yet more patients across the bridge leading to the huge hewn oak double doors, which, even at this hour, were standing open. "Looks to me as if they're fixing to scarper," said the driver. "We'd better see what's going on."

"Excuse me," Violet asked as she dismounted the vehicle and walked across. "What is happening?" The nurses stopped what they were doing and turned to her, chattering excitedly and fast in French. In normal times it would have been at the limit of Violet's understanding, but now, in their excitement and with her hearing impaired by the blast, it just became an incomprehensible jumble of sound.

The driver tried. "Where are you all going? Who's in charge here?"

"I am in charge," said a loud voice, and both Violet and the driver turned to it. A sister approached. "You must not to stay here. Les Alle... the Germans are coming. All who can must go."

Violet crossed to her, her hand held out in greeting. "Sister, we are sorry to bother you but we are lost. Our station was bombed last night..." Her words trailed off as the sister put her hand up to her ears.

"You have blood here."

"I'm afraid I cannot hear properly... the sounds seem to come and go."

"Were you near with the bomb?" the sister asked in a louder tone.

Violet looked down at the floor, the tiredness and strain of the past hours now beginning to tell on her. "They were all killed. All of the nurses and doctors... I fell down but..."

"Your ear could be broken. You have to see a doctor when you get back."

"The problem is that we don't know the way back," the driver explained.

"Where do you try to go?" The sister took her arm and started to lead her back towards the bridge.

"Camiers Base Hospital," said the driver.

"Pah, you will not be able to go direct to there I think. The Germans are in the middle of here and there."

Violet heard these words and gasped. "What?! Have we lost the war after all this?" She put her head in her hands, tears springing to her eyes.

"Non. Not lost. But there is a big problem." She took hold of Violet's arm. "Come."

Violet pulled her arm away. "Sister we have wounded men in the ambulance. They must have some attention."

The sister put her hand to her mouth "Oh mon dieu. La-bas?" She pointed to the ambulance.

Violet nodded and the three of them went back over to the ambulance. "This one here is dead," Violet whispered to the sister, who nodded and then turned her attention to the remaining three, examining them briefly before summoning a couple of passing orderlies and ordering them to assist the driver in unloading them into the chateau. Then she once again took Violet by the arm and guided her across the bridge.

"What are you going to do?" said Violet as they entered the huge entrance hall.

"We are taking the one who are able, south to Paris. But some of us will stay here with all the one who cannot go."

Violet turned to her, her eyes wide. "But... but you will be captured."

"Perhaps, but we cannot leave them."

Violet nodded. "No I can see. But surely... no you are right..." She gasped as a familiar figure walked slowly towards her, leaning on the arm of an orderly. "Armand!"

He looked up at the sound of her voice and raised his arm to shield his eyes, trying to make out the face framed in the light from the doors. Violet he thought... Violet here? He shook off the hand of the orderly and walked slowly across to her. "Violet? Is that you Violet?"

"Armand it's me!" she cried, and to the astonishment of the sister she broke free and ran across the hall, stopping just in front of Armand, fearful of knocking him down, marvelling at the fact that he was walking now unaided. He was taller than she had imagined, even though he still stooped slightly and leant heavily on a stout stick. "You are walking?"

He raised his free hand expressively. "As you see. Slowly yes, but walking."

She waited no longer, and taking the last step hugged him gently, burying her face in his chest. "Armand. Armand."

He stroked the back of her head and then cupped her chin in his hand, turning her face up to his as he bent slightly to kiss her on the lips. Her eyes closed as she responded to its sweetness.

Across the hall the astonished sister coughed politely. Armand released Violet, who turned her head to look back, smiling shyly at the sister. "We are friends."

The sister snorted and then, to Violet's relief, smiled back at her.

"More than friends I think."

Violet lowered her eyes before looking back up into Armand's. A soft smile played on his lips. "More than friends I think." He cupped her chin in his hand again and stared down into her eyes, an enquiring look on his face.

She nodded imperceptibly, reading his lips and whispered back. "Much more than friends." He bent and kissed her again. At length, conscious of their audience, he released her and she shot a guilty glance at their onlooker. "Oh I'm sorry sister."

"Do not be sorry. L'amour ou la guerre. Love or war. Which is best... love I think. Yes?"

Violet put her arms around Armand. "Oh I'm so glad to see you Armand. Oh we shall...?" She stopped. His face had a stricken look and she pulled back a little. "What's the matter? Why are you looking at me like that?"

"Because..." said the sister, taking Violet's arm and speaking close to her ear, "...because he is leaving here with the others as soon as they are in the..." She seemed to search for the word.

Violet turned back to Armand. "No! Surely not. Oh no you mustn't."

He held her then, looking down into her face. "I have to go Violet. I am still in the army and I have to go where they tell me. I think I go now to Paris and then to Orleans to be close to my home." He stroked her face with the back of his hand. "Come with me."

The tears welled in her eyes. "Oh Armand. Armand. You know I want to but... but I can't just run off now. I have to go back until October unless the war is over by then." She buried her face in his chest and sobbed.

The sister tapped her on the shoulder. "Mademoiselle, he must go now. They will be waiting for him and we have to see to you and your men."

"You have men with you?" Armand asked.

"Yes, that's why I'm here. The casualty clearing station was destroyed and we just escaped. There are three wounded and one dead in the ambulance. Oh here they are now." She turned and the orderlies paused as she placed her hand on the first man's chest and looked enquiringly at him. "How are you?"

"Fine thank you nurse." He craned his neck to the others standing there in the hall. "Thanks to this nurse we're here you know. She made the driver wait to take us." He coughed and the orderlies hefted their load and carried on through the doors at the far end of the hall as the next two stretchers came in.

"We will attend them," said the sister, moving to follow them. "You say your goodbye and then come to me and I will look to your ears before you go." She left the room.

At her words, Armand turned quizzically to Violet and put his hand up to her cheek, noticing the blood for the first time. "You are hurt?"

She touched her ears. "Oh it's nothing apart from the fact that I can't hear very well just now. Sister will fix me up I'm sure."

The orderly who had originally accompanied Armand into the hall, and who had quietly stood aside throughout this reunion, now took Armand's arm to gently guide him to the door. Violet took the stick from Armand and crooked her arm in his. There was a small desk by the door and, as they reached it, Armand bent down to a small pad that was lying on it. He reached inside his jacket and took out a pen, took a sheaf off the pad and wrote carefully on both sides. Then he folded the paper and handed it to Violet. "The hospital in Orleans where I think I will be going, and on the other side my home address." He looked meaningfully at her and bent close to her ear so that he could be sure she heard. "Come and see me when you are free. I will be there for you and for..." he winked, "...for anyone else you love."

"Oh Armand." She flung her arms around him and kissed him again, full on the lips. He nearly overbalanced, and would have fallen had it not been for the orderly who moved forward to steady him.

"Careful my love, do not break me."

"Oh I'm sorry Armand, it's just... it's just that..." She looked across at the orderly. He stared back unabashed and slightly amused. She averted her eyes from his gaze and back to Armand. "It's just that the time will go slowly 'till we meet again."

"We will meet again, and I will be stronger then. Come, I must go now."

They walked slowly out and over the bridge, Violet and Armand now arm in arm, with the orderly following behind carrying the stick. The walk to the camion, though short, tested Armand's strength to the limit, but it was a walk that both of them wanted to string out as much as they could. Nevertheless, by the time they got there he was quite exhausted and had to stop and gather himself before attempting the climb up. He turned to Violet. "You will go back to Camiers?"

"Yes I will. Write to me there and I will write to you in Orleans."

"Take care my Violet."

"And you too. She hugged him, unwilling now to release him again. "Don't go home until you are well enough."

"I will be at home when you come I think." A moment of doubt seemed to cross his mind. "You will come?"

She smiled. "Of course I'll come, but I may have to go home first. I'll write to you Armand. Don't worry." They kissed then for the final time, accompanied by whistles and calls from the other men in the camion. When he released her she backed away, both hands clenched to her lips as the orderly helped him climb up into the back before raising the heavy tailgate and calling around the side to the driver. As the lorry started to move off, the orderly grabbed hold of the hand ring, put his foot in the step and swung himself aboard.

Violet stood waving until they were out of sight, the smile frozen on her face, the tears coursing down. She stood still in the open for some time, alone and dejected. He had gone from her life again, just as Frank had... no not like Frank, for Armand had gone to await her coming. Was he then as Frank had been to her? Could anyone ever be? They were different these two men, and her feelings for each of them were different. With Frank it had been the love of a girl for a boy, as they both had been. Impatient, urgent love that they both had shared. With Armand it was the love of two people who had known pain and loss... a mature love, growing from friendship. She smiled to herself, wiping the tears from her eyes. Did she love Armand now? Was that a betrayal of Frank? No it was not. Frank had told her to make a life for herself, and she knew now that she always would have. She was not the kind of woman who would ever want to be alone and unloved, especially now that the guilt and pain were taken from her. Did Armand love her? Surely yes. He had not proposed or anything that formal, but he had set out the path which they both could take to that end. 'When this is over and things are sorted at home I will meet Armand again and we will be free to explore our feelings for each other,' she determined. Her eyes lit on the ambulance and brought her thoughts back to her predicament. Carefully folding the piece of paper he had given her, she placed it in her apron pocket and turned back to the chateau.

The place seemed empty. She called but there was no response, so she went through the doors at the far end of the hall. They opened out on to an area of formal gardens with beautifully kept gravel pathways leading through the flower beds of an open-ended horseshoe formed by the chateau. There were French doors open on the wing at the left-hand side and she walked towards these. As she got there she could discern that the room was laid out as a ward and two nurses were quietly attending about thirty bed-ridden patients who were obviously too ill to be taken in the transports. The atmosphere was calm and ordered and no one would have guessed that they were awaiting a conquering enemy. Violet called out to one of the nurses without entering the ward. "Do you know where the sister is?" She nodded and came over to the doors to beckon across to a matching set on the opposite wing. "Thank you," said Violet.

She walked across, knocked and went in. Inside the sister and another nurse were attending to the three surviving British wounded. The driver sat on a chair in the corner, his head in his hands, exhausted. "How are they?" Violet asked as she entered.

"This one and this one are not so bad. They have legs hurt and we have..." She searched for the word. "...bandaged. Yes bandaged."

Violet could only just hear her. "Your English is very good."

"Thank you. I have been in England before the war since one year."

"It is very good." She lowered her voice and leant closer. "How is the other one?"

The sister looked rueful. She didn't reply immediately but leant across, talking directly into Violet's ear. "I think he have to stay here."

Violet nodded. "What did you do with the boy that was dead?"

"The morgue. Now, I look at your ears." She indicated a chair and Violet sat as instructed whilst she fetched a scope. She came back across to her and examined each ear. "I think the pressure may have done this. You are very close with the bomb?"

"Yes. Very. It's a miracle I wasn't hurt badly."

"I clean them and put some drops in." Violet relaxed in the chair, her eyes closed as the sister cleaned out the dried blood as best she could and plugged both ears with a soft dressing. "Bon," she said as she finished. "You must see the docteur when you get home." She turned to the driver still sitting in his chair. "Some food, then you must go. Yes?"

"Yes please sister," he said, enthusiastically rising to his feet.

"And you too nurse? You must be hungry."

"I could eat a horse," said Violet, pleased that she could now hear a little better.

The sister burst out laughing. She tugged the other nurse's arm. "Elle faute manger un cheval." She turned her smiling face back to Violet. "That is funny, no? English people do not eat horses."

"This one would," piped up a voice from the stretcher. They all laughed.

"I will arrange for some food to be brought to you my friend," said the sister. "Come. You two come with me." She led them from the room, out into the gardens and along to the dining rooms.

"Will you stay until the Germans come?"

"I will stay if they come or no."

"You are very brave," said Violet as she sat where indicated. The driver sat self- consciously at the far end of the same table.

"Brave? What is brave? All who live now are brave." She bustled away and came back with a dish of ham and some long loaves of bread. "Eat. I will take some to the two men who will go with you, and we will take the other one to the ward. If you want some cafe help yourself, or you can have wine or water." She went back into the kitchen and came out shortly with another tray of food and a large jug. The driver got to his feet to let her out of the door. Violet watched her leave and then resumed the meal. She had not realised until then just how hungry she was.

"Do you want anything to drink nurse?" said the driver before he sat down.

"Oh yes please. Water for me."

He poured her a glass and filled his own with wine before re-joining her at the table. When the two of them had eaten their fill, he stood, wiping his mouth with the back of his hand and belching. "Beggin' yer pardon miss, but I think we should be going if we're to get back before night."

Violet agreed with him and the two of them made their way back to the room where the two men lay on their stretchers. "Have you both had something to eat and drink?" said Violet as they entered. "Only we're off now. Back to the hospital."

The sister entered the room and the driver turned to her and asked, "Is there any way of driving around to here? Only they're a bit heavy and presumably all the blokes is gone now."

"We will have to manage with the four of us, I'm afraid," she replied. "It is not possible to cross the moat."

It took the four of them about half an hour to carry the two men to the ambulance, but eventually, after the driver had scrounged some petrol, they were all ready to depart. Violet turned to the sister. "Thank you for everything sister and good luck. Bon chance."

"Good luck for you. Go to the south through two villages, then a droite... right to the west and you must come home before it is night."

"Thanks a lot sister," said the driver, and his words were repeated by the men in the back. Violet gave her one last hug before she climbed into the passenger seat.

"I hope you meet your man in Orleans."

Violet smiled at her. "I will," she said quietly, as they started off. "I will."

They drove off down the driveway and turned right at the gate, heading south where the road ran straight between its avenues of trees. With no other traffic they soon began to make good time, and within the hour they entered a village and slowed down, searching for signs of life in the squat earth-coloured houses. Every window and every door was firmly shuttered. The place seemed utterly deserted.

"Where have they all gone?" Violet mused.

"The question is why have they all gone?" said the driver in a worried tone.

"I don't know," Violet replied, "but let's get going. I don't like this."

"Me neither." He dropped a gear and accelerated through until they gained the open road again, where he slowed and stopped. Violet looked at him, enquiring. "I need... well I need a pee miss. Must 'ave bin the wine."

"Me too" came a voice from the back.

"And me nurse, but how are we going to do it?"

The driver got out and went over to a tree, where he stood nonchalantly urinating against the trunk. 'I need one myself,' thought Violet, but I'm not doing it out here in full view. She went around to the back of the ambulance. "I'm afraid all we can offer you two chaps is a mug and I'll have to throw it out for you."

She leant in and helped first one and then the other urinate in the mug, flinging it each time into the dust by the roadside. As she threw away the second filling she became aware of a series of vibrations in the air. "Do you hear that?" she called to the driver as he walked back to the van, buttoning his flies.

He cocked his ear in the direction she was indicating. "Gunfire and shelling." He glanced up at the sun. "I reckon that must be due west of here."

"What does that mean?" said Violet in a worried tone. "Are we cut off?"

He shook his head. "Nar can't be. Must be some sort of training or maybe our chaps shelling them."

"Sounds more like incoming than outgoing mate," one of the men called out from the back of the van.

Violet turned. She hadn't really wanted to bother the injured men with their fears. "Don't worry. He's probably right."

"All the same miss, I reckon we should get going soon and get away from here," said the driver, starting up the engine again and getting into the driving seat.

"Agreed," said Violet, deciding that she would after all postpone her own call of nature.

About half an hour later they entered another village, situated on a crossroads. At the junction there was a fountain and Violet asked the driver to stop in order that they could replenish their water bottles and wash out the only mug they had. "I also need to... well you know."

"Well I wouldn't be too fussy nurse. The place looks deserted anyway."

She looked around. It did indeed look deserted. Doors were closed and all the shutters on the windows of the few houses were fastened. "Honk your horn. See if there's anyone about," she asked.

The driver gave two short blasts on his horn, followed by a longer one. There was nothing. Nothing except... except that Violet thought she saw a flicker of movement from one of the windows. But then it was gone. If there was anyone around they were not intending to show their faces. She looked around. 'Where on earth can I go to the toilet,' she thought, and then seeing that the barn door adjoining the house was open, nipped in there. She squatted down, grateful at last for the chance. A rustle in the straw startled her and she stood up quickly. A small calf lowed at her. She laughed at her fears but adjusted herself as fast as she could and ran from the barn back to the ambulance.

"There must be people here," she called as she approached the van. "There's a calf in the barn. But they obviously don't want to show themselves."

"Well that's their lookout," said the driver. "I vote we get out of here and get going. It'll be dark soon."

"Seconded," said a voice from the back. "I'm getting hungry again."

They took the right turn out of the village, glad now to be heading west again towards home. They approached a double bend on a slight rise in the land, took the first of the bends and crested the hill. Ahead was a gate leading up to an open barn. As they went into the bend, Violet was conscious of a sharp cracking sound and the glass in front seemed to craze and fall back into her lap. She looked across at the driver. He still held the wheel with his hands but his face had a puzzled, frozen expression. A trickle of blood ran down his forehead, and as his head dropped forward a gaping chasm was revealed in the back, from which blood and brains now slipped easily.

Her scream was cut short as the van, its wheel held rigid by the dead driver, failed to take the bend and instead careered into the narrow gateway, hitting it on the driver's side, snagging the tarpaulin from the stanchions and tearing it away. The vehicle swerved into the hedge and rolled over completely, throwing Violet first into the well underneath the driver's lifeless legs and then up and back into the roof as it came to rest upside down. The tearing, wrenching noise of metal scraping on hard earth was replaced by a silence, broken only by the whirring noise of the bearings as the rear wheels continued to turn.

Violet had finished up upside down, her head bent forward on her chest as her body pressed down. Her legs above resting, one against the steering wheel and one through the broken windscreen. Blood from a shallow cut sustained in her right calf ran slowly up her leg and she shifted her weight to gingerly extract it, taking care not to cut herself again. Once free, she collapsed in a foetal heap on what would have been the roof of the cab, snuggled up now to the limp form of the driver pressing almost indecently into her. She wriggled free through the open window and lay for a few moments face down in the dirt.

A moaning sound came from the rear of the van and she crawled around to investigate. One of the soldiers was dragging himself from the wreckage on his elbows, his useless legs trailing behind him. She pulled at him and carried on pulling until he was clear of the vehicle, then she went back for the other chap. There was little she could do for him. His body lay on the ground in the centre of the upturned van but his head was invisible, trapped between the ground and the inefficient guillotine of the side panels. She didn't have to feel for his pulse to know that he was dead. Poor boy, all that he had gone through and now this.

Shouts could now be heard and it was quite obvious that the snipers who had caused this mayhem were even now making their way across the field towards them. Nothing could be seen and thankfully Violet and the soldier were hidden from the approaching enemy. She grabbed hold of his arms and dragged him backwards, face up towards the barn and in. He opened his mouth to speak but she silenced him. "Quiet, we have to hide. They're coming."

"You go nurse," he whispered, but she shook her head and carried on pulling, backing into the straw. She dropped him and proceeded to fling aside large armfuls of straw until she had created a cavity, into which she quickly dragged him before covering him over. She stood back for a moment and examined the spot. Then, satisfied that he was invisible, she dived into the straw herself, pulling it back around her as she burrowed inwards until she judged that she too was invisible, trying as hard as she could to still her heavy breathing.

She could clearly hear the approaching troops now as they marched through the gate, their heavy boots scraping and thudding on the hard earth. She heard their guttural voices as they examined the upturned vehicle and prodded the bodies within it, laughing as the driver fell backwards through the window.

A different voice, speaking the same language but with more authority, started up and Violet heard the men run into the barn. They talked to each other as they methodically moved along the edge of the straw, stabbing inwards and upwards with their bayonets, throwing them forward almost as a lance and withdrawing them on the shoulder strap. Violet put her hand in her mouth to stifle her breathing, which sounded so loud, even in her damaged ears, that she was certain that she would be discovered. The razor-sharp bayonet sliced through the flesh of her thigh, cutting deeply, but thankfully withdrawing without the resistance that would have given her presence away, and she bit down on her hand trying not to scream, praying that the blood would not be noticed.

The soldiers carried on talking to each other as they worked towards the middle of the heap. The one working her side continued to move towards the centre and she realised that he could not have seen anything untoward and that the straw must have cleaned off any evidence. She concentrated as never before on keeping still and lying quietly, despite the searing pain in her leg.

There was a shout as the wounded man, unnerved by the approaching danger, threw aside the covering of straw, calling out, "All right mates I'm here."

The soldiers barked an order to him to come out and Violet could only imagine him trying to indicate that he could not comply.

Eventually they must have understood, because she heard the sound of him being dragged from the barn, his protests and his cries of pain as they threw him forward in a crumpled heap in front of their commander. She heard his pleading. She heard the shot as it rang out, its echo reverberating into the barn, searing into her terrified mind. She buried her face deeper and stifled her sobs as she heard them march away.

She lay there until nightfall, alternatively wide awake with terror or dozing fitfully. Only when she was sure it was fully dark did she stir herself to crawl painfully from the straw. She stood holding on to the stone pillar to support herself, but the pain in her leg made walking impossible and an alarming stiffness had set in. Leaning up against the end wall was an old pitchfork. She hopped across to it thinking to use it as a walking stick. She tried to walk holding on to it but the prongs went into the ground and their curve made it impossible. She reversed the tool and slipped her arm through the prongs so that she could use it as a crutch, and that seemed to work much better. The thin metal cut into her armpit and she searched around for something to bind the crook. Nothing.

She hobbled outside, aware now that her dress and apron made her highly visible, even in the dark. In front of the barn lay the crumpled body of the poor boy whose death she had heard. Further forward she could just make out the dark outline of the upturned ambulance, from which tumbled the lifeless body of the driver. She crossed to the nearest body and painfully lowered herself to the ground beside him. Needing his dark jacket, she reached out and gently undid the buttons, trying all the while not to look into his face. She pulled the jacket open and tried to feed the arm through. It wouldn't go so she forced the straightened arm into a crooked position, tugging and pulling the sleeve and eventually freeing it. For a while she lay beside the body, panting from the effort and the horror of the situation, trying desperately to keep her head. Then, by levering herself against the body, she managed to turn it over. Part of the freed side of the jacket went over with the body and became trapped as it flopped face down. She leant right across and on the body, feeling with her hands to release the jacket. The air in his lungs expelled by her weight let out a low moaning noise and she recoiled in horror, scrabbling backwards away from him, trying not to scream out loud.

'He's dead,' she reasoned. 'Is he really dead? Am I mistaken? Of course he's dead. Pull yourself together Violet or you'll never get out of this alive.' She crawled back across to him and prodded him with the pitchfork handle. Stiff. No movement. Dead. Grabbing hold of the jacket she tugged it free and pulled it from his other arm. She made her way back towards the barn post, and with her back to it, holding the pitchfork in one hand and the jacket in the other, pushed with all her might with her one good leg, shuffling her way up the post until she was upright.

Leaning the pitchfork carefully against the post she pulled on the jacket, jerking herself forward to bring it back down behind her. She reached for the pitchfork and cried out as she realised that she'd knocked it over. It lay at her feet, yet for all the world it might as well have been the other side of the yard. She shuffled her way back down the post into a sitting position, crying with frustration and grabbed it. Then as soon as she had recovered her breath she repeated the process, back up this time, holding firmly to her crutch. 'Where am I to go,' she thought. No point in carrying on westwards. It's quite obvious that the Germans have broken through at this point and outflanked the front. She thought carefully. They had gone on towards the village. Maybe they had gone on through. They were obviously moving fast and may not have stopped there. If she could get to the village she could see from the outskirts if the Germans were there. More likely they had taken what they could and moved on.

In any event she couldn't just stay here. There was no water. Yes there was. In the van. And there would be a first aid kit in there as well. Where would it be? Under the driver's seat? She hobbled across to the vehicle and tried to get around to the other side. She stopped halfway, disappointed that the hedge prevented her. Crying with frustration, she banged her free hand on the tyre and then stopped. Silly girl, she thought. It's upside down. The driver's seat's on the other side anyway.

Leaning the crutch against the van, she lowered herself painfully down. Then, lying on her stomach, she crawled into the upturned body of the van and felt around for the water bottles she knew must be in there. Her hand touched the body of the dead soldier in the darkness, and for an instant she had to fight the impulse to get out, but she persevered and eventually was able to crawl from the wreckage with the treasured bottles. One felt full and the other seemed to be half full only. She reached up and put them into the mudguard, where she could recover them later.

The pain in her leg was getting worse now and she pulled up her skirts and felt for the wound. The bayonet had sliced through the outer side of her thigh, leaving a cut about four inches long but deep. So deep that she shuddered as she felt along it, trying to judge its extent. Blood still oozed from it, though now it had thankfully started to congeal. Too much movement, she thought, would open it up. She must bind it before long. She shuffled backwards towards the cab and pulled and tugged at the driver until he was clear. She reached up and under the upturned seat and felt for the first aid kit. Thank God it was there.

The box was heavy but she made sure that she didn't drop it. Enough time had been wasted. She needed to get going and get to some form of safety. She felt for the dressings and selected a long wide one, which she proceeded to wind around her leg, wincing as the material came into direct contact with her exposed flesh. 'Must bind it tightly,' she thought. 'No point in it coming undone on the way, even if it's only a temporary binding.'

When it was done, she pulled her skirts down and raised herself

painfully upright, edging along the van until she reached the rear
wheel. She retrieved the bottle and continued on around to where
she had propped up the pitchfork.

The journey back to the village, a distance of about a mile and a
half, was perhaps the longest and most painful she had ever made.
Several times she had to stop and rest as waves of nausea threatened
to overcome her. The pitchfork now seemed to dig into her armpit
with increasing ferocity, to the point where it was difficult to
determine which hurt the most, her leg or her arm. Once she thought
she heard the sound of an approaching vehicle and panicked at
the thought of being caught out in the open. Getting off the road at
that point was impossible and she just had to stand in the darkness
hoping. Was she behind the lines? Had the patrol just been a probing
force, or was the line broken completely and would she find herself
trapped irretrievably in enemy territory? Eventually, after what
seemed an eternity and as no vehicle came, she breathed more
freely and continued her painful progress.

She approached the village and moved away from the centre of the
road, hiding in the shadows, looking in, listening hard for any sign
of life or occupation. All was quiet. No lights could be seen and there
were no vehicles parked in the street. To all intents and purposes the
place looked deserted. She moved closer, keeping to the edge of the
buildings, trying all the while to be as quiet as she could. The barn
door she had been in before was open, as indeed it had been then.
She could see the deeper blackness even in the dark, feel and smell
the warmth emanating from its straw-filled interior. She hobbled in
and tripped up on something soft, throwing her hands forward to
save herself as she fell. The pitchfork clattered to the ground beside
her with a noise she was sure would have woken the dead, and for
some time she lay there expecting the sound of marching feet and
guttural voices.

None came and eventually she began to take stock of where she
was. She lay now against something soft. Well not soft, but certainly

not hard either. What is it? She felt forward and touched the object. Furry. It was... it was the calf. Dead now, it lay there, and as she moved its opaque eyes reflected the dim starlight. Poor thing. Why? She felt along its flank and pulled her hand back quickly as she realised why. The hind quarters had been hacked off roughly at each hip joint and presumably carried off to be cooked over some camp fire, leaving the balance of the carcass there to rot. She shuddered and painfully raised herself to first a kneeling and finally a standing position, clutching all the while to her pitchfork, aware now that she might need it as a weapon as well as a crutch.

Sheaves of straw and hay were stacked up neatly in ledges and she dragged herself up on to the first one and lay back thankfully, pulling the jacket tight. Her ears throbbed painfully and the wound in her leg was beginning to feel as if it was on fire. Blood seeped through the bandaging and she dabbed it with her skirt, too tired to do much else.

She lay thinking about all that had gone on over the last few days. Armand. Was he all right? Surely he must be. He had left quite a while before she had and he had gone due south rather than turning west. He must be all right. Please God make him all right. 'Don't take another man from me,' she thought as sleep came at last, and she lay there oblivious of the rustlings of a thousand tiny creatures going about their lives around her.

......

Daylight flooded through the curtains in her room, the sun carving out visible beams of light, which illuminated her bed. She raised her head a little and looked out through the window. Funny, she couldn't remember it ever being low enough to see out from whilst in bed. Never mind. Oh there's young Frank and mother playing with the dog.

She stirred and reached for the sheets to throw back. She looked around for her slippers. They weren't there. Where on earth could they be? "Have you got my slippers Frank?" she called out through the window.

The two figures stood up quickly and stared in her direction. They had a knife in their hands. What were Frank and mother doing with a knife and the dog? She tried to raise herself off the bed and looked down startled as her hand pushed against not the mattress but hard sharp straw. What was straw doing in her bed?

The small boy hid behind the woman's skirts and she put her hand down and back, holding him protectively behind her.

"Mother," called Violet. "Is that you?"

The old woman put down the knife and, ordering the small boy to stay put, approached Violet. She said nothing that Violet could hear but stood there for some time, examining her from about ten feet away. She looked around the rest of the barn trying to gauge if they were alone, and satisfied that was the case came forward to stand just below Violet.

Violet stared at her. It's not mother, she thought. What was this strange old woman doing in her bedroom? She looked around, seeing now for the first time the piles of straw, the oak beams reaching up and over from the sunlight into the dark recesses. She felt the hardness of the straw upon which she lay and, as she attempted to turn over, she cried out as a searing pain shot through her leg.

A hand touched her shoulder and she looked up into the concerned face of the old woman. Her lips moved but Violet couldn't make out any of the words, which seemed to come at her as if from under water. She put her hand to her ear and felt the dressing, stiff now and forming a plug. The pain in her leg seemed to rise to a crescendo and her head dropped back on to the straw.

The small boy climbed up on to the level that Violet lay on, sitting cross-legged about a yard away, his grubby face cupped in his hands. Dark eyes stared at her inquisitively. The old woman's lips moved again and the boy nodded but remained seated.

The woman turned and made as if to leave. Violet called out to her, stretching her arm towards her. The woman turned and held out both hands with the palms out, motioning her to remain. Then she hurried from the barn.

A few minutes later the old woman came back accompanied by a worried-looking younger woman. They stood in front of Violet for some time arguing, before the old woman obviously insisted on being obeyed and the two of them climbed up on the straw ledge. The boy now stood up, and taking hold of the pitchfork hurled it up into the main body of the straw. Then he bent down and retrieved the water bottles before jumping down to wait expectantly.

The two women took hold of Violet under the arms and pulled her over to the edge of the straw ledge, holding on to her as her legs swung down to the ground. The younger one jumped down and, when she had Violet safely supported, the other one joined her. Pain and dizziness swirled within and around Violet as they inched forward out of the barn and into the sunlight. They passed the mutilated calf and the old woman pointed to the knife they'd been using to retrieve some of the carcass lying beside it and grunted something at the boy, who picked it up.

Between them, the two women carried her down the street to the corner and round to the first door. Seeing the fountain, Violet vaguely remembered that she had stopped here before. She had thought then that perhaps there was someone still here and she had obviously been right. Now they carried her through into the wrecked interior with broken tables and chairs and shattered glass and china littering the bare floors.

On the wall the simple pictures of Madonna and child hung crooked yet unbroken, as though those who had perpetrated this mess could not quite bring themselves to defile the icons. How can they live here like this, thought Violet. Then, as if in answer to her question, the small boy ran forwards and carefully lifted and pulled up a panel in the simple staircase, revealing a boarded wooden floor within. He bent down and felt for the edges before lifting a whole section of flooring. A winding staircase led into the darkness, down which the two women carried Violet, one standing in front of her whilst the other crouched down behind, supporting her under the arms. The trapdoor banged down, shutting out the light, and she could hear the small boy putting back the panelling. How did he get in, she wondered.

The gloom gave way as her eyes grew accustomed to it and she could see that they were in a small cellar about fifteen feet square. A door at one end presumably led on to another underground room and the little light that there was seemed to come from two eyebrow-shaped windows high in the far wall. As she looked, the small boy appeared at one of these, pulling aside the vegetation as he squirmed through. The younger of the two women ran forwards to help him down, leaving Violet supported only by the old woman.

The mother, for that is what Violet presumed her to be, hugged the child to her as she looked across at Violet. Violet smiled and she smiled back, before ruffling the boy's hair and releasing him. She stood up on a small box, reached through and rearranged the weeds to hide any sign of entry.

The room swam before Violet's eyes and she slumped in the old woman's arms, causing her to call out. The younger one jumped down from the box, reaching her just in time to stop her slipping unconscious from the old woman's grasp, and the two of them laid her down on a straw-filled palliasse and covered her with a rough blanket.

......

Ernest heard the clack of the letterbox flap and the soft sound of the letters hitting the floor. He crossed the hall and stooped to pick them up, idly shuffling through them as he walked back across and into the dining room. "Anything interesting dearest?" said Elsie from her place at the other end of the table.

"I don't know yet. I don't think so," he said as he sat down at the table. "There's one with a red cross on it. Must be from Violet, although it doesn't look like her handwriting."

"Well go on dearest, open it, see what it says. Is she coming home?"

He opened the envelope and proceeded to read. Suddenly his face went white and he slumped down, burying his face in the envelope, silent sobs wracking his body. Alarmed, Elsie stood and rushed around to his end of the table. She shook his shoulder crying out, "What's happened Ernest? What is it?"

Alice came in from the kitchen dressed in her hospital uniform and stood just inside the door. "Oh my lord what's happened?"

"I don't know. Ernest please show me the letter." He raised himself slightly and handed her the letter before burying his head once more in his crossed arms. Alice crossed the room and stood just behind Elsie, with one arm around her waist and the other resting on Ernest's heaving shoulder.

"What is it?"

Elsie put down the letter and stared into space. "It's Violet."

"What? What is it? Is she ill?"

Ernest raised his head, pushed up against the table and stood. He turned and encircled one arm around Elsie's slim waist, supporting her frail frame. With the other he reached out for Alice, who slipped within his grasp. He held them both. "Violet... she's missing... presumed killed or captured." His voice broke and he hung his head. The three of them stood there for some time, united in their grief and disbelief.

"May I see the letter?" said Alice. Elsie wordlessly handed it to her and crossed over to the easy chair by the fire. Ernest remained standing, leaning against the table as Alice held the letter in front with both hands and scanned the contents, skipping the opening paragraphs, concentrating on the pertinent ones.

"The casualty clearing station in which she was serving was attacked and destroyed before being overrun by the enemy," she read aloud. *"We*

have no reports of any survivors from this outrage, but it is possible that your daughter, along with others, was taken prisoner..." Alice put down the letter, not bothering to read the usually expressed condolences which followed. "Oh I'm so sorry." She crossed to Elsie and knelt down on the floor in front of her, taking her hands and looking up into her face. No tears were visible, but the thin pale features had suddenly taken on an almost transparent pallor and the eyes, always deep set, seemed now to almost retract into the depths of their despair. The illusions of wellbeing that had existed of late dissipated, and before her sat the woman she had known for all those years before.

There was silence in the room as each of them remained deep in their own thoughts. Eventually it was broken by Elsie. "You must find her Ernest. Wherever she is... dead or alive... you must find her."

He nodded, unable to speak for the emotions churning around within him. He looked down again at the letter, offering despair yet at the same time a strange sort of link. His heart thumped in his chest and his eyes filled and swam.

Was she dead? Surely not... he would have felt it... he would have known. Surely he would have known? How could she leave this world and him not know?

He remembered the anger he had felt when she first mooted the idea of going away and how he had given in. If only he... oh what was the point. She had been right to do what she did and none of them had dreamt that she would be in any danger.

"What will you do Ernest? Will you go to France?"

He remained silent for a while, thinking of his response before giving it in a cracked and broken voice. "I think perhaps it would be better to remain here for further news for the time being. That there is trouble in France is quite clear, and if I go straight into a war zone without any clear idea of what I'm going for or... even where I'm going it would achieve nothing."

"But surely we just can't sit and do nothing," said Elsie.

"I'm afraid that for the moment that is all we can do my dear..." He shook his head despairingly. "Wait and hope and pray."

"I think I shall go to my room and lie down for a while," said Elsie as she raised herself to her feet. Both Ernest and Alice moved forward, offering to help, but she brushed them aside gently. "I can manage on my own thank you. I shan't be long... I just... I just want to lie down for a while on my own."

They watched her leave the room, waiting until the door was closed. "Oh Ernest," sighed Alice as the door finally shut. "Oh Ernest I'm so sorry."

"Alice," he said, and he opened his arms as she slipped into his embrace. Anybody seeing them there would have known that the intimacy they now shared in this moment of grief was nothing new.

......

Time meant nothing to Violet as she lay there on that pallet in fitful nightmares. What horrors the blade had inflicted on others and what unspeakable filth it had embraced before entering her none could have guessed at. The leg swelled to half as big again and the wound seeped green and yellow pus. Dark red lines radiated from it, carrying the poison to her very being, infecting even her brain with their dark despair.

Visitors came and went within her thoughts and she cried out as they left her. Frank knelt beside her bed, his gentle face concerned at her plight. She smiled up at him and reached out to touch him, withdrawing her hand in horror as his face disintegrated, the skin peeling back to expose the flesh and then the very bones. Her mother and father stood there beside her bed, looking down at her pleading with her to come home, to get up. She tried to raise herself but only succeeded in rolling off the pallet.

Reality flooded back briefly as her face buried itself in the choking dust of the dirt floor and the old woman, clucking her disapproval, pushed and worried her back, covering her up once more. Baby Frank. Was he here as well? How did he get here? He stood there looking down at her. Why wouldn't he come to her? Did he hate her that much?

The small boy looked away from the imploring gaze of the sick woman on the bed and reached up to his grandmother's skirt. She placed her hand on his head, muttered a few words to him and he ran off.

He came back with a large bottle containing a greenish-yellow liquid, which he handed to her. She nodded and sent him off again before kneeling slowly down on the floor beside the now unconscious Violet. Picking up the end of the blanket, she folded it back on to Violet's torso, exposing her legs. Carefully she eased the skirts up until the wound area was visible. The rough bandaging was caked with blood and pus and she eased it from the wound and threw it aside. Taking a rag from her skirt pocket she tore it in half, placing one half on her shoulder, then picked up the bottle and unscrewed the cap. The faint smell of the absinthe mingled with the odours of sickness as she soaked the rag in the spirit. Gently at first, then with increasing vigour, she sponged the wound clean, finally pushing the rag into the very depths of the wound with her index finger. Violet stirred and then let out a scream from within her nightmares. Her arms went rigid at her sides and her eyes opened wide. The old woman stopped, waiting until the spasm had subsided.

The daughter came across. "Qu'est-ce que tu fais?"

The old woman held up the bottle for her to see, and the enquiring look turned to one of recognition. She nodded, and the older woman resumed her task in silence. When the wound was as clean as she could get it she threw the rag over to the old bandages and took the other half off her shoulder. Soaking this in the liquid she placed it over the wound and pressed it down. She turned as her daughter approached and handed her a strip of material torn from a petticoat, which she used to wrap around the leg to secure the dressing.

Her daughter helped her to her feet and the two of them stood for a few minutes looking down at Violet, before leaving the cellar by the stairs to continue their constant search for food in the surrounding houses and fields.

Time held little meaning for Violet, but gradually the fever began to break and she became more aware of her surroundings. She watched, when she was awake, the comings and goings of the two women as they went about their disjointed existence. Clinging to their home, exiled within its subterranean rooms, foraging and scavenging within its vicinity for scraps that would keep them alive. She became well enough to take food, although not yet strong enough to feed herself. Sometimes one of the women, but often the small boy, would patiently sit beside her on the bed, spooning a thin cool soup into her mouth, wiping her chin clean with a napkin. She tried to summon up even the limited amount of French that she had gleaned, but in her weakened state her mind could not seek that far and she had to make do with nods and carefully phrased expressions of thanks in English.

One unfortunate side effect of her better health was the increased need to use some sort of toilet facility. To attempt the stairs to the outside toilet was of course out of the question, and it was therefore a true testament to their dedication that these impoverished people attended to these, her most personal needs. The business of getting into a position so as to be able to even use the bucket required the help of both women, and sometimes even the small boy. Dignity had long since been discarded, and as the days and then weeks slipped by, all thoughts of privacy and decorum faded.

Violet lay alone on the palliasse, looking up and out at the thin arch of daylight coming from the window at the foot of her bed. Across the room against the other wall, but barely three feet from where she lay, was the large straw-filled mattress that the two women shared with the small boy since she had taken up the only other. Between the beds stood one small chair, upon which sat a tin jug of water, and underneath was the toilet bucket covered over with a cloth. The silence in the cellar seemed almost palpable and she stirred uneasily, disturbed by a feeling she could not express.

Suddenly she heard screams and gun fire. The small boy rushed down the stairs. For a moment he stood at the bottom looking up in terror, before scrabbling through the opening to the next cellar to hide. Violet raised herself up on her elbows as far as she could, but could not summon up the strength to do more than just stare open-mouthed at the staircase, her mind racing, appalled at the obvious and impending danger. There was a sound on the stairs and the legs of the younger woman came into view. Violet heaved a visible sigh of relief, but then her hopes were dashed as the woman turned on the stairs, looking back up them as she inched down.

A deep laugh seemed to rent the air and the boots of a German soldier came into view. The woman backed away from the stairs and stood between them and Violet. The soldier came into the cellar, his rifle held before him, its gleaming bayonet fixed. He jabbed it at her and shouted something. She moved aside, and for the first time he saw Violet lying there on her pallet, the blankets drawn around her throat. He moved forward and the woman backed away and stood beside Violet's bed. He pushed her aside with the edge of the bayonet as he looked down lasciviously at the young girl laid out before him.

The French woman shouted at him to gain his attention. "Elle est malade!" As if in confirmation, Violet's stomach contracted in fear and she vomited violently over the edge of the bed into the dust, before falling back in a swoon. The German wrinkled his nose in disgust, kicking his boots into the dirt to remove the spatterings. He raised his rifle and prepared to spear Violet, but before he could do so the woman threw herself forward and stood between them.

She smiled up at the man, and reaching for her dress at the neckline tore it open to reveal her bosom. She threw her head back to accentuate her vulnerability, forcing herself to smile. The dress slipped to either side of her breasts and they swung full and free before him. He looked down at her and transferred his rifle to one hand. With the other he reached forward and grabbed her left breast, squeezing it roughly, violently pinching the nipple between his index finger and thumb. His breath started to come in hoarse gasps. He let go of her and walked across to the wall at the head of the bed, where he leant his rifle. The woman watched him, the smile fixed on her face as he returned to her. Standing in front of her, he took hold of the dress with each hand and pulled sharply downwards, releasing it to fall to the floor around her feet.

She stepped naked from its ruins and moved slowly around him to stand before her bed. He followed her, turning as she did, watching the movement of her body, smelling the odours of her peasant womanhood. He watched as she squatted and then lay across the bed before him. He gasped as she opened her legs wide to reveal herself fully to him.

Unbuckling his belt he let his trousers fall to his knees, fumbling within his drawers for his penis. He brought it out, swollen now with his animal lust, and letting out a strangled cry, he literally dropped down on to and within her in the same movement.

Violet awoke from her swoon and was aware of frantic movement on the bed, almost within arm's reach of where she lay. At first she was unable to interpret what was going on, but gradually made out the dark shape of the German's uniform accentuating his white bottom pumping up and down. His boot soles kicked against the edge of her bed as he sought to thrust himself deeper and deeper within his pleasure. And below his heaving body she could make out the lower legs and feet of the woman.

He ceased his thrusting for a moment and withdrew, looking down at his knees, which were becoming sore on the dirt floor. He brushed them off as he rested on his elbow, exposing the naked woman below him. Then he picked her up from underneath him, almost as if she were a rag doll, and turned her over on her face along the length of the bed. Moving behind her, he knelt between her opened legs and reached under her belly, bringing her up into a crouching position. He grunted in satisfaction as he entered her from the rear, burying her face in the bolster with the force of his thrusting.

Violet let out a cry, which he didn't hear. The woman turned her face to her, eyes wide open in fear and pain. She raised herself on to her wrists, looking across at Violet, and in between thrusts put her finger to her lips in a gesture for her to remain silent. Their eyes held each other. Violet's wide with terror and disbelief, the woman's hooded with pain and humiliation.

The soldier seemed now to be in a world of his own at the end of the living being that had become his plaything. His eyes were closed, his face red and sweaty, as he reached his climax and shuddering finish within her, accompanied by a great shout. He slumped down on her back and the weight forced her arms and then her legs to give way. He shouted his displeasure as the straightening of her body withdrew him from her and turned her over to lie there once more before him exposed, and totally within his control. He grimaced lewdly as he toyed with her breasts, slapping them from side to side, laughing at their linked reciprocal movements.

That he was getting aroused again was quite apparent, but now he began to look from the victim he had taken across to the next object of his insane lust. Violet.

The woman, realising that her ploy was not after all going to work, frantically tried to distract his attention. She pushed up against him and grabbed his buttocks, moaning all the while, but he seemed to take no notice of her advances and instead slapped her down and made ready to cross the floor. Violet saw what was coming and began to try to mentally prepare herself for what she perceived now to be inevitable. She closed her eyes.

A wailing sound rented the air, followed by the crunch of a shell hitting the outbuildings to the rear of the house. The German swore violently and stood quickly, pulling up his trousers and buckling his belt. He rushed over to his rifle and hefted it. Turning round as he reached the foot of the stairs, he pointed the gun at the woman on the bed.

He smiled at first, then he began to laugh. He spoke to her then in his own language before he fired straight into her helpless body. Violet screamed as the body arched upwards in a last obscene gesture, held for a moment, and then relaxed back down on to the bed.

Her scream drew the beast's attention and he swung his weapon towards her, firing as he did. The bullets went high, just above Violet's prone body, and splattered into the wall as he prepared to fire again. She saw her death standing there before her in all its grinning bestiality and she shut her eyes tight, breathing her last prayer as the sound of gun fire split the room. She waited for the bullets.

Funny, she thought, how time seems to be standing still. Why could she still hear, still feel? Was there, after all, no threshold between life and death? Was it all just a seamless whole? Would Frank now be within her world?

She opened her eyes to see the German falling backwards, coming to rest sitting open- legged on the floor at the foot of the dead woman's bed, his rifle beyond his grasp.

A new set of legs came into Violet's view. Black boots with dirty cream puttees. English? No surely not. Wrong colour. What then?

"Kamarade?" the German called out to the advancing figure, his arms held up in surrender.

An American soldier came into full view. He stood at the bottom of the stairs surveying the scene. He looked across at Violet cowering beneath the blanket, her face half hidden, her eyes beseeching. He looked long and hard at the naked body of the dead woman on the bed.

"Kamarade," whispered the German as the soldier slowly turned towards him.

"Kamarade eh?" He pointed to the body. "Kamarade?" He sneered. "You filthy bastard." He looked down at the supplicant, noticing for the first time the open flies. The German saw his gaze and smiled guiltily. The American pointed his rifle at the man's head.

The German screamed for mercy, his voice pitched high by his fear, his hands held open in supplication. The American lowered his rifle and the German's voice changed tone and his hands dropped to his sides.

The burst of fire crashed around the small room, and as it died away it was replaced by the high-pitched screaming of the German as he clutched the tangle of gore that had once been his lower abdomen and genitalia.

"Help me," Violet called out above the din. "Help me please."

The soldier turned towards her in utter amazement. "Christ you're English. Beggin' yer pardon ma'am." He called back up the stairs. "Joe get yer butt down here there's a limey... English woman down here!"

He was joined by another soldier, who took in the scene of carnage with one glance and spat in the direction of the now jibbering German soldier. Between the two of them they gently lifted Violet and carried her up the stairs and out into the daylight.

Below in the cellar the small boy crawled from his hiding place. For a moment he stood, looking at his dead mother, then at her killer sitting there helpless on the floor. He crossed to the gun, picked it up and walked towards the stricken man, who looked up at him, pleading. The boy smiled. A long cruel smile of recognition and hate. He left the cellar and let down the trap, leaving the beast to die there alone in his agony and terror.

As Violet came out into the sunshine, supported between the two American soldiers, the light blinded her. The air, despite the lingering smell of cordite, felt fresh and good and she breathed it deep within her lungs, seeming to gain strength from it.

Smoke curled from the outbuildings at the rear, and as her eyes got used to the daylight she could see that the ground and the road in front of the house was littered with the bodies of dead Germans.

Sprawled there in the dirt she could feel no real enmity for them. The one closest to her was just a boy, lying there on his back, his arms thrown behind his head, his eyes closed as if in sleep. The man dying in the cellar she could hate, but this boy... no not this boy.

Her eyes lighted upon the prone figure of the old woman lying dead. Her outstretched arms had released the pail of scavenged roots and they lay scattered before her. A sudden movement caught her attention and the soldier on her left stiffened in anticipation, then relaxed as the small boy walked slowly forward to the body. He knelt down in front of the woman and Violet thought he was about to embrace her as he bent forward. But he simply picked up the bucket and proceeded to place the spilled vegetables back in it, all the while holding on to the German's rifle. When it was full, he stood and looked around at the assembled men regarding him with horror and pity in their eyes. Then he threw back his head, shouldered the heavy rifle and, picking up the pail, turned and marched off south down the road. They watched him go in silence.

The two soldiers on either side of Violet looked around for somewhere to lay her. They shouted to one of their group to lay one of the dead German's jackets on the stone step of the fountain and carefully sat her on it, leaning her back against the parapet. She was so weak that even seated thus she found it difficult to remain upright, so they stacked two empty ammunition boxes beside her to lean on and placed a tin cup of water in her hands. The sun warmed her face and she sighed, glad to be safe at last.

"What's the date today?" she asked the soldier filling his billy can beside her.

"May first ma'am," he replied cheerily. "And ain't it just a fine one."

May the first. May the first. Good lord, she thought. I've been here for nearly six weeks. What on earth will my family think has happened to me? There can't have been any news from the chateau because... well surely that had been taken. "Is this the front line?" she enquired.

"No ma'am, that'd be a few miles north of here if you could call it a line." He hesitated. "Say, you are English aren't you?"

She laughed wryly. "Yes I'm English. Don't worry I'm not a spy. I'm not brave enough for a start."

"Sorry ma'am, but you can't be too careful, 'specially with all these Boche going about the country." He finished filling his bottle and stood in front of her. "How long you bin here?"

"Well if you're correct about the date it's nearly six weeks... very little of which I can remember."

"Well you is just plumb unlucky then ma'am, 'cause this is just about as far as they done got. If'n you'd bin just a few miles further south you'd have been in our camp and they sure as hell... beggin' yer pardon ma'am... didn't git that fur."

She smiled to herself at the unaccustomed richness of his speech and reflected as he walked away on what he had said. A few miles south. If only they'd not turned right they would have been safe. Armand. Thank God, Armand would have been safe. He had gone on south. Where would he be now? In Orleans? She hoped so. She started as the realisation came to her that he too would probably think her dead or captured. She needed to get back as soon as possible but... well she felt too weak to do too much just yet.

A soldier wandered over to her. "Chocolate ma'am?" He proffered her a lump and she took it, gratefully mumbling her thanks. She broke off a piece in her mouth and laid her head back as she savoured the sheer joy of its taste and texture. She had eaten virtually nothing except the odd bowl of thin vegetable soup for so long now, and the feeling of real food in her mouth felt so good.

A Sergeant walked over to her. "Ma'am we've got to be gittin' along now. There's a column comin' up behind us and they'll have the means to git you back to a hospital. I want you to take this here pistol and keep it beside you." He saw her reaction and held up his hand to forestall her. "Now I don't guess you want it ma'am, but I'd feel right better if'n you took it." He placed it beside her on the stone bench. "An' here's some more chocolate and some beef. I've opened it fer you." He placed both down beside her and she looked at them wonderingly... lovingly. "Is there anythin' else you need ma'am?"

She looked away from the food, shaking her head. "No. Nothing thank you... except... do you have a blanket... only I'm a bit chilly in spite of this sunshine."

"Sure thing ma'am. Joe!" he called. "Joe can you rustle up a blanket fer the lady?" He turned back to her. "Well good day ma'am." He turned away to re-join his men, who were forming up in a line ready to depart.

"Sergeant," she called.

"Yes ma'am."

"Thank you."

"T'ain't nothin ma'am." He saluted her and turned away to busy himself with the business of war. Joe came over carrying a rolled-up blanket, which he draped over her knees.

"Thank you Joe," she said. "Good luck."

"Good luck to you ma'am, and I'm sorry about yer friends."

"I never even knew their names and..." She looked up into the sky. "They looked after me for nearly six weeks and... then this." A tear appeared at the corner of her eye.

"There's plenty to cry about here ma'am. Ain't that a fact." He saluted her, then turned to join his comrades, leaving her sitting there alone in the square. A quiet descended, broken only by the singing of the larks and the trickle of the spring in the fountain behind her. She turned her face up to the sun and savoured its warmth on her skin.

Another sound distracted her. It came from the direction of the house. Faint and high-pitched like the distant wail of some machine. She wondered at it for some time before realising with a thrill of fear and guilt that she was listening to the ending of the insane life in the cellar.

......

Ernest sat alone in the front room, his head in his hands. It had been weeks now, and still there was no news except that which gave him the greatest fear. The offensive in late March had been cunningly planned to strike at the intersection of the lines of both the British and French, dividing them and thrusting through into the hinterland beyond. The objective had been achieved, there was no doubt, with the British curling back to protect the channel ports and the French doing likewise in the opposite sphere to protect Paris.

The advance that had penetrated this breach had pushed all before it, opening up the logjam of all the previous years. Within its cauldron somewhere, alive or dead, was his daughter. The pain he felt was real in all respects. His hands shook if he allowed them to, so he had taken to holding them both together. 'Violet... oh Violet, where are you? What am I going to do?'

Even though she had been away for so long now, she pervaded every facet of his life. She always had. She always would. She would always mean more to him than any other person. Elsie. Dear Elsie. He had treated her abominably throughout their marriage. He had almost despised her for her illness during those long years, and then for these last years when she had been in some sort of remission and had taken on a new lease of life they had become friends... companions. Now of course all that was gone. Since the news she had rarely been seen outside her room and the illness and lack of vigour had returned to claim her. No tears had passed her eyes, but the hurt and pain lay trapped within them and within her.

'Oh Violet,' he thought. 'If only you knew what we are going through. Silly man. Don't be ridiculous. Of course she knows if... if she's alive, then what we are suffering may be nothing to what...' He stood quickly gasping for breath, the full horror of his train of thought thundering in his brain. What if she is injured, alone. The thoughts tumbled about in his mind and he held his head to stop the madness.

The door opened and Alice came in. She was dressed in ordinary clothing as she had called the hospital and told them that she would not be able to make it that day. She stood just inside the door, looking at Ernest standing there, his head in his hands, the sobs wracking his body. "Oh Ernest," she said as she crossed the room to him. "Ernest this won't do. Oh my poor dear." She embraced him and he buried his face in her shoulder, sobbing. She patted his back as if he were a child, making soothing noises in his ear. His sobs subsided.

"I'm sorry Alice. It's just that I feel so hopeless... so, so helpless. I just don't know what to do anymore."

"There's nothing you can do for now except be strong for yourself and for the mistress."

"Dear Alice," he said, releasing himself from her embrace to put his hands on her shoulders and look down into her face. "I am so glad you are here with us... with me."

"I always will be," she said. "As long as you want me... and the mistress puts up with me."

He smiled. A guilty secret smile, but on that tragic face a smile nonetheless. "She understands, I know. She... well there's no problem as long as we're discreet."

The sound of letters coming through the box broke into their conversation and he rushed from the room and out into the hall. Alice followed and watched as he bent down and flicked through the letters before coming up with one bearing the red cross. He held it out in front of him and discarded the rest back on to the floor. Slowly he walked back into the front room, staring all the while at the envelope in his shaking hands. He stopped in the centre of the room and continued to stare at it.

"Aren't you going to open it then?" Alice asked.

"What?" He turned to her, his eyes troubled. "Oh yes. Yes." He pulled at the flap and took out the letter. She moved around to stand in front of him, watching his face intently as he read.

Dear Mr Matthews,

We have received some news about Violet, which I feel we have to share with you, even though it does not tell us anything conclusive about her present whereabouts.

A letter arrived for Violet the week after the incident and we held this letter here in my office until it became clear what had befallen her. When the letter was not answered the sender, a Monsieur Taillefer, wrote to me directly enquiring about Violet's whereabouts.

It would seem that this gentleman, who was previously a patient at this hospital, had struck up a friendship with your daughter before he was transferred to a convalescent hospital about forty miles away. From his letter and from subsequent correspondence it has become clear that he met Violet at the other hospital, the day after the casualty clearing station was destroyed, and that she was in the company of a British ambulance and driver with wounded soldiers she was attempting to bring back to us.

Their meeting was brief, as at the time of Violet's arrival he and other wounded were being evacuated to safety. But we now know that Violet was not killed with all of the others and her last known whereabouts is the Chateau de Fontere, from which she was departing for here. Unfortunately, the chateau was overrun by the Germans and either she was taken prisoner there or had left before they arrived.

I am so sorry that I have not got any firm news of Violet's present situation, but we all felt here that you would want to know what we have discovered.

The letter was signed by the matron.

Ernest put down the letter and stared out into space, tears coursing down his face.

"What is it Ernest? What is it? Bad news?" said Alice desperately.

He shook his head. Unable to speak, he handed her the letter and she moved across to the window to read it, leaving him standing there in the centre of the room, wrapped up in his own silent thoughts.

She put down the letter and turned to him. "We must tell the mistress."

He regarded her as if he was waking from a dream and mouthed her words to himself, seeming only then to understand them. "Tell the mistress. Yes! We must tell Elsie." He reached out for the letter, which she was holding out to him, turned and ran from the room and up the stairs, calling out his wife's name as he went. Alice followed a little more sedately.

Ernest burst into Elsie's room. She was sitting on her chair near the unlit fire, staring into it. The curtains were drawn and the whole room was gloomy and dark, despite the sunshine. Ernest rushed over to the curtains and flung them open. "Great news," he shouted.

She stood up and faced him, but standing in the light from the window his face was invisible to her. All she could detect was his shape and his outstretched arms raised in triumph.

"Is she safe?" she enquired, as Alice too entered the room.

"His arms dropped and he moved forward. "Well no, but there's news of her after the fall of the hospital." His shoulders slumped as the realisation came to him that the news, whilst welcome nonetheless, was not at all conclusive and he began to feel a little foolish at his entry and the interpretation that had been taken from it. He stepped forward and took Elsie by the shoulders, looking down into her pale, frightened face. "We've received a letter from the matron of the Base Hospital telling us that a friend of Violet's... a French man, saw her the day after the hospital was bombed and she was at another hospital... which... which has been captured. Oh but don't you see Elsie... she wasn't dead. She was alive and that means that she probably still is, even though she may be... well captive."

Elsie stood there looking up at him, her face registering little emotion, but her eyes searching within his for more information, more hope. He stared down at her, seeing the workings of her mind, and as the first tears began to flow he scooped her up in his arms and held her frail body close to his whilst the grief wracked her tiny frame. Alice watched quietly from the doorway and then silently closed the door and went downstairs. They needed to be alone and she knew it. It was not that either one would want to cut her from them at that moment. She knew that. But it was their daughter and the emotions of that moment that were theirs alone.

Ernest saw the door close and understood. Elsie regained her composure and made her way back to her chair, assisted by Ernest. She sat and he stood just in front of her, holding her hands. "Now you must go Ernest," she said. "Find her and make sure she's safe. Find her for me... for us both. Please."

......

The day wore on and Violet began to shift uneasily on the increasingly hard stone. Her bottom, thinned by weeks of near starvation, ached horribly. She longed to stand but knew that she was too weak to do so. In front of her, on the dusty street, lay three dead bodies plus that of the old woman. Their weapons had been removed by the Americans and all lay on their backs in a prone imitation of surrender. Flies gathered around their eyes and open mouths and Violet shuddered at the sight.

She looked around to check that she was not about to be joined by the promised relief column and, satisfied that she was entirely alone, pulled up her skirts to examine her leg. The livid purple scar ran straight down the outside of her thigh. Almost an inch wide at its centre point it reminded her of a scar on a tree trunk, with the bark slowly growing over as a permanent reminder. She felt around the wasted muscle and winced as even the slight pressure sent shocks of pain through her. The lines of red radiating from it were obviously only shadows of their former intensity. She caught the scent of aniseed. What had the two women put on it? Well whatever it was, it had saved her life.

She remembered her ears and felt them, noting that the dressings had long since been removed. They felt tender, but apart from that there didn't seem to be any noticeable damage.

A movement distracted her from her self-examination and she quickly rearranged her skirts. One of the supposedly dead Germans was moving. She watched, appalled and fascinated, as his arms folded at the elbow and the head rolled slightly to the right to greet the hand, which cupped the brow. The eyes opened and examined the blood on his palm from the wound creasing his temple.

Violet held her breath as he rolled over, oblivious to his audience, and she rocked back when he cried out as the motion audibly jarred the broken sections of his shattered legs. He lay still for a while, struggling to come to terms with the pain, his head, facing Violet now, resting on his forearm. The eyes opened and she saw the pain and the fear within them. He made no movement, but his eyes held hers, staring at her.

"Wasser," he croaked.

She reacted then. Still holding his gaze, she felt beside her for the pistol and pulled it towards her. It was heavy... too heavy for her to hold up with one hand, but she managed to get both hands around its thick cold butt and unsteadily raised it to point in his general direction.

He smiled the lost smile of defeat and submission and buried his face once more in his forearm, mumbling to himself. A self-deprecating laugh came from him and she lowered the weapon slightly to wonder at him. "Don't move or I'll shoot," she called in a voice as strong and as authoritative as she could muster. It sounded, even to her, pathetically weak and she had little doubt that were he able and were he willing she would have little or no defence against him.

"You are English," he stated without looking at her, his head remaining buried in his arm.

"Yes. You speak English?"

He laughed again. The ironic laugh of a man who knows that he has nothing to gain. "As you hear, I speak English. I should do. I went to Cambridge."

She relaxed a little but then raised the gun again. "You're still the enemy, and I warn you to keep away from me or I'll... I'll..."

"Kill me? Is that what you're trying to say? Well go on then. For my part, I've had enough of this disgusting war... filth, blood and... oh to hell with it." He opened his eyes and looked directly at her. "Get it over with please."

She lowered the gun and rested it on her knee, still holding on to its butt with one hand. "I can't... I can't just shoot you in cold blood. I'm a nurse, not a killer like you." He laughed again, but it was cut short by a cough, the movement of which sent shock waves of pain through his body. His brow creased and he squeezed his eyes shut, burying his face in his arm.

In the silence, she craned forward as far as she could, examining him, searching him for any threat. "Are you all right?" she enquired at last in a tremulous voice.

"Please give me some water."

"I can't."

"Why on earth not, for God's sake? I'm not going to hurt you. I can't even walk."

"Nor can I." She heard herself use the words and immediately regretted them. Now he would know that she was helpless. Like a rabbit caught in the stare of a stoat she stared transfixed as he raised his head from his arm and looked quizzically across at her.

He smiled. "I'm sorry. How did it happen?"

"One of your patrols ambushed our ambulance several weeks ago."

"I'm sorry."

"Sorry! Sorry! You're sorry! You Germans blow up the hospital, killing all my friends. You ambush a clearly marked ambulance and kill the wounded men in cold blood, then weeks later you turn up here and kill that poor woman over there and... and that despicable creature down there rapes and murders the other girl and tries to rape me. And you're sorry." Her voice trailed off as the effort she had put into this tirade clearly taxed her strength and she hung her head.

"I am sorry. I didn't do those things," he said quietly. "But I'm still sorry for everything. Sorry for the men I've killed, sorry for my dead friends, sorry for you, sorry for me, sorry for this whole damned war. How much more can I be sorry?"

She lifted her head and looked across to him, her expression softening. "I didn't mean... oh you know what I meant."

He nodded. "I'd still like some water."

"I still can't walk. You'll have to come over here."

He dug his elbows into the ground and pulled himself forward. The effort and the pain made him call out involuntarily and he had to rest before trying again. Sweat stood out in beads on his forehead and the locks of blonde hair that fell across it dampened and stuck. "Are you alright?" she asked gently.

He gritted his teeth and nodded. Inch by inch, foot by foot, he covered the ground between them. Teeth gritted against the pain he struggled on, stopping from time to time to recover his breath and senses. She held the gun loosely on her lap, but as he neared she put it aside and reached out to touch him, finally leaning forward to pull as hard as she was able. He collapsed, leaning half against the edge of the stone and half against her leg. She cried out at the pressure and he jerked himself aside, muttering his apologies.

"Can you get up here?"

He shook his head. "No, that's as far as I can get."

Setting the pistol aside completely, she picked up the tin mug and reached back into the well to fill it. She handed it down to him with both hands, gently nudging him back into wakefulness. He took the mug awkwardly from her, spilling much of its contents, but greedily consuming the rest.

"Would you like some more?" she asked, and he nodded as he handed it back to her. She refilled the mug and handed it back down to him. He drank again, savouring the liquid as it eased his parched throat.

"Thank you," he said as he passed it back up to her and slumped back down in exhaustion. The two of them remained silent for a while and Violet found herself examining the man, who now lay before and beside her. His legs were horribly and possibly irretrievably broken, the feet indicating by their unnatural position the extent of his injuries. She marvelled at the endurance and fortitude that had, in the face of these terrible wounds, allowed him to crawl across to her and she shivered at the realisation that such strength could still represent a threat.

She looked around for the gun and realised that since his arrival it now lay beyond his head, leaning against the stone, and that she would have to lean across him to get it. He noticed her gaze and, turning slightly, reached up for and picked up the gun. Her heart stopped as she realised her mistake.

He passed the gun back up to her. She took it in silent incredulity. "Better keep it your side. You never know who's about."

Her laughter was the laughter of one who realises they have been trumped in no uncertain terms, and it only increased when he joined in laughing, alternating with grimaces of pain as the movement jarred his legs. At length their laughter petered out, and they sat still and silent, each in their own thoughts.

"You should try to bind your legs a little to stop the bleeding," she advised.

He looked up at her and shrugged his shoulders. "What with? I'm not in a fit state to go looking for..." He searched for the word, the first time he had done so in a conversation that so far had demonstrated his perfect command of the language. "I don't know, what do you call a bandage such as that?"

"A tourniquet... a French word. Well try not to move too much now and see if you can tighten your trousers around the wound to staunch the blood.

He reached down and pulled the legs tight about his thighs, wincing at the new pain. "My name is Dieter."

"Pleased to meet you Dieter. My name is Violet. She extended her hand down to him and he took it and shook it gently.

"Violet," he mused. "Violet. Such a pretty flower. Tell me about this flower."

"About the flower?"

"No silly, I meant about you. Tell me about you."

"Me? Why me?" She handed him down a lump of the chocolate and he looked at it appreciatively before breaking off a piece and putting it in his mouth. He chewed thoughtfully for a moment before replying.

"Because I want to hear about things that are not of this war... things... tell me of your life before all this. Please."

She frowned and looked down at him. "I can't... I can't tell you much about me that isn't affected by or caused by this war. My whole life... everything I am and everything I know seems to be wrapped up in and around this war."

He nodded sagely. "Tell me anyway." She sighed and proceeded, sometimes against her better judgement, to tell him everything. She went through her life up to and including Frank and even the baby. She told him about her experiences through the war and about Armand and her fears for his safety. She told him of her new found love for Armand. He sat there before her, silent like a confessor, and she wondered if he had nodded off into unconsciousness. How much had he heard before he fell asleep. All of it? Nothing?

He opened his eyes and reached into his inside breast pocket to fish out a small brown leather wallet, which he handed up to her. "Please look inside and you will find some cards with my address. Tell my wife, Gisela, that you met me. Give her my love and to my son, Gunther."

She took the wallet and searched through it until she found some cards with what seemed to be an address on them. "I'm sorry I don't know any German. Is this it?"

"Yes that's it."

She handed back the wallet to him and pocketed the card. "Why can't you tell them yourself?"

He looked up at her and smiled weakly. "You'll see." She didn't, but she let him relax into silence again and she too, weakened by all the activity and stress, dozed off in the pale sunlight.

A sudden shout awoke her and she found herself staring straight into the point of a bayonet, the wicked dark eye of the rifle muzzle beyond it and beyond that the determined face of a young American soldier.

Dieter, at her feet, faced with a similar threat, threw his hands in the air, knocking her thigh as he did, and she cried out at the pain of his touch. "I'm sorry," he said quietly.

"I am English," Violet cried out to the soldiers now milling around in front of them.

"What the hell you all doin' sittin' there with this Boche then?" sneered the soldier nearest Dieter, as he flicked his bayonet forward to pierce his jacket and nick into his chest. Dieter drew himself up as far as he could to relieve the pressure and cried out at the pain of his action. The American misconstrued his cry and drew back his weapon, preparing to thrust deep.

"He's wounded and he's no threat," Violet cried out. "Leave him alone."

The soldier holding his bayonet at Violet jerked it at her. "He's Boche, and I say again ma'am what is you doin' with him?"

"Your Sergeant and Joe... yes Joe... you must know Joe came here. They said you'd be along and they told me to wait here for you. They gave me..." She scrabbled around on the bench beside her. "...they gave me this chocolate and this tin of beef and told me to wait for you."

"And the German. Did Joe give him chocolate?" snarled the other soldier.

She turned to him. "No, I gave him that when he recovered. You see they... we thought they were all dead... but he wasn't. He was..."

"He was only unconscious and the lady was gracious enough to take pity on me," piped up Dieter.

The face of the American nearest him contorted with rage. "The lady was gracious enough to take pity on me," he mimicked. "You filthy Boche!" He reversed his rifle and swiped Dieter across the side of his head with the butt, knocking him sideways to the ground. Dieter rolled over with the force and lay there looking up into the horrified face of Violet.

"Now do you see?" he hissed through broken teeth.

"Please don't hurt him anymore," pleaded Violet, searching desperately from face to cruel face.

The soldier took no notice and instead grabbed hold of Dieter by his jacket and dragged him away on to the open ground, from where he had crawled earlier. "Is this gracious enough for you," he cried as he forced the bayonet deep into his chest, putting his whole weight on it. Dieter half sat up, his hands reaching out for and grasping the rifle before the American twisted it and withdrew. He fell back, shuddered and was still.

Alone among the grinning, jeering audience, Violet watched, her eyes wide with terror, her mouth open in a silent scream. A blackness seemed to fold in on her and a loud buzzing seemed to break out in her head, blotting out all senses as she swooned and fell to the ground.

......

"Could you please direct me to the matron's office," Ernest enquired of the orderly walking towards him.

"Certainly sir," he said, stopping and indicating behind him to his left. "It's that one there on the corner."

Ernest thanked him and crossed to the hut. My God, it all looked incredibly primitive, he thought. What must it have been like when it was all just tents? He knocked on the door and entered. There was a sort of counter just inside the door, behind which stood another orderly carefully writing on a list. He looked up as Ernest entered.

"Good day to you sir. May I help you?"

"Yes please, my name is Ernest Matthews and I would like to see the matron."

"I'm afraid she's with another..."

The door behind him opened and a large uniformed lady came up behind him, stopping him in mid sentence. "Mr Matthews. Hallo. You've come about Violet? Do come through." She reached for the counter top, raised it up and swung the door within it open, ushering him through and into her office.

Straight in front of him was a desk piled high with paperwork, and in front of it were two chairs, one of which was occupied by an elegant-looking and well-dressed gentleman with a prominent moustache. He leant heavily on his cane and rose unsteadily to his feet as Ernest entered the room.

The matron brushed past Ernest and took up position behind her desk. "Mr Matthews, may I introduce Capitaine... Monsieur Armand Taillefer. He is also here about Violet."

Ernest shook the hand that was proffered to him and then turned to the matron. "What news Matron? Do we know where she is yet?"

"Sit you down Mr Matthews, and you too monsieur." She waited until they were both seated and then sat herself. "Now we do not have anything definite, but we do have a report of the ambulance you last saw her with, Monsieur Taillefer. It has been found upturned with all the occupants dead..." Ernest jumped to his feet and Armand leant forward, placing both hands on the desk. The matron held her hand up. "No wait please gentlemen. There was no sign of Violet. She was not amongst the dead."

"Mon dieu," said Armand, relaxing back into his chair. "Thanks God for that. But where can she be?"

Ernest looked across at the Frenchman, wondering to himself quite what he was there for, and at the same time feeling grateful to be apparently sharing the concern for Violet with someone. "Yes thank God for that," he said. "But it still doesn't answer the question about where she is."

"I'm afraid we can shed only a glimmer of hope on that Mr Matthews," volunteered the matron. "It would seem that an injured woman suffering some sort of shock, but speaking English, has turned up at an American field hospital. There is no indication from them as to who she is, as indeed they inform us that there is little or no information or identification available with the exception of the rather curious possession of a card with German writing on it." She looked up quizzically at both men and they both shrugged their shoulders, unable to shed any light on this particular fact. "We do have Violet's small private bag with her personal belongings here. It was found near the crashed ambulance. She reached down behind her desk and brought out a bag, which she placed on the table. "You will no doubt wish to take charge of this Mr Matthews." He nodded and reached forward to touch the bag. Tears welled in his eyes and he hung his head.

Armand reached across and handed him a clean handkerchief. "Monsieur," he said quietly. Ernest nodded his thanks and dabbed his eyes.

The matron coughed. "There is the matter of this letter addressed to Violet." She turned to Armand. "Your original letter, which when there was no reply alerted you to the fact that she was missing... and us to the realisation that she had not been killed at the casualty clearing station. It is addressed to Miss Matthews, but as the writer you will presumably wish to retain it." She passed the letter across and Armand reached forward and took it.

Ernest watched this latter transaction with increasing curiosity. What precise interest did this chap have in this whole affair? Armand saw his look and interpreted his question. "Monsieur, your daughter was a nurse to me when I was at this hospital. She was very kind to me for so long a time and we have become... friends." He looked across at Ernest's face. "Very good friends, you understand?"

"I think I do sir," said Ernest, a little more brusquely than he really wanted to sound.

Armand picked up the tone of his voice. "I assure you sir that I have only honourable... how do you say...?"

"Intentions?" queried Ernest, helpfully this time.

"Oui, c'est ca. Intentions. Honourable intentions. She is a very wonderful woman."

"I think I can say Mr Matthews," matron intervened, "that nothing of any impropriety has taken place."

Ernest looked at her and back to Armand, who smiled slightly. "I have not been very well you understand." A faint smile played at his mouth's edge.

Despite himself, Ernest could not disguise his amusement. 'I like this man,' he thought. He seems a gentleman. "Monsieur, I would like to know how you know that my daughter was not at the casualty clearing station." He looked across at the matron. "Is that the correct expression?" She nodded the affirmative and he continued. "Tell me please what happened."

"Mais oui. I was taken from this hospital to another one, a French one after Christmas, and although Violet wrote to me and I wrote to her we did not see each other again while the war has not finished. You understand?"

"Yes of course."

"In March, the Boche make the offensive and we are told at the hospital that we have to go to Paris and then for me to Orleans to be safe. As I was being taken out to the lorry it is my surprise to see Violet arriving with an ambulance and some men who have been wounded. I was very happy to see her you understand, but I cannot stay long as the camion is waiting to go. She told me that the hospital she was at had been hit by bombs. Her ears were bleeding from the..." He mimed an explosion.

"Blast?"

"Oui, blast. She could not hear very well, but the sister says she will look at her before she goes. She was coming to here but... she never arrives."

Ernest turned to the matron. "Could you please tell me where this American hospital is and I will go there and see if it is my daughter."

"Certainly," said the matron. "Here is the address and the name of the sister who has sent this information. I do hope you are successful Mr Matthews. Violet was very popular here. She had many friends, and if it is her please be sure to let us know she is safe."

"I will indeed matron, you can rest assured. Now I wonder how can I get there?"

Armand perked up. "Ah, there I think I can help monsieur. I have a car and a driver."

Ernest looked at the man. There was certainly a lot more to this chap than met the eye. It would be interesting to find out more about him. The two of them bade their goodbyes to the matron and left the office. Ernest, rushing ahead, keen to get going, stopped as he realised that the other man was walking very slowly, leaning heavily on his cane. "Are you all right?" he enquired.

"Oh yes. I am sorry. I have been in the hospital until two days ago, when I left to find Violet. I am good but a little slow. It is only some weeks since I walked."

"I'm sorry, I didn't think. When were you injured?"

"Last year... vers... about August I think."

"What? And you're still like this. It must have been an awful injury."

"It was not good and I am lucky I have not died. Violet and the others, but most of all Violet, help me to be as you see... still not good but alive and... getting better."

"I had no real idea of how it was here. At home we grumbled when something was not available... silly things you know. Here I can see that we knew nothing. I got some idea of course from Violet of the horror but... well what can I say."

"You can say that you have a wonderful daughter."

"I know that. She has had some... well sadness but... but we are going to put it right."

"I know of her sadness."

"You know?"

"Yes I know. I know of Frank who was killed. I know of baby Frank."

Ernest stopped in his tracks. He didn't know what to feel. Ashamed? Guilty? Apart from Crowe and that awful woman Court, he had never discussed the subject, never admitted the subject to anyone but himself and Violet. Yet here he was discussing it with a perfect stranger. He couldn't resist the thought that for her to tell another was in some way disloyal. "Why has she told you all of this?"

"To understand it. To try to forgive herself."

They reached the entrance gate and Armand indicated a large motor car with a driver standing beside it. "Ca va Philippe," he said to the driver as he approached. Ernest looked at him askance. A large car. A chauffeur. What was this man Violet had taken up with?

"Monsieur Armand," the driver said as he came forward with a slight limp to assist Armand and take his cane. He led him to the rear door, opened it and stood by ready to assist him in.

Armand turned. "Mr Matthews. Please to get in."

The driver, realising that they were to have company, apologised and stood aside for Ernest to enter the vehicle. When he was seated, Armand gave him some instructions on directions before he was helped up the step and in. He relaxed back into the sumptuous leather seating and closed his eyes in exhaustion.

The car set off and after a little while Ernest felt able to continue their conversation. "You say my daughter has discussed her... her... secrets with you."

Armand opened his eyes, turned his head and looked the older man straight in the eye. "She has told me of her love for a brave man who gave his life in France. For my country, you understand."

"Yes, I can see that is how you would view the subject," said Ernest.

"She was... how do you say... keeping all of it inside her. She was feeling sad and ashamed and... yes guilty, but for what?"

"Well her behaviour at the time was... well it was not correct, even in your eyes surely... not that we haven't... not that I haven't forgiven... no that is the wrong word..." He looked out of the window at the passing countryside before continuing. "I was very angry and... well hurt for a long time but now I am reconciled to it and when Violet is ready and home we will make arrangements to take back the child... my grandchild."

"I know and I am very pleased for the two of you."

"That's a funny way of putting it. Pleased for the two of us. You realise of course the tongues that will wag when all of this comes out in the open."

"Tongues will wag? What does that mean?"

"Sorry. What I meant to say was that some people will be scandalised, angry, and they will say... well bad things. You understand?"

"I understand. If they do that for a person so good as her they are stupid." Armand made a dismissive Gallic gesture and Ernest could not contain his amusement. Armand caught his mood, and the two of them laughed for a short while in the car before the seriousness of their mission once again weighed down on them.

"One last question," said Ernest. "Presumably my daughter's history does not offend you in any way."

"Your daughter's history is of love and care. Why have I to be offended?"

"And what precisely is your relationship with my daughter? Sorry, another question, I know, but I am interested in why you should discharge yourself from hospital when you are obviously not completely well, to travel around France looking for her."

"I hope to gain the love of your daughter. C'est ca seulement. She was there for me and I have to be here now... when she is in danger."

Ernest nodded his understanding and they each subsided into their own thoughts and let the countryside roll by. The evidence of war was all around them in the lack of inhabitants and the destroyed buildings. Happily, however, the tide of the German advance had now turned and the road they were travelling on, in the opposite direction to that which Violet had been attempting all those weeks ago, was firmly in allied territory. Occasionally they had to stop to let military convoys go past, mostly consisting of Americans tramping north to shore up the defences and continue the build-up for the counter-offensive that this time would push the invaders from the soil of France. At times they were stopped and questioned, but Armand had a signed pass and they were able to proceed without hindrance.

Once more, Ernest found himself wondering at the calibre and connections of his companion. That he was well associated there could be no doubt. That he was quite well off was also quite apparent by the car and the driver, but the man himself, though well dressed and elegant, had no airs about him. He had declared himself for Violet in no uncertain terms, yet he felt none of the antipathy towards him that he had felt for Balfour. Why not? Was it purely a matter of class? Surely not? If Violet had announced all those years ago that she was going off with a foreigner he would have been apoplectic, yet now he felt only a vague sense of pride. 'Is it me? Have I changed that much,' he thought. Perhaps it was time.

He had decried her relationship with Balfour as unwise and immoral, yet he had... yes, go on admit it, Matthews... he had taken up with Alice, their maid. He felt his face flush at the thought of it and he stole a sideways glance at his travelling companion to assure himself that his thoughts were not read. Alice. Ten years his junior. A thousand years his social inferior. The scandal, should their affair become public knowledge, would be monumental, yet still he persisted. 'And I had the effrontery to judge Violet's young love for Balfour. I can't... no I won't give Alice up,' he determined. 'Eventually

I'll have to admit it to Violet and ask her forgiveness but... she makes me feel so whole again. Maybe she even takes the place that I filled with my love for Violet... not that I love Violet any less... Violet! Oh God, please make her all right. Please keep her safe until we get there.'

Elsie came into his thoughts. That she had gone into remission was without doubt. She had fought so bravely to stay well and on top of things throughout the long years of the war and Violet's absence and now... now the shock had set her right back. He remembered the years of indifference he had had to her sufferings, the years of loneliness when he had absorbed himself in work. Strange, how on her recovering some of her wellbeing they had formed an affection for each other which allowed and even created his ability to form the affair with Alice. Nothing direct had ever been said, but he knew she knew of it and he knew also that as long as he was discreet and her position in the household was not threatened, nothing would be said. Nothing to feel guilty about, he reasoned. Then why did he?

For his part, Armand was also examining his thoughts and impressions of the man he had so recently met. He seemed a likeable enough fellow. Quite obviously he was very fond of his daughter and so he should be. That the bond between the daughter and the father was an uncommonly strong one was not in doubt. She had tortured herself with feelings of guilt for all those years, more from a sense of having betrayed her father than anything else.

He examined his own feelings. Was he hoping for too much? He had not known Violet for very long. They came from different countries and backgrounds and they had found solace in each other's company in the unreal surroundings of a war. 'Am I fooling myself,' he thought. No, surely not. The affection she had shown when they met at Fontere had been undoubtedly genuine. He remembered also the Christmas by the bridge. Yes, he had every reason to hope that he could gain the love of this man's daughter, as he had so pompously put it. He smiled to himself and hid his smile from his companion.

After a few hours driving, passing through various small villages, Armand began to take a more detailed interest in the road and their actual position. He leant forward and slid open the glass partition between the passenger compartment and the driver and conducted a conversation with Philippe, which was way beyond the comprehension of Ernest. The car slowed down and Armand kept a close look-out on the scenery.

"What are you looking for?" Ernest asked.

"We are getting near to the village where she may have turned off. If I am right the ambulance should be near here. I want to see."

They approached a double bend, a strange occurrence in any event in this flat country of open and straight roads. The remains of a barn could be seen on the bend nearest to the direction they were travelling and, as they got to the entrance, the driver slowed down and stopped.

Beyond the gateway they could clearly see the upturned ambulance, and for a few moments they sat in silence looking at it, all of them with their hearts in their mouths. Eventually Ernest opened his door and slid out, followed by Armand, assisted by the driver, who had rushed around the vehicle to his master. They walked slowly in and up to the vehicle. Armand began, immediately, to look around for clues as to what precisely had happened, bending down to look beneath the upturned vehicle and swishing his stick in the long grass beside it.

Ernest regarded the scene impatiently, unsure of exactly what they were looking for, fearful of what, exactly, they might find. "Should we not be getting along to the hospital," he suggested.

Armand seemed preoccupied with examining the area but he looked up, his face thoughtful. "Yes, we must go now but..."

"But what?"

"Monsieur, if it is not Violet, we have to come back to here and look from here for her."

The fact that the girl in the hospital might not after all be Violet and the fact that Armand was preparing for such an eventuality struck home and the shock registered on Ernest's face. Oh God, what would he do?

His hopes had been rising steadily ever since the second letter, and to have them dashed now was more than he could bear. "It has to be her," he muttered as he waited, whilst Armand was helped back into the car. "It has to be her."

They started off again and very soon reached the village, where they had to turn south. The road here was busier than the one they had been travelling on and they were slowed down to a crawl as they battled against the tide of war going the other way. At times they had to stop as large vehicles and mule wagons blocked the narrow road, and several times they were forced to back up. It took over an hour to cover barely ten miles, but at last they reached what was quite obviously an American field hospital, the Stars and Stripes fluttering proudly from a flagpole set up outside.

The driver stopped the car and switched off the engine. Armand and Ernest sat still in the back, looking over to the entrance. That they were now here and that their hopes and fears could very soon be realised weighed heavily upon both of them. The driver slid back the partition. "Qu'est-ce que vous voulez monsieur?" he enquired.

Armand pulled himself together. He looked across at Ernest and touched his arm gently. "Shall we go monsieur?" Ernest nodded and Armand leant forward for the door handle. The driver got out and came around to hold open the door. For a moment the two men stood beside it, but then Ernest led the way into the entrance and through to the orderly room.

An orderly passed them on to an officer from the Medical Corps, who listened to their explanation as to why they were there and then led them out and down the walkway to a hut. He knocked, and the door was answered by a sister. The two of them had a hurried and whispered conversation whilst Ernest and Armand stood back.

"Mr Matthews!" the sister called out.

"Yes that's me, and this is... this is Violet's friend Monsieur Tie... Tie..."

"Taillefer," Armand volunteered. "May we see Violet? May we see the English girl?"

"Why yes of course," the sister replied. "We've bin expectin' you an' I can tell you that Violet is now talking some. Enough fer us to know she's your daughter."

"Oh thank God," Ernest breathed, and the two men exchanged a look of triumph.

"What precisely is wrong sister?" Ernest asked.

"Well," replied the sister, letting them into the hut and leading them along its length to a curtained-off end. "We're not entirely sure. She's had some sort of wound and that has led to a sickness. But she was gettin' better from that and physically she's quite strong. Trouble is that she seems to have had some sort of a shock which has made her sort of withdraw inside herself."

"Is she senseless?" queried Ernest.

"Oh no, not in that way. I mean she's eatin' fine and she's puttin' on weight since she got here, but she just won't talk apart from to finally tell us her name. She seems to just be locked in some sort of misery. Maybe you can perk her up some."

They reached a bed with the curtain drawn around it. The sister pulled it aside.

Violet was sitting quietly on a chair beside the bed, staring straight out into space. Her face was pale and drawn and she made no particular movement as they approached. But her eyes followed their progress.

"Violet darling. It's daddy," whispered Ernest. "How are you?" A small tear appeared at the corner of her eye and trickled down her cheek.

Her expression didn't change. He dropped to his knees in front of her and took her hands in his, looking up at her. "Please try to think Violet. It's daddy and..." He turned around and motioned Armand forward. "...and your friend Armand. We've come to take you home."

Armand came forward now and stood beside her chair. He bent down stiffly and kissed her on the cheek, tasting as he did the salty tear. "C'est moi cherie. Armand."

She looked down at her hands, noticing as if for the first time that they were being held. She raised her eyes and looked into Ernest's eyes. A flicker of recognition crossed her face and he smiled up at her. "Daddy?" She turned her head and looked up at Armand. His face, serious and concerned, looked down at her. "Armand?" she whispered.

"Oui, c'est moi. We have found you my Violet." He bent down and kissed her on her upturned lips. She reached up one hand and pulled him down towards her, but the pain of such a movement caused him to wince and he had to hold on to the back of her chair to prevent himself falling over.

"Careful darling," laughed Ernest, standing quickly and moving forward to support him. "He's a bit fragile you know. He should by all accounts still be in hospital. If it wasn't for wanting to find you he still would be." He assisted Armand across to the vacant bed and up on to it. Armand sat there, his legs dangling, looking at her in wonder.

"I thought everybody was dead," she whispered.

"No my love. Alive, as you see, but worried for you."

"I... I... how long have I been here?" said Violet.

"About a week and a half," piped up the sister, who had watched all of this from a distance, "and them's the first conversational words you've done spoken miss. Welcome back to the world."

Violet searched each face, trying to discover what had gone before. They observed her struggling with her memories and waited for them to flood back. Suddenly her face crumpled and she started to cry. Ernest moved forward to cuddle her but Armand put out his hand to stop him. "Let her remember," he whispered. Ernest gave him a look, questioning his judgement, but in the face of his determined stare stood back.

"They killed them all," she sobbed.

"Killed who? Who did they kill?" asked Armand. "Tell us Violet. Please."

Her head hung low as she began her story. Slowly at first, but then faster as she got into it. She told them of the ambush and the murder of the soldier. How she had made her way to the village and how the two women had saved her life. Her voice faltered as she described the rape and murder of the unknown woman and the emasculation and death of the assailant. The two men took a certain amount of grim satisfaction from her description of this, even though Ernest, unused to such matters, found it difficult to hear such words on his daughter's lips.

She reached the part of her rescue, and at that stage collapsed into uncontrollable tears. Both Armand and Ernest, and indeed the listening sister, feared then that something had befallen her following her rescue and jumped to the conclusion that perhaps she too had been raped. It was with some relief therefore that they heard out the rest of her story, when she finally managed to recover her composure.

"That explains the German card," Ernest whispered to Armand.

She heard and looked up. "You have it? Do you have the card? Only I promised Dieter I would write to his wife." She looked across at Armand. "He was such a nice man and they... they shouldn't have treated him like that. They really shouldn't." She stared at him, her eyes awash with tears, and he leant forward and took her hand.

"No, they should not have done that Violet. C'est la guerre." He shook his head sadly. "C'est la guerre."

The sister came forward now. "Come on now my dear, dry your eyes and have a little drink of this here orange juice. It'll make you feel better." She busied herself with tidying Violet up and getting her to drink and Ernest and Armand backed away slightly to talk.

"What shall we do now?" asked Ernest. "I can't take her back to England like this. It seems to me she still needs to recover her health."

"I have been thinking of this," said Armand thoughtfully. "I think it would be best to take her tomorrow to my house. Both of you to have a rest and recovery. Do you agree?"

"How far is it?"

"If we leave in the morning, we will be in Paris by the middle of the day and to my house by the night. After, I can take you to Le Havre for a boat to England."

Violet had obviously been listening, for she now intervened. "Please may we go tonight?" She looked up at the sister. "I am sorry sister, but I want to get away from soldiers and war. I've had... I've had enough."

The sister nodded her understanding. "Ain't that a fact girl. Ain't that a fact."

"Are you sure you're well enough to travel?" Ernest asked.

"I want to go," she pleaded. "Take me home please Armand. Take me home."

He walked across to her, and for the first time she noticed and realised that he was stiff and as yet not completely well himself. "Oh Armand you're naughty. You've discharged yourself, haven't you?"

He shrugged his shoulders guiltily.

"Yes he has Violet, and a good job too," said Ernest. "We would never have found you were it not for him. First of all his persistence and now his motor car."

"You have a car here Armand?"

"He has a car, and a chauffeur my dear," said Ernest.

She looked quizzically at him and then back to Armand. "A car and a chauffeur?" She smiled now for the first time. "A farmer?"

He grinned shyly and Ernest, watching this in amazement, realised that perhaps Violet knew nothing about this man's apparent wealth. Why should she? After all, in a hospital all were ostensibly equal apart from rank and... well, he had obviously been a bit secretive.

"I am a farmer," said Armand in a little boy hurt voice. "Several farmers. I have six farms and a few... some other things." He shrugged his shoulders again, returning her faintly taunting smile with a look of innocent guile. "Come! We must go. We can be in Paris tonight. We will make messages to the hospital and your mother and then we will go to my house."

"Have you anything with you?" Ernest asked.

"Only the clothes I stand in... stand in?" She turned to the sister. "Can I stand yet?"

"I don't know, let's try shall we, otherwise we'll get a wheelchair. Come to think of it, that would be best anyways. Come on let's try." She held out her hands and beckoned Violet to stand.

Violet pushed down hard on the arms of the chair and tried to raise herself. Her arms shook with the effort but gradually she managed to stand. She jerked forward the last little bit and stood for a moment, swaying before the sister grabbed and held on to her. "I think maybe you'll need a bit of time. Do you think you should see a doctor before you go? He may not want you to leave."

"Whether he wants me to leave or not I'm leaving," said Violet in a voice that brooked no argument. "But I think a wheelchair would be a good idea. Just to the motor car."

Armand smiled a proud smile at her and moved forward with Ernest to take over her support as the sister went off to fetch a wheelchair.

......

The journey south to Paris was fairly uneventful, and the only stops they had to make were for food, drink and the calls of nature. As Paris got closer, the signs of war lessened until, at the outskirts, the only clue to the momentous events to the north were the convoys heading in the opposite direction. Soldiers in the vehicles, most of whom appeared to be Americans, waved happily as they passed. Armand and Violet, who had witnessed at first hand what they were heading into, found it increasingly difficult to respond and took refuge in fitful sleep, whilst

Ernest, and to some extent Philippe, never seemed to tire of returning their greetings.

As they approached Paris, and the Eiffel Tower came into view, Ernest could not resist a thrill of anticipation. He had never before been abroad, and now here he was in Paris. Elsie and Alice would clamour to hear his descriptions when he got home, and he paid particular attention to every detail and impression, willing it all to memory for them. Elsie and Alice! He must let them know everything was all right and that Violet was safe. He must tell them where they were going.

"Er, Armand?" he said to the younger man sitting on the other side of his daughter, holding her hand.

"Um yes... oh I am sorry I was asleep. Shhh, Violet is sleeping, I think we should not wake her."

"Yes. Sorry," Ernest whispered. "It's just that I need to send a message to my wife and to the hospital to tell everybody that she's all right."

"I had thought of that and Philippe will drive first to the Ministry and I will make the message."

"Thank you Armand. Sorry to wake you." Ernest sat back in his seat. Damned fine fellow this Armand. Damned fine fellow, he thought.

The streets of the capital were alive with civilians and large groups of off-duty soldiers of all nations mingling there in the warmth of the evening. Far from giving the impression of a city which several times in the last few years had been threatened by conquest, it seemed more to revel in the frisson of war and delight in the entertainment of its off-duty participants. At times they had to slow down to a near stop, not for convoys of war machinery but for bands of laughing and singing soldiers, usually accompanied by bevies of glamorous young ladies.

Ernest beamed and smiled joyfully at them all, but Armand and Violet, awoken by all of the clamour, could not bring themselves to such jollity in the midst of what they had both experienced and knew continued. Besides which, both of them had to admit that they were by now extremely tired and their respective wounds were starting to hurt.

They slowed and turned into a side street and thence through an archway and into an open courtyard.

"Your father will want to send some messages to your mother and the hospital from here and then we will go to the hotel," Armand said to Violet. "Do you want to stay here or do you want to come inside?"

"I think I'd better stay here even if your driver... sorry, what's his name?"

"Philippe."

"Philippe. Yes. Well he might be able to help me just stand for a bit by the door."

"He will," said Armand. Philippe came around and helped him out as Armand whispered some instructions to him. He nodded his understanding and Armand joined Ernest and walked into the huge building.

Violet sat in the car with the door open, watching them go. She noticed Armand's tired, stiff gait and felt a pang of pity for this brave man who had so selflessly taken himself from his own sick bed to find her. The horror of the past few weeks seemed to be receding fast in the presence of, and with the help of, both him and her dear father. She wondered at her mental weakness over the past weeks. She had seen so many horrible things. And yet it would seem that she had a breaking point and the... the death of poor Dieter had obviously been it. She felt slightly ashamed now, but at the time and afterwards she had felt that she really had had enough and could take no more. Dear daddy. He must have been distraught when she was missing. Pride in him and their love for each other overwhelmed her. He had come alone to this foreign land to search for her. He hadn't known that Armand would be here to help and that he would have a motor car and driver. Now there's a thought. Armand was a naughty man.

A farmer he had said. Growing asparagus he'd said. Did he think that she would think any less of him if he were a wealthy man. Surely not? She would have to have a talk with him. Dear Armand.

It was perhaps no more than half an hour, but it seemed longer before the two men returned to the car and, by then, a very tired Violet. They were accompanied by a large besuited gentleman who shook Ernest's hand warmly before turning to Armand. He bowed slightly before proffering his hand and bidding them all "bon voyage".

"Who is this man Armand?" thought Violet. She exchanged a look with her father and he shrugged his shoulders, returning her questioning with his own.

They drove for a short while before crossing the Seine to the Boulevard St. Germaine. Just past the junction with the Boulevard St. Michel the car pulled up in front of a hotel and a uniformed doorman came forward to open the doors.

"Ah Monsieur Armand," he said as he peered in. "Bon soir."

"Bon soir Jean," Armand replied as he painfully dismounted. He directed him to the luggage and called across to Philippe to fetch a wheelchair from the foyer. In the next few minutes and hours, Violet and Ernest found themselves whirled into a world of luxury such as they had only previously dreamt of. A maid assisted Violet into a hot bath and waited patiently as she lazily scrubbed and splashed herself, the hot water freeing her from all those years of privation and discomfort. When she had finished she helped her out, towelled her dry and then dressed her in a towelling robe before supporting her as she hobbled to one of the two comfortable-looking chairs beside a small table, where she sat quietly for a while, lost in her own quiet thoughts. There was a knock at the door. "Come in," she called. The door opened and Armand came in followed by Ernest. She made as if to rise but they both motioned her to stay where she was.

"We are going down to have a meal in the restaurant," said Ernest. "But we thought that you will prefer to have your meal in your room."

"Yes, I would like that thank you. I'm very tired and besides I've nothing to wear that would be at all suitable."

"If you will forgive the liberty Violet, I have asked that somebody come and take some..." He made the mime of stretching out a tape measure, searching for the word.

"Measurements?"

"Oui. Measurements, and to show you some pictures for some dresses and coats."

"But Armand why should you?" said Violet.

"Why should I not?" He smiled and she smiled back up at him.

The two men left the room, and before long another knock at the door revealed a waiter with a tray of food, the like of which she had only previously imagined. Wartime Paris certainly didn't stint on the creature comforts. When her meal was finished, a small wizened old man knocked and entered and showed her books and patterns, from which she picked two dresses, two pairs of new boots, undergarments and a hat and coat. They were promised for the morning, and at last Violet was able to call the maid and get to her bed, where she fell into a deep, dreamless sleep.

As morning broke she lay there, reluctant at first to leave the vast bed's warmth and comfort. The maid came in and assisted her to the bathroom and then helped her to dress in her new attire. As she put on the new clothes and examined herself in the mirror, her sense of wonder at what was now happening to her increased, and by the time she was ready she could hardly contain her anticipation for the journey ahead.

......

That they were getting near to their destination became apparent through Armand's increasing excitement as he pointed out landmarks and buildings of distinction. They entered Chateauneuf from the direction of Orleans, the narrow winding street opening dramatically out into the wide expanse of green in front of the majestic iron gates leading through into the park and gardens by the Hotel de Ville. The road turned slightly and they passed the beautiful church by the old market before turning down the narrow street with its pretty shops on either side. Down through the town they drove, past the new market, past the road up to the station and on out into the countryside again, with Armand keeping up a running commentary on all they were witnessing. At the next junction they turned right towards Sully and ran down the hill and on to the level floodplain of the Loire, with its neat patchwork of carefully tilled fields displaying patterns of various crops, some of which Violet could recognise but others of which were new to her.

"Where is the Loire river?" Ernest enquired. "I thought that we would see it from here."

"It is just behind those trees, but you cannot see it because of the... I don't know what it is in English. We call it a levee. Napoleon made it dug, a long hill all along to prevent the floods."

"Must have taken some digging."

"Yes, but it stops the floods and it is far enough from the river to leave it to be wild."

"You love this country, don't you Armand?" said Violet, touching and gripping his arm.

He turned to her, his eyes bright with excitement like a small boy. "Yes I do. As I love life and..." He glanced across at Ernest and hesitated before adding, "...as I love you."

Ernest felt a bit of a gooseberry, especially as Violet, unselfconsciously, leant forward and kissed Armand full on the lips. Although, to his amazement, he felt no particular embarrassment. He simply felt as if he were intruding on their privacy, and the revelation of his feelings added to his wonder at the whole turn of events. He recalled how days ago he had been in the depths of despair, terrified that his daughter was dead or lost to him. The anguish that he and Elsie had shared was still palpable to him. He experienced a pang of guilt that he was now here with Violet enjoying her company and the... yes, it had to be admitted... the man in her life, whilst at home Elsie remained in her ignorant misery. When would she get the message? Today? No, surely not possible. The Ministry they had called at had promised to see that it was sent with all speed, but it would surely be several days until the good news reached home. Would she understand the course of action they had taken? He had told her in the message that Violet had been ill but was recovering, and he had explained that they were going to a friend's home in order that she could recuperate. But none of that could possibly give the full explanation, and in reality would raise as many questions as were answered. He would not stay long. He must go back soon. But what of Violet? That she and this man were forming a deep attachment was perfectly obvious. That Elsie would expect Violet to return as soon as she was able was also quite apparent. What to do?

If Violet went with him to England in the next few days, would that jeopardise any burgeoning relationship with Armand? Probably not. But was it worth the risk?

After all, it wasn't the same situation as had led to his daughter's indiscretion with that poor chap Balfour. You bloody hypocrite Matthews. Poor chap Balfour? You hated him and... yes, you drove him away. Well he would have gone anyway eventually. 'I don't hate him anymore. I don't... even if I ever really did,' he thought. However, the result of their affair rendered Violet... well it made the prospect of marriage in the normal sense difficult... especially as the child would have to be acknowledged. Finchley would be buzzing with gossip over that one and... well let it! 'I nearly lost the love and affection of my daughter. I nearly damned well lost my daughter. and by God I'm not going to risk that again.'

His jumbled thoughts were interrupted as, just before the village of Germigny-des- Pres, the car slowed almost to a stop, before taking a sharp right-hand turn on to a very narrow lane which snaked through two double bends, over a narrow bridge and on to the hamlet of Le Mesnil. They swept through and then on and to the right, towards a belt of trees. A brick wall rose alongside the lane and then merged into a range of barns and outbuildings presenting small fortified windows to the lane. A driveway led through an archway in the central towered section, and for a brief moment, as the car slowed, Violet and Ernest thought that they were going through. But the car swept past and on to another set of huge wrought iron gates set between two rounded ivy-covered towers.

The car swung left and then right and in between the gates. Violet gasped as the short tree-lined driveway revealed the building before them. Ernest was stunned into silence.

Before them the chateau stretched out to either side and up and beyond their immediate view. Huge French doors, their shutters thrown wide open, marched in symmetry along its flanks, which were contained at either end by square towers, standing like giant architectural bookends. Violet craned her neck to look upwards. Three floors rose majestically to the slated roof, from which, at various points, dormer windows projected. Her gaze travelled back down, noting the mellow pink bricks, the creamy stone detailing and the iron cage hanging flower baskets planted with cascades of trailing greenery and flowers, matching the planting in the window boxes below. To either side of the smooth gravelled driveway there were green lawns interplanted with beds of sculpted box and yew.

"Oh Armand it's lovely," Violet gasped. "You never told me. You never so much as hinted, you rascal."

"It was not so beautiful to me before. With you here the crown has its jewel."

"Armand you're a one. You really are." She dug him playfully in the ribs, this time carefully avoiding the sensitive areas. "All that business about being all alone when you went home. You wicked fellow."

He threw his hands in the air in surrender. "But I am alone without you. I did not say I would be helpless... I just have told you that my sister was in the next village and my parents were dead." She laughed now and Ernest joined in, picking up on the tale that was being revealed. "All alone with an army of servants. Mr asparagus farmer?"

He resigned himself to his guilt, jutting out his bottom lip like a small boy caught out in his deceit. "It is possible to be alone with many people. Anyway there is asparagus."

She giggled playfully. "You're forgiven Armand dear... but on one condition. That you promise to show me everything in this wonderful house."

"I promise. As soon as you are well we will explore together. Now we arrive."

The car stopped in front of the entrance doors and an older couple flung them open and descended the few steps, the woman leading with her hands raised in the air in joyous greeting and the man coming forward, a broad welcoming smile on his face. The woman reached the motor car first and opened the door, crying out Armand's name. She seemed to realise at the last moment that he was not alone in the car and stood back slightly, still beaming as Philippe came around the car and made ready to assist. Armand took his hand and alighted from the vehicle to be embraced by the woman, whilst from behind her the man reached forward to grab his hand. At length, when the greetings were over, Armand released himself and turned back to the car, from which Violet was being helped.

Ernest got out of the other door and came around just in time to help Philippe with Violet, and the two of them stood either side, supporting her as Armand prepared to make the introductions. "Jean-Claude et Marie. Permettez-moi de presenter mes chers amis, Mademoiselle Violet Matthews et son pere Monsieur Matthews." He turned back to Violet and her father. "This is Jean-Claude and his wife Marie, who look after me and my house."

He was virtually brushed aside by Marie, who now bustled forward, brushing Ernest and Philippe aside to envelope Violet in an embrace, kissing her twice on each cheek as she continued a stream of excited conversational greetings. Left without support and in the face of this onslaught, Violet nearly collapsed within her grasp and would have fallen if Ernest had not grabbed her around the waist and pulled her close. Marie's hand flew to her mouth as she realised Violet's frailty. She turned and issued a stream of instructions and exhortations to both Jean-Claude and Philippe. Jean-Claude obediently relieved Ernest, and he and Philippe virtually carried her within the chateau.

Ernest stood by the car watching his daughter being taken through the doors, and for a brief moment felt a little left out. Suddenly the woman seemed to regain her awareness of him. She turned, and to his astonishment he received the same attention as his daughter, right down to the ritual, and to him totally unfamiliar, kissing. She released him as Jean-Claude, relieved of his burden, came out again. For one panic-stricken moment Ernest thought that he too was going to kiss him, and it was with great relief that he accepted the proffered hand, responding to the incomprehensible greetings with smiles and nods of agreement. A smiling Armand rescued him and the two of them mounted the steps together and entered the house.

......

"I really should have gone with him, you know," said Violet as Armand came back into the room and took up the seat beside her on the couch.

"You are not well to go yet. He wanted to go and you can go when you are better."

"But Armand, I *am* well enough. I can walk... oh I can't run yet, but I could have gone."

He leant across, took her hand and raised it to his lips. "Do you really want to go from here now. From me?"

She smiled and caressed his cheek. "No my dearest, I do not want to leave you but I am... well I am being a little irresponsible. I'm still a

VAD. My mother must be beyond her wits with worry. There's still a war on and I just stay here as if... as if I'm on holiday."

"Do you not believe that you deserve a holiday?"

"Armand they all deserve a holiday. You know that, but there's a war on and the men have to fight as you did and the women have to do their bit as well."

"Even the married women?"

"Even the married women. What's that got to do with it?"

"Will you marry me?"

She stared at him in disbelief. Whatever turn she had expected the conversation to take this was not one she had remotely envisaged. She knew the answer of course, but she just hadn't been expecting the question. "Armand... I don't know what to say... I..."

"Say yes, of course." He took both her hands in his, holding them firmly in his lap and looking intently into her face.

She smiled at him, her mind in a whirl of delight and... what was it... fear? No, not fear but... well, yes, it was in a way. She thought she knew all there was to know about him, but she had thought that before at the hospital and she had been wrong. And him? Did he really know what he was taking on? He was a respectable man and she was... well she was a fallen woman really. She released her hands from his grip, stood with difficulty and crossed to the light.

She stared out through the window to the grounds beyond, one part of her brain registering the view before her of the lawns rolling gently down to the lake and trees at the bottom, whilst the other struggled to come to terms with the enormity of what had just happened.

"Am I rejected?" His voice sounded strained and betrayed the fear he undoubtedly felt. At the sound and tone of it she snapped out of her own turmoil. She turned, her features still invisible to him.

"Oh Armand. No you are not rejected. I love you but... are you sure? I'm not the best you could expect. I... I have a history, which you know of and..."

"...and you are the woman I want to marry."

She crossed to him and sat beside him, taking his hands and looking earnestly up into his concerned face. "Armand you are a rich man and I am from... well... we're not poor by any means but we have nothing to even approach what you have and..."

"You do not have to pay me to marry you. It is free."

For a second she struggled to ascertain what he meant. Then she laughed out loud. "Silly, you know what I mean. Your life here and your connections are very grand, very important, and are you sure I am the right person to be..."

"My life here is nothing... it is empty without you and I am sure of what I want. I want you to be married with me."

"What about your family? What will they say about me, a foreigner with a baby?"

"They can say what they wish to say. My sister has not been to see us here since we are back. She does not care for me and I do not care what she thinks. It is what we think that is important and I think that we must be married."

"Yes."

"Pardon?"

"Yes. I will marry you Armand."

He gasped and pulled her up as he too stood. They kissed then, long and tenderly, in the soft light of the huge room. Eventually they separated and walked hand in hand across to the window. "What about my father?"

"I asked him if he was happy for this before he went away." She turned to him, laughing up into his face, which bore once more that boyish guilty look he adopted when caught out.

"You old rogue Armand. You've been planning all of this, haven't you?"

"Is it so wrong to do?"

"No. No it's not. It's just that... oh never mind. And what did my father say?"

"He said that he was happy if you said 'yes'. He wished me the luck."

Violet looked out into the gardens again. Dear daddy. That's why he had insisted she stay, saying that she could come when she was fully better and that mother would understand. He had been hoping that the romance would... had it been a romance? Not in the conventional sense... not even in the same sense as that which she had had with Frank. With Armand it had been... well it had been as if they were both lost in the world and had come home to each other. Fireworks had not gone off, but the home fire was lit and they had both come to it.

"Will we marry here in France or in England?"

"I do not know. Where would you prefer?"

"I would prefer not to be married in Finchley, but I would like my parents to be with me and..."

"You would like the little boy to be with you. Yes?"

She nodded silently and he cupped her chin in his hand and looked into her eyes. "Wherever we are married your son must be there." She flung herself into his arms and the two of them stood holding each other in silence for some time, each lost within their own thoughts and happiness.

......

Armand lay awake in his bed, looking out into the dark empty space of the huge room. His back ached slightly as it nearly always did, as if a small worm was turning within him, and he reached behind and rubbed the area lightly. The room was hot and the heavy draped curtains framing the deep shuttered windows hung still. He flung the top cover from him and lay on the bed naked, except for the thin sheet.

In the gloom he could make out the features of the huge room. The windows. The door to his dressing room and toilet and the door to the long passageway leading across the front of the building and on to the room where Violet lay.

The weeks since his proposal had flown by in a whirlwind of romance, discovery and anticipation. They had told the staff first, and the delight of them all, but in particular Marie, had been an additional joy to him and a great relief to Violet, who had strangely expected some resistance from others. If she had expected it from his sister then she was not to be disappointed. Her reaction had indeed predictably been hostile. On her one visit she had taken virtually no notice of Violet, insisting on speaking colloquial French very fast in an obvious effort to exclude her from any conversation, as she objected to the whole idea of her brother marrying a foreigner.

He had of course given her short shrift and she had collected her silent and docile husband and departed, leaving Armand and Violet convulsed with laughter as soon as Jean-Claude had shut the door on them.

He smiled now and chuckled to himself in the darkness at the memory of it. If she objected now, what would she say when it became known that there was a young boy.

The young boy. Not a baby, as they had always discussed. He would be four years old next birthday and his character would already be developing. What would he be like, this child of Violet and Frank? His age would mean that he would probably be very unhappy at first, separated from the family he had grown up with. Violet had, he knew, not addressed that probability, and really at this juncture he did not want to spoil her happiness, a happiness that had increased immeasurably with the news that at last the war was over.

That the war was won in official terms meant little to them, but that it meant that Violet was therefore free of the nagging feeling of guilt at her absence was a massive relief. Oh they tried to share the joy with all about them, but privately they agreed that for them, at least, there could never really be a winner. A huge chapter was ending in history and in their own lives, and the only real sense they had from it all was that they could now, at last, move forward into that new era together.

They had decided that they would go to England for Christmas and that Armand would stay with her parents whilst she travelled on to Devon to collect the child. Then he would travel back to France and she would follow two weeks later with her parents for the wedding, which would take place in Germigny.

The door squeaked on its hinges as it opened, and he sat up in bed to see who was coming. A dark shape moved quietly across the room and stood to the side of the bed, outlined against the thin light filtering through the slatted shutters. "Armand," she whispered.

"Oui c'est moi Violet. What is the matter?"

He held the sheet up to his naked chest. She moved closer and stood immediately beside the bed. He could smell the scent of her body and hear her soft breathing.

She reached up to her throat and unlaced the neck of her nightdress. Her hands dropped to her sides and she stood there silent for a few moments. He felt the constriction in his throat and the fire rush into him as he reached down and held the sheet aside.

Violet lifted the nightdress over her head and let it drop to the floor. Naked, she stood there for a moment before slipping in beside him, moaning softly as she felt the heat of his body and the excitement in his loins.

"Armand," she breathed. "Armand."

He cuddled her close and then held her as he rolled over, covering her body with his in a gentle flood of passion, which rose until it eclipsed all reason, memory, pain and doubt.

In the morning as day broke, she kissed his still sleeping form and stole from his room. All her wars, around her and within her, were now over.

January 1919

Frank knelt on the cold leather of the back seat of the taxi, staring helplessly through the oval rear window at the receding figures of Florrie and Joe. He wiped his eyes with the back of his hand to clear his distorted vision, but in moments the tears came back to ruin his last sighting of them. Tight-chested, his head pounding with fear and unhappiness, he gave up and buried his head in his crossed arms on the rear shelf. A hand touched his shoulder and he flinched and drew away.

"Frank. Frank darling... let me help," said Violet, quietly through her own tears.

He turned his head, exposing one tearful eye. "I want my mummy."

"I know you do darling but... there's nothing to be..." She hesitated, unsure of her ground and unwilling to be seen by him to be laying down too many strictures. "Do you want a cuddle?"

"I want my mummy to cuddle me," he wailed.

"Frank?" she asked.

"What?" came the muffled response from a face buried deep within his crossed arms.

"I want a cuddle." He looked up. She was crying. Why was she crying? She hadn't just lost her mummy and daddy, had she? "I need a cuddle Frank." She held out her arms to him and he turned and buried himself in her lap, sobbing. 'How strange,' she thought. 'The first time I have held him since he was a tiny baby and yet... and yet. Oh it is so wonderful. Here am I, the cause of all his misery, and yet we can still take comfort from each other.

She had deceived herself and others when she had so easily given up the child four years ago, and to have continued that mistake could never have been right, whatever the short-term grief that they all must now face. Armand... dear Armand. He had tried to prepare her for some rejection and a good job too, otherwise she would have given up at the first onset of the boy's enmity. She was not going to be distracted in her purpose. The guilt that had haunted her through the long years of the war was assuaged and she would not allow it to return. Armand would support her and he would win over Frank as much as would the very adventure of their journeys.

Thinking of Armand brought on a feeling of calm, and she gently stroked the boy's head as he lay there on the seat, his head buried in her lap. Armand would be waiting for them at Paddington with her dear father. The two of them seemed to have become the firmest of friends and Ernest had purloined Armand for much of the time to take him around the capital, showing him the sights. That is, when he could be released from the clutches of Elsie and, to some extent, Alice, who had immediately adopted and embraced him as their own superhero who had, as far as they were concerned, won the war single-handed.

What they would think of him when they eventually got to France and saw just how important he was defied imagination. If his Gallic charm and exotic accent alone had won him, their undying devotion, then the sight of the chateau, would have him elevated to a deity. Her brow furrowed a little. He had been very tired in the evenings and she had had to speak to her father on one occasion and remind him of his frailty. At times she would notice his grimace of pain and he would instinctively clutch at his renal area before recovering his composure, looking around to check if his actions had been noticed. Maybe there was a slight infection? She would arrange for him to see Doctor Crowe when she got back. Maybe she was worrying unduly? Maybe he was just tired? Maybe it was all part of the healing process? Still, better be safe than sorry. They had a pretty big journey ahead of them and then the wedding.

The wedding! Her heart leapt at the thought of it. Elsie, who had responded to her safety and then to her eventual arrival with a new lease of life and health, had thrown herself, with Alice's help, into the preparations for the journey to France and the wedding itself.

Initial disappointment that Violet would not be married in Finchley had dissipated when Armand had arrived, and been replaced with the excitement and glamour of the occasion.

Violet ruffled the boy's hair anew. He was awake but just lay there. Dry-eyed now, thank God, his thumb stuck firmly in his mouth. She would have to see if she could break that particular habit. But not just yet. Frank would be an important part of the wedding. He was to be her pageboy and he would remain at her side for the whole of the ceremony. Armand had insisted on that one. "We should make him feel very important," he had said.

Elsie. She still had to be told about Frank. Should they have told her before she left to collect the child? Maybe. Maybe her father had changed his mind and given her warning of what Violet would be bringing? How would she take it? Oh she would dote on the child, but she would be hurt that she had never been told. How could they have told her? When the child was born the intention had been to hide his very existence, and when they had decided otherwise they had not felt her well enough for the responsibility she would undoubtedly have insisted upon.

The countryside gave way to the city, and as the boy became aware of the noise and the buildings obscuring the skyline, he lifted his head and finally sat up, looking out from side to side at the unfamiliar sights and sounds. They pulled into the station forecourt and he held her hand in wonder as they passed through the gates and over the bridge to the London-bound platform. "Which way does it come from?" he asked excitedly.

She pointed down the track in the direction the train would be coming from. "If you keep a look-out down there you'll see it coming very soon, but don't go near the edge. When you see it coming let me know."

She went across and sat on the bench. Quite frankly she would have been a lot happier in the waiting room out of the chill, but at that stage in their relationship felt it important to keep the young boy amused. As long as he had something to excite him he seemed able to lift himself from any despair.

She watched him standing there on the platform in front of her. A good-looking boy... not pretty, but ruggedly boyish. His jacket was buttoned up neatly, but his cap was already askew on his head and his socks had slipped down his calves and rucked up at the top of his boots. "Pull your socks up Frank," she called softly. He looked across at her and then lifted first one leg and then the other to hoist the offending garments as he continued to scan the tracks.

"It's coming! It's coming!" he cried as the steam and smoke of the approaching train became visible in the distance. He ran back to stand by Violet and she held on to his hand as he stared in wonder at the approaching beast. It passed them in a thundering, roaring cloud of steam and smoke, with Frank standing there transfixed by this vision. He turned his wonder-filled face up to Violet's. "Cor that was smashing. Can we see it again?"

She laughed lightly and pulled him closer. "We have to get on now, but you'll see it when we get off at Paddington."

"I thought we was going to London."

"You thought we were going to London," she corrected, "...and we are. London is a very big city and it has... I don't know... well five or six big train stations with trains going in all directions to all parts of the country. The one we are going to is called Paddington."

He looked at her, understanding her words but unable to fully comprehend the enormity of them. All of his senses seemed heightened by this unfolding world before him, banishing all sadness. He watched as she instructed the porter to place the heavier bags in the van and excitedly mounted the steps and entered the carriage.

As the whistle blew and the train jerked forward and then gradually picked up traction and moved off, he clasped her hand and stared out of the window, his mouth open, his eyes alight. She squeezed his hand back, pulled him to her and kissed his forehead as she took off his cap and unbuttoned his jacket. Not for one moment did he take his eyes off what was happening all around him, as his old life slipped away on the tracks behind them.

......

"Let me and Frank go in alone first please daddy, and then you and Armand can follow, in say... ten minutes."

Ernest smiled at her and squeezed her shoulder. He pushed open the parlour door and stood back as Violet and Frank went through, before quietly shutting it again.

Elsie was sitting in her chair by the fire reading the newspaper. She looked up as Violet approached and put down the paper. "Oh darling you're back. Come in and sit down. Does Alice know you're here? I'll ask her if she'd mind..." She stopped, noticing the small boy for the first time. "And who's this little fellow?" she enquired, rising to her feet and coming forward. "Do we know you young man?" She bent down and placed her thin hand on his cold, rosy cheek, smiling down into his slightly troubled face.

"Mummy," said Violet quietly. "Mummy this is Frank."

"Pleased to meet you Frank. We don't often have gentlemen callers... well leastwise not until recently." She turned and winked up at Violet. "Come over here young man and sit by the fire and let's get those outside clothes off you while we have a cup of tea with us or you'll never feel the benefit when you go back out."

She took his hand, as Violet released him, and led him gently across to the fire, where she proceeded to unbutton his coat. "And where have you sprung from my lad?" she asked. Frank looked up at Violet and his bottom lip began to tremble. He didn't know what to say. Why did they ask him all the questions? They were the grown-ups and they should know, shouldn't they? Violet went forward and held him tight in front of her as Elsie sat down, unsure of why her warm greetings to this young visitor should so unnerve him.

"Mother..." There was a long pause, during which time seemed almost in suspension as eyes flicked from one face to another seeking answer, aid and understanding. "Mummy. There's no way of saying this other than to... to just tell you right out." She swallowed hard and looked down. Elsie stared back at her, her hands frozen in the act of unbuttoning the boy's coat. Violet forced the words from her mouth, desperate to have them out in the open now. "Frank is my child... my baby."

There was a silence in the room as the two women stared deep into each other's eyes, one scanning, searching for truth and comprehension, the other willing the former to believe and understand. Frank stood between the two of them, feeling the buttress of Violet's supporting legs behind him, whilst in front the thin hands of the older woman dropped, at last, from his coat buttons and into her lap. Why didn't she know about him? If Violet was his mother, why didn't her mummy know about him?

The door opened and Alice came into the room with a tray of tea. "Ah there you are Miss Violet, Ernest... your father said you'd be in here and suggested you might like a pot of... hallo, who's this?" She put the tray down and stood in front of Frank, looking down into his face. "Well hallo there little one, what's your name then?"

"My name's Frank."

"Frank, is it? Well Frank, how about you come with me and we'll get that coat off you and see if we can't find something nice in the kitchen for you." She looked at Violet and Violet understood that she knew and that she had been sent in for this very purpose. Elsie remained seated, still staring at the boy.

"Yes Frank, why don't you go with Alice and she'll see if you... well she'll look after you while I talk to my mummy here." The boy looked up at her, a worried look on his face, unwilling now to be passed on to someone else, yet attracted by the thought of goodies in the kitchen. Violet reassured him. "Just for a moment Frank. She'll bring you back in a moment, won't you Alice?"

"I most certainly will. Come on Frank my love, come with Alice for a moment." She held out her hand to him and he took it and followed her. "I expect you need the toilet as well young man, don't you?" He nodded as they left the room.

Violet knelt down in front of her mother and took her hands. "I'm sorry mummy. I wanted... meant to tell you before but... well we thought it best not to..."

"You hid him from me. Why?"

"I hid him from myself mother."

"But why? Why didn't Armand tell me you had his son? I've... I've made him welcome in my house as your future husband..."

"He's not the father!"

"Not the..."

"No mummy. Frank's nearly four years old. I only met Armand for the first time in late 1917."

Elsie looked down into the fire, thoughts tumbling about in her head. She looked back up at Violet. "Well that's... that's before you went... no it's before... when you went away." Realisation began to dawn on her.

She swivelled in her chair and faced Violet directly, leaning forward to look deep within her eyes as she spoke, searching for the full truth. "It's when you went away to the country after your fall, isn't it? Did you... were you... did something happen to you whilst you were away ill?"

Violet clasped her mother's thin hands and shuffled closer to her. "No mummy, it was before that. I went away because I fell, but I fell because I... because I had received notice that Frank was dead."

"Dead? But he's here. I've just seen him. What do you mean dear, I'm getting quite confused."

"Frank Balfour, the man who worked in daddy's office was baby Frank's daddy. He was killed... he was... you remember mummy, I told you he was killed when I came home."

"Why yes dearest, but I didn't know that he was..." She looked up at the ceiling as if searching for some sort of help and then back down at her daughter. "I didn't know that you were... oh Violet, how could you?"

"I loved him mummy and he was going off to war. We were going to be married when he came home but... well you know the rest."

"And your father. What on earth is he going to say? He'll... well I don't quite know what he'll do when..."

"He knows mummy. He's always known. It was he who arranged for me to go to the country to have the child, and it was he who arranged for the fostering of the child until I reclaimed him yesterday."

"He knew? He knew without telling me?"

"He felt it was for the best mother. When he first knew he was very angry and he would not acknowledge the child and would have nothing to do with him. I... I went along with that. That's why I went away again, why I went into nursing. Trying to hide my shame and guilt... until Armand made me..."

"Armand knows of this child?" Elsie's face grew even more perplexed, and her darting eyes betrayed the emotions within her.

Violet's tone softened. "Yes he knows, and he has been looking forward so much to meeting him and to being a father to him."

Elsie smiled. "He's a lovely man. Such a gentleman, even though he's not British."

"Mother," Violet chided.

"Oh I'm sorry dear. I didn't mean to be disparaging. It's just... well you know."

"I know," said Violet, rising back into her chair and leaning forward to attend to the tea, "but it's not that far away mummy. You'll see when you come." She handed a cup to Elsie, who then noticed for the first time that there were three more cups on the tray.

"I see that the others are obviously waiting to join us," she said conspiratorially.

Violet looked a trifle guilty. She stood, crossed to the door and opened it. "You can come in now. Tea's in here," she called.

Both men came into the room. Armand hung back by the door with

Violet, but Ernest crossed to his wife and stood before her looking down at her.

"Why did you not tell me beloved?" she asked quietly.

He dropped to one knee in front of her and rested his hands on her lap. "Because at first I did not want anyone in the world to know and later... later I was worried that you would take it all upon yourself when you were not well."

"But Ernest, he is my... our grandchild."

"I know my dear. I know. Please forgive me and let us try to make amends."

"The fault is mine," interjected Violet from the door. Elsie and Ernest both swivelled round to observe her, pity and pain mixed in their expressions.

"No! No! I'll not go down that road again Violet," protested Ernest as he stood up clumsily. "It damn near tore us apart before and I'll..."

"Where is my lovely grandson?" Elsie interrupted. "He must be quite confused and I think it behoves all of us to make him feel at ease and as happy as we can." Violet and Ernest looked at her in wonder.

Armand, standing by the door, coughed. "Bravo. If you do not mind me saying, it must be a strange thing for you to find out this news Mrs Matthews."

"Elsie please. Please call me Elsie."

"Elsie... it must be a shock for you, but I think it can be a very nice shock to find you have a so nice little grandson... and for me there must be no blame. We are all here together... alive thanks God... and we all must to be a happy family and to look forward now to our wedding and our future. Yes?"

Elsie rose and crossed the room to him. "Yes," she said. "Yes, yes, yes." She hugged him and he kissed her on both cheeks.

Violet held her breath as she turned to her. Elsie stood for a moment, scanning her daughter's face, then she smiled and the two of them embraced silently, rocking from side to side. For almost the first time in her life, certainly the first in her memory, Violet found comfort, sanctuary and loving forgiveness in her mother's arms. Across her mother's shoulder she could see Ernest, watching the two of them with tears in his eyes. Armand crossed the room and stood beside him, holding his arm.

There was a soft knock on the door, which opened to reveal Alice standing there with Frank held before her. Elsie released Violet, and taking her hand the two of them crossed to the door. "Hallo again darling," said Elsie. "Come on in. Come over here and tell me all you saw today." She held out her hand and Frank took it.

......

The train pulled into Tenterden station and Frank was first at the door, impatient to be out, to run along the platform and see the engine. "Be careful Frank," Violet called. "Don't lean out, and wait until the train stops before you open the door."

"Yes Violet," he called back, his hair and voice swept away in the wind. They had decided that Violet was the best name for him to use, even though Ernest had expressed some surprise. Mummy was still reserved in Frank's mind for Florrie, and Violet had no desire to supplant his feelings for her. The train stopped and Frank fumbled with the handle, trying to turn it with both hands as he reached out over the cill. He couldn't do it, but stood back as the station master stepped forward and opened the door, carefully swinging it back to its full opening before standing back and calling out, "Tenterden. All change. Tenterden."

Violet smiled to herself. It seemed a lifetime ago that she had heard those same words from this same man. Would he remember her? She hoped not. Oh, all Tenterden and indeed Rolvenden would know very shortly. But for now all she wanted was just to get to Jesse's front door with the minimum of fuss. She picked up their two large bags, placing them by the door before alighting and helping

Frank from the train. Then she reached back into the carriage and pulled out the bags and placed them on the platform.

"Tickets please," said the station master. Violet handed him the two tickets and the ritual he had carried out all those years ago was re-enacted in front of her fascinated and amused face. When he had finished and the void tickets were safely disposed of in the bin, she turned to him. "Is there any chance of a taxi?"

"Yes ma'am," he replied. "You should be able to get one outside, or else if you go up to the top of the road."

She looked down at the heavy bags. "Is there anywhere I can leave these while I search for one?"

"Yes ma'am, in the ticket office."

She thanked him and, picking up a bag in each hand, called Frank to follow her. "Can I help?" the small boy asked, turning away from staring down the platform at the engine and running back to join her.

"Yes," came the reply, but in truth his assistance when it came was more of a hindrance. Still, she let him try and was glad that he had offered. They stowed the bags in the office and walked out into the open and along to the end of the station yard to the road. The engine huffed and wheezed at the end of the platform in front of the closed level crossing gates and she slowed down to let the small boy look up at it in wonder.

Hand in hand they walked up the hill, and she marvelled at how little everything had changed. At the top she looked through the windows of the public house. No revellers there today. How many of those laughing souls were forever extinguished in the mud of Europe? How many were back now, broken in body and spirit?

She shivered and the boy looked up at her, seeing the sadness in her face. "What's the matter Violet?"

"Nothing darling," she said, hugging him close to her. "Nothing. Only a bad memory. Come on, let's look for that taxi. Can you see one?"

He looked up and down the street searching, trying hard to be of use to this woman he was undoubtedly becoming very fond of and who had shown him more in a few days than he could have imagined in all his dreams and games of the past. He saw a black motor car across the road, parked outside the other public house, and pointed excitedly. "There. There's one there."

She followed his gaze and indeed it was a taxi, and sitting in it was a driver lazily reading a newspaper whilst he awaited a fare. They crossed the road and she knocked on the window. "Are you for hire?"

"Where to ma'am?"

"Rolvenden Hill, only first we have to collect our bags from the station."

He got out of the cab and opened the rear door. "Hop in ma'am... and young sir," he said as he helped the two of them in.

Ten minutes later, Violet sat in the rear seat as the taxi made its way back down the High Street after picking up their luggage. She noticed every detail of the passing scenery, remembering that hot July and how she had trudged along this very road. Then, as now, she had been filled with doubt over her mission. Then she had feared rejection from a lover who had unwillingly deserted her. Now she was retracing her route to a meeting which she hoped for and dreaded in equal measure. She had not warned Jesse of her coming. Indeed, she had only decided a few days after Armand's departure that she wanted to make this journey... had to make this journey. Panic rose within her breast as she contemplated possible rejection. Jesse had every right to hate her for ignoring her all these years... but she had as much right as anyone to know that young Frank existed.

What if she would not let them in, would not accommodate them? What then? Her parents were expecting to meet her in Newhaven in seven days time, ready to take the boat to Dieppe, where Philippe would be waiting with the motor car. If Jesse rejected them she would either have to make her way back to London in ignominy or travel on to Newhaven and stay until they arrived.

Her face flushed at the thought. Would Jesse do that? No, not the Jesse she had known. She could explain if she was given the chance... she could explain the shame and the guilt she had felt and the mistake she had made. She could even explain the fact that she had not written after she had finally received her letter. No she couldn't! Nothing could ever really make up for the wrong she had done Jesse. 'What would I have said,' she agonised. 'How could I have just told her in a letter what had happened virtually under her roof, behind her back? How are you Jesse, and by the way, I had Frank's illegitimate son.'

She smiled at the thought. No. Better to do it this way now, face to face. She could show her the boy and she would know. Oh yes she would know. Elsie had known, even though it had been so difficult for her to take in at first. Alice had known straight away. Had daddy told her? She assumed not. Alice and her father. Was Armand correct when he had said that he felt that there was more to their relationship than that of master and servant? She had watched carefully after that but had seen nothing to indicate any improper relationship, other than the fact that when she had overheard them talking together, Alice had, rather curiously, addressed him as Ernest. At all other times she had called him Mr Matthews, but Violet had put the matter to the back of her mind. Interesting though. She would watch them when they were all in France. If there were anything in it she sincerely hoped it would not hurt her mother, who she had grown increasingly fond of in the past few weeks.

The taxi rumbled across the level crossing at the bottom of the hill and slowed as it began to tackle the steep rise. Guiltily, she glanced off to the right, along the valley towards the spot where Frank had been conceived, hidden now by the bend in the valley. She closed her eyes and imagined the place. If she got time she would try to go there just once.

Oh she wouldn't say anything to a soul, but if young Frank stood just once in the place of his conception then maybe, just maybe

Frank would know from wherever he was and be happy that his seed remained on Earth.

The taxi slowed as it reached the turning into Pudding Cake Lane and the driver reached back and slid open the glass partition. "Which house do you want ma'am?"

"Lilac Cottage. Jesse Long's house. But driver, can you please stop here and we'll walk the last few yards?"

"Are you sure ma'am?"

"Yes I'm very sure. Just here will do, and then you can turn around in that entrance." The taxi stopped and the driver got out and helped them from the vehicle. He reached in and retrieved their luggage, placing it down beside them. Violet paid and thanked him and the two of them stood watching as he drove off with one last honk and a wave.

"Who are we going to see now?" said a tired Frank.

"We are going to see Jesse. She was your father's... well she was like a mummy to him really."

"Like my mummy was to me?"

She laughed lightly. "No darling, Florrie was your foster mummy, she wasn't actually related to you. Jesse was really your father's auntie. Only when his mummy and daddy died she looked after him and... well she became like his mummy."

Frank looked at her. He thought he understood, but she had used several words that he couldn't quite grasp. What was the meaning of the word 'foster' and why wasn't Florrie related to him if she'd been his mummy?

He shrugged his shoulders in a gesture so reminiscent of his long-dead father that it was perhaps a good job that Violet didn't notice at that vulnerable moment.

She hefted the two bags, one in each hand, and they walked the few yards to the cottage gate. As they got there, Frank skipped ahead and opened it for Violet, who manoeuvred her way through it before putting the bags down just inside. She called Frank to her softly and smartened him up as best she could. "Socks please Frank," she said smiling, and he pulled them up with a grin.

Violet took a deep breath and knocked on the door. At first there was no sound at all and she feared that Jesse was out, but after a few moments she could make out approaching footsteps and the door was opened.

Jesse stood there in the doorway, blinking in the light, peering at Violet who stood silently, holding her breath, not knowing quite what to say or do.

"Violet?"

"Yes Jesse, it's me." She paused and held her breath, waiting for some signal to let her know whether she was welcome or not.

"Oh my darling you're safe. I've been so worried about you. Rosie and Keith said that you'd bin injured or captured and that you never came back to the hospital." She flung her arms open and Violet rushed into them and buried her face in her shoulder, crying freely.

"I'm sorry Jesse. I'm so sorry for what I've done to you. How can you ever forgive me?"

"Hush love. What's to forgive?"

"I didn't get your letter and... and after... after."

"After Frank's death you had to make your own way. But you're here now my love and welcome."

Violet realised then that the shorter woman had not seen Frank, who was standing behind her wondering quite what to do. She moved aside to reveal him, releasing Jesse from her embrace.

Jesse's arms dropped to her sides and she examined the small boy on the pathway. She moved forward and placed a hand on each shoulder, looking down into his face intently. "How old is he?" she enquired softly.

"He will be four in a month's time."

The small boy looked up into the soft, warm face of this large, white-haired woman. Her eyes filled with tears. "What is his name?"

Violet went to answer but Frank piped up. "My name is Frank."

"Of course it is my love," said Jesse lovingly. She bent slightly, swept the boy off his feet and hugged him. "Of course it is my love." She turned with her burden and smiled through her tears at Violet. "Thank you my darling. Oh thank you."

Violet stood under the small porch, the tears falling freely from her eyes as Jesse put down the boy, and taking each one by the hand led them through and into the little cottage.

......

Frank stepped proudly down from the large car as Philippe held open the door. He stood to one side and watched intently as Violet descended from the vehicle, resplendent in her cream wedding dress. Her veil blew up slightly in the breeze and revealed her face, smiling with joy. He drew himself as erect as he could and glanced down at his socks. They were still up, thank goodness, and as she noticed his glance she laughed lightly.

He fingered the gold cufflinks and pulled down his shirt sleeves so as to display them beyond his jacket. Pure gold they were. Jesse had given them to him. They had belonged to his real father. They had his initials on them and Violet had told him that they were very valuable and that he must look after them very carefully.

Ernest appeared from the other side of the motor car and joined them. "Are you all right my darling?" He smoothed down her veil.

"Yes thank you daddy," she whispered. Across the sun-dappled square they could see the Mairie, outside which, amongst the crowd of assembled guests and well-wishers, they could distinguish Armand standing proudly. Ernest took Violet's arm in his and prepared to move across.

Violet reached out for Frank's hand. "Stay with me Frank darling, whenever you can... unless grandfather tells you otherwise." He nodded, and taking her hand marched proudly beside her across the square. As they approached, Armand bowed slightly to them. Ernest and Frank stood back as he took Violet's arm, turned and led her up the steps to the first-floor chamber.

The assembled guests followed excitedly, noisily climbing the narrow winding stairs and into the room, above where they either sat down on one of the many arranged chairs or crowded about the table at the end in chattering groups. Formality seemed a long way off and several shorter individuals and children stood on chairs in order to get a better look. Some wore suits showing signs of age, and in many cases little or no evidence of any cleaning or pressing, whilst others had simply attended in their normal day to day working clothes. One old woman, one of Armand's tenant farmers, stood there bent nearly double, her rubber-booted legs showing the effects of rickets, even through the heavy skirts. Her hands, callused and grimy, were piously clasped and her demeanour, in the midst of all this clamour, was one of silent respect. Beside her stood her two slightly more erect daughters, similarly attired apart from the fact that their headscarves were dirty white instead of the black she wore. No man was apparent and, in truth, the overwhelming ratio of women to men bore testament to the greed of the battlefield.

To the right of the table sat the group of immediate family and friends, staring at the bride and groom intently and trying hard to ignore the pressing and smelly throng. Elsie and Alice, now, joined by Ernest and Frank, sat surveying the scene around them with not a little amusement, their eyes wandering from the couple standing in front of the desk to the other guests and back again. In the seats immediately beside them sat Armand's sister and her husband, Henri. He stared uncomfortably down at the floor, whilst she stared ahead frostily, her eyes fixed on the window beyond the desk, her presence there by the demand of duty rather than desire.

The Maire walked importantly into the room and the assembled throng parted as he made his way behind the desk to perform the civil ceremony itself. Ernest and Violet moved forward slightly and the seated adults stood, completely obscuring Frank's view. He sat back on his hands and looked around. For the first time, he noticed that amongst his group of more important guests there was a boy of similar age to his own who also remained seated as his mother, a large handsome woman in a grey suit with an intricate hat, stood to observe the ceremony. The boy saw him and smiled his greeting. A good-looking boy with clear blue eyes and fine, carefully combed blonde hair, Frank made a mental note to search for him afterwards and see if they could play some games together. He could show him the chateau grounds and even the dungeons. Well, the cellars really, but in his imagination they were dungeons.

Oh no! The boy would want to speak French and it was so difficult to make up any really good games when your companion could not understand the rules. He had tried with some of the boys back at the chateau, who often found themselves hanging around whilst their parents either conducted business with Armand or carried out some task or other around the estate. Signs and grunts had to suffice where language failed, but gradually, ever so gradually, he was beginning, even after these few short weeks, to comprehend the odd words.

Pierre-Luc was his favourite new friend. His father had a small farm, which he owned rather than tenanted, just outside the main village. He grew roses, which were sent to market in Paris, and whenever he came over to see Armand, Pierre-Luc was free to play with Frank and had taken him and shown him many of the secret places and wonders of his new home.

The blonde boy smiled again and, as his mother seemed entirely preoccupied with the proceedings, he slid along the row of chairs towards Frank. "Guten morgen," said the boy.

"Hallo," replied Frank, rocking on his hands and smiling back at his new friend.

The boy pointed to his chest. "Gunther. Ich heiße Gunther." He jabbed his chest again and repeated the name. "Gunther."

Gunther, Frank thought. That didn't sound like all of the other funny names he'd heard since he came to France. The boy's speech sounded different as well, not at all like the words Pierre-Luc used and had tried to teach him. He pointed to the boy and said his name. "Gunther?"

"Ja Gunther." The boy pointed to Frank, his eyes open wide, questioning.

Frank smiled. "My name is Frank." He pointed up and over towards the happy couple. "That's my mother being married."

Gunther, who Frank could now see was a little older than he was, drew in his breath. "Ah Engleesh und... Violet is your... mutter?" He pointed over to the front of the assembly. "Ja?"

"Yes and my name is Frank."

"Ah ja." He made as if to continue, but just then a loud burst of applause broke out and the throng separated to reveal Armand and Violet hand in hand facing their audience, returning their good wishes and greetings. Violet, the veil thrown back on her head, her face wreathed in smiles, searched through the crowd for him and Frank ran towards her outstretched hand as those in front stepped aside to let him pass. Gunther looked up and, catching his mother's glance, returned to her side. He would seek out his new friend later.

Armand and Violet, arm in arm and with young Frank clinging proudly to her hand, marched from the room, down the stairs and out into the open. The noisy assembly followed them, spilling out into the square to form up behind them in the semblance of a procession. Once ready, the couple led the throng across the square, up the short flight of steps, through the churchyard with its neatly clipped yews, to the main entrance in front of the church.

A beaming priest stood there waiting to greet them. "Rene," Armand whispered as they approached.

The priest nodded. "Armand, mon cher ami." He stretched out his hand and shook Armand's warmly as they reached him and then, holding his bible high in the air, leant forward to kiss Violet twice on each cheek before turning to lead the way into the church.

Within the church, many of the pews were already occupied

by people who, in the main, seemed fairly well heeled and who had chosen not to attend the noisy civil ceremony. Heads turned expectantly as the happy couple followed the priest down the aisle, nodding greetings to those that they recognised. Frank kept hold of his mother's hand until, at the end of the lines of pews, Ernest stepped forward from behind and guided him to the left to join Elsie and Alice as they arrived.

The rest of the crowd from the Mairie came into the church and fanned out on either side, searching noisily for suitable seating, calling to each other and waving their friends to the available pews. The English group watched this display of informality with disbelief and Violet sneaked a look back at her father, who returned it with a broad grin and a wink.

René waited patiently in front of the standing couple, talking quietly to them, murmuring encouragement as they waited for the hubbub to die down. Frank sat on the hard wooden pew swinging his legs and looked up at the vaulted ceilings of the church. He imagined that he was upside down and tried to visualise what it would be like if the roof was the floor. The congregation commenced singing as he wandered in his imagination through the curves and hills of the vaults and climbed laboriously over the buttresses. His neck cricked and he clasped it and rolled his head from side to side.

"Are you all right Frank?" Alice whispered.

"Yes thank you," he replied and she squeezed his hand, beside her on the pew.

He looked behind him and caught the smile of his new friend Gunther, which he returned. Gunther's mother saw the exchange between the two and bent down to whisper in her son's ear. He nodded and she cocked her head in order that he could whisper back. She nodded, and noticing that Frank was still watching, smiled at him and gave a little wave, which he returned shyly.

Frank searched the rest of the church looking for someone else he knew. He wished so much that Florrie and Joe were there. At moments like this he missed them so much, and in spite of Violet's constant attempts to make him feel wanted, he sometimes longed to be able to just throw himself into that warm embrace of his childhood. A lump came into his throat and he felt a tear start in the corner of his eye. Alice, and then Elsie, noticed and both leant forward assuming that he was overcome by the emotion of the occasion. Alice took out her handkerchief and dabbed his eyes before swinging him up and sitting him between herself and Elsie, who immediately bent her face down and looked enquiringly into his.

"Are you all right little man?"

He nodded and tried to smile as she took his hand in hers and held it firmly in her lap, paying attention once more to the ceremony. Alice placed her arm around him and he leant into her body and sought the warmth he so craved. He closed his eyes and concentrated. He tried to remember the farmhouse, but each time a picture of it came into his head it became confused with the chateau. He tried to imagine Florrie's face, but again each time he thought he could see her the face became confused and he was never quite sure if it was her face he was seeing or that of Jesse.

He concentrated on the memory of his brief visit to her little cottage and the memory of the myriad of hugs and kisses that he had received. He pictured her standing there with Violet, laughing happily as Rosie and Keith playfully hoisted him into the air. Oh, if only they too were here. He leant still further into Alice and dozed fitfully, fidgeting from time to time as the hardness of the pew made him uncomfortable.

A cheer awoke him and he sat up bleary-eyed, wondering what had happened. Armand and Violet stood facing back down the church, smiling at the assembled crowd, man and wife now in the eyes of the church as well as the state. They started to walk forward and Frank slid off the pew to make his way to Violet's side but Ernest held him back, whispering for him to remain behind and let the couple progress alone down the aisle to the door.

The priest followed the couple and Ernest stood aside to let first Elsie and then Alice join him and Frank before proceeding down the aisle. Gunther waved at Frank as they passed and Elsie whispered. "Oh I see you've found a new friend Frank."

"He speaks funny," said Frank.

"That's because he's German," Ernest interrupted. "He is the son of a German soldier Violet met in the war."

Frank looked around and up at his grandfather. "Cor did she kill him?"

"No Frank, he was her friend but he died. It is very sad and you must be careful what you say."

"But grandpa, if he's a German..."

Ernest held his finger to his lips. "He's a young boy and his mother is a very nice lady and the war is over now Frank. I want you to promise me. Will you promise me Frank?"

"Yes grandpa," said Frank reluctantly. Cor, what games they could play now, he thought. Real Germans, real Frenchmen and him as the English hero. They could have great fun back at the chateau.

"Ah, there you are darling," cried Violet as Frank came through the doors. "Everything all right?"

"Yes thank you Violet." Ernest let go of his hand and he ran across to stand beside her.

Armand reached across Violet to take his hand. "How is the little soldier?"

"I'm all right," he replied as Armand chucked him playfully under the chin.

A large dignified and black-suited man came forward with his equally large wife on his arm and commenced talking to Armand, bowing stiffly to Violet as he was introduced.

"Violet, this is Monsieur and Madame Leclerc. Monsieur Leclerc is the manager of the factory in Chateauneuf, the ironworks I showed you on the other side of the station."

"Ah pleased to meet you Monsieur, 'dame," said Violet, extending her hand. "Armand showed me the factory when he picked me up at the station. Such a big factory and so much movement and noise."

The woman obviously understood not a word of Violet's gushing conversation, but the man translated the gist of it to his wife. She nodded and he turned back to Violet. "You must to come one day and I will show you."

"I'd be delighted," said Violet, and beaming politely the man bowed again before escorting his wife to the back of the crowd.

"He looks very important," giggled Violet.

"He is important. It is that factory which provides nearly all of our money. Without it the chateau would be too expensive as the farms do not make for us any money."

"Well we will have to visit this important man and his factory as soon as possible then, shan't we?"

She caught sight of Doris in the crowd, craning to get a better view, and waved to her. Doris jumped up and down and blew a kiss to her, which Violet returned with a wink.

"Monsieur Armand," called the photographer from behind his cloaked tripod. "Excuse moi si'l vous plait." Armand drew himself erect and clasped Violet's arm to hold the pose. She smiled at the lens and they waited. "Le garcon?" called the photographer.

"Il reste avec nous," Armand called back. He bent down to Frank. "Come closer Frank and be with us in this picture."

"You're wonderful," whispered Violet through her fixed smile. "Thank you darling." She rested her hand on the boy's shoulder as they stood there as a family.

Eventually, when all the combinations of photographs had been taken that were either expected or could be thought of, the cry went up for everybody to return to the chateau. Philippe opened the door of the larger car and Violet, Armand and Frank got in to shouts and waves from all still present. Jean-Claude brought up the other motor car and immediate family got into that, whilst others with transport called out to various acquaintances and friends in order to fill their vehicles. In a cacophony of shouts and blasts from the motor car horns, the cavalcade set off.

The first sign of any division between the classes of the various participants became noticeable, not through any design, but by dint of the method of transport they now employed to return to the chateau. Those who did not possess or were not invited into the motor vehicles made their way across to the flat, horse-drawn carts lined up on the other side of the street and clambered up upon them. Shouting and singing, and, in one exuberant case, firing a shotgun into the air, they crowded on to the carts and sat around the perimeter, their legs swinging freely over the sides as the horses took up the strain and lumbered forward and out of the village.

In the limousine, Armand turned to Violet and kissed her. "Thank you my darling Violet for making me so happy a man."

"And thank you Armand. Thank you for everything. I've never been so happy. I have you and I have my little boy." She put her arm around Frank and drew him to her. "And I have my whole family."

"Will you be going away tonight?" asked Frank.

"No darling, we will be going tomorrow, but you are not to worry. Grandpa Ernest and Grandma Elsie will be staying here until we get back and they'll look after you. You'd like that, wouldn't you?"

"I'd rather go with you. Can't I?"

She smiled down at him and then looked up at Armand, wondering quite what to say. He bent forward and leant across her, taking hold of the little boy's hands. "Frank I have something to ask you. Something I would like you to do for me."

Frank looked up into his face, a face he had only known for a very short while but a face, nevertheless, which he was beginning to know very well and trust. "What is it? What do you want me to do?"

Armand's expression grew serious. "I am going away for one week with Violet on our... on our honeymoon." He looked at Violet and smiled broadly before adopting again the serious expression and redirecting his gaze to Frank. "I will be away for one week. Now, you are my family... you are like my son. Do you understand?" Frank nodded and he continued. "I want for you to stay here to be in my place and to look after all my things."

The boy's eyes opened wider. "Will I be in charge?"

"Mais oui... certainement... you most certainly will... with the help of Philippe and Jean-Claude... who will do all of the work of course. But... and Frank this is important... if they need you to be the patron you must be ready. Can you do that?"

Frank pulled his face into the most serious and grown-up expression he could possibly imagine. "Yes Armand."

"I can trust you?"

He glanced at the pride-filled face of his mother, who nodded silently at him. He looked back at Armand. "You can trust me," he said proudly.

"Oh my darlings," said Violet. "Oh my two darlings."

The car turned into the driveway and came to a halt outside the doors. Philippe alighted and hurried around the vehicle as quickly as his limp would allow as Jean-Claude approached, both hoping to be the first to open the doors and welcome the couple. In the end they had to share the task and stood there side by side, red-faced and smiling broadly as first Violet and then Armand came out of the motor car. Armand put his arm around his bride's waist as they stood there looking about themselves, watching the driveway gradually fill with the arriving guests.

Noisy and expectant they poured out from and off the various vehicles that had transported them to the chateau. The more well to do stood stiffly, presents in hand, as they were buffeted by the more exuberant peasants eager to get to the food and especially the drink they knew would be available in plenty inside.

Violet and Armand mounted the steps and stood either side of the door to welcome them all in, shaking each one by the hand as they passed by. At times the throng of people threatened to dislodge Violet from her position and Philippe, returning from parking the car, moved forward and placed himself beside and behind her to buttress her, whilst Jean-Claude did the same on the other side for Armand. The strain of shaking hands and repeatedly kissing an endless succession of cheeks began to tell, and it was with some relief that the last guests were finally ushered through to the great hall.

Tables had been laid out in lines below a top table, to which Armand now led his bride. The seated throng clapped and cheered as they passed. Elsie and Alice beamed their pride and pleasure as Violet arrived, and Ernest stood and assisted her to her place. At the other end of the table, Armand's sister and her husband stayed seated, although he tried to rise, only to be pulled back down by her.

Armand took his seat and looked out over the assembled crowd, who had by now, for the most part, reverted back to attacking the copious quantities of food and drink spread out along the tables. "Where is the boy?" he whispered to Violet.

She looked around seeking him out amongst the guests, but there was no sign of him. "I don't know. The last time I saw him was as we got out of the car."

Armand signalled to Jean-Claude, who left his place to rush around and behind the top table to his master's bidding. He bent his head close to Armand's and listened intently. Straightening, he looked out over the assembly before signalling to Philippe, who joined him as they made for the door. One or two of the guests noticed the interchange and wondered at the mission, but most were too busy indulging themselves to pay too much attention.

Ernest leant across to Violet. "What's happening?"

She smiled. "It's Frank. He seems to have gone missing."

"Oh, shall I go and help look for him?"

"No need daddy. Jean-Claude and Philippe have gone. They'll find him better than any of us." She laughed. "They should do, they showed him most of his hidyholes and secret places."

The party continued, with great plates being carried in to much applause, heaped high with charcuterie. More wine was carried in and distributed along the tables, only to be seized upon almost before it was down. Hunks of bread were torn from the loaves and handed around, oblivious of the knives set out for the purpose. On the top table, Elsie and Alice looked with suspicion and not a little trepidation at the array of unfamiliar food laid out before them and opted for that which most resembled what they were used to. Ernest, on the other hand, fortified by liberal quantities of wine from a glass that mysteriously never seemed to empty, experimented with some of the more outlandish-looking items whilst acknowledging the barrage of good wishes and salutations directed from the tables below.

The doors opened and Philippe entered, carrying Frank in his arms. A cry went up and hands reached out to touch the infant as he was carried through to the top table and sat on a tall chair between Violet and Armand, who both bent to him, caressing him and whispering to him. Philippe muttered a few words in Armand's ear and he announced to the crowd that the boy had been found asleep in the motor car, where he had stayed to avoid the throng. A concerted "Aah" was uttered by all, and Frank lowered his gaze shyly.

For Frank, seated up there between his new parents, the object of so much attention and praise from so many people he could barely, if at all, understand, the rest of the afternoon blurred into an endless cacophony of noise, which stayed most of the time at one level but occasionally rose to an almost deafening volume as some particular joke was told. Sometimes one of the guests would rise to his feet and propose a toast to the happy couple, and for a moment the noise would die down before rising again as the whole assembly repeated the cry and joined in the salute.

At the table just below and in front of Frank sat Gunther. He had smiled up at Frank several times, and they had carried on a wordless conversation through all of the other noise and activity. As the afternoon wore on, and the adults showed no sign of any let-up in their merrymaking, he caught Frank's eye and motioned his head towards the door. Frank nodded, and Gunther leant across and whispered to his mother, who nodded. She stood and leant across the table calling to Violet. Violet nodded and whispered to Frank that he could go with Gunther, and the two boys gratefully left the room to play.

June 1926

The monk swung open the large iron gates of the small school at Saint Benoit and stood back into the shade of an acacia as the doors of the schoolhouse opened and the boys came tumbling through. Folding his hands in his sleeves, he stared meaningfully at them as they approached in a noisy gang, reducing the front ranks to a quieter, if still hurried exit from the yard.

As Frank and his two companions drew alongside, he looked up into the darkness of the cowl, searching for the stern face within. "Goodbye father."

The head raised and the light was let in to reveal dark, aquiline features. A small smile played briefly on the lips and the eyes flashed from beneath dark eyebrows. Then the head was lowered again and the light extinguished. From within came a sonorous voice with little or no emotional content. "Be good for the holidays boys."

"Thank you father," said Pierre-Luc.

"Are you staying in France for the holidays Frank?" the monk asked.

"Yes father," Frank replied, halting now in front of him. "Gunther's coming from Germany with his mother. But then we may go to England. I'm not sure."

The hooded head raised again and the light shone now on fully exposed features. The lips curled back to reveal stained and broken teeth and the voice, raised in pitch, lost its monotone. "Never trust a German," he hissed with such venom that Frank stood stock still for a moment, rooted to the spot by the strange hatred from this normally colourless man. Pierre-Luc and their other companion, Marcel, instinctively drew alongside Frank and stood either side, pressing into him.

The father stared down at the trio of boys in front of him. At first they shuffled uneasily and stared down at the ground. But then Frank raised his head and returned the glare of the man. His face broke into a wide, open smile. "Oh father, Gunther's all right... he's our friend." The spell was broken and the face receded once more into a cowl, with little more than a grunt of disapproval. "Come on you two, Philippe's waiting for us and we've got to get to the station." He guided his two friends out through the gates and across the square to the waiting motor car.

"Goodbye father," Marcel called over his shoulder.

He did not wait for a reply. Which was just as well, for otherwise he would have heard the hissed "Jew", given with the same venomous hatred reserved for the Germans.

The boys separated now and ran through and under the trees and into the vehicle. "Good afternoon Philippe," said Frank as the three of them settled down in the back seats.

"Good afternoon yourself Master Frank. Are your friends coming home with you, or are we to drop them off somewhere?"

"No Philippe, they're coming home with us to have tea and then we're all going to the station to meet Gunther." Philippe nodded his understanding as the car started off and the three passengers proceeded to hang out of the windows, waving at other school friends as they passed them on their way out of the square. They reached the main road, where they stopped alongside two slightly older boys standing on the corner. Marcel leant out as far as he could and tipped off the hat of the nearest boy.

"Get back inside the car," Philippe called back. "Sit down all three of you and behave, otherwise I'll tell Monsieur Armand."

"Sorry Philippe," they chorused together with little or no remorse in their voices. Philippe smiled to himself as he glanced into the mirror. He wouldn't have told on them anyway. It was perfectly understandable that they should be excited at the start of the holidays and they were only being boys. He searched from left to right, looking out along the narrow street to make sure that all was clear before slipping the car back into gear and pulling out.

The boy who had been relieved of his hat ran up to the departing car. "I'll get you Fleisch," he called, waving his fist.

Marcel smiled back as Frank pulled him aside and leant once more from the window. "Have a nice holiday Serge," he called mockingly, and ducked back in as the freshly retrieved hat was flung in his direction.

"Boys," called Philippe.

"Sorry Philippe," came the concerted reply and the three of them relaxed back into the seats, giggling and pinching each other.

Their arrival at the chateau was a noisy and exuberant affair, with the boys excitedly chasing each other around the front grounds before finally rushing up the stairs, through and down to the huge kitchens. Marie turned from her range as they came tumbling in. "Steady boys. Calm down now," she shouted with as much authority as she could muster behind her broad, welcoming grin.

"Anything to scoff Marie," said Frank.

"Yes we're starving," said Pierre-Luc. "Aren't we Marcel?"

"Yes we are," said his breathless and red-faced companion. "Starving."

"Starving is it? Well we can't have that, can we? Three dead boys, what would the master say?"

"It'd be terrible Marie," moaned Frank in mock agony. He writhed and clutched his stomach as he bent and swayed. His two companions grinned at him and then clutched their own bellies and joined him in the pantomime. "We're dying," gasped Frank as he sunk to his knees.

Pierre-Luc joined him, and then Marcel, kneeling in supplication, his arms outstretched, pleaded in a weak and tremulous voice. "Please feed us kind lady. Please!"

"Oh get away with you. Come on now." She dragged Frank to his feet. "I don't know, the three of you are a turn. There's bread and saucisson on the table over there, but mind you don't eat too much or you'll not want your dinner tonight when your friends come."

The boys rushed over to the table, where Frank swept the bread above his head and parried the outreaching hands of his companions. Pierre-Luc grabbed hold of the bread knife and the two of them danced around the table in a mock sword fight, urged on by Marcel.

"Boys!" came a call from the door and Violet entered the kitchen. She looked across at Marie and returned her grin with a skywards rolling of her eyes. "Settle down now boys... and Pierre-Luc put that knife down before you injure somebody. Now come on be good, the three of you. Have something to eat and then go upstairs and smarten yourselves up a bit before we have to go to the station."

"Sorry mother," said Frank in English as he sat on the bench, flashing a glance at his two friends as they too sat, stifling their giggles.

"Sorry madame," the two other boys intoned.

Violet switched back to French. "That's all right. Now Frank, you cut the bread and I'll cut some saucisson for you all. Do you want anything to drink?"

"Lemonade please," said Frank. He turned to his companions, his eyes alight, "Do you want some of Marie's home-made lemonade? It's delicious."

"Yes please," said the two boys, and Marie, smiling, put down her spoon and bustled off into the pantry to fetch the drink.

"How many slices for you Pierre-Luc?" said Violet as she struggled with the hard sausage.

Three please Madame," came the reply.

"And you Marcel?"

There was a short silence before the boy replied. "I cannot eat saucisson madame."

Violet rested her hand from sawing through the hard meat. "Oh of course. I'm sorry Marcel. Would you like some cheese or a tomato?"

"A tomato please madame."

"Marie," Violet called.

"Yes madame."

"Bring a tomato when you come please."

"Yes madame."

"Why don't you eat saucisson Marcel?" Frank asked.

"Now Frank, that's enough. You know that Marcel doesn't eat any meat from pigs because of his religion," said Violet sternly.

"Yes but..."

"Yes but nothing Frank."

"But if it's bad for him why can we eat it?"

"Frank! You're embarrassing Marcel. Now stop it please."

"It's all right madame," said Marcel.

"Sorry Marcel," said Frank. "Only..."

"...only nothing Frank. Now come on all of you, eat up." She looked up as Marie approached with a jug of fresh, cloudy lemonade and three stout mugs, which she set in front of the boys.

"Cor smashing," said Frank as he held his mug up to her and waited until the sound told him that it was nearly full. He quaffed the drink and looked across the rim of the mug at his two friends as they too greedily drank the sweet liquid. He gasped for breath, grinning over at the two of them. "Told you it was good, didn't I?"

Pierre-Luc and Marcel merely nodded as they drank, then they too came up for air and the three boys put down their mugs and attacked the food set before them.

For a short while peace reigned, but within a few minutes of Violet's departure the games had recommenced and, as the food was finished, the play-fighting resumed until finally they were all shooed out of the kitchen by an exasperated Marie.

The car swung into the station forecourt and stopped in front of the tall square building. So imposing, yet so alike to all other stations throughout France, its only real claim to separate identity lay in the bold arch of lettering on each gable end, 'Chateauneuf-sur-Loire'. The dust clouds swirled into the evening air as the motor car drew to a halt and the doors opened to release the boys, who ran straight up to the double doors and into the hall.

"Wait for me boys," called Violet as she dismounted. "Oh those boys will be the death of me," she said to Philippe as he waited for her to step clear before closing the car door behind her.

"There would be no life without them madame."

"That is true Philippe," she said laughing. "But you have to admit they are exhausting."

He smiled back at her and followed her into the station hall and up to the barrier, where the boys now stood peering expectantly out and on to the platforms.

"Wait there boys," Violet called as she went over to the ticket office. "Is the train from Orleans on time?" she enquired. The man behind the glass told her it was and she returned to the barrier. "Now boys, I want you to behave on the platform and stand clear as the train arrives. We don't want an accident, do we?"

"No mother," said Frank.

"Well, hold on to my hand then and we'll go out on to the platform." He reached out for her offered hand but withdrew it as the other boys giggled. "You two boys, hold on to either me or Philippe, whichever you prefer. Otherwise stay here in the hall until we come back through."

Reluctantly, the three boys each took the hand of an adult and the five of them crossed the railway lines to the platform opposite and stood looking down the tracks searching for the coming train. The boys stretched as far as they could from Violet and Philippe, without actually letting go of their hands, and it was Marcel who first spotted the signs of the approaching train. "There it is," he cried, jumping up and down. "I saw it first."

"Did not. I saw it at the same time," said Frank.

"It doesn't matter who saw it first," said Violet. "Now behave boys and keep a watch out for the doors as they open... and stand back."

The great engine passed the small group in the usual cloud of hissing steam and smoke, its brakes squealing on the iron wheels as it drew to a halt. Doors banged open and faces peered out, looking down the platform. "There they are," shouted Frank as he broke free from his mother's restraining grasp and ran forward to where Gunther was already halfway down the steps. "Gunther we're here!"

"Be careful Frank!" shouted Violet and then, seeing that there was no further danger, she released Marcel's hand and he and Pierre-Luc ran up and joined Frank. Gunther reached the platform and, grinning broadly, was swept into a mass embrace by his three friends.

"Is nobody to help me?" came his mother's voice from the open doorway, speaking in English.

She stood there smiling down at them all and Violet returned her smile with an open-armed expression of welcome. Approaching her mid-forties, she was nevertheless still a handsome and imposing woman, although her blonde hair was beginning to show signs of white. The seeds of their friendship may have been sown in sadness, but the companionship they felt for each other over the intervening years was intense. For Violet, this older woman represented a joy that she looked forward to each summer. "Hallo Gisela," she called.

"Violet. Oh Violet. It is wonderful to see you."

"And you too. Come down and let Philippe get your bags."

"We have more in the baggage carriage."

"Don't worry." She turned to the boys. "You boys go and see to the other luggage and make sure they are all off. How many are there Gisela?"

"Two only. One trunk and a smaller brown suitcase. Gunther knows which ones."

"Yes I know," called Gunther as he, followed by the other three boys, sped off.

Violet and Gisela embraced as she reached the platform. "So good to see you," whispered Violet. "So good to see you."

"And you too."

"How long can you stay?"

"I can stay only a few weeks. But Gunther can stay longer if you don't mind."

"Mind? Of course we don't mind. You know you are always

welcome. Oh, it's so good to see you. I can hardly believe it's a year since we last saw each other."

"Yes it is, I am afraid."

"How are things in Germany?"

Gisela gave a wan smile. "Not good. Fights. Communists and Nationalists. It's as if we are no longer one country." She sighed.

Violet took her arm and held it as first of all Philippe and then the boys joined them. They stood in a group as the train departed, leaving the way clear for them all to cross the tracks back to the station building, with Philippe carrying the hand luggage whilst the four boys between them manhandled the heavier trunk and suitcase through and into the motor car.

......

"Pull tighter!" cried Frank.

"I am," shouted Gunther. "I can't pull any harder. It's as tight as I can make it."

"Marcel, you put your finger on the knot then," said Frank, "and Gunther and I will lock it."

"I'm not doing that. You trapped my finger last time and I couldn't get it out. You do it," Marcel protested.

"I can't you clot. I have to hold the rope tight, otherwise, if it's loose, the whole thing will fall apart like it did last time."

"It wasn't my fault."

"I'm not saying it was, but go on Marcel, put your finger on that knot. Come on, I can't keep it tight forever."

"Oh all right then," Marcel grumbled, "but give me time to get it out before you pull it completely tight."

"We promise," shouted Gunther, "but get on with it please, this string is burning my hand."

"Mine too," said Frank.

Marcel leant across the oil drums and quickly placed his finger on the knot meant to tie the plank across it. "Press hard now. Ready?"

"Yes," came the reply from them both.

"Then pull hard now Gunther." They both pulled hard on the rough string, trapping Marcel's finger once more. He yelled in protest and they slackened off. Gunther attempted to pull again but Frank shouted out, "No, it's no use like that, it's just not tight enough." The drum rolled and the plank slipped off it and into the shallow water with a soft splash.

"I'm sorry," wailed Marcel, "but..."

"It's not your fault," said Gunther. "We'll have to think of another way."

"I know," said Frank. "We can use a stick. Marcel can hold it down on the knot and then pull it out at the last minute."

"I wish I was clever like you," Gunther said, adopting the pose of a monkey and rolling his eyes back into his head. "Go and get a stick Marcel, as our mighty engineer has ordered."

"Certainly captain," said Marcel saluting.

"Hey, who said you were captain. I might want to be."

"My dear Frank," said Gunther with mock civility. "How can you be the boat builder and the captain?"

"Quite easily, thank you sir," replied Frank in the same vein.

"I'll fight you for it."

"I don't think that will be necessary... captain." Frank laughed as he lifted the plank back on to the drum. "Now where's that stick?" Marcel came splashing through the shallows with a stick in his hand, from which he peeled the bark. The two bigger boys pulled tight on the first knot and Marcel placed his stick down on it to hold it tight whilst the locking knot was tied. They pulled tight. "Pull the stick out... now!" Frank shouted, and the knot was finally home with the plank secure.

The boys danced about with satisfaction, whooping for joy at the final success of the operation. A call came from the willow trees on the bank and Pierre-Luc came into sight. They all waved. "I bring food and drink," he called as he ran down the sandy bank and paddled across to them, a bag held high above his head.

"Leave it on the bank for now and help us with the last planks," said Gunther. Pierre-Luc aeroplaned his arms and reversed direction to the bank, where he deposited the bag before re-joining them.

The remaining planks were duly lashed to the drums and the raft began to take on real shape. "We need a mast," said Marcel.

"No we don't," scoffed Gunther. "We've got galley slaves to row us."

"Where?"

"There and there and there," laughed Gunther, pointing to the other three in turn.

"Oh you think so do you?" cried Frank. He splashed water up at Gunther and the other two joined in. Soon all four of them were soaked to the skin and then, fed up with that game, they retreated to the bank and stripped off, laying their clothing out flat on the warm grass to dry. "What's in the bag Pierre-Luc?" asked Frank as he crawled across to it.

"I don't know. Marie gave it to me when I went to the house to see if you were all there." They opened the bag and drew out the wrapped-up bundles of sandwiches and stoppered bottles of lemonade. Gasps of joy and delight were followed by a relative silence as the four of them tucked into the grub before laying back in the sunshine. It didn't last long. Before many minutes had passed, one boy had thrown a clump of grass across at another, and when that was returned the others joined in and soon the peaceful picnic had turned into a scrap, which ended up with all four of them tumbling down the bank and into the shallow water.

Anyone seeing them playing there and hearing their cheerful, colloquial banter would have taken them all for French. Frank, of course, used French with an ease that can only be attained by the young, who, when brought up in a bilingual environment, seem able to switch almost seamlessly from one language to another. Gunther, on the other hand, had picked up his knowledge of French on his now annual holidays at the chateau, and whilst he could speak with relative fluency he had a greater difficulty when it came to reading and writing, and for the first few days, and often when he was alone with Frank, he would revert to English, a language that he was extraordinarily proficient in.

They all lay there laughing in the shallows for a while before Gunther ordered "All hands on deck", and they all climbed aboard their raft and set out for the small island out in the main channel. The Loire was wide and deep here, reflecting the wide, bright sky above and between its high willow-clad banks. Winter floods had scoured out the outside bends of the banks and deposited sand and uprooted trees to form islands, which would survive for the summer and perhaps even another mild winter, but very rarely any further.

In summer the waters flowed slowly, opaque with their constant burden of silt. Here and there, the current below the surface showed itself in fierce eddies and swirls where jetsam coming down the river interrupted its path to turn within its grasp. The boys knew these waters. They knew the currents in the main stream beyond the islands could take a man unawares and they kept within the slacker waters, using its power to transport them to their island but never beyond.

If Violet ever gave the impression that she didn't care or worry about the boys playing on the river, then anyone believing it would have been seriously mistaken. Every time they went out to the river she worried, but Armand assured her that the four of them knew the dangers and that they would not come to any harm. At times, his dogged belief in the certainty of providential protection enraged her, but at others his very calmness within that certainty stifled her protests. Even so, from time to time, when no one else was about, she would creep to the edge of the willows just to see that they were alright, and whenever they finally came home from their play she breathed a sigh of relief.

If she had done so this day, she would have never allowed any further unsupervised visits to the river, for as the raft neared the island the current caught it, sweeping it along its banks towards the tip.

"Pull!" screamed Frank as they all paddled frantically, trying to stay in the lee of the island as the current threatened to sweep them out into the main stream.

Gunther dug his wooden board deep into the water and pulled with all his might. The plank snapped and the release of pressure sent him reeling backwards, to somersault into the water. He called out as his fingers clawed at the sides of the drums but slipped on their painted surface.

Marcel discarded his paddle and threw himself across the raft to grab Gunther's outstretched hand. He missed the hand but managed to hold on to the wrist and Gunther locked his hand around his whilst swimming with the other and kicking out with his feet to keep himself alongside. Frank and Pierre-Luc, left to the rowing, paddled for all they were worth and gradually the raft began to move back towards the island. "Hold on Gunther," Marcel shouted, "we're nearly safe."

The raft grounded on the coarse sandy beach of the island and Pierre-Luc jumped off and secured it to a tree with a length of trailing rope, whilst Frank clambered across and helped Marcel to lift Gunther up on to the decking.

For a while they just lay there catching their breath, before all four of them dragged the raft up beyond the water.

"Cor that was a close shave," panted Frank. "We nearly lost the captain."

"If it wasn't for Marcel I would have been swept away," said Gunther.

Marcel sat up grinning. "You owe me your life," he announced. "I have you in my power."

"I'll show you who's in whose power," yelled Gunther, launching himself across at Marcel and knocking him flat on the sand. The two of them rolled over and over, giggling as they tickled each other, but stopped as they reached the water's edge. They sat up and Gunther put his arm around the smaller boy's shoulder. "Thanks for saving my life," he said quietly.

"Don't mention it captain," grinned Marcel.

Frank joined them, having detached the rope. "Come on you lot, let's drag the raft along the island a bit out of the current, and next time we come we'll bring a longer length of rope and tie it to the trees on the main bank so that we don't get swept on past by the current."

"Good idea from the engineer," shouted Gunther. "Now backs to the rope men."

Large trees, which had been deposited on the sand and continued to grow, dominated the centre of the narrow island, and once the boys had tied up the raft to one of these they spent the rest of the day climbing amongst them and even managed to construct a platform from driftwood and branches.

"If we come back tomorrow with some more wood and some tarpaulin we can make a proper tree house," suggested Marcel.

"And then we'll have our own island," Frank mused.

"Our own country," said Gunther. "We could call it Allemance and have our own flag."

"Allemance?" queried Frank. "What about my country having its share?"

"Whoops. Sorry I forgot," said Gunther. He muttered to himself. "Anglmagne... Frankalle... lais..."

"Anglefrankalle," suggested Marcel.

"Anglefrankalle Anglefrankalle," they all repeated. "Anglefrankalle. Alleanglefrank. Frankanglealle."

Every combination was tried but none seemed to find favour.

There was a short silence, broken by Frank's whoop of delight. "I know, I've got it. Allemanceterre!"

Frank looked from face to face, seeing their gradual acceptance.

"It still doesn't have all of the big bits in it, does it?" complained Pierre-Luc.

"It doesn't really matter. We know who we are and we know that we are the citizens of Allemanceterre," said Gunther.

"Brothers in arms," cried Marcel.

"Brothers in arms," they all cried.

"Swear on the sand of Allemanceterre that its citizens will never take up arms against each other," cried Frank.

"We so swear," they all cried, grabbing handfuls of the coarse white sand and hurling it into the air with blood-curdling whoops whilst they ran and chased each other around the entire circumference of the island.

......

"Stand still please Frank," said Violet, speaking to him in English. "I know you don't want to wear a tie, but this is an important occasion and it is very important for us all, especially dear Armand."

Frank glanced across at Gunther sitting by the French windows, watching his discomfiture. "How long will we be?" he asked his mother.

"We should be back by the middle of the afternoon." She looked across at Gunther. "We will be back by the middle of the afternoon, Gunther. You'll be alright here, won't you?"

"Yes of course. Pierre-Luc and Marcel are coming after lunch and we'll probably go down to the river."

"Oh," moaned Frank, "I'll never find you."

"Of course you will dear," said Violet. "Now hold still please Frank, otherwise I shall get cross."

"Can't Gunther come with us?" said Frank in English.

"No dear. Armand wants you to himself on this occasion and I agree with him. It's no small matter we're dealing with and it's a great honour... an act of love on his part."

Frank sighed. "Oh I know. It's just... oh never mind."

"Never mind what?" said Armand as he came into the room, dressed in a splendid suit and carrying a tall and important-looking hat in his hand. He crossed to Violet and kissed her. "You look lovely my dear."

"Thank you Armand. We shan't be long. I just need to get this tie right and I... can't seem to..."

"Let me," he said, moving in front of her and taking up the task. He laughed at the grimacing face of Frank before him and cuffed him playfully on the cheek as the tie was finally knotted home. "I'm proud of you my boy, and I shall be even prouder of you this afternoon." He bent down and kissed Frank on the cheek and then turned to Violet, missing the embarrassed look that Frank shot across at Gunther. Armand noticed the German boy sitting quietly. "Ah Gunther, there you are. Where's Gisela?"

Gunther stood to address the adult. "She will be down in a minute sir."

"Good. Well we'd better be off then." Armand stood aside to let Violet pass, then clapped his hand on Frank's shoulder. "Ready my boy?"

"Yes sir."

"Good. Let's go."

"Where will I find you Gunther?" Frank enquired as he neared the door.

"We'll be on the island building the tree house," said Gunther.

Frank nodded. Damn. They would start it without him and he'd so wanted to be there to supervise the construction. Still, at least he'd know where to find them all. "I'll see you all there then."

As they arrived in the hall, Gisela came down the main staircase. Violet and Armand stopped and looked up at her as she reached the last but one step and each in turn kissed her. "You look lovely my dear," said Violet.

"Lovely," echoed Armand.

"It is very nice of you to say so monsieur 'dame," replied Gisela in French, rolling her eyes and crossing her hands on her knees coquettishly. They all laughed happily as she descended the last step, adjusting her hat. Violet donned her own hat and pursed her lips in admiration as Armand swept his on to his head, giving himself an air of added stature and importance.

Philippe now appeared to hold the door for the party and they descended the few steps and got into the open doors of the motor car. As they sat down, Gisela took hold of Frank's hands and held them, looking into his eyes. "You are a very lucky boy," she whispered.

"I know," replied Frank, looking across at Armand.

Armand smiled shyly. "It is me who is the lucky one. I have gained a family and today will complete that happiness for me."

The three adults chatted amongst themselves as the car sped on its way through Chateauneuf and on towards Orleans. Frank daydreamed as he watched the familiar and now much-loved countryside roll by. He tried to think of England. He tried to think of Devon, of Florrie and Joe. But truth was that the memory of them was now only really kept alive by Violet's reminders, and in pictorial thought they had long since faded. Jesse he could still remember, as they had visited her on several occasions en route to his grandparents' house in London. He smiled to himself at the memory. The warmth of her greeting, the attention she had lavished on him and the sadness she had shown so openly when they finally had to leave.

And now here he was, on his way to Orleans to be formally adopted by Armand. He looked across at the man who had become his father in so many senses of the word. A quiet yet strong man... well, strong in character but sadly weakened by the terrible injuries he had received in the war.

The car pulled up in front of an imposing stone building, and as it stopped Frank was the first out to hold the door open whilst the others alighted. Philippe, as usual, came around as fast as his bad leg would allow and took over the duty just as the last person, Armand, stepped out. They stood for a few moments in a small grouping as Violet adjusted first Frank's and then Armand's ties and checked that all else was in order. Then they all marched into the building to be greeted by Monsieur Leclerc. Following the usual pleasantries, they all filed into a large room, at the end of which was a desk, behind which sat three official-looking gentlemen.

"Is this the boy?" the one in the middle asked. Armand ushered Frank forward and stood beside him with his hand on his shoulder.

"This is the boy... and this," he indicated Violet, "is his natural mother, my wife, Madame Taillefer.

"What is the boy's name?"

"Frank Balfour," said Violet.

"Balfoure. And where is the boy's father?"

Armand stepped forward slightly and leant towards the desk. "The boy's father is dead. Killed in the Great War on the soil of France, in defence of France." He stepped back and stood erect and proud beside his wife.

"The boy may sit down over there," the official commented and Frank, escorted now by Gisela, retired to some chairs set out to one side of the large room.

"Where is the boy's birth certificate?"

Violet fished in her handbag and withdrew the document. She handed it to Armand and he unfolded it and placed it in front of the man, who scrutinised it carefully.

He summoned Armand and Violet closer, and lowering his voice asked, "Madame was not married to the boy's father?"

"No she was not," said Armand. Violet looked at the floor, feeling the crimson creeping up her face and the smarting behind and within her eyes.

"No matter. Eh, your name was Balfoure before your marriage madame?"

"No, my name was Matthews. The boy's father was Balfour."

"And we are here to give the boy French citizenship and for

Monsieur Taillefer to formally adopt the boy as his son. By what name is the boy to be known?"

Armand looked at his wife and then across at the boy. He coughed and then spoke clearly and loudly so that all in the room could hear. "The boy will continue to be known by the name of the hero. Even though I take him as my son. His name will be Frank Balfour."

Frank looked up at Armand, who returned his gaze. The older man smiled encouragement and Frank returned his smile with the openness that Armand had grown to love.

"Who is the witness to this document?" asked the official, and Leclerc stepped forward and stood beside Armand. Frank watched from his chair as the signing and swearing continued. He felt excited, elated and very proud, but above all, if he was honest, he wanted to get back to his friends. It seemed an eternity before the men behind the desk finally stood up and leant, one by one, across the desk to shake the hand of first Armand and then Violet. The centre man then handed Armand a document and gave him some instructions as to what would be necessary to complete the registration and obtain the 'carte d'identite' for the boy.

Armand thanked him profusely and they all left the room in silence, walked to the main entrance and stood on the top steps. Armand summoned Frank to come closer, and as he did so he seized him with both hands and planted a kiss on each cheek. "You are my son now Frank and I am so proud of you." He turned to Violet, his eyes alight with joy, and she slipped into his arms.

"Thank you my love," she whispered in his ear. "Thank you for everything." She looked past him at Frank standing there with Gisela and Leclerc. "What have you to say Frank?"

Frank felt every eye on him and felt the importance of the occasion. He thought quickly, knowing that what he said now would be remembered by all of them for all time. "I... I... thank you Armand. Thank you... father."

Tears flooded down Armand's face as he held out his free arm and Frank slipped into its embrace. They stayed like that for several moments before Gisela tapped Violet on the shoulder. She embraced her friend as Armand brandished the paper in the air. "You are a citizen of France and you are my son," he cried.

Frank looked at the paper in Armand's hand. He couldn't make out all of it, but he could see his name near the top. Frank Balfoure with an 'e' on the end was clearly written. He had gained a letter as well as a father and a country.

......

"I know it's there. I'm telling you it has to be there," whispered Frank as he and Gunther came through the dining room. Gunther glanced back through the French doors at Armand, Violet and Gisela sitting on the patio, under the shade of a large umbrella.

"Shouldn't we tell them where we're going?"

Frank followed his gaze. "No, we're not doing anything wrong. We're only exploring." He tugged at his friend's arm. "Come on, I'll show you the way." He led him through and into the hall, across and behind the staircase, where, feeling along the panelling, he found a carved rosette. He turned it slowly before pushing gently on the panel, which moved slightly, creaking as it did. Frank stopped and looked at Gunther's excited and incredulous face. "Told you, didn't I? You didn't believe me, did you?"

"How did you know? Did someone tell you?"

Frank smiled. "No silly. No one knows except us. I just read about it in a book and figured out that it could happen here, so I tried every knob in the place and this one worked." He pushed harder at the panel and it opened like a door on to steps leading down into the gloom. "We need some light. It's jet black down there."

"There's a hurricane lamp in the outer kitchen. Shall I run and get it?"

"Yes," said Frank, "and light it first. I'll shut this and wait here."

Gunther ran off and returned several minutes later, walking slowly with the lit lamp, its glass still up.

"What do I do now?"

Frank took the lamp and lowered the glass gently as he turned up the wick. It spluttered a few times and smoke blackened the glass before he turned the wick back down and it shone out clear and bright. He handed the lamp to Gunther and turned once more to the rosette. Frank opened the door and ushered Gunther through and down the first few steps. He followed him, closing the panel behind them and locking it shut with a knob on the inside. They looked at each other apprehensively for a moment before Frank took charge of the lamp and led the way slowly down the steep steps. At first they held on to the walls at either side, but as their hands picked up more and more cobwebs they plucked up the courage to walk in the middle of the steps, which in any event seemed to be stone and quite substantial. Thick spider webs brushed against their faces as they went on down and Gunther began to get quite frightened. "How deep have we gone?" he whispered.

"I don't..." Frank's voice, spoken in normal tones, echoed and reverberated in the long, cylindrical chamber. He lowered his voice to a whisper. "I don't know, but I think that we must be below the level of the cellars now." As he spoke they reached the foot of the long, straight flight. A tunnel, just over the height of a man, ran off level at a right angle, its construction a continuous curve of brickwork except that here and there along its length there were square shafts which led upwards. In the walls of these shafts irons were set, and the two boys stopped at the second one and looked up.

"Where do you think they lead?" said Gunther.

"I don't know, but I guess that they lead up into the main cellar passages. Probably up to those iron covers in the floor which I always assumed were drains."

"Then this tunnel would give access to the whole chateau if anyone knew about it."

"Yes, but it's our secret, isn't it?"

"What about Pierre-Luc and Marcel. Will you tell them?"

"I might, I might not. Here, we could play some mighty tricks on them before we told them, couldn't we?"

"We could if we could find a way out other than crawling up through those covers, which I don't really fancy."

Frank looked at his friend in the light of the lamp. "Yes, we need to find where it leads to. It stands to reason that it must lead somewhere, otherwise what's the point of it?" He held the lamp higher to see as far as he could down the tunnel. It ran on in a straight line, on and beyond the reach of the light they held. "Come on," said Frank, we can't leave it here. Let's find out where it goes to."

Gunther looked at the eager face of his friend. He didn't like it down here, so far below the ground. A slight feeling of panic gripped him. Nobody knew they were here and if... if anything happened then how would anyone ever find them. "We could be lost down here forever," he whispered to himself.

"Frank turned to him. "Eh, what did you say?"

"I said we could be lost down here forever. Nobody knows we're here."

Frank grinned and made a ghoulish face, raising the lamp to accentuate his features. "Lost forever," he intoned in a sepulchral voice. "Lost forever," came the echoing reply.

"Shut up Frank," urged Gunther. "Shut up or I'll go back up."

"Sorry," grinned Frank. "Oh come on, it's a straight passageway from the bottom of the steps. I tell you what, if it starts twisting about then we'll pack it up until another day. Alright?"

"Alright," said Gunther, "but mind if it gets any different I'm off."

"Me too," laughed Frank. He hoisted the lamp aloft and the two boys crept carefully along the tunnel, hand in hand.

"We must be beyond the walls of the chateau by now surely," said Gunther after another few minutes of careful but steady progress.

Frank stopped for a moment and thought. "Yes, you must be right.

We must be under the patio area by now." They carried on, and after about half the distance they had already travelled, they came to what seemed to be a dead end.

"Well that's that," said Gunther, disappointed. "We'll just have to go back up. What a silly thing to do. Fancy going to all that trouble of building a passage if all it does is go nowhere."

Frank said nothing. He approached the seeming dead end and held the lamp close. It was stone at the end. Smooth stone that seemed to have no features at all except for an iron knob set at about waist height. He reached out and tried to turn the knob. It didn't move. It was fixed firmly into the stone. He looked down at his feet. The flooring here was also stone, smooth like the end wall. Featureless. But was it? He knelt down, and the diminution of light made a nervous Gunther gasp. "What are you doing?"

An excited Frank motioned him forward to look at the floor. Set in the stone leading away in a quarter circle from the left-hand side of the end stone panel was an iron track. "It must be a door. It has to be a door," he said excitedly as he stood up. "The knob doesn't turn because you have to pull on it." He turned and put the lamp down on the floor just behind them. "Here, help me pull on the knob."

The two boys grabbed hold of the knob and pulled hard. At first nothing moved. They pulled harder and the stone end panel moved ever so slightly. "It's moving," shouted Frank, and the echo of his excited cry ran off down the passage and came back again. "Pull as hard as you can."

They pulled and tugged at the door and gradually it came open, moving with greater ease as it gained momentum. A chink of brilliant light showed on first the left-hand and then the right-hand side as the stone swung in on its hinges. The outer face became visible and they could see that it was carved into a platform or shelf, upon which was the stone figure of the Madonna. "It's the figure in the grotto on the ha-ha below the patio," whispered Frank in amazement. "We've come out below and beyond the patio."

The two boys scrambled through and stood in the light, gazing at each other.

Frank was pleased and excited at the seemingly marvellous discovery, but Gunther was just pleased to be safe and sound. "Mustn't forget the lamp," said Frank, diving back in to retrieve it, "and we must shut it again." He raised the glass and blew out the lamp.

On either side of the Madonna there was an ornate knob, which outwardly seemed to serve no useful purpose other than decoration. Now, however, the actual purpose intended by its makers was revealed and the boys were able to easily and quietly pull on them to shut the door to their secret passageway. They made their way along the lower patio to the steps, through and up to the upper patio.

"Good heavens," said Violet as they came up and on to the sun patio. "Where did you two spring from? You went into the house, didn't you?"

"Yes... well we... we've just been mooching about," said Frank, trying to hide the lamp behind his back.

"Yes just... shall we go back inside Frank?" asked Gunther.

"Yes coming," said Frank, and the two of them rushed past their elders, making for the French doors.

Armand reached out and held Frank as he passed. He motioned him down and Frank bent his ear to his mouth. "Did you shut the panel?" he whispered. Frank nodded. "And the Madonna?" Frank nodded again. Armand winked at him. "Good boys."

......

"Whose serve is it?"

"Yours I believe, Gisela," said Violet.

"Who's winning?" called Armand as he came down the steps to the court.

"Violet of course," Gisela moaned.

"Only just," Violet laughed. She skipped to the edge of the court. "Armand darling, how lovely to see you. What brings you home at this hour of the day?"

Armand walked on to the court and kissed her. "Nothing really. There was nothing much happening at the factory and I fancied some fresh air. I may change and go out and help Jules."

"Oh do you have to darling? Why not stay here," said Violet, cuddling up to him.

"Yes, stay with us," called Gisela, walking up to the net. "You can play the winner."

He laughed lightly. "No thank you ladies. I think I would be better employed in the fields this afternoon."

"Well don't get all dirty and don't get too tired," said Violet.

"No madame," he said, saluting.

"And take plenty to drink in this heat. You know your kidney has been playing you up recently and I don't want you to get sick just before I go off to England."

"I'll be alright."

"I'll be alright," she mimicked.

He laughed lightly and slapped her on the bottom as he turned away. "See you later."

"See you later," the two women chorused as they made their way back to their respective ends of the court.

A little while later Armand, dressed now in a stout pair of boots and some equally robust moleskin trousers, left the chateau. He wore an open white smock shirt and a wide-brimmed hat and he carried a walking cane. He whistled as he descended the steps and swung his cane idly as he walked down the path, through the gates and out into the road beyond.

Philippe, washing the motor car just under the arched entrance to the farm yard, saw and heard his master. He straightened up and called out, "Do you need me monsieur?"

"No Philippe," called Armand over his shoulder. "I'm just going for a walk over to the fields to Mesnil to see how Jules is getting on. You carry on there."

Philippe shrugged his shoulders and waved at the departing man before resuming his work. Armand walked on, whistling quietly to himself. The day was hot and sultry. Even the birds had stopped singing in the heat and the day's chorus was left to the crickets, scratching away their tuneless little songs in the short grass beside the road. As he walked they flew up in front of his feet and landed ahead until a crowd of them preceded him.

He rounded the corner by the farm tenanted by the old woman and her two daughters. The buildings were laid out in the familiar horseshoe arrangement, with the centre section nominally given over to human occupation whilst the two outer wings housed the animals, together with stores and machinery which needed to be under cover. In practice, the division of occupation was extremely blurred and livestock of all sorts wandered in and out of all parts of the building.

He smiled to himself as he thought of his last visit, where they had bustled about trying to clear chickens off the table, brushing hay from a chair as they begged him to be seated.

"A pastis patron?" the old crone had croaked as she rummaged in the piles of dusty old sacks in the corner, much to the annoyance of a sitting hen. She had turned from her search, bottle in hand, and held it aloft triumphantly. Aloft? With a back as bent as hers, the horizontal plane of the bottle had barely altered, but it was duly transported to the table along with cries for a daughter to fetch a glass. Armand laughed to himself as he remembered the production of the cracked and frosted glass. He shuddered as he recalled the gnarled, blackened hands of the old woman reaching out for it and wiping it 'clean' on her filthy apron before setting it before him with as much of a flourish as she could muster. The pastis, when it came, was cloudy as it left the bottle and he wisely refused water, which in any event would have made little or no difference to its consistency.

He had told Violet of his visit and she, of course, had laughed along with him, but admonished him for taking the drink. "Oh I doubt it would have harmed me very much," he argued. "A drink of plain water: now there's a different matter. That would have killed me for certain!"

The gates to the enclosed yard were shut, and through their heavy ironwork he could see little or no human activity. Presumably they were all out in the fields. He walked on and turned left past the farm on the right, which they referred to as Mesnil itself. Untenanted at the moment, the buildings lay quiet and empty but the land still had to be worked. He had thought, once, of looking for another tenant to take it on, but if he was honest with himself he rather enjoyed the responsibility and though he didn't need the money as such, the returns from working the land himself with hired labour were far greater than if it were let out.

Besides, it gave him something to do, something to plan for and something to get him out of the office at the factory whenever he felt like a breath of fresh air. He stopped and stood looking out over the flat fields leading up to the levee. In the plots beyond, he could see the old woman and her daughters bent into their daily toil, pulling away at the weeds that threatened to choke their living. A clump of trees stood alone amongst the flat fields and he smiled to himself as he recognised the remains of a tree house high in the crook of the tallest one. Last summer's great adventure quietly decomposing, the boys having moved on to greater ones on the river.

Freshly turned-up soil on the long lines of asparagus showed up now, and at the end of the field he could see Jules struggling behind the plough, seeking to keep it in the furrows as he urged the horses on. Light work, this, in the fertile sand of the flood plain, but back-breaking nonetheless. The plough stopped and Jules called to the horses to stand as he released the handle and walked forward to the plough. He bent down and then knelt on the ground as Armand arrived. "What's up Jules?"

Startled, Jules stood and turned to the voice. "Oh patron it's you. You gave me a start." The horses lurched forward. "Whoa!" he cried.

Armand went forward to their heads and held on to their bridles. "What's up?"

"Bloody stone."

"A stone? They're rarer than hens' teeth here surely."

"Usually, but every so often one turns up from the deep and it's usually me that hits it. Back them up a bit can you and I'll pull it clear." Armand clucked to the horses and pushed back on their harnesses. They resisted, worried at the strange man forcing them into this equally strange manoeuvre. Armand persisted and succeeded in backing them up a couple of steps. "Hold them there while I roll it clear," called Jules as he pulled at the large stone.

He tugged at it, scrabbling away at the surrounding soil. Then he knelt down on one side of the mound and, bending forward, pulled and rolled the stone towards himself, up the slope of the haunched-up soil.

"Nearly got it," he shouted. "Hold them still now." He gasped as the weight of the stone pulled on his arms and his knees slipped in the soft earth. The boulder broke from his grasp and rolled back down, crashing into the ploughshare with a loud crash. "Damn," he yelled as he fell backwards into the next trench.

The horses felt the blow on the plough, heard their master's shout and lunged forward, knocking Armand off balance. He lost his grip on the harness and fell backwards into the path of the frightened animals. A heavy knee clipped him hard on his chin, knocking him practically senseless as he slipped further under their legs. Alarmed at the fact that they were now standing on the figure of the man, the horses reared up and rushed forward, trying to get clear of this unusual obstruction. Ironshod hooves thudded down on to Armand's chest in a jumble of unrecognisable sensations. A brief moment of peace as they passed over his body was interrupted forever by the cruel cutting edge of the guide wheel and then the ploughshare itself.

Jules struggled to his feet and stood aghast at the scene before him. Armand lay crumpled up like a discarded rag doll half buried in the soil. His dead eyes stared up at the clear blue sky and his white shirt soaked up the startling red blood that gently oozed from the terrible gashes in his torso.

......

"Are you alright madame," whispered Leclerc.

Violet nodded but kept her head bent down, staring at the floor with the monogrammed handkerchief held to her mouth. It had been a week now and still she could not contemplate... could not countenance the event that had so shaken her life. Tears welled in her eyes but she let them fall freely, splashing into her lap. Gisela came into the room. She looked at Leclerc and he went across to her. She whispered in his ear and he left.

"There my love," she said, kneeling in front of her distraught friend. She took the handkerchief from her hand and dabbed Violet's eyes. "Your father is attending to your friends but I think that the notaire is ready now for the reading of the will... that is if you are well enough."

Violet looked into the eyes of her friend. "Oh Gisela, he's only been in the ground for an hour and now we have to dissect his assets in public. I don't know... I... oh..." She buried her head in her hands.

"Let's get it over with my love, then you can relax." Violet sighed and nodded her assent. She stood and Gisela took her arm and guided her to the door, out into the hall and across and into the library, where they entered by the large double doors. A desk had been placed at the end of the room, and at it sat the notaire with his assistant. Chairs had been set out in front and most of them were occupied except for the front row. The notaire rose to his feet, whilst trying at the same time to hold on to the piles of papers, and stood whilst Violet came forward with Gisela to sit down, alone, on the front row. Gisela retired to the rear of the room as Ernest entered with Frank. He nodded to various people as the two of them passed down the aisle. To Elsie, sitting with Alice in the centre of the room, he mouthed the words "Are you alright?" She nodded her reply and he and Frank took the chairs beside Violet.

Frank looked through his own tear-blurred eyes, up into his mother's grief-stricken face. She stared straight ahead, seemingly oblivious to the proceedings, and he sought out her hand and held it. He glanced to the back of the room at Gunther, sitting beside his mother, and his friend returned his wan smile. In between them sat people and friends of various classes from Leclerc and his wife through to the various tenant farmers. Philippe, Jean-Claude and Marie sat towards the back of the room, pain and grief written large on their still shocked faces. Immediately behind his mother, looking stony-faced, sat Nicole, Armand's sister, with her husband Henri, looking uncomfortable and out of place.

The notaire coughed and ostentatiously opened up a large document, holding it up for all to see. "This monsieur 'dames is the will of the late Armand Henri Taillefer. You may all examine it separately if you wish, but I felt that it would be better if I ran through the principle contents for you all." He stared out at the congregation looking for approval or dissent, and having found none of either proceeded.

"The bulk of the estate including the chateau, the shares in the factory and the vacant farms are left to Monsieur Armand's adopted son, Frank Balfoure." A gasp ran around the audience and Nicole barely stifled her exhaled explosion of dismay. Her husband grabbed for her hand and held it tight, hoping to avoid a scene in this company. The notaire acknowledged the effect of his words on the assembly by lapsing into silence briefly before continuing.

"A fixed income from the shares in the factory is to go to Madame Violet for her lifetime and then revert to Frank upon her death. The balance of the income, after maintenance, upkeep and payment of other beneficiaries..." He paused and looked around the room. "...is to be held in trust to the benefit of Frank."

"My God this is intolerable," shouted Nicole, rising to her feet. "Come Henri, we are leaving."

"I would suggest that madame remains,", said the notaire. "There are some benefits within the will which she may be interested in."

"Sit down please my love," whispered Henri. Nicole looked down at him, looked around at the faces staring at her. She raised her hands in a dismissive gesture and sat. Violet's head in front of her remained stock still, seemingly unaware of the outburst.

"We come now to the tenanted farms," said the notaire. "Monsieur Armand was at pains to stress that this next bequest was in no way a reflection or a slight to any of the main beneficiaries. He felt that the income from the factory would be sufficient... he felt that this next bequest was a debt he wanted to repay." He cleared his throat. "The tenanted farms are left to their current tenants to hold free."

Stunned silence greeted his last words and the notaire looked around the room waiting for some other reaction.

Very soon couples and groups began whispering to themselves, and as he remained silent the hubbub of conversation grew louder as excited people discussed their good fortune.

The old woman and her two daughters, alone, showed no emotion and continued to just sit, hands held together, staring ahead. Any change of ownership would not bring any alteration to the grind of their lives.

The notaire waited for a while to further the effect and then called for silence, as he wished to continue. "Monsieur Armand's faithful and devoted servants and friends, Jean-Claude, Marie and Philippe, are to receive their wages for the remainder of their lifetimes, irrespective of whether their services are required, and in addition all three are to be permitted to occupy their present quarters in the chateau and on the estate for as long as they so desire."

Nicole threw her hands in the air. "Why have I had to sit here and endure this? Surely there is now nothing left for me to have any interest in?"

"On the contrary madame," said the notaire firmly. "We now come to Monsieur Armand's last bequest, apart from a few minor ones which I have listed here. The jewellery which has remained in the family, handed down from his parents and grandparents is, with the exception of the listed pieces referred to in this document which have already become the property of Madame Violet... the jewellery is to be passed to monsieur's sister Madame Nicole."

Again a silence hung in the room. Then Nicole stood. She pointed at the notaire. "You! You have... you have made me sit here for all this time in order to be fobbed off with a few baubles!" She tugged at her husband's sleeve. "Come Henri, we will leave this place. We have lost everything, our honour, our family name and value to these... these foreigners..." Her spluttering rage left her finally speechless as Henri stood and they made their way into the aisle and along to the back of the room. Philippe stood and moved ahead of them, and as they approached the door he held it open for them.

All eyes were fixed on the departing couple as Violet stood and called down the aisle. "You could have it all if it would only bring me back my husband." Eyes swivelled round to Violet. Nicole stopped dead and Henri bumped into her. She turned and looked down the room at the widow, sniffed disdainfully, turned back again and swept through and out.

January 1927

"**W**hen are we going home Violet?"

"Home? We are at home," said Violet, looking up from the book she was reading.

"I meant home to France," said Frank. "I miss all my friends."

Violet put aside her book and patted the seat next to her on the sofa. "Aren't you happy here?" she said, taking hold of both his hands and guiding him down to sit beside her.

He looked away from her and into the fire. "It's not that I'm not happy here. It's just that... just that... well our home is in Germigny, isn't it?"

Violet let go of one of his hands and cupped his chin, turning his face to hers. She stroked his smooth cheek. "I know you miss it darling but... but it's just... it's just that without Armand..." She fought the tears that threatened. "Without Armand there I feel so alone."

"But how can you? You'd have me and there's Marie and Jean-Claude, Philippe and everyone else. Aren't we ever going home?"

She looked away, unable to face him now directly, unable to lie. Did she want to go back? She felt torn. Armand had left everything to them and now they were absentees. The chateau he had loved so much was cold and empty, and the only real contact they had had with France for some time had been the monies she regularly received from the notaire with a list of the accounts and details of deductions made. She would have to go back soon of course. She knew that. There were things that would need attention, decisions that would have to be made. But live there alone without... without him... without Armand?

Could she do that? She turned and faced the boy. "Darling we must go back soon." His eyes lit up and she held her hand up to stifle any comment. "But only to sort things out. After that we must find you a place in a school here and we must try to make this our home."

"But Violet I can't go to school here. I don't want to go to school here. I want to go back to my school in Saint Benoit. Please can I?"

"Darling you can't live there alone, can you?"

"Why not? It's my house. Armand left the chateau to me, didn't he?"

"Yes I know he did darling..."

"Well then it's my home, isn't it?"

"Yes it's your home but... darling don't you see that you cannot simply live there alone at your age."

"Then come with me."

Violet looked at the earnest face of her son. She sighed. She hadn't wanted to move back into her parent's house at first. Having been mistress of her own home it was not easy to become a daughter again, and at first she had told herself that it was only a temporary arrangement whilst she recovered from her great loss. Now she knew that for her, France had been Armand and that without him it was a foreign land in which she, in spite of having mastered the language, felt herself to be a stranger.

"I... we are English Frank. We belong here and you need to go to an English school to learn about... about being English for a start. For goodness sake you've got a slight French accent."

"What's wrong with that?"

"Nothing darling, except that you're not French, you are English."

"I don't want to be anything. I just want to be able to live in my own house... chateau, and be with my friends."

"I know you do darling, but I've decided that this really is for the best."

She saw his look of horrified despondency. "We'll go there quite often. We can spend all or part of the summer holidays there, but my mind's made up, we will live here and you will go to school here."

The boy stood up, brushing away his mother's outstretched hands. "I wish... I wish I'd stayed in France."

He saw the hurt in her eyes but pushed the barb deeper.

"I wish I'd stayed in Devon and not come to live with you."

The shock registered on her face and she stood suddenly, knocking her book to the floor. She raised her hand to strike him but he stood in front of her, defiant, and her hand stayed. They stared at each other, the anger flying from their eyes, pain and betrayal written on each countenance. Time seemed to have stopped, before her face gradually began to crumple and the tears blinded her. She lowered her arm and felt him grasp her and cuddle into her body. "I'm sorry Violet," he sobbed. "I didn't mean those horrid things. It's just... it's just that I miss him so much."

She buried her face in the top of his shoulder, stroking the back of his head. "It's alright my love. I know. I know. I loved him too you know."

They remained locked in each other's arms for some time before he spoke again. "I can't even remember Devon really."

She laughed through her tears. He kept his head buried in her body, but she could feel that he too was laughing and crying at the same time. "We'll not forget France Frank. We'll go in the next few weeks and we'll spend as much of every holiday there as we can. I promise."

He didn't reply. Instead he held tight to her, his face still buried, hiding his shame at the way he had tried to hurt her.

Ernest came into the room. "What's this?" he asked.

Violet looked up at him and shook her head, warning him against further comment. "We're just a bit sad, daddy. We're both missing Armand and Frank is missing his home and his friends." Ernest nodded his understanding. He strode across the room and clasped them both within his arms. Then he released them and left the room quietly.

......

"Honestly mother I don't want to meet people. I'm quite happy as I am," said Violet, exasperated by her mother's insistence.

"Nonsense dear, you're a young woman and you should meet suitable people."

"Mother, I'm not a penniless widow. I have a wholly adequate income of my own and I don't need to meet anybody else."

"I know dear. I'm not saying it for any reason other than... well I think you should have more fun out of life. I mean Frank's at school now during the day and all you do is just stay here. You need to see some life my dear."

Violet laughed then. A rueful, almost embittered laugh. "Life? Life mother? I've lived a thousand lives. I've loved and lost two men. I've watched hundreds more die in a stupid war I still can't understand to this day... I... oh what's the use."

"What's the use of what?" said Ernest, coming into the room.

Violet turned to her father. "Oh father it's mother. Tell her I don't need to... to get out and about and meet people."

"Of course you don't my dear. There is a gentleman coming to dinner tonight, but I can assure you it's not simply for your benefit darling. I am hoping he will take the lease of the Stanmore shop so I want you all to make him feel at home." Violet shrugged her shoulders, defeated by his good humour. She left the room muttering that she was going to change and would see them later.

Out in the hall she ran into Alice. "She's driving me mad Alice," Violet complained. "Can't she see that I'm happy as I am, just me and Frank." Alice smiled and Violet continued. "Does she do the same to you?"

"No dear," said Alice, seriously. "I think she knows I've made my bed, if you see what I mean."

Violet wasn't quite sure that she did, but returned Alice's smile nonetheless.

"Oh well," she said, "I'd better go up and get ready to impress. Are you attending this dinner, or are you lucky enough to be otherwise engaged?"

"I'm the maid tonight."

"Lucky thing," called Violet as she mounted the steps. "You wouldn't like to swap would you?"

"I don't think your father would like that," said Alice to her departing figure.

A little while later the doorbell rang. Violet crept to the top of the gallery as Alice opened the door. She heard the deep male voice of the entering guest and her father's welcoming tones as he bustled out of the study to greet him. She tried to peer down the steps but was afraid of being seen. "What are you doing?" whispered Frank.

She turned, surprised and not a little embarrassed at being caught out. "Oh Frank... I... I," she giggled. "I was trying to get a look at father's dinner guest without being seen."

"Why don't you want to be seen? Aren't we going down in a minute?"

She straightened her face. "Yes. Yes of course we are darling, it's just that... it's just that I wanted... well to see what he was like before I actually had to meet him." She changed the subject. "How was school today?"

"It was alright I suppose. We didn't do very much. We haven't done very much all term really, but I've made some friends."

"Oh darling," said Violet crossing to him and hugging him. "That's wonderful. Are they nice?"

"Well one of them, Philip, he's quite good fun and he helps me with my English spelling whilst I help him with arithmetic."

"Just wait until you start French. Then you'll be popular."

He smiled wryly. "I doubt it. I expect the teachers will tell me I'm saying it all wrong and the boys will laugh at me and call me sissy."

"Don't be silly dear," she said. "Come on, let's get ready to go and help your grandfather impress his business colleague."

About fifteen minutes later, Violet and Frank entered the parlour. Elsie was seated on the sofa whilst Ernest and his guest were standing over by the window, looking out into the garden. "Ah there you are darling," said Ernest, breaking away from his guest and coming over to the door. "Come on in and meet Jim Slater. Jim, this is my daughter Violet and her son Frank."

Slater observed this handsome woman standing by the door. A son? Was she then married? Surely not? Matthews had given him the distinct impression that she lived at home with him. A widow? Ah, the war. Definitely the war. He stepped forward. "Pleased to meet you Mrs...?"

"Taillefer," said Violet, leaving it at that for effect to see how this man handled discomfiture.

"Taillefer," the man said in a passable imitation of the pronunciation. "Taillefer. That's not English, is it?"

"French," said Violet. "My husband's... my husband was Monsieur Taillefer."

"Was?"

Ernest interjected. "Violet's husband, Armand, was killed in a tragic accident last year. Tragic."

Slater took hold of Violet's hand and held it. She felt powerless to refuse... powerless to retrieve it. "Oh forgive me. I didn't mean to pry." He looked at the boy standing protectively beside his mother. "And the poor boy, what is his name?"

"My name is Frank," said the boy, the slight accent registering in Slater's mind.

"Come and sit with me here my dear," called Elsie. Violet nodded to the man and went across to sit with her mother. Frank followed and sat on the arm of the sofa to be close to her. Slater turned and continued his conversation with Ernest.

Violet chatted quietly with her mother whilst observing the man. Of just under average height, he obviously had a tendency to overeat, as was evidenced by the bulge in his waistcoat. His eyes were grey, hooded by enormously bushy eyebrows matching his full head of grey hair, which was in contrast perfectly cut and parted in the middle. He was what... about in his mid-forties, and his manner indicated a self-assurance that would come with comfortable means.

He turned, seeming to notice her attention, and tipped his head to her and smiled whilst carrying on his conversation with Ernest. 'God I hope he hasn't misinterpreted my interest,' thought Violet, seeking to control her tendency to blush. She noticed then that his complexion was a little ruddy and the lips on his small mouth had a hint of blue. He will need to be careful of his health in later years, she thought.

Alice came into the room and sidled over to Elsie. She bent down and whispered in her ear. "Ernest dearest and Mr Slater..."

"Oh do call me Jim, Mrs Matthews," he said jovially.

Elsie smiled. "Then you must call me Elsie."

"Certainly I shall."

Elsie blushed. Violet watched her mother, amazed. She was actually playing up to this man and enjoying the whole thing.

"Well... Jim... and Ernest, dinner is served if you'd like to go on through."

Slater assisted Elsie to rise from the sofa and held her arm as Alice held the doors open for them to pass through. Ernest held back a little, and taking Violet's arm together with Frank's he propelled them through into the dining room. "Seems like a jolly nice chap, doesn't he?" he said quietly under his breath. Violet said nothing, but she caught Frank's look and a silent message passed between them.

In the dining room, Elsie indicated which seat was hers. Slater guided her to it and held the chair for her as she was seated. He looked up expectantly as the others entered. "Where do you want me to sit?" he enquired.

Ernest let go of Violet's and Frank's arms and came forward into the room. He indicated the two chairs set out on one side of the table. "You sit here old chap, next to Violet, and you, Frank, you can sit on this side opposite your mother." He waited until they were all seated before sitting himself.

"Is Alice not dining with us tonight?" asked Elsie.

There was a short, pregnant silence before Ernest, looking slightly embarrassed, broke it by laughingly saying, "No dear, she's a bit busy tonight." Slater seemed not to notice the conversation at all as he attended to the careful placing of his napkin. Alice entered the room with a large soup tureen and proceeded to ladle soup into each bowl in turn. Slater leant aside as she got to him and addressed Frank.

"Where do you go to school Frank?"

Frank started at the unexpected question. "I, eh... oh I go to the school in Finchley sir."

"And do you like it?"

"Well it's... it's alright I suppose but..." He looked at his mother before continuing. "...I preferred my school in France."

Violet looked up. "Now Frank, you know that's not possible." Frank looked across at her and caught the intended warning. He looked down and concentrated on the soup, which had just arrived in his bowl.

"I should think not," said Slater. "Far better to attend a decent school don't you know." Violet cringed inwardly at this unlooked-for and unwanted support, but the man continued. "Need to know you're British you know."

Frank's spoon froze in mid air. "But I am..."

"Armand left an estate in France which includes a magnificent chateau," interrupted Ernest, fearing that the boy might say something which could be construed as rude by Slater. "That and a large ironworks." Violet shot a look at her father, but he didn't seem to notice. "Produces a handsome income for the both of them, don't you know."

"Daddy dearest, I'm sure Mr Slater isn't the slightest bit interested in all of this," said Violet, her eyes pleading with him to shut up.

"On the contrary dear lady, I am most interested," Slater interrupted.

'I'm sure you are Mr Slater,' Violet thought. 'I'm sure you are.' She looked across at Frank, who continued with his soup whilst still smarting from the implied criticism of his beloved France. Slater, too, took another slurp of his soup before continuing. "You see much of my business revolves around contact with France."

"With France?" queried Violet. Frank looked up, interested. "But I thought you had shops."

Slater laughed. "Yes, wine and spirit shops. We also have cellars and we import wine from France and bottle it ourselves with our own label. Slater's Wine Limited."

"Ah I see," said Violet. "And how many shops did you say you had?"

"Four, spread throughout north London."

"Soon to be five, eh Jim?" said Ernest jovially.

Slater looked around at him and returned his smile. "Indeed yes. Soon to be five!" He turned back to Violet. "Excuse me, but are you able to speak French?"

"Why yes of course. Well quite well. Not as well as Frank of course, who is bi-lingual. Why?"

Slater brought his hands together in a praying position and held them up to his lips. "I don't speak a word of French, and since the departure of one member of staff we have enormous difficulties with correspondence in French and increasingly with telephone calls. You couldn't help, could you?"

Violet held her hands up defensively. "Oh no. No Mr Slater..."

"Call me Jim please."

"Mr... Jim I don't mean to... it's just that I don't... I have no wish to take on employment at present. Or come to that any need."

"Heavens no Violet, I didn't mean that. I merely hoped that you could perhaps help me out sometimes with translation. If you didn't want to come to the office I could perhaps bring letters here for you?" He waited expectantly and there was a silence that Violet felt impelled, yet reluctant, to fill.

"Surely you could do that for Jim, dearest?" said Elsie. Violet turned to her, her eyes flashing a command of silence. Her look was returned with an innocent smile.

"I'm sure Violet would be only too happy to help out," said Ernest.

Violet, beaten, fixed a smile on her face and turned from her mother to face Slater. "Why yes Mr... eh... Jim, yes of course I could, from time to time." She caught Frank's look of pity, mixed with a little scorn at her defeat. "And... and of course there's Frank. If I'm not here Frank could help you... couldn't you Frank?"

Frank shot a despairing look at his mother before lowering his eyes and hiding his emotions.

"Splendid," announced Slater. "Goodness me Ernest, this evening is turning out to be a good one, eh?"

"Glad you're enjoying it old man," said Ernest, pleased as punch at how things had panned out. Alice came back into the room and proceeded to clear the bowls. "That was lovely my dear," he said smiling up at her as he handed her his bowl.

"Yes indeed... lovely," repeated Slater, leaning aside for her to take his bowl from the table.

"Have you had any Alice?" questioned Elsie. Slater's face took on a slightly quizzical expression.

Her reply, whispered to Elsie, was lost to him as Ernest, seeing the question perched on his lips, sought to change the subject. "Eh, I wonder if any wine comes from your chateau Frank?"

The mention of wine diverted Slater's attention and he turned and looked first at Ernest, then across at Frank. He made as if to pursue the question with the boy, but decided instead to address it to Violet. "Where exactly is your chateau Violet?"

"Oh it's not mine... Jim... it was left to Frank. The whole estate was left to Frank. The chateau, the farms... those that were kept within the estate and indeed the factory. I merely receive an income for life."

"And a pretty handsome one at that," interrupted Ernest. Violet shot him a look of reproach, but he seemed unaware of any misdemeanour.

Slater, meanwhile, was staring across the table at Frank as Alice entered the room again, bearing a huge tray on which were perched various dishes and tureens. Ernest rose to his feet and went across to the sideboard to help her put it down. Slater's gaze shifted from Frank and took in the strange sight of the master of the house assisting his domestic servant. Ernest returned to his seat carrying a large flat meat dish, upon which were laid out succulent slices of roast beef.

He turned to Slater, oblivious to any query over his actions. "Roast beef. My absolute favourite." Alice placed a pile of heated plates in front of him. "Jim, you first," he said.

"No. Oh no, Ernest, please serve the ladies," said Slater.

Ernest obliged as Alice placed the dishes and tureens down the centre of the table. "Could you pass that along to your grandmother," he said to Frank, handing him the first plate. Frank delivered it and returned to his seat.

"Where did you say the chateau was?" Slater asked Frank as he accepted a tureen and ladled potatoes on to his plate before passing it on.

"Germigny-des-Pres, Chateauneuf-sur-Loire," said Frank, deliberately rolling and luxuriating in the music of the names.

Slater picked up the first word only, and even then misinterpreted it. "Germany did you say? Where's that?"

"It's in the Loire Valley about twenty miles from Orleans," said Violet, fearing that Frank would probably seize upon and continue to take the advantage of language to confuse the man he so obviously did not like.

"Really? And you say you grow wine there... well vines?"

"I don't really know." Violet turned to Frank. "Do we darling?"

"We grow some in fields," replied Frank, "but the grapes are harvested by Monsieur Fichot."

"Yes. Yes that's it... Monsieur Fichot." She turned back to Slater and took the tureen he had just finished with from him. "Our neighbour takes the grapes, and in payment he gives us back wine, although quite what happens to it then I don't know."

"It's in the cellars," piped up Frank. "Hundreds of bottles when I last saw."

Slater's eyes lit up. "Hundreds of bottles. Is it a good wine?"

"I wouldn't know," said Violet, "...and neither, of course, would Frank."

Slater turned to Ernest, who was at that moment standing beside him, filling his wine glass. "Have you tried this wine Ernest?"

Ernest thought carefully as he moved across to first Violet and then Elsie, both of whom refused his offer, Elsie holding her hand over the rim of her glass. "I can't say if I have or if I haven't, old chap. I seem to have drunk quite a bit when I've been there, all of it good, but whether it was the estate wine I can't really say."

"Well my dear, if you ever want to sell it just let me know," said Slater.

Nodding in Frank's direction, Violet said, "It's not mine to sell, Mr Slater."

"Jim, please."

"It's not mine to sell Jim. It belongs to the estate and the estate is in trust for Frank until he reaches his majority."

Slater looked disappointed. "Ah well, what a pity. It would have been interesting to market a wine from an English-owned French vineyard."

"I am French," said Frank.

"Yes dear, you are French but you are English too," said Violet.

Frank has dual nationality, don't you know," said Ernest.

"Did you serve in the war Mr Slater?" asked Violet, immediately wishing she hadn't by the heavy silence that seemed to thump down on the little grouping. Ernest and Elsie sat rooted to their chairs, dreading the embarrassment that could follow. Frank looked up from his plate, sensing blood.

Practice had made perfect with Slater. He gave a light laugh. "Alas no my dear. Not at the front... if you get my meaning, but there were other duties that had to be carried out... all of which had their importance." He let a tiny moment pass before jumping back to preclude any questioning. "You were in France with your husband I suppose, Violet?"

"My mother was a nurse," said Frank proudly. "She got bombed and blown up and captured and everything."

"Really?" said Slater. "How very interesting."

"She was ever so brave," Frank continued, "just like..."

"That's enough now Frank," said Violet quickly. "Lots of people did lots of brave things in the war. I know I raised the subject, but I would prefer it if we didn't pursue it... if you don't mind."

"Not at all," said Slater, glad that he had got through that infernal subject yet again... and relatively unscathed at that. They ate in silence for a few minutes, each intent on finishing the course, maintaining the conversation by means of smiles and expressions of appreciation of the meal. Slater put down his knife and fork as he swallowed the final morsel and turned to Ernest. "How is your business Ernest. Picking up?" Alice entered the room and proceeded to clear away the dishes.

"Yes, it seems to be holding steady and we are moving more into the agency side of things, which has considerably less..." He stopped as Alice took his plate. "Thank you my dear. That was delicious. ...which has considerably less risk involved in it for us."

"Ah, so are you the agent rather than the landlord for the Stanmore shop?"

"Yes, we will be agents for the landlord and you will deal through us."

Slater rocked back in his chair. "Ah, I see. I see."

"Is that not what you understood?"

"No... well yes... yes I suppose it really makes no difference. It's just that I hadn't appreciated that you didn't own the building yourself."

Ernest leant forward. "Well we do own some buildings, but we are also agents for other landlords. That is the situation here."

Slater cocked his head to one side, staring down at his place setting. He chewed the corner of his lip for a moment and seemed to be thinking hard, exploiting the silence for effect before saying, "No matter really. No matter at all."

"Precisely," said Ernest, trying not to sound too relieved. "It makes not one jot of difference."

"Do you two men have to talk about business at the table?" said Elsie from the other end. She wagged her finger in admonishment.

"So sorry my dear," said Ernest. "Ah, here's the apple pie we were promised. Now I can tell you Jim that you have never tasted apple pie the like of that which Alice makes."

Slater laughed. "I'm sure it will be delicious, but I have to warn you that my dear mother, God rest her soul, made a truly superb pie."

"Well, let us hope that this will remind you of that blessed comfort," laughed Ernest.

Alice placed a bowl in front of each diner, filled with a goodly portion of pie, a large knob of clotted cream on top.

"Has your mother been gone for long Jim?" enquired Elsie.

"Alas, too long Elsie," replied Slater, pausing in his tasting of the pie. "She passed away nearly three years ago after a swift but distressing illness."

"Oh I'm so sorry. You must miss her terribly."

"I do, dear lady. I do." He raised the back of his hand to his eye, still clutching the desert spoon, and made as if to brush away a tear.

Frank looked closely but couldn't see sign of one.

"No matter," continued Slater. "You were correct my dear Ernest. This apple pie is delicious."

"I said it would be," replied Ernest, and for the next few minutes there was little or no active conversation as they all paid due attention to the food.

Slater put down his spoon with an ostentatious flourish. He leant back in his chair, raised his hands in the air and brought them back down to pat his ample stomach. "Superb. Elsie and Ernest you've done me proud. That was delicious."

"Don't thank us," said Elsie putting down her spoon. "It is our own dear Alice who should be thanked."

"Quite so," said Ernest. Slater looked at them both, the nagging question in his mind.

"Gentlemen you will excuse me please," said Elsie, making as if to rise from her chair. "I am a little tired, and if you'll forgive me I'll retire to the other room for a while."

Slater stood and Violet too rose from her chair and went across to her mother. "I'll come with you mother dearest."

"Nonsense Violet. You stay here with our guest. Frank will come with me and keep me company, won't you darling?" Frank, of course, jumped at the chance and immediately went to his grandmother's side. Slater turned back to his seat and sat once more as Frank assisted Elsie from the room.

"You'll have some stilton and a glass of port, dear chap," said Ernest as the door closed.

Slater rolled his eyes skywards and patted his belly yet again. "Does a duck like water... eh old man?"

Seizing the opportunity, Violet, who had remained standing, volunteered, "You sit there daddy and I'll go out and get the cheese." She made for the door to the kitchen.

"No hurry," called Slater. "Why don't you sit down. We can surely wait for your maid to bring it in?"

Violet stopped at the door. She thought rapidly. "Eh, well, I expect Alice is having her meal now."

"And damned well deserved," cried Ernest, "after doing us so proud."

"Yes," agreed Violet, "It's no trouble. I'll be back in a moment." She pushed through the door.

"Well I must say you are damned lenient towards your staff old man," said Slater.

Ernest looked at him briefly before getting to his feet and going across to the corner cabinet, from which he took out a decanter of dark, lustrous port. "Alice is like a member of my family. I... that is we are all very fond of her. Very fond."

Slater decided not to pursue the matter, but he made a mental note to watch and observe this interesting relationship. "That looks a fine port."

"It should be, it came from your shop, as of course did the wine we had with the meal."

"Well I can't complain then can I, and nor shall I need to I've no doubt."

Violet came back in with the cheese on a large plate, surrounded by slices of apple. Slater raised his hands in salutation as she placed it between the two men. "Would you like biscuits or bread with your cheese?" she asked.

"Why biscuits of course my dear," said Slater.

"They eat the cheese before the dessert in France, don't you know?" said Ernest as Violet left the room once more. "And they eat it with bread or sometimes with nothing at all."

"Strange habits these foreign fellows have I must say," said Slater, lowering his voice as Violet returned. "Ah lovely. Are you joining us my dear?"

"Alas no Jim. I will see you later, but for now I feel I should be getting Frank off to his room and seeing how mother is." Slater began to rise from his seat but she was gone from the room before he got halfway up. He sat back in his chair.

"Damned fine-looking daughter you've got Matthews."

"Yes she is, isn't she?" beamed a proud Ernest. "She's been through some pretty bad patches though, but she seems to be pulling through and Frank is of course a tower of strength for her."

"Don't know how I missed her all these years. I'd've come courting myself I've no doubt. No doubt at all."

"Have you never married Jim?" said Ernest quietly.

Slater threw back his head and laughed.

"Nearly been caught a couple of times but I've escaped so far.

Course there was mother and... well the business took up most of my time."

"I used to let mine take up all my time, but you suddenly realise your own mortality you know and there's a lot you can miss out on," Ernest revealed wistfully.

"Maybe so. Maybe so," mused Slater. "Perhaps it's time for a change." He raised his glass of port to Ernest. "To your health sir, and to change!"

July 1927

"**B**ut why does he have to come with us?" moaned Frank.

"He's not coming with us darling," said Violet. "He's got to be in France on business and I've invited him to call on us at the chateau."

"I don't want him there."

Violet stiffened in her seat and looked out of the train window at the Kent countryside rolling by. That the boy had continued to dislike Jim Slater was becoming more and more of an embarrassment as time went on. Oh she hadn't liked the man very much herself at first, but she had developed a sort of neutrality on that front now. Just as well, really, as since that first meeting the original offer of help in translation had been expanded to an almost regular task. At first she had resented it, but then she began to look forward to the break in her domestic routine.

Occasionally she even found herself in deep discussion with Slater over some aspect of the business and was surprised at first, and then gratified, when he appeared to value her opinions.

Ernest and Elsie, of course, encouraged his visits to the house, and if he was ever there at or approaching meal times would invariably invite him to join them, to the point where there was a danger of his presence at the dinner table becoming regular. In time, that meant that Slater had to understand a few things about their household, and one of the first of those was that although Alice was nominally the servant, she was thought of and treated as more of a family member and companion. That of course extended to her being seated with them at some meal times. Violet smiled to herself, remembering the first time Alice had sat at the table when Slater was there. Although he had endeavoured to carry on talking and eating as normal, his eyes would keep wandering back to examine, almost to verify her presence. Alice of course had felt his interest, and after that, as often as not when he was there, she excused herself on one pretext or another. The only real problem with that was that Frank, too, contrived to be absent from the table, preferring to join Alice in the kitchen. She turned from the window and addressed Frank. "What is it about Jim that you get so angry about darling?"

"I just don't... I don't like him. Jesse said that he didn't sound a very nice man."

"She only had your opinion to go on and I don't think Jesse would pass such a judgement on anybody without knowing them."

The boy bridled defensively. "She did. She said so."

Violet smiled weakly. "Yes dear, but I expect she was only trying to please you. After all, she does love you so much."

The memory of the last few days flooded in like a warm tide. No trip to France would ever be complete without the stop-over at Jesse's little cottage and the welcome they both received. This trip had been especially eventful as they had, for the first time, seen Rosie and Keith's new baby and Violet had become the little mite's godmother at a simple ceremony in the church in Tenterden. She closed her eyes for a moment to recall the baby, the smell of him, the warm softness. It had awoken longings within her that up to now she had either subjugated or forgotten. How wonderful it must be, she thought, to know your baby's development through every day of his life, to luxuriate in his very being. She looked across at Frank, remembering how she had held him for a few brief days when he was a baby. She recalled the pain, the empty void that had filled her heart and her whole life for so long. She closed her eyes to blank out the thought and deliberately concentrated on the memory of their reunion. Oh there had been problems, not least the terrible upheaval that the little boy had undergone, but nothing could detract from that feeling of wholeness, that sense of being complete... and since then... and especially since the death of dear Armand, he had been such a wonderful son, companion and friend. She had hoped so much that she and Armand would have had children, and although he had never said a word about it she knew that he too had longed for a child of his own. That there was unlikely to be any issue had become clear to them both when - she shot a glance at Frank and turned her face to the window to hide her flushed cheeks - despite an active and thoroughly enjoyable sex life she had not fallen. It was in no way a reflection on Armand that his tacit recognition that he was to remain childless had been implicit in him wholeheartedly embracing Frank as his son, adopting him formally and making him his heir.

"When's he coming then?" Frank persisted.

She started, drawn back from her reminiscences to the problem at hand. "Eh... oh it's in a couple of weeks. His meetings are in Paris and I have said that I will attend them with him. Then after that he will come back for a few days before heading off home."

Frank stared at her from his seat opposite. "Why does he have to come to the chateau? He could go home from Paris on the boat train?"

"I really think you're being unfair Frank. The chateau is my home as well and surely I've got the right to ask who I want to visit. Anyway you'll not be alone, Gisela and Gunther will be there."

"They're already there."

"I know they are darling, and they'll still be there whilst I'm away, and when Jim comes I expect that you and all your friends will be out and about all the time anyway."

"So I won't have to be nice to him?"

"Of course you have to be nice to him Frank," said Violet, annoyed. "We are not rude to anybody."

Frank saw that she was getting cross and backed down by saying, "So I don't have to stay in and help entertain him?"

"No dear you don't," said Violet, relieved that perhaps this particular episode of discord was now coming to an end. Now rapidly approaching his teenage years, young Frank was a handsome young fellow, and if she wasn't much mistaken he would turn a few hearts one day. His resemblance to his father was uncanny, and at times, when he shrugged his shoulders or adopted some pose, the sight of him would give her quite a start. How Frank would have loved him. She closed her eyes and thought of him. Would it have worked out with him if he had survived the war? Who could tell. That she had loved him dearly she had no doubt, but people change, love changes, and in no way was she the same woman. How different had been her love for Armand? The same passion, the same intensity of feelings, yet with Armand they were coupled with that wonderful sense of... well comfort... security that he gave out. They had both been wonderful men in their own very different ways and she knew in her heart that she would never again find love as she had with them.

"He's courting you, you know."

The shock of Frank's statement breaking into her thoughts made all the colour drain from her face. "Who's courting me?"

"Slater. Slater's courting you."

"Don't be ridiculous!" She felt the blood come back into her face, felt the warmth in her cheeks and cursed inwardly at the realisation that the process of recolouration was going too far and that she was blushing. She burst out laughing, more to mask her embarrassment than any expression of genuine humour. "Courting? What do you know of courting?"

"I know enough to know when a man is... well interested in a lady."

"Well I can assure you that nobody's interested in this lady," said Violet lightly.

"Why not?"

"Well because... because."

"I would be if you weren't my mother."

The laughter gave way to an inner joy at the beauty of such a protestation.

She opened her arms. "Come here and give your mother a cuddle... that's if you're not too big for one now." He didn't hesitate. He wasn't too big for that. Not in the privacy of a railway compartment, leastwise.

After changing at Ashford they caught the train for Dover and took the lunchtime ferry for Calais. This wasn't their usual route and they had therefore persuaded Philippe that it would in turn be better for them to catch a train to Paris, stay the night and then catch another the next day to Orleans, where he would collect them. Violet had booked into the same hotel that she had stayed at when Armand and her father had first rescued her. She had thought long and hard about how it would make her feel to be there without him, but came to the realisation that they had never really been there as man and wife. They had indeed not only had separate rooms, but she had been confined to hers. It would be interesting, however, to discover the full joys of the hotel and there was no doubt that carrying the name Taillefer would ensure that her stay was made as comfortable as possible.

She was not to be disappointed when they arrived. The doorman, remarkably, recognised her immediately as the young lady who had accompanied Armand all those years ago. He expressed his shock and dismay at his untimely death, as did every member of staff that she came across. Frank was assumed, amusingly enough, to be Armand's son, even though his age meant that he had to have been born out of wedlock. Being France, and with Armand's name being held in such affection, Violet simply introduced Frank as "my son" and let them draw their own conclusions.

Before leaving the following morning, Violet booked herself a room for a fortnight ahead, when she would be meeting Slater. She toyed with the idea of booking him a room as well but decided against it, as not only would that have stirred up all of Frank's antipathy again but also because she did not want to appear too presumptive.

The journey south was uneventful and it was about midday when the train pulled into Orleans station. Frank was at the door as the train ground to a halt, the window open, eager to be off. Violet smiled to herself, remembering how as a little boy he had been so excited by the actuality of being on a train and had rushed forward on the platform to examine and marvel at the engine each time they arrived anywhere. Now, here was this older boy of hers who, whilst still excited by the prospect of travel and vast engines, couldn't wait to get away and off to his beloved chateau.

If Armand had wanted the house to go to someone who would treasure and value it, as he had done, then he couldn't have picked anybody better than Frank. If there is a heaven, she thought, then pray God Armand and Frank are together, friends at last, looking down on the boy who was in so many respects a son to both of them.

Frank spotted Gunther first and whooped out a welcome from his perch high up in the doorway. Gunther saw him and tugged at Gisela's arm, pointing excitedly. He left her and ran down the platform, waving both arms in the air.

"Welcome home," he said formally, in impeccable English, as he stopped at the foot of the steps.

He saluted and Frank returned the salute, trying to keep a straight face.

Violet came up behind him. "Come on Frank, down you get and fetch the luggage, there's a good boy." Gisela came to the foot of the steps and Frank kissed her on both cheeks before rushing off with Gunther to the baggage car.

"Hallo darling," said Violet to her friend. "How are you?" She descended the steep steps to the platform and the two embraced. Violet registered the fact that Gisela seemed to have lost a lot of weight and she determined to question her about it when they were alone.

"I'm fine," said Gisela. "I'm fine. How are you? Was it a good journey?" She looked down the platform expectantly. "Philippe said he was going to look for a trolley."

"Oh it doesn't matter that much. We haven't got very much luggage really." She laughed. "Having a house in each country means that, to a large extent, we have separate wardrobes to suit the different climates."

"Oh I know what you mean, and the weather since we arrived has been wonderful."

"How long have you been here?"

"About... well just over a week now. How was Jesse?"

Violet sighed. "Oh she was wonderful, and guess what? I'm a godmother to Rosie's baby. Oh you've never met her but she was a nurse in the war with me and she is married to Keith, who was Frank's best friend." Gisela looked blank for a moment and Violet realised that she was muddling Frank up with his father. "Frank's father. He was Frank's friend and he was with him when he died."

Gisela nodded her understanding, but the mention of the war and death had thrown a cloud over their joy. She hugged Violet, looking down the platform. "Ah there he is," she said as Philippe came towards them, wheeling a large flat trolley.

He greeted Violet effusively, kissing her twice on each cheek and then once more for good measure.

"Philippe," said Violet laughing and switching into French. "We've only got a few bags, we don't need that great big thing." Philippe shrugged his shoulders and left the trolley beside them as he spotted the two boys struggling down the platform with the bags. Violet watched him go, a look of affection on her face. A gruff single man whose only real joy was the motor car he lavished such care on. He seemed to have adopted Frank and Violet as his true family since the death of his beloved master and, though he was no blood of Armand's, he would have laid down his life for either of them.

Violet faced her friend. She examined her. Care and worry seemed to etch their wicked lines on her face and her eyes, once so sparkling and blue, seemed to have lost some of their light. Her skin, once so healthy and clear, seemed to have taken on a grey pallor, reminding Violet of the waxed material used in lampshades. Something was wrong. "How are you really my friend?" she whispered.

Gisela looked up startled. She saw the concern in the younger woman's face, read the thoughts in her mind and knew that with this friend it made no sense to try and hide her problems. "Does it show that much?"

"It shows." A tear appeared in Gisela's eye and a moment later she was crying freely. Violet swept her into her arms and held her there, swaying slightly.

Philippe and the two boys came back to them. "Are you crying mother?" Gunther asked.

Gisela raised her head from her friend's embrace. "No." She wiped her eyes and smiled as broadly as she could. "I am just so pleased to see Violet." She let go of Violet and cupped Frank's bemused face in her hands. "And you too my Frank. You too."

"Cor you can give me a ride on the trolley Frank," said Gunther excitedly. He swung the bags on and then mounted it himself, standing near the front and pointing dramatically towards the exit.

Frank looked around from Gisela's embrace and saw the opportunity. "Me too. There's room for me as well." He leapt on to the trolley. "You can push us can't you Philippe?" Philippe shook his head. "Oh go on... please?"

Philippe smiled, shrugged his shoulders and picked up the handle. He tugged and the trolley started forward with a jolt, causing Gunther to fall back into Frank's arms. "Careful," Violet called out. "Hold on tight."

The two boys held on to each other, giggling, as Philippe manfully dragged them off down the platform and through the exit. Violet linked her arm in with Gisela's as they walked behind. "Tell me all about it when we get back to the chateau," she whispered. "When we've got a bit of peace and quiet to ourselves."

Gisela nodded and they made their way through and out to the motor car, where Philippe and the boys were busy loading the bags. The journey back to the chateau was a noisy one, with the two excited boys laughing, swapping stories of home life and planning all sorts of expeditions and adventures for the holidays, some of which made Violet's hair curl. As they pulled into the driveway, the excitement reached some sort of crescendo and the motor car had hardly stopped before the boys were out of it and running off, up the steps and into the chateau.

Jean-Claude and Marie appeared on the top step, smiling broadly, torn between attending to the two boys who had just rushed past them and greeting Violet properly. As the boys seemed to have disappeared into the depths of the house, they raised their arms in resignation and proceeded down to greet their mistress. Violet received their kisses and embraces and allowed herself to be led up and into the chateau and through into the drawing room, where they left her, promising to return in a moment with some refreshments.

Violet looked around at the familiar sights and breathed deeply of the well-loved and remembered fragrances. She glanced out of the room and out down the rolling lawns to the lake beyond. He had proposed to her in this very room and now... now he was gone. She heard the door close quietly and turned to Gisela.

"Oh Gisela."

Gisela moved to her and held her hands. "I know," she said softly. She led her to the sofa beside the tall French windows and the two of them sat quietly for a moment looking out over the grounds. The figures of the two boys appeared far down the lawn, tumbling and cartwheeling as they yelled their joy to the skies.

"They are so happy here," said Violet, "...and yet... oh Gisela, every time I come back I feel as if he should be here. I know he won't be... but I just... I just..."

"Hush my dear." Gisela drew Violet's head down to her breast and held her tenderly.

The doors opened and Marie stepped through carrying a large tray of food, which she placed on the table just in front of them. She stood back smiling broadly before catching their mood and understanding what the problem was. "Monsieur will always be here madame," she said quietly, "as long as we, who loved him, remember him."

Violet looked up at her broad, kindly face.

"Thank you Marie. Thank you."

Jean-Claude entered with a smaller tray of tea. "English tea just as you like it," he said, putting it down in front of the two women. He stood back smiling affectionately at them. Marie took his elbow. He looked at her and caught the meaning in her eyes. She guided him out of the room.

There was silence for a few moments as the doors closed, then Violet composed herself. "What's the matter?"

"The matter?" feigned Gisela.

"The matter," said Violet sternly. "What is wrong?"

Gisela stood up and walked over to stand in front of the French window, looking out. Her body was outlined against the light and Violet saw clearly now how thin she was. She turned to face Violet, her face and features invisible against the brightness. "I am ill," she said softly. Violet put down her cup and rose to her feet. She moved towards her friend but Gisela held up her hand to stop her. "I am very ill and I think that this is the last time that I will be here with you."

Violet cupped her mouth in her hands and stood facing Gisela, her eyes wide and questioning. "Oh Gisela no... surely..."

"No Violet, there is nothing that can be done, I know that now."

"But... in London or Paris... surely there is... what is wrong exactly?"

Gisela went back to the sofa and sat down. Violet stood in front of her waiting. "I have been to the doctor because I have been unwell and I have lost a lot of weight. They... they tell me that I have... that I have krebskrank... cancer."

Violet stood, her hands falling uselessly down to her sides as she stared incredulously at Gisela. "Cancer?"

Gisela nodded. "Why, there was an article in the newspapers earlier this year warning of the dangers but... well I never expected... Where is it?"

"It started in my breasts. I felt the lumps but I did not... now they say it is everywhere." She put her head in her hands and Violet quickly sat down beside her, put her arm about her and drew her into her embrace.

"How... what do they say?"

Gisela buried her head in her hands. "Six months. Maybe not as much."

"Does Gunther know?"

"No, I cannot tell him until... until..."

"Hush now," whispered Violet. "We'll work something out."

Gisela raised her head from her hands. Violet saw the suffering then, the loss that registered deep within her tired, hollowed eyes. "This friendship we have is the most... the best thing of my life except for my boy." She choked on the rising tide of her tears. Violet pulled her closer and hugged her tight.

"We can... did your doctors not object to your coming here?"

"They did, but I told them I had to come for this last time to see you my friend."

"Then we must make this time a happy time, and when it is over we must see exactly how I can help. I can help you know Gisela. You are my friend and you were Armand's friend and I am sure that he would want me... and Frank, to help as much as we can."

Gisela smiled weakly at her friend. "I... it is no use Violet, I know what will happen to me. It is just my poor Gunther. He is to go to a school. The money is arranged from his father for that, and his uncle Helmut will take him in, but... I would like it if he could see you... come here when... when..."

"Hush now," Violet whispered. "He will always have us. Both of you will always have us."

Gisela reached into her skirt pocket for a handkerchief and wiped her eyes. "Thank you Violet. I am sorry to be a nuisance... to spoil your holidays."

"Nonsense," said Violet. "What are friends for if not for times like this? Now what about Gunther? He must be told you know."

Gisela sighed. "I know but how... when?"

"We will both talk to the boys tonight," said Violet firmly. "Frank should be there to help his friend and I am sure that he will say what I have said." She reached out for a plate and handed it to Gisela. "Come on now, have something to eat. After all, it's a shame to let this food go to waste, especially as Marie has obviously taken so much trouble to make English sandwiches for my homecoming." She stopped. "Are you taking any medicines?"

"I have some, yes, but they are very strong, and although they help with the pain... that is all."

Violet grimaced. "You must be careful with them you know, they are probably a strong opiate."

"I will... I will be very careful with them."

Later that evening, Violet called Frank and Gunther into the drawing room. "Oh do we have to Violet?" wailed Frank. "We were going out to see Pierre-Luc."

"Yes you do Frank. This is important," Violet insisted, trying hard not to sound irritated.

"Oh alright then," he grumbled as he came through the French windows into the cool of the room. "Oh you're here as well Gisela... your mum's in here as well Gunther," he called back to the other boy as he too entered the room.

"Sit down here please Frank," said Violet, indicating a chair opposite the sofa. "And Gunther, you sit next to your mother please."

"This is all very formal," said Frank as he sat down puzzled. "What have you been up to Gunther?"

"Gunther has been up to nothing, but it does concern him." Violet looked at Gisela. "Shall I continue?" Gisela nodded, her hands in her lap, holding and fiddling with her handkerchief. "Gisela has been given some very bad news about her health," said Violet softly. She stopped and looked straight at Gunther. "She is very ill and she is going to need all our help for... she is going to need all our love and all our help."

Gunther stared at Violet, his face seemingly void of emotion. He turned to his mother and she looked up and into his eyes. He saw then what he had not noticed before. The pale dry skin, the eyes set deep in dark hollows. "Mutti?" he whispered. She nodded and opened her arms to him, stroking the back of his head as he buried his face in her meagre breast.

Violet moved across to stand beside Frank, with her hand resting on his shoulder. He reached up and clasped it without taking his eyes off the couple on the sofa. "Your mother has a very serious illness Gunther," Violet continued softly. "She is going... she will need all our help and she... you both will have it, won't they Frank?"

Frank went to speak, but all that came out was a croaking sound. He cleared his throat. "We will help as much as we can," he said strongly and in as manly a voice as he could muster, in spite of the large lump that seemed to have lodged in his throat.

Gunther raised his head and looked once more into his mother's eyes. "Are you going to die mother?" he said, unconsciously continuing to speak in English, even at this tender, private moment.

Gisela looked down at her son. Tears fell from her eyes as she nodded, unable to utter the words.

......

Violet put down the letter and stared out of the porthole at the sea. How beautiful it looked at this time of the year... at this time of the evening. Its normally rough surface was flat and calm like a misty mirror reflecting the blue, grey and gold of the low sun's rays. The steamer cut into this unblemished plane, sending its wash in ever-diverging lines. She watched idly for a while before lying back on the bunk to stare up at the ceiling.

What a time this summer had turned out to be. The memory of Gisela's death still weighed heavily upon her, but at last she was coming to terms with the decision her friend had made. Violet shivered as she remembered her first sight of Gisela's body, the

evening she had rushed back from Paris. She had been laid out on
the bed in her room, and to all intents and purposes she had looked
as if she were merely asleep until one noticed the crossed hands with
the crucifix placed in them and the deathly pallor of her still face.

She had entered the room with Gunther and stood beside the bed
with both hands on the boy's shoulders. They had stood there for
some time in complete silence before she had drawn him to her, and
only then had he allowed himself to cry once more. Violet had led
him from the room and into the small sitting room just along the
corridor. She guided him to a chair and sat him down in it, kneeling
in front of him and taking hold of his hands. "She is better now
Gunther," she had said.

"Why did she die?" the boy had sobbed. "Why did she leave me?"

"She had to leave you Gunther, she was ill and she was dying and
we all knew it."

"But she wasn't going to die now was she? She was going to die...
she didn't have to die now." The anger flared in the boy's eyes and he
looked Violet straight in the eye, accusing, challenging her to defend
his mother.

Even though she was, herself, having the greatest difficulty
coming to terms with the sense of betrayal she felt over Gisela's
actions, Violet realised that she really was going to have to face her
own feelings at the same time as she attempted to explain them to
Gunther. She cleared her throat. "Well you see darling, Gisela knew
that she was dying and she wanted to... well she felt that she had the
right to choose for herself where she died... and how."

"She didn't have the right to leave me alone," the boy had cried.
"She is horrible. I hate her."

"No you don't. You're just angry and frightened," Violet had
protested.

The boy had persisted and continued to rail against the injustice
and betrayal he felt. Violet had done her best to calm him down, but
it was so difficult when coupled with her own feelings. That Gisela

had planned her exit and chosen to do it there and then, she could in many ways understand. Violet had seen too many people die in agony, despair and utter degradation to argue with Gisela's logic on that one, and... well, to be honest, if she could have prevented her from doing it she would have. But... but still there was this sense of betrayal. Gisela had gone behind her back... waved her goodbye, knowing that she would not be there... would be dead when she returned.

What despair could lead to those feelings of utter detachment from the continuance of life. Violet raised herself from the bunk and looked out of the porthole again, wanting to see the world to reassure herself that it was still there. Gisela had cut herself from this world as a deliberate action. Cut herself off from her friends and family. She sighed, feeling the empty pit in her stomach, the rising of anger in her breast. Oh what was the use in feeling like this? Gisela was right. What future had her poor friend had? What did she have to look forward to?

Gradual deterioration in her physical being, loss of faculties... dignity... all that the rest of us take for granted. Friendships and fellowships being subjugated by pity... memories being forever coloured by her final condition.

Violet sighed heavily. Poor darling Gisela, perhaps she had been right. Perhaps it was the last act of choice open to her in a life that had held far too few pleasures and far too many griefs. "I will be with my beloved Dieter," she had said. 'Well let's hope so my darling Gisela,' thought Violet. 'Let's hope so, but... oh I do miss you so.'

Gunther had retreated into a world of his own for some days after the death, and really the only people who could approach him had been Frank and, to a slightly lesser extent, Marcel and Pierre-Luc. At the funeral, which had been widely attended, the three boys had supported and attended their chum throughout and friendships, which had been strong anyway, had been firmly cemented for all time.

Violet recalled the tearful goodbyes when Helmut, Dieter's brother, had departed with Gunther a few days after the funeral. She had promised him that he was free to come to them in England and that he would certainly continue to be expected at the chateau for the summers, and his uncle Helmut, who didn't seem a bad sort of a chap, had acquiesced. She visualised Gunther's lost face as he waved from the train, backed up by Helmut and Slater. Yes, Jim Slater had stayed on until the funeral was over and, to be honest, although he had understood little or nothing of what was going on around him, in so many languages, she had been grateful for his support.

Her thoughts went back to the funeral. God they had been lucky that Jacques Brouillard had been the doctor attending when Gisela had died. If it had been anybody else, they would have certified that her death was suicide and that would have made it next to impossible for René to allow her to be buried in the consecrated ground of the family plot at the chateau. As it was, when he had arrived, long before Violet and Slater had got home, he had assessed the situation immediately and removed the letters and any other evidence pointing to suicide, including the empty bottle of medicines.

He had briefed Jean-Claude and Marie not to mention the exact circumstances and quietly handed the letters to Violet later that evening. Violet had read hers immediately, but Gunther had taken his letter up to his room and read it alone. To this day, Violet had no knowledge of the contents of the letter and the boy had never once mentioned it.

Helmut, it seemed, had received a separate letter by post a few days later, and therefore when Violet had finally contacted him he was aware of what had transpired. Funny situation really, thought Violet. He had not seemed at all distressed by his sister-in-law's death and seemed perfectly resigned to the fact that he was now the guardian of a small boy he knew next to nothing about.

Violet had begged that Gunther be allowed to visit them in England and continue his visits to France, and the man had simply agreed without question. It would seem that the relationship he planned with his nephew was going to be a very distant and hands-off one. Just as well really, because to imagine any kind of emotion in the man was difficult.

Slater had, strangely enough, got on awfully well with Helmut, partly because he spoke a little English but... really more than that. They seemed to have an affinity that transcended race... a sort of male bond that allowed them to... well, stand back from all of the grief and despair all around them that week. Business had raised its head of course, as it always would when Jim Slater was around. Any opportunity that presented itself to him would be seized upon and dealt with. "Hocks. They grow damned fine hocks in your country old man," he had said, dragging Helmut out on to the patio. Violet laughed to herself at the memory of the two of them out here, each with one foot up on the parapet, in earnest and deep discussion, oblivious to the quiet and hushed nature of the conversation amongst the other mourners.

The door opened and she turned as Frank entered the cabin. "About another hour and a half I reckon," he said, "and then we'll see the coast."

"Oh that's nice darling."

"It'll be nice to see England again, won't it?"

She looked at him, examining his face for a hint as to whether he was serious. "Do you mean that?"

"Yes," he said. "Of course I do. Nice to see Jesse and granddad and grandmother and... and Alice and everybody."

She smiled at him and opened her arms. "Come and give your mother a hug." He moved into her embrace. "You'll still miss France though?"

"Of course, but really..." He raised himself from her embrace and looked her straight in the eyes. "...really it's good to have two countries, isn't it?"

"It certainly is my darling," said Violet, cuddling her son to her.

March 1928

"I just don't know how to tell Frank," wailed Violet. "What do you think daddy?"

"I think that you are a big girl now and that Frank must accept that you have a life of your own," said Ernest seriously.

"I know. I know but... well he's never really liked Jim has he? And now... now if I do marry him... well I don't know what he'll say."

"Do you love Jim Slater?"

Violet swung round to look at her father. He leant forward, an enquiring expression on his face. She looked away, out of the window. "No, I don't love him." She looked back at her father quickly and crossed to him, sitting beside him on the arm of his chair. "I don't dislike him, but I have loved two men before and I can never love any other man as I loved them."

"Then why marry him?"

"Because I still need... I am still a young woman and I want to be... I miss the companionship of marriage and I don't feel ready to remain a widow for the rest of my life, however well provided for... and because he's asked me." She swivelled round on the arm of the chair and swung her legs over his until she was sitting on his lap. "You understand, don't you daddy?"

Ernest hugged his daughter, looking over her shoulder. 'Oh I understand my darling,' he thought. I understand the needs that we both feel. But to have those needs without love, could that work?'

"Would you grow to love him?"

She raised herself from his embrace and stared down into his face, laughing. "Why daddy, you old softie."

"Old softie be damned Violet, I just want your happiness, that's all," he said gruffly.

"I am going to be happy daddy. I'm not giving anything up, am I? I've still got you and mummy and my darling Frank."

"Ah yes, but will you not lose a bit of Frank? After all, for the last few years he's had no competition for your affections... and now..."

"Now he still has no competition. Nothing could ever supplant my love for him. Nothing."

She stood and paced around the room. "But how do I make him see that?"

"Do you want me to talk to him?"

Violet pondered this suggestion for a few moments, then she turned back to her father. "No, it has to be me. I'll just have to talk to him tonight after dinner. I'll just have to make him understand."

Ernest sighed. "Well, get it over with before Slater comes again because if I know Jim Slater he won't want to hide the facts or keep quiet about it at all."

"I haven't said yes yet."

Ernest snorted. "Don't think that'll make any difference my girl."

"But I told him that I would have to think about it and discuss it with Frank and... well all of you... oh surely not?"

"Speak to Frank, Violet."

She sighed and lowered her head. "Yes... yes I must." She looked up at him. "By the way, where's mummy?"

"Oh, she had to go to her room earlier. I'm a bit worried about your mother. She seems to be getting... well weaker somehow, almost as if she's slipping back to how... to how she was before... you know."

"Is anything upsetting her?"

Ernest shifted in his chair. "No. No... I don't think so... it's just... I just think that... she picked herself up so much during the war years and now... well she seems to have let go again."

Violet patted him on the shoulder. "I'll go up and see her daddy, and then I'd better talk to Frank." She left the room, shutting the door behind her, and went upstairs to her mother's room. She knocked on the door before entering. Her mother was sitting in the chair by the fire. She looked small and frail, just as she had for all those years before. Her shoulders were hunched into the blanket that draped them and she leant forward to gather up every last ray of warmth from the small fire.

As the door opened, she looked up and smiled at her daughter. "Ah, there you are darling. I was just having a little sit here by the fire."

"Are you alright mummy?" said Violet, concerned, as she crossed the room."

"Yes, I'm just a little tired these days my dear, and cold, so cold." She picked up the small poker on the hearth and poked at the fire, causing it to flame up.

"Here let me," said Violet, kneeling down and picking up the small scuttle. She knelt up straight and prepared to throw some more coal on the fire.

"No!" Elsie cried, throwing out a thin arm to prevent her. "Don't do it like that darling, it makes it so cold for so long." She rested back in her chair as Violet put down the scuttle. "Put a few lumps on at a time, there's a love."

Violet picked up the tongs and selected a few lumps, which she placed amongst the flames. "Are you often this cold mother," she asked.

"Always lately. It's just this winter. It never seems to go."

"It's not that cold mummy. It really isn't. Do you think you should see Doctor Crowe?"

"No, there's no need to bother him. I'll be alright when the weather gets better... you'll see." She shifted her position and stretched up to pull the blanket tighter around her shoulders. Violet stood and assisted. "And how are things with you my darling?" she sighed as she settled back in the chair. "Everything alright?"

"Yes mummy, everything's alright, it's just that... it's just that... well Jim Slater has asked me to marry him and..."

Animation leapt back into the old woman's face and she leant forward excitedly, reaching out for her daughter. "He has! Oh my dear that's wonderful."

"Do you really think so mother?"

"Oh yes. Yes, of course I do. You're too young to be alone and a widow forever and... well let's face it, many girls would jump at the chance of such a man." She sighed. "So many lovely men dead."

"I'm not thinking of getting married because there's a shortage of men mummy," said Violet laughing. "Jim Slater has asked me and, well I have said that I will consider it."

"What's to consider?"

"Frank for one, mummy. He doesn't really like Jim and I fear he never will."

Elsie sighed. "Yes, I've noticed."

"You have?"

"Why yes dear. I may be unwell again lately, but I do notice things you know. There's not much goes on in this house that I miss."

Violet looked seriously at her mother's eager face. 'Yes I believe you,' she thought. 'I can well believe you and... well never mind about that for now.'

"What should I do mummy?"

"Elsie sat back in her chair again and contemplated the fire. "You should decide what's best for you and the boy and make your decision as an adult. Do you love this man?"

"No mummy..." She held her hand up to stifle any comment. "...but I don't think that's necessary. I've known love and what I want to try and achieve is some sort of stable home for Frank and myself and... well for whoever else comes along."

"Without love?"

"Is it really necessary mother?" Violet looked meaningfully at her mother, who held her gaze for some moments before smiling.

"No dear, it's not always necessary."

"There we are then, and really it would be good for Frank not to be so cosseted by all of us women and to have a man to look up to as well as daddy."

"There's your answer then," Elsie concluded.

Violet sat down on the vacant chair beside the hearth.

"I must talk to Frank then."

"He was here a few moments ago. I think he's gone to his room."

"I'll go and see him straight away. Thank you mummy."

"What for?"

"For helping me make my mind up."

"Is it made up?"

"I think so."

Her mother lapsed into silence, gazing once more into the flickering fire. Violet stood, kissed her on the top of her head and stole from the room, out and across the landing. She knocked on Frank's door. "Come in," he called.

She entered. He was sitting on his bed reading a huge leather-bound book chronicling the Great War.

"Oh hallo Violet, it's you," he said closing the book as he swung his legs off the bed. "What do you want?"

"To have a chat," she said as she slipped up on to the bed to sit beside him. "What's that you're reading?"

"This? Oh, it's the book Slater gave me for Christmas."

"Yes of course it is. That was nice of him, wasn't it?"

"It would have been better if he hadn't given it in the presence of Gunther."

"Well I don't expect that occurred to him darling."

"Oh I think it did Violet. I think it did."

"I can't imagine that you're at all right darling, but never mind. It's Jim I wanted to talk to you about."

Frank narrowed his eyes and waited for her to continue. She didn't, so he prompted her. "What about him?"

"He's asked me to marry him."

Frank snorted violently, slid off the bed and walked across to the window, his back to her, his features hidden from her. "I hope you said no."

"I haven't said anything yet. I wanted to talk to you."

He turned and his face became visible to her. The eyes pleaded, but the mouth remained firm. "Please say no."

"Frank I'm a young woman."

"Then find someone else. Anyway, why do you need a husband? Armand has left you well provided for. Why? He would hate this."

"He would never have expected me to live my life alone."

"You are not alone. You have me and... and you have... well everybody else." He came towards the bed and stood right in front of her, the anger showing now in his every feature.

She reached up and took his hands, dragging him back down to the bed to sit beside her. "Please Frank, try to understand. Jim Slater can never replace Armand... or Frank for that matter, but I do feel that we need a proper sort of family life. You need a father figure to..."

"If you think that man will ever be a father to me then... then..." He turned to her, his eyes blazing. "Never. You can marry him, but he will never be my father. I have a father. Armand was my father. I was adopted by him and I will never have another but him."

Violet pleaded. "Frank please! Nobody said that he was going to adopt you... anyway you'd have to consent to that... I merely say that you need... we need a proper family life." She tugged his hands, trying to make him look at her and pay attention. She lowered her tone. "Frank darling, we live here in my parent's house. It's as if I'm still the child, it's not my house and I want my own house. I want to be mistress in my own home."

"You can be," the boy said excitedly. "We can go back to France and stay there."

"No Frank, I cannot live in France without Armand. I go there with you every summer, but all the time I am there I feel... it feels wrong without him."

"You always seem happy there."

"I am... I was... apart from... well Gisela... but... you've got to admit that for me the chateau is now full of ghosts."

He looked at her incredulously. "Ghosts? There are no ghosts.

Armand and Gisela loved it there, as I do, but there are no ghosts."

"For me there are... and there's another thing Frank."

"What?"

"I want a baby..." She tried to stop him, but he tore from her grasp and ran to the other side of the room. "Frank, what's wrong with that? I'm not an old woman."

"You're disgusting," he sneered.

She rushed over to him and raised her hand to strike him, but he stood there defiant, daring her to hit him. 'We have been here before,' thought Violet. Her arm lowered and the two of them stood there facing each other, breathing heavily. After a while, she turned from him and walked slowly back to the bed. She sat on it and looked up at him. In a quiet and measured voice she told him, "Frank, you are my beloved son but I never had you as a baby. Florrie had you. I was alone and... from the first few days I never held my own baby until you were a little boy." She stood and walked slowly across to him to stand once more in front of him. "I held Rosie's baby and I knew then that I wanted to have my own baby... I want you to have a brother or a sister."

The anger still burned within him. "But why Slater? You could have any man."

She laughed, mimicking him. "You could have any man. I don't want just any man. I want a man I know, who I think I can trust and who can give us both a home."

"So you're going to do it?"

"I want your blessing." She waited, seeing the workings of his mind.

"Will I have to live with you in his house?"

"Why yes, of course darling, but you'll still see granddad and granny whenever you want."

"And France? Will I still be able to go to France for the summers and when I want?"

"Yes dear. We'll come with you."

"I'd rather not go with him."

She saw the enmity in his eyes, the determination in his face. She would have to fight this particular battle again at another time, but for now... well one thing at a time. "As you please darling, but you'll surely not deny me a holiday there from time to time."

He didn't answer. Instead, he turned and looked out of the window once more, seeing nothing in particular, simply unable to face his mother directly at that moment. Violet got up from the bed and went across to him. She slipped her arms around his waist from the rear and hugged him. "It'll be alright darling I promise," she said as she kissed the back of his neck. She released him and crept from the room, turning one last time to observe him standing there rigidly, looking out of the window. She sighed and shut the door.

September 1928

Violet sat alone in the conservatory, looking out over the small neat garden. Carefully manicured lawns and flower beds set out in unimaginative lines and squares ran away from the house on either side of the narrow plot, leading the eye, directly and without any deviation of sight or spirit, to the rear wall. A garden devised and maintained by an orderly mind, convinced in his superiority over both nature and beauty.

She sighed and shifted in her chair. Two months. It was two months since she and Frank had come to live in this house. Two months since her marriage to Jim Slater in the church at Enfield, attended in the main by business colleagues and immediate family, together with, at her insistence, Jesse, Rosie and Keith. Violet smiled ruefully to herself remembering the scene afterwards, when the guests had all departed.

"Who on earth were those dreadful people from Kent?" Slater had demanded.

She had told him then of Jesse's relationship to Frank and the association with Keith. She shuddered as she recalled the fury in his face, the contempt in his eyes, as he'd stood there in front of her, shaking with rage.

"Do... do you mean to tell me madam... are you telling me that the boy is a bastard?"

She had flushed crimson then. Oh, not that time with shame, but with anger. Anger at the use of the word as a denigration of her son. How dare he seek to use her past misfortunes and mistakes against Frank. "Frank is my son and I see no point in dragging all of this up after all this time... after all it was long, long before I met you and..."

"Time makes no difference. The boy is a bastard and you have foisted him upon me."

"I have foisted nothing upon you. You have freely married me and

I have not sought to hide anything from..."

"Not hide anything! Not hide anything! You... you lead me to believe that you are a widow with an orphaned son and..."

"I have not misled you!"

His eyes had narrowed and he had stepped menacingly towards her. "Do not... do not raise your voice to me madam," he had instructed in a cold, icy tone. "At no time have you so much as hinted that the boy's father was not your late husband. Why, the boy himself has even referred to the man as his father."

"He was his father by adoption. Armand adopted Frank as his son and heir..."

An explosion of derision had issued from Slater. "And you think that makes him less of a bastard?!" He had moved towards her, wagging his finger in her face. "I will not have my name besmirched by you. Do you hear? Do you hear?!"

He had turned from her then and gone to the foot of the stairs, leaving her alone there in the hall, wondering quite what to do and where exactly to go. As he reached the first steps he had stopped and turned back to face her. "What was your father thinking of for God's sake?"

Violet faced him. "I would be obliged if you would leave my father out of this, if you don't mind."

He had sneered. "Oh I mind madam. I mind and I'll not leave him out of this as, after all, he has connived with you to deceive me."

"There has been no deceit Jim, please believe me."

"Please believe me," he mimicked, "please believe me. If you expect me to ever believe you again madam then you are much mistaken." He had turned and continued to climb the stairs.

"Am I to go then?" she called up.

He had stopped dead and stood there for a few moments, his back to her. Then he turned and slowly descended the stairs to halfway. "You are my wife madam and I will not have you leave this house to impeach my good name. It is bad enough that you have deceived me, but I will not have the whole world appraised of the fact."

Violet had looked up into his angry face. A tingle of fear had run through her. What had she got herself into? She could hardly run back to her parents' house at this time of night... or even the next day come to that. She had never loved the man, but she had felt that he would make a husband. Now... well... oh God what now? She had tried appeasement. "Jim... Jim this is our wedding night. We shouldn't be arguing like this over something that is... well long, long in the past."

She held her arms open to him, pleading with her eyes for him to come into them and forgive her.

Slater had looked down at his wife, standing there in the hall at the foot of the stairs, cold rage creeping through his heart. There she stood, beckoning him with her charms... her bodily charms, or so she had thought.

"I have lived alone without the company or need of a woman for all of my life," he said slowly, driving the words into her like a cold dagger. "It would seem that I am destined to continue in that vein. Your room is at the end of the corridor. I shall not trouble you tonight, or for many a night to come for that." He had turned and continued up the stairs, leaving her stranded there in the strange house.

Violet sighed to herself and adjusted her position in the wicker chair. Thank God Frank had not been there to witness the scene. Thank God he had left with her parents after the reception. That something was wrong in her marriage was next to impossible to hide from him. After all, when he had finally come to the house during the following week he had not failed to notice the fact that she and Slater had separate rooms, and when her father had departed the coolness between them would have been perfectly apparent.

Slater had buried his anger in a civility which he extended to both of them whenever it was absolutely necessary to have anything to do with them, which was, thankfully for all parties, not very often. The only meal that he regularly took with them was breakfast, and even then he confined himself to his end of the table and busied himself with the careful reading of the newspaper.

Frank had been late for breakfast one morning and had arrived in the dining room just as Slater was rising and preparing to leave for work. He had looked at the boy as he entered. "And what time do you call this sir?" he demanded.

Frank had grinned. "Sorry, I overslept."

"Perkins!" Slater had called. The door had opened and the servant entered. Slater addressed her whilst looking straight at Frank. "Perkins, please clear away the breakfast things immediately. Master Frank will not be taking breakfast this morning or any other morning, come to that, when he does not have the decency to rise on time."

"But Jim surely..." Violet had pleaded.

"But Jim nothing madam," he had said without taking his eyes off the boy standing there, returning his gaze. "Be good enough to retire to your room and prepare for your schooling," he instructed the boy.

Frank had stood there a few moments, but then he simply turned on his heel and left the room. Perkins had picked up the tray on the sideboard and backed out.

"Jim, there was no need to..." Violet had whispered.

"No need madam? I will decide whether there is a need in my house, and I have decided that I will have discipline and I will have manners displayed in my house. Do you hear?"

"Yes Jim, but please," she had protested. "Let's not take things that are between us out on the boy."

"I am not taking things out on the boy, as you put it. The boy lives in my house and must respect my rules. That is all there is to it."

"That is not all there is to it and you know it. How long are we to go on living like this?"

He had looked at her as she sat there at his table. In the place where his beloved mother had sat. God she would be disappointed. He coughed into his hand and sat back into his chair. Might as well get this over with now, he had thought. "I have made arrangements for the boy to attend a boarding school."

"What?"

"I said that I have made arrangements for him to go to a boarding school."

"Without consulting me?"

He had laughed then, a bitter, sarcastic laugh. "Did you consult me before foisting a bastard upon me?"

Anger swept over her as she rose in her chair. She leant on the table and shouted down at him. "For the last time, I have foisted nothing on you and I will not live the rest of my life in this purgatory because you cannot accept a simple fact." Violet had stood and swept out of the room, along the corridor and into the same conservatory in which she now sat.

Slater had remained seated for a while, stunned at the ferocity of her attack. Would she leave? He couldn't allow that. Why, if people heard of her leaving then he would become a laughing stock, and if they heard... if they heard the reason for their incompatibility, well that would be even worse. He had placed his folded paper on the place mat before him, adjusted his tie and followed Violet out to the conservatory.

As he entered, she had moved across to the doors to the garden and stood facing out, her back to him. "Please sit down Violet," he asked quietly.

Violet turned to look at him. Those were the most civil words he had spoken to her since their wedding night. Was he, she had thought, seeing sense at last? She sat and waited for him to speak again.

"I feel that the boy cannot be happy in this house and that it would be best for him to be away at a school where he will be well educated and... given some discipline."

He crossed the conservatory to stand in front of her. "I believe it to be for the best."

Violet stared up into his flushed face. "And when is this to happen?"

"Next term, at the beginning of September."

"You have arranged it all without any consultation with anybody else?"

"I have advised the boy's solicitor in France and he has agreed that it is for the best."

Violet stood up in front of him, barely two feet from him. "Do I understand that you have written to the notaire without any word to me or to Frank?"

Slater's gaze had shifted uneasily for a moment, and then the temper within him rose again and he'd raised his finger and wagged it at her. "I have to make the decisions in this house and I have made them and consulted the boy's legal guardian."

"He may be the boy's guardian, but you forget Jim that I am also the boy's legal guardian and his mother."

"And you are also my wife, which means that I will be obeyed in this." His breath came in gasps and his face became flushed. He looked around and took a seat in the other chair. Violet remained standing.

"You have no right."

"On the contrary madam, I have every right. I have decided that the boy is to go to boarding school and so he shall."

He will not go unless I say so and he wishes to," shouted Violet.

"I want to go," a voice had interrupted from the door. Violet and Slater had turned to see Frank standing there. Violet walked towards him, her eyes questioning. "I want to go to boarding school," he had repeated.

"There you are," snorted Slater triumphantly. "The boy wants to go."

Violet took Frank's hands in hers. "Frank. Frank. You cannot be serious?"

"Why not Violet? Gunther goes to boarding school."

She swung his hands and pulled him towards herself. "Frank, Gunther's mother is dead. That's why he goes."

"Nonsense," said Slater, rising and standing beside her. "It is perfectly normal for a boy to go away to school. Matter of fact he should have gone long ago."

"Are you sure Frank?" said Violet, hoping even now that the boy would relent.

"I'm sure Violet," he said.

She had turned to Slater, defeat in her voice. "Where have you arranged for him to go?"

Slater drew himself up to his full height, pleased now with the success he was experiencing. "He is going to a very good school in the New Forest and he will be going there as soon as he gets back from France."

She gave a short, derisory laugh. "Ah yes, the problem as you see it will be well and truly swept under the carpet and I'll have little or no time with my own child."

"Again, nonsense madam. You will have the holidays with the boy, and anyway what's unusual? I went off to school long, long before his age."

"It's alright Violet," said Frank. "Honestly it's alright. I'm perfectly happy to go."

"There you are, the boy's happy," said Slater as he brushed past. "I must get to work." He went to the door into the house and made as if to go through, but just as he'd got to the threshold he had stopped. He turned and addressed Frank. "I'd thank you not to eavesdrop on my conversations in future."

Frank had said nothing and Slater had swept from the room and off to work.

Violet stood and walked across to the doors deep in thought, remembering what had taken place in this very room all those weeks ago. Frank and she had gone off to France at the end of July, thankfully unaccompanied by Slater, who had protested that he was far too busy to go gallivanting around Europe. They had had a lovely time at the chateau, and it was only with the greatest regret that she had returned alone after three weeks, leaving Frank and Gunther in the charge of Marie and Jean-Claude.

Now, after just one full day with him back at home, they were to take him to his new school. Why, she thought, did everybody but her believe that it was all for the best? Her father had professed himself delighted with the fact, and she had had to endure Slater's smirk of "I told you so" as he extolled the virtues of a good schooling. Frank had become very enthusiastic about the whole affair, egged on by Gunther, who had trumpeted the delights of his school, describing the fun he had there.

She had tried talking to Frank, but he was absolutely determined. "Look mother, I cannot be happy in Slater's house and he doesn't want me there."

"Nonsense," she had said, but she knew that her lie convinced nobody, least of all Frank. He knew that he was the problem between her and Jim and he had said as much when he told her that when Frank was away, she and Slater could make their own lives. Fat chance of that, she thought. She had been back in England for over a month now, and apart from the usual words that two people sharing the same house would have to speak to each other, there had been little or no contact. Oh, whenever her father came round, Slater put on a veritable display of jolly normality, but she guessed from Ernest's sideways looks at her that even he was not totally convinced.

The two men were part of some sort of club or association that she didn't quite understand. They were to attend some sort of meeting this very evening, she thought. She knew that whatever sort of club it was, it was an exclusively male one and she knew also that it had some sort of secret ritual.

Violet heard the doorbell. That would be her father. She walked from the conservatory, into the hall and across towards the front door. As she neared it, Slater came down the stairs and beat her to the door. He opened it himself to reveal Ernest standing there, dressed as was usual for these meetings in a dark suit with a black tie and carrying a small, highly polished wooden case. Slater was dressed in similar fashion, if a trifle more ostentatiously. He greeted Ernest effusively. At these times, a comradeship seemed to exist between them that transcended the normal and they would both look, for a moment, as if they were naughty schoolboys caught in the middle of some secret prank. What was strange, too, at these times was that Slater seemed to treat her father with a deference which, at other times, was less apparent. It was as if, for the purposes of these meetings, her father assumed a position, which Slater respected and aspired to.

Ernest let go of Slater's hand as Violet approached. "Ah, there you are my darling. Alright?"

"Fine thank you daddy," she lied, kissing her father on the cheek. "How's mummy?"

"Not so good I'm afraid," said her father. "I think it would be nice if you could visit her in the next couple of days. It'd cheer her up."

"Certainly," said Violet. "I'll come tomorrow."

"Oh that would be splendid. She'll be so pleased. Come for lunch and then perhaps Jim could come over after work and have dinner with us. It'll be just like old times."

"Err, you've forgotten, Violet," interrupted her husband.

Violet turned to him, her eyes questioning. "Forgotten what?"

"We're taking Frank to his new school tomorrow."

She put her hand to her mouth. "Oh of course. Yes I'd completely forgotten daddy. Frank's going to his new school tomorrow. It'll have to be the day after."

"That's alright. Yes, I'd forgotten as well. Is he in? I'd like to wish him well and... well give him a little something for the tuck shop."

"Yes of course," said Slater. "Wait there and I'll fetch him. I'd invite you in Ernest but we really should be going soon, don't you know." He turned to Violet. "Where is Frank?"

"I think he's in his room."

Slater went off in search of the boy, leaving Ernest and Violet standing in the hall.

"Is everything alright darling?" Ernest whispered.

Violet looked at him. She felt her face start to flush and she had difficulty looking directly into his eyes. Damn it, she could hide nothing from him. She fought to contain the tell-tale symptoms. "Of course it is daddy." She changed the subject to avoid further embarrassment. "I'm worried about mummy. What exactly is wrong?"

Ernest sighed. "I don't know. Crowe thinks that it's some sort of blood disorder that comes and goes, causing weakness and debilitation."

"She was so well that time I came back from Southampton and now..."

"Now she's back as she was before, only older and even weaker."

"Oh poor mummy. I wish I could come tomorrow instead of having to take Frank to this beastly school."

"Never mind," Ernest said putting his arm around her shoulder. "The next day will do I'm sure." He looked up and took his arm from her as Frank, followed by Slater, approached. "Ah, there's my fine boy."

"Granddad," said Frank, smiling as he offered his hand.

Ernest took it, but pulled him closer and kissed him on each cheek. Slater looked on, puzzled. Ernest saw his look and laughed. "Boy's just back from France, don't you know." He put his hands on each of Frank's shoulders, looking down into his fresh, clear face. "All ready for your big day tomorrow?"

"All ready granddad," he replied.

"Good. Well here's a little something for you to take with you." He pressed a note into the boy's hand.

"Thank you granddad," said Frank. He kissed him on the cheek, hugged him, then stood back into Violet's arms. "How's granny?"

"Not well I'm afraid," said Ernest sadly. "Not well at all. She'll be sorry to have missed you."

Slater interrupted. "She'll be well enough the weekend after next, I trust?"

"I fear not," said Ernest. "I fear not."

"But ladies night. You have to have a consort," said Slater, concern written all over his face.

"I know but who?"

Slater thought for a few moments. Then he looked at Violet. "Would you do it Violet?"

"Do what?"

"Be your father's lady on Saturday week."

"What's on Saturday week?"

"Ladies night. Your father is the... well, as the master of the lodge, he must have a lady to sit with him on ladies night and..."

"Jim, I have no idea what you're talking about," said Violet, not knowing whether to be amused or angry. "You have never spoken to me of your... well yours and daddy's club."

"Never?" Ernest looked from his daughter at Slater.

Slater shrugged his shoulders apologetically. "I've never actually spoken to Violet about... well about the Masons."

Ernest looked away from him and back to his daughter. "Weren't you coming?"

Violet held her hands open in front of her, palms out. "I'm sorry daddy, I don't know anything about this. It's all news to me. Perhaps it would be better if Jim and I talked about it tomorrow."

Ernest stood for a few moments, totally bemused by this revelation. How could she not know of ladies night? Was Slater originally intending to come without his wife? What was going on? Slater interrupted his thoughts. "Well Ernest, old chap, we must be getting along or we'll be late." Ernest nodded. He put his hat on and kissed Violet and Frank once more, before moving to the door. Frank stepped forward to open it as Slater bustled across to the hat stand, took up his small case and adjusted his hat. He came back to the open door. "Don't wait up," he called as he left.

Don't wait up. Don't wait up. Who was he trying to fool? They occupied separate bedrooms, they lived separate lives within the same house. Don't wait up. How would he know the difference? The door shut and she and Frank were left alone.

"What was that all about?" said Frank.

"I'm not quite sure. It would seem that their club has some sort of... well social event planned and daddy assumed that Jim would be taking me. But I've never heard anything about it."

"Well he really let the cat out of the bag, didn't he?" Frank laughed. "He offered you to granddad and you didn't know you were going anyway."

Violet started to giggle. "Yes, he didn't know how to get out of it did he, and now he'll have to take me whether he likes it or not." They both started to laugh and Violet put her arm around her son as they retired to the sitting room.

......

The car turned into the gravel drive and drove slowly up between the high rhododendron bushes, which shielded the lawns and gardens beyond. Like a long tunnel, the driveway wound through the grounds of the school, transporting Frank from one life to another. They turned a corner and the school buildings were revealed.

This was the boarding section of the school. The main part of the school, with all the classrooms and playing fields, was some half a mile away across the common. They had driven there first, only to find the gates locked. Slater had angrily dismounted from the car and stormed into the small shop on the opposite side of the road, just a bit further down into the village. As he left, Violet drew Frank to her and squeezed him tight. "Are you sure about this Frank? It's not too late you know."

He nodded. "Yes I'm sure Violet. Honestly." He indicated the returning figure of Slater. "I'll not miss him and he'll not miss me I'm sure."

"But I'll miss you darling. What am I going to do alone in that house with him?"

Frank looked at her. He didn't say anything. He didn't have to; his face showed his reply. 'I told you so' was written all over it. "I know," she murmured. "I know." Then it was his turn to squeeze her, releasing her as the car door opened and a red-faced and flustered Slater got back in.

"The boarding section's round the back of the village in an old house," said Slater as he sat down heavily. "Driver!" he'd yelled. The glass slid back. "Back out of here and go across the road and down beside that grass and left behind those houses to the end of the road. Then right and it's on your right." The driver nodded his understanding and slid back the partition before setting off as instructed.

Violet looked around Frank at her husband. "Did they not show you where the boarding section was when you made the arrangements?"

Slater had looked at her, exasperation in his face. "I've never been here before."

"Never? But surely." She swallowed hard, trying to contain her rising anger. "Surely you inspected the school before making all these arrangements?"

"No need," he replied.

"No need? Frank is to go to a school which you have no knowledge of... know nothing about."

"I do know about the school. I made suitable enquiries and received suitable replies." His face got redder and his small mouth grew tighter as his temper also began to rise.

Frank, seeing that this was going to develop into some sort of altercation, had jumped in. "It's fine. Honestly." He turned to his mother. "Honestly Violet, it looks fine. Lovely countryside... the forest." He indicated outside the car and both adults involuntarily followed his gesture with their eyes. "I shall have such fun here I know it and... well it will be Christmas before you know it and then we'll be together again."

Violet had returned her gaze to the interior of the car. Slater looked across at her with undisguised triumph in his face. She tossed her head dismissively and concentrated her attention on Frank. "Are you sure darling?"

He nodded and the party remained silent as the car slowly made its way down the lane and turned into the driveway, drawing to a halt in the large turnaround in front of the house. Just ahead of them another car was pulled up, and from it stepped a man and a woman. They turned to address the inside of their motor car, the woman reaching out with both hands, the man gesticulating and pointing alternatively within the vehicle and down to the ground. Eventually a hand reached out from within the motor car and was seized by the woman, who half dragged, half coaxed the reluctant occupant out. A boy of about Frank's age, but smaller, stood there in the sunlight, blinking back his tears. His father shouted some command at him and the boy stiffened, flinched and turned to him. The mother went up behind her son, obscuring him from view, sandwiching him between their bodies.

Frank looked away from this scene and caught Violet's concerned eyes. "Looks a bit homesick already, doesn't he?" he said lightly.

"We'll not have to endure a similar scene I trust," said Slater gruffly.

"You will not," said Frank firmly, looking him straight in the eye. Slater grunted and sat back in his seat, reluctant to get out of the vehicle.

"Are you coming in?" Violet enquired.

"No, I don't think so," he replied. "I'll wait here while you say your goodbyes."

"As you please," said Violet, reaching forward for the door handle. Frank leant forward to do it, but before his hand touched the handle the door was opened from the outside by the driver. Frank sat back in his seat and allowed Violet to brush past him. He turned to the figure of Slater. "Goodbye," he said simply.

Slater merely grunted again and turned his face. Frank cocked his head in recognition of the dismissal, smiled to himself and left the vehicle. Outside in the sunlight he turned to his mother. "Right then Violet, let's see where we're supposed to go," he said cheerfully.

Violet followed him around to the rear of the motor car, where he took the large suitcase from the driver. "Can you manage it darling?" she asked.

"Of course I can," said Frank, hefting the case and heading towards the building, which had obviously been a substantial family home before it had been taken over. One step led up to a large open porch, from which double oak doors opened on to the hall within. Frank, followed by Violet, mounted the first step and stood just within the porch, catching his breath whilst resting the heavy case.

Another car scrunched on the gravel of the driveway and the doors swung open, barely before it had come to a halt. Frank and Violet turned to look as a boy leapt from the car, shouting his goodbyes into its interior before slamming the door shut again. He made his own way around to the boot and took out a small suitcase. He shut the boot and banged on the rear window before heading off towards the open porch without so much as a backward glance. The car reversed and departed.

Violet glanced at Frank and smiled weakly before stepping aside quickly as the other boy arrived within the porch. He swept past her and on towards the double doors. Frank attempted to stand aside but was prevented from doing so by his heavy suitcase. The boy, apparently oblivious of any obstruction, pushed past, catching his suitcase on Frank's bare legs. "Careful," Frank shouted.

The boy turned briefly, seeming to notice Frank for the first time. He was about a year older than Frank, roughly the same height as him, but of a heavier build. His hair was ginger and his face blotched and marked with freckles. His eyes, pale green under their ginger lashes, were rimmed with pink in a slightly effeminate manner, which was dispelled immediately by the menace within them. "Name?"

"Pardon?"

"What's your name boy?"

"Apologise to me and my mother first."

The boy looked astounded and made a move towards Frank. Violet joined her son and the bully, faced with the presence of an adult, backed away. He turned on his heel and entered the hallway.

"What a rude little boy," said Violet. "I've a good mind to report this to whoever is in charge."

Frank put out a restraining hand. "Please leave me to fight my own battles Violet. I can handle him. Heavens, if I can handle Serge I can deal with that ginger top."

Violet smiled. "Well if you're sure darling."

"I'm sure Violet. Now let's see where I've got to go and then you can get going. I'm sure Mr Slater will be getting impatient."

Violet winced. Frank would insist on referring to her husband as 'Mr Slater' and it grated with her every time she heard it. She had questioned him once about it, but when he had asked just what was he supposed to address him by, they had both been stuck for suggestions. Jim would have been totally inappropriate, even supposing Slater would have agreed to it, and Slater was at once too formal and yet at the same time too familiar as it brought him down to the same level of address as was reserved for school chums. So it was that Frank avoided direct reference to his stepfather wherever possible, and if forced to would address him directly as 'sir' and, to third parties, as Mr Slater. She touched him on the cheek with the back of her hand, then stood back a little as he once more hefted the heavy suitcase.

They both entered the hallway and stood for a moment to accustom themselves to the relative gloom of the interior of the building. A line of three older boys stood at the other end of the hall, carrying clipboards, upon which they had lists of names. Frank put down the case and stepped forward.

"Name?" said the first boy in the line.

"Frank Balfour."

The boy scanned his list. He looked up. "No, not in Red House." Frank stood, not knowing what to make of this statement. The older boy looked up again at him. "Not in Red House. Try Green."

"Green?"

The boy pointed at his neighbour. "Green."

Frank examined the other boy, noticing at last that he did in fact have a small green badge on his lapel. He turned back to the first boy and noticed that he wore a red badge, which he had failed to see when they had first entered. "Thank you so much for your help," said Frank, with heavy sarcasm and a thick smile. The boy glared at him, but by now Frank had turned away and was standing in front of the second monitor.

"Name?" he asked.

The boy must have heard the exchange with the other boy. Frank opened his mouth to say something, but Violet's cough at his shoulder stopped him. He shrugged his shoulders. What the hell. "Frank Balfour."

The monitor scanned his list. "Frank Balfour?"

"That's me," said Frank, grinning.

The older boy looked up, a total lack of humour in his face. "Green dormitory. Down the hallway on the right, ground floor." Frank nodded and turned to pick up his suitcase once more. He stopped as the boy continued. "Assembly in the main dining room in two hours' time."

"Where's that?"

"Somebody will show you."

"Oh how kind."

"Frank," Violet warned. "Frank darling, let's go and see your dormitory, shall we?" Frank looked at his mother and grinned. She knew him so well, knew when he was annoyed, when he was about to explode. He lifted the suitcase and set off down the hall, followed by Violet and the gaze of two older boys memorising his features for later.

Frank and Violet entered the dormitory through the double doors off the hallway. It was a huge room, which had obviously been used in the house's previous incarnation as some sort of ballroom. High-vaulted ceilings stretched up to individual pinnacles at various intervals down its length, where they were crowned with elaborate chandeliers looking strangely incongruous given the poverty of the furnishings below.

To one side there were high-level windows only, set about six feet apart, but to the other side of its length there were French doors set at the same spacing. These opened on to a gravel terrace, which gave way to a low stone wall holding back the neatly manicured lawns. Beds, which reminded Violet instantly of the hospital beds she had known for so long, were spaced out along both sides of the room, leaving about four feet between each. At the end of the room there were three beds set across at right angles. No chairs were visible except between these three beds at the end, and instead a simple locker was the only division.

At the foot of each bed there was a name tag, and closer inspection revealed that many already had names written on them, denoting that they had been allocated. Most of the beds on the side with the high-level windows seemed to be taken, as were the three beds at the end.

Frank, being a lover of fresh air and the countryside, couldn't quite understand why the beds furthest away from the French doors seemed to be the favourites. He would have preferred one of the beds at the end of the room, where he could have been close to the window and been able to see out, but as these were all taken he plumped for what seemed to him to be the next best thing, one just beside the doors themselves.

It was a pity that when lying in bed he would see into the room rather than out, but he could always roll over on his tummy and look through the bars of the bed head, he supposed. He lifted his suitcase on to the bed and its weight was greeted by a musical twanging. Frank pulled a wry face and felt the mattress, barely two inches thick, stuffed with horse hair or some such like. He bent down to look underneath. Strings of weak-looking linked metal ran side to side from the iron frame, and even with nobody in the bed they gave away a history of previous occupation in sags and shapes.

"Doesn't look that comfortable, does it?" he remarked. "Still it'll have to do," she said yet again.

Violet pulled a face. "Oh Frank I'm sorry. Listen, it's not too late you know."

He made a brushing-off motion with his hand, and then seeing the hurt it caused put his arm around her. "I'll be alright Violet. Honestly mother I will."

He had not often called her mother before, and the shock of the word on his lips ran through her like a thrill. Frank either didn't seem to notice, or having used the word deliberately chose now to make light of it. Violet put both arms around him and held him tight. "Oh I shall miss you."

Frank smiled at her, brushing her hair back from her face where it had fallen forward. "And I'll miss you too, but you wait, it'll be half-term before you know it and then it'll be Christmas and we'll be together again."

In the bed next door, the reverse situation was taking place. There the boy from the car that had been in front of them was being comforted by his mother, who was trying to soothe him by expressing exactly the same reasoning. However, the milestones set out by Frank, which seemed to have satisfied Violet, seemed only to represent unattainable goals for this small boy and, oblivious to any audience, he simply dissolved into tears. His embarrassed and exasperated father, standing at the foot of the bed, announced that he was going to wait outside and that his wife should say her goodbyes and leave in a few minutes. With that he turned on his heel and marched off down the dormitory and out.

The mother attempted to mollify the crying boy, remarking all the while that she must go. His father was waiting and he would be annoyed if she took too long. The boy took no notice at all and clung ever more tightly to his mother, his cries getting louder and more and more insistent. Eventually his mother managed to prise him free of her body and hold him at arm's length.

Frank looked at Violet as she watched this scene. Tears rolled down her cheeks and she brushed them aside. "Violet?" he asked. "Violet are you alright?"

She turned away from the small boy and his mother. "Oh Frank, it's just like... it's like when I took you from Florrie," she whispered.

Frank looked at his mother. The memory of their first meeting and the wrenching of his life away from Devon were faint now, but at times a strange yearning came over him for something lost and barely recalled. He felt that pull in his heart now. Florrie and Joe. What would they look like? What did they ever look like? He should have seen them before now but... well life didn't always work out as planned and... well they had never been in the right area at the right time. He observed Violet's grief-stricken face. She had been strong then. She had not given way and she had taken what was hers.

Now she was seeing again... knowing once more the pain of a child being wrenched from its mother. Frank went forward to her and hugged her close. "It's alright mother. It's alright you know."

"Oh Frank," she sobbed into his ear. "I'm sorry."

He pulled back a little to look into her eyes. "Sorry? What for?"

"For everything. For Florrie, for... for marrying Jim. I'm so sorry."

"Hush now," he said, smoothing her cheek. "It's done and... well who knows, with me out of the way for a while it might be alright."

Violet smiled weakly. "You're a good boy Frank. I should have listened to you but... but I felt... oh what's the point now." She reached in her coat pocket and drew out a handkerchief. She blew her nose and dabbed her eyes dry before carefully refolding it. As she made the last fold, the monogrammed 'V' came to view. She laughed wryly.

"What's funny?"

Violet pointed to the 'V'. "This. Your father, Frank, gave me a set of these one Christmas."

Frank looked at the letter. He reached out and touched it gently, almost reverently. "They're always with us Violet."

She nodded. "I know. I know." Sharp words from the woman at the next bed distracted their attention from each other and they both turned to witness again the sad drama taking place.

Frank touched Violet's arm briefly. "You go now Violet and I'll see if I can... well you know."

Violet turned from the other couple. She hugged Frank one last time and kissed him on both cheeks. Frank smiled reassurance at her and she backed out into the main body of the dormitory. He waved his hand and grinned. "See you at half-term."

"See you at half-term," she mouthed, unsure of her ability to actually speak without her voice breaking. Frank motioned for her to go and she turned and walked off down the room.

Frank came around his bed and stood beside the small boy and his mother, who seemed oblivious of his presence. "Hallo I'm Frank," he said cheerfully. "Looks as if we're to be neighbours."

The woman looked up and held her son at arm's length. She recognised the gesture that Frank was making and smiled her appreciation and thanks. Cupping the boy's chin in her hand, she drew his face up. "Look Simon, you've found a friend... err." She looked urgently at Frank, trying to remember the name he had only just given them.

"Frank. My name's Frank. Frank Balfour."

The woman smiled again gratefully. "Frank. Oh yes, this is Simon. Simon Blake. Simon say 'hallo' to Frank."

The small boy, his face held up by his mother's hand, muttered a 'hallo', his lips trembling. Frank moved closer and held out his hand. The woman released her son and stood back a little, leaving him no alternative but to slowly extend his hand to return the greeting. At the end of the dormitory, Violet smiled to herself. Her Frank. She drew herself erect with pride, turned and left.

"Where are you from?" Frank asked.

"Salisbury," the woman replied for her son.

"Salisbury. Well that's not far away, is it?" Frank turned back to the boy. "Perhaps on some weekends we could catch a bus and go to your home for tea."

The woman tried not to show her visible sigh of relief as the thought of this registered immediately and very noticeably in her son's mind. He looked up at her. "Could we?" he said in a croaking voice. "Could we really mummy?"

She smiled down at him. "I don't see why not Simon. I don't see why not at all."

The boy's face lit up and he brushed his cheeks with his cuffs to wipe away the tears. His mother reached into her pocket and drew out a handkerchief, which she handed to him. He took it and blew his nose before offering it back to her. "You keep it darling," she said. "Give it back when you bring your friend to visit."

Frank looked up at her. He slapped his new chum on the back and sat down on his own bed, swinging his legs up and over to dismount on the other side. As he did so, just avoiding the case at the end with his feet, the springs groaned and complained. He laughed ruefully. "Bet yours is no better."

Simon smiled and jumped up on his. The bed obliged with similar sounds and the two boys laughed together.

Simon's mother coughed discretely. "I really should be going Simon. Daddy will be getting quite cross." Simon ceased his laughing immediately. His face dropped and he sat there on the bed, looking as if he was going to cry again. "I must go," his mother insisted. She looked across at Frank. "You'll look after him, won't you?"

Frank nodded and jerked his head towards the door. "Yes we'll be fine, won't we Simon?"

Simon nodded his head dejectedly, torn between making friends with Frank and running once more to his mother's embrace. His mother swept forward and kissed him on the cheek. "Goodbye Simon," she breathed hurriedly, backing away before he could grasp her. She shot a look at Frank before turning and making off down the dormitory. Simon followed her progress through his tear-blurred eyes. He stood off the bed and made to move out of the aisle between the beds, but by then Frank was at the foot of it, blocking his exit.

Frank put his hands on the boy's shoulders. "It'll be alright Simon."

Simon looked away from his mother for a moment and up into Frank's face, seemingly unable to comprehend. He looked away again towards the door, searching for the figure of his mother. She was gone. He turned back to the boy's face in front of him and it dissolved from his vision as the tears flooded into his eyes. A deep pit of loneliness and pain tore through him, and he broke free from Frank's grasp to throw himself down on his bed, face down, clutching the pillow and sobbing within its slender comfort.

Frank stood for a moment and watched his new friend. Then he sighed, turned away and busied himself with the emptying of his suitcase into his locker.

"So here you are then."

Frank turned at the sound of the voice. The ginger-headed boy stood at the foot of his bed. Frank straightened up and turned to face him. "You've come to say sorry, I presume."

The boy grimaced with incredulity. "Come to say sorry, I presume," he mimicked. His face took on a menacing expression. "I don't say sorry to new boys."

"Then I have nothing further to say to you," said Frank, turning back to his locker.

"Nothing further to say to you? Who the hell do you think you are?" shouted the boy.

Frank turned again, slowly, and walked towards the older boy. "I am Frank Balfour," he said. "If it's any of your business."

"I'm making it my business." He turned towards the top beds. "Horsfield!" he called. "We have a fellow here that doesn't seem to understand his place."

A figure rose languidly from one of the beds and came down the dormitory. Frank recognised the monitor from the hallway. "Ah yes," Horsfield remarked. "We've met. Cheeky little sod, isn't he?"

The ginger head grinned an evil greeting to the older and much larger boy. "What shall we do with him?" he asked salaciously as he flicked items of clothing from Frank's suitcase. "Shall we... shall we initiate him Horsfield?"

"Leave my things alone," shouted Frank, moving forward to retrieve a shirt before it tumbled to the floor.

"Or what?" said the ginger-headed boy.

"Yes or what?" asked Horsfield.

Frank drew himself up to his full height, which although equal to the smaller boy was considerably below the senior monitor. "Or we'll have to fight," he said. "I don't want to, but if I have to I will."

The bigger boy laughed derisively. "You can't fight me. I'm a monitor and you have to obey me. He has to obey me, doesn't he Cartright?"

The other boy smiled up at his guardian and obvious hero. "He has to obey you," he repeated. He turned to Frank. "Otherwise it's the strap, isn't it Horsfield?"

Horsfield stood importantly, his hands clasped in front of his body. "Otherwise it's the strap," he intoned.

Frank bristled. "What for? I've done nothing wrong and you can't..."

"But I can," said Horsfield. "If I say you've done something wrong then you've done something wrong. Do you understand?"

"No I don't," said Frank, annoyed and clearly getting desperate at his predicament. Their attention was broken by a muffled cry from the bed next door as Simon turned over, obviously frightened by the menacing turn of events.

Cartright left the foot of Frank's bed and moved towards Simon. "Well what have we got here?" He grinned back at Horsfield. "A cry baby. We've got a cry baby. A disrespectful one and a cry baby side by side. What shall we do with this one?"

Frank vaulted the bed and stood between Cartright and Simon. "You'll leave him alone, that's what you'll do."

Cartright laughed out loud. "And who's going to make me?"

"I am," said Frank, jabbing forward with his fist into the diaphragm of the other boy. Cartright doubled up and Frank grabbed hold of his shoulders, turned him around, still bent double, and pushed him out of the space between the beds into the main body of the dormitory.

Horsfield gave out a roar and went to rush at Frank, but checked himself as an adult voice shouted out. "Stop!"

All eyes turned to observe a master standing there. A smallish man with jet black hair smoothed across his head from a razor-sharp parting on one side. He wore thick round pebble glasses and a black gown hung from his thin shoulders, partially obscuring the dark, crumpled suit beneath it.

"What is going on here?" he demanded.

Cartright turned, still doubled up. He pointed at Frank but could not get any words out. Horsfield stepped forward to stand in front of the teacher. "This boy," he said, indicating Frank, "hit Cartright in the stomach, sir."

The teacher smiled at the monitor. He turned to Frank. "Name?"

"Frank."

"Frank what?" said the master, his voice rising slightly.

"Frank Balfour," replied Frank, beginning to feel that far from the situation getting better it was in fact deteriorating.

The teacher drew himself up and clutched the book he was holding to his bosom. "Frank Balfour what?" he asked in a slow, measured voice.

The boy beside him sniggered, but stopped as the teacher shot him a glance.

Frank felt the hairs on the back of his neck rise. His mind raced as his temper cooled, and reason began to replace anger. "Frank Balfour sir," he said.

"Frank Balfour... sir," the man repeated. "Well Balfour, what is the meaning of this disturbance?"

Frank pointed to Cartright, who by now was erect and standing expectantly beside Horsfield, pleased at his opponent's discomfiture. "He was bullying Simon sir," said Frank.

An eyebrow raised quizzically. "And who's Simon, may I ask?"

Frank indicated the bed beside him. "This is Simon, sir."

"And cannot Simon speak up for himself?"

"No sir, he's upset."

The master laughed then. A thin, reedy laugh with no real humour, intended only to mock. "Oh he's upset, is he? Well perhaps he and you could find time to attend me in my study in half an hour's time and we'll see if we can think of something which will help you both with the rules of this house."

Frank swallowed hard. "Yes sir... err, where is your study sir?"

The man, having issued his order and turned to leave, stopped. He turned back to Frank. "My name is Mr Hattersley. You will find my study along the corridor on the right, on the other side of the entrance." He turned and marched off down the room and out.

As the doors closed, Cartright turned and sneered at Frank. "Well Balfour, now you'll get what for... and afterwards..."

"Afterwards we'll have a little chat," said Horsfield. "Won't we?" The two boys laughed and walked back to their beds.

......

Frank and Simon stood outside Mr Hattersley's study. "Ready?" whispered Frank.

Simon nodded his head bleakly. "What will he do?"

"To you? Nothing I should hope, after all you had nothing whatsoever to do with it."

"But you hit him for my sake."

Frank shook his head. "No, I hit him for my sake. I didn't like him from the moment I set eyes on him. You were just the excuse." He grinned. "Come on, let's go into the Mad Hatter's tea party." Simon stifled a nervous giggle as Frank knocked on the door. There was no reply. "Perhaps he's asleep with the dormouse," whispered Frank. Simon burst out laughing. The door opened and Mr Hattersley stood there, observing the two boys.

"And precisely just what do you find so amusing?" he demanded of Simon as the laughter died instantly.

All colour drained from Simon's face. "Eh nothing... nothing sir. It's just... nothing sir."

Hattersley stood aside and beckoned the two boys into his study. He pointed to the front of his desk and then brushed past them in the small room in order to stand behind his desk, his back to the window. He reached into a drawer and withdrew a thin cane, which he flexed. "I will not have fighting in my dormitory. Is that understood?"

"Yes sir," the boys chorused.

"So, if I will not have fighting in my dormitory, why was I forced to witness your violence?"

Simon edged closer to Frank until the two boys were touching. He looked at his new friend, who, far from seeming scared, stared straight at the teacher. 'Oh my goodness,' he thought, 'he's going to get us in even more trouble.' He tore his eyes away from Frank's resolute face and back to the teacher. "We're sorry sir," he stammered.

"No I'm not," said Frank. Simon shot a horrified glance at him and instinctively inched away from him.

"Not?" screeched the teacher, leaning forward over the desk. "Not sorry! In that case I will have to *make* you sorry then."

"Do you not want to hear my side of the story, sir?" said Frank resolutely. Simon wished with all his might that the ground would open up and swallow them. Tears came unbeckoned to his eyes and he hung his head. 'I want my mummy,' he thought. 'I want to go home.'

Hattersley moved around the desk, swishing the cane through the air with a wicked sound. Simon hung his head and cringed away from him. "Your side of the story? I saw you hit Cartright with my own eyes."

"Yes sir you did. Because he was bullying Simon."

"Simon," sneered the teacher. "We do not refer to each other in this place by Christian names." He turned. "What is your name boy?"

"B... B... Blake s... s... s... sir."

"Well Blake, perhaps you can tell me why you were fighting."

Simon was struck dumb, but Frank answered for him. "He was not fighting sir. He never moved from his bed. He was crying and Cartright was tormenting him."

"Six strokes for you!" shouted the master, pointing at Frank. "And three for you." He pointed at Simon, who seemed ready to dissolve.

"That's not fair sir," said Frank. "He had nothing whatsoever to do with it."

Hattersley checked himself. A cruel smile played on his lips. He moved to stand directly in front of Frank. "I have allocated nine strokes of the cane... six to you and three to Blake. That makes nine strokes in all eh... doesn't it?" He flicked the cane under Frank's chin and Frank cursed himself inwardly for his involuntary flinch. "Nine. Do you make that nine?"

"Yes sir," said Frank

"Then would you like to take all nine?"

"No sir, but if I have to I will."

"If I have to I will," Hattersley mocked. "Well young man, you do have to." He indicated the desk top. "Bend over."

Frank stepped forward and bent over the desk. Hattersley forced his head lower until his face touched the desk top. He flicked

Frank's jacket up and stood back. The first stroke caught Frank by surprise, even though he had braced himself for it. Involuntarily he straightened up a little. Hattersley cursed under his breath and forced his head back down. Again and again the strokes landed on his buttocks, shielded only by the thin material of his shorts. He counted them to himself, biting his lip, trying not to cry out, not to give this man any satisfaction.

Eight. Thank God only one more. His rear felt as if he had sat on the stove, but there was one more to come. He turned his head sideways so that he could see Hattersley's face. The eyes twinkled cruelly behind the glasses and a thin bead of perspiration showed on his top lip. He was smiling, and as a slick of spittle escaped from the corner of his mouth, he licked his lips. Good God, thought Frank, the man's enjoying this. He braced himself for the last stroke.

Hattersley struck down hard, missing Frank's bottom completely and instead striking across his bare upper thigh. The pain screamed through Frank and there was nothing he could do to stop himself crying out and standing up straight. He stuffed one hand in his mouth as he turned to face his tormentor, whilst rubbing his thigh with the other. A gleam of triumph lit up the master's face.

'Damn him,' thought Frank, fighting his way through the pain screaming through him. 'He'll not reduce me to this.' He withdrew his hand from his mouth and stood up erect. "Thank you sir. Will that be all sir."

Hattersley, panting a little from his exertions, looked down at the boy. He flexed the cane in his hands, running his fingers almost lovingly down its length. "Yes I think so," he said. "That will be all for now."

A bell rang and he looked up. "Assembly," he announced. He opened the door and shooed the two boys out. "Hurry up now or you'll be late for assembly, and lateness begets a punishment." He chuckled. A thin, humourless sound meant to reinforce his mastery over the boys. He shut the door.

Simon looked at Frank. "Are you alright?"

Frank rubbed his bottom. "No," he hissed under his breath, through clenched teeth, "but I don't want him to know it."

"Where do we have to go?"

Frank looked down the corridor. Boys were passing by at the end. He pointed to them. "I suggest we follow them."

The two boys moved off. As they walked, Simon touched Frank's arm. "Thank you."

Frank looked at his new friend. He smiled ruefully. "It's nothing."

"I'm sorry I got you involved and I'm sorry you took all those... all that beating."

"I told you before," Frank said. "Cartright and I had already crossed swords. If it hadn't of happened then, it would have happened some other time."

"Yes, but the teacher might not have been there."

Frank laughed now. A full laugh which caught the attention of the boys passing at the end of the corridor, who stared at the two small boys, wondering just what was so funny. "Next time I'll keep a look out," said Frank.

They joined the throng of boys making their way to the main hall and filed in. Seats were set out in rows on either side, and on the floor at the end of each row there was a coloured dot painted on to the boards, which they correctly assumed referred to the respective houses. Frank and Simon hesitated for a moment, trying to decide whether within the house allocation of seating there was any order of seating according to seniority. There didn't appear to be, so they slipped into some seats halfway down one of the middle rows.

Frank looked around. The gentle hum of conversation died down as a large man in a gown and wearing a mortarboard came into the room from a side door and mounted the small stage. He stared out across their heads, for all the world as if he was just looking out to sea. Nothing in his immediate view seemed to register with him, and no recognition was given that these were in fact individual human beings in front of him. He walked to the centre of the stage and placed both his hands on the lectern.

"Good evening boys." The voice was deep and seemed to possess a gravity which reminded Frank very much of the monks at Saint Benoit.

"Good evening headmaster," the audience intoned, the newer boys taking their cue from the old hands and following the address so that it petered out rather than finishing crisply.

"For those of you who are new to the school, we bid you welcome and we hope that you will enjoy your school days here and look back on the time spent with us with fondness." Frank glanced sideways at Simon and smiled. Simon smiled back. In the row in front of them a head turned round. It was Cartright. He grinned and stuck out his tongue. His companion too, turned briefly and repeated the gesture. Frank stared straight ahead.

"Turn to the front Cartright," boomed the headmaster.

Cartright's head whipped round and faced the stage. Frank stifled his giggle, thankfully hidden by the taller form of Horsfield. "Just what is so interesting behind you Cartright?" the headmaster demanded.

Cartright stood. "Sorry headmaster," he whined. "I was just turning to welcome the new boys behind me to our school."

The head smiled and looked around and across the assembly. "There we are," he said, his tone rising with pleasure. "That's the spirit of the school that we engender. Thank you Cartright. Sit down."

"Thank you sir." Cartright sat but did not turn around again. If he had done so, he would have encountered one pair of eyes burning with fury and another with an expression of puzzlement.

That first night Frank could not sleep. In the bed beside him he could hear Simon weeping, sniffling back the tears. "Are you alright?" he whispered. There was no reply apart from a slightly louder sniff. Poor Simon, Frank thought. If he didn't get a little more gumption, life was going to be very hard for him at this school.

The rules that governed the school were probably no more or less oppressive than Frank had known at other schools. It was their interpretation and enforcement which was obviously going to be the problem. The headmaster seemed a kindly, even unworldly chap and he probably went through life actually believing that boys like Cartright and men like Hattersley could have honest and decent sentiment within them.

There had been no further incidents that evening to unduly disturb the new boys. Supper had been a quiet affair, taken in the main hall, where the presence of the headmaster together with all of the house masters and the matron had served to preserve order. Not a memorable meal. Cabbage that had probably been boiling all day lay limp and drained of all and any goodness on the plate beside a dark brown viscous mixture of gravy with some sort of indeterminate meat buried within it. From beneath this green and brown layer two off-yellow boiled potatoes stood proud, unsalted and tasteless. Frank shuddered and grinned to himself at the memory. What on earth would Pierre-Luc and Marcel have made of all this? And the pudding. Stodgy, tasteless something covered in a thin yellow liquid. 'Oh Marie,' he thought, 'send me a food parcel.'

He lay there listening to the sounds of the dormitory. Boys snored and coughed. Others farted occasionally, a sound guaranteed to produce a low chorus of sniggering. Simon's sniffling seemed to have stopped, but from a bed further on down the line the sound of another's crying could be clearly heard. Bare feet pattered on the boarded floor, making their quiet and secret ways to different beds. What on earth was going on there, Frank wondered. Eventually, of course, sleep came.

......

Church parade on Sunday meant that all the boys had to be ready after breakfast, dressed in their finest uniforms and lined up in the driveway in twos. The masters would walk up and down the line, inspecting them as if they were troops going into battle. Boys whose ties were crooked or whose shoes did not shine to the requisite level were hauled out of the line by their ears and either straightened out there and then or sent off to remedy their ills. Hattersley stopped as he got to Frank and Simon, standing stock still in the line. He looked them up and down, searching for something to single them out for, but Frank, fearing this, had taken extra special care with his appearance and had made sure too that Simon was extremely presentable.

He kept his eyes fixed to the front as he felt the searching gaze of the man. Simon could not help looking at his would-be accuser, his eyes making brief and fearful contact with the teacher's before he turned away.

They marched down the driveway and out into the lane, stopping briefly at the main road for a master to make sure that no traffic was coming. Then across and up the winding lane, leading up to the small church at the top. There was, thankfully, no requirement for them to keep in step, but they were expected to keep in line and refrain from talking. Glancing around him as he walked, Frank could see the forest and heathland stretching away into the distance. Apparently, after lunch the boys were free to wander off into the forest or down to the village and he was looking forward to exploring his surroundings.

A herd of wild ponies grazed peacefully in the late summer sunshine and he allowed his imagination to wander. One pony was a light grey with darker tail and mane and he imagined capturing it and training it as he had read in books. He made a mental note to save some titbit from lunch in order to tempt the animal closer.

"Halt!" came the command from the back of the column and Hattersley ran forward. He stood at the head, his hand held out as if he was a policeman directing traffic, and waited for the head and the other masters to overtake the column and sweep through the lychgate.

When they had all passed through, he waved the boys on and they filed up the pathway and into the cool of the church.

Frank had, of course, been to church quite often at home, but he was by no means a regular churchgoer as Violet's faith, although not totally destroyed, had been severely shaken. The service droned on and on and he stood and sat automatically as everyone else did, without paying too much attention. The back of the pew in front of him bore the initials of boys from down through the years and he determined that his would adorn it before too long.

Simon paid meticulous attention to all that was going on. He sang lustily without reference to the book and bent his head, with eyes firmly closed, for each of the prayers. It was quite obvious to Frank that for Simon this was very serious business. Better not make any blasphemous remarks, he thought, even in jest.

There was no doubt that Simon was not Frank's usual choice of companion. He was the same age as Frank but considerably smaller and weaker. A bit of a weed really, he would probably excel at school work and revel in his studies. He had probably never even thought of the games and adventures that Frank was used to. Still, necessity made strange partners, and at this juncture in their boarding school career both found comfort in their new friendship.

After lunch, Frank suggested that they go for a walk in the forest but Simon declined, saying that he wanted to write to his parents. 'No matter,' thought Frank, 'I'll probably enjoy myself more exploring alone.'

He wandered first of all into the village. All the small shops were closed, so despite the fact that he had money on him he wasn't able to buy anything. On corners he could see gaggles of boys in the school's uniform, but he determined to avoid them all for now. He kicked a stone idly along in front of him as he walked through the village and out into the country.

The trees gave way to open heath and he wandered along between great gorse bushes towering in large clumps. Some had openings

in them which led into their centre, and within these there was
evidence that the horses used them as shelter. They reminded Frank
of the thorn bush koraals he had read of in African adventure stories
and his imagination stretched to encompass games that could be
devised in this terrain. What a pity that Gunther, Pierre-Luc and
Marcel weren't here to join in.

But there we are, he thought. Gunther will be at his boarding school
and Pierre-Luc and Marcel... now they were the lucky ones, would be
at home in Germigny preparing to go to school in Saint Benoit.

'How I wish I was there,' he thought. 'Why can't Violet see that
for me to be there is no different to me being here, apart from the
fact that among friends and in my own home I would feel better.'
He sighed. Oh what was the use? She hadn't wanted him to come
here. He hadn't really wanted to himself, but if the alternative was
to live, unwanted, in Slater's house, then perhaps even this would be
preferable.

He crested a ridge and looked out over the expanse of heather
interspersed with the gorse. A lark flew up from the ground in front
of him, singing as it rose higher and higher. He shielded his eyes and
followed its progress up into the clear sky before it was hidden from
view by the sun.

"Hallo, and what have we here then?" said a familiar voice.

Frank turned to the sound. Cartright and Horsfield stood just down
from the ridge, looking up at him. His heart thumped and he turned
to see if flight was possible. Another boy, one that he hadn't seen
before, came up on his right, cutting off any escape towards the
village, and as he turned back, Horsfield ran out to the left to cut him
off.

Frank darted looks in each of the three directions as the boys
closed in. He glanced behind him at the open heathland, now his
only chance of escape. Could he outrun them on this terrain? Well
now's the time to find out, he reasoned, the only alternative being to
stand and fight against the odds. He turned quickly and dashed out

into the open country. The three boys whooped with joy and gave chase.

Frank bounded from tussock to tussock, swerving in and out of the gorse clumps. He made good ground, but the three boys were able to keep turning him so that gradually they gained on him. His breathing became laboured as the effort of jumping and running began to tell. He swerved off line once more to counter one of the boys coming up on his right and ran straight into Horsfield.

Frank bounced backwards off the larger boy's chest and fell back on the ground. Horsfield, winded, bent double and sank to his knees on the ground just in front of Frank's splayed legs. He fumbled forwards to grab one of Frank's feet, but Frank kicked out sideways and went to stand and run again. He rolled over on to his side and prepared to stand, but as he did so Cartright arrived and made a diving tackle, catching Frank around the neck.

As Frank went down again, Horsfield regained his composure and reached forward again for Frank's legs, managing to hold on to one foot. With the other free foot, Frank kicked wildly back, catching the bigger boy on the side of his head. He screamed but continued his hold.

Frank struggled wildly trying to free himself, lashing out with his only free limb as Cartright continued to hold on to his upper torso, pinning his arms to his side. He twisted almost clear, and for one moment thought that he had actually freed himself, before the other boy arrived and grabbed hold of his free leg.

For several moments all four, by now, exhausted boys rested, each trying to regain his breath.

"Let me go you cowards!" Frank shouted. He kicked his legs but the two boys held tight. Squirming in Cartright's vice-like grip, he tried to free his upper torso but to no avail. The two boys at his feet stood up, still holding on to his legs, and Frank decided that further struggle was useless. Cartright finally let go and rolled back out of his reach before joining his companions holding on to Frank's legs.

Frank looked up at their grinning faces. "Well what now?" he yelled furiously.

"Now we have a little ceremony to perform," sneered Cartright. He reached forward and grabbed Frank's tie, pulling the knot clear of the collar before tightening it back round his neck as a noose. Frank struggled for breath and Horsfield noticed.

"Careful Cartright. Don't strangle him." He pointed to Frank's reddening face and Cartright slackened off the hold.

"Well if he didn't struggle so much he wouldn't get hurt so much, would he?" He jerked the tie. "Stop struggling or else."

Frank went limp and then his eyes flew open as Cartright, still holding on to Frank's tie with one hand, began to undo the buttons of his shirt. "What do you think you're doing?" he screamed.

Horsfield laughed. "We're going to strip you... naked."

"Strip me? What for?"

"You'll see," said Cartright, pushing Frank over as he pulled the jacket and shirt off his back and hurled them away into the bushes. He jumped back, leaving Frank naked from the waist up, lying on the ground with his legs held up by the two older boys. Cartright came forward again and stood between the two boys as they stretched Frank's legs apart. He reached forward and grabbed at Frank's belt, undoing the buckle.

Frank screamed with all his might and twisted and bucked, but he could not free himself. His back scuffed on the ground and his elbows and the back of his head started to hurt. Cartright tore open his fly buttons, and with one deft move pulled Frank's trousers and underpants down to his ankles.

Horsfield switched his grip to take in both of Frank's legs with the assistance of the restricting garments. Cartright and the other boy, meanwhile, grabbed hold of each of his wrists. "Grab his cock," Cartright whispered at Horsfield, grinning lewdly and nodding his head down at Frank. Horsfield tentatively let go with one hand and stretched forward but Frank, seeing what was coming, threw his body into a convulsive twisting movement and the older boy had to resume his double-handed holding of his legs. Frank relaxed slightly, and for a while the four of them rested, but all too soon Horsfield gave a command and they picked Frank's naked body up between them.

"That one will do nicely I think," said Horsfield, indicating a clump of wicked-looking gorse about six feet across and four feet high. They carried Frank across to it and stood about a yard from it, holding Frank's body between them.

"What... what are you going to do?" Frank yelled, knowing deep down exactly what they were planning.

"We're going to introduce you to the forest," shouted the other boy.

"Yea. We're going to initiate you," said Cartright, "and teach you to respect your elders and betters."

"Ready lads," Horsfield said. "On the count of three." Frank squirmed in their grip but they swung him out and away from the bush three times. "One... two... threeee!"

On the last big swing, they released Frank and he hurtled into the centre of the bush, landing face down in the prickles, which seemed to reach in and stab every part of his anatomy. He screamed with pain and rage within the grip of the stinging branches. His private parts felt as if they'd been ripped off, and he lay there unable to move without causing himself more pain.

His three tormentors stood aside laughing and pointing at him. "Damn you," Frank yelled. "Damn you to hell."

"Ooh, temper temper," Cartright taunted. "Don't you like your new bed?"

"I'll get you," Frank shouted. "All three of you had better watch out."

"Oh dear, I'm frightened," jeered the other boy, whose name Frank didn't know.

"Me too," mewed Cartright. "Ooh, let's run away shall we?"

The three boys ran off together laughing, leaving Frank alone, crying with pain, frustration and shame. Any movement seemed to cause even more hurt and he stayed as still as he could, trying to think of what to do next. Eventually he determined that there was nothing else for it, he would have to make a move of some sort or he would be there all night.

He gathered all his strength together, and breathing deeply prepared to hurl himself over on to his back. With one convulsive move he managed to turn over, but screamed as the needles tore into the flesh on his back. Still, his most tender areas were now free. He lay there for a while looking down at his body. Thousands of angry red needle-point marks showed up all over him, and in places long red scratch lines seemed to join them up like the dot pictures he remembered from childhood books.

His short trousers and underpants had ended up halfway down his shins and both boots had, thankfully, stayed on. Gently he eased himself into a semi sitting position and reached forward to grab the waist. He pulled upwards and jerked into the air as best he could, easing the shorts up his legs and on to his bottom.

For a few minutes he lay there, gasping with pain and exhaustion, whilst slowly and carefully doing up his fly buttons. The tie, which had remained on as the only article of clothing above the waist, seemed to have snagged on one of the branches, which were now below him, and he reached for it with both hands and tugged it free. Then with one final effort, rewarded with yet more stab wounds from the bush, he jerked himself upright and for the first time was able to take his whole weight on his shod feet, free of the needle's support.

In the distance he could see the three boys nearing the edge of the heathland. He cursed as they entered the trees. Had they taken his shirt and jacket? He couldn't see them.

He had to get free of the bush now, and gathering every last reserve of strength he jumped up and leapt once, twice and out on to clear ground. Free at last, he searched for his clothing and found the shirt and jacket soiled and crumpled down at the bottom of the bank. His cap had been flung into another bush, and he was only able to retrieve it with the aid of a long stick.

Shaking out the clothing, he tried as best as he could to smooth out the wrinkles and creases. His tie was torn and frayed at the end and he undid it and laid it aside. Gently... gingerly he got dressed, cursing as the cloth aggravated the reddening marks all over his body. He reached down for the tie and put it around his neck. The extra pressure on the stings made him wince, but he persisted and eventually he was able to do it up to the point where, if he met a master, he could still claim to be in his Sunday uniform.

Wearily and painfully he made his way back to the school.

......

"That was the strangest event I have ever been to."

Slater turned in his seat to the sound of Violet's voice. "How so?"

"Well it was a very nice meal and there were some awfully nice people there, but... well, all that jumping up and down and toasting this, that and the other... well it's a wonder everybody hasn't got violent indigestion."

Slater chuckled. "Yes. Yes I suppose you're right. It must seem pretty peculiar to an outsider."

Violet looked across the taxi at her husband. Even though they had not sat together during the evening, he had been unusually affable, seeming to bask in the reflected glory of his wife being consort to the master of the lodge. At every opportunity, from his position at the head of the table just below the top table, he had sought to draw the attention of his companions to her presence, with smiles and much raising of glasses.

For all the world it had been as if there'd never been any differences between them. Come to that, she thought, he's been strangely appreciative all week. It was almost as if Frank's absence had brought back the man she had agreed to marry. Gone, in a few short days, was the heavy-jowled bore, and in its place was the jolly man that she had grown so used to seeing at her parents' dining table.

It didn't excuse his behaviour of course. She could never really like the man; certainly never love him. But some sort of accommodation might be possible. 'Oh what a fool I've been,' she thought. 'Why did I not take notice of Frank? We were fine. Just the two of us. We had money and possessions. What did I do it for?'

His voice broke into her thoughts. "I thought you looked uncommonly good tonight."

A compliment! She couldn't let that go without some reposte. "I'm the same as I've always been. The same as before our wedding. It's just that since then you haven't been looking."

He coughed. "I'm sorry but... well you gave me quite a shock. I..."

"Let's not go over it all again please, Jim. I have never meant to deceive you and I am sorry that you feel that I have done so in some way."

"Yes but..."

"Please Jim. Please can we not bring the subject up again. I'm sorry if I've disappointed you and there's nothing more I can add." She searched in the darkness for some clue as to his expression, but his eyes were hidden from her.

For some while there was silence and she thought that perhaps he had taken offence and that the coldness between them was to continue, but then out of the darkness came his voice, speaking quietly. "I think that perhaps we should... perhaps we should try to... well forget the disagreements and..."

"And what about Frank?" she asked. "Yes, we can agree our differences but Frank... Frank has had to go away."

"All boys go away. There's nothing unusual in that."

"Under those circumstances?"

"Under any circumstances. Look, let's not row about this. The boy is at boarding school. He is welcome home in the holidays if he wishes, or he can go to his own house in France. What is wrong?"

She sighed. "What is wrong is that he feels that he was driven away by your enmity."

"I'm not the boy's enemy."

"I didn't say you were, but you have to admit that... well when you found out about him your attitude towards us both changed dramatically."

"I thought you didn't want to talk about it?"

"I don't really, but perhaps now we're talking we can at last settle things between us and try to become a family."

"Is that what you want?"

She laughed. "Of course it's what I want. Otherwise why would I have married you. I'm not exactly destitute am I?"

Slater sat looking out of the window. The darkness of the open countryside gave way to the lit-up streets of the city. They would be home soon. He'd had a fair bit to drink that evening and was acutely aware of his wife, barely two feet away from him on the other side of the taxi seat. She had looked marvellous tonight. Everybody had remarked on her vivacity, and he had been able to inform many an enquirer that the beautiful lady sitting next to the master was in fact his wife.

He recalled their envious glances. 'Lucky fellow' had been written all over their faces. And when he had told them that she had property... well. His whole being swelled with pride at the memory of their congratulations and he stole a sideways look at her. Not a conventionally handsome woman but beautiful nevertheless and he... he had never laid a finger on her.

Oh if only she didn't have the boy. That he disliked Frank had a lot to do with the boy's antecedents. But it went further than that. He'd wanted a wife but the boy was extra baggage and when... when he'd discovered that he was a bastard... well what man would have behaved differently? Still, he had effectively removed that little problem, and if he was careful then things would work out just right.

The income that Violet received was of no major importance, but it certainly was useful... and then there was the rest of the estate. Oh, it was in the boy's name, but Violet was his guardian and he seemed to get on fairly well with the boy's other guardian, even if the blighter didn't speak a word of English.

'All in all Slater,' he told himself, 'you've got quite a lot to lose here.' He took a deep breath. "I am sorry."

"I beg your pardon?"

"I am sorry for the past... for how I have behaved towards you since our wedding night."

The taxi turned into their road and drew to a halt outside their gate. Violet sat still in her seat, her mind racing. Sorry. He had said sorry. What on earth did she do now? She had grown almost accustomed to their living separate lives under the same roof and now... now what would happen? Slater got out of the vehicle and stood outside the driver's door, negotiating and then paying the fare. Violet could just see him in the light of the street lamp. Not the nicest of men, she was sure, but hardly the worst.

Many had remarked that she had been extremely fortunate to find not one but two men since the war, and both of them well heeled to boot. Countless women who had given their all during the war years were destined to remain alone, whereas she... she had found Armand and now Slater. She smiled to herself. It was hardly fair really. The mother of an illegitimate child, a fallen woman taking not one but two respectable men whilst all those good souls remained as spinsters.

Slater came around to her door and opened it. She gathered her dress and stepped out. He held his arm out for her to take. Good God, she thought, things had changed. Before, he would have simply marched up to the front door, leaving her alone on the pavement. A tingle of alarm ran through her. Would he want more from her? Would he want to...? How could she deal with that?

The man had become her husband, and on their wedding night she had prepared herself to share his bed... his body, but... but now? Now they had become virtual strangers and the thought of intimacy with him was... well it was very difficult.

Would he understand? Would he accept that to try and put all the weeks since their wedding night aside would be next to nigh impossible, or would he take offence? She stole a glance at him as he ushered her through the door. His face, usually puffy, was showing an extra hint of ruddiness tonight and his eyes seemed to be sandwiched even deeper than usual beneath the steel grey eyebrows and the rise of his cheeks.

He smiled warmly at her and she contrived to smile in return. He caught the scent of her, the nearness of her, and, for a fleeting moment, the feel of her body as she brushed past him.

Violet felt his eagerness and concluded that she would either have to accept or reject his advances tonight, or at some time very soon.

"A nightcap?" he asked as he took her coat.

"No thank you Jim," she said. "It's been a long night and I think I'll get to bed."

He nodded. "Yes. Yes I quite understand. Eh, I'll eh... I'll just have one myself." He pointed into the drawing room and made his way to the door. "You're sure?"

"I'm sure," she said, mounting the bottom step. "Good night Jim."

"Good night," he said. She turned and he stood and watched her as she climbed the stairs to the half landing, before turning out of sight. He sighed and entered the drawing room.

Violet made her way to her room. She shut the door and sat on the bed, kicking off her shoes and reaching up to remove her earrings. Then she flopped back on to the bed and lay there looking at the ceiling. What a night. All the time she had lived in her father's house he had never once mentioned to her that he was a freemason. And here he was, not only a mason but the... what did they all call him... the worshipful master. She chuckled to herself. Dear daddy. He had sat there beside her, basking in all the formalised adulation that had flowed up at them from the assembly in front of them, at times stealing a sideways glance at her and smiling a lop-sided, embarrassed sort of smile. She had squeezed his hand under the table reassuringly.

She rose from the bed and removed her clothing, hanging the dress carefully in the wardrobe and laying her slip and petticoat over her dressing table stool. She would deal with them in the morning. She opened her door and stole a look down the landing. No sign of Slater. She dashed naked across to the bathroom, carrying her night dress.

Some minutes later, she repeated the process in the other direction and slipped gratefully into her bed. For a short while she lay there staring into the darkness, thinking of the evening that had just gone, but after time she nodded off.

The door opened quietly. Violet did not wake, but the disturbance caused her to roll over in her sleep with her back to the entering figure. As the sheets were gently lifted, her eyes sprang open and she stiffened. The bed sagged as Slater, naked, slipped in beside her, pressing up against her back. A hand reached in under her night dress. It slid up her side and around to cup her right breast as he pressed closer to her back. She could feel his hardness pressing at her buttocks as his hand kneaded her breast, the fingers reaching around to pinch her nipples.

She jerked her body around intending to face him, but as she did he pushed closer and all she could manage was to lie on her back. In the darkness she looked into where she imagined his face would be. "What do you want?"

His reply, smelling strongly of the whisky he had drunk, was a hoarse chuckle. "What do you think I want?

One arm was trapped by the weight of his body, but her right arm was free. She reached across and touched his face and he interpreted the movement as a caress. Violet's mind raced. She was not really prepared for this. She had, in a way, anticipated it, but that had done little or nothing to ease her burden. What was she to do? How could she refuse this man who was so obviously aroused and had come to claim what he felt was his by right and which he evidently thought he was to have?

His hand reached down and grasped her night dress, wrenching it up her body and exposing her loins. In one move he was on top of her, his legs held close together, the knees slightly bent to force hers apart. She raised her hands and he grasped them both and pushed back, trapping them beside her and raising himself from her torso.

She felt her legs part and gave up any token of resistance, however unnoticed. He was at her and she could feel him pushing as he gyrated his hips, seeking entrance. She felt her dryness and the restriction it created but he only pushed harder, his breath coming in gasps and moans. Suddenly she felt wetness and almost simultaneously he slipped within her and collapsed down upon her, breathing heavily.

She cursed her weakness, the betrayal of her body, before realising that he had in fact ejaculated, and it was that which had enabled him to enter. He raised himself slightly and rolled off her, seemingly completely satisfied. "Well that was good, wasn't it?" he gasped.

Good? she thought. Good? The actual sex had lasted seconds. He had shown no consideration for her whatsoever and he imagined it was good!

She opened her mouth to speak and then thought the better of it. What was the point? He was happy. It was unlikely that the event would be repeated too often, and if it served to keep the peace then it was a small price to pay.

For a while he lay there breathing heavily, but then he sat up and swung his legs over the edge of the bed and on to the floor. He stood, hesitating for a moment before feeling his way to the door. He stopped, holding it open for a moment before mumbling "good night". And then he was gone.

Violet turned over in the bed and pulled the sheets tight around her. She felt used, almost abused, but at the same time she felt a calmness. The marriage was consummated at least and she now possessed a key. If she could excite him once she could do it again and she could use that to gain what she most cherished: peace.

......

Frank lay awake in his bed. Half-term tomorrow, and he had decided, after a lot of thought, that he wanted to visit Devon to see Florrie and Jim.

Violet had pleaded in her letter for him to come home, but he had insisted that he had wanted to do this for some time and now seemed the perfect opportunity. In a very short time it would be the end of the Christmas term and he would be home for longer. She relented, reluctantly, but asked that he, firstly, write to Florrie to tell her he was coming and secondly, that he contact her on his return to school to tell her all that had gone on.

That she, in some way, feared his encounter with his past came through in her letters and Frank had the foresight to write back, telling her that he wanted to just take this opportunity and that it made no difference whatsoever to his feelings or love for her. He was just tying up a few loose ends and satisfying a long held curiosity.

He hadn't written to Florrie. He had decided that he had little or nothing to say in a letter. He was thirteen years old and he had last seen them when he was four. If truth be known, he couldn't even remember them properly and it was only by borrowed reference to Violet that any sort of memory was kept alive.

He rolled over in his bed, hearing the now familiar sounds of the dormitory full of sleeping boys. He didn't like the place. He never would, but since those first days he had come to some sort of accommodation with his tormentors, who perhaps felt a little guilty about how they had treated him and perhaps also felt some respect for the fact that no word of his ordeal had passed his lips.

A couple of days after his particularly painful initiation he had gone to the showers and found Simon suffering his, which took the form of being stripped naked and held whilst black boot polish was applied to his private parts. Cartright and two other boys held on to the wriggling boy whilst Horsfield stood ready to apply the polish. Seeing Frank enter, Cartright had called over to him to come and help but Frank had declined, although he stayed just inside the door, fascinated and appalled.

Simon's call ended in a laugh, as he was clearly enjoying being the centre of attention. He gave up his struggling and Horsfield moved forward to stand between his legs, held open wide by the other two boys. Cartright grinned down at him. "Now you're going to get it," he had gloated.

Horsfield rubbed the rag into the open tin and flourished it in front of Simon. Then he leant forward and began to deliberately and thoroughly rub it into the boy's groin. Simon squealed and wriggled as the cold wax was worked into his private parts. Frank looked on silently.

Suddenly Horsfield had stepped back and the three other boys let go of Simon, letting him subside to the floor, where they stood around him pointing down at him, giggling. Horsfield had obscured Frank's view and he moved from the door to get a better look.

Simon lay grinning up at his persecutors, his naked white body a perfect contrast to an incongruous black erection. Cartright sniggered, his hand over his face, and the other two boys backed away laughing. Horsfield had just stood there looking down at his victim, a slow, easy smile playing on his lips.

Simon arched his back, a sensuous, almost contented smile of pride on his face. Horsfield reached down and took his hand, hauling him to his feet. For a second, the two boys stood close together as if about to embrace, but then the older one propelled him to the showers, smacking his bottom as he pushed him under the faucet. "Get yourself cleaned up," he had said grinning. He turned to Cartright and winked as he pointed out of the door and the three boys had left the room.

The shower came on. Simon turned in the water and saw Frank standing by the door. He grinned, pointing down at his still erect penis. Frank had turned and left him to his pleasures.

Frank sighed. Since that day he had not really spoken to Simon about the incident, and more and more the smaller boy had moved into the sphere of influence surrounding the monitor. As if in confirmation, the sound of bare feet on the wooden floor caught his attention and he raised his head from the pillow as Simon came back to his bed from the direction of the end beds. He caught Frank looking at him in the moonlight and grinned a guilty grin. Frank turned over and looked the other way.

He directed his thoughts quite deliberately to the day to come. The train to Exeter was at nine o'clock in the morning, and when he got there he would have to get a taxi to the farm. Would they be there? Of course they would be. They were farmers. They would always be there. They had to be there. What would he say? How would he introduce himself? The endless permutations ran around in his mind until he finally found sleep.

......

The taxi wound up the driveway with Frank sitting on the front of his seat, eagerly looking forward to the approaching farmhouse. Did he remember? 'Is it how I have always imagined it?' he thought. The tyres scrunched on the gravel of the driveway as the vehicle stopped outside the front door. Frank reached forward, opened the offside door and stepped out. He reached back in and slid his small suitcase out on to the running board and down on to the ground beside him.

The driver's door began to open, but Frank stepped up to it and handed him the money. "I believe this is what we agreed on," he said.

The man pulled the door shut again and counted the money. He nodded. "Will you be wanting me to wait for you?" he asked.

"No. No I'll be fine here," said Frank, standing back. The driver slipped the car into reverse and Frank watched as it backed across the face of the house and beside it. It stopped briefly before pulling out and disappearing down the driveway. Frank continued to gaze after it, until it was out of sight.

He turned and looked around him. In front of the house the trout pond lay unbroken, save for the slight disturbance on its mirrored surface as the water swirled through the grate and on into the stream. His eyes followed its course down the hill to the other ponds, past the sentinel rock and on to the river down below. Memories of puzzling whiteness came back to him.

He turned to look at the house, standing there in the autumn sunshine. Solidity emanated from every stone, every pore of this house. The faint gnawing sensation he had felt before came back to him, only now it was coupled with a feeling, a sensation of... what was it? Fear? No, not fear, there was nothing here to frighten him.

He was aware of the strangeness of the situation. Here he was, visiting people who had established so much importance in his life, yet of whom he had only received memory. He couldn't even put a face to Florrie... or to Joe, for that matter. Every time he thought of Florrie, Jesse's face came into his mind.

The front door opened to reveal a girl a few years younger than he was, blinking out into the light, her hand shielding her eyes. Frank picked up his suitcase and stepped forward. "Hallo, is anyone in?" The girl dropped the hand from her brow as he stood just in front of her, on the bottom step looking up. "Lizzie?" he asked.

She started. How did he know her name? "Yes," she said. "How do you know?"

Frank laughed. "It's a long story. Is Florrie in?"

"Yes. Yes she's out in the kitchen."

Frank looked at this girl. He'd remembered the name, hadn't he? Or could Violet have mentioned it? No, he'd remembered it surely. She was a pretty girl. Her dark blonde hair, all curls and ringlets, framed her fresh face with its perfect little features. A small sweet nose, blue eyes... startling blue eyes that gazed inquisitively down at him.

"Could you tell her I'm here."

Lizzie stopped staring back at him and grinned. "Yes. Yes wait there... no come on in and I'll run and tell her. Who did you say you were?"

"Frank. Just tell her it's Frank."

She turned and ran down the passageway towards the kitchen. Frank mounted the steps and placed his suitcase on the top step, just beside the door jam. He stepped in through the door and then thought the better of it and retreated to the top step. He could hear voices from down the long, dark passageway and eventually a door opened and Florrie came out.

She walked slowly down the passage, her hands behind her, striving to undo the ties of her apron. Her face, barely visible to Frank in the gloom, bore an incredulous expression as she peered forward. "Frank?" He stepped through the door as she stopped briefly to pull the apron over her head, casting it on to the sideboard.

"Hallo... mum... Florrie."

Her hands flew to her mouth and she stood stock still, her eyes staring out over them at the young man standing before her. Tears sprang into them and she opened her arms. Frank did not hesitate. He walked straight in and was enveloped in an embrace, the like of which he had only previously experienced from Jesse. It felt like walking into a dream.

For some time she gently rocked him in her arms, murmuring his name. After a while, she released him and held him at arm's length, staring into his face. He looked up into her eyes and smiled. "I've come to visit for a few days if you don't mind."

Florrie looked beyond him at the still open door, wonder in her eyes. "Where's Violet?"

"She's at home."

"At home? But how... what..."

"I'm at boarding school in Dorset and it's half-term. Violet said I could catch a train to visit you." He stood back, his face troubled. "You don't mind do you?"

Florrie reached forward and placed her hands on his shoulders. "Mind? Of course I don't mind. I'm delighted... it's just... well I just wasn't expecting it. You've given me quite a turn young man, but that doesn't mean that you aren't the best sight these eyes have had for... oh come here my darling." Saying that, she enveloped him once more and held him, rocking from side to side, humming tunelessly to herself.

A discreet cough distracted both their attentions and Florrie released him and turned to its sound. Lizzie stood there, amazement and wonder all over her face. Florrie beckoned her and she moved to them and was swept up into the same embrace as Frank. She had little alternative but to put her arm around the stranger and the three of them stood locked together for some time.

Eventually, Florrie recovered herself enough to let go of them both and the two of them stood in front of her looking up into her beaming face. "Lizzie... this is Frank. You know, the Frank I was always telling you about. He lived here with us when he was a little baby and... oh Frank it's so wonderful to see you." Her hands flew to her face. "Oh my goodness you must be tired. Dorset you say, and you've come on your own. Oh you poor mite, you must be starving."

She took each of the children's hands and led them through to the kitchen. Frank entered the room and looked around. Faint memories flooded through his brain. The large table. The flagged floor. He looked across to the range and breathed deeply. The smells of the room flooded into him, awaking forgotten dreams. Home. Home like Jesse's. Home like Germigny. Another place to call home. Tears sprang unbeckoned into his eyes and he wiped them quickly with the back of his hand. Florrie saw the gesture, and he was swept once more into her embrace.

The afternoon passed like a dream time with Florrie asking him questions about Violet and his life, whilst Lizzie sat across the table from him, enthralled, hanging on his every word. He told them of Armand and his death and the inheritance that had come to him as a result, and as he described it Lizzie butted in. "So you're rich then?"

"Lizzie!" Florrie admonished.

Frank smiled at her and then turned to Lizzie. "Well... well yes I suppose I am but..."

"Cor I've never met a rich person before."

"Lizzie," warned Florrie. "Don't be rude."

"I'm not being rude mum, it's just that he is rich, aren't you Frank... he's got a big chato in another country and farms. Are they as big as this farm?"

Frank smiled. It didn't seem right to tell them that the farmland he owned was three, no four times the acreage of their beloved farm. "They're big but they are very different from this farm. It's mainly fields of vegetables, all flat. No hills like this."

Lizzie looked disappointed, although she wasn't quite sure why. He had tried to make them out to be not as grand as their farm, but she felt sure that he was not being entirely truthful. She stared deep into his eyes and saw in them a person she felt instinctively for. He had once been her brother, so mum said, and even though she had no memory of him, she could well believe it. Still, he wasn't a brother really, was he, and he was ever so exciting.

"Do you know George?" she asked.

Frank looked across the table at her. George. George. He should know him. His face betrayed his lack of memory. "Auntie Kate's boy."

George. A memory stirred. White. Why white? He shook his head slowly. "No... no I'm sorry. I feel as if I do but..."

"Hush now my dear," said Florrie, coming up behind his chair and putting her arms over his shoulders, her face close to his. She looked across the table at Lizzie and silently entreated her to let him be.

The kitchen door opened and Joe walked in, carrying Frank's suitcase. "The door was open with this..."

He stopped, amazed at the sight of Florrie embracing a seated young man.

She smiled up at him. "See who's here."

Joe stood still. He put down the case and advanced a little, his gaze intent on the face of the seated boy. Frank stood up and took a pace towards him.

"Frank?" Frank nodded and held out his hand to shake. Joe took it in both of his and pulled him towards him into an embrace. He held tight for some moments before releasing him and standing back, a slightly embarrassed look on his face. "I'm sorry... I just... oh it's good to see you lad."

Frank smiled. "It's good to see you too." He saw the discomfiture on the man's face and stepped forward to embrace him in turn. Joe accepted him in his arms and Florrie joined them.

The two adults looked at each other, tears in their eyes, smiles on their faces. Happiness radiated from the little grouping and Lizzie shyly got up from her seat to join them.

The next few days passed in a whirl. Frank accompanied Joe all around the farm and revelled in helping out with all sorts of tasks. At all times Lizzie would be there, gazing adoringly at her new acquisition, her new-found hero. And when they finally returned to the farmhouse, Florrie was always there to greet them, a smile on her face and with lashings of cakes and tea to feed them.

The evenings were taken up with Frank telling them all about his life, about Armand and the chateau, about Gunther, Pierre-Luc and Marcel. They listened enthralled, marvelling at the adventures in foreign lands that had befallen the boy since he had left them, even if secretly Joe felt that places outside England were not to be totally trusted.

On one evening Kate turned up with George, and Frank was able to finally remember, even if only vaguely, his old chum and playmate. White kept on coming back to him in flashes and he mentioned this to Florrie at the breakfast table one morning. She looked at his face, wondering, then a smile broke out. "It was snowing when you left here. You were sledging with George when your mother arrived. Everywhere was covered with snow."

Frank sat back, a smile on his face. So that was it.

"How is Violet really... do you always call her Violet?"

Frank laughed. "Nearly always. I think it comes from the fact that I used to call you mummy and... well... she's fine. She's married a man called Slater."

Florrie looked at the boy perceptively. "And how do you get on with this man?"

Frank smiled. He couldn't hide anything from Florrie any more than he could from Jesse. "Not very well. That's why I went to boarding school."

Florrie crossed the room and sat down beside him, holding his hands on the table. "Is Violet happy?"

"Not really, but she's done it and... well she... you know."

"Why did she marry him if... I mean from what you've told me your adopted father... Armand, was that his name?" Frank nodded. "...Armand left you enough to keep her, didn't he?"

"He left her an income as well. She didn't need to marry him for money."

Florrie sighed. "Then why?"

"Because I think she was lonely after Armand and she... she..." He stopped.

"She what?"

Frank swallowed. "She wanted a baby of her own. She said that she'd never had me as a baby and she wanted one."

Florrie's face opened up. "Oh the love. The love. And has she had one?"

Frank looked embarrassed. Talking of babies in connection with his mother... with Florrie, an adult despite the obvious intimacy between them, was getting near to his limit. "I... err... I..."

Florrie cursed herself for her insensitivity. He was a boy, however grown-up he seemed. However much he had experienced and for all the fact that he had made his own way here. He was a boy and here she was talking about intimate personal things with him. "I'm sorry Frank, I didn't mean to pry."

He looked at her and smiled. "I'm not embarrassed... not really, it's just... well it's just that I don't know and well... they didn't really... they haven't really got on very well since..."

Florrie looked concerned. "Since what, Frank darling?"

"Since he found out about my father."

"Your father? What about your father?" She laughed. "Don't tell me he's jealous of what he left you?"

Frank looked confused, then he understood. "Oh not Armand... I mean my real father Frank."

"Your real father? What's he got against him? He never met him, did he?"

Frank looked embarrassed. "No... he never met him... it's just that well... he and Violet..."

"Oh... oh I see." Florrie cuddled the boy. "You mean they weren't married... silly man. What's that to do with you?"

"I don't know really. It's just that... well he thought that Violet hadn't... he thought she should have told him, and when he found out he was furious."

Florrie looked seriously at Frank. She cupped his face in her hands. "You're a good boy Frank and I want you to promise me that you'll never think badly of yourself, or of Violet for that matter, just because your father was killed when he was. They were both good people tied up in a stupid war."

Frank gulped. Jesse had said as much to him and he understood entirely, but it was marvellous to hear it confirmed by this woman, who, though not related to him in any way, seemed almost her twin. If only she and Jesse could meet some day, he was sure that their friendship would last forever.

Lizzie came in. "You two again," she laughed.

Florrie turned and stood. "Us two again." She opened her arms and Lizzie walked into the expected cuddle.

"George is here Frank," said Lizzie brightly.

"I'll nip out and see him," said Frank, rising and going to the door. In truth, he would rather have stayed in the kitchen with Florrie and Lizzie but felt that perhaps he should go out and see George.

It wasn't that he didn't like George, it was really that despite everyone going on about him being his old chum, his old playmate, he had very little in common with him. He couldn't remember George of old apart from the odd snatch of conversation. No doubt when they had been small boys he had hero-worshipped the older boy but now... now... well he was just plain boring. Like a playful lamb that had ceased its gambolling to point its face forever to the ground.

And then there was Lizzie. For some reason George seemed to resent the rapport that he had struck up with her. He seemed to react as if Frank was seeking to take away her affections from him. Oh, there was nothing serious, but nevertheless there was something there.

Frank opened the back door and stepped out into the yard. He saw George idly kicking a stone around. "Hallo there George," he called with little enthusiasm as he joined him.

November 1928

Frank trudged back across the common from the school in the direction of the boarders' house. His large leather satchel was slung over his shoulder, and in both arms he carried the heavy carpet bag containing his sports kit.

He didn't really like organised sport, but at least it got him outside and into the fresh air, and this afternoon the air was fresh. His face felt flushed in the cold wind and already the mist was rolling in as dark threatened. He turned into the lane and walked slowly down towards the gates and up the driveway.

Other boys filed in from various directions, and as he neared the door Cartright joined him. They had never been friends... never could be really, but it did seem to Frank that, of late, Cartright had been overtly courting his friendship.

He had little or no doubt what had brought this about.

When they had first started French lessons he had sat next to Simon as Hattersley, their teacher, had fired French words across them, seeking to impress them all with his cleverness. Frank had exchanged looks with Simon and his other classmates in silent and universal agreement that the task being set, of understanding this foreign language, was going to be next to nigh impossible.

When questions were asked, in excruciatingly bad French, he had winced inwardly but refused to raise his hand or volunteer any answers.

That is, until one day when Hattersley, recognising him at last, seized upon him as he gazed longingly out of the window. "Mr Balfour," he hissed as he came down the aisle. "I'm sorry to disturb your sojourn but..." He thwacked the cane down on the desk, causing Frank to jump involuntarily. "...do you think you could give us some time to attend to this French lesson?"

A nervous titter had run round the class as Frank faced up to the intense gaze of the teacher staring down at him through his round, thick glasses. "I'm sorry sir," he said. "What would you like me to say?"

"Say Mr Balfour? Say?" He seemed to think, his index finger tapping on his lip. "I would like you to give me the full conjugation of the verb... 'to have'."

"In French?"

The little man bridled and whacked the cane down on the desk top once more. "In French? Of course in French Mr Balfour. This is a French lesson, is it not?"

Frank had stood up. He was not as tall as the teacher, but even at his age he exuded more physical presence than the older man. Unthinkingly, the teacher had stood back a pace but continued to stare at the boy, gloating at what he had thought was his obvious discomfort and soon to be humiliation.

Frank switched into fluent French. He conjugated the verb and then went on, in his boyhood language, to explain that he was of dual nationality, that he spoke perfect French and that he owned a chateau and several farms in France as well as an ironworks, all of which he intended to return to as soon as his schooling was finished.

Hattersley's mouth had fallen open as he struggled to keep up with and understand what was being said to him, and Frank sat down relishing the total silence that had befallen the room.

In the headmaster's study, later on, with a clearly indignant Hattersley present, Frank had to explain his background. The headmaster was clearly very impressed at the material substance that one as young as Frank was fortunate enough to possess, but Hattersley kept on trying to establish that Frank had in some way been insolent.

"The boy attempted to make a fool of me in front of my class," he protested.

"That is a very serious misdemeanour," counselled the headmaster. "Were you attempting to... well you know?"

"No sir. Not at all sir," Frank had innocently protested. "Mr Hattersley asked me a question and I answered it. I merely went on to try to explain to him... well that French is my second... no perhaps my first language."

The headmaster coughed. He looked at Hattersley. "Is there any point in the boy attending classes at a level at which he is obviously far beyond?" The teacher was staring at Frank intently and seemed not to hear the headmaster. "Mr Hattersley?" the headmaster repeated.

He turned. "Eh... yes... sorry headmaster, you were saying?"

"I was saying, is there any point in the boy attending classes which... well to put it mildly, are beneath him?"

"I hardly think it right to belittle my classes headmaster, especially in front of a pupil."

"Oh no! Oh no, Mr Hattersley. I was not in any way trying to... eh... denigrate your excellent classes. I was merely saying that as the boy is obviously at a level which is far beyond his classmates it may be better if we can find something more suitable... an alternative for him which would be equally productive."

"Yes headmaster, but what?"

Frank sat there quietly watching the two men deliberating. He coughed politely. "Excuse me headmaster, may I make a suggestion?"

The two men stopped talking and turned to him. "Yes," said the head.

"Perhaps I could help some of the other boys with pronunciation and... well general conversation?"

"Excellent!" the headmaster almost shouted. "Excellent. Capital idea, don't you think Mr Hattersley?"

The headmaster missed the look of pure enmity that Hattersley had shot Frank. All he had seen was the smile that Frank gave back. An open, winning smile accompanied by "Glad to be of help."

Trudging through the cold, Frank grinned at the memory. "How's it going Balfour?" Cartright enquired.

"Fine. Fine thank you," Frank replied.

"Err, I was wondering..."

Here it comes, thought Frank. Here it comes. "Yes?"

"I was wonder..." He stopped as Frank held up his hand to silence him. Cartright followed his gaze.

"That's my stepfather's motor car," said Frank incredulously. "What on earth's he doing here?" Cartright merely shrugged his shoulders. Frank moved forward, leaving him standing. He entered the door and searched both ways along the corridor, looking for a clue as to why the motor car was there. Was it his mother? Surely Slater would not be here alone unless... unless there was something wrong with Violet! He ran down the corridor towards the housemaster's office and knocked.

A muffled sound came from within which he couldn't quite interpret, but he entered nonetheless. The master was sitting at his desk and Slater was seated in the armchair to the side. As Frank entered, the master half rose but Slater remained seated. "Ah Frank. Eh your father..."

"Stepfather," Frank interjected.

"Yes... your stepfather has... some... well perhaps it would be best if I left him to explain." He rose and nervously shuffled past Frank and out of the room.

For a moment there was a silence, then Slater indicated the small hard chair directly in front of the desk. "Sit down a moment please Frank," he said. "I've got something that I have... some bad news I'm afraid."

Frank remained standing. He stared at the man. "What? What has happened to my mother?"

"Your mother? He gave a little laugh, glancing sideways at the master. "Oh no, your mother's fine. It's not your mother."

"Then what? Who?"

"I'm afraid that your grandmother has been taken ill and..."

"How is she?"

The man looked serious, and for a moment Frank saw that he genuinely regretted being the bearer of bad tidings. "I'm afraid, Frank, that your grandmother died the day before yesterday."

Frank stood there looking at him. Grandmother, that frail, sweet woman. She was dead? Oh poor Violet, poor grandfather. "Have you come to take me back?"

Slater looked up at him. "Yes, your mother... naturally your mother wishes to have you with her... you will not need to stay long... a few days perhaps... until the funeral at least, but it would be better..."

"I'll get my things ready."

Slater nodded and Frank left the room.

The journey home was a strange one, and for the most part was completed in relative silence. The only conversation revolved around stopping points for relief and refreshment. As the evening wore on, Slater became increasingly conscious of the passing of his regular mealtime and eventually insisted that they should stop at an inn on the Hog's Back.

Frank was half inclined to argue that they should press on, but after a moment's consideration decided that the man was going to stop in any event, and to tell the truth, by now he too was famished. It was therefore late at night, approaching the early hours of the next morning, when they finally pulled up outside the Highgate house.

"Why have we come here?" Frank enquired.

"Why not?"

"Well is Violet here?"

"I don't know. She may be, more probably she may be over at her father's house, we'll have to see."

Frank looked at him as he got out of the motor car. He watched him come around the front and got out to join him on the pavement. "If she's not here, shall we go there?"

Slater let out a dismissive laugh. "At this time of night? I should think not. We'll go in the morning." He turned and stalked up the pathway and into the front door.

Frank watched for a moment. Then he ran up the path and grabbed Slater's arm. The man turned, amazed. He said nothing at all but stared down at Frank's hand as it clutched his jacket sleeve. Frank removed it.

"Why can't we go now?"

Slater looked down into the boy's face. He could see that he was tired. He could see that he was pretty overwrought. Don't want some silly scene here Jim, he thought. He smiled as warmly as he could. "Let's see if she's here, shall we?"

She wasn't. They called through the house and Frank ran up to her bedroom, but the only person that surfaced was the maid, Perkins, who peeked out from the basement room she occupied. Frank saw her. "Is my mother here?"

She shook her head. "Gone to her father's house." She pulled her shawl around her and retreated.

Slater came down the passageway, a large drink in his hand. "Not here?"

"No, she's at grandfather's house. Can we go?"

Alarmingly for Frank, the man came right up to him and put his hand on his shoulder, bending down, bringing his face close. Frank could smell the drink on his breath now and see at close quarters the flush of his face and the slight pinkness of his eyes. The face contorted into a semblance of concern. "Frank. Frank dear boy, we'll go in the morning. It'll be best you'll see."

Frank pulled back. "But she'll want to see me tonight."

"She'll be asleep."

"Asleep? No she won't."

"She has to have her sleep now."

Frank searched the man's face. Has to have her sleep now? Why now? Was Violet ill? "Is my mother unwell?"

Slater laughed now, and standing up took a large swig from his glass. He drew himself up to his full height and addressed Frank in a proud and booming voice. "Never fitter. She's carrying my child."

The colour drained from Frank's face. His child? This man's child... his mother was pregnant. He stared up into his stepfather's face, and the pride it displayed was all the confirmation he needed. So, she had achieved what she had wanted. Well let's hope that whatever came out of it owed more to Violet than Slater.

Slater's expression grew less jovial and more serious. He looked down at Frank standing there, his thoughts tumbling within but his voice silent. "Are you not going to congratulate me?"

Congratulate him? 'Do I have to,' Frank thought. The silence seemed to hang in the air and he was aware that the man's grin was in danger of deteriorating into a scowl. "Congratulations," he said quietly. "Congratulations to you both."

"Thank you boy," said Slater, taking another swig from his drink.

Frank turned and looked up the stairs then back to the man, who was obviously gearing himself up for the next drink. "I think that I'll go to my bed now," he said. "At what time will we be leaving for Finchley?"

"Straight after breakfast."

"I'll see you at breakfast then," said Frank, turning and making his way up to his room.

Christmas 1928

"**D**o you actually understand what was going on there?" said Slater, glaring at his wife in the passenger seat. "Do you understand?"

Violet looked across at him. His face was flushed and angry, his eyes wide, staring through the windscreen as he gripped the steering wheel tightly, jerking into every corner. "Why yes Jim dear, but... surely... well we've both suspected something of the sort for some time."

An explosion of derision came from Slater's lips and he clapped his hand to his forehead. "But... surely," he mimicked. "Good God, he... he now flaunts the situation in... in front of the whole world. It's just... just too much!"

Violet sighed. "Please don't upset yourself so Jim. It really doesn't affect us, does it?"

"Doesn't affect us? Doesn't affect us? I'll be a laughing stock."

"I don't see why you should be. After all..."

"Oh you don't." He snorted. "Well let me tell you madam, it is well known that he is my father-in-law and it is equally well known that he was to be my master of ceremonies during my year in the chair."

Violet put her hand on her husband's arm. He glanced down at it and then quickly back at the road ahead, shaking her grip loose with a flick of his elbow. She spoke softly to him as if he were a child. "Really Jim, please don't take on so. Please try not to upset yourself. I'm sure everything will be fine."

"Oh you think so do you? Everything will be fine." He raised his hands off the steering wheel in exasperation. The car hit a pothole and he replaced them quickly, jerking it back into line. Violet gripped her seat and braced her feet down hard. "And just how will everything be fine? Have I not been shamed enough by your family and its loose morals?"

Violet flushed. A cold, steely feeling crept into her breast and she felt her temper rising. She clutched her stomach, swelling now from the pregnancy. Keep calm, she thought, keep calm. "I take it that you are referring to me."

"You're damned right I'm referring to you." He stared across at her angry face. Caution was gone now. The barb was in and he would turn it.

"How can you say that?!" Violet exploded. "I have been a dutiful wife to you and I bear our child. How can you say that?"

The car drew into their road and Slater stopped outside the front gate leading up the straight path to the front door. He pulled violently on the handbrake and got out, slamming the door behind him as he stalked around the front of the vehicle and straight through the gate. Violet sat still in the seat, watching his back. He opened the front door and went in, pushing it shut behind him. Fury rose up in her. She would not be treated like this. She scrambled out and ran up the path to hammer on the closed door until it was finally opened by Perkins. "Thank you," she breathed as she rushed past the startled and slightly alarmed woman.

Entering the drawing room she, as expected, found Slater standing in front of the sideboard, his back to her. He held a bottle in one hand and was drinking from the other. "I asked you, how can you say that?" she shouted.

He kept his back to her but put the bottle deliberately and carefully down on the top. He raised the glass to his lips once more and drained it, placing it down in front of him, out of her view, as he turned. "I will say what I want in my house."

"You have no right to question my morals just because..."

"Your morals! What morals? The mother of a bastard!" he screamed.

Violet clutched her breast and reeled back, a sick feeling rising in her stomach. She turned and sought a chair, and finding one, slumped across to it and sat down holding her belly. She breathed deeply and tried to stare back at him defiantly, refusing to let him see the full effect of his outburst. "The mother to be of your child sir," she whispered meaningfully.

He turned around and deliberately filled his glass again. Violet sat watching him, waiting for his reposte. He turned, the glass in his hand, raised it to his lips and made as if to drink. At the last moment he lowered the glass slightly and hissed over the top. "So you say madam. So you say... the word of a strumpet."

The shock registered on her already stricken face. Her eyes flew open and then filled with tears of shame. Her mouth refused to work and her brain could summon no words to place within it. Slater smiled cruelly. He drained the glass and stalked from the room. At the door he crashed into Frank, who having discovered that they were home was coming down to greet them. Frank was thrown back against the jamb as Slater pushed past, before turning back to Violet, addressing her from the hall. "And you can tell him to get out of my house," he said indicating Frank. He turned, ignoring the shocked look on the boy's face, and walked up the stairs and out of sight.

There was a stunned silence as Frank leant back against the frame, looking after the departing figure of his stepfather. Eventually he turned to look at Violet. "What was that all about?"

"He's angry at your... at your grandfather."

"What about grandfather?" Violet opened her mouth to speak and then just couldn't find the words. She shut her mouth again, a stricken look on her down-turned face. "Is it about grandfather and Alice?"

She looked up quickly. "You know?"

"Of course I know."

Violet smiled ironically. Of course he knew. They'd all known, hadn't they? Only none of them had ever dared to admit it to themselves. She started to laugh and cry at the same time, bending forward in the chair, the tears rolling down her face.

"Violet?"

"Yes Frank," she said, looking up at him as she wiped the tears from her eyes with the back of her hand. "What are we going to do?"

"Do?"

"He's thrown me out."

Her face straightened. "This is my home now as well as his."

"That's as may be, but it isn't mine. What am I to do?"

Her face took on a worried expression and he crossed the room and knelt down before her. Violet ran her hand through his hair and he leant on her lap. "I'm sorry darling," she said softly. "I'm so sorry. I should have listened to you."

"It's alright," he said. There was silence as she played with his hair. After a while he stirred. "Should I go to grandfather's?"

She thought carefully. Quite obviously the poor boy could not be expected to stay in Slater's house for the rest of his holidays, yet... yet if he went to her father's, any rift between him and Slater would be cemented and that would make her position untenable. She was, after all, pregnant with the man's child, and quite frankly she did not relish the thought of having to leave and have the child at her father's house with all the tittle-tattle that would provoke. Her mind raced. Her father and Alice had announced that they were intending to spend actual Christmas in Essex, and effectively that removed them from the scene. Where could Frank go? Oh the poor darling. 'What have I done,' she thought. Christmas and he's... it came to her. Jesse!

"Jesse," he said.

She started. "I just thought of that." She gave a little nervous laugh. "I just thought of that this minute... how did you..."

"I don't know, but it's a great idea, isn't it? We'll go to Jesse's and have a really great Christmas with her." He looked up at her, his eyes shining with happiness and expectation.

Her face dropped. "I can't go Frank."

"You can't go? What do you mean you can't go? You can't stay here."

She smoothed his hair and stroked his cheek. "I have to stay here.

This is my home and I'll not give it up... not when... the baby."

He looked at her in horror. "You cannot possibly mean that you intend to stay in his house as his..."

"...wife? Well that's what I am, isn't it Frank? For good or ill."

He shook his head in disbelief. "I can't believe that you'd do this."

She laughed weakly. "Nor can I, but I'll not be driven from here with my tail between my legs as if I've something to hide. Don't you see that then he would be able to parade his stupid fantasies as if they were the truth?"

He nodded silently. "I'll go alone then. Will you be alright?"

She leant down and kissed him. "I'll be alright. When we're alone I can handle him. I promise. He'll not risk the child's health and... well we'll see."

For a while the two of them sat there quietly, each with their own thoughts but both thinking of each other. At length she roused him and they got to their feet and went up to their beds. In the morning, Frank was packed by the time he came down for breakfast. Slater had gone out without mentioning where, and to be honest neither of them very much cared. They sat close to one another, a luxury that were Slater there they would not have been able to enjoy as he always insisted that they space themselves around the huge table, making quiet conversation next to impossible. They chatted quietly, trying to reassure each other that everything would be alright, whilst listening out for the sound of the doorbell and the arrival of the taxi that they had ordered to take Frank to the station.

"It'll be a bit of a shock for Jesse when I just turn up."

"Yes it will be, and I'm afraid there'll be a bit of explaining to do. I've written a letter telling her that... well I've told her that you and Jim aren't getting along very well at the moment and..."

"Why not tell her the truth?" Violet laughed. "I don't need to. I know you'll do that well enough and I know she'll understand... and besides she'll be so pleased to have you that all else will pale into insignificance."

The doorbell rang and her face dropped with her tone. "Will you be alright?" He got up and hugged her. "Of course I will. It's you we've to worry about, left here with... well you know."

"I'll be fine. He's got visitors coming to dinner this evening and... well when he's in company he always puts on a good show."

Frank laughed. "I know that. They must go away thinking I'm his favourite person, the fuss he makes."

Violet laughed with him and allowed him to help her to her feet to see him to the door. "When do you have to be back at school?"

"On the fifth of January. The Saturday. Why?"

She thought for a moment. "Come back to grandfather's house on the Friday and stay there the night and you can go on from there."

"Don't come here?"

She looked at him, the pain and embarrassment clear in her face. "If the coast is clear then you can come here, but otherwise we'll tell granddad that you want to stay there as... well you won't have seen him over Christmas."

Frank nodded. "I understand. I'll see you though, won't I?"

Violet hugged him close. "Of course you will my darling. Of course you will, and don't worry, I'm going to sort this out one way or the other, but first..." She patted her stomach. "...I have to sort this out." The two of them walked down the path hand in hand.

Seeing them coming, the taxi driver got out and loaded up the case as Frank and Violet hugged each other. Eventually they separated and Frank mounted the running board and pulled the door shut. He slid open the window to wave as the gears crunched and the taxi set off. Violet stood at the gate, waving at the departing vehicle. Long after it had disappeared, she was still standing there, before she realised that she was getting quite cold. Shivering, she made her way back and into the front door. She had felt this wretched before. Oh yes she had, and that time... all those times it had been when she had let Frank down. Damn you Violet, she thought, that the boy still loves you is a miracle.

March-June 1929

The spring term went slowly for Frank and his feelings of isolation from his family were barely assuaged by the stream of letters that Violet kept up. It was obviously impossible for him to go home at half-term and he wrote to her saying that he was quite happy to stay at school for the few days it involved.

Violet gratefully accepted his decision, and Frank therefore spent the most boring holiday of his life mooching around the practically empty school, his only company those few boys who habitually stayed as their parents were posted abroad. The great house, usually so full of life, seemed hollow, its halls and corridors silent beyond reverence, echoing every passing footfall or softly spoken word.

He had seen Violet only briefly at his grandfather's house after he had spent Christmas at Jesse's, and that meeting had been a tense one. His grandfather was, quite naturally, curious about why Frank had not gone straight home and indeed why he had suddenly decided not to spend Christmas with his family. "I had no idea. I... we would not have gone away and just left you."

"You didn't leave me grandfather," Frank had protested. "I wasn't left. I went to Jesse's and I had an absolutely wonderful time."

Ernest snorted. "Well it still doesn't explain why you had to go off and leave your mother like that at a time when... well at a time when families should be together, don't you know."

Frank had looked across at Violet, his eyes pleading for help. She flashed back her understanding before turning gently to her father. "Daddy, Frank went to Jesse's with my blessing. Jim... Jim and I didn't have anything much planned for Christmas, what with the baby and... well you know... we just all thought that Frank would have a better time with Jesse... and... and with Keith and Rosie. And he did, didn't you Frank?"

"Rather," said Frank enthusiastically.

Ernest had looked from his daughter to his grandson and back again. "And there's nothing else to it?"

"Nothing daddy, I assure you."

Frank returned Ernest's inquisitive gaze with a blank face and the whole incident passed off without further discussion. Alice, however, had shot a look at Violet, which told her in no uncertain terms that once again she guessed the truth. Unseen by both Frank and Ernest, who by now had gone on to talk of other things, Violet had blushed, angry at herself for this tacit admission of the lie.

As the end of term holiday approached, Violet's letters to Frank became more and more desperate about what he was to do and where he was to go. She tried to reassure him that everything was back on an even keel at home and that it would be quite alright for him to go there. But Frank read between the lines and concluded, quite rightly, that an uneasy truce existed between Slater and his mother and that his presence might well unsettle that balance.

He wrote to Florrie asking if he could go there for the holidays, and when he received the reply, which of course told him that he was more than welcome, he wrote to Violet telling her that Florrie had invited him to Devon for the holidays and that he had accepted. Whether Violet saw through the little white lie or not he was never really sure, but it seemed to let her off the hook as she wrote back telling him that as he was nearer, as she was now heavily pregnant, as it was only a short holiday in any event, and as they would be together for the whole of the summer holidays, perhaps it might be a nice idea.

Frank smiled ruefully to himself as he read the letter. He loved Violet very much but he could see, hidden in her words, the relief she must have felt that her home life was not to be disturbed. 'Roll on the time when I'm able to leave school and live my own life in France,' he thought. Then Violet would not be dependent on anybody and she could live with him. He paused in his thoughts. No, Violet had refused to live in France after Armand's death. That was the problem. That was the reason... the cause of both of their current predicaments.

Well, come what may he was not going to stay away from Germigny for one moment longer than he needed to, and when he was there, if she needed somewhere, it would be there for her as well. In point of fact, he had asked her if he could go back to France permanently and attend school there, but she baulked at the idea, refusing to countenance him living away in another country. He guessed that she was afraid that once there, they would gradually lose contact and that just having him in England was important to her and in some way gave her some security.

He thought guiltily about the forthcoming holiday and how he had tricked her. The truth was that despite his love for Violet, in the current situation he felt a greater affinity for Jesse and Florrie and felt more comfortable, more at home, when he was with them.

Violet had always tried to make him aware that he was her dearest son and, for a while with Armand, they had enjoyed the proper relationship that should exist between any normal mother and child. That she felt a great guilt over his original fostering was always apparent, and that came up whenever Florrie was mentioned. It was almost as if she sometimes wished that the contact had not been made by him... that she would have preferred him to deny that period in his life when Florrie was his mother, even though his memories of that period were very hazy.

He didn't want to cause any pain to her, but the fact was that at a time of his life when his home environment was far from happy, if he could gain some feeling of stability by harking back to his previous life, then so be it.

In any case, even if Florrie, Joe and Lizzie had not had anything to do with him, even if he had never been fostered by them, had he met them he would have been instantly attracted to them all. They were his kind of people, and he felt that he was certainly theirs. One short visit, out of the blue, and he felt as if he had known them all his life.

It pained him that Violet could not fully share his joy at finding such friends. That she could never completely divorce her feelings of having her relationship with him threatened worried him, and he sought to reassure her that she was and always would be a special part of his life. She was his mother and she would always be unique, no matter how many others he found love and friendship with. He sighed. Perhaps it was the very insecurity that she felt that had driven her into the disastrous relationship with Slater. Perhaps she realised that with her marriage to Slater she had thrown away all those years of happiness and effectively destroyed Frank's home life. All Frank knew was that the Violet he knew was not the Violet of old.

School had settled into its normal routine and Frank had resigned himself to being a part of that routine until the end of his schooling. The day began when the first bell rang in the dormitory. There would be a mad scramble to get out of bed and along to the showers before the hot water ran out. There, monitors would shout and bully the pupils into line, letting favourites and seniors in ahead of lesser mortals, who would shuffle forward dejectedly knowing that, by the time they got there, the water would be freezing but that they would be made to get underneath it nevertheless.

Frank had established himself quite well in the pecking order by virtue of his ability to help certain senior pupils with their French homework, although he always had to be careful not to make it too obvious that he had done it for them. He took the favours and enjoyed the privileges, knowing all the while that however well the fools did in their homework, if they couldn't translate that into an ability to pass an exam, all was for nought. It wasn't his problem if they refused to capitalise on his help.

When all were washed and dressed, the bell for breakfast would ring and they would file into the dining hall, where they would pick up a bowl and spoon to queue up in front of a large table in front of the kitchen door. Great ladles of glutinous porridge would be dumped unceremoniously into the bowl and they would pass on to the next urn. Here, a minute ladle was dipped briefly in and its contents of watered-down milk poured on top to form a thin halo, which could be stirred in to make the mix edible.

Absolute quiet had to be maintained at the breakfast benches in case the masters were disturbed in their contemplation of the daily newspapers. They would sit at their table eating, ostensibly, the same fare as the boys, although from the consistency and colour of the mixture being spooned out from the smaller pan on their table, it was obvious to any observant human being of whatever age that theirs was an altogether finer brew.

The same went for the tea, which the boys drank out of battered, enamelled mugs filled from a huge tea urn, manhandled by a large and constantly sweating woman with arms as thick as many a boy's legs. Theirs was a thick, dark liquid clogged with floating tea leaves of dubious vintage, thinned out by a dash of milk. The masters, meanwhile, drank from a fine bone china teapot, poured gently into their equally fine cups through a strainer.

The trudge to school itself was a chore to some, but for Frank it provided some of the most delightful moments of the day. There were two ways to the actual school buildings. One, the shorter route, was taken by the majority of the boys, as it meant going through the centre of the village, past all the shops and the railway station, where they would be joined by the arriving day pupils. If there was time, they could stop off at the sweet shop to buy tuck from their allowance, and outside that establishment a queue of boys would form, anxious to get inside and make their purchase without being late for school. Around that queue a satellite group would form, seeking to barter either place or purchase, and in many cases to swap or borrow loans and favours.

Some boys who were good at managing their affairs became, in effect, money lenders, either at extortionate rates or more usually in return for promises which they, in turn, would barter on. Thus it was that a monitor wanting to get out of, say, gardening on Saturday mornings would arrange to have his place taken by a boy who wanted to be counted in when he was out. That boy would, in turn, get the rota for gardening filled by some unfortunate lower on down the scale of things who had placed himself into virtual slavery for a few sweets or a packet of five cigarettes.

Frank had no need of this system. He was well known for his ability to help with French and, therefore, was always in direct demand without any need of intermediaries, using his knowledge to free himself from the tyranny of the monitors.

In that quest for freedom and separation he chose, more often than not, to take the longer route to school, around the outskirts of the village, across the common and down the small lane with the stream running beside it, to the junction opposite the school gates themselves.

Here, in the quiet of the morning, he would breathe deeply of the forest air, taking in all the sights, sounds and smells that so many would ignore or simply be unaware of. He alone would spot the fox slinking back along the hedge to her daytime lair, the buzzard quietly quartering the open ground at the forest's edge and the families of early morning rabbits nibbling away in groups.

Once, as he rounded a gorse bush, he came across a pony giving birth. She lay there on her side, her eyes wide and staring, raising and lowering her head in a great arc from ground to flank in her birthing agony.

With short puffs of steamy breath issuing from her nostrils, the mare seemed oblivious to his presence as he squatted behind her, watching intently as first of all two front feet and then the head of the foal became visible.

He gasped as she lumbered to her feet and stood splay-legged, head down with the foal protruding from her, and as it slipped suddenly from her in its wrapping of membrane and thumped to the ground, he held his breath in fear at the damage it must have suffered. He had, in fact, held his breath for so long that, when he eventually did breathe, he did so with a force that rivalled the indrawn breath of the horse and she wheeled around to him.

Frank had stayed down on his haunches and the mother, perhaps aware that the boy meant her no harm, had bent down and begun the task of licking her foal clean.

When he finally, and very reluctantly, had to leave, Frank had noted every detail of the young pony's colouration and resolved to try and locate the pair after school, and beyond, to monitor their progress.

School itself followed the pattern of more or less every school, with a rotation of lessons throughout the day. That there was a mixture of day boys and boarders served to provide normality during the day, and it was only as the school day ended that the differences emerged.

Day boys would wander out from school planning all sorts of activities for their evenings, all of which could be boasted of the next day, whereas boarders knew full well that their evening was set out in tablets of stone.

As soon as they got back to the boarding house, there would be a tea consisting of jam sandwiches, one round per boy, plus a mug of tea, almost certainly warmed up from the morning's brew. After that would follow two hours of homework, and then finally it was supper time, an altogether jollier affair compared to breakfast, as talking was allowed. Even so, by that time of night, the boys were usually so hungry that the only real sound to be heard throughout most of the meal was the clattering and scraping of knives and forks on the crockery as every last morsel was greedily consumed. As the last cutlery was placed neatly on the plates, the buzz of conversation would gradually rise until the order was given to collect up the plates and dishes and pass them through to the kitchen, after which they were dismissed.

Following the meal there was about an hour of free time before the bells rang for washing and bedtime. And that, in effect, was each and every week day for Frank and his fellow students.

Weekends were different of course, and Frank took advantage of the free time allowed during the day to roam at will in the forest. Sometimes Simon would ask if he could go with him, and on occasion Frank would allow him to. Most times, however, Frank preferred to be alone, as then he could follow up the various trails and quietly watch, from a hidden vantage point, the animals he so loved.

It didn't seem to matter how often he told a friend, especially Simon, to keep quiet. It always seemed to be impossible for them. Frank would lie there in a brake, spellbound at the sight of a hind with her fawn, and suddenly his companion would sneeze or cough... or worse still, start to whisper. Up would come the deer's head, round would come the enquiring eyes and ears, and with a snort she would be off.

All of this is not to give the impression that Frank was a loner. Far from it. Once he had realised that as he was probably going to have to see out his school days at that school, even though it was not his choice, he recognised that he had to make the best of it.

His popularity had gone up immeasurably since his wealth had become known, and the respect that he earned from pupils and teachers alike for his contribution to the French lessons brought him many friends... with the exception of Mr Hattersley.

Hatters had grudgingly accepted the headmaster's joyful embrace of Frank's offer to assist, but that did not mean that he had forgotten or forgiven the sleight that he felt he had received. At every opportunity he sought to denigrate Frank's value and belittle his abilities. He took to producing volumes of obscure French manuscripts, which he would flourish as masterpieces and pass to Frank for translation.

The fact that the French contained within them was ancient and unintelligible to virtually any normal person, let alone a fourteen-year-old boy, seemed to escape him. When Frank struggled to understand them he would hoist the book aloft, praising its value and deploring Frank's inability.

"What have you to say to that eh... eh boy?" he had gloated in front of a class one week.

Frank had looked at him. He knew what he was up to but there was little he could do without being rude, and for him to be rude was just what the man wanted. He coughed and looked around at the class of expectant boys, all staring at him waiting for his answer. "I... err... well sir, it's very old French... not at all like it's spoken today and..."

"And you don't understand it, do you?"

Frank swallowed hard. "No sir I don't, but..."

"But nothing. Sit down boy and we'll carry on with our normal lessons." Smirking in an 'I told you so' sort of fashion at the rest of the class, Hattersley had turned from Frank, who had no alternative but to just sit as told and attempt to study the book, aware all the time that the eyes of his fellow pupils were upon him. 'How strange,' he had thought. 'They all want my help and yet they are so pleased to see me humiliated.'

When the lesson was finished, Frank had expected that he would be singled out, or at least called before the headmaster to explain his failings, and he had spent the rest of the lesson rehearsing his defence. He was, perhaps, a little disappointed, therefore, when Hatters had gathered up his papers at the bell and simply swept from the room without a word. Boys crowded around Frank, some openly scornful, some a little more circumspect in the knowledge that he could still be of help.

"Cor he laid into you Balfour," one said.

"Yeah, he doesn't think much of your French, does he? 'spect he'll see the head about you and you'll have to do the lessons just like us."

Frank looked at the circle of expectant faces around him. "I don't care what he thinks, or what he does."

"But you couldn't read 'is book could you?"

Frank smiled. "Ask him if he can." The boy's smirk wavered as

Frank continued. "I take it you won't be requiring my help any more Smith?" He looked from his face to the others around him, seeing the doubt settling in.

"Err... well no... I... I mean yes... of course old chap. Of course I will," Smith had said hesitantly.

"Me too. You'll still help, won't you Frank?" said another.

"We'll see," said Frank, picking up his things and pushing through the circle towards the door. He was followed by a group of boys all eager to make amends, and if Hattersley's plan had been to undermine Frank's status with the boys, then the plan backfired. Later that night in his bed, Frank had mulled over the events and come to the conclusion that Hatters could only take the matter so far, otherwise he would risk the ire of the other teachers, who had, quite frankly, found Frank's assistance useful.

At long last the holiday arrived.

Frank had packed his suitcase in the morning, and when school was over he ran the short route to the boarding house to collect it and get back to the station. As he got there, Mr Johnson, the geography teacher, called to him to stop running in the corridors.

"Sorry sir, it's just that I've a train to catch. I'm going to Devon for the holidays."

"Devon is it? I thought you came from London, and what takes you to Devon instead of home?"

"Friends sir."

"Friends? Not family?"

Frank hesitated. "No, not family... well not exactly. I eh... I used to live there when I was a baby and my mother was away in the war."

The man's eyebrows raised inquisitively. "In the war?"

"Yes sir. After my father was killed in the war, she went as a nurse."

"Really?"

"Yes sir. She was ever so brave and..."

The teacher interrupted him. "Did you say you had a train to catch?"

"Yes sir. Sorry sir."

The man smiled. "Well cut along then, you don't want to miss it, do you?"

"No sir... yes sir... excuse me sir, may I..."

"Go on boy," the man said kindly, "...and just this once you'd better run."

"Yes sir. Thank you sir," said Frank, scarcely believing his ears. He ran off. Behind him, Mr Johnson watched him go. Almost unconsciously he reached down to his thigh and fingered the lumpy scar tissue through his trousers. He smiled thoughtfully. Maybe he had met the boy's mother. Maybe, maybe not, but they shared a bond nevertheless.

That holiday was one of the happiest times that Frank could remember in his life... at least since the death of Armand. He joined in the farm and family life, and for the all too brief period he felt as if he really belonged.

Florrie and Joe were keen to show him off to all their friends and relatives, many of whom remembered him from when he was a baby. The trouble Frank had was that they all expected him to remember them as well, and in truth there wasn't one of them that he did.

"He was a baby," Florrie would exclaim, coming to his rescue and sweeping him up into her arms. "You don't expect him to remember everybody, do you? Isn't it enough that he's here?"

Frank grew to love them all more and more. With Florrie, he shared an intimacy that made it difficult for him to imagine a time when they had not known each other. Joe? Joe was solid and dependable and Frank felt that with him, although he didn't say much, he thought of him as if he were still his son. A son that had returned after a long absence. Frank was truly humbled by the love this simple couple seemed able to give, and at times he envied Lizzie her parentage. Kate, too, had virtually taken over where she had left off all those years ago and slipped into her role of auntie as if nothing untoward had ever happened.

The only fly in the ointment was George, who for some reason had taken it into his head that Frank formed some sort of threat to him and his position within the family. Secretly, although nothing had ever been said, he had always assumed that he and Lizzie would, one day, be man and wife and that he would therefore inherit the farm, upon which he lavished so much time and effort.

He resented the fact that Lizzie, of all people, even though she was still a child, seemed attracted to the glamour of this interloper... this foundling who had suddenly turned up in all their lives. Oh, he was careful not to express his feelings or to raise the stakes but Frank, perhaps alone, felt his enmity.

That Lizzie was besotted by Frank there could be no doubt, and Frank had to get used to her wanting to be around him all the time. Not that he minded too much. She was a bright girl who didn't behave at all childishly and she didn't, above all, seem to resent his relationship with her parents, and especially her mother, in any way. It was almost as if she too just accepted that he was family and that he had returned after a long, long absence.

Frank toyed with the idea of tackling George but decided against it. He had very little in common with the young man, and he felt that if a heart-to-heart talk went wrong the older boy would resort to violence, and if that happened it would complicate any future visits. There was no way he wanted to risk that.

He confided in Florrie though. "I don't think George is very pleased that I've turned up again."

She stopped what she was doing. "You pay him no mind Frank, do you hear?"

"It's just that..."

"It's just that nothing. George's nose is out of joint a little for the attention you've bin gettin'. T'isn't any more than that."

"I know but... well I haven't done anything to annoy him and..."

Florrie wiped her hands and crossed to him. She picked up his face in her hands and held it, forcing him to look at her. "George is my nephew and I love him very much... but I know what he is and I know what he hopes for. You were my baby, and as long as I draw breath you are welcome as a member of my family. Do you hear?" Frank tried to nod in her grip and her face broke out in a wreath of smiles. "Do you hear?" she repeated laughing.

"I hear," he mumbled through squeezed cheeks. "I hear." She let go of him and they embraced, laughing.

Lizzie came in. "You two again," she cried, her eyes dancing.

"Us two again." They laughed and made room for her within their embrace.

......

All too soon the holiday came to its end. On the last full day the sun shone brightly in the Devon sky, and by mid-morning the day was warm. One could almost hear the life running through the trees, and the air was full of the sound of birdsong. Lizzie sidled up to Frank and took his hand in hers. "Come with me."

"Where?" he whispered.

She smiled up at him. "I want to show you my secret places." She tugged at his hand, pulling him towards the back door.

He looked around the empty kitchen. Oh why not, he had little else to do. Florrie had disappeared into the house with a pile of laundry and Joe was long since away, out on the farm somewhere. He squeezed her hand. "Oh come on then, let's go."

She led him out of the back door, around the side of the house and across the drive to the small bridge across the stream, leading into the sloping field beyond. "Where are we going?"

She pointed down the hill towards the river bank. "I want to show you my river."

"Your river?"

"Yes, my river... and my friends."

"Come on then," he shouted, letting go of her hand and running off down the field. "Show me your river."

She giggled and ran after him, catching him up by the sentinel rock and pushing him in the small of his back. He stumbled and tumbled over in the grass. Over and over he went as she held her hands to her mouth, hoping that he would not be hurt. He came to rest as the slope of the hill gentled out and she ran up to him, concern written all over her face. "Oh Frank I'm sorry. I didn't mean to hurt you." His eyes remained shut tight and she knelt down beside him and shook him gently. Suddenly his eyes flew open and he wrestled her across his body and the two of them rolled over giggling. "Frank, you're awful. I thought you was hurt."

He sat up laughing. "Serves you right for pushing me." He playfully punched her upper arm and she rubbed it ruefully.

"Well I didn't think you'd fall over like a dummy."

"Like a dummy, is it? Like a dummy! I'll give you dummy!" He reached for her again, but she put her finger to her lips.

"Shhh. They'll hear."

"Who'll hear?"

"The river people."

He looked puzzled. "The river people? What river people?"

"The river itself and the people who live in it."

"People?"

"Yes. The birds and the small animals. The people."

He laughed. "They're not people, they're animals."

Her face took on a hurt look. "They're not. They are the river people." She stood up. "And if you're going to be horrid then I'm not going to show you."

Frank looked up at this small girl. Her face was flushed and angry now and her hands were on her hips. Her mouth was set firm and her eyes blazed with indignation. He smiled and reached up to her hand. "Here, take me and show me your people." She took his hand and hauled him to his feet.

As they approached the river bank she motioned him to crouch and once more held her finger to her lips. Frank understood well her need for silence. How often had he tried to insist on it, in vain, from his friends in the forest. They crept forward to the old willows and, lying flat on their bellies, inched on their elbows to the river's edge.

Frank gazed down into the rushing waters. He knew this place. He had been here before. His eyes lit up and he turned to her and smiled, motioning her towards him. She put her ear to his mouth and he whispered. "I know this place."

Lizzie switched her mouth to his ear. "I thought you would. Can you hear her?"

"Who?" he mouthed silently, his eyes questioning.

She put her mouth to his ear again. "The river. Can you hear her singing to the stones?"

He pulled his face away from her, his eyes holding hers. How old was she? Ten? No, she was nearly two when he had left with Violet so that would make her coming up to... well twelve. He saw her brow furrow, the question repeated on her face, and he turned from her to look down into the river. The waters tumbled and swirled over and through the rocks, and at each one they curled in the lee and turned over in a froth. He closed his eyes, cocked his ear and listened. The water did indeed sing to the silent stones within its midst. A low murmur, interspersed with a higher tinkling sound. His eyes flew open and he nodded to her.

"You hear it?" she whispered almost inaudibly. He nodded and her face lit up with happiness as she bent towards him and kissed him.

Frank was taken aback, but as Lizzie had by now turned back to the river, seemingly oblivious of anything untoward in her actions, he shrugged it off.

She was a strange fish, this girl. She showed no resentment at his close relationship with her parents and now here she was with him, showing him things and expressing thoughts that belied her age. She pointed and he followed her direction.

From beneath a curtain of moss hanging in front of a small hollow, halfway up the opposite bank, a head peered. A bird's head, dark but with its white chin and breast just visible. A dipper. She pushed through the curtain and flew on to the large rock just in front of them, dipping as she landed. Frank and Lizzie held their breath as she turned on the rock, dipped once more and ran down and into the water on the upstream side, disappearing beneath the surface.

Lizzie's finger pointed upstream of the rock and there, in the clear distortion of the rushing waters as they swirled between two rocks, they could see the bird, half flying, half walking on the bottom as it searched for food. "River people," Lizzie whispered, smiling.

Frank nodded. "River people," he agreed.

She edged backwards away from the bank and he followed her. When they were clear she stood up and then sat on the gnarl that he had sat upon all those years ago.

"Thank you," said Frank. She turned and looked quizzically at him. "Thank you for showing me your river."

She smiled. "Do you have a river?"

He thought carefully before answering. "Yes... yes I have a river, though I share it with some very dear friends."

"Is it like this river?"

He glanced back towards the river and then faced her. "No. No it's not like this river. It's big, very big, almost as wide as from here to the house."

She gasped, looking up to the house at the top of the hill, trying to imagine a river that big. "Like the sea?"

He laughed lightly. "No, not like the sea. The sea's not like any river."

"I've never seen the sea."

"You've never seen the sea... well, imagine the water in a huge lake and imagine it goes on and on and on until it gets to the horizon. That's what the sea is like."

Lizzie tried to imagine such a scene, but there was nothing in her experience that could prepare her for such a vision. "Does your river sing?"

Frank shook his head. "No, it doesn't sing. Matter of fact it's silent most of the time."

"Silent?"

"Yes, it just... well it sort of moves silently for the most part but it... well it sort of reflects the sky."

He turned to her, the enthusiasm rising in his voice. "The light's the thing. At times it seems to just run into the sky... they seem to merge together... and it's always changing. Every year there's a new island or an old one's gone, 'cept our island. That's been there for years now."

"Your island?"

He looked at her and grinned. "Your river... so why not my island? Well mine and Gunther's... and Pierre-Luc's and Marcel's, of course. We call it Allemanceterre."

"Aly munch what?"

"Allemanceterre. We call the island that after all the names in French for England where I come from, Germany where Gunther comes from and France."

"And these boys are your friends?"

"They're my best friends, and we spend every summer together at the chateau." She fell silent, pulling gently on a shaft of grass and sucking its soft end thoughtfully. He prompted her. "What's the matter?"

"Won't we be seeing you again this year?"

"Of course you will. I'll be in France for the summer holidays but I'll come and see you all next half-term, if I'm welcome."

Lizzie smiled. "Of course you'll be welcome. Will you show me your river one day when I'm older?"

Frank stood and bowed to her, sweeping his arm forward and down in a long arc. "I'd be delighted mademoiselle." She laughed and held up her hands to him so that he could pull her to her feet.

"Come on," she said. "I'll show you another place." She ran off along the river's edge and he followed her. The track disappeared into the woods and he chased after her as she bounded from rock to rock and scrambled around tree roots. At last she stopped and he caught up with her, panting from the exertion. She pointed at a wide, deep and clear pool.

He looked and then crept forward quietly, expecting at any moment to see some secret beast within its waters. He saw nothing and was just about to turn and ask just what exactly he was looking for when, with a shriek, she brushed past him and dived naked into the water. Her slim white body cut through the dark waters and broke the surface in the middle of the pool. "Come on silly," she cried, sweeping her hair back from her forehead as she trod water. "Come on in."

He looked aghast at her. "But... but I haven't got any..."

"Then come in bare," she called.

"I can't."

"Scaredycat," she taunted. "Scaredycat."

"I'm not."

"Then come on in then."

He watched her for a few minutes. She upended and dove down in the water, resurfacing closer to the bank, where she splashed water at him. "I'll get you," he shouted, backing away.

"You'll have to catch me then, won't you?"

"I will," he said as he sat down and untied his laces. He stood and stripped off first his upper garments and then his trousers, down to his underpants. He hesitated for a moment after taking off his socks, and then with a yell tore off his underpants and rushed into the water. As he hit it the cold seemed to grab hold of him, constricting his chest.

He thrashed around, trying to regain his breath as Lizzie came up to him. "It's freezing," he gasped.

"Swim about a bit. You'll get used to it."

Frank swam fast across the pool and back again to where she now stood, knee deep in the water, her arms held in front of her, elbows pinching together, hands clasped to her chattering lips. "It's no good," he cried. "It's too cold for me."

Oblivious to her exposure, she held out her hand for him to grasp and pulled as he clambered up the slippery rock. For a moment the two of them stood facing each other, taking in the details of each other's bodies. Then Frank, shivering, rushed across to his pile of clothing. He picked up his shirt and jumper and slipped them on as one, hugging the garments to himself. He heard a light laugh and turned to face her standing there, her clothes in her hand. "Put your clothes on," he yelled through chattering teeth. "You'll get your death of cold." He turned and sat upon a log to put the rest of his clothes on as she casually draped her dress over a branch and slipped her knickers on.

He hurriedly pulled on first his underpants and then his trousers, grateful as much for the privacy they afforded as the warmth. Lizzie, unconcerned, turned around to face him. He saw the budding nipples, the swelling breasts of the pubescent girl. A strange tingle ran through his loins and yet he felt no particular shame. She smiled at him and lifted her arms as she slipped the dress over her head. "Now we know all about each other's secret places, don't we?" she giggled.

Frank tore up a clod of moss and hurled it at her, but she dodged it and, picking up her shoes, darted off through the woods, back towards the open field. He smiled to himself. The minx. He pulled on his socks and boots and followed her out into the sunlit field and on up the hill to the house.

As the two of them entered the kitchen giggling, Florrie looked up at her daughter's wet hair. She smiled. "Bin swimming?"

"Yep," said Lizzie, before seeing George sitting at the table. "Hallo George."

George said nothing. He looked across at Frank and Frank knew that he knew. "Cor it was perishing in there," he said, ignoring the dagger-like look of the older boy.

"I should think it was," said Florrie. "That water's straight off the moor. If'n you're wet I'd get some dry clothes on if I were you."

"I'm alright," said Lizzie. "Uhm fresh made biscuits." She sat down on the bench and grabbed one.

"I think I'll put some dry clothes on," said Frank. He made for the door, aware that George had not taken his eyes off him. 'What do I care?' he thought. 'I've been swimming with Lizzie. So what?'

"Frank wants to come for half-term. He can, can't he mummy?" Lizzie blurted out. Frank stopped and turned, a look of embarrassment on his face.

"Frank's welcome here whenever he wants and he knows it," said Florrie smiling.

Frank felt his face flush, as much with pride as anything. "Thank you," he said. "I'll see if I can make it." He turned and went on upstairs to change.

At school, he often cast his mind back to the farm, to Florrie, Joe and Lizzie, and at night, as his body changed and his voice got deeper, increasingly he would remember Lizzie's white slim body, her breasts and her wet hair, and the same thrill would run through his loins.

That summer term went slowly for Frank, impatient for its end and his forthcoming trip to France. The only significant interruption to the normal routine, apart from a blissful few days' half-term holiday in Devon, came when he received a letter from Slater informing him that Violet had given birth to twin boys, Ian and George.

Frank didn't know quite what to feel. Twin brothers. Wow! But look who their father was. Still, all in all, they had to have some of Violet in them... didn't they? He itched for the end of term and the chance to meet them and then get to know them during the holidays in France.

July 1929

"There's a huge foreign motor car in the drive with a chap driving it dressed in a grey uniform," a small boy shouted down the dormitory.

Amidst the general hubbub of boys clambering over beds, and each other, to get a better look at this phenomenon, Frank quietly picked up his case, walked to the door and on down the corridor. At the entrance door he was met by an excited-looking head. "Ah Balfour, your chappie appears to have arrived. Caused quite a stir."

"I'm sorry sir."

"Sorry? Sorry? Oh I didn't mean... eh have a nice holiday Balfour and we'll see you no doubt next term."

"No doubt. Thank you sir," said Frank, picking his case back up and making for the exit. He pushed through the crowd of boys surrounding the motor car. "Philippe!" he called to the figure of his friend, bent down ostentatiously polishing the headlamp. "Que fais-tu?"

"Ah Monsieur Frank," shouted Philippe joyously as he pushed through the circle of onlookers. He swept his cap off his head and bowed before an incredulous Frank, before taking his suitcase and stowing it in the huge boot. Frank stood surrounded by his now silent schoolfellows as Philippe came back around to the side of the vehicle and opened the door. He stood to attention and indicated the interior. Frank sheepishly stepped inside. "Philippe," he whispered as he passed the man. "Qu'est ce que tu fais?"

"L'apparence, M'sieur Frank. La plus belle impression pour vous."

"Ce n'est pas necessaire."

Philippe's eyebrows raised and he shut the door. He smartened his lapels and deliberately brushed off his jacket as he crossed around in front of the motor car and got in. Gently he let off the handbrake and eased out the clutch. The great vehicle slid forward and on down the winding drive as the crowd of boys parted in front of it. As they got to near the gate, Frank leant forward. "What was that all about?"

"About, Monsieur Frank? I don't know what you mean," said Philippe, a picture of innocence.

"You know what I mean you old rascal, and stop calling me monsieur." He paused. Hattersley was just entering the gates on his bicycle, and at the sudden and unexpected sight of the huge vehicle he wobbled and dismounted. He stood aside to let them through, a quizzical expression on his thin face. "Stop here Philippe, for just a minute please," said Frank urgently.

He slid open the window. "Sorry about that Mr Hattersley. I do hope we didn't frighten you. I'll have to have a word with my man to be more careful next time." He slid the window shut and tapped Philippe's shoulder through the partition. "Go!" The car sped off, leaving Hatters standing there open-mouthed, his hand raised in a gesture halfway between a wave and a summons. Frank rocked back into his seat, laughing.

Philippe observed him in the mirror and understood. "He's the teacher you don't like?"

"He's the one."

"Good."

Frank leant forward. "Philippe, I don't want to ride back here. Stop and let me in the front now, can you?"

"When we are away from this town I will stop," said Philippe, and at the next passing place in the forest he stopped to let Frank join him in the front.

"Now tell me all about what's been happening in Germigny," he said as he settled into the front seat. From then on, the journey to London seemed to fly by, with Philippe telling Frank all about the goings-on at the chateau and in the village. By the time they got to Slater's house, Frank knew all about who had married who, who had had whose baby, and exactly what scandals had occurred in the whole region.

As they drew into his mother's street, Frank grew quiet. "What is it?" asked Philippe.

"I don't like this man my mother's married to."

"I guessed," said Philippe. He leant across. "Guess what else?"

"What?"

"I don't like him either." Frank laughed, and they were both still laughing as the car drew to a halt at the gate behind Slater's somewhat smaller vehicle.

The door opened and Violet was there, smiling as she ran down the path. She swept open the gate as Frank dismounted and rushed into his arms. "Frank, oh Frank, it's so good to see you after so long." She pushed him back a little, still holding on to him, examining him. "Are you alright? My how you've grown, quite the young man about town." She hugged him again. "Oh Frank, my Frank."

A discreet cough reminded her that Philippe was there, holding Frank's case. "On reste ici madame?" he asked.

A frown crossed her face. "Mais oui, bien sûr Philippe. Pourquoi pas?" She smiled and changed the subject. "Avez-vous fait bonne route? Est-ce que la carte etait utile?"

"Bien sûr, madame. La carte de monsieur était parfait."

"Oh good." Another cough from the gateway told her that Slater was now here. She turned, a smile on her face. "Look Jim, it's Frank."

An uneasy silence fell, which Frank broke. "Good afternoon sir."

Slater, obviously ill at ease, coughed again. "Good journey?"

"Fine thank you sir."

"Found your way then, did you?" Slater shouted across his shoulder to Philippe.

"Yes, map very good. Merci," said Philippe as he carried the suitcase through the open gate and on up the path. "I put in Monsieur Frank's room, oui?"

"Oui," said Violet to his departing figure. She turned. "Come along in darling and meet the twins."

"Yes, come and see my boys," said a proud Slater. "Finest pair you'll ever see, don't you know." He stood aside and let first Violet and then Frank precede him up the pathway.

Frank felt strange. The last time he had been here he had virtually been ejected from the premises, and yet here he was being invited in as if none of that had ever occurred. He wished he could see Violet's face, speak to her privately, find out exactly what was going on. Thank goodness they were due to leave for France in a few days and thank goodness Slater was, as far as he was aware, not coming on until much later in the holidays.

They entered the house and Slater ushered them towards the stairs. "You go on up with your mother. I'll just fix myself a little drink and I'll see you when you get back down." He went past them and into the drawing room, shutting the door behind himself. Frank looked at his mother. "At this time of day?" he whispered.

"At any time of day," she whispered back. "Still, it keeps him quiet." They both giggled, holding their hands to their faces to stifle the noise. Violet jerked her head towards the staircase and the two of them rushed up to the top landing outside the nursery door, where they stopped, breathing heavily, trying to recover their composure. Violet held her finger to her lips. "Let's try not to wake them just yet." Frank nodded. Violet quietly opened the door and they both slipped in, closing it silently behind them.

They crept arm in arm across the room to the two cots set side by side and peered in. The first boy was fast asleep. "That's Ian," Violet whispered. She crossed to the other cot, in which the baby was awake quietly staring up into space. "And this little man is George."

Frank looked down at his little half-brother. He tickled George under his chin and the head swivelled around from side to side, searching vainly for the source of the touch. Violet bent closer and the mouth opened and a small gurgle issued forth.

"He's... they're both smashing Violet."

She looked up from the baby, proud and pleased. "They are, aren't they?"

"Smashing. What does Slater think?"

"Proud as a peacock."

"No more... well silly imaginings?"

She shook her head. "No. The minute he knew they were twins he knew that ran in his family. Apparently his father was a twin. The moment he saw them he... well he sort of knew." She giggled. "You can see the resemblance anyway."

Frank laughed. He held his hand to his mouth to stifle the sound for fear of waking the other baby. "Fat pink cheeks, a propensity to drinking..."

"Smelly both ends." Violet collapsed in a fit of giggles and fell into Frank's arms.

The two of them reeled across the room and sat down together on the couch in the corner, hugging.

"No mistake," Frank managed to squeeze out before he too was rendered speechless with mirth. The two of them held each other, rocking with laughter for some time before she stood wiping her eyes with her handkerchief.

"Come on," she said. "We'd better get down or he'll only wonder where we are."

"Or drink himself into the ground."

"Frank," she half admonished. "It's not quite that bad."

"But it's bad enough, isn't it?"

"It's bad enough," she agreed. "But, as I said before, it keeps him quiet and allows me to get on with my life... and the twins." Frank hugged her and they made their way downstairs and into the drawing room.

As they entered, Slater turned to greet them, a glass in his hand. "Fine lads eh Frank?" he said, his voice betraying the drink he had taken.

"Yes, lovely boys," said Frank, stepping further into the room. "Congratulations to you both."

Slater looked pleased. "Well thank you Frank."

"Jesse will be pleased to see them and so will Marie when we get to France."

Slater's expression changed. He had been about to take a swig from his glass, but now he let his arm fall. He looked across at Violet, an inquisitive expression on his face. "You haven't told him?"

Violet looked embarrassed. She wrung her hands as Frank turned to her, puzzled. "Why? What's the matter? You are coming, aren't you?"

"Frank," Violet began. "Frank... Jim feels... we both feel that the boys are... well..."

"They can't go gallivanting off to foreign climes at their age... it just ain't healthy, don't you know." Slater took a pull from his glass and turned to sit down. Frank's eyes swivelled from his mother to the man and back again.

He saw the warning in Violet's eyes, begging him not to pursue the subject in front of Slater. Stifling the sense of betrayal he felt, he forced out the words. "Yes... well that's a pity... another time maybe?"

"Yes, yes another time," said Slater as he sat heavily in the large chair.

Violet put her hand on Frank's elbow. "You must be hungry?"

Frank had been staring at Slater slumped in his chair. He tore his gaze away from him and looked at his mother, trying to read the frantic signals in her eyes. "Yes... yes I am quite hungry."

"Well dinner is at eight o'clock," said Slater from his chair. Frank's eyes broke free from his mother's and he turned again to look at his stepfather.

"Yes. Yes dinner's at eight, but I expect you'll want to get washed and changed before that," said Violet lightly.

"Yes," said Frank absent-mindedly, his gaze still fixed on Slater. He felt her touch. "Eh... yes. Yes I'd like that. I think I'll go to my room for a while."

"I'll come and see you've got everything darling." She steered him towards the door, turning briefly as they got there. "We'll see you at dinner dearest," she called back to Slater, shutting the door quickly before he could reply.

Out in the hall, Frank turned to his mother. "Why didn't you tell me?" he hissed.

"Oh I'm sorry Frank," she moaned softly. "I was going to of course but... oh he made such a huge fuss about it that I had to give way and... well to tell the truth he's probably right. They are very young for such a journey." She propelled him back to the staircase and they mounted it side by side.

"It's not the end of the earth. It's only home to Germigny."

"I know dear, but he doesn't see it like that and well..."

"Well what?" Frank was getting annoyed now. He hadn't seen Violet for months and now, at the last minute, his plans for the summer were being swept away.

Violet sensed his rising anger. "I know you're upset darling. I'm upset too, but think about me please."

"I am thinking about you. I'm thinking how much of your life that man controls."

Violet felt anger now, the heat rising to her breast. She raised her finger and wagged it in his face. "I don't think you're being very fair Frank. I know you're disappointed but the boys are very young and it's only six weeks since I... well it was and is quite a strain on me you know, and it still is."

Frank saw that he was being unfair. He hadn't considered Violet's physical state in all of this and her angry admonishment brought him up sharp. He stopped on the step. "I'm sorry Violet. It's just..."

She put her hand on his arm. "It's alright darling. I know how it must look and... well I know that he's right this time and I should have considered it earlier. Look, let's make the next few days special, and when you get back we can have a few days together before you go back to school."

She hugged him and he returned her embrace.

"Can we go and see grandfather?"

"Of course. We'll go first thing after breakfast tomorrow morning. Philippe can take us."

"Philippe!" He put his fist to his forehead. "We've brought him all the way over here to take us all and now you're not coming."

"Oh, I shouldn't worry about that darling. Philippe is just pleased to be able to take you back and, to tell you the truth, he's probably had a wonderful little holiday himself driving across England."

"All the same it's a bit ostentatious, just me in that big motor car."

Violet laughed. She dug him in the ribs playfully. "Lord of the manor," she joked. Frank looked sheepish and squirmed out of her reach, running up the stairs ahead of her to his room. As they got to the door she stopped and cocked her ear, motioning him to be quiet. Frank listened hard but could detect no sound. "The boys are awake properly," she said resignedly. "I'll have to go and see to them and probably feed them."

Frank observed his mother. She was looking tired and drawn. "You got your wish," he said softly.

"My wish darling?"

"To hold your own baby."

She smiled at him. "Yes I did, didn't I... times two."

"Times two," he repeated. He kissed her on the cheek. "I'll see you later."

Frank spent the next few days with Violet and, amongst other things, they visited his grandfather, who, surprisingly, was at home when they called rather than at the office. Violet asked him why, but he merely shrugged his shoulders and brushed off her enquiries with a garbled explanation about business not being so good at the moment and something about not being prepared to waste any more of his life on it.

Both Frank and Violet were quite surprised by his attitude and seeming indifference to what, after all, had always been the single most important aspect of his life. Violet, of course, immediately suspected that her father's involvement with Alice had something to do with it, but Frank felt that perhaps there was more to it than that.

He had no particular interest in business and finance, but in view of the ironworks he had made a point of reading the newspapers whenever possible in order to keep abreast of how things were in the world in general. From that, he knew of the depression that was sweeping the country and indeed the world, and it was a short leap of the imagination from that to the conclusion that his grandfather's business would also be suffering. He knew, as well... they all did... that Ernest had made some pretty speculative land deals and that perhaps his lack of attention since Elsie's death had let quite a few things slip.

Violet tried to raise the issue again during another visit, but each time she did so, Ernest either brushed the matter aside or they were interrupted by Alice entering the room, whereupon he immediately changed the subject. In the car on the way home, she expressed her worries to Frank and the hope that everything was alright. Frank wasn't quite so sure that everything was as it should be. But he also felt that it really wasn't his place to be discussing his grandfather's finances. Nevertheless, he couldn't help but be worried, even though there was little or nothing either of them could do... especially if grandfather refused to discuss things with them.

A few days later, Frank and Philippe left for France, via Jesse's house. Violet tearfully waved goodbye to her son from the gate and then trudged wearily back into the house and up to the nursery. She wished with all her heart that she could have gone after all, but knew that to have done so would have caused a terrible row with Slater. 'Once more I've let Frank down,' she chided herself. 'But what else could I have done?'

What have you got yourself into Violet? You were so strong. You dominated every relationship and forged your own life, and yet now here you are in thrall to a man you cannot love, the mother of his children. What went wrong? She sighed as she entered the children's nursery. All her life she had fought for what she wanted. She had refused to let Frank go and followed him to Kent; she had gone off to war, where she had seen and suffered privation and injuries that would have daunted many a person.

She bent down and adjusted the blanket, which had slipped over George's face, covering his little mouth. His head moved and his lips smacked but his eyes remained shut and he carried on sleeping. Perhaps with the shock of losing Armand she had given up. For the first time in her life she had felt secure, cocooned in his love, protected by his wealth. And then... and then he was gone and she had found herself alone again in a foreign land.

The tears started in her eyes at his memory and she had to clear them to see that Ian was alright. He lay there fast asleep, his cherubic face a picture of sweet repose. Funny how different the twins were, even at this age. Ian was sweet and quiet, and for the most part he just slept. At times she had to wake him up to feed him and change him, all of which was usually accomplished with little or no crying or protestation. George was altogether a different matter. He was always the first to wake and would lie there in his cot, giggling and waving his arms in the air, his little legs kicking away under the covers. He cried of course, all babies cry, but when George cried the whole household heard it. He would lie there, red-faced and angry, until he was picked up, and then his little head and mouth would search the air blindly for the nipple he knew would be there, his hands clasping and unclasping in his eagerness.

Violet smiled to herself. It would be necessary to try and temper that spirit before it got out of hand. That George was going to be the dominant twin there was no doubt. The thought brought her back to her own predicament. Why had she married Slater? Had she just given up? She'd thought, before their marriage, that he would be an easy man to control, and that after all she had been through, marriage to him would just allow her to coast through life. In reality, it had turned everything upside down and threatened all that she had and loved.

What to do? She cupped her hands in front of her mouth and breathed deeply. 'What can I do?' she thought. 'I've made my bed, so to speak, and now... now I'm stuck with it. But it can't go on.' A sound from Ian's cot caught her attention and she quietly crossed the room and looked in. He was only dreaming. She caressed his little cheek. So young. So vulnerable.

She drew in her breath. The fact was that Jim was right. The children were too young and she herself was not really fit enough to make the journey. Even if she had tried to insist, Slater would, almost certainly, have forbidden her to take the children. Why? Oh why didn't you think that it would be impracticable, she thought, cursing herself for leaving matters so long, ending up with Philippe having a wasted journey and Frank upset.

For his part, once he was over the initial disappointment, Frank put his mind to the summer ahead. He would have liked to have had Violet to himself for a change, but as it was not to be, he determined that he would make the best of his stay in his beloved chateau.

In so many ways he could not understand just why his mother had seemingly thrown her life away on a man she so clearly didn't love. Oh he had warned her, but she had insisted on marrying him and now... now it seemed that she was trapped, and with the arrival of the children, the trap had closed tighter.

How could she ever leave now, even supposing she really wanted to? If Slater refused to let her take the children on holiday, then for certain he would prevent her taking them away if she ever did leave him. He considered talking the problem over with Jesse when they arrived, but decided that it really wouldn't achieve anything other than to make Jesse unhappy. He explained Violet's absence with the simple yet plausible excuse that she was tired and the babies were too young for the journey. In the end, Jesse's ready acceptance of the reasoning made him think that perhaps, although he was loathe to admit it, Slater had been correct this time.

On the way through France there was a visit that he had long wished to make, although he had kept quiet about it up until then, and when Violet had not come he had not thought to mention it to her. He had confided to Philippe, by letter, that he wished to find his father's grave, and on the way through to England, Philippe had made it his business to seek out the cemetery. Just south of Compiegne they turned off the main highway in the direction of Soissons, and after several miles the motor car slowed down as they approached a hedged-in section of land standing out on the otherwise featureless landscape.

"This is it," Philippe said quietly to Frank as the car stopped by the white gates set in the hedge. "Do you want me to come in with you?"

Frank shook his head, strangely unable to speak. He opened the door and stood beside the car for a few moments, listening to the sounds of the summer's day. He looked back into the vehicle at Philippe, who smiled encouragement and waved him towards the gates. Frank nodded and turned and walked through them.

Inside the hedge the air was still and quiet, the only sound being the larks up above and the crickets buzzing in the long grass at the edge. Row upon row of simple white stones marched in perfect line across the carefully manicured turf. He turned and called through the gate. "Where is it?"

Philippe leant out of his window. "Towards the back right-hand corner."

Frank turned and walked slowly down the line of silent stones. He read the names to himself as he walked. They were all English or English-sounding names and he tried to imagine the occupants and the lives they had led. Men and boys, some of them scarcely older than he was, lay there far from home. He felt a lump rise in his throat and a constriction in his chest as he neared the far right-hand corner.

With a shock he read the name 'Balfour F.W.' and the rank 'Sergeant'. He stood still, rooted to the spot, his gaze fixed on the lettering, his mouth silently mouthing the name.

Here lay the father that he had never known, the father who had never known of him. Salty tears smarted in his eyes and he wiped them away. What had he been like, this man? Violet didn't talk much of him, but Jesse and Keith had spoken of him. 'Oh I would have liked to have known you Frank Balfour,' he thought. 'I would have liked to know you... father.'

He knelt in front of the grave and wiped his eyes with his hand. For a second he examined the wet of the tears on his fingers, then he gently wiped them off on the cool stone. He looked down the line of headstones standing silent in the summer sun and then back at the one that marked his father's passing. Silent stones. No river here to sing to the silent stones, only the larks. One rose in fluttering, vertical song and he wished it well. "Sing little person, sing," he mouthed quietly. "Sing to the silent stones."

"Goodbye father," he whispered. He stood for a moment, contemplating the grave, then he turned and walked to the gate, out through it and into the car.

Philippe reached across and squeezed his hand as he got in. "Alright?"

Frank nodded, unable to speak for a moment. He raised his hands in a gesture of helplessness and shook his head as he looked down. He waved his hand, indicating that they should move off. Philippe put the car in gear, turned around and headed back the way they had come.

It was some time before Frank had recovered his composure sufficiently to talk. "I never knew him you know," he said quietly.

"I think that you do know him," said Philippe.

"How so?"

"He lives within you."

"Do you really think so?"

Philippe nodded. "They all live within us."

Frank looked sideways at this man, his friend, his employee and his protector... as he had been for Armand. How one can underestimate people, he thought. He turned his attention to the journey ahead and the holidays to come, and before long the atmosphere of gloom had lifted and it was a jolly, if tired, pair who eventually arrived at the chateau, to be greeted warmly by Marie and Jean-Claude as if they were kings returning from conquest.

The strange part about that summer's holiday was Gunther. On the morning of his arrival, Frank, Pierre-Luc and Marcel stood impatiently at the station waiting for him.

The train pulled in and they searched the carriage doors for sight of their friend and leader. Normally he would have been at the window waving at them and calling, but this time there was no sign of him until the train had pulled up to a complete halt. They wondered for a moment whether he had missed his connection and searched each other's faces for some sort of explanation. Then Marcel saw him at the top of the steps. He pointed excitedly and they all ran over and stood beneath the steps, looking up expectantly.

Gunther was dressed in some sort of uniform. Well, it seemed like a uniform, but apart from his belt buckle there was no sign of insignia. He wore a sort of peaked cap with a black leather hatband, pulled low down on his head, touching his ears. Even in the July heat of the French summer he wore a thick brown shirt, buttoned at the cuffs, with a black tie carefully knotted and tucked behind the diagonal leather strap running across his right shoulder and clipped on to his black leather belt.

He acknowledged his friends with a nod and a strange, straight-armed salute and placed his foot to the first rung of the steps. His high black leather boots with the trousers tucked into them rang out the sound of metal on metal.

"Good God Gunther," cried Frank. "What on earth are you got up like that for?"

"It is my party uniform," Gunther replied stiffly in French.

"Party?" shouted Marcel. "Are you going to a party?"

Gunther looked at his friend almost disdainfully. "No stupid, I mean the party uniform."

"What party?" asked Frank, clearly amused.

Gunther, by now halfway down the stairs, stopped and drew himself erect before answering. "The National Socialist Party." He swung his bag out to Pierre-Luc, who caught it and stood back.

"Socialist... you mean you're a Communist?" ventured Marcel.

Gunther visibly bristled with rage. He reached the platform and put his face up close to Marcel's. Marcel backed off a little as Gunther spat out, "We fight Communists. We are National Socialists and we are against Bolshevism and the Jewish conspiracy."

"Sorry... here listen Gunther I'm Jewish," spluttered Marcel. "Does that mean you're against me?"

"Yeah, careful Gunther," said Frank, "we're all friends here you know."

"Allemanceterre," Pierre-Luc volunteered. "Remember our oath."

"Yes Gunther, remember our oath. You're not at home in Germany now, you're here with friends," said Marcel.

Gunther turned from one to the other as they spoke, his face, at first showing anger, softened as each boy's criticism struck home. There was a silence as he observed his friends, one by one, standing there looking at him in concerned anticipation. He raised his hands in submission. "I'm sorry... Allemanceterre."

"Allemanceterre!" they all chorused as they came together in a hug.

"No more politics and no more uniforms when we get back to the chateau," said Frank, and Gunther nodded his acceptance.

No more was said when all four were together that year, but Frank and Gunther did discuss things when they were alone at the chateau in the evenings. Sitting out on the patio, Gunther described his boarding school. He told of how his uncle had introduced him to the party, and how he had joined the cell at the school. Frank listened, clearly fascinated and appalled as Gunther told of meetings followed by running battles in the street with both police and Communists.

"Why do you want to fight?" he asked.

"I don't want to fight, but we can't let our country be taken over by Communists and Jews, can we?"

"Gunther, Marcel is a Jew. Are you against him? He wouldn't do you any harm... he's not interested in politics at all, let alone taking over anybody's country." Gunther looked away, unable to answer properly. Frank prompted him, unwilling to let the question remain unanswered. "Well... what about him?"

There was a silence, during which Gunther stared out across the lawns towards the spot where his mother had died. Frank followed his gaze and realised that his friend was clearly troubled. After a while, Gunther broke his silence. "Marcel is my friend and I have no fight with him..." He turned to Frank. "...any more than I can have with you."

Frank reached out and touched the arm of his friend. "We are both of us alone in this world, aren't we?"

Gunther looked puzzled. "You are not alone." He glanced again to the spot down by the lake. "You have Violet."

Frank laughed with heavy sarcasm. "I have Violet. You think I have Violet? I have seen my mother for two days since last Christmas and I spent Christmas itself with Jesse."

"How so?"

Frank threw his hands in the air in a deprecating gesture. "She is married to that man Slater and he hates me because... well because of my father."

Gunther turned to him. "Your father? What's he got against Armand?"

Frank looked at him for a moment, seeming not to comprehend what he was saying. Then the penny dropped. "No, my real father silly, my father Frank."

Gunther looked puzzled. "But what can he have against him? He died in the war, didn't he? Surely he never met him?"

Frank laughed bitterly. "No, he never met him. It's just that... well it's a bit difficult really."

"Go on, you can tell me."

Frank swallowed hard. "My father... Violet and my father were never married."

There was a long silence, during which the two of them stared out into the deepening gloom. "I never knew my father," said Gunther. "Dieter... Violet met him. My mother never spoke of him and my uncle Helmut hardly mentions him."

"I said I am a bastard," said Frank bitterly.

Gunther turned to him. "No Frank, you are Frank Balfoure, adopted son of Armand Taillefer and my friend." He raised his finger and pointed it at Frank. "Never forget that."

Frank was taken aback by the ferocity of the admonishment. For a moment he recoiled from the wagging finger, but then he smiled. "Thank you Gunther."

"It's nothing," his friend replied. "Anyway, us orphans have got to stick together, haven't we?"

"We certainly have," agreed Frank. "We certainly have."

April 1930

Violet held George tightly as the taxi swung into Etchingham Park Road. She glanced sideways at Perkins holding Ian and smiled briefly as the woman returned her look, nodding to indicate that all was well.

"They certainly didn't think about little mites like this when they invented motor cars," said Violet to herself more than anything.

"You alright in the back there ma'am?" called the driver.

"Fine thank you. Eh... it's just up here on the right... there by those gates."

"Righty ho," said the cabbie, pulling over and stopping. Perkins reached forward for the door handle and dismounted, turning to wait whilst Violet, having paid the still sitting driver, got out. The two of them stood briefly as the taxi drew off.

"Time was when the cabbie would have helped us out and carried everything to the door," Violet mused.

"Time was when lots of things was different," said Perkins, turning and making her way up the path. Violet watched her go, a small smile playing on her lips. She had never really struck up much of a relationship with Perkins, who had been at Highgate long before she arrived. Not that the woman's relationship with Slater was any closer. For Perkins, the Highgate house was the home of the late Mrs Slater, and her son and his wife were merely lodgers in the mistress' house.

But then the twins had arrived and something about them softened the old woman's heart. Although her principal duties were meant to be the kitchen, she had pitched in and helped with the boys to such an extent that at times Violet felt as if her own position in the nursery was reduced to that of a wet nurse. Recently, much to the annoyance of Slater, meals had even been late, and the only excuse had been that she had been busy with the boys.

"Busy with the boys!" Slater had railed at Violet. "What do you think you are doing taking household staff away from their duties?"

Violet had tried to explain that Perkins had taken the tasks upon herself and that she had given her little encouragement but Slater had stormed off, shouting that if she didn't have a word with her about it then he, most certainly, would.

Violet held the baby close as she bent her knees to pick up the bag and follow Perkins up the pathway. Slater would not be pleased when he discovered that Perkins had come with her, but how else was she to manage two small boys in a taxi?

The door opened and Alice stood there, a welcoming smile on her face. Violet could still never quite get used to the fact that although she answered the door as she always had done, she now did so as mistress of the house, dressed as a lady of quality.

Perkins, as usual, refused to acknowledge any change of status and pushed straight in past her and on through to the front sitting room, where she deposited the child on the sofa. plumping up the cushions around him to support him.

Violet smiled her greeting and stood for a moment as Alice bent down to examine George, tickling his chin. "Hallo little man," she cooed." She raised her eyes. "And how's mum faring?"

"Mum's alright," said Violet. "Daddy wants to see me about something urgent."

Alice's face dropped. "Yes, I'm afraid he does."

"Bad news?"

Alice looked stricken, and for a moment Violet thought she was going to burst out crying, but then she recovered herself. "He'd best tell you himself." She took hold of Violet's arm and guided her through to the sitting room. "Here, plonk the little mite down beside his brother and I'll go and sort a cup of tea out for everybody. Tea Mrs Perkins?"

The older woman thought for a moment before replying. "Yes. Yes I'd like a cup."

"Good," said Alice lightly. "You stay here and keep an eye on the boys... and Violet, your father's in the drawing room. I think he'd like to see you in there alone."

Perkins opened her mouth to protest at being ordered around by the likes of Alice but was stopped by Violet's reply. "Good. Thank you Alice, I'll go through... you'll be alright with the boys for a while, won't you Mrs Perkins?"

Perkins could only nod her agreement as Violet and Alice left the room. They crossed the hall together, separating at the drawing room door. "Tell me why he needs to see me?" begged Violet as she hesitated before entering.

Alice nodded. "Like I say, best if he tells you." She indicated Violet to open the door.

Violet knocked briefly and entered without waiting for a reply. Although it was the middle of the day, the curtains were half drawn and the room was in semi darkness. For a moment Violet had to stand and adjust her eyes to the gloom, but then she made out the figure of her father sitting at his desk, his head slumped in his hands. "Why daddy, why are you sitting in the dark?" said Violet, walking across to the curtains and preparing to pull them.

His head raised slightly. "Leave them please Violet," his voice croaked.

She stopped and let the curtains fall back into place, turning to look at him. He remained at his desk, his head held in his hands, his face invisible to her. In front of him, strewn all over the desk, lay papers and documents, the top one of which bore some sort of seal. "Are you ill daddy?" Violet asked as she crossed to stand behind him. "Is everything alright?" There was silence, so she repeated the question. "Is everything alright daddy?"

She noticed then, as her eyes continued to adjust to the light, that he was crying. Great silent sobs wracked his body and he removed one hand from his face and reached back to her.

She took his hand and knelt down beside him, looking up at him trying to discern his features. "Tell me what is wrong daddy," she pleaded.

Ernest lifted his head from his hand, took back the other from Violet, and reached into his jacket pocket for a handkerchief, upon which he loudly blew his nose. He wiped his eyes at each corner and turned in his chair to face his daughter, kneeling on the floor in front of him.

"Daddy?"

Ernest cleared his throat. "Gone," he said in a cracked voice. "All gone."

Violet stood. "Gone? Who's gone?"

He looked up at her, picking up the top document and waving it at her. "All gone, I've lost everything."

"Lost everything?" She reached out for the document and carried it across to the light. "How? What is this?"

"It's a petition for bankruptcy."

"A petition for what?"

"You heard. Bankruptcy."

Her eyes opened wide, her gaze flew from him to the document in her hand and back again. "How? Why?"

He shrugged his shoulders and turned away from her. "I mortgaged everything to pay... and I..." He buried his face in his hands again. "They'll take everything, the office, the house. We'll be on the street..." He broke down and wept openly. Violet scanned the document briefly, half taking in its contents, unable to fully comprehend its import. She put the papers on the small table at the end of the sofa and crossed to stand behind her father, placing her hands on his shoulders.

"It can't be that bad daddy," she said, leaning down and kissing the side of his neck. He turned in his chair and buried his face in her lap.

"It is I'm afraid darling. It is. I'm ruined." He gripped her tightly, his face buried in her dress.

Violet stood there staring out into the room, her hands idling with the hair on top of her father's head. She glanced around the room at the furniture and effects that her parents had accumulated over all the years of their marriage. Very little had changed since Elsie had been there. The same pictures adorned the walls, the same ornaments were displayed in and on the furniture. Was all of this to be lost?

"What can we do daddy?" He shook his head in the folds of her dress, mumbling something which she could not interpret. "Sorry?" she said.

He raised his head. "Nothing. There's nothing we can do."

"Nothing?"

"Nothing. I have to appear in court next Tuesday, and if I cannot satisfy the court and my creditors, the mortgages will be forfeit and I will be declared bankrupt."

Violet reached down and took hold of his chin, forcing his tear-stained face to look up at her. "Then we have 'till then to find the money."

Ernest smiled wanly. "I don't think it's possible this time, Violet darling."

"Of course it's possible daddy. I've got some money from my income, you can have that." She stopped. "How much do you need?" Ernest didn't answer. Instead he got to his feet and walked across to the small table and picked up the document. He leafed through it and handed it silently to her, pointing at a figure halfway down the page.

Violet took the papers from him and squinted down at where he had pointed. There was a sharp intake of breath. "How much? Oh no, surely daddy... how did this happen? I... I haven't got anything like... I can't raise this much."

"I know. I told you it was hopeless." He sat on the sofa, burying his face in his hands once more. Violet stood, the papers held down by her side, her mind racing. Frank! Frank would have the money. No, it was in trust and there was no way the notaire would allow him to... Jim! Jim Slater would have the money. She would ask him to help, and he couldn't refuse his children's grandfather... could he? He could, but she would still ask.

"I'll ask Jim if he can help."

"He won't."

"What do you mean he won't?"

Ernest raised his head from his hands. "I mean, he's hardly having a good time of things himself. Think of it Violet, he's a wine merchant in the middle of a depression when nobody's got any money."

Violet looked puzzled. "He's never mentioned anything."

Ernest laughed, a shallow despairing laugh. "I doubt he would. With Jim Slater everything has to appear proper and correct, but I bet your allowance is all that's keeping him afloat, and if anything ever happened to that... which is of course possible, then... well..."

Violet stood stock still, the shock registering on her face. "What do you mean if anything happened to that?"

"I mean, darling, that the whole civilised world is suffering and it's quite possible that the ironworks is suffering with it."

Violet's brow furrowed. "How would I know?"

"You won't. Your income is fixed. It's Frank who'll have to find out how things are when he visits the trustees." He noticed Violet's worried expression. "Look, everything's probably quite alright. You'd have heard if there was serious trouble. I was wrong to worry you, but I meant what I said about Jim."

Violet looked across at her father for a moment, then went and joined him on the sofa. She put her hand on his elbow. "I can still talk to Jim, he may have some ideas."

Ernest studied his daughter's face. "I know you want to help darling, but please don't think I don't know."

"Don't... know what?" said Violet hesitantly.

Ernest took her hand. "I know that things have not been very good between you and Slater, in spite of the twins."

"Nonsense," said Violet, a little too lightly to be convincing.

"Violet, you don't have to pretend to me. This is daddy, remember," said Ernest as if talking to his little girl again.

Violet looked into his eyes. She saw the suffering and the humiliation he was going through, but she saw also the concern he felt for her. She dropped her gaze then raised it again, looking him straight in the eye. "He... he feels I betrayed him... that I tricked him into marriage by not telling him that Frank... that... well you know."

"That Frank is illegitimate?" She nodded. Ernest rose from the sofa and crossed to the fireplace. He turned, his hands on his hips. "But you didn't ever seek to deceive him, did you?"

"No! No, not at all. He never asked and it never occurred to me. I felt... it was as if Frank was Armand's son. That's not to decry Frank, his father, but... well it never crossed my mind, and then on the night of the wedding he asked who Jesse was and... oh daddy it was awful, and it hasn't ever really got better."

"And you expect me to throw myself on this man's mercy?"

Violet stood and joined him by the fireplace. "What choice do we have?"

Ernest regarded his daughter, her anxious face turned up to his. The hollow, empty feeling that had overwhelmed him of late came flooding back. She was right. Who else was there? Even if Slater could not prevent what was almost certain they would need somewhere to live, and for the moment Violet's home was the only place he could think of. He nodded silently and held her tight as she slipped into his embrace. There was a timid knock on the door. Before either of them could answer, it opened and Alice poked her head round. "Excuse me," she said hesitantly. "I... eh the ..."

Ernest waved her in. "It's alright Alice dear, I've told Violet about our situation." Violet raised her head from her father's shoulder.

"Oh... well it's just that the twins..." The sound of George crying wafted into the room and Violet released her father. "It's alright Alice, I'll come. You stay and talk to... to daddy. He'll tell you what we're going to do."

Alice looked grateful, but in these circumstances felt the ambiguity of her situation. She had to physically stop herself from acting as if she were still the maid, yet felt unable to assume the full role of mistress of the house when with relatives. She mumbled something to Violet and side-stepped her as she swept through the door and on to attend to the children.

Violet didn't stay long, and when the twins had been fed and quietened down she and Perkins took their leave. The ride back in the taxi was a silent one, with Perkins longing to know just what was up, sensing that some sort of disaster had befallen Violet's family. Well whatever it is, it serves that jumped-up madam right, she thought. Who does she think she is pretending she's the mistress of a house when all she is is a maid who's taken to whoring.

Violet rehearsed what she was going to say to Slater, running it over and over in her head. Each time she felt that she had it word perfect, another thought came into her head, and in trying to incorporate it she lost the thread of her argument. She gazed out of the window and held tight to the infant in her arms. What on earth would Jim say? How would he react to a situation which, if her father was correct, could engulf all or any of them at any time?

They arrived home, and when she had paid the driver they walked up the front path to the door. Violet put down the bag and held Ian to one side as she fished in her handbag for the key. She retrieved it and stepped forward to place it in the lock. As she turned it the door was opened suddenly, wrenching the key from her grasp. A furious-looking Slater stood on the doorstep, barring their way.

"And where do you think you've been madam?" he demanded.

"Please Jim dear, you know I went to visit my father," said Violet, as sweetly as she could muster.

"Your father! Your father! You take my staff to your father's house?" He raised his arms dramatically. "And I suppose that my staff have had to cook his meal so that he can bed his."

There was a sharp intake of breath from Perkins and Violet shot a glance backwards at her, warning her to keep silent. The woman dismissed her look and stepped forward. "Beggin' yer pardon sir. I have not been cooking for anyone else. I have been looking after your children whilst the mistress spoke with her father."

"You are not retained by me to look after children. You are retained to cook my meals. Do you hear? My meals!"

"But the mistress..."

Slater's face now became bright red, and a small trickle of spittle appeared at the corner of his mouth. "...but the mistress nothing. Either you will confine yourself to the normal household duties or you will pack your bags and go. Do you understand?"

"Perfectly sir," said Perkins. She handed George unceremoniously to Violet, who struggled to hold the two babies, one to each arm. Then she pushed past them both and through to her rooms.

Violet looked up at her husband. "Really Jim, there was no need for that. She was helping me with the twins when I needed help."

Slater snorted. "Help to go off visiting your precious father and his strumpet."

Violet felt the anger rising. "Help with our children whilst I made a perfectly proper visit to my father and, if you hadn't been so hasty, help with getting them back up to their nursery on my return." She looked down at the two infants in her arms, one asleep, one looking around trying to decipher where all the noise was coming from. "Really Jim, are you simply going to stand there? I cannot carry them both."

He sneered and put his face close to hers so that she could smell the drink upon his breath. "Well you should have thought of that before you took them out. Shouldn't you?" He turned on his heel and made his way to the drawing room, slamming the door behind as he entered.

Violet stood there for a moment. She hefted the babies in her crooked arms, feeling their weight beginning to tell on her muscles. She mounted the last step and kicked backwards to shut the front door, leaving the bag outside. Her handbag dangled loosely from her arm and banged against her leg as she slowly mounted the stairs, leaning heavily on the balustrade, sliding her combined weight upwards, step by step.

It took her some time to reach the nursery floor, and by the time she got there both boys were awake and crying and she was exhausted. She pushed open the door and placed each child in its cot. As each one realised that he was being released, rather than fed, his cries got louder.

Violet sat down on the sofa and put her head in her hands, holding the palms tight against her ears to block out the sound.

Eventually she got to her feet, removed her coat and got down to the business of feeding and changing them. It was therefore about an hour later that she tentatively crept downstairs.

She went first to the kitchen, hoping to apologise to Perkins. The room was in darkness, which surprised her. She had expected to find Perkins and the kitchen maid hard at work preparing the belated meal Slater was so incensed about. Perhaps, she thought, they had all eaten and had not waited for her to come down. She shut the door and walked along the corridor to the drawing room. The door was closed and she put her ear to it, trying to discern any movement or occupation. There was the faint sound of a glass against glass.

Violet took a deep breath and pushed the door open. Slater turned from the sideboard, a recently filled glass in his hand. She observed his face, bloated and red from the drink, his eyes sunk deep. He raised the glass unsteadily to his lips and slurped from it. The arm dropped and a little of the liquid spilt before he recovered himself. Violet felt her eyes follow its progress to the floor. Consciously, she raised her gaze to his face once more, noting the dribble from the corner of his mouth.

His eyes blazed furious from their hollow sockets, and as he took a step towards her, she instinctively retreated backwards to the door. He found himself in free space. His eyes swivelled down to the floor and back up, sweeping the walls, seeking to fix his position. He stepped back and leant heavily on the sideboard.

"Have you had dinner?" Violet ventured.

"Dinner?" he slurred. "Dinner? And who's to cook it? You?"

Violet pulled the front of her dress down, aware that in her rush to get back downstairs she had not tidied herself up. "Me?" she enquired.

"Yes you madam, being as how the staff have all left due to your stupidity."

She bridled. "My stupidity? It was not me that insulted Perkins on the doorstep. It was not me who gave the woman an ultimatum."

He went to step forward again, but then thought the better of it and this time she did not retreat, safe in the knowledge that he probably could not reach her, even if he wanted to. He raised the arm with the glass in it and pointed at her before releasing the glass, which shattered on the floor in front of him. "You! You led my staff against me. You have brought my name and household into ridi... ridi..." He struggled with the word and then gave up. "Strumpet," he hissed.

Violet stood for a moment, rooted to the spot. There was no point in continuing this conversation. The man was dead drunk and no purpose would be served. Equally there was little point in giving him the satisfaction, for that is what it would be, of knowing of her father's circumstances when he was in this particular frame of mind.

"I think I'll go to my room early," she said. She turned on her heel and left the room, firmly shutting the door behind her.

It was later that night that she was awakened by a strange noise in the hallway. She raised her head from the pillow and contemplated the door. Was it Slater? It didn't sound like him. It sounded more like a sawing sound... the rasping of a coarse file. She reached for her dressing gown at the foot of the bed and slipped it over her shoulders before crossing to the door.

What time was it, she thought? She switched on the electric light and glanced at the clock. Three o'clock in the morning. What on earth was going on? She put her ear to the door, listening carefully for any clue. Faintly she could distinguish words amongst the other strange sounds, words which she could not interpret.

She opened the door a crack. The landing light was on and she could see Slater, bent practically double, holding on to the railings with both hands. He appeared not to have noticed her and she stayed silent, staring, fascinated and appalled by what she saw. She could just make out what he was saying now, the words sliding out of his lips amidst the froth of spittle and vomit that ran down his chin. "Help mother, mother." He swallowed and drew back, inhaling deeply. "Mother!"

She recoiled, holding tight to the door, unwilling to be seen by him as she tried to come to terms with the scene before her. He was dressed only in his shirt and trousers, bare-footed and with his braces hanging loosely at his side. His shirt, open halfway down his chest, was stained from his vomit and his collar hung loose behind, flapping by the rear stud.

Violet gathered herself together and forced herself to open the door fully, revealing herself. "Jim?"

He turned towards her, his eyes wide, his mouth hanging slack and open. She noticed then that his fly buttons were also open and the trousers gaped wide, revealing yellow-stained underpants. He let go of the railing with one hand and stretched out to her. The effort unbalanced him and he quickly replaced his grip, bending his head, fighting for the next breath.

Violet advanced a few steps towards him. "Jim what's wrong? Are you ill?"

He turned his face up towards her. "Can't breathe," he rasped. "Can't breathe." He clutched at his chest with his closed fist, beating at it.

Violet knew then that he was having a heart attack. She had seen similar symptoms in the tents during the war, but then there was always help at hand whereas here... here there was none. She moved to stand beside him and placed her arm around his shoulder. "Jim, you must remain calm," she said into his ear. "Try to remain calm and come and sit down in your room whilst I get the doctor." She tried to prise him from the railings but he gripped all the more tightly.

"Mother," he gasped. "Get mother."

"Mother's not here, Jim. You know that," she chided, still trying to coax him back into his room, her arms around his heaving shoulders. Suddenly he let go of the banisters and turned in to her, gripping her tight. She struggled to contain the revulsion she felt as she was imprisoned in his embrace. His face turned up to hers and she lifted her chin as high as she could, seeking to avoid his smelly, vomit-ridden breath. "Mother," he cried, tears welling in his eyes and tumbling down his cheeks. A sudden seizure wracked his body and he relaxed his grip on her, allowing her to slip free.

For an instant he remained more or less upright, but then he slowly crumpled in front of her like a puppet that had just had all its strings cut. He sagged to his knees, looking beseechingly up into her horrified face. Violet cast around in desperation. Where could she put him? She moved behind him and put her arms through under his armpits, trying to support his upper torso. Bent double, her face just behind his head, she tugged but his weight was too much for her and she had to stop.

Another spasm gripped him. His head dropped forward and she felt his chest expand as he drew in a mighty breath. Then his head jerked back, cracking into her chin, driving her front teeth through into her lip. She let go of his body and recoiled back, feeling and tasting the fresh blood in her mouth. Aghast, sick with the pain, she leant against the balustrading, trying to stifle the retching nausea.

For a moment Slater stayed on his knees, and then his body fell forward. His face smacked on to the floor, and for a few seconds he remained in this incongruous position, his bottom in the air, before he rolled over sideways. Violet felt him go, heard him go, and forced herself to look up and across at him. His eyes bulged wide, and then suddenly they closed and he seemed to just relax. He breathed out slowly, and as the breath continued to escape from his body a rattle came from his throat.

She watched, horrified, as his eyes flew open once more. They flickered from side to side and then the life just seemed to die within them and he was still, apart from a bubbling yellow froth, which appeared at each corner of his mouth and silently grew.

Violet wept openly, holding her heaving stomach with one hand whilst trying with the other to stem the flow of blood from her lip. She wasn't crying for Slater, she knew that. She was crying for this final act of humiliation that she had undergone at his hands, and mixed with that was an awful feeling of... well relief. She was free of the man at last, and no matter how sacrilegious it was in the presence of his still warm corpse, she could not contain that feeling.

A sound from the nursery brought her back from her thoughts. She hauled herself to her feet, adjusted her dressing gown, frowning slightly as she encountered the stains he had put upon it, and walked wearily up the next flight to the nursery.

The morning found her still there, sitting on the sofa with Ian in her arms as she stared out of the window. George lay in his cot on the other side of the room, his arms and legs free as he waved them all above himself, giggling at the sight.

Violet started as she heard the doorbell ring. She placed the sleeping infant in his cot, paused briefly to cover George up and left the room.

As she got to the first landing, she came across Slater's by now rigid body, lying blocking her passage. Gingerly, she stepped over his outstretched arms and then over his folded legs, trying all the while not to look into his face, with its still open eyes.

A feeling of revulsion swept over her and she had to rest just beyond his body to recover her equilibrium. The doorbell rang again and she hurried on down the stairs and opened the front door. Ernest stood there. For a moment the two regarded each other, her face a blank, his one of concern, then slowly, almost imperceptibly at first, her face crumpled and she fell into his arms crying.

......

When Frank received the summons to the headmaster's office, he guessed at once that some disaster or other had occurred at home. As he entered the room, the headmaster adopted exactly the same expression he had on when he had informed Frank of the death of his grandmother, and for a long moment Frank feared what was to come. Was it grandfather? Surely not? Oh not Violet?!

He stood expectantly as the headmaster cleared his throat. "Eh... once again Balfour, I'm afraid I have some distressing news for you." He stopped and regarded the boy in front of him, letting his words sink in.

"Yes sir, what's happened now sir? Is it my mother?" said Frank, afraid of the answer.

"No Balfour, it's not your mother. I'm afraid that your stepfather has had... he has passed away suddenly..." He continued talking, but Frank never heard another word of what he said. He was so relieved, so inordinately pleased that Slater had gone from his life and that nobody that he loved or cared for had died, that the rest of the speech of condolence went straight past him. He recovered his senses as he perceived the headmaster looking closely at him, repeating his name. "Balfour? Balfour, do you hear me? I'm so sorry to have to bring you this obviously distressing news."

Frank looked at the man. He wanted to dance and sing, yet this man thought that he was distressed! He smiled, unable to control his emotions, and then forced the smile into a semblance of a grimace, which the headmaster happily took for an expression of distress.

"I... thank you sir... May I please arrange to take the train back home to be with my mother?"

"Certainly," said the head. "Your grandfather has specifically requested that we make all possible arrangements for your return home, and I suggest that you take the early morning train and we will telegraph your parents... your grandfather to appraise him of your arrival times."

Frank thanked the man and left the office. He had to fight hard to control himself for the rest of the day, and on through to the evening he had to work hard to keep up the appearance of a bereaved person. He felt that not only would he be misunderstood if he showed his true feelings but that perhaps in some way they would question the necessity for him to go home. And to go home was exactly what he wanted to do. If possible, now that Slater was gone, he never wanted to come back to this school. As he packed his things for what was supposed to be a few days away, he made sure that what he left behind were possessions that he would not miss if they took a long time to be forwarded.

Ernest met him at Waterloo. His face was sad and drawn, and for a while Frank felt that in some ways the death of Slater had adversely affected him. "You look very unhappy grandfather," he ventured in the taxi.

Ernest seemed to recover from some sort of daydream. "Eh what... oh I'm sorry Frank. What did you say?"

"I was asking if everything was alright," said Frank.

Ernest looked at him for a moment. "Yes... yes." He saw the boy looking at him. "No, not really," he admitted.

"Surely it's not Slater?" asked Frank.

"Slater? No, not him... well his going was my last hope... if hope there was."

He lapsed into a moody silence, which Frank allowed for some time before asking again. "Can you tell me what's wrong grandfather? Is anything the matter with Violet or the twins?"

"Violet? No, not Violet. It's me. Look, you might as well know... after all the whole world will know tomorrow... I've got into financial difficulties and..."

"Well surely we can help. I'm rich... well in France I'm rich, and Violet has her income and now she'll have Slater's money and house."

Ernest smiled. "Yes, but not by tomorrow she won't. Assuming, that is, the man even left anything to her."

"Why, what's so important about tomorrow?"

There was a heavy sigh. "I have to appear in court tomorrow. If I do not have the money... and it's an awful lot of money... I will be declared bankrupt."

Frank leant forward in his seat, looking into his grandfather's face. "Bankrupt? What does that mean?"

"It means, Frank, that I will lose all my possessions, my house, furniture... everything I possess, and that I will be penniless and destitute until or unless I can ever repay my creditors."

"Will you go to prison?"

Ernest smiled. "Prison? No... no they stopped sending one to prison in seventeen hundred and something... although sometimes that seems preferable."

"And how exactly was Slater involved in this?"

"Slater? Oh no, he wasn't involved, it's just that he was my last hope. Violet was going to ask him for financial help, but he died before she could broach the subject."

Frank sat back in his seat. "Did he know of your problem?"

"No. No I don't think he did." Frank laughed, and the sound of his laugh surprised Ernest. "Why are you laughing?"

"Because Slater would have been so pleased that you were at his mercy, and now I know that he never had that pleasure." He laughed again, and this time Ernest joined him. The taxi driver, hearing the sound of their laughter, glanced back. Funny, when the boy and the old man had got into the cab they had appeared sombre, yet now they were rolling around with mirth.

At Highgate they were met at the door by Violet. "Oh Frank," she gushed, "I'm so glad you could come."

Frank smiled up at her from the bottom step. "Come? Do you think I'd miss burying that man?" He grinned at her and Ernest dug him in the ribs in playful admonishment.

Violet's face dropped and she glanced inside and upstairs. "Shhh," she said. "We mustn't speak ill of the dead."

"Is he in there?" said Frank, appalled and fascinated in equal measure.

"He's upstairs in his bedroom," said Violet.

"Well he can't hurt any of us anymore can he?" said Frank decisively.

Violet turned from staring up the stairs. She looked at the face of her son, eager and fresh, and she smiled back at him. "No he can't, can he?"

"No he can't. He's ruined my life for some years now and now he's dead I, for one, am glad."

Violet couldn't help glancing back up the stairs, but it was Ernest who spoke next. "Come on now Frank, in you go. I don't know about you but I'm famished."

It broke the tension and it certainly dispelled some of the dread that Violet felt. Even though she knew that he was dead, she could not help but feel that his physical presence upstairs was some sort of threat. That feeling lingered right through to the funeral, but first, in spite of all that had occurred, they had to deal with Ernest's court appearance.

Violet felt unable to attend, but Frank insisted on accompanying his grandfather to the court. He watched and listened as the debts were read out and the creditors produced their accounts and mortgage documents. He witnessed his grandfather's humiliation as he had to admit that he had no immediate way of satisfying his creditors.

The judge picked up the papers and pronounced that henceforth Ernest James Matthews was bankrupt. He prepared to sign the documents passing all his property and rights to the official receiver acting on behalf of the creditors, but as his pen poised over the papers, Frank jumped to his feet.

"Please sir, can I help?"

The judge looked at Frank and then at the clerk to the court. "What business does this boy have in this court?"

The clerk shrugged his shoulders and struggled to formulate a reply. Ernest broke in. "I beg your pardon your honour, this is my grandson. He has accompanied me to the court as... well as support."

"Well will you kindly instruct your grandson to respect this court and to keep quiet, or I shall have him forcibly removed. Is that understood?"

Ernest nodded and then his heart sank as Frank stood once more. "I am not trying to be disrespectful sir. I have money and property and... and my mother will have more property at the end of the week."

The judge looked across at Ernest. "Is this true?"

Ernest wrung his hands in front of him. He looked across at Frank. "Frank, I know what you're trying to do but..." He turned back to the judge. "The boy is indeed wealthy, your honour. He has a great deal of property in France, but it is held in trust for his majority and can be of little assistance to me, whatever the boy's motives."

The judge held up his pen and prepared to sign but, once more, Frank stood. "Your honour, my mother's husband died on Saturday. She may be able to help."

The judge looked exasperated. He looked across at Ernest, raising his eyebrows in a silent question. Ernest desperately motioned Frank to be seated. "It is sadly true your honour. My daughter's husband passed away on Saturday."

"And do you know for certain that your daughter will inherit from her husband, and that if that is the case she will wish to pledge her inheritance to your cause?"

Ernest shook his head and then hung it. "No your honour, I have no such certainty."

"Perhaps then we can proceed," said the judge sternly. He turned to Frank. "Young man, I appreciate your outbursts were well intentioned, but I must warn you to keep quiet and not to interrupt the proceedings of this court. Am I understood?"

"Yes sir, but..."

"Am I understood?!" the judge thundered.

"Yes sir," said Frank, sitting dejectedly. He listened as the order was made and Ernest was bound over to await the bailiffs to accompany him to his home and relieve him of all his possessions. He watched as his grandfather, a broken man, was led from the court to await the dismemberment of his life's work and achievements.

Frank asked to see his grandfather but was told that perhaps it would be better if he went home as Ernest would be detained for most of the rest of that day. He offered to wait, to accompany his grandfather, but was firmly and politely put off and told to go home.

It was well into the evening when there was a knock at the door and Violet and Frank answered it together. Ernest and Alice stood on the doorstep with two suitcases between them. "Are you alright? We were so worried," said Violet, ushering them in.

"Alms for the poor," joked Ernest.

"Come on in silly," said Violet. "Welcome home."

Despite the trauma of that day's and the preceding day's events, they all spent a jolly evening, which the brooding presence of the body upstairs did little to dispel. For her part, Violet felt as if she were free once more, and Frank felt that he, at last, now had a chance to regain his family life and his relationship with his mother in particular.

Ernest, despite his great loss, admitted that now it was all over... now that the worst had happened... it felt as if a great load had been lifted from his shoulders. He was barred from his home and his possessions, from his office and from all his properties, pending their sale and the realisation of his assets. And yet he still felt a sense of freedom that he had not known for some considerable time. He had to admit to himself, in all honesty, that having the cushion of Violet's home was a considerable benefit, without which he would have been in great difficulties, and he thanked her profusely for taking them in. Violet blushed for the first time in years but admitted in return that she was honestly glad of the company and glad to feel part of a proper family again.

For Alice's part, she felt that she had started with nothing and that was how she had finished, only this time, in some strange way, she felt more secure than she had felt before. She had of course always been aware of her delicate position, but now with Ernest reduced in social and financial status she felt that all the barriers to their relationship were removed. "The only way from here is up," she had joked to him on the way over to Violet's, and he had squeezed her arm in reply and kissed her on the cheek.   On the Thursday there was the funeral. For the three of them, Violet, Frank and Ernest, attempting to look suitably sombre, the service and the eventual incarceration was a particular trial, especially as, almost to confound their expectations, it was attended by so many people.

"Where have they all come from?" Frank whispered to Violet as they stood in line at the cemetery gate, shaking hands.

"I don't know," she whispered back, before turning to accept yet another condolence.

"The masons," Ernest said quietly. "I don't think he had any other surviving family."

"Then why are they not greeting you grandfather?" said Frank. "You're a mason, are you not?"

"I am but..."

"But they don't want to know you now. Is that it?"

Ernest nodded his head. "They say that all masons are brothers who must stick together through thick and thin..." He broke off as a middle-aged couple stopped in front of them and the man offered his hand to Violet. The man doffed his hat and moved off, his wife in tow, and Ernest continued. "We even have a toast to poor and distressed masons everywhere." He laughed thinly. "Everywhere as long as it's everywhere else and not nearby."

A tall man in a high black hat approached. He took off his hat and extended his hand to Violet. "Mrs Slater?"

"Yes, so glad you could come," said Violet automatically.

The man coughed. "Dreadful business. Dreadful... eh my name is Maxwell... err Charles Maxwell of Maxwell, Stuart and Maxwell."

Violet acknowledged him. "Pleased to met you Mr Maxwell. Did you know my husband well?"

What passed as a smile played on the man's thin lips for a moment, but was replaced with a suitably grim expression befitting the occasion. "I am... I do beg your pardon Mrs Slater, I was your husband's solicitor."

Violet smiled. "Ah good, then you'll be wanting to see me about my husband's estate and what is to be done about it?"

Maxwell coughed politely and replaced his hat on his head. "I will want to appraise you of the contents of Mr Slater's last will and testament. Yes madam, I will indeed."

"Would you like to come back to the house or... well what would you suggest Mr Maxwell?"

"I would suggest a meeting in my offices at this address." He handed her a small slip of paper. "At... shall we say eleven o'clock tomorrow morning?"

Violet hesitated. "Eleven o'clock?" She turned to her father. "Do you think Alice would mind looking after the children again tomorrow if I attend Mr Maxwell at his office?"

Ernest laughed lightly. "I would think that she'd be delighted."

Violet turned back to the solicitor. "That will be fine Mr Maxwell." He bowed ever so slightly, and placing his hands behind his back walked away.

Violet called after him. "Is there anything I need to bring Mr Maxwell?"

"Nothing Mrs Slater," he said, pausing in his progress and turning back to her briefly. "Everything I need is in my office. Until tomorrow then?"

"Until tomorrow," Violet repeated as she watched his receding figure. She turned to her father. "What a strange man."

"Strange or not," he said. "We will find out what Mr Slater's intentions are for you tomorrow."

Violet shrugged. "I'd hazard a guess from that man's demeanour that it's not good news." Ernest raised his eyebrows in silent agreement.

There was no wake. They had not thought to invite anybody in particular back to the house, and in truth once the funeral was over they were glad to get back home and remove not only their mourning clothes but the pretence of their loss. That evening Violet, in the knowledge that Slater was physically out of her life forever, felt as if she could fly.

The following day the three of them attended Mr Maxwell's offices, arriving just before eleven o'clock. They were ushered into a small waiting room and kept waiting in there until nearly a quarter past the hour, by which time Ernest was becoming more than a little agitated. "What on earth does the man think he's doing, keeping us waiting like this," he exclaimed.

Violet sought to calm him down, but as the door opened and a clerk stepped in, he rose to his feet. "We have an appointment with Mr Charles Maxwell," he exclaimed. "Is he ready to receive us yet?"

"He is free now sir," said the clerk, "but he gave me the impression that it was to be a Mrs Slater I was to fetch."

"I am Mrs Slater," said Violet, standing. "This is my son and my father. I wish them to accompany me."

The clerk looked uncomfortable. "Well... well I suppose you'd all better come along," he said. He turned and led the way out of the room and along the corridor to a large wooden door, outside which he stopped. He knocked, and on hearing a voice from within he opened the door. "Mrs Slater," he announced.

Maxwell stood as Violet entered, but his smile froze as he perceived the other two. "I do hope you don't mind Mr Maxwell," Violet said breezily as she took one of the seats in front of his desk, "but my father and my son have agreed to accompany me on this sad mission." She did not wait for the man's reply, but indicated the chair beside hers for Ernest and waved Frank over to one by the wall.

Maxwell watched them all sit and then sat down himself. "No... no not at all," he said as he shuffled his papers. "Err shall we proceed?"

"By all means Mr Maxwell," said Violet. "Unless you are expecting others."

"Others? Oh... err others. No... I was expecting you alone madam." He looked down at the document in his hand. "The last will and testament of Mr James Slater," he intoned. He looked across at Violet. "Do you wish me to read the whole document?"

"I think that perhaps you could just read out the pertinent bits," said Ernest.

Maxwell's eyes switched from gazing at Violet and fixed on Ernest. There was a long silence, which he eventually broke. "Quite." He turned back to Violet. "Are you in agreement with that Mrs Slater?" Violet nodded. "I need to hear your agreement Mrs Slater."

"I agree to you reading out the relevant details," said Violet.

Maxwell nodded. "Thank you. The details are quite simple, and you may take away this certified copy." He handed a separate document to Violet. "Mr Slater has left all his worldly goods in trust for the benefit of his two sons, Ian and George, upon their majority."

There was silence for some moments before Violet spoke. "Is there no mention of me?"

"Hmm. Yes... yes I'm sorry, there is mention of you. You may live in the house during the upbringing of the children, until such time as you remarry or the children reach their majority, whichever is the sooner."

Violet looked across at her father. He looked perplexed and she addressed Maxwell again. "Is there no mention of income... I mean what is to happen to the income from the business. What are the children supposed to live on?"

Maxwell coughed. "The business has not been doing too well of late and... well Mr Slater felt, quite rightly I suppose, that in the event of his demise, the... err there would be nobody to run it... properly." He looked around the room, avoiding direct eye contact with the others and, in particular, taking care not to get caught by Ernest's intense look of annoyance. "I am instructed to sell it and all other properties, except the house, and to put the proceeds of any sale into a trust fund for the benefit and schooling of the children."

"I repeat," said Violet a little more firmly, "what is to pay the household bills and provide for the upkeep of me and my children in the intervening period?"

For the first time Maxwell looked uncomfortable. He picked up the main document and opened it, partially shielding his face behind it for a moment. He put it down on the desk and smoothed out the page. "I am instructed to agree the appropriate household bills and expenditure with you each month, and to advance you the relevant amount."

Violet went to stand but Ernest restrained her. She stared across the desk at Maxwell. "Do you mean to tell me that I am to come cap in hand to you each month for basic living expenses?"

Maxwell's voice grew cold. "I think you misunderstand me Mrs Slater. I am authorised to defray those living expenses directly related to the upbringing of the children. I am not empowered to advance any monies for your own living expenses or for any other members of your family... in particular Mr Slater mentions your... your son... one..." He studied the document again. "...one Frank Balfour." From the other side of the room, Frank began to laugh. He stood and crossed over to stand beside his mother, his hand on her shoulder. "Really Mrs Slater, I hardly think this is a time for mirth," Maxwell spluttered.

Violet stood and leant across the desk. "Not a time for mirth?"

she said. "Well Mr Maxwell, the funny thing is that despite what you may think, both Master Balfour and myself are of independent means and the funny thing is we never really needed or wanted a penny of your precious Mr Slater's money and he knew it."

"I am aware that you are in possession of your own income, Mrs Slater. Perhaps that is why your late husband felt that it would be better to distribute his estate in the way that he has," said Maxwell, clearly aware that the whole pantomime of the distressed widow had been an act.

Violet smiled as sweetly as she could. "I shall look forward to our monthly chats. When may we expect your first visit?"

Clearly taken aback by this turn of events, Maxwell fumbled around on his desk looking for his diary. Frank saw it first under a pile of paperwork and handed it to him. "Is this what you're looking for?"

"Yes... thank you," said the man. He looked through the book, making mental notes of the appointments set out within it. "Err... let us see... will... no that won't do... will next Wednesday at eleven o'clock be suitable?"

"It will indeed," said Violet. "Come daddy and Frank, let us leave Mr Maxwell to his work. She smiled sweetly as Ernest rose from his chair. "Until next Wednesday then Mr Maxwell." The three of them left the room and made for the front door and the street.

For some minutes they walked in complete silence, each deep in their own thoughts. Then Frank spoke up. "Do you think he didn't like us?"

"Who?" said Violet.

"Slater. Your Jim. Do you think he didn't like us?"

Violet started to giggle. "What us? The bastard, the strumpet and the bankrupt? What on earth gives you that idea?" She started to laugh out loud, and very soon both Frank and Ernest joined in. Soon they were in hysterics, and passers-by crossed the street to avoid contact with this trio, who were so obviously drunk with happiness.

On the following Wednesday, Maxwell duly arrived at eleven o'clock sharp and was shown into the study by Frank, who, rather disarmingly for Maxwell, immediately placed himself in the chair next to Violet.

Just as the man was about to start the meeting, the door opened and in walked Alice, carrying a tray of tea, followed by Ernest. Alice placed the tray on the small coffee table and then, to the complete surprise of the solicitor, they both sat down on the sofa and prepared to take part in the meeting.

"Err... it's not at all necessary or usual to have the staff present at this sort of meeting," said Maxwell.

Alice made as if to rise, but Ernest put his hand out to restrain her. "This is, as you know Mr Maxwell, my father Mr Ernest Matthews," said Violet, "and the lady sitting next to him is Alice. They are our house guests."

"House guests?"

"Precisely. They live here with us, with Frank and myself and the twins. We have no staff now, we do not find it necessary."

Maxwell shifted uneasily in his chair. "I... eh I cannot think that it was in Mr Slater's mind that the house would be occupied by persons other than yourself... eh his children and any staff."

"Can you not Mr Maxwell? From what I understand you to have said the other day in your office, I may live in this house. Surely that means that whilst I do so it is my home, and surely, if it is my home, then I may have friends and family to stay in the normal course of events?"

Maxwell looked around at the eager faces staring at him. He swallowed. "Yes... well... but..."

"Mr Maxwell, is this my home or is it not?" said Violet, ramming home her advantage.

"It is your home Mrs Slater... it is just that..."

"...that Mr Slater, in his desire to make life as uncomfortable for me as possible, forgot to address this particular issue, and that if he had foreseen it, he would have entered something in his will which prevented it. Am I correct Mr Maxwell?"

"I hardly think..."

"Am I not correct Mr Maxwell?"

He shifted again in his chair. "Well to a point. I do think that Mr Slater imagined that it would only be you and his children that lived in the house."

"Well Mr Slater imagined wrongly, Mr Maxwell. My son Frank will be living with me permanently and attending a local school, and for the foreseeable future my widowed father and Alice will be staying with me to help in the upbringing of the children. Until and unless you can demonstrate that there is a specific clause in the will prohibiting this, that arrangement will pertain."

Frank looked across at his mother, undisguised pride and joy written all over his face. This was really his mother, the Violet of old who fought for and got what she wanted and he... he was not going back to that awful school. He would spend the rest of his school days at home, and then when he was ready he would take up his inheritance in France. The future looked wonderful.

Violet sat back in her chair and watched the workings on Maxwell's face.

She had him stumped and it felt good. It felt as if, at last, she was taking on and beating Slater, repaying him for the wasted years of humiliation and unhappiness. At one point she had almost felt sorry for Maxwell, thinking that perhaps he was only the messenger and that it was unfair to badger him so. But now she could see that he had, in fact, actively connived in the preparation of the will and that he was, in fact, cursing himself for not foreseeing this eventuality.

There was a long silence as Maxwell leafed through the will. Then he looked up. "Of course Mrs Slater, you will appreciate that I can only agree to household expenses that relate specifically to the care and upbringing of Mr Slater's children and..."

"Mr Maxwell, we would not have it any other way. We are, as you know, of independent means and we would wish to defray our own expenses."

Maxwell fidgeted with his collar. "Well, shall we get down to the main point of the meeting... eh... the discussion of this month's expenses?"

"By all means Mr Maxwell. Tea?"

The rest of the meeting was a sedentary affair, which the others, having taken their tea, left Violet and Maxwell to. They discussed all the household expenditure and he studiously calculated and divided each and every item in an attempt to exclude any payment that could benefit either Violet or her family. Finally they arrived at a figure for that month and he promised that he would make the monies available on the following day.

Violet showed him to the door, shook his hand politely and shut the door behind him, leaning against it, breathing heavily. Frank, Ernest and Alice appeared from the other room, convulsed with laughter, and the four of them hugged each other, laughing until the tears ran down their cheeks.

"We should have said I was the maid," said Alice, laughing. "Then we could have got my wages."

"And have him divide them up to make sure that we didn't get a part of you? I wouldn't give him the pleasure," said Violet.

THE END

SING TO SILENT STONES
Volume Two: Frank's War

First Chapter Sample

September 1939

Frank sat up in the canoe and dipped the paddle to take him closer to the bank, beneath the shade of the overhanging willows. A strong smell of fish made him wrinkle his nose, and he could see now that the bank and branches above were coated with white from the night time roosts of the flocks of cormorant that wheeled and dived in the wide waters of the Loire. He grimaced in disgust and guided the canoe back out into the current.

He settled back, the paddle across his lap, his face up to the sun to let the world slip by. My, what a week it had been! Gunther and Lizzie had only left this time last week, but it felt as if it were ages ago. On the Monday he had restarted work at the factory, expecting that after the summer recess things would be relatively quiet, but at the gate he had been met by an excited Leclerc, waving a piece of paper in his hands.

"Look Monsieur Frank! Look at this, we have got it."

Frank had waited for the man to reach him before taking the papers from him. "What have we got Monsieur Leclerc?"

"The order for the new railings for the Mairie and park in Chateauneuf."

Frank had looked at him, his mouth falling open. He glanced down at the papers and quickly ran his eyes over them. "We got that? But that's... that's just wonderful." He handed the papers back to Leclerc. "That's a massive order, isn't it?"

Leclerc beamed. "It most certainly is my dear fellow. It most certainly is, and it means that with the confirmation of the new gun carriage wheels we have now fulfilled our targets for the next two years."

Frank put his hand out and Leclerc took it. "It is your victory, Monsieur Leclerc," said Frank. "We... all of us owe you so much."

Leclerc bristled with pride. He drew himself erect as he shook Frank's hand. "Thank you Monsieur Frank... thank you very much. I do my best."

"As you always have Monsieur Leclerc. As you always have." He had let go of the man's hand and transferred his arm to his shoulders, turning him back in the direction of the gates. "Now how can I help? What have we to do?"

Lying back in the boat, Frank smiled to himself. What a silly question. How can I help? Well, he'd found out alright! And the result had been a week of non-stop activity. Late into each evening, right up until the Saturday night, they'd been in the offices pouring over plans and designs. The factory floor had to be rearranged to accommodate the new lines. Castings and moulds had to be perfected and duplicated, and while Frank had busied himself with these in-house tasks, Leclerc had got on with the ordering of materials.

The activity in the factory throughout that momentous week had all but blotted out what was happening in the big wide world. Oh, Philippe had tried to keep him abreast of what was going on, but, to be truthful, by the time he got back to the chateau each night, he'd been so tired that he could barely comprehend what the man was trying to tell him.

The war clouds were looming once again over Europe. Ultimatums were being bandied back and forth, and only the day before had come the rumour that Hitler had finally invaded Poland. Frank had sighed to himself as he listened. The consequences of that were tremendous. A German invasion of Poland would, almost certainly, mean that Britain would declare war on Germany, and France was sure to follow, and where on earth would that lead?

"Tell me it won't happen," he'd said to Gunther in August.

"It won't happen," Gunther had said. "Our two peoples will never fight each other again."

"Which two peoples, Gunther?" Frank had asked. "Are you talking of France or of England?"

Lizzie had leant forward eagerly. "Yes Gunther, surely you could not contemplate being at war with any of your friends?"

Frank had watched Gunther's face as she spoke. It was funny. Gunther had never before exhibited any real feeling for women, but on meeting Lizzie all that had changed. He had danced attendance on her as if she were the most beautiful woman in the world. He had, Frank laughed to himself at the memory, really worn his heart on his sleeve for the vivacious English girl he had met for the first time that summer.

At times, Frank had felt something almost akin to jealousy. This was his Lizzie, and although he had always thought of her as a little sister, something was different this time. Perhaps it was the fact that for the first time they were away from Devon. Perhaps it was just the joy of having her here at the chateau at last.

Frank opened his eyes and squinted along the bow. He steadied the canoe's passage and then lay back to think once more.

More likely, it was that, for the first time, he had really appreciated just how beautiful Lizzie was and that she was definitely, most definitely, no longer a little girl.

"Show me your river, Frank," she had said mischievously the week before. "Show me your secret places."

Her eyes danced with wickedness, and Frank's mind had raced back to that spring day in Devon, the cold waters and the white of her body.

"Yes, let's go for a swim," Gunther had said, jumping in, clearly excited at the prospect.

"Yes let's," said Pierre-Luc and Marcel, almost together. Frank had looked across at Lizzie, a resigned smile on his face. She had smiled back sympathetically, knowing, he had no doubt of this, where his thoughts had been, and when they had all got to the river's bank, no swimsuit could ever hide the fact that the child's body he recalled was miraculously changed.

His friends' faces as Lizzie emerged from changing in the bushes! Admiration would be a polite word, but from three... no, to be fair, four boys, the looks she had received amounted to a lot more than that. God, she had looked wonderful! Slim legs and waist. Full bosom, scarcely concealed in her costume. Her hair, long, dark and shining... flying free. Frank shook his head at the memory.

The day after that, Marcel and Pierre-Luc had left to re-join their regiment and Frank, along with Gunther and Lizzie, had gone to the station to wish them goodbye. Lizzie had remarked how smart the two young men had looked... how handsome. Gunther had merited a frown of disapproval when he had tried to say that, in his opinion, the uniform of the German army was considerably smarter. "How could you say that?" Lizzie had complained.

"Yes, explain yourself man," Frank had interjected, slightly amused at his friend's obvious discomfiture... at his suddenly finding himself at odds with Lizzie when he had tried so hard for weeks to impress her.

Gunther floundered. "Well... well it's just that... well... oh alright, have it your own way."

"I think all men in uniform look wonderful," said Lizzie lightly. Frank and probably Gunther too, at that moment, had earnestly wished that they too were in uniform. Frank had even toyed with the idea of dressing up in his when they got back to the chateau but decided, in the end, that it would be a little silly... and very, very obvious.

He had elected to do his Service a couple of years before, as he had not wished to bother with higher education. "Go to university, you'll love it," Violet had pleaded. Love it? Why should he love it? What he loved was right here in Germigny and Chateauneuf. No amount of schooling or university would change that. Why should he waste time on higher education when what he really wanted to do was to learn how the factory worked and be ready to take it on full-time when Leclerc finally retired. Leclerc had been his teacher, his friend, and in the years since he had finally returned full-time to France, he had listened and learnt from the older man. What more could he ever aspire to?

He rounded a bend in the river and drew near to the old quayside at Saint Benoit. This was one of his favourite places. Gone now were the quays and berths that trading gabare of old had tied up to, and in their stead the stately willows held the bank and tickled both sky and waters with their silvery green. What had once been a place of noise and activity now slept quietly in the summer sun. A small circle of houses and cottages lay back up to the top of the levee, and from them, half hidden now in the long grass, you could still discern the steps leading down to the water's edge.

The river ran straight for a while and then curved gently to the left before running on down past the road leading back to the chateau. As it turned, the waters slowed and deposited sand and silt to form the chain of islands to the right-hand side of the river, culminating in their boyhood island of Allemanceterre. Frank drifted quietly by these, staring intently up the banks for signs of life. Terns roosting on the shingle rose into the sky, protesting as they wheeled around his head, before settling again as he passed.

The river now ran faster as it drew level to where he had arranged to meet the ever-faithful Philippe, and Frank scanned the bank for sight of him. The glint of well-polished paintwork caught his eye and he powered the canoe to the edge and beached it. He got out, calling Philippe's name as he did so, and then lay back on the grass, his eyes closed, savouring the sounds and smells of this river that he loved so dearly. A footfall beside him told him that his friend had arrived. "That was lovely," he said without opening his eyes. "I've waited all week for that."

There was no reply. Philippe sat on his haunches, gripping his knees and staring out across the waters. For a few moments there was silence between the two of them, but then the older man spoke, slowly and quietly. "The British have declared war on Germany."

Frank sat up slowly. He didn't look at Philippe. Rather, the two of them just sat quietly, staring out across the moving waters. They must have sat like that for five to ten minutes, each locked in his own thoughts, before Frank finally spoke. "And France?"

"Today, maybe this evening... but for certain."

"It begins again."

"It begins."

The silence resumed. Frank thought of his father, the rows upon rows of silent white stones. Was this now his destiny? Philippe stared straight ahead, lost in his own world of memories. At length Frank turned, and resting on one elbow touched his companion. "What should I do?"

"Do?"

"Yes, what should I do? Should I go to England and enlist or should I stay here?"

Philippe sat back on the grass and stretched his legs out before him, leaning back on his hands. "Do you want to go to England?"

"Not particularly, but I can't just sit and do nothing, can I?"

"You are not doing nothing. The factory is making parts for the guns of the French army. That is important, no?"

Frank thought for a moment. "It is important, but is it all I can do?"

"I think," said Philippe, turning to face Frank at last, "that you are already a reservist in the French army and that you should wait for orders if they come. If you went to England would you enlist?"

"Yes... yes I would."

"And you'd be sent to France to fight?"

Frank smiled. "Yes, I suppose you're right."

"Then why waste the journey?"

Frank laughed now. The clever old fox. He got to his feet and dragged the canoe further out of the water. "Here, give me a hand to pull this to the top," he called, "and then we'd better get back home." The two of them dragged the canoe up the steep bank and tied it to a tree at the top. "I'll come back for it later," said Frank, walking off to the motor car. "I know you wouldn't want it near this thing."

"Certainly not," agreed Philippe. He paused as he noticed Frank going to the driver's side, then shrugged his shoulders and got in the other side at the front.

Frank reversed the great car away from the top of the levee and did a three-point turn behind the willow tree, with Philippe watching anxiously to check that his beloved vehicle was not scratched. Frank smiled at him in recognition of his fears. "Don't worry old man," he said, laughing as he slipped into forward gear. "I know how to do it you know."

They rode back to the chateau in silence, each deep in his own thoughts. As they pulled into the driveway, Jean-Claude came down the steps, his face serious, the traces of tears still showing on his cheeks. He waved his hands in the air, shaking his head silently.

"I know Jean-Claude, I know," said Frank. He reached up and pulled down the older man's hand and held it. "Let's wait and see shall we?" Jean-Claude nodded. He glanced up at Philippe coming around the motor car to join them, and the three of them retired to the house.

All Europe held its breath for the next few weeks in the general expectation that the Blitzkrieg that had destroyed Poland would be repeated throughout the continent. When it did not come, a semblance of normality crept back into life in the French countryside and towns, despite the restrictions which were gradually being imposed. The order for the new railings, so joyfully gained, was cancelled at short notice but was replaced by a larger one for gun carriage carcasses, and Frank and Leclerc were kept extremely busy reorganising the factory for this new production.

Pierre-Luc and Marcel, finding themselves in uniform at the outbreak of war, were confirmed in their regiments and posted north of Paris, but Frank received a letter telling him that he was in a reserved occupation and that he should stand by to receive further orders if the necessity arose.

As expected, there was a long letter from Violet agonising over whether he should stay in France or come back to the safety of England. Frank could scarcely resist a smile as he read the letter. Poor Violet. In spite of the fact that she had lived for so long in Germigny, she still clung to the idea that it was a foreign land and that the only real safety lay in England. She had been to the chateau only twice since he had finally moved back there permanently, and although she and the children had enjoyed themselves immensely, she had been quite happy to go home. For Violet, the chateau meant Armand. All the time she was there she half expected him to come through the door, and when he didn't the disappointment built up to such a degree that eventually she felt that she just had to go.

Frank understood her feelings. He had loved having her there and had revelled in his twin half-brothers. What characters they had become and how amazing it was that two, so alike in looks, could be so different in every other respect. George was loud and jolly... always the first up in the morning, always the keenest to get out and get on with whatever activity had been arranged for him. If nothing special had been laid on, then he would sulk and moan until, eventually, by dint of his sheer determination, either something would be organised or he would end up in some sort of trouble, which served to enlighten his day just as well.

Happily, even though the driving forces in his make-up quite obviously sprang from Slater's tree, there were subtle differences in character brought about by environment. Whereas Slater's personality had been honed by loneliness and an unrequited craving for the love of his mother, George was surrounded by affection. If Violet was not available then, at home, there was always Alice and, if they visited, it was to Jesse in England or Marie in France.

Ian, on the other hand, was a quiet and gentle boy who one day would aspire to all things learned, but for now was content to bask in the company of his brother and the love they felt for each other.

When Frank had first taken them down to the river, George had rushed straight down to the water's edge, shouting out his joy. He had picked up stones and hurled them as far out as he could, whooping as they splashed into the current. Ian, however, had stood quietly for a moment at the top of the bank, taking in the view. He had smiled up at Frank, and although no words had passed between them, Frank had understood that the little boy was telling him that he liked this place as much as he did. After that, and only then, he had run down to the water's edge to join his brother in their game.

As the phoney war continued and the autumn wore on, Frank wished that he could go to England and visit them, but it simply wasn't possible. The work at the factory continued apace, and as the year drew to a close, increasingly he was called upon to don his uniform and report for duty at weekends.

He received several letters from Lizzie. In the first she thanked him profusely for the wonderful holiday she had spent with him at the chateau, and in the subsequent letters she went on to bemoan the division of the friendships she had so obviously enjoyed. She passed on her love to Pierre-Luc and Marcel and hoped that they were safe. Most especially she mentioned Gunther and expressed the same fears that had been growing in Frank's mind.

How could he regard his boyhood friend as an enemy? Yet that is what he now was, and the possibility remained that they might well find themselves pitted against each other in the future. How could he cope with that? They all knew that Gunther had gone home in August with the specific intention of joining his regiment, and the thought that he was somewhere out there, in the uniform of the enemy, was a terrible one. Night after night Frank ran all the various scenarios around in his mind, and when Pierre-Luc or Marcel visited on leave they discussed the problem endlessly.

But it was the other part of her letter that disturbed him the most. George, cousin George, that lumpen yokel, had proposed to Lizzie just before he had enlisted. She wrote quite candidly to Frank that she didn't... couldn't ever love the man, but that she had not felt able to turn him down and send him off to war grieving. Oh she hadn't accepted, thank God for that Frank thought, but she had left the matter open and George was expecting an answer when he got back from initial training. "What should I do?" she had wailed in her letter. "I can't hurt him and I can't hurt Auntie Kate. He's told her... and mum and dad... and it really has put me on the spot. Auntie Kate is so excited, you'd think it was all arranged."

Frank tried to analyse his own feelings. Were they those of a concerned brother, or was there something more? Even though he had noted how beautiful she was... even though he had revelled in her company and delighted in her friendship... there was nothing else between them... was there? How could there be, they were practically brother and sister. But George? Why him? If she had to be married, then surely to God she could do better than that.

Frank determined to write to Lizzie, urging her not to throw herself away. He sat down one evening, tired after a hard day at the factory, and started the letter. Four times he got half way down the page before he tore it up and threw it in the waste paper basket. Sometimes he thought he was being too patronising. Another time he read what he'd written and decided that if George ever came across the letter, it would be impossible for them ever to be in the same place. And on another occasion he realised that what he had written could be upsetting to either Kate or Florrie or both and that was something he could not... would not risk.

Eventually he nodded off in his chair and put off the letter until another day, but as he did he wished with all his heart that he could write in a completely different vein. Oh, don't be silly Frank, he thought, as he drifted into sleep, she'd think you a fool and just where would that leave you?

He never really wrote the letter that he wanted to... felt he should have written. In the end he combined the simple message, "Think carefully", with his letter of Christmas greetings, and that in turn was put in the same envelope as his greetings to the rest of the Devon family. No mention, in turn, was made by Lizzie of any decision having been reached, and Frank finally put the matter to the back of his mind to concentrate on the tasks in hand, namely the constantly increasing orders for arms-related fabrications from the factory.

Leclerc was cock-a-hoop. "If this is what the threat of war brings then it's not so bad," he said jovially.

Frank wasn't so sure. The fact that no actual hostilities had, as yet, taken place on French soil did not convince him that Leclerc could possibly be right in his theory that the Germans would never actually dare to attack the might of the French army. A theory that was certainly weakened when the Germans invaded and conquered first Denmark and then Norway. "It's coming," he insisted to Leclerc.

"Nonsense my boy," the older man had replied, clapping him on the back. "They'll never get through, and if they did try it then our chaps and the British would crucify them."

"I do hope you're right," Frank had replied without enthusiasm, but all the while a feeling of dread was growing within him.

On the 10th of May, the Germans invaded Belgium and Holland, and for Frank that sealed his convictions. As he received the news from a stunned and clearly upset Leclerc, he felt no sense of vindication. Instead he felt a profound sense of sadness and, something he could, of course, never tell anybody else, a distinct fear for Gunther. The thought of his best friend lying dead and mutilated in some field haunted him, and he remembered how Violet had recounted the story of Dieter's death. Could that same fate await the son? That evening he made a point of visiting Gisela's grave in the family plot behind the chateau and placed a bunch of flowers upon it.

In the days that followed, the news from the north got grimmer and grimmer, culminating in the invasion of France, with the German army driving a wedge between the British and French forces.

"The British are trapped on the beaches," Philippe informed Frank. "The channel ports are lost."

Pierre-Luc and Marcel had last been heard of with their regiment north of Paris, and increasingly Frank found that he now had all his friends to worry about. He visited their parents and shared with them the hope and expectation that the two young men would soon be home. Marcel's parents could not bring themselves to believe that the French army, the greatest army the world had ever seen, could possibly be defeated. Pierre-Luc's parents, on the other hand, were a little more realistic. They knew of the Blitzkrieg tactics that had overwhelmed country after country and saw no reason why France, alone, should be immune to such warfare.

As the British and French armies scrambled off the beaches at Dunkirk, in the last days of May and the early days of June, Frank reported to army headquarters in Orleans. Assigned to the 57th Regiment, who were preparing to move north in company with the 4th Regiment and a battalion of the 17th Senegalais, what did this presage for family and friends?

TO BE CONTINUED

Register for a pre-publication offer and
news about part two of this story –
Sing to Silent Stones: Frank's War at
frankswar@hornetbooks.com or visit
www.hornetbooks.com

The Author

The story within *Sing to Silent Stones* is largely fictional but it does, nevertheless, incorporate very many true tales from David Snell and his wife Linda's families.

Both of David's parents were wartime pilots in the RAF and he and his brother, Peter, spent much of their childhood on RAF bases in the UK and the Far East, where the talk often revolved around the war and flying. Peter became a pilot but unfortunately died, aged 38, doing aerobatics in his own Second World War Harvard. David has spent a lifetime in the property/building industry and is a well-known writer and speaker on the subject of self-building.

Without prejudice to his parents, the phrases 'The only good German is a dead one' and 'The frogs are hopeless at fighting' were a constant theme. But David always questioned these assumptions.

He is a lifelong anti-war campaigner.

David's interests revolve around history and bird-watching. He has been married to Linda for 45 years and he has three children and three grandchildren